HEARTSTOPPER

VOLUME 4

Heartstopper: Volume 4 was originally published in England by Hachette Children's Group in 2021.

This book is a work of fiction. Names, characters, places, and incidents are either the product of the author's imagination or are used fictitiously, and any resemblance to actual persons, living or dead, business establishments, events, or locales is entirely coincidental.

Library of Congress Control Number: 2020946440

ISBN 978-1-338-61756-6 (hardcover)
ISBN 978-1-338-61755-9 (paperback)

16 15 14 13 12 11 10 9 8   22 23 24 25 26

Printed in China 62
This edition first printing, January 2022

[redacted]

ALICE OSEMAN

HEARTSTOPPER

VOLUME 4

graphix

An Imprint of

SCHOLASTIC

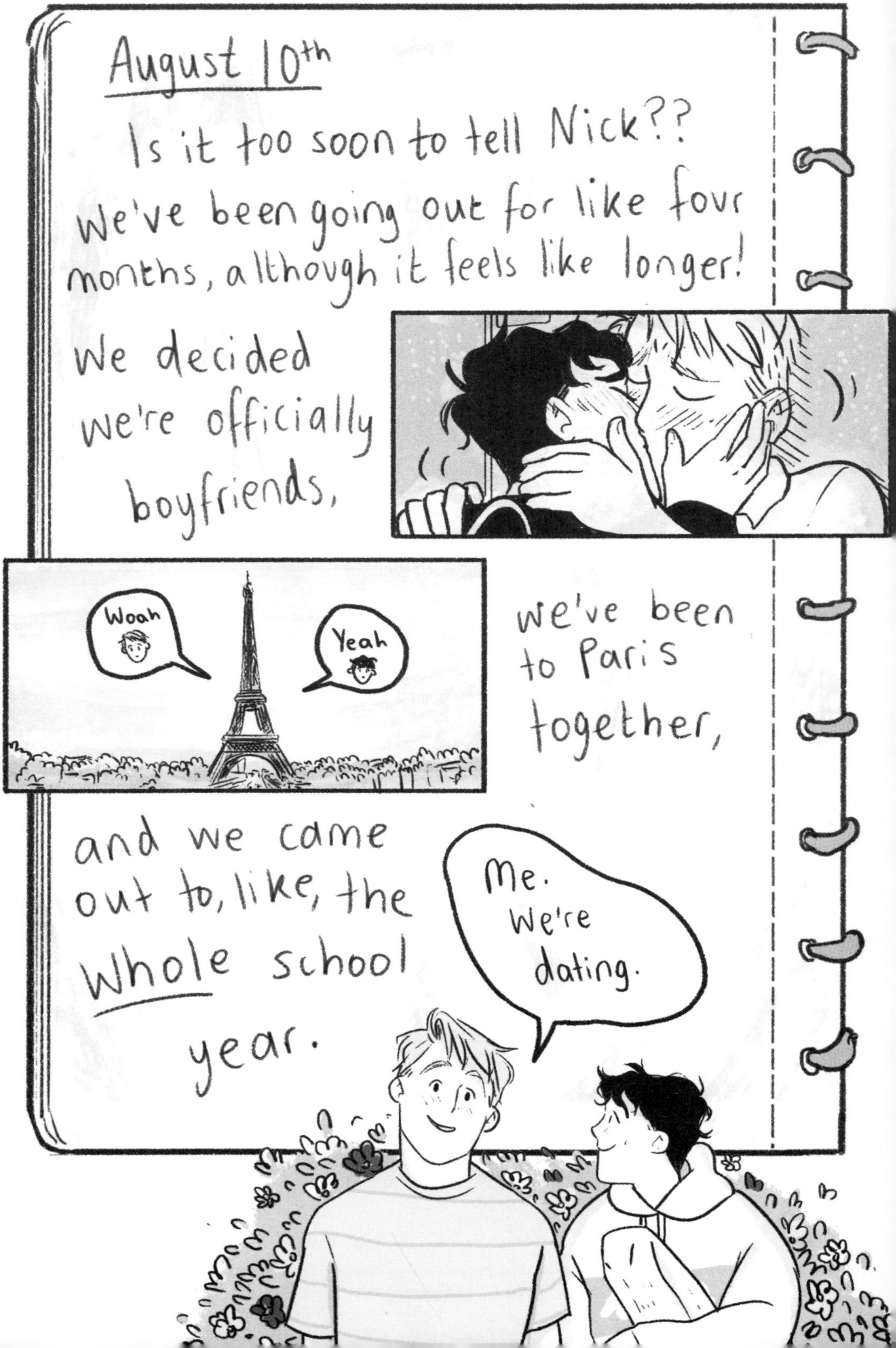
August 10th
Is it too soon to tell Nick?? We've been going out for like four months, although it feels like longer!
We decided we're officially boyfriends,
Woah
Yeah
we've been to Paris together,
and we came out to, like, the whole school year.
Me. We're dating.

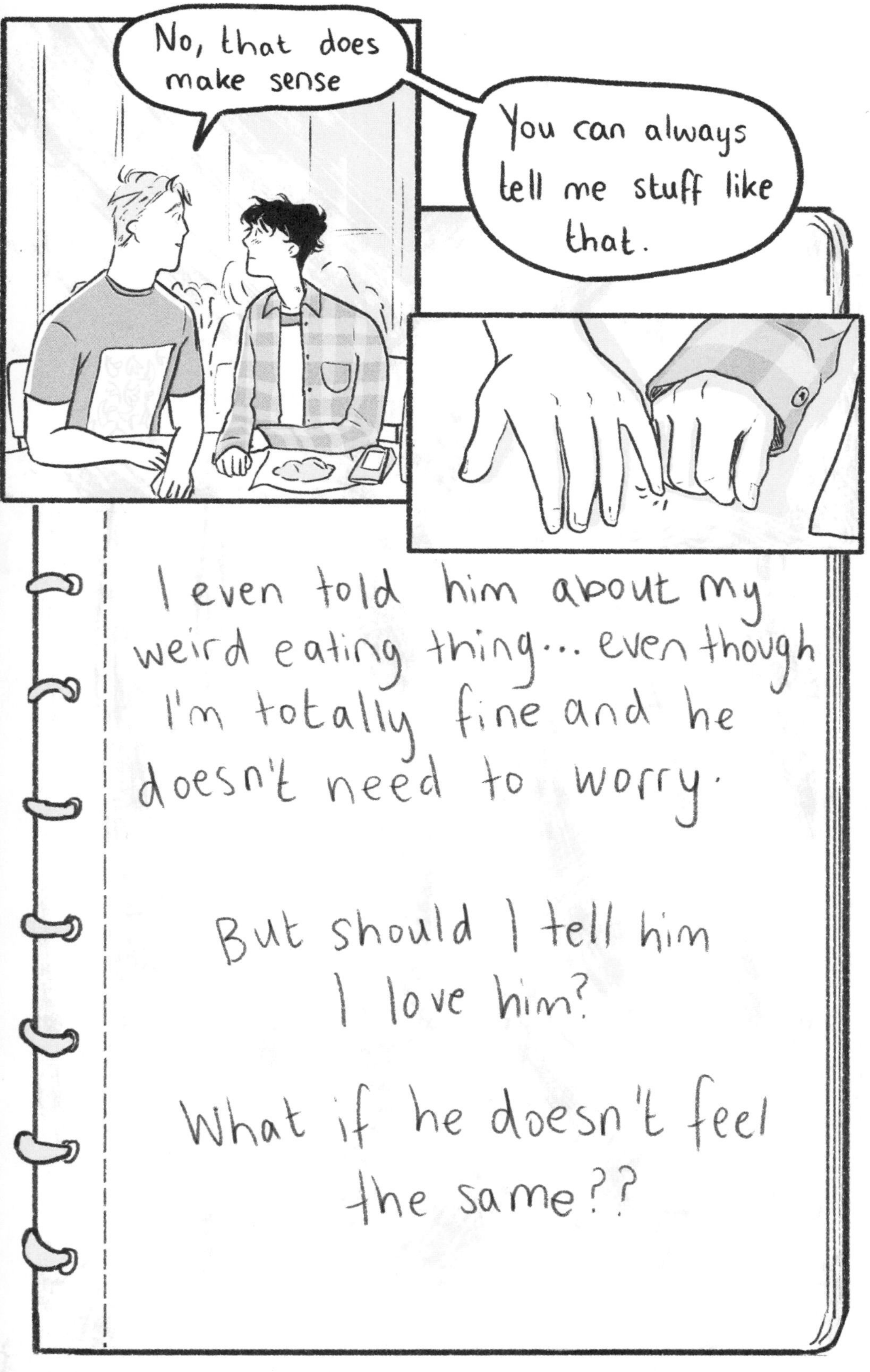
No, that does make sense
You can always tell me stuff like that.
I even told him about my weird eating thing... even though I'm totally fine and he doesn't need to worry.
But should I tell him I love him?
What if he doesn't feel the same??

5. LOVE

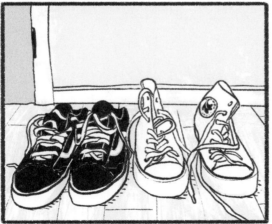

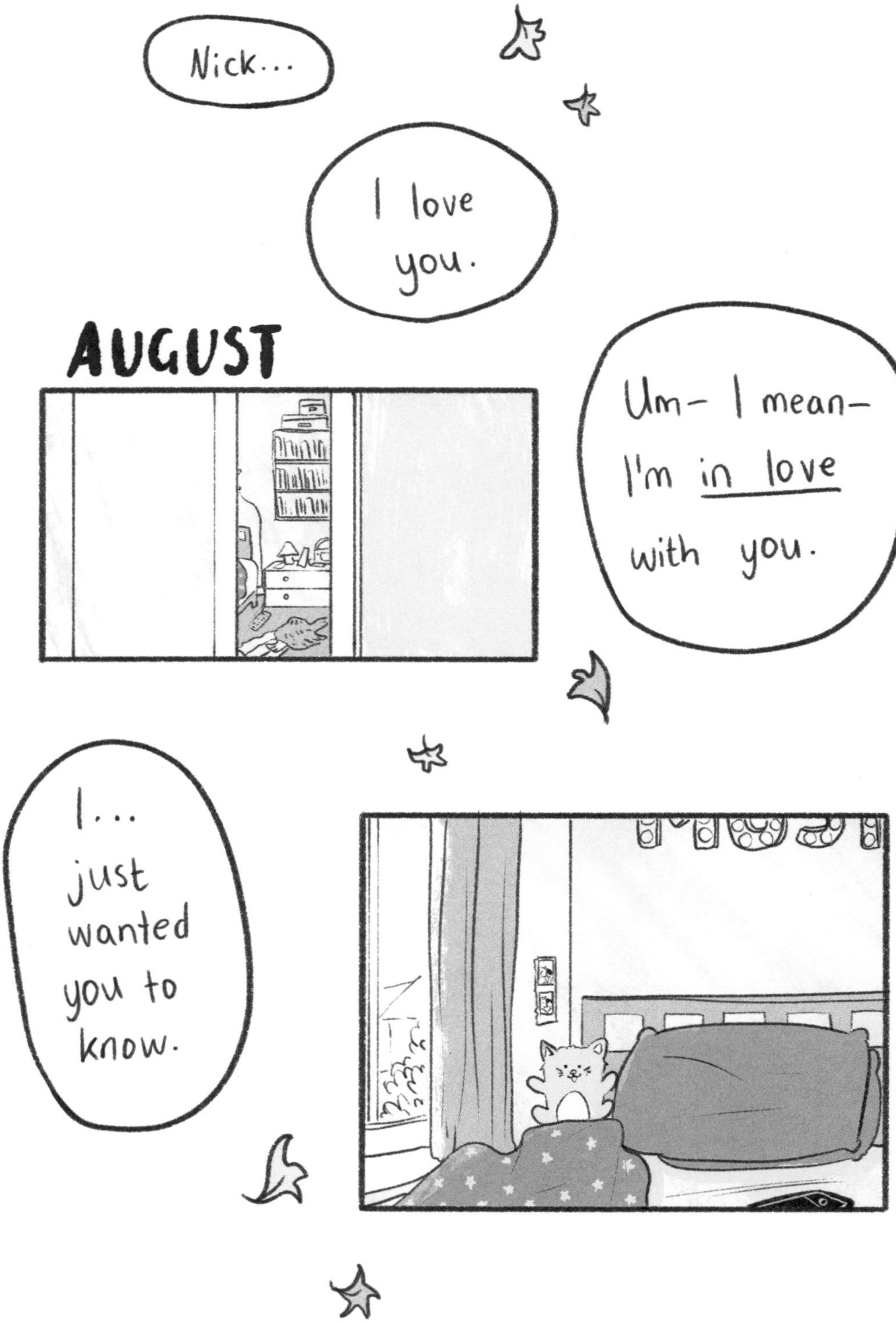
Nick...
I love you.
AUGUST
Um- I mean- I'm in love with you.
I... just wanted you to know.

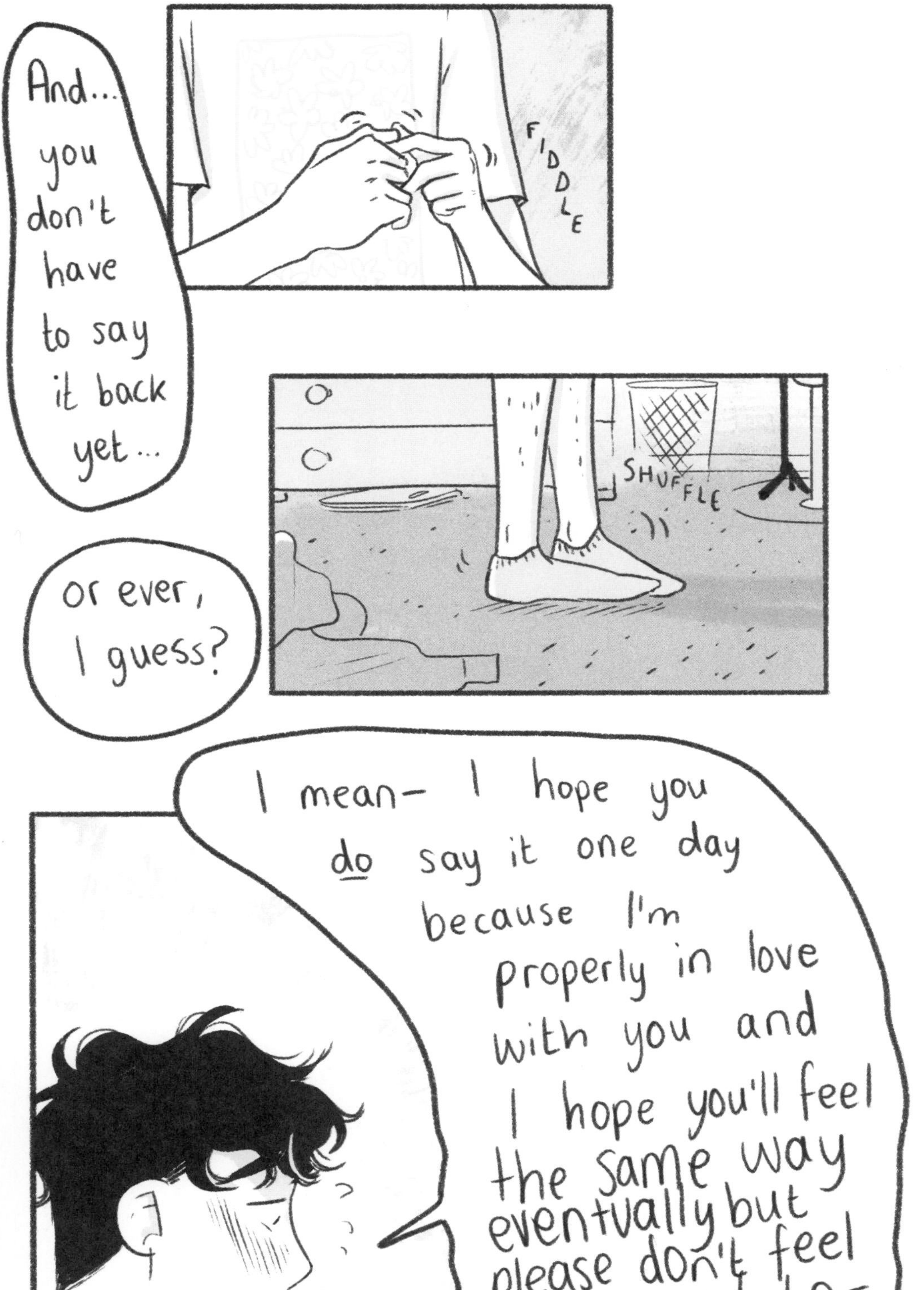
And... you don't have to say it back yet...
FIDDLE
or ever, I guess?
SHUFFLE
I mean- I hope you do say it one day because I'm properly in love with you and I hope you'll feel the same way eventually but please don't feel pressured to-

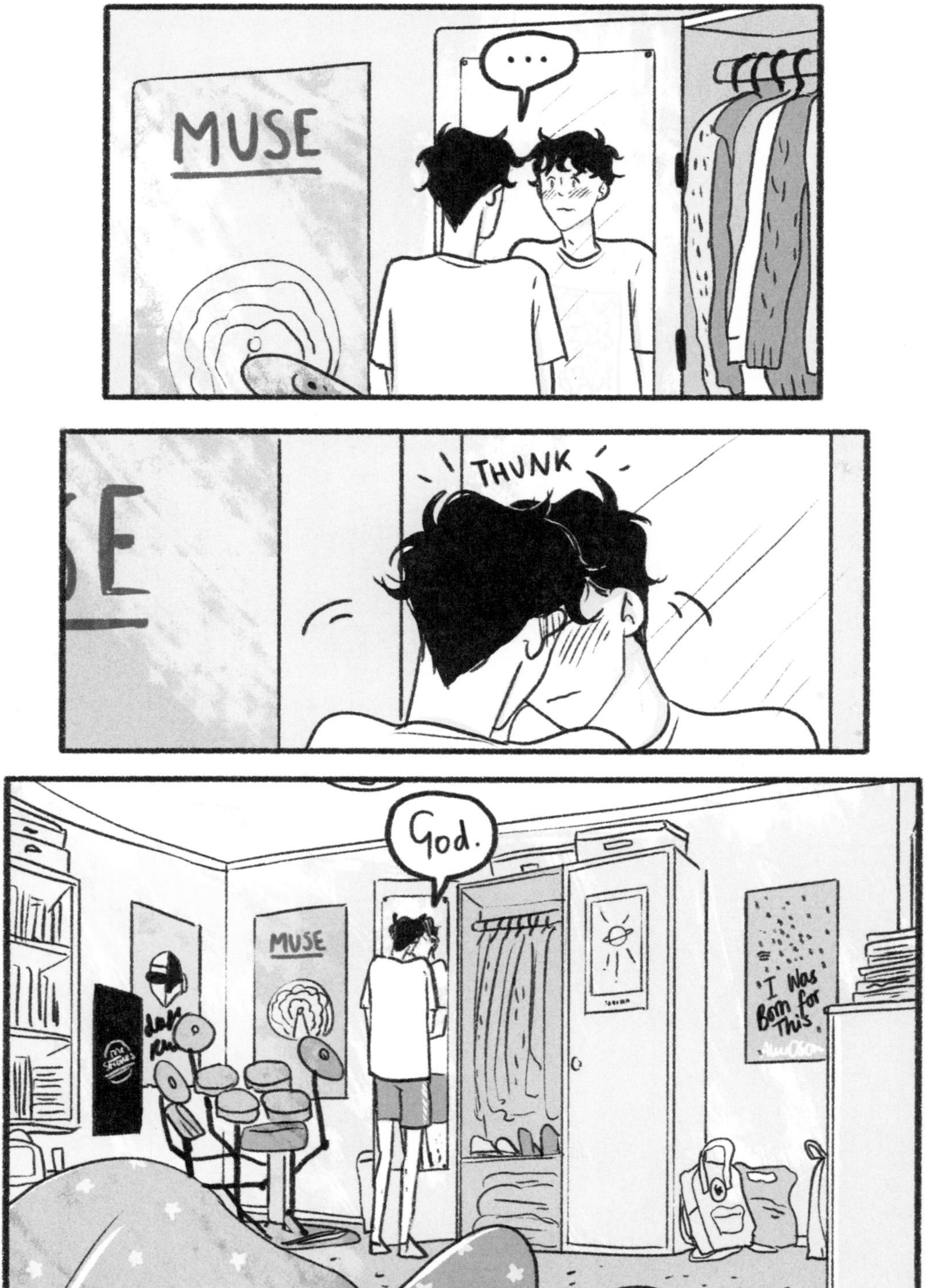
MUSE
...
THUNK
God.
MUSE
I Was Born for This

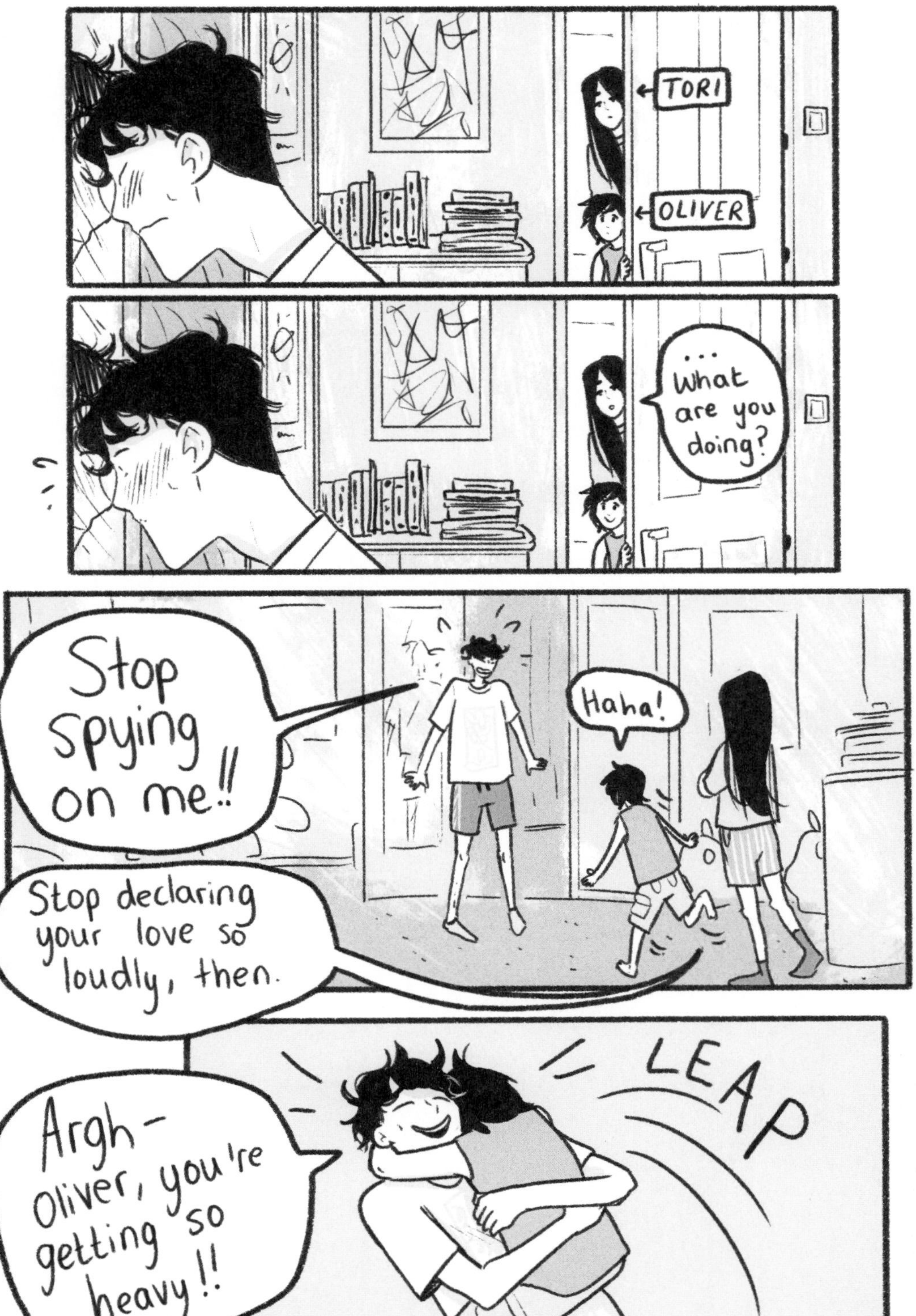
TORI
OLIVER
... What are you doing?
Stop spying on me!!
Haha!
Stop declaring your love so loudly, then.
LEAP
Argh- Oliver, you're getting so heavy!!

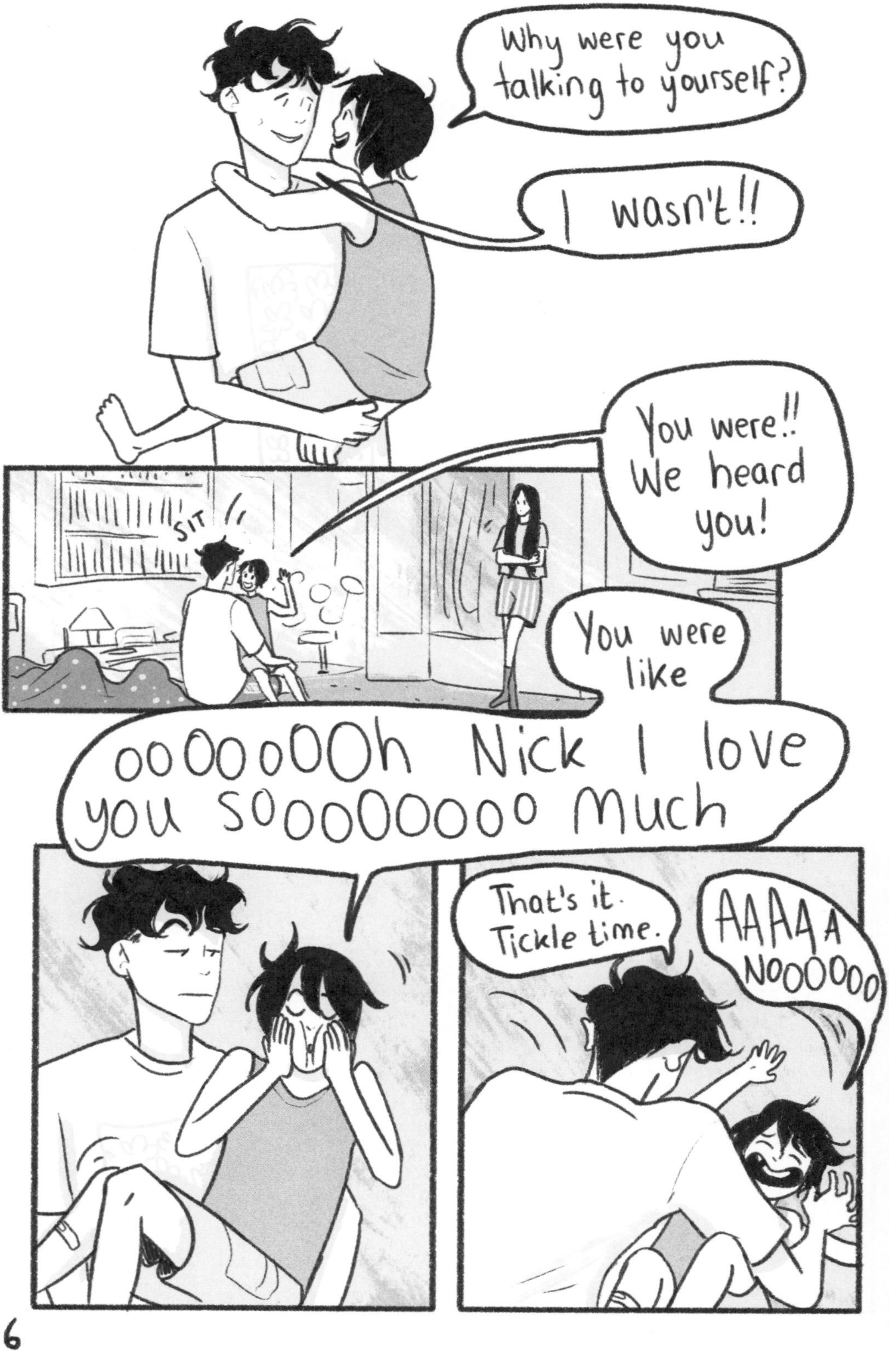
Why were you talking to yourself?
I wasn't!!
SIT
You were!! We heard you!
You were like
ooOOooOOh Nick I love you soooooooooo much
That's it. Tickle time.
AAAAA NOOOOOO

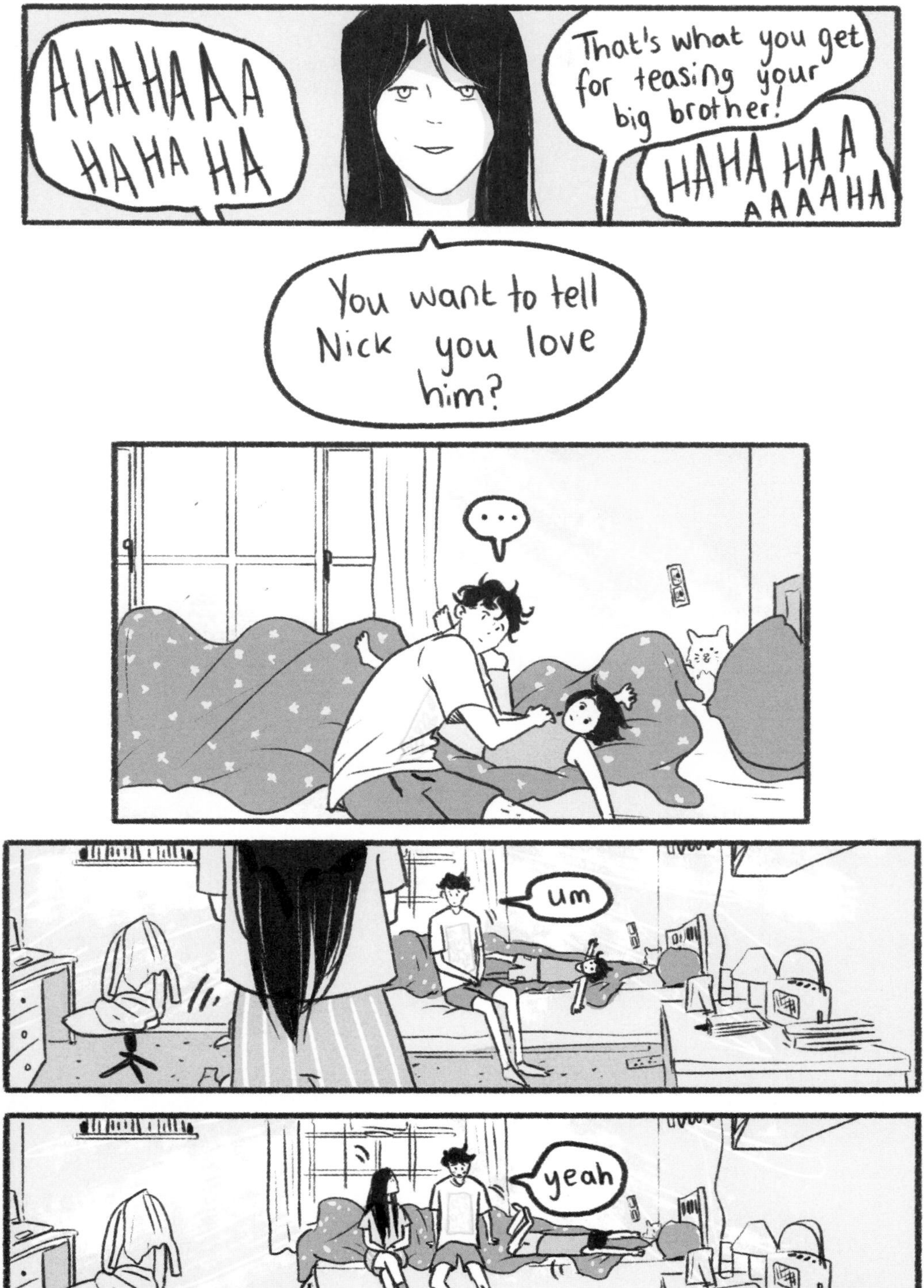
AHAHAAA HAHAHA HA
That's what you get for teasing your big brother!
HAHA HA A AAAAHA
You want to tell Nick you love him?
...
um
yeah

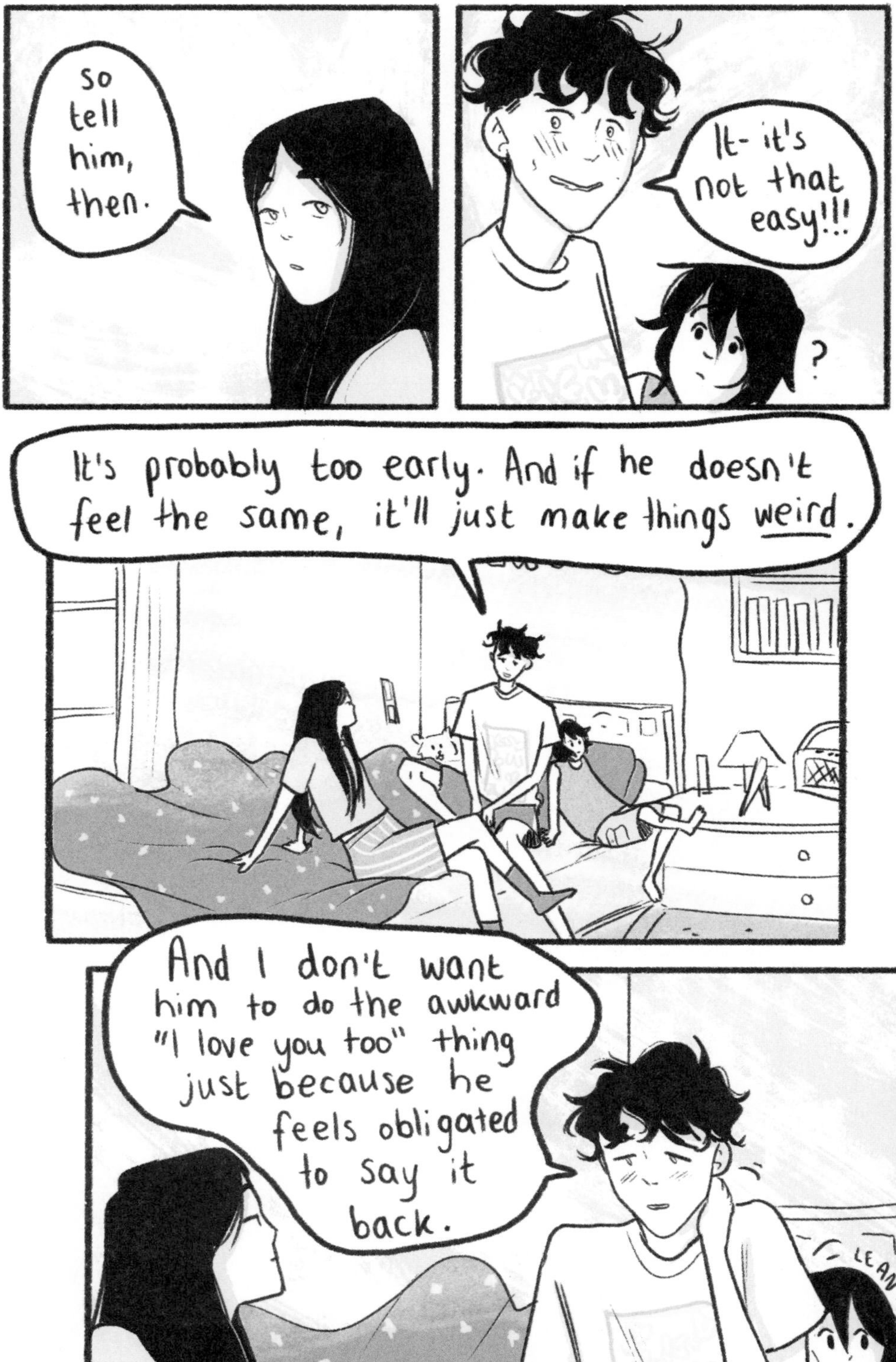

So tell him, then.
It- it's not that easy!!!
?
It's probably too early. And if he doesn't feel the same, it'll just make things weird.
And I don't want him to do the awkward "I love you too" thing just because he feels obligated to say it back.
LEAN

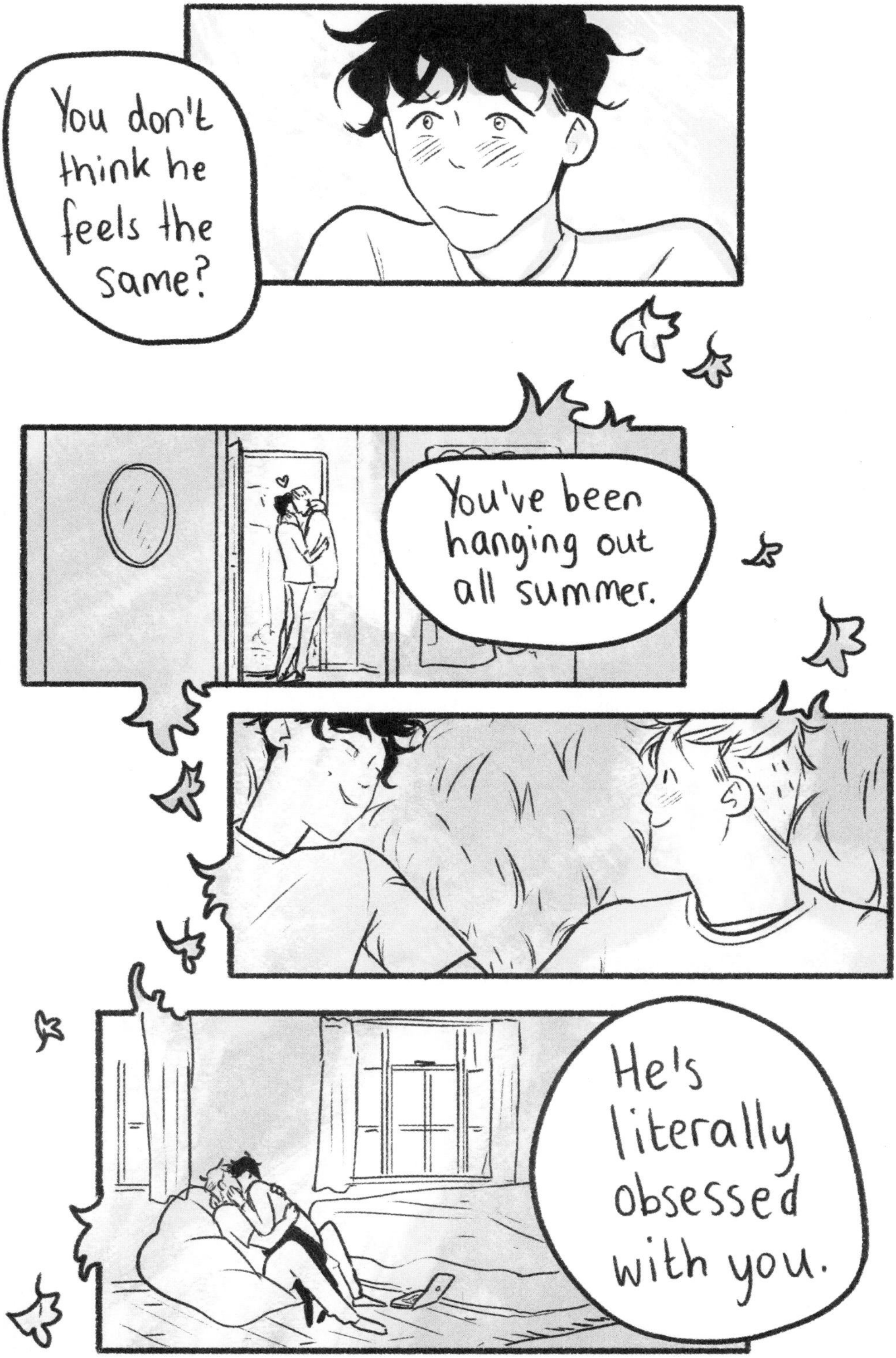
You don't think he feels the same?
You've been hanging out all summer.
He's literally obsessed with you.

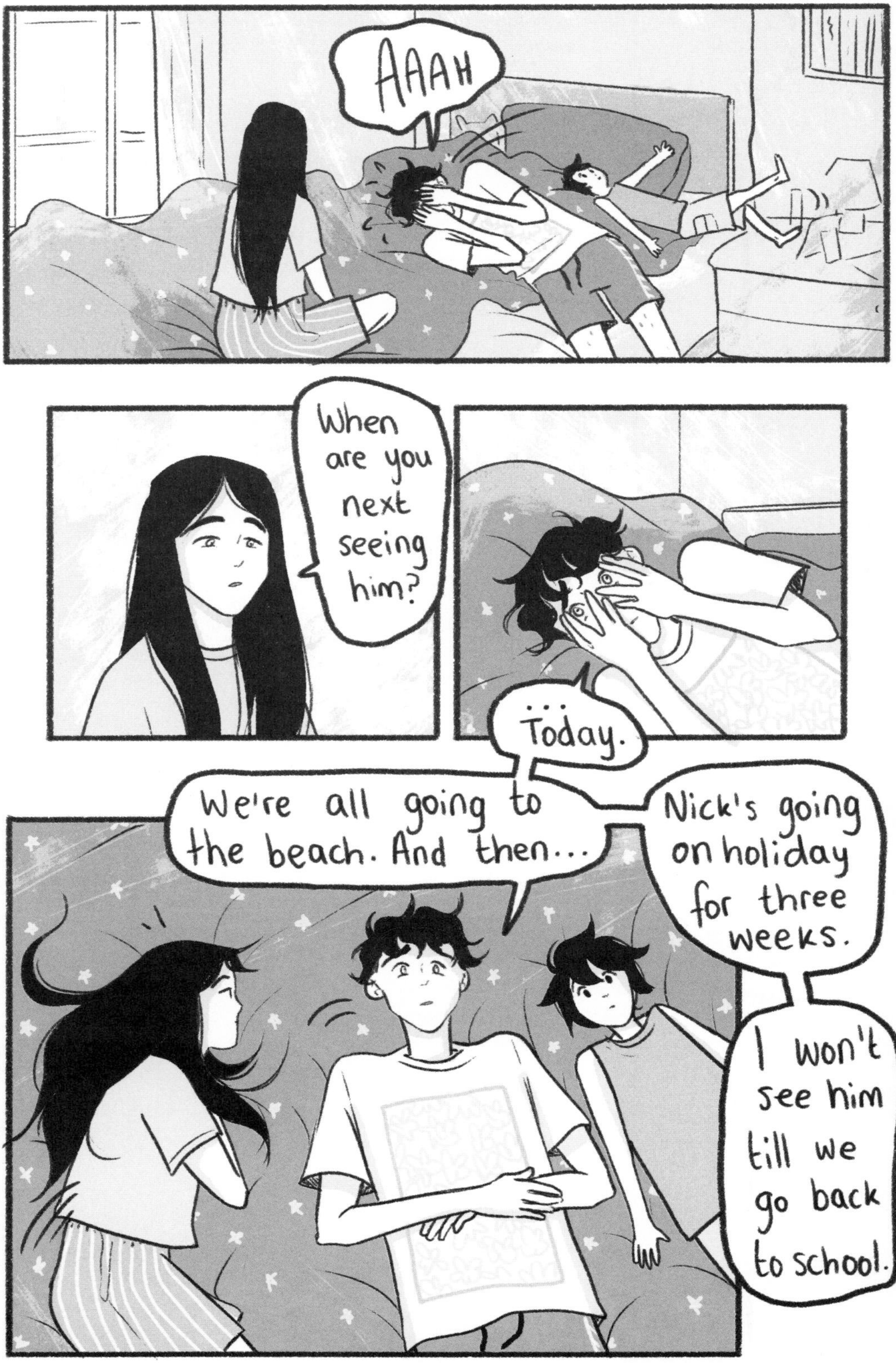
AAAH
When are you next seeing him?
... Today.
We're all going to the beach. And then...
Nick's going on holiday for three weeks.
I won't see him till we go back to school.

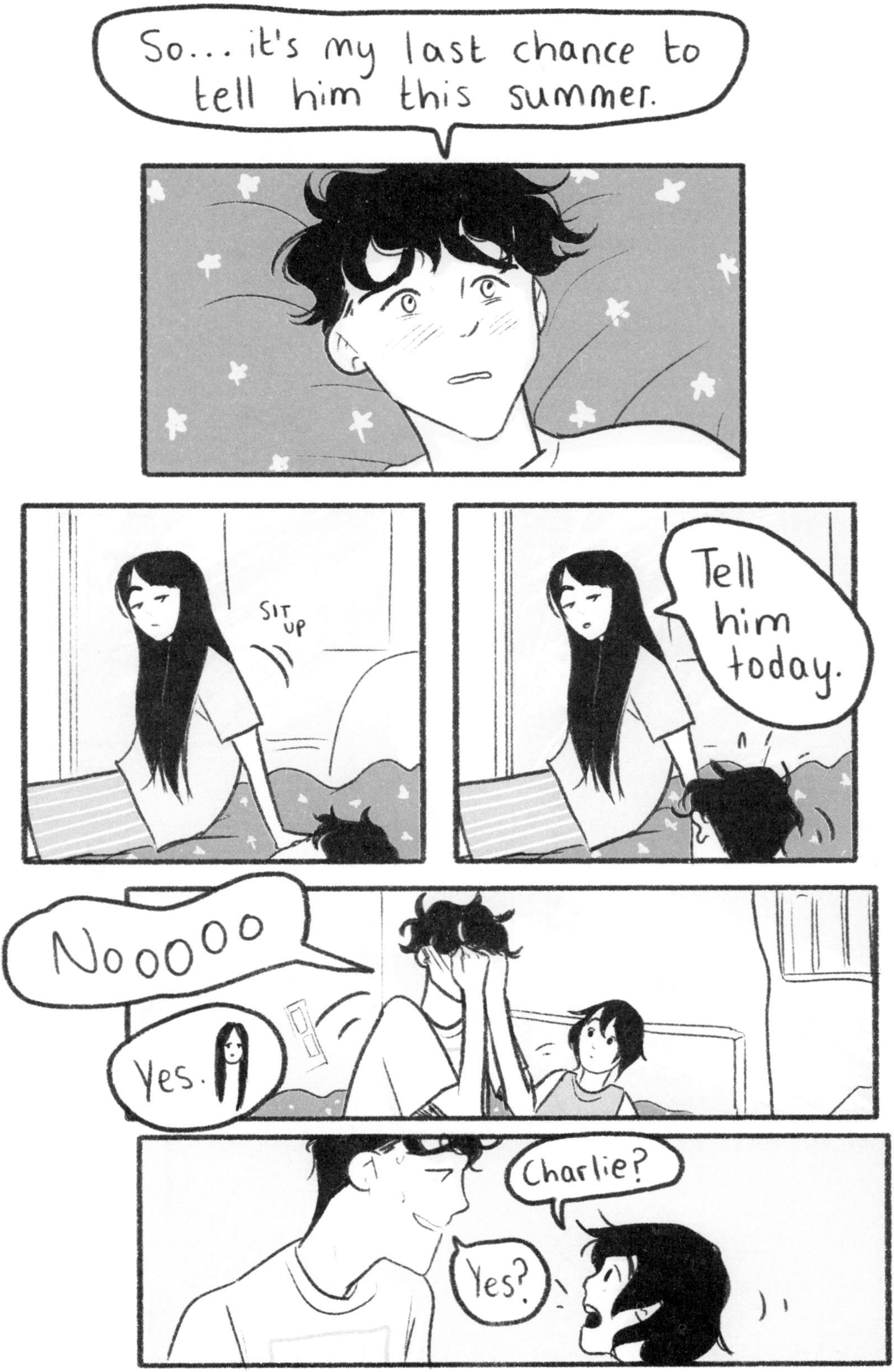
So... it's my last chance to tell him this summer.
SIT UP
Tell him today.
Nooooo
Yes.
Charlie?
Yes?

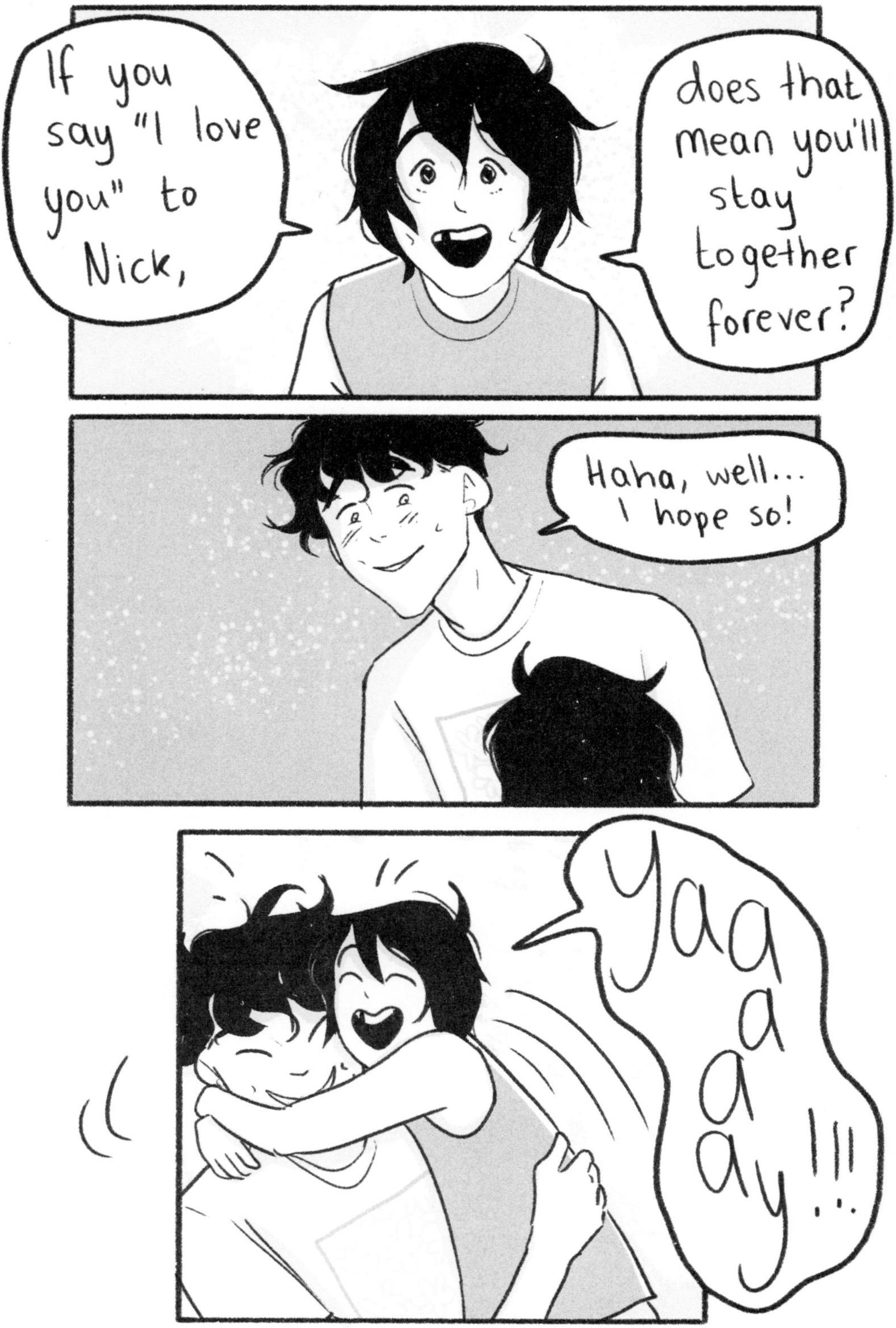
If you say "I love you" to Nick,
does that mean you'll stay together forever?
Haha, well... I hope so!
Yaaaaay!!!

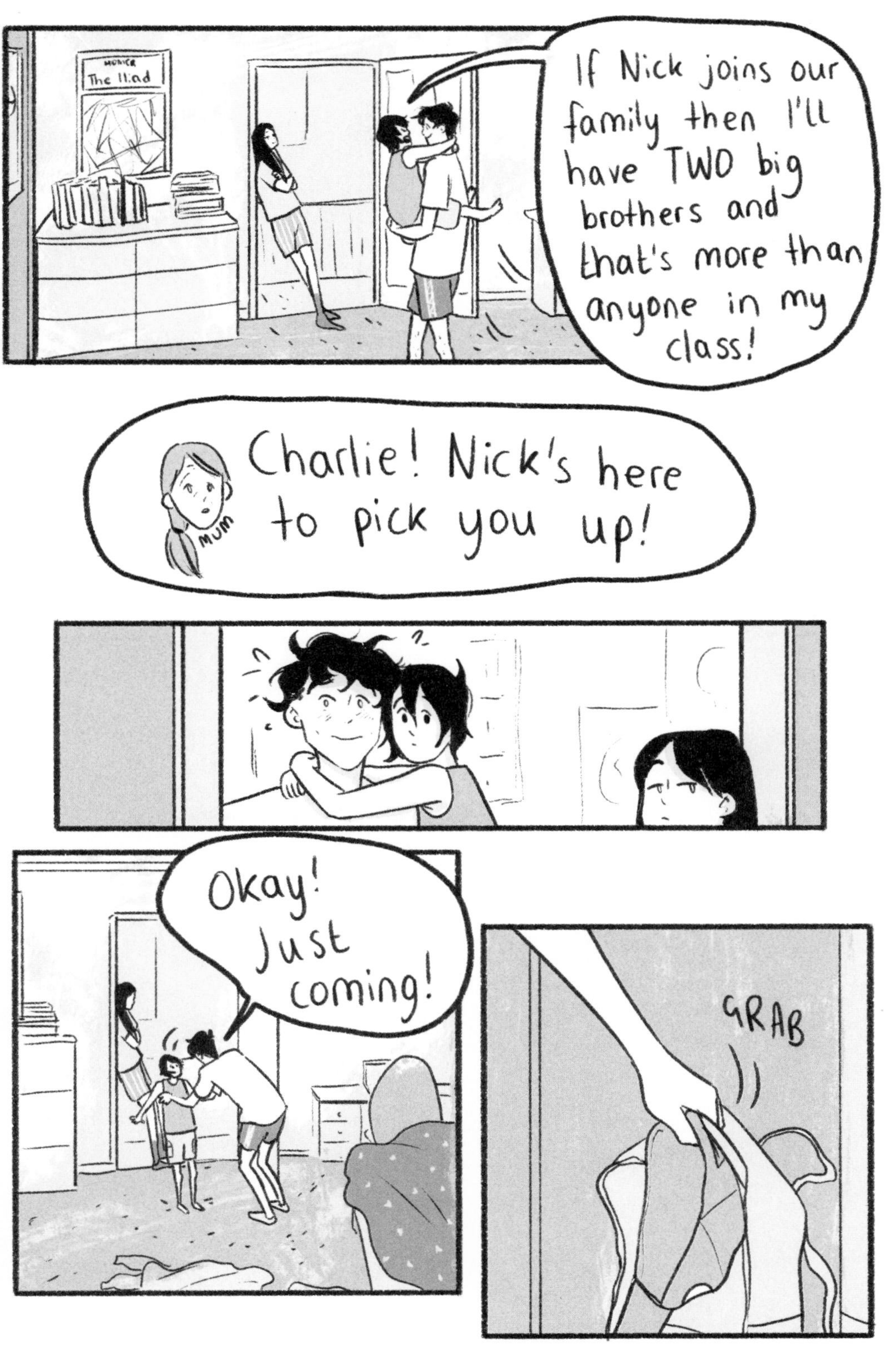
HOMER
The Iliad
If Nick joins our family then I'll have TWO big brothers and that's more than anyone in my class!
Charlie! Nick's here to pick you up!
MUM
Okay! Just coming!
GRAB

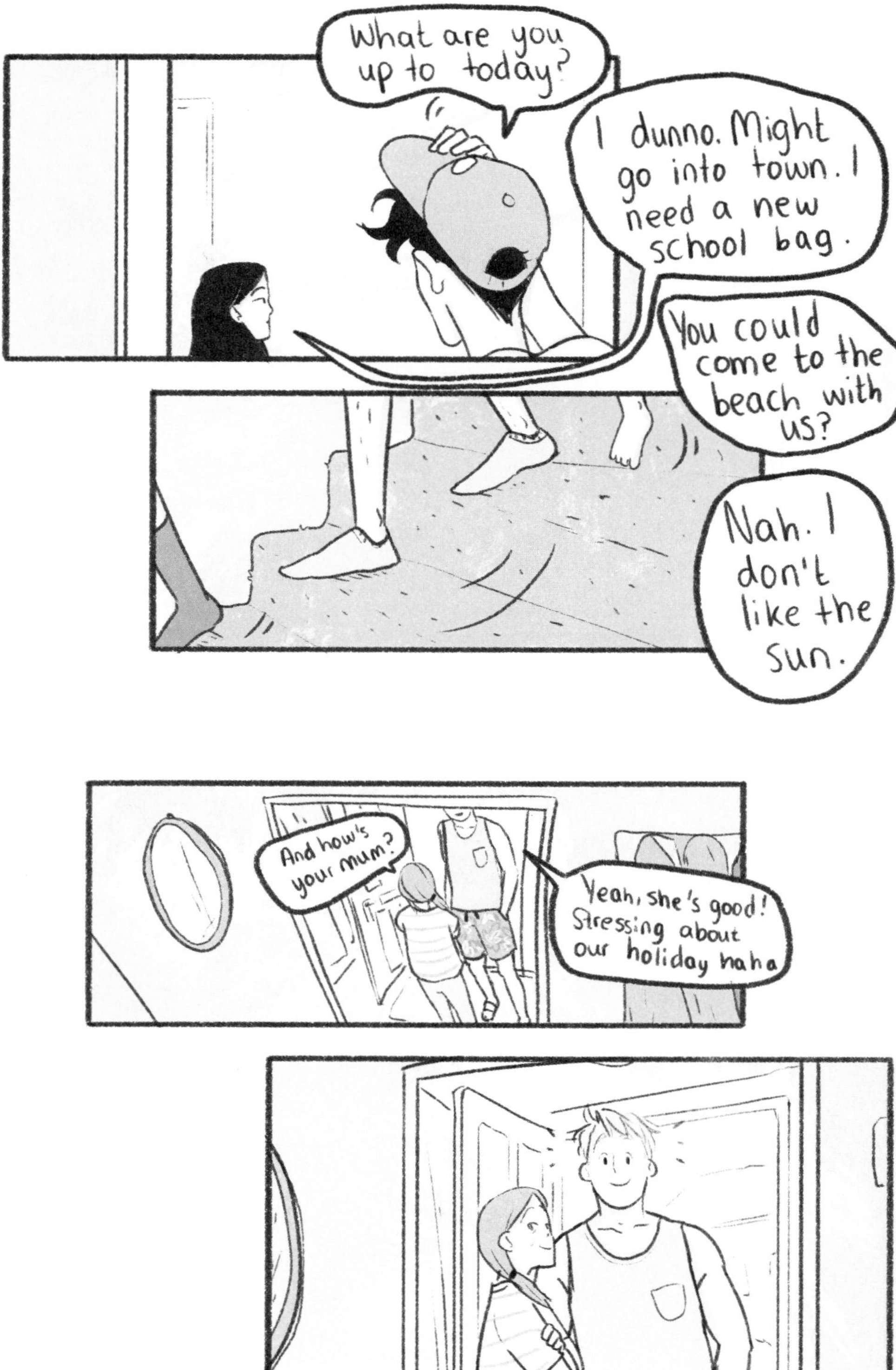
What are you up to today?
I dunno. Might go into town. I need a new school bag.
You could come to the beach with us?
Nah. I don't like the sun.
And how's your mum?
Yeah, she's good! Stressing about our holiday haha

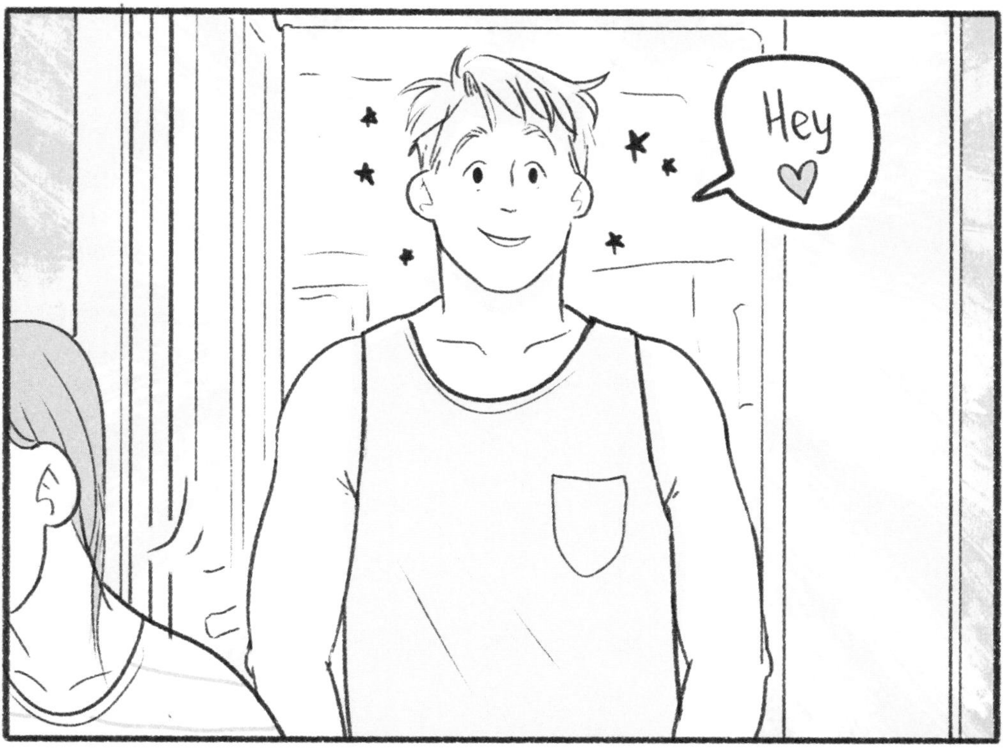
Hey ♡

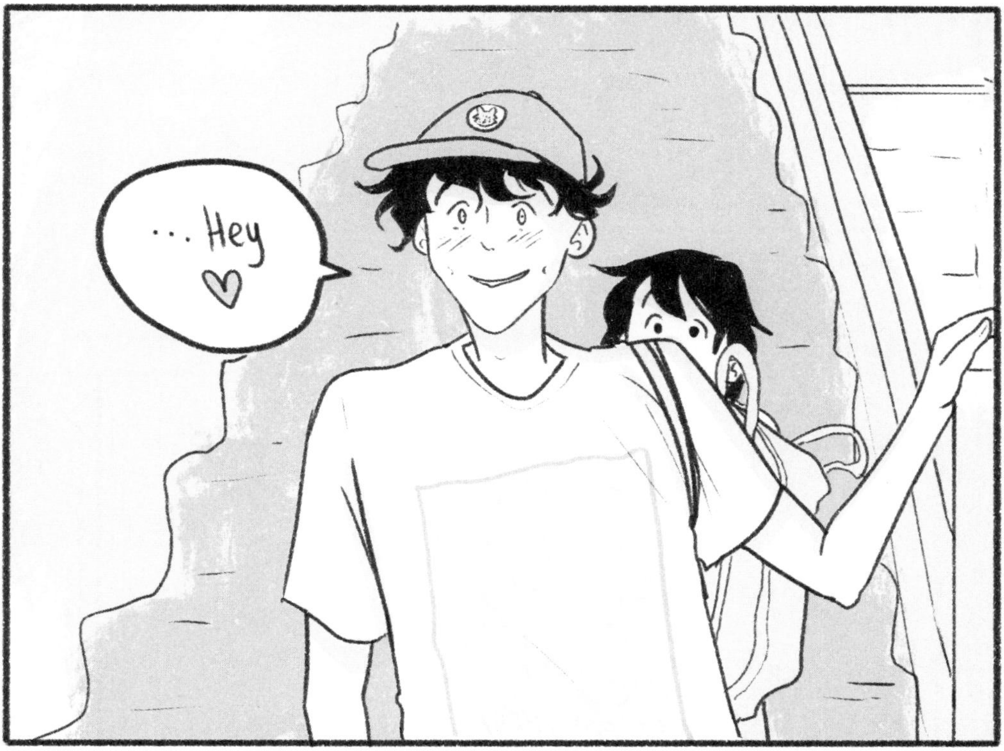
...Hey ♡

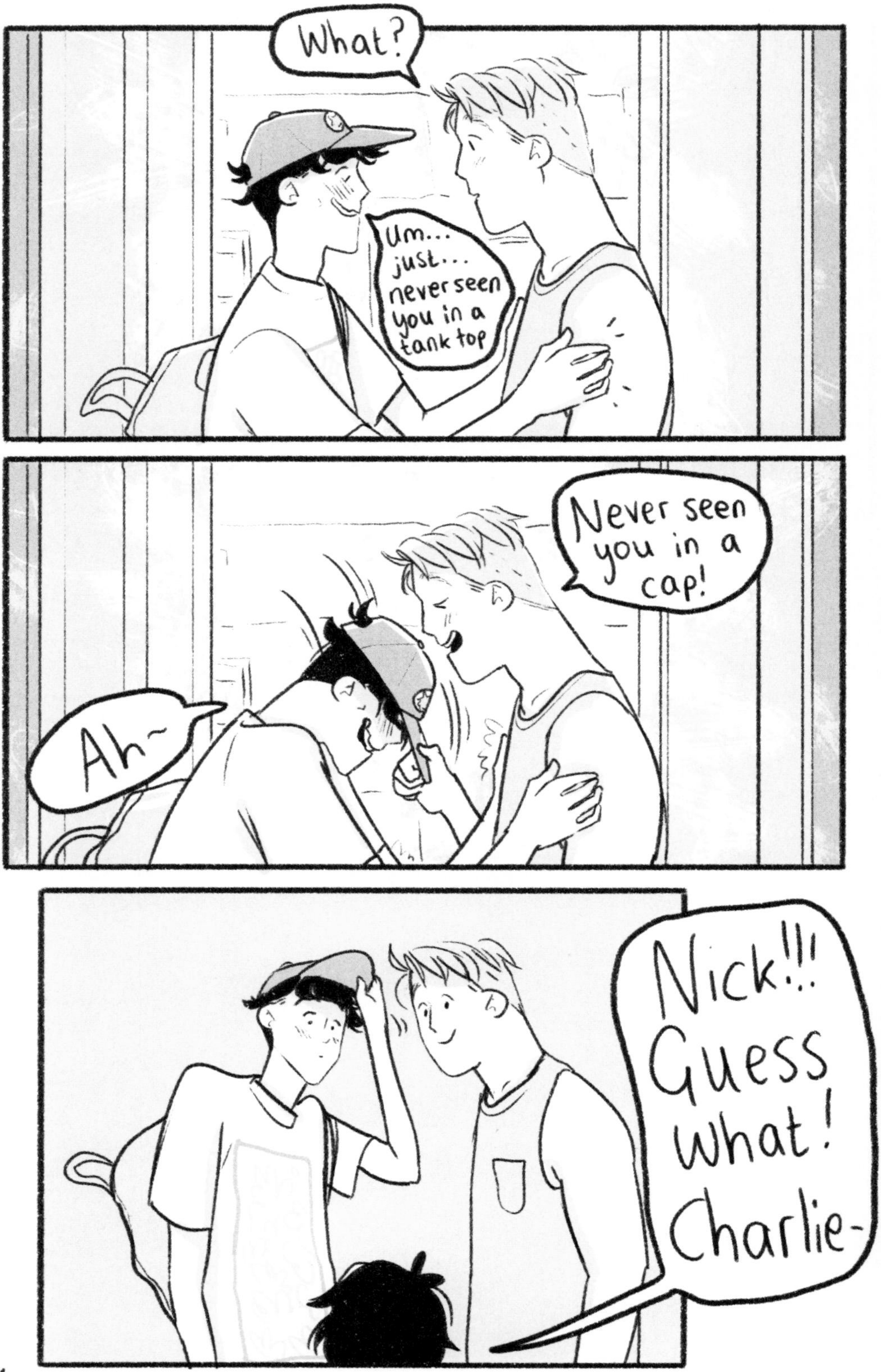
What?
Um... just... never seen you in a tank top
Never seen you in a cap!
Ah~
Nick!!! Guess what! Charlie-

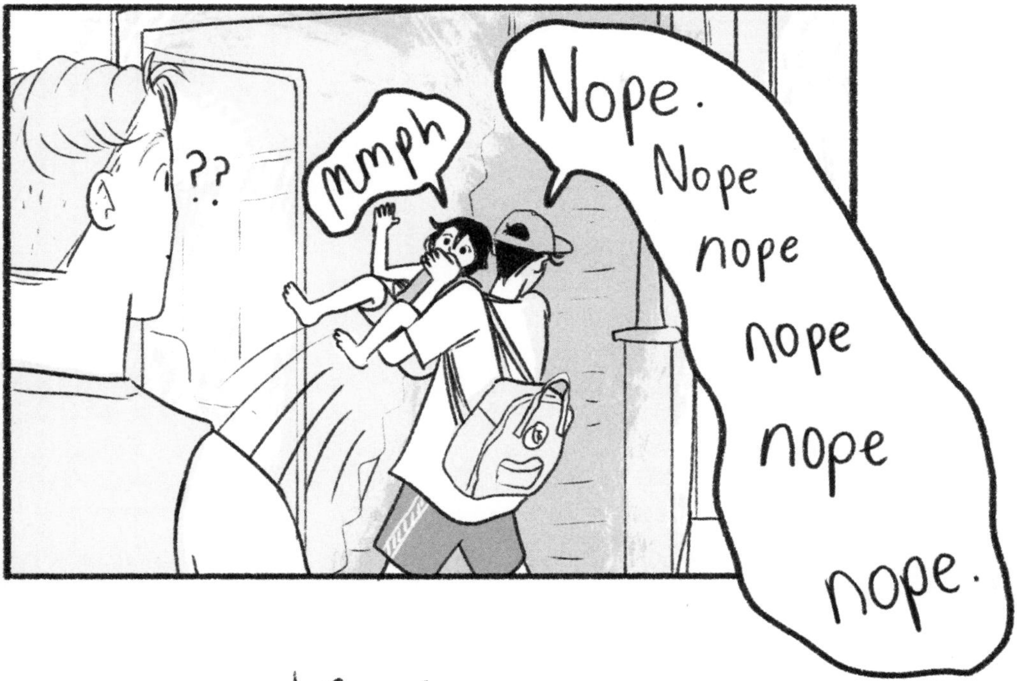
??
mmph
Nope.
Nope
nope
nope
nope
nope.

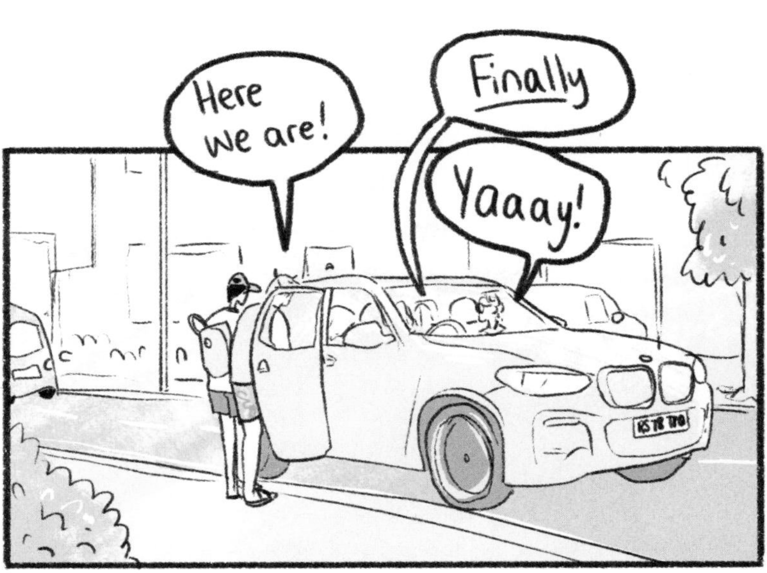
Here we are!
Finally
Yaaay!

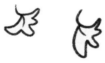

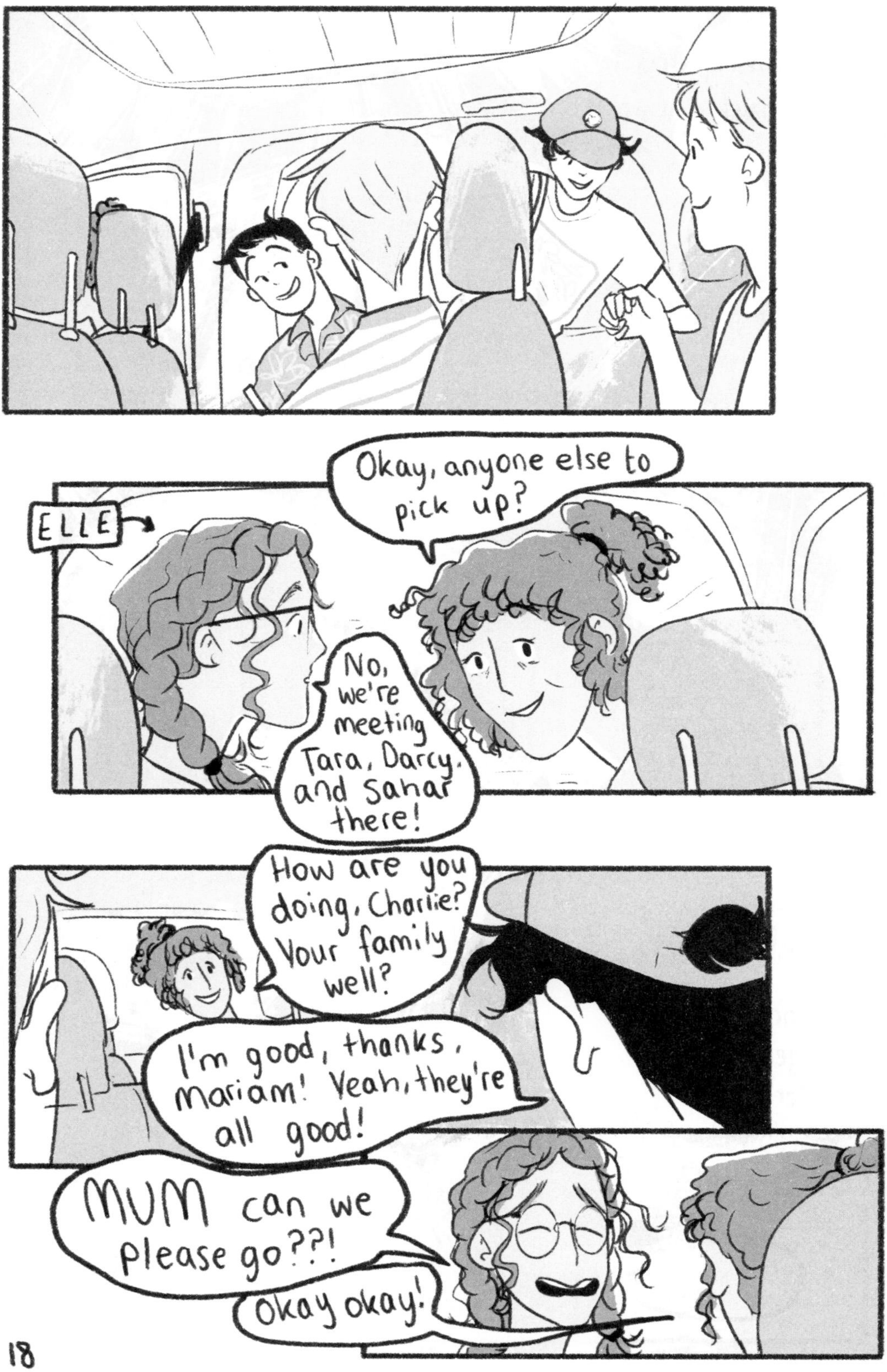

ELLE
Okay, anyone else to pick up?
No, we're meeting Tara, Darcy, and Sahar there!
How are you doing, Charlie? Your family well?
I'm good, thanks, Mariam! Yeah, they're all good!
MUM can we please go??!
Okay okay!

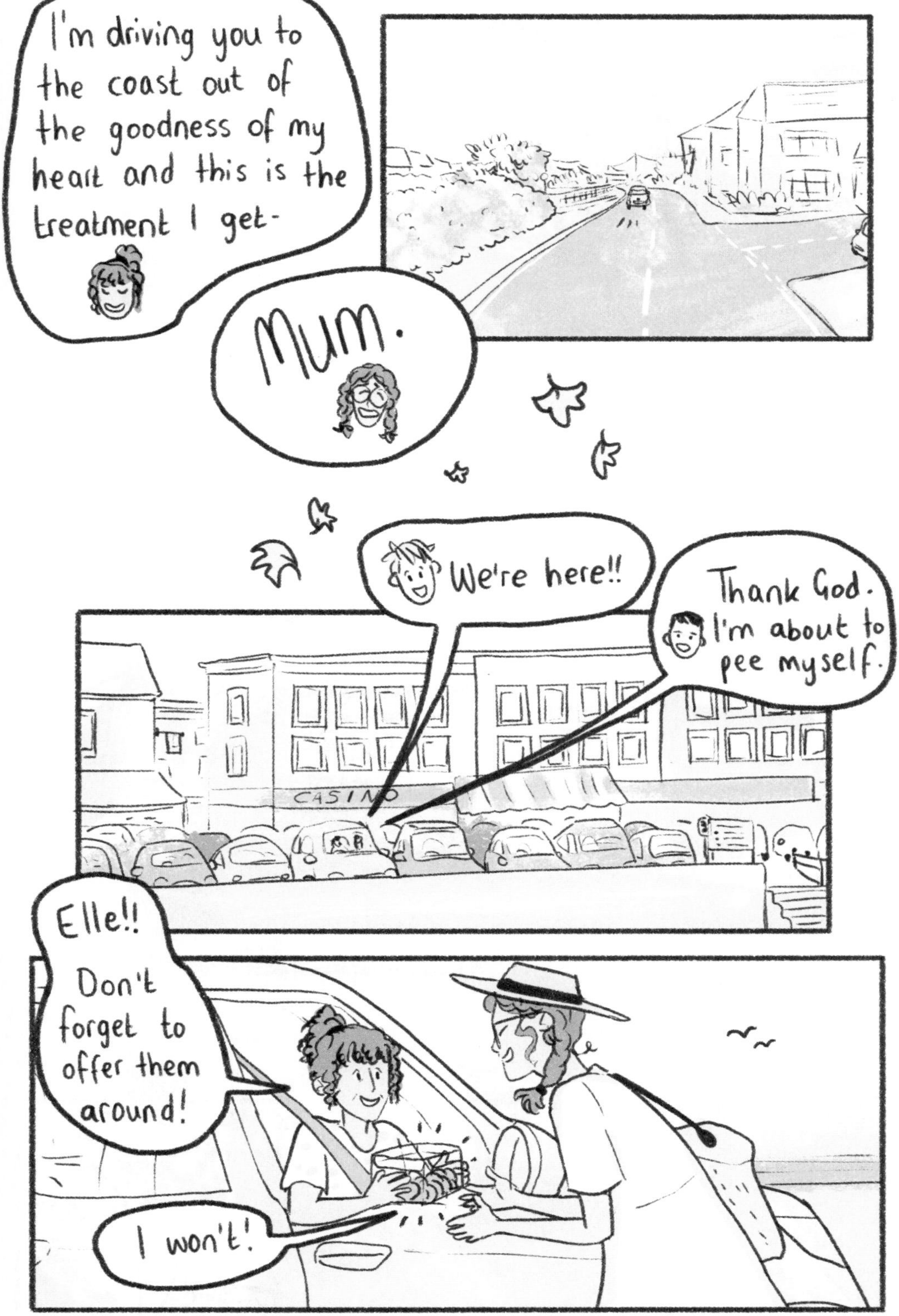
I'm driving you to the coast out of the goodness of my heart and this is the treatment I get-
Mum.
We're here!!
Thank God. I'm about to pee myself.
CASINO
Elle!! Don't forget to offer them around!
I won't!

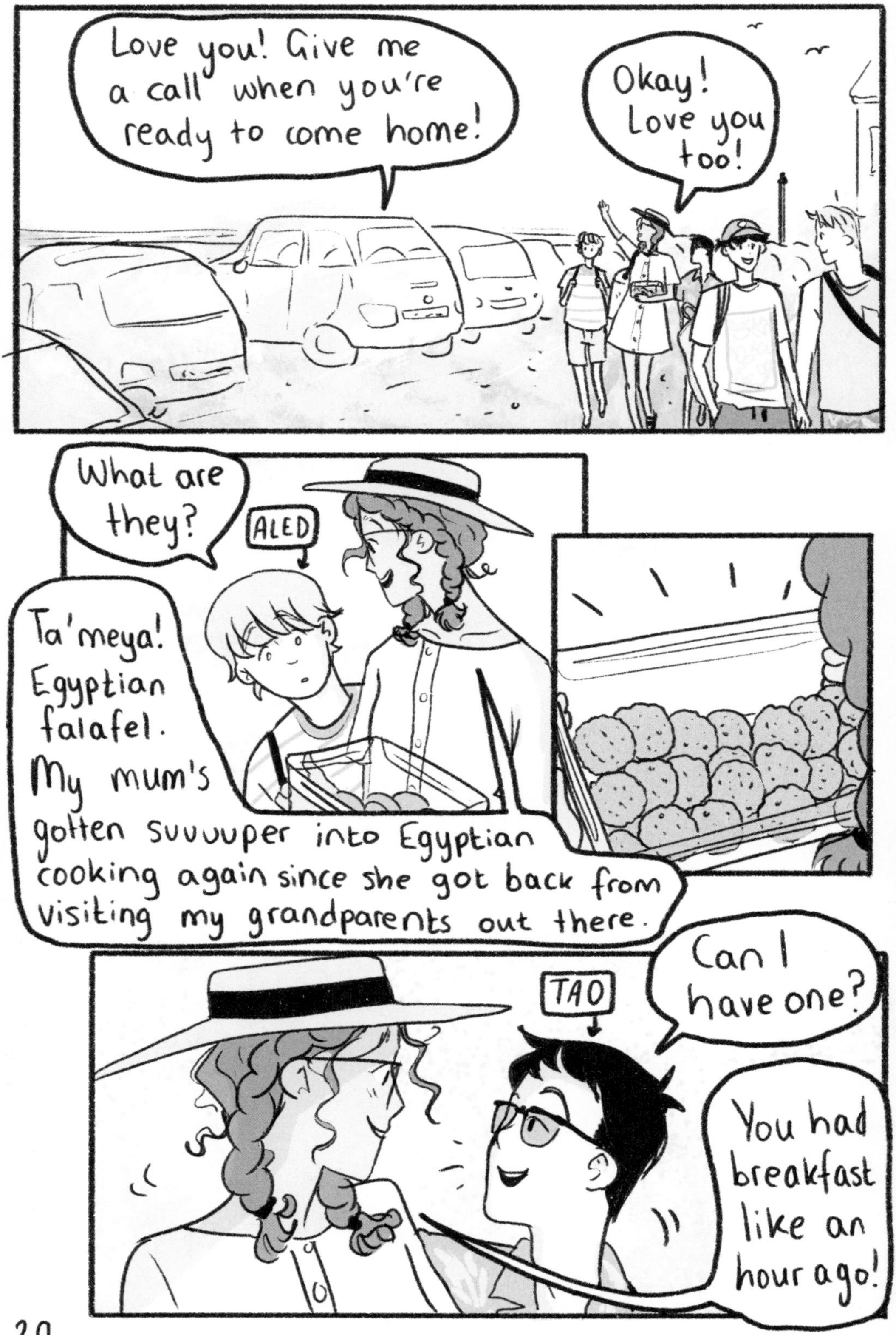
Love you! Give me a call when you're ready to come home!
Okay! Love you too!
What are they?
ALED
Ta'meya! Egyptian falafel. My mum's gotten suuuuper into Egyptian cooking again since she got back from visiting my grandparents out there.
TAO
Can I have one?
You had breakfast like an hour ago!

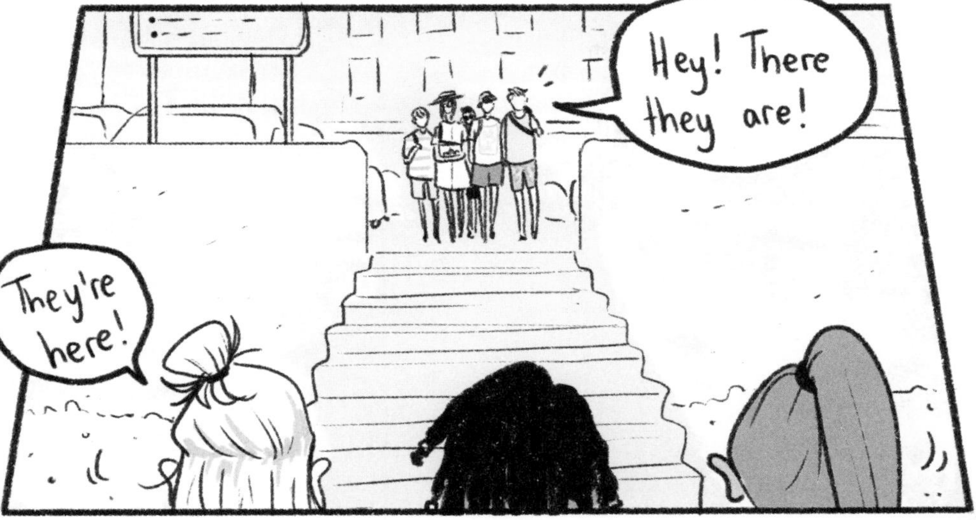
Hey! There they are!
They're here!

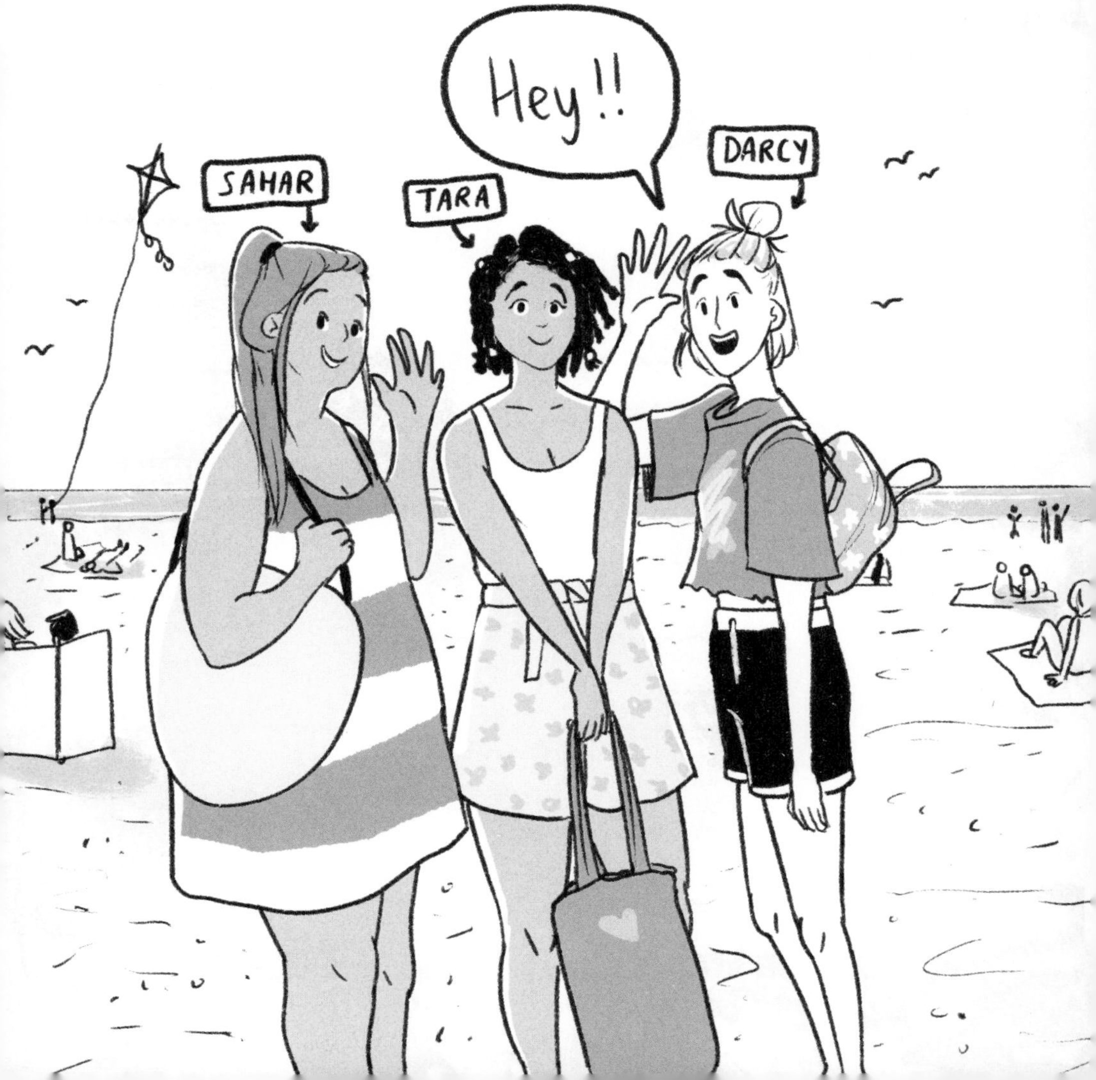
Hey!!
SAHAR
TARA
DARCY

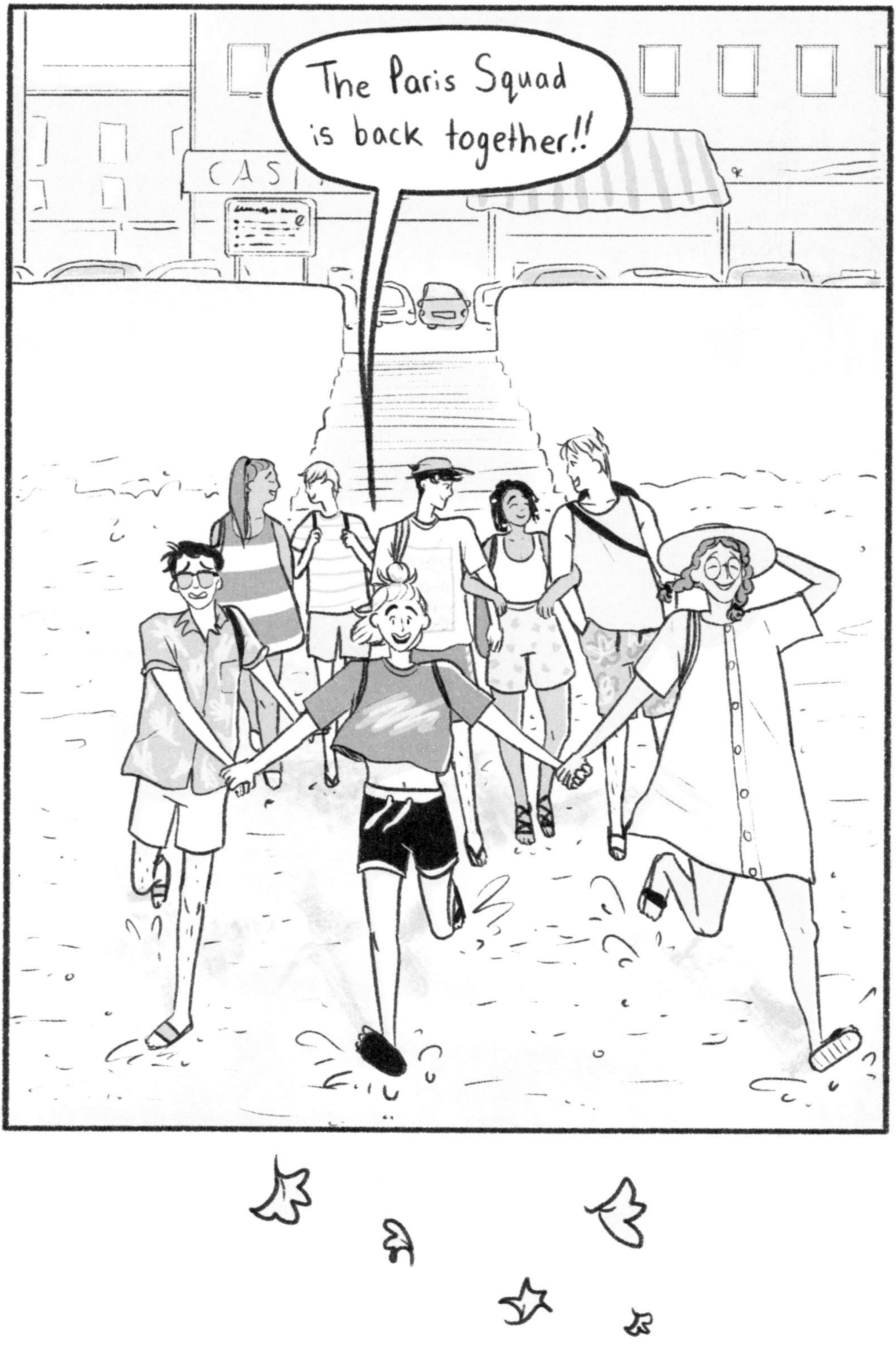
The Paris Squad is back together!!

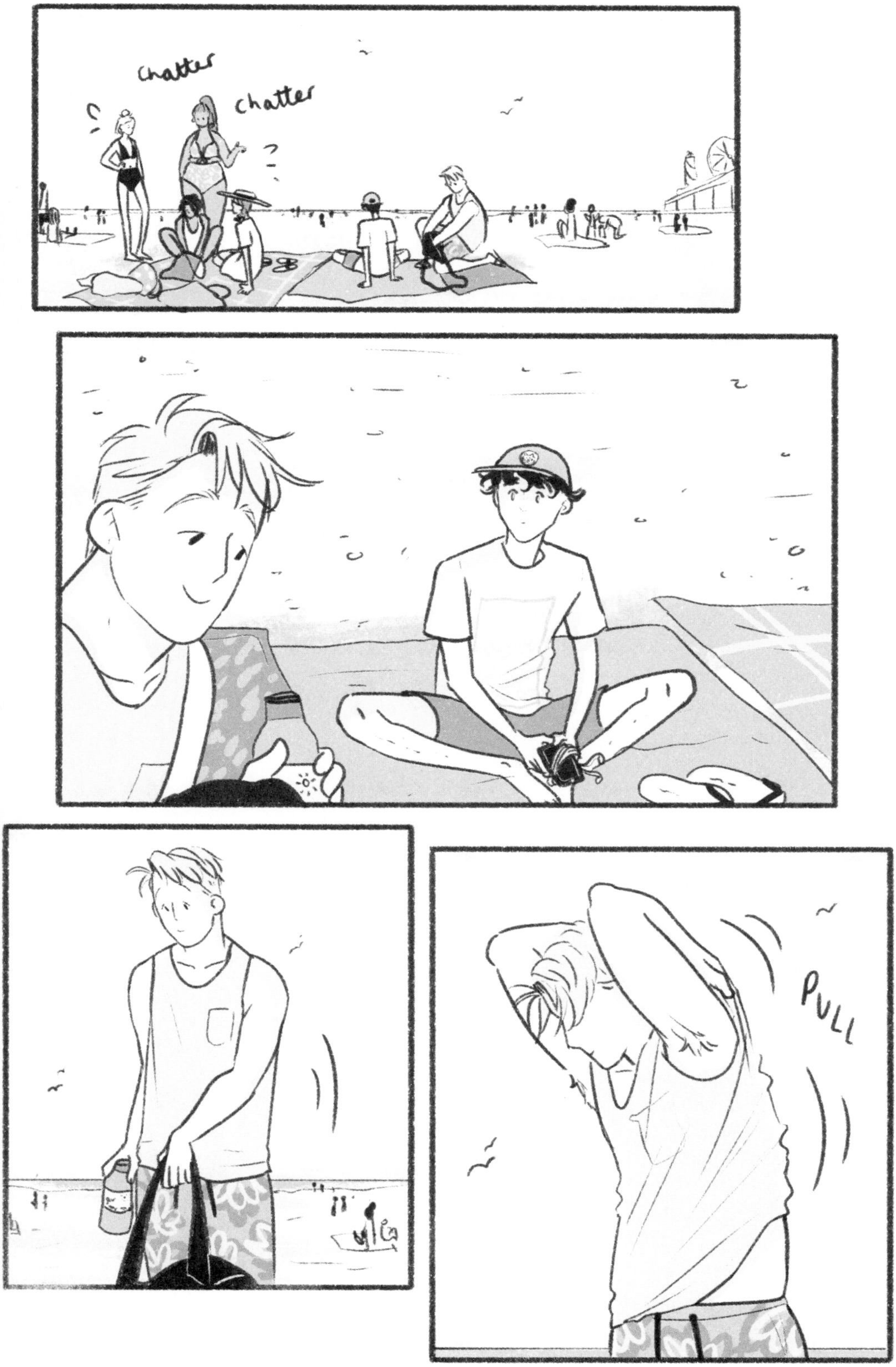
chatter
chatter
PULL

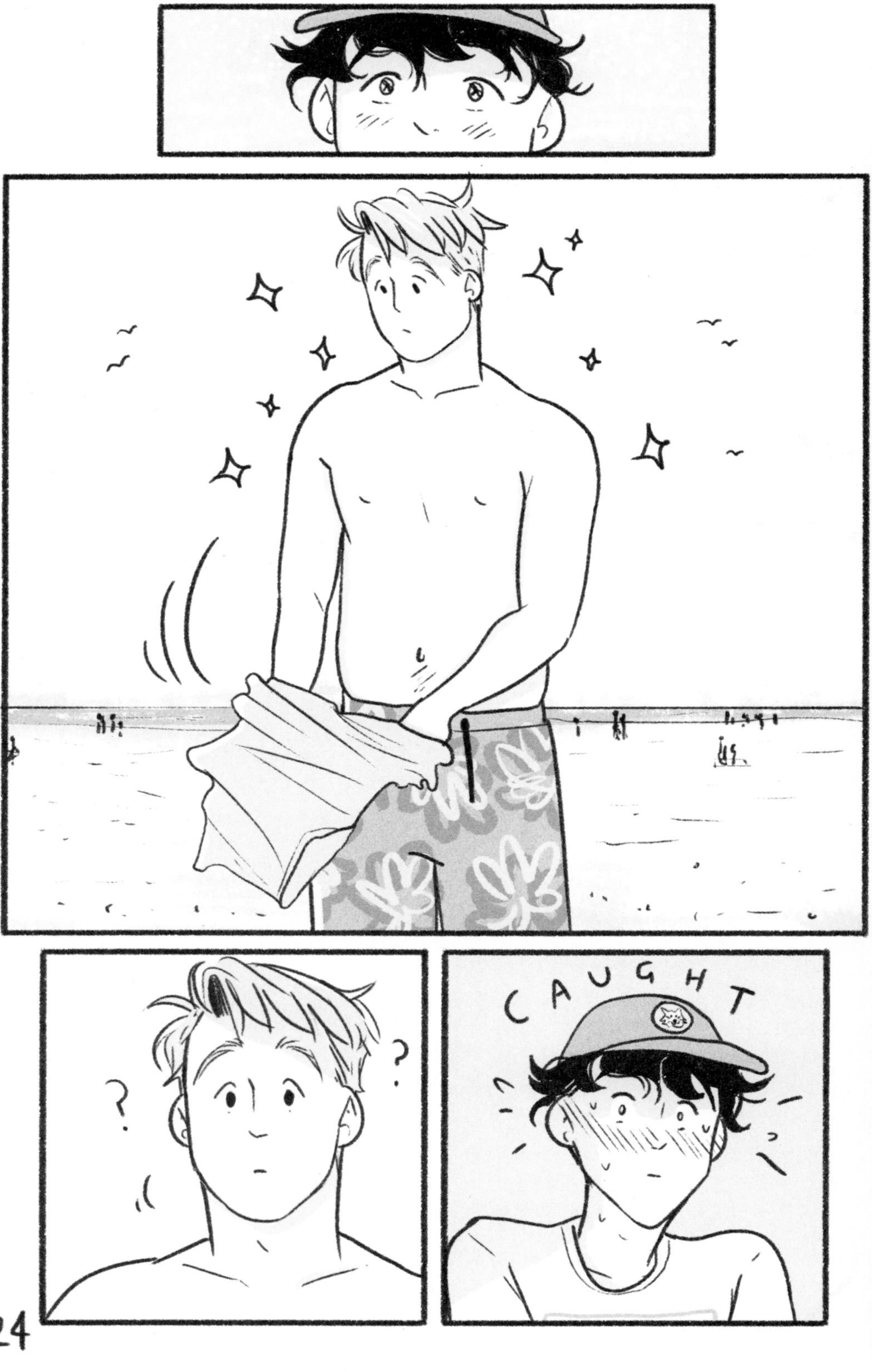
CAUGHT

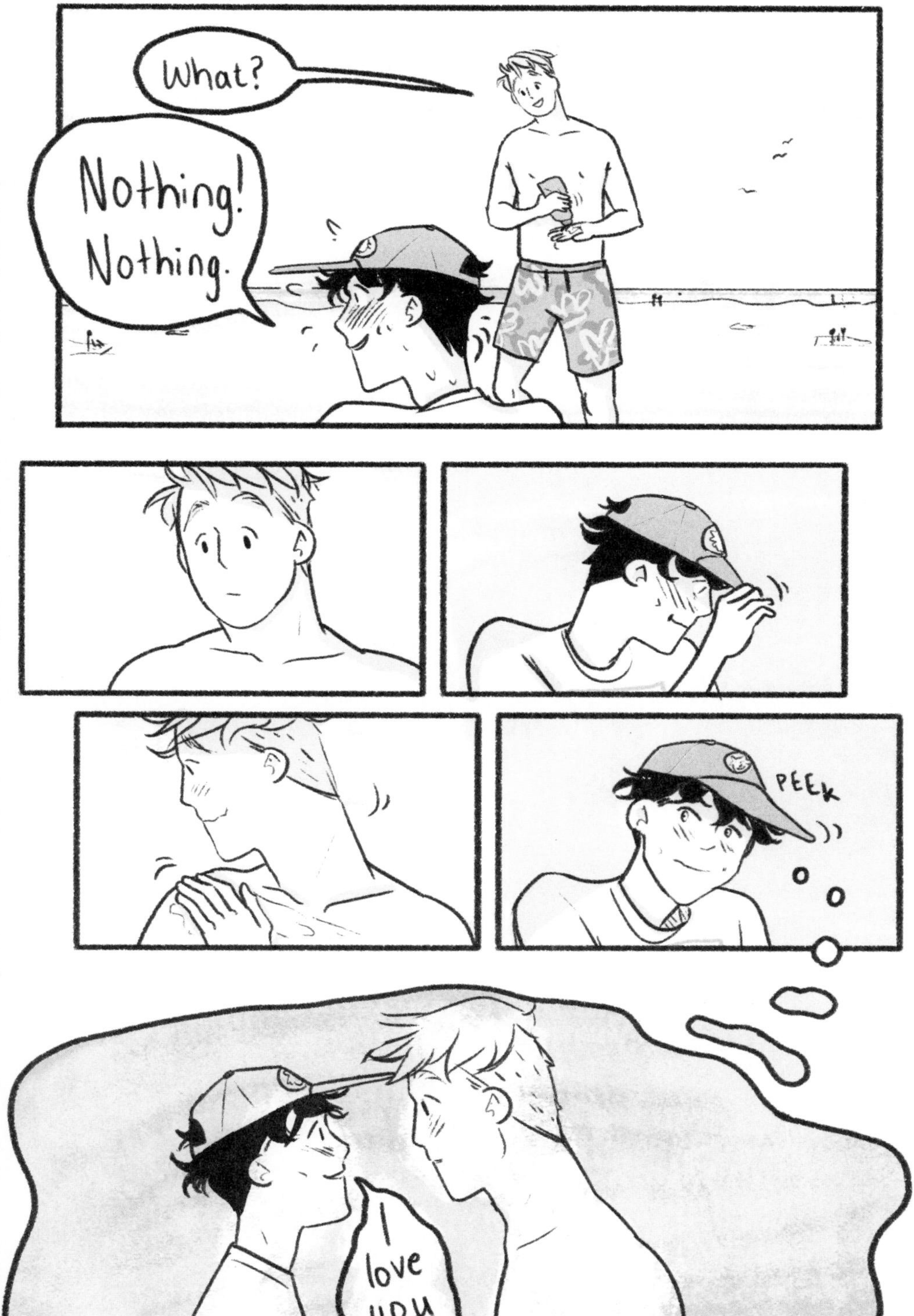
What?
Nothing! Nothing.
PEEK
I love you

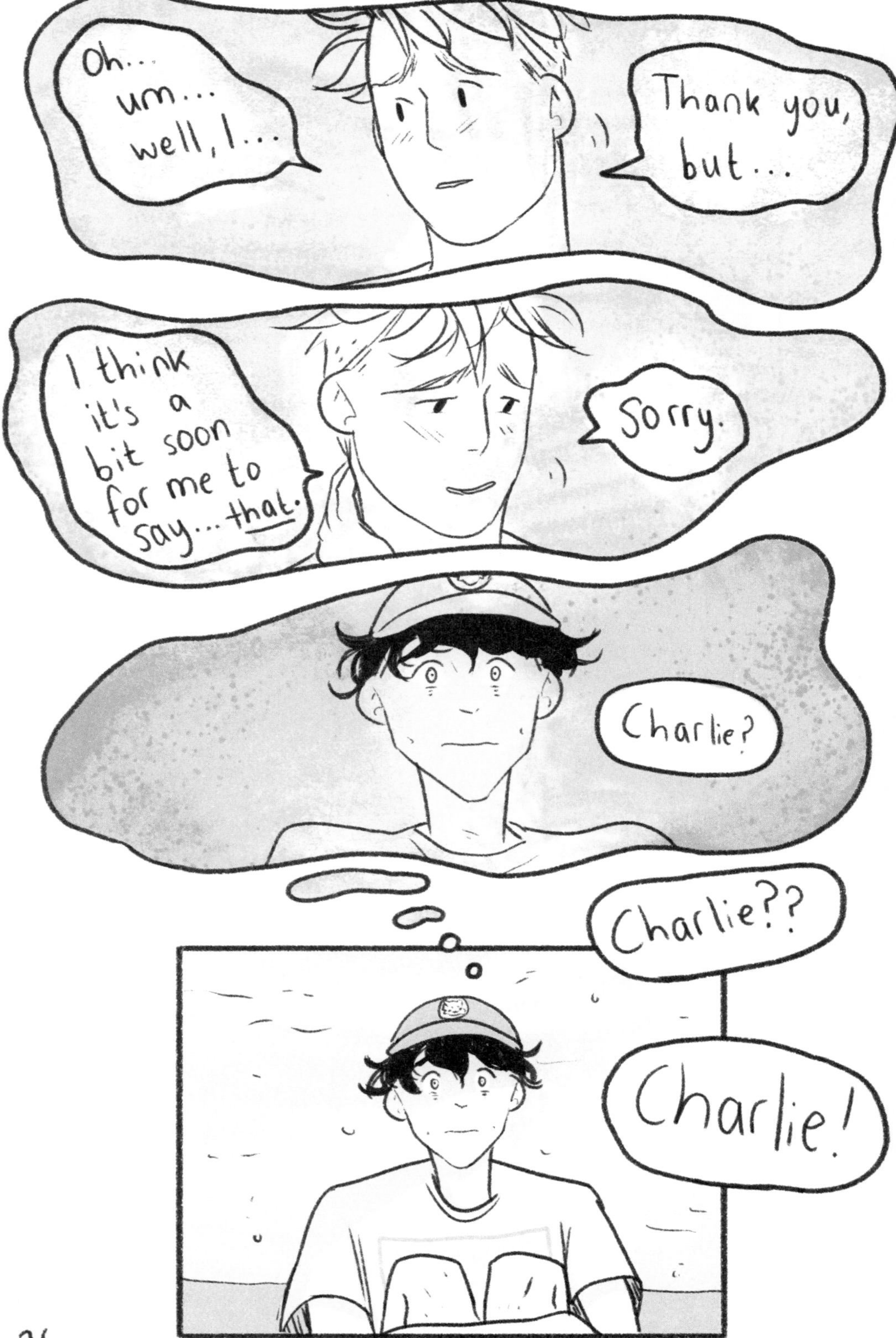
Oh... um... well, I...
Thank you, but...
I think it's a bit soon for me to say... that.
Sorry.
Charlie?
Charlie??
Charlie!

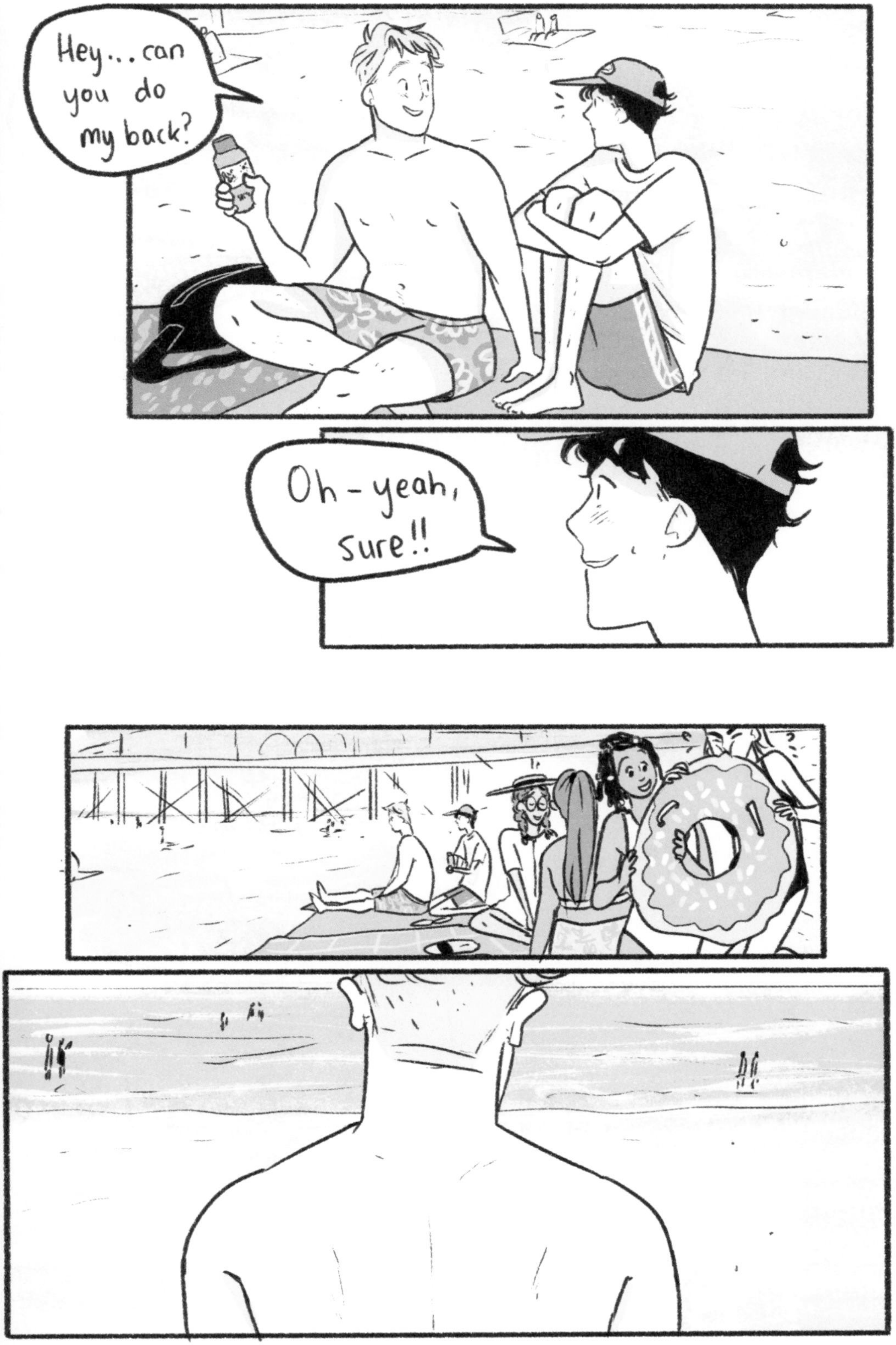
Hey... can you do my back?
Oh - yeah, sure!!

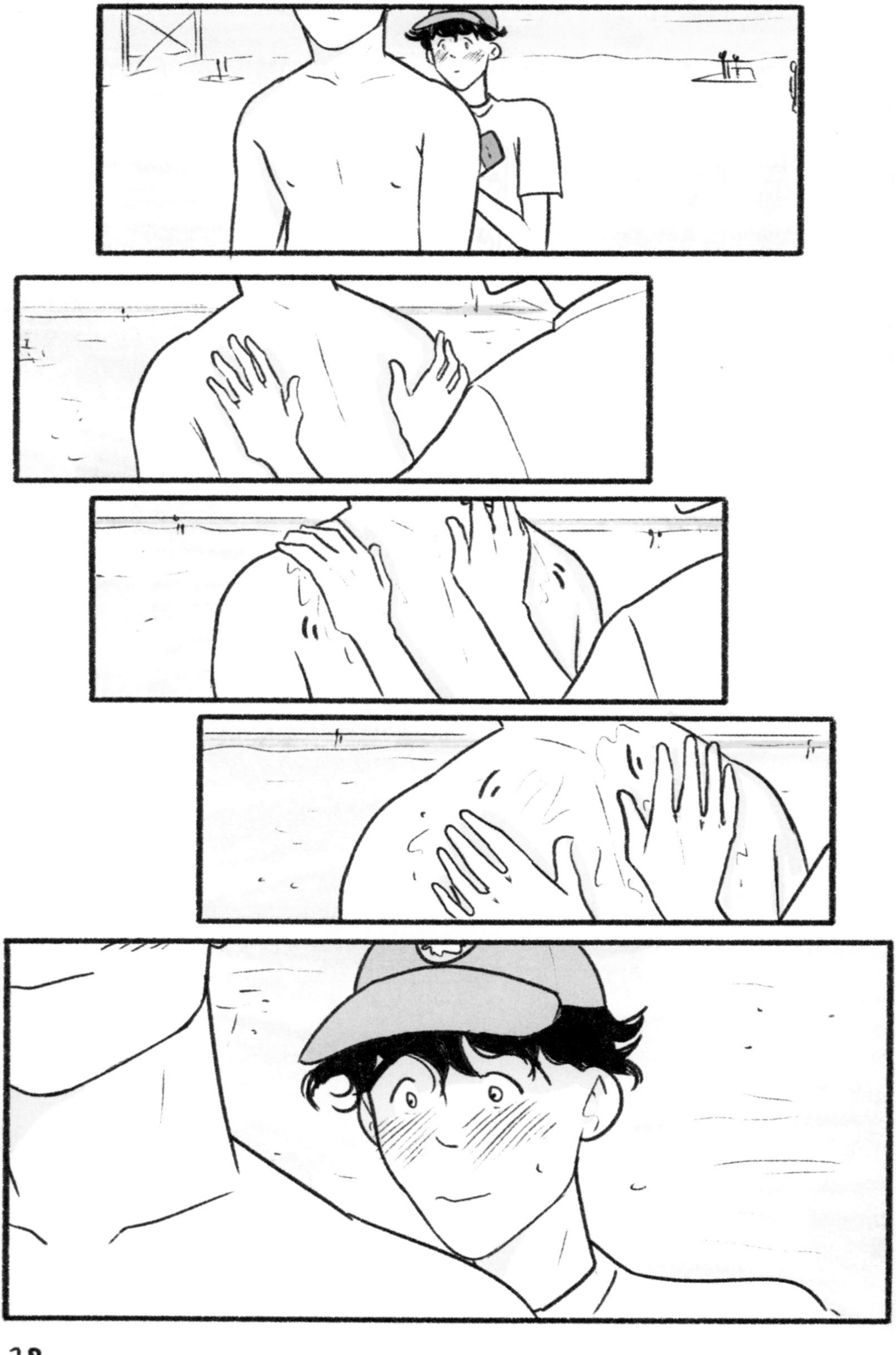

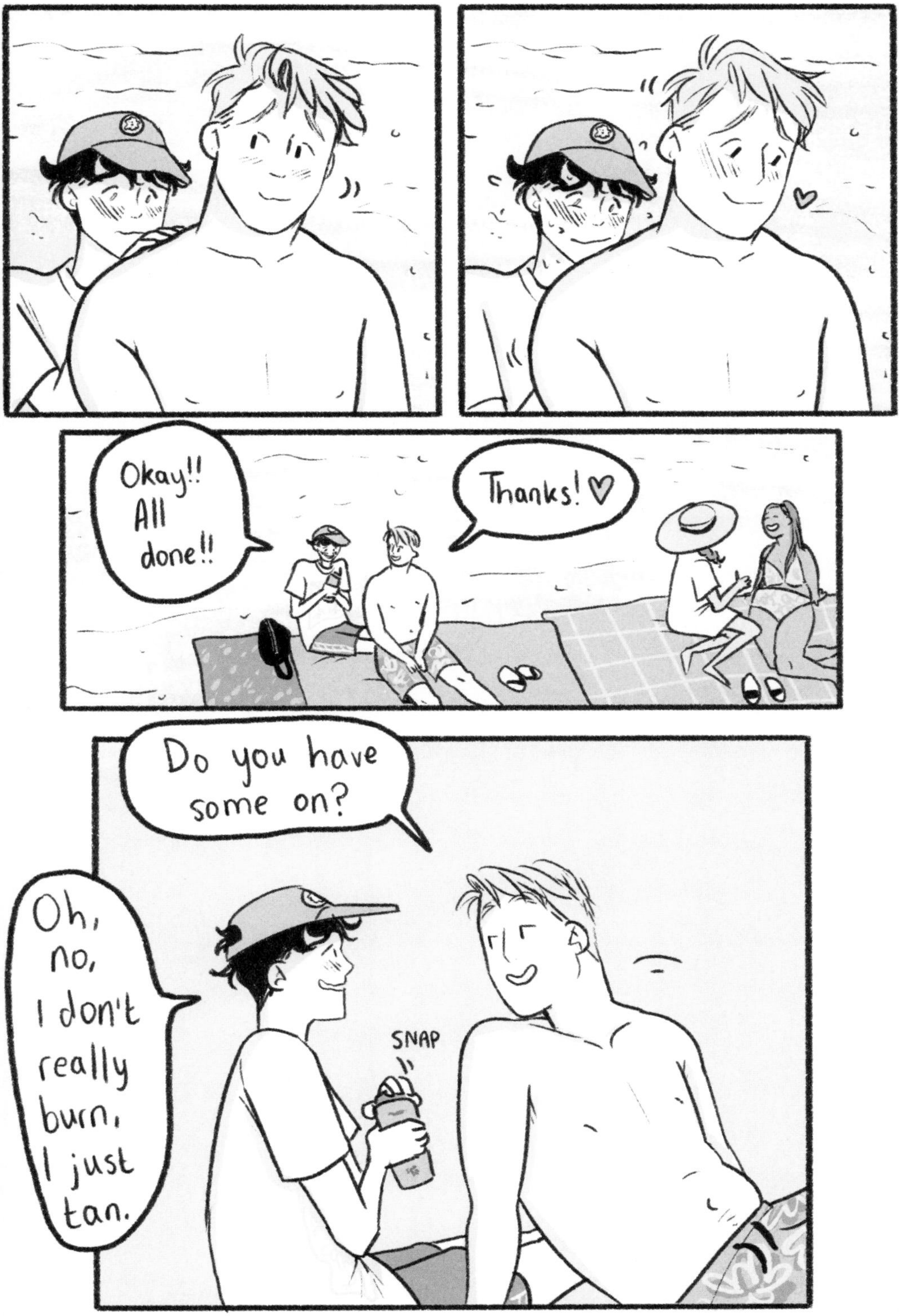
Okay!! All done!!
Thanks! ♡
Do you have some on?
Oh, no, I don't really burn, I just tan.
SNAP

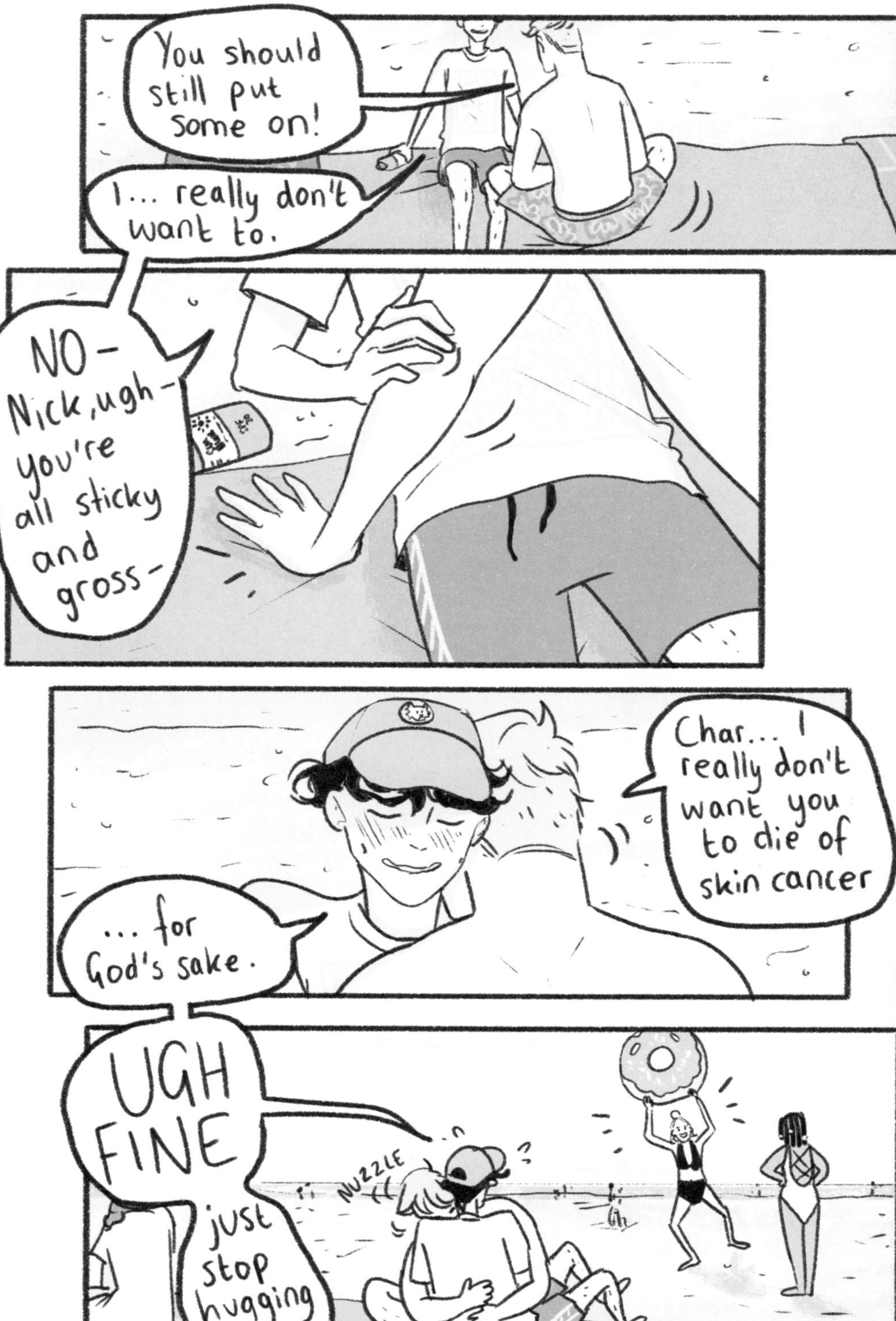
You should still put some on!
I... really don't want to.
NO- Nick, ugh- you're all sticky and gross-
Char... I really don't want you to die of skin cancer
... for God's sake.
UGH FINE
just stop hugging me
NUZZLE

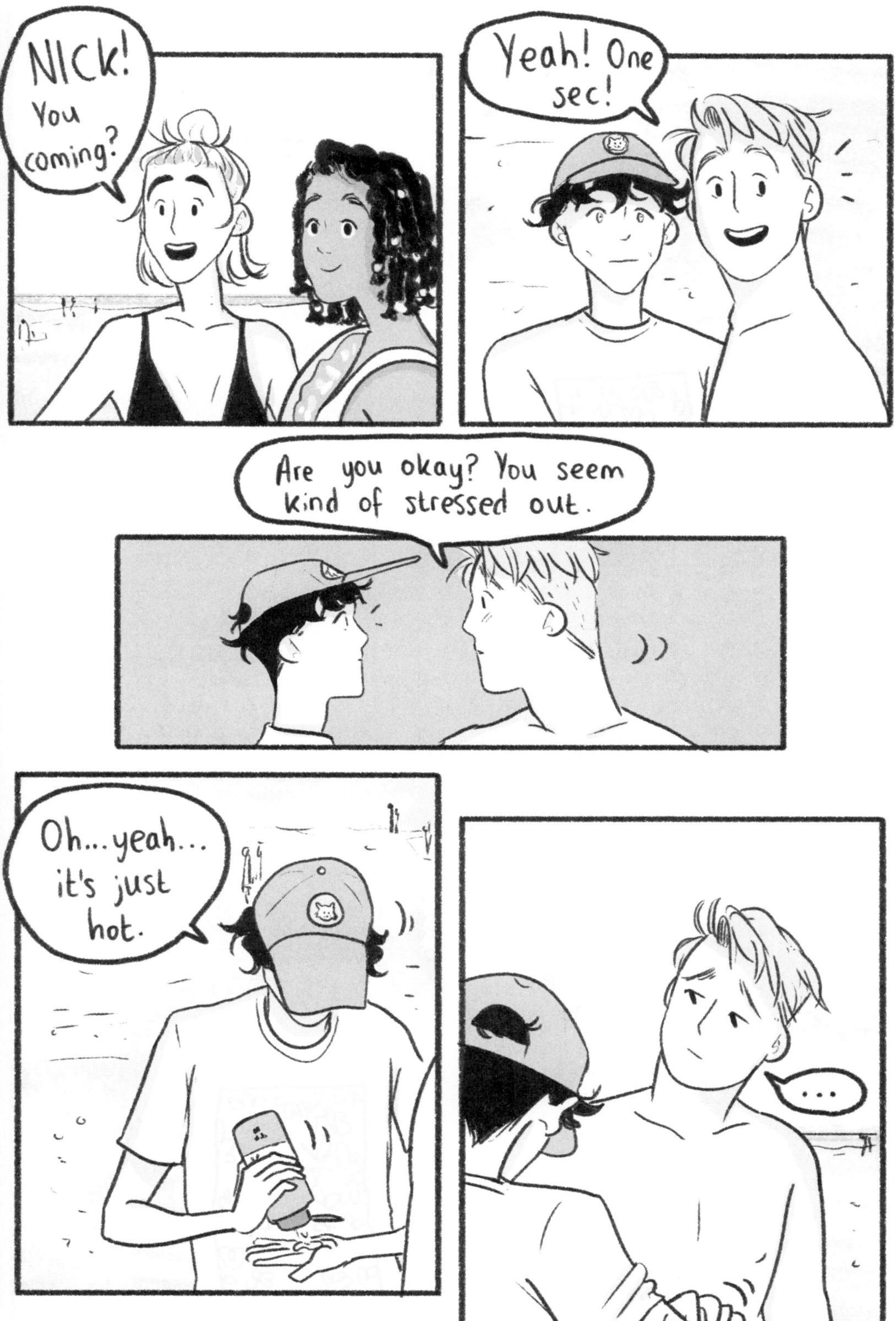
NICK! You coming?
Yeah! One sec!
Are you okay? You seem kind of stressed out.
Oh... yeah... it's just hot.
...

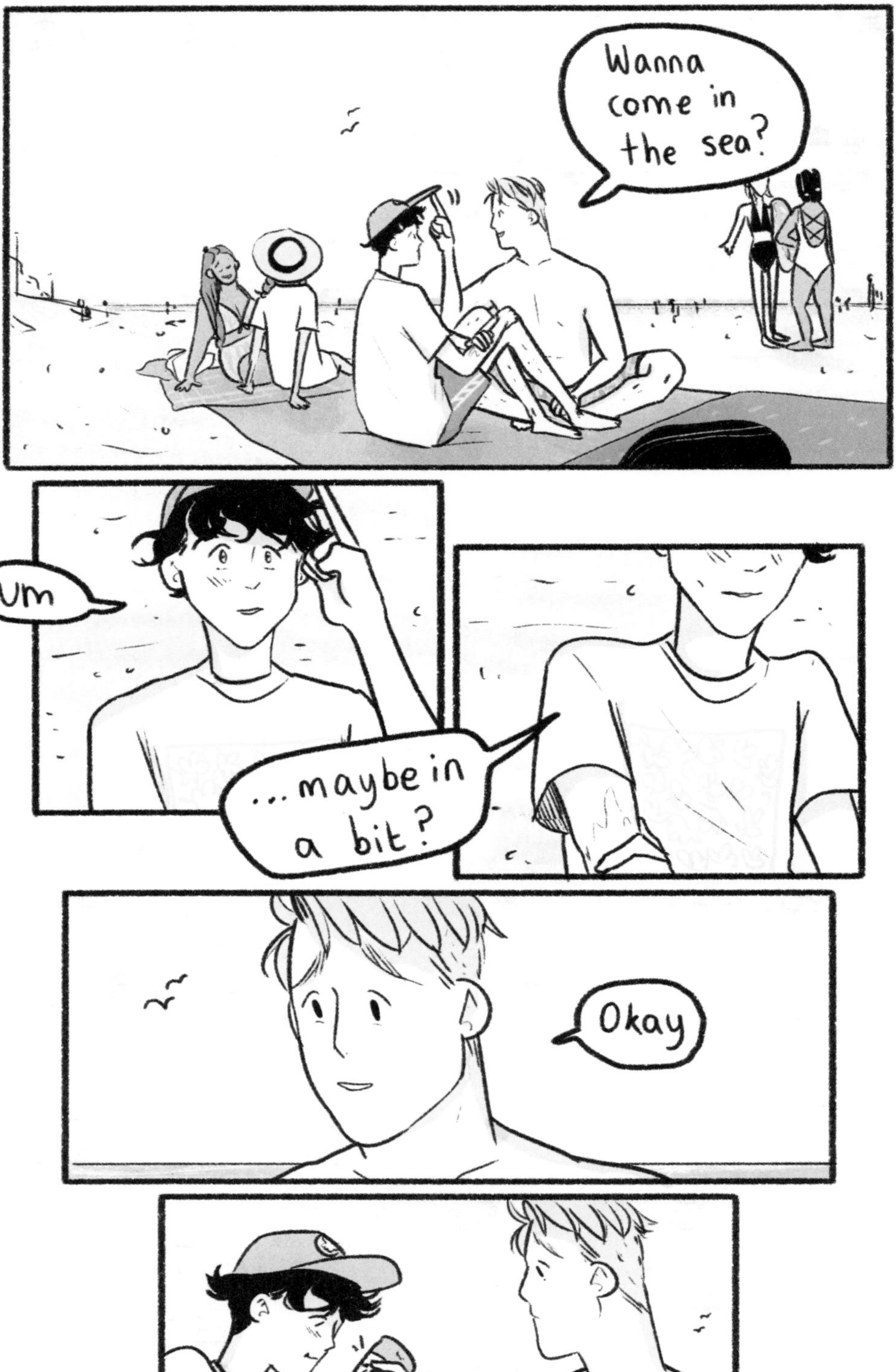
Wanna come in the sea?
Um
...maybe in a bit?
Okay

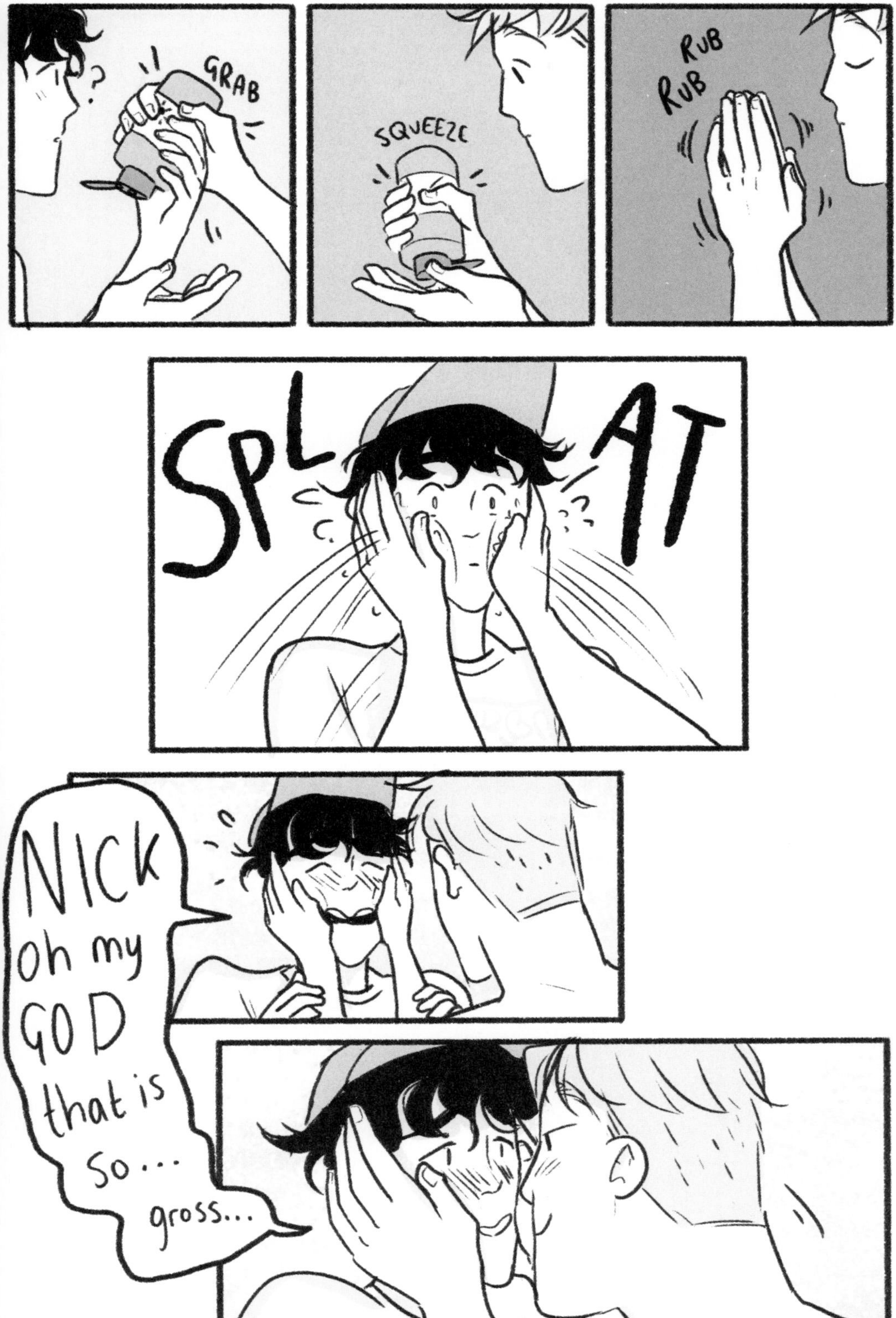
GRAB
SQUEEZE
RUB
RUB
SPLAT
NICK oh my GOD that is so... gross...

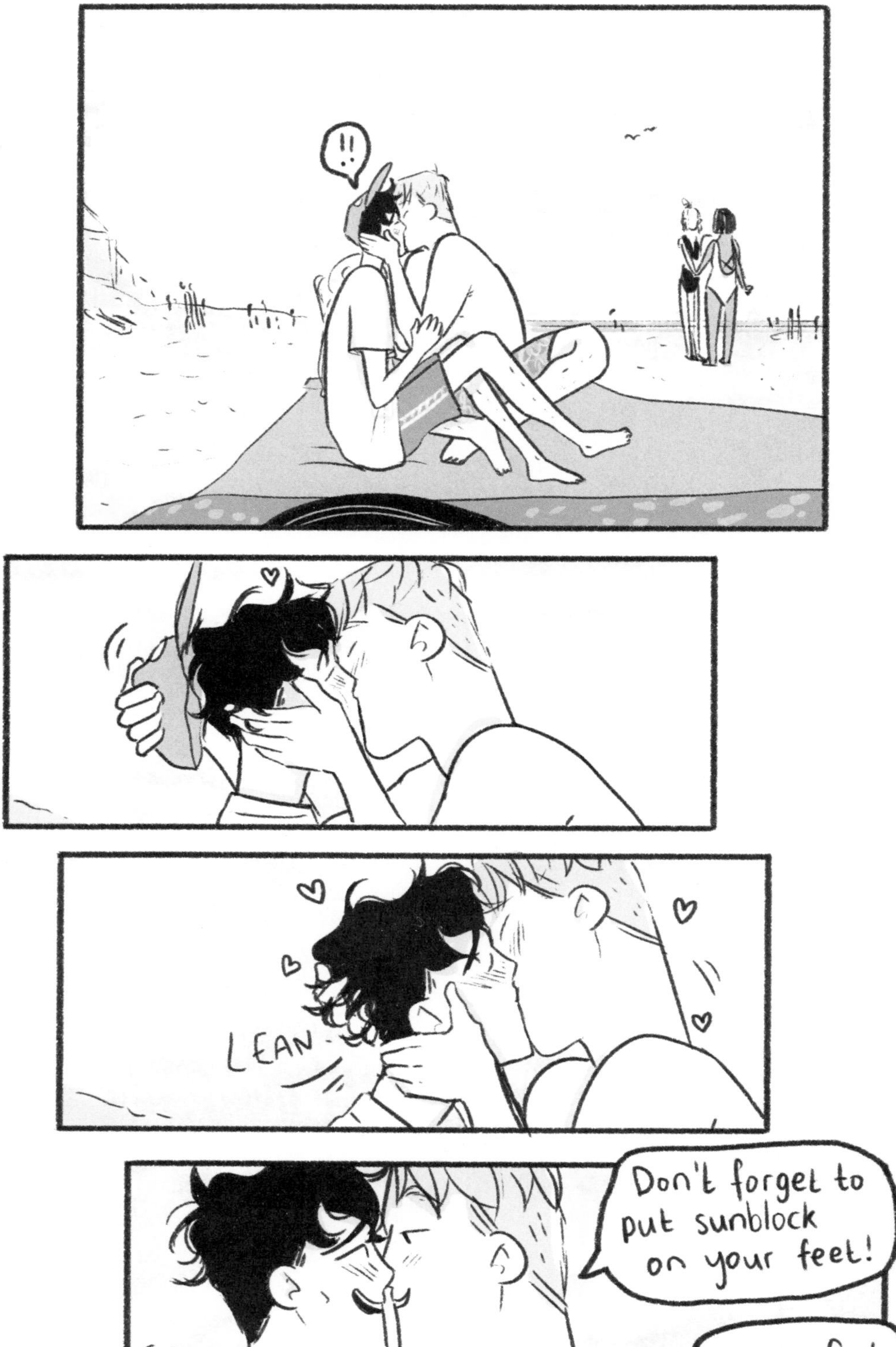
!!
LEAN
Don't forget to put sunblock on your feet!
Oh my God

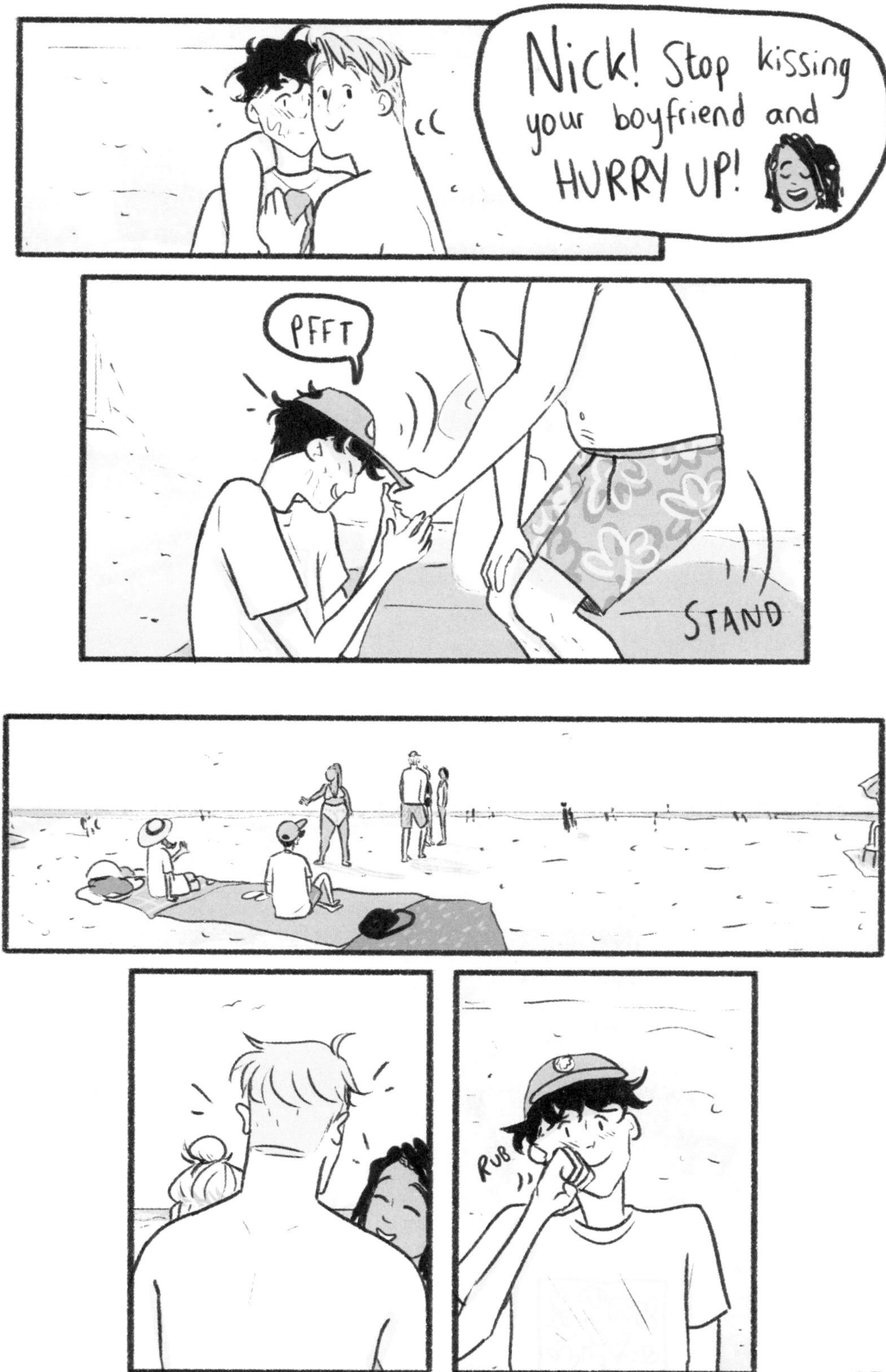
Nick! Stop kissing your boyfriend and HURRY UP!
PFFT
STAND
RUB

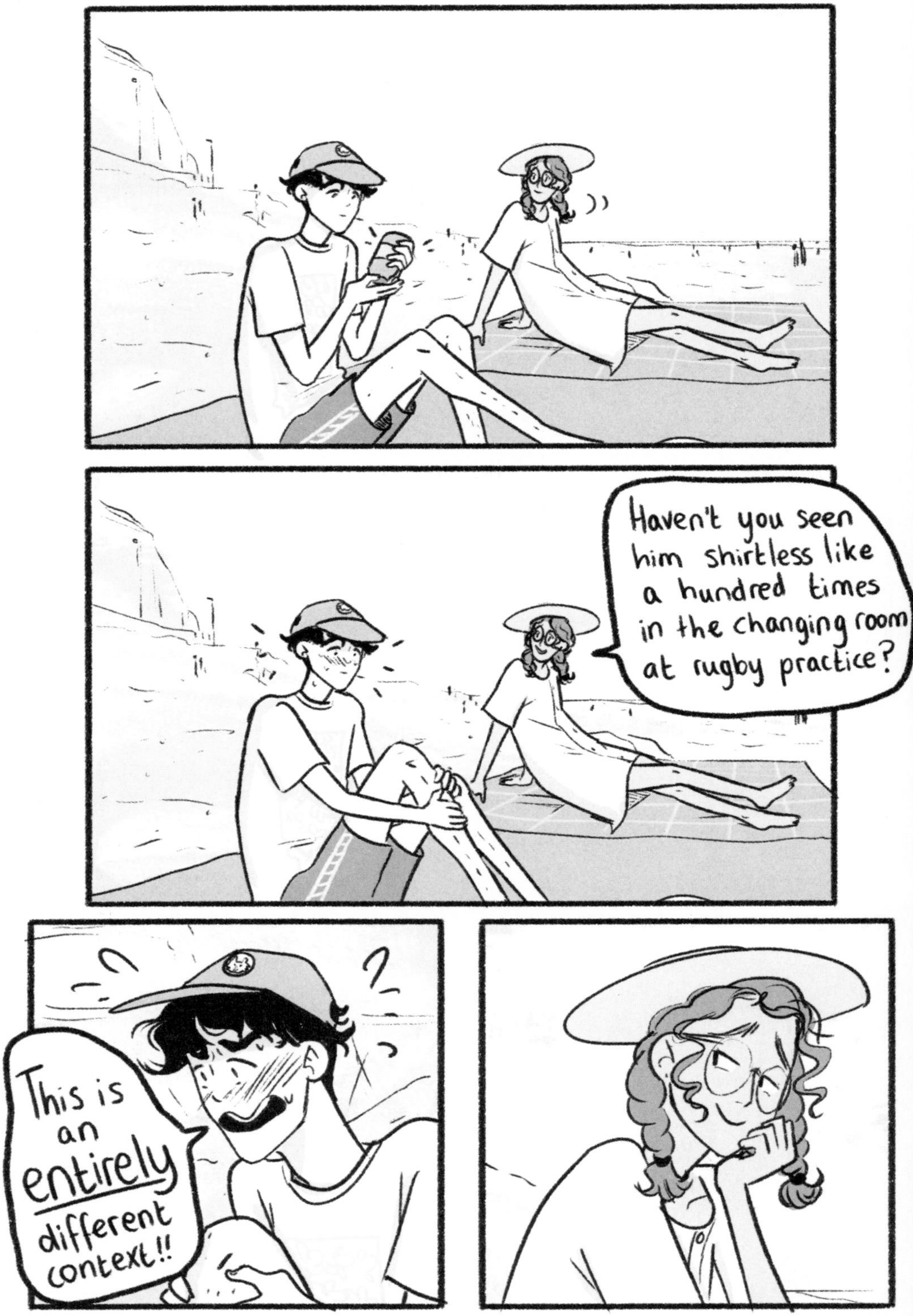
Haven't you seen him shirtless like a hundred times in the changing room at rugby practice?
This is an entirely different context!!

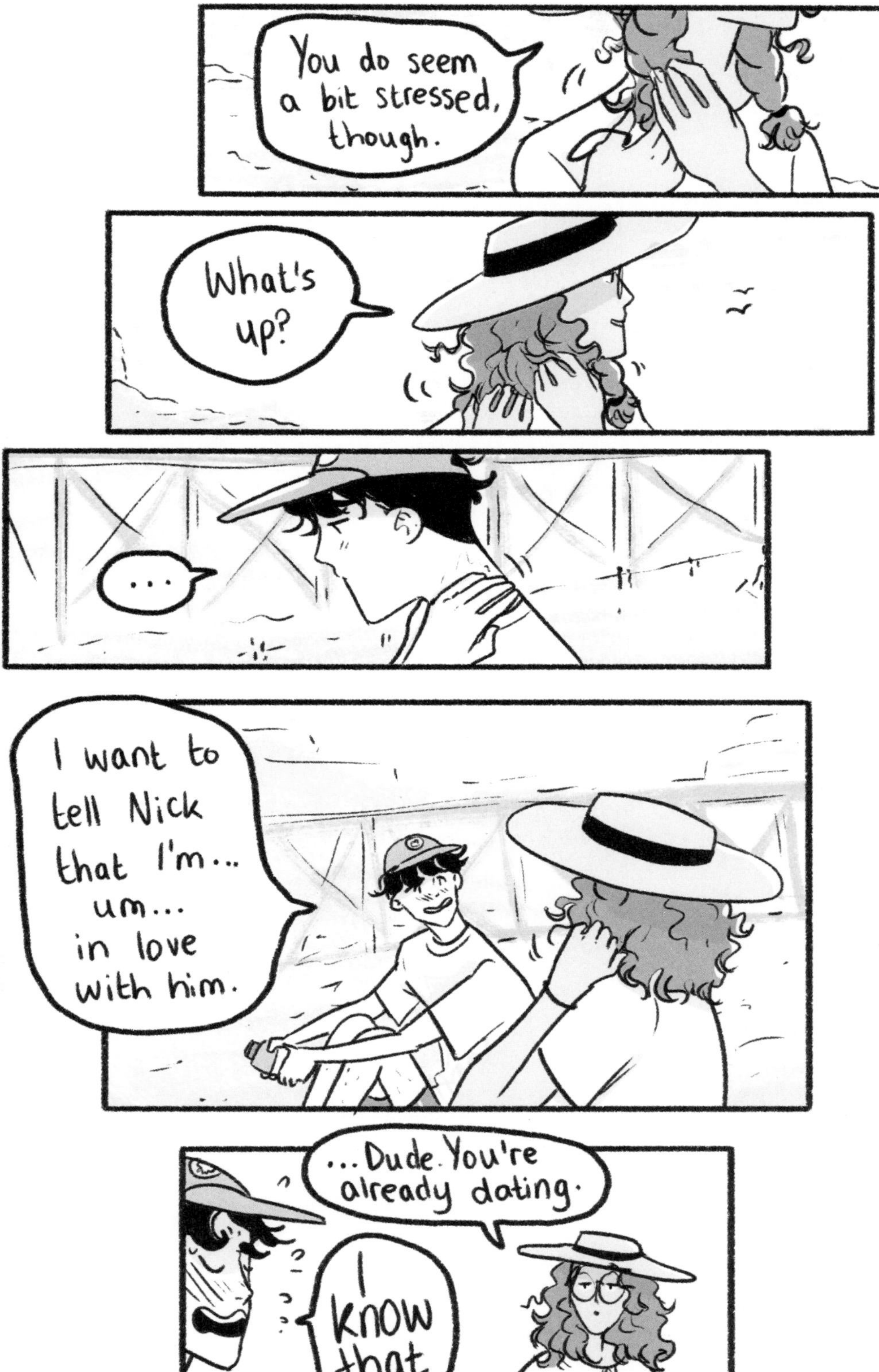
You do seem a bit stressed, though.
What's up?
...
I want to tell Nick that I'm... um... in love with him.
...Dude. You're already dating.
I know that

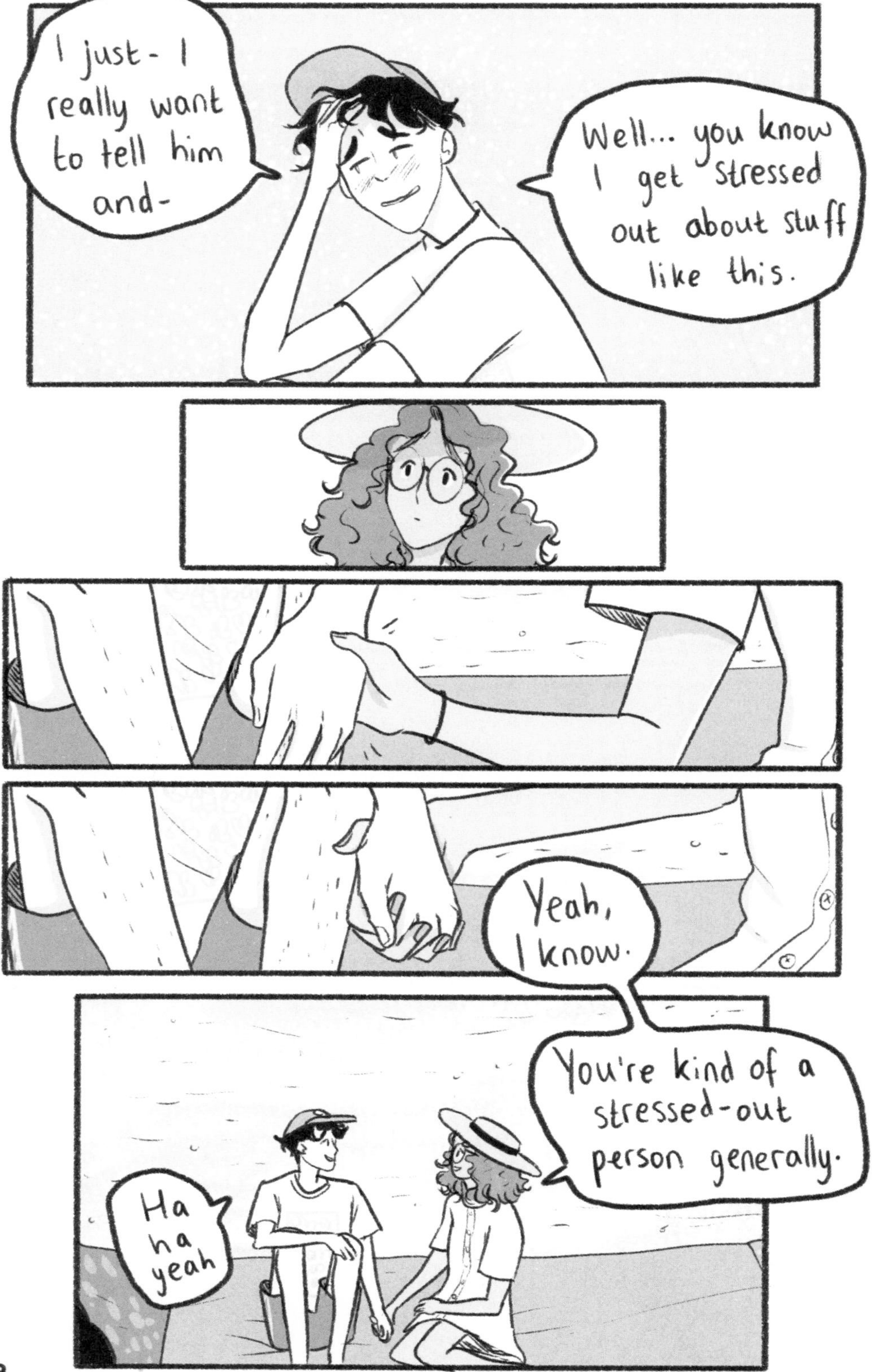
I just- I really want to tell him and-
Well... you know I get stressed out about stuff like this.
Yeah, I know.
You're kind of a stressed-out person generally.
Ha ha yeah

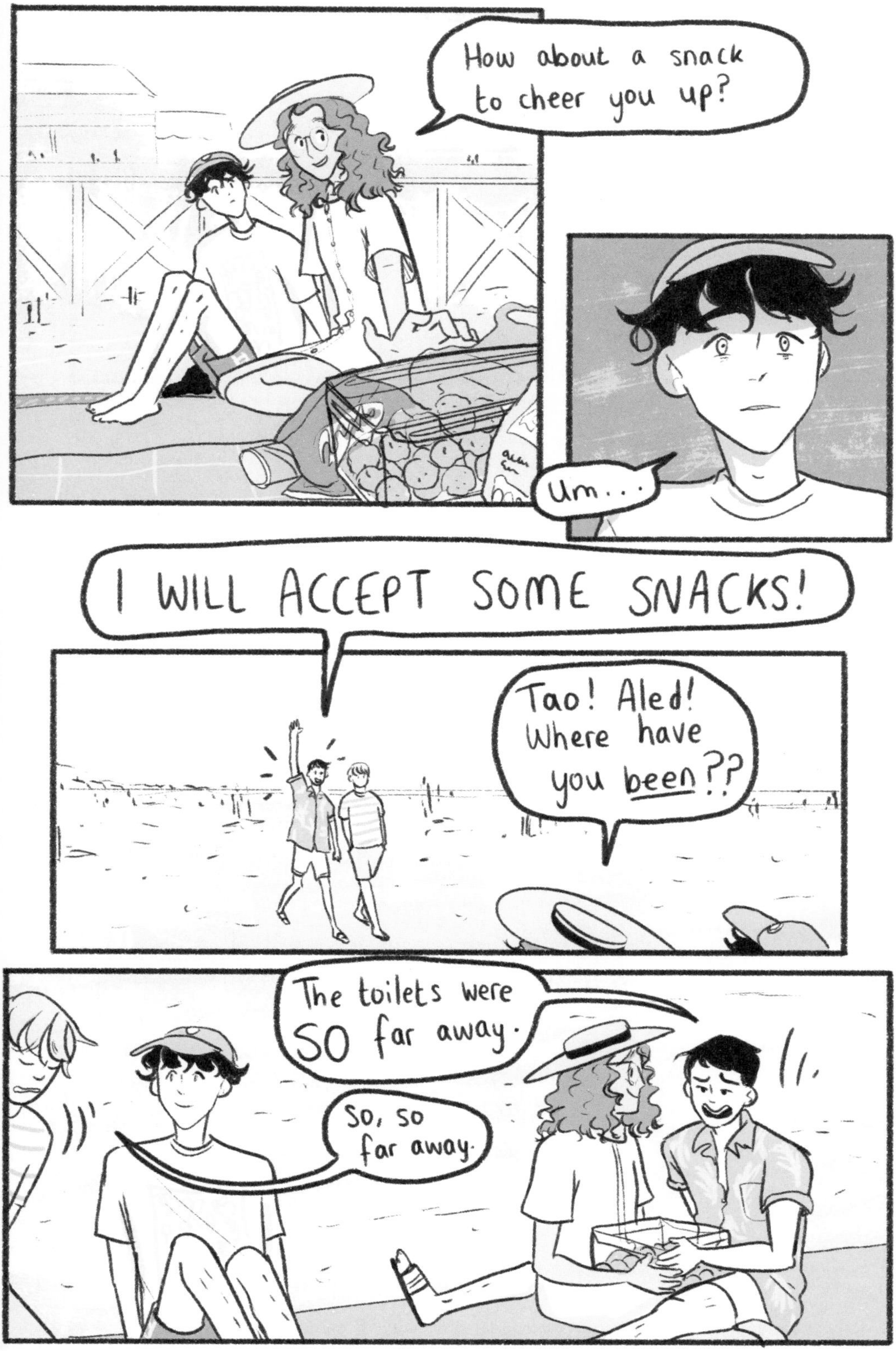
How about a snack to cheer you up?
Um...
I WILL ACCEPT SOME SNACKS!
Tao! Aled! Where have you been??
The toilets were SO far away.
So, so far away.

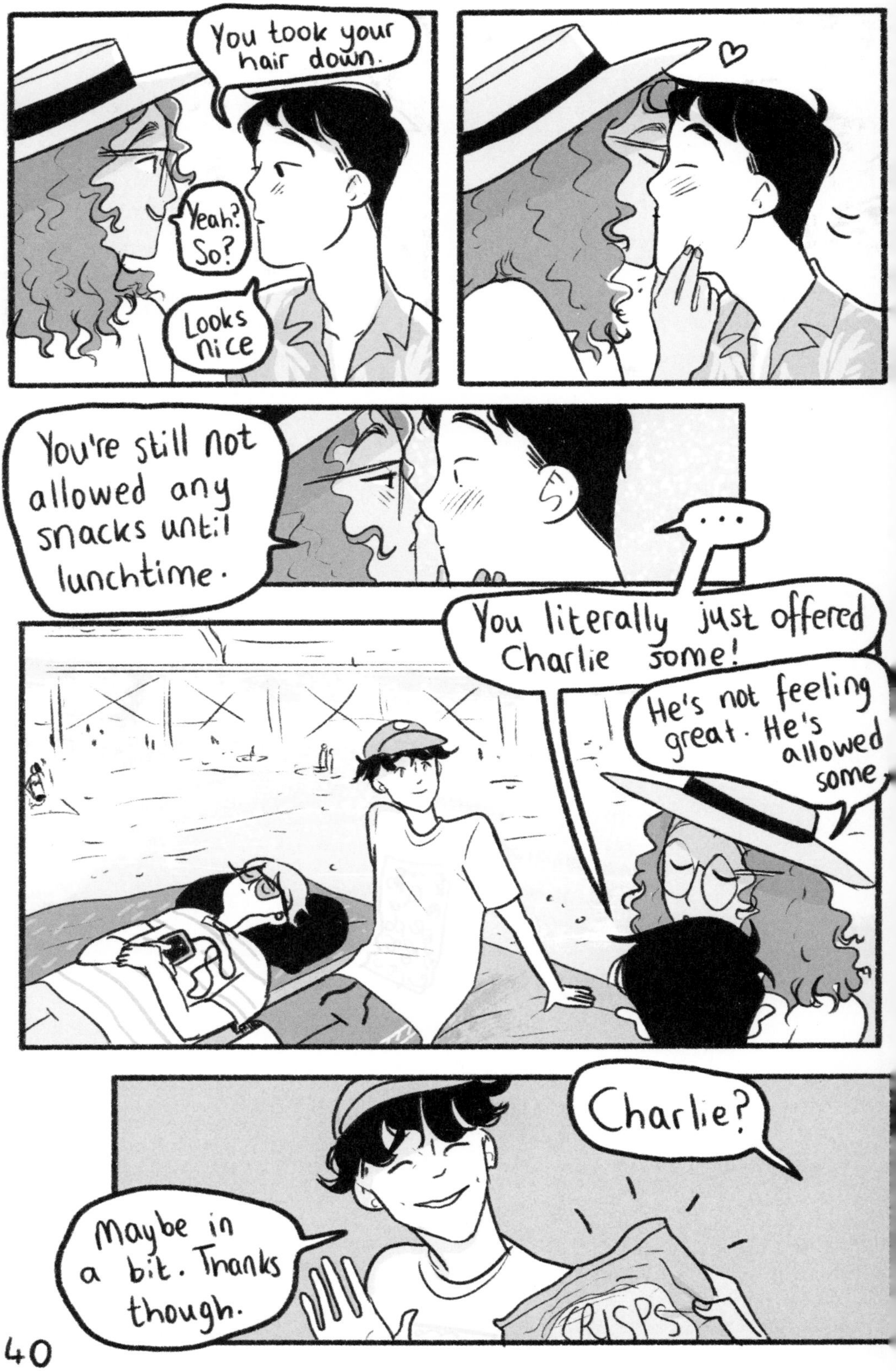
You took your hair down.
Yeah? So?
Looks nice
You're still not allowed any snacks until lunchtime.
...
You literally just offered Charlie some!
He's not feeling great. He's allowed some
Charlie?
Maybe in a bit. Thanks though.
CRISPS

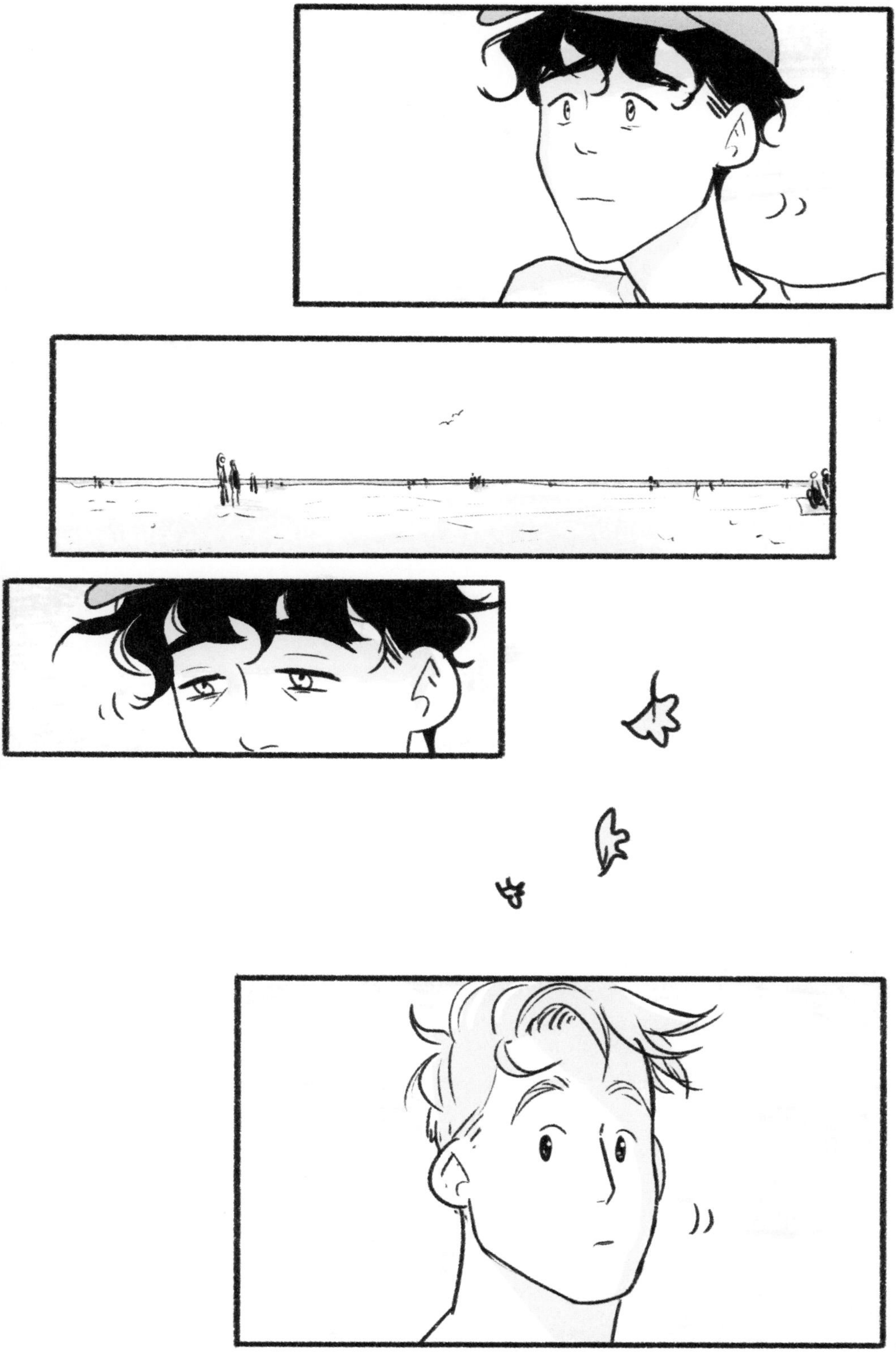

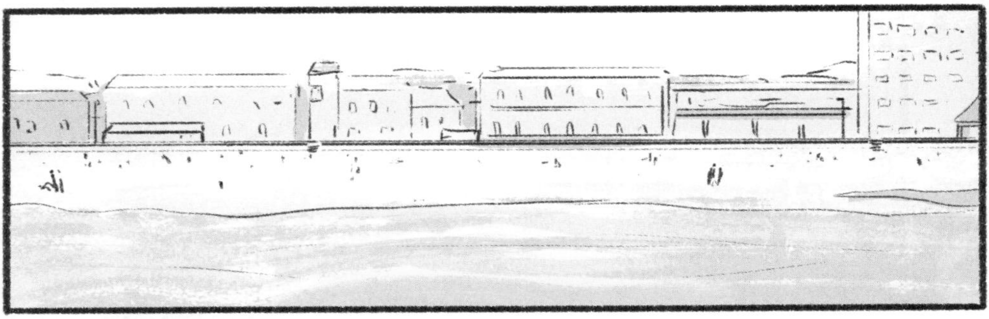

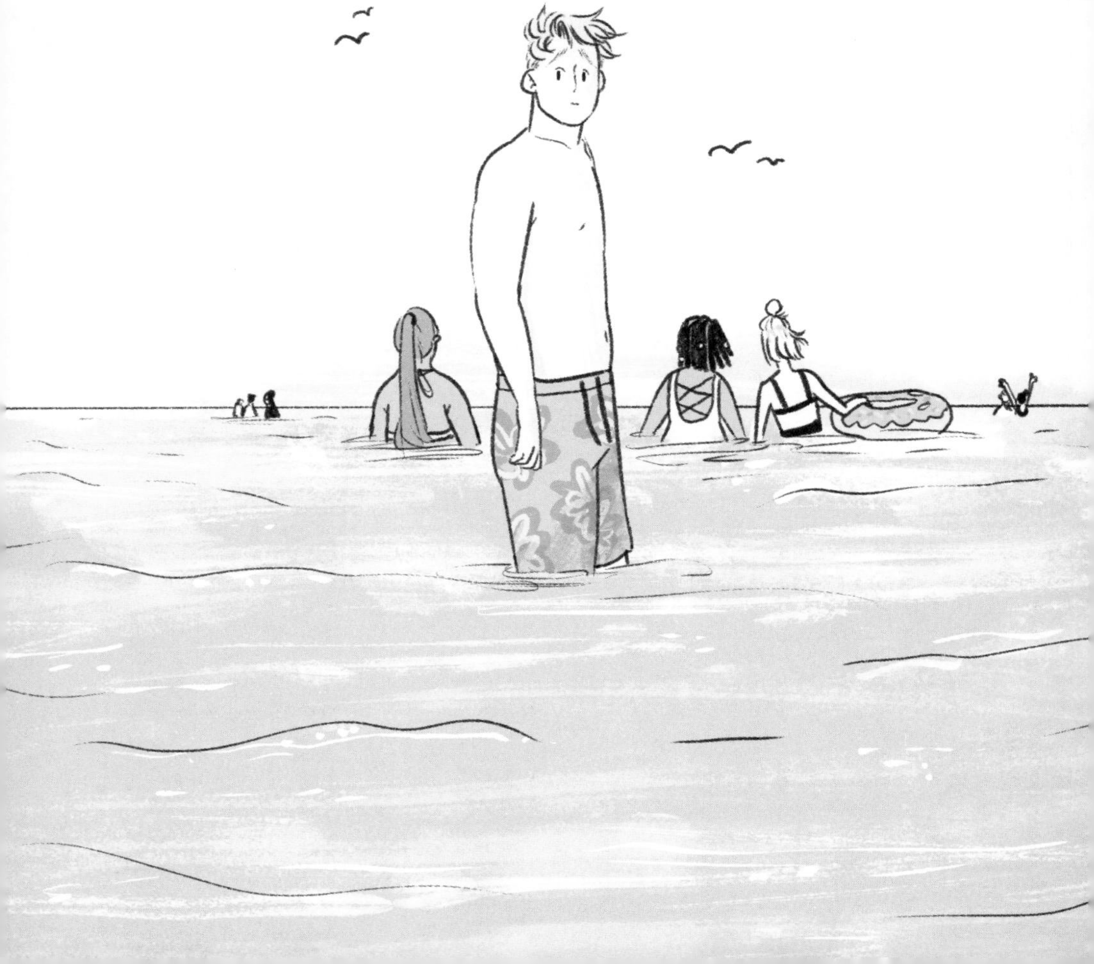

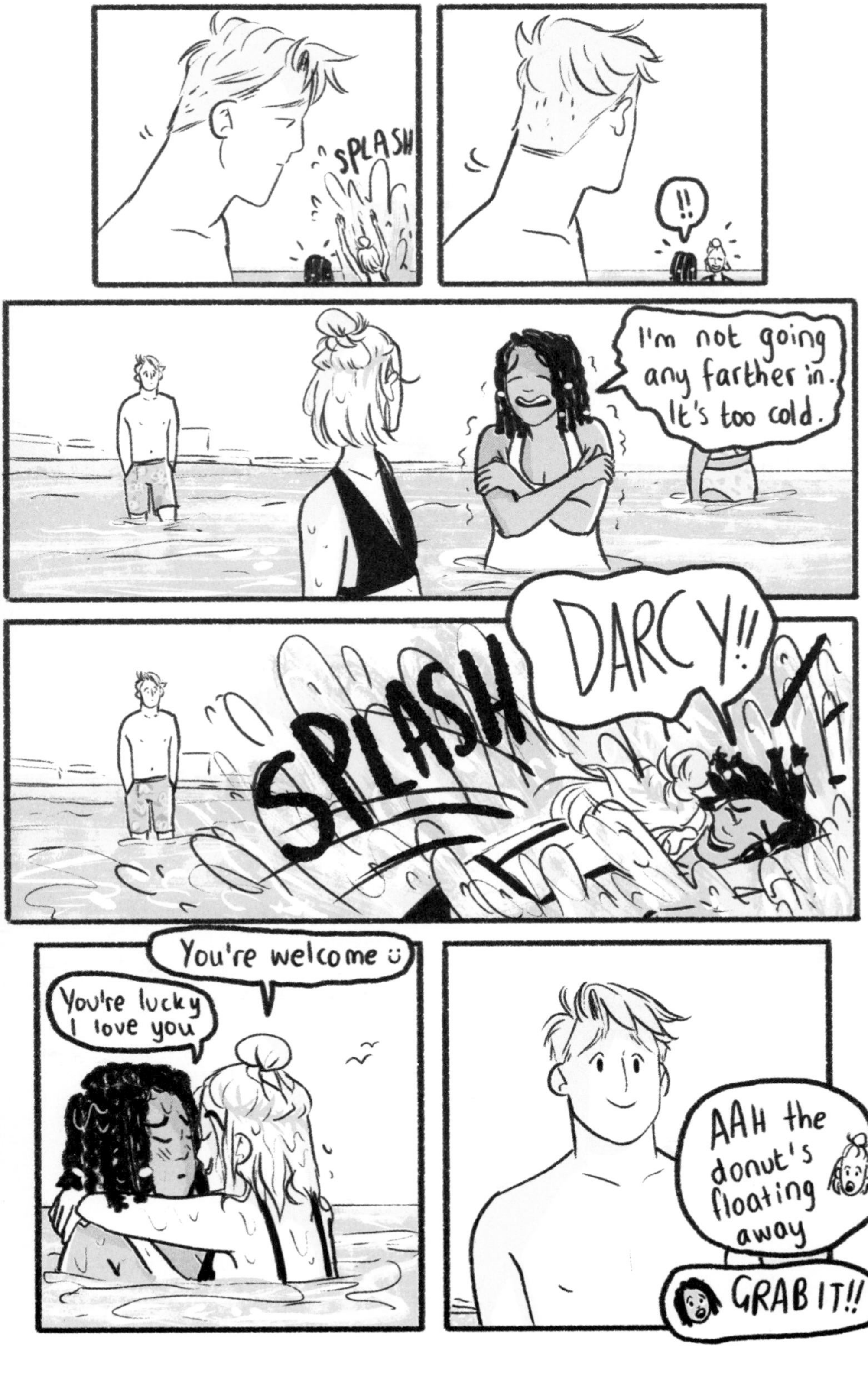
SPLASH
!!
I'm not going any farther in. It's too cold.
SPLASH
DARCY!!
!
You're welcome ☺
You're lucky I love you
AAH the donut's floating away
GRAB IT!!

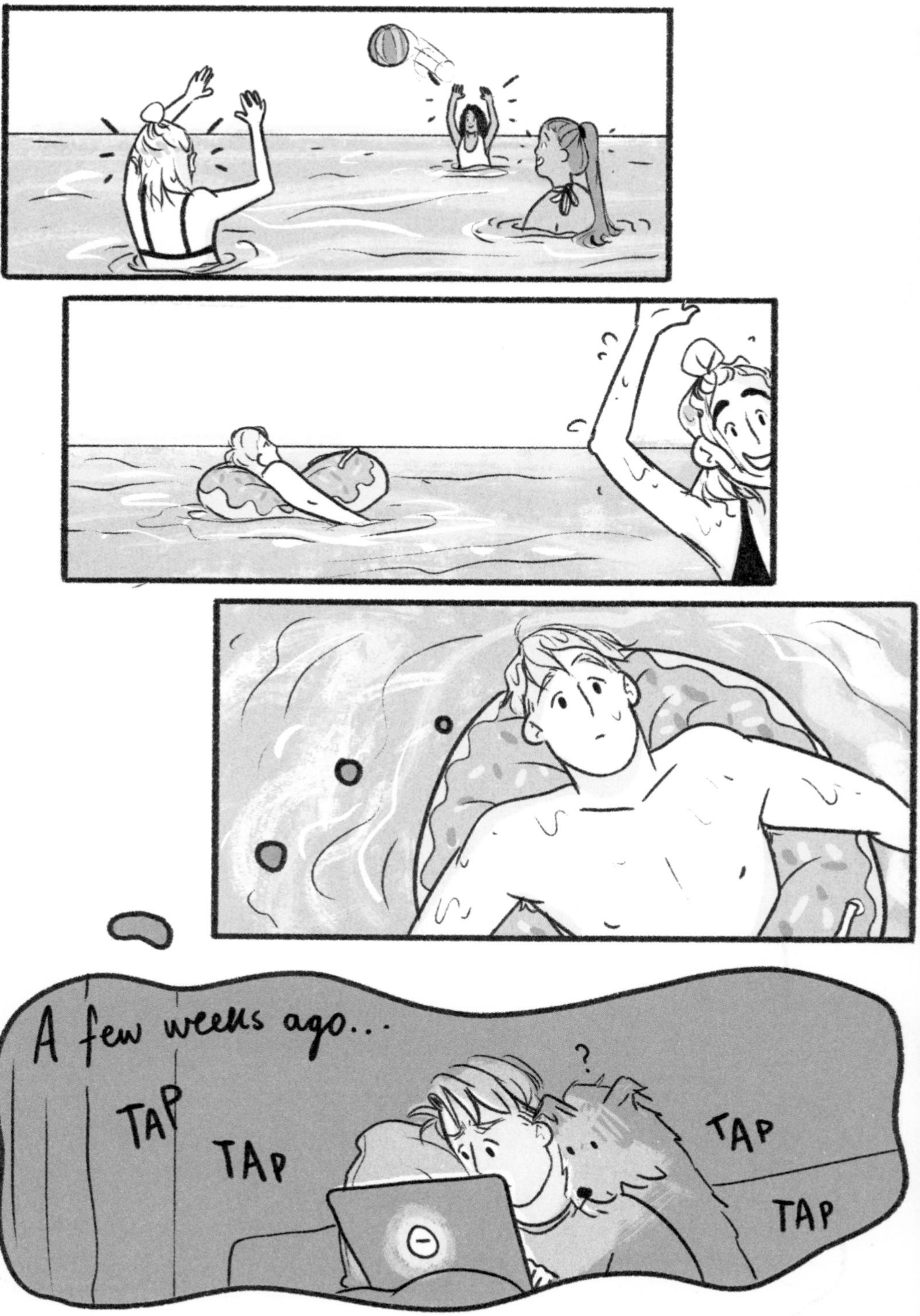
A few weeks ago...
?
TAP
TAP
TAP
TAP

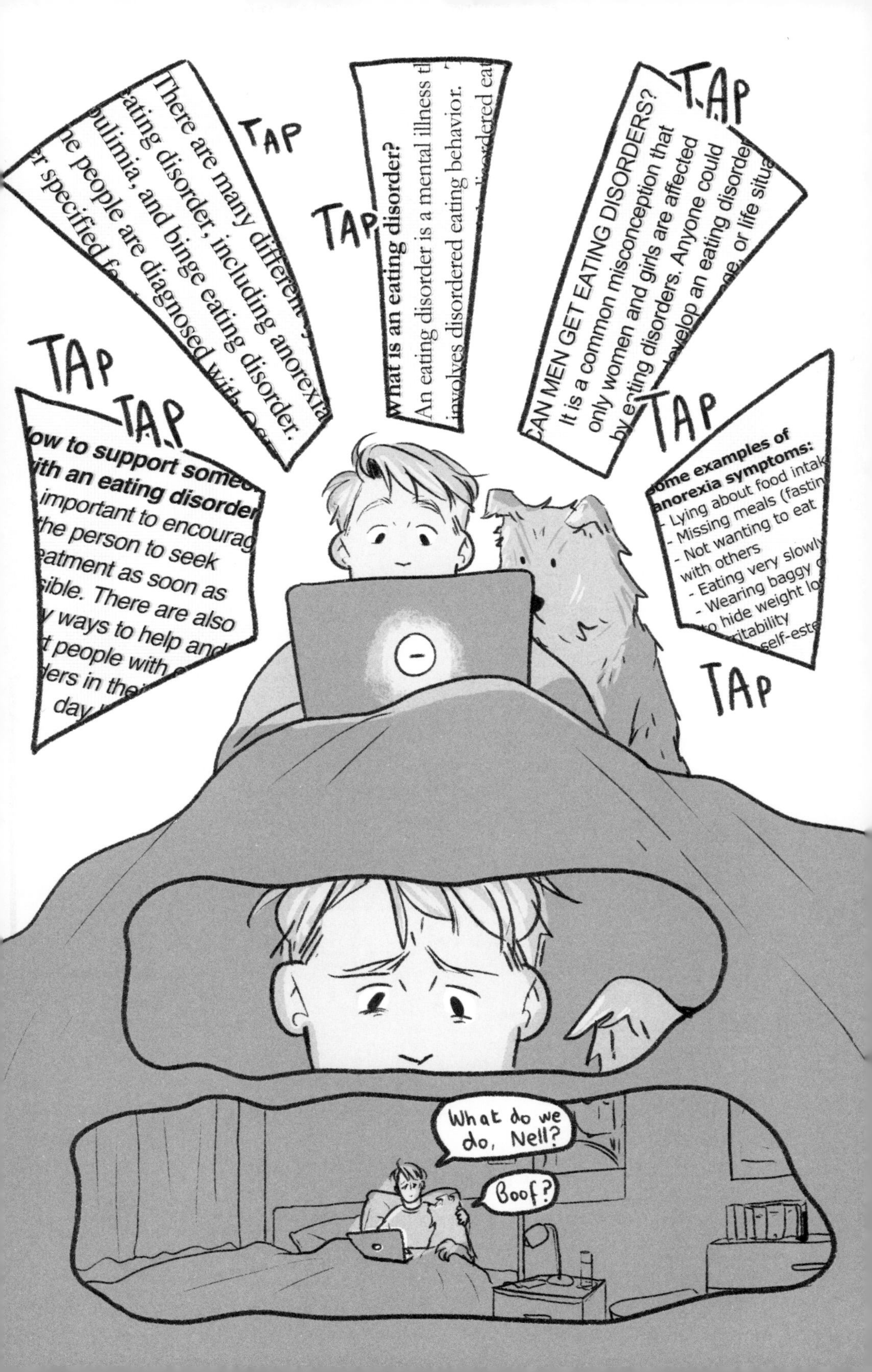

TAP
TAP
ow to support some
ith an eating disorder
important to encourag
the person to seek
eatment as soon as
sible. There are also
y ways to help and
t people with
ders in the
day.
TAP
There are many differen
eating disorder, including anorexia
bulimia, and binge eating disorder.
ne people are diagnosed with
r specified f
TAP
TAP
What is an eating disorder?
An eating disorder is a mental illness t
involves disordered eating behavior.
T.AP
CAN MEN GET EATING DISORDERS?
It is a common misconception that
only women and girls are affected
by eating disorders. Anyone could
develop an eating disorde
TAP
ome examples of
anorexia symptoms:
- Lying about food intak
- Missing meals (fastin
- Not wanting to eat
with others
- Eating very slowly
- Wearing baggy c
to hide weight lo
ritability
self-este
TAP
What do we do, Nell?
Boof?

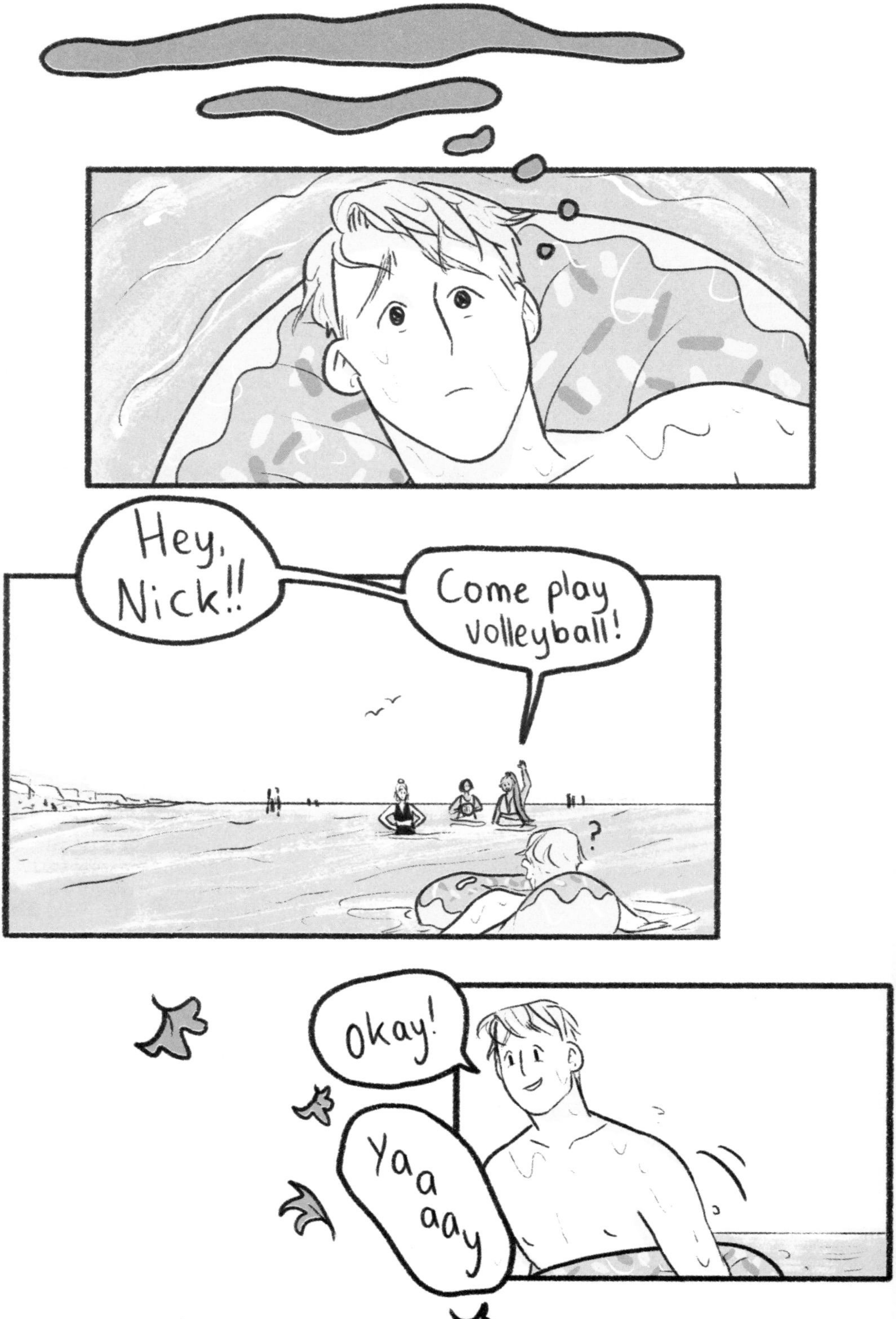
Hey, Nick!!
Come play volleyball!
?
Okay!
Yaaaaay

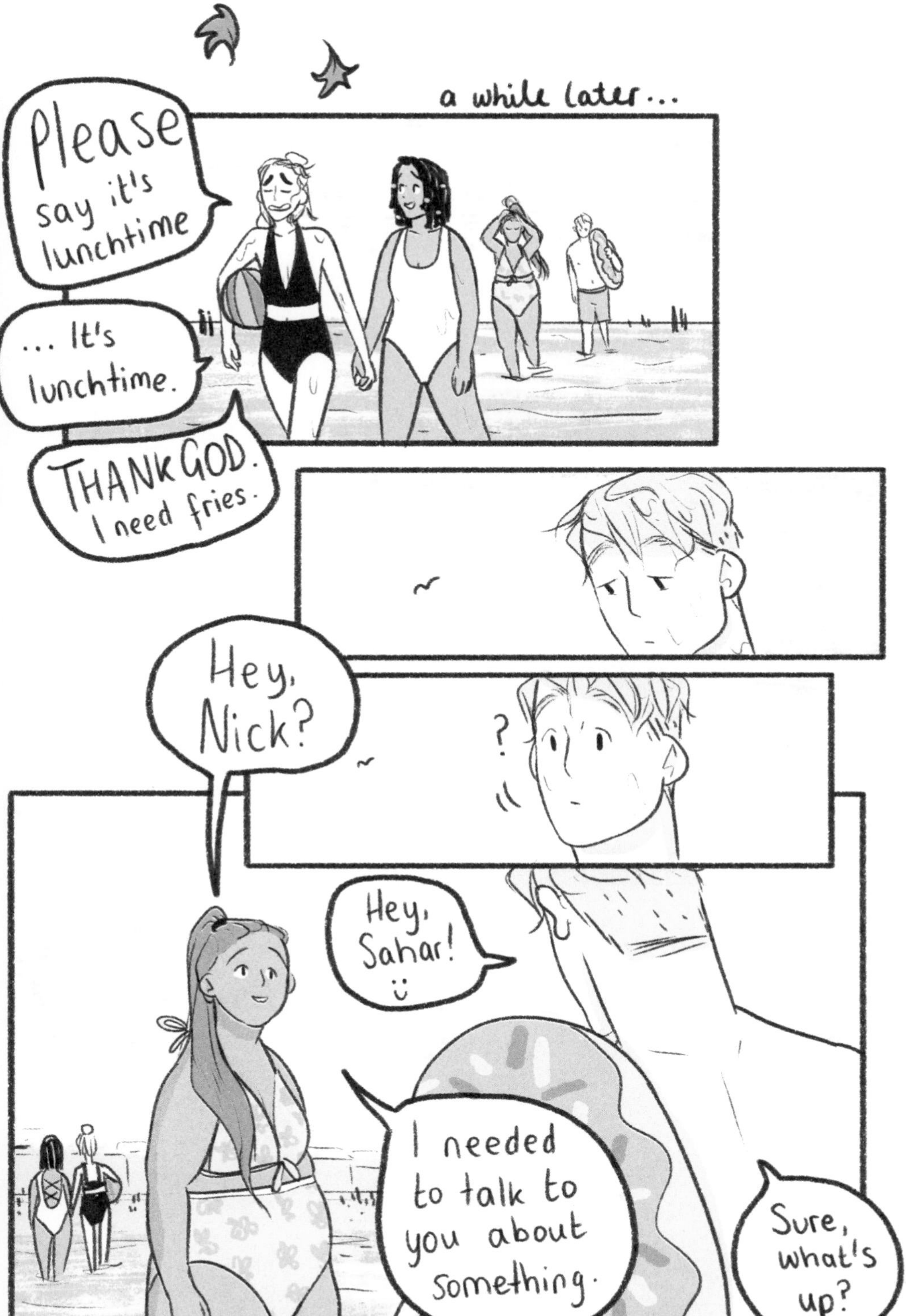
a while later...
Please say it's lunchtime
... It's lunchtime.
THANK GOD. I need fries.
Hey, Nick?
?
Hey, Sahar!
I needed to talk to you about something.
Sure, what's up?

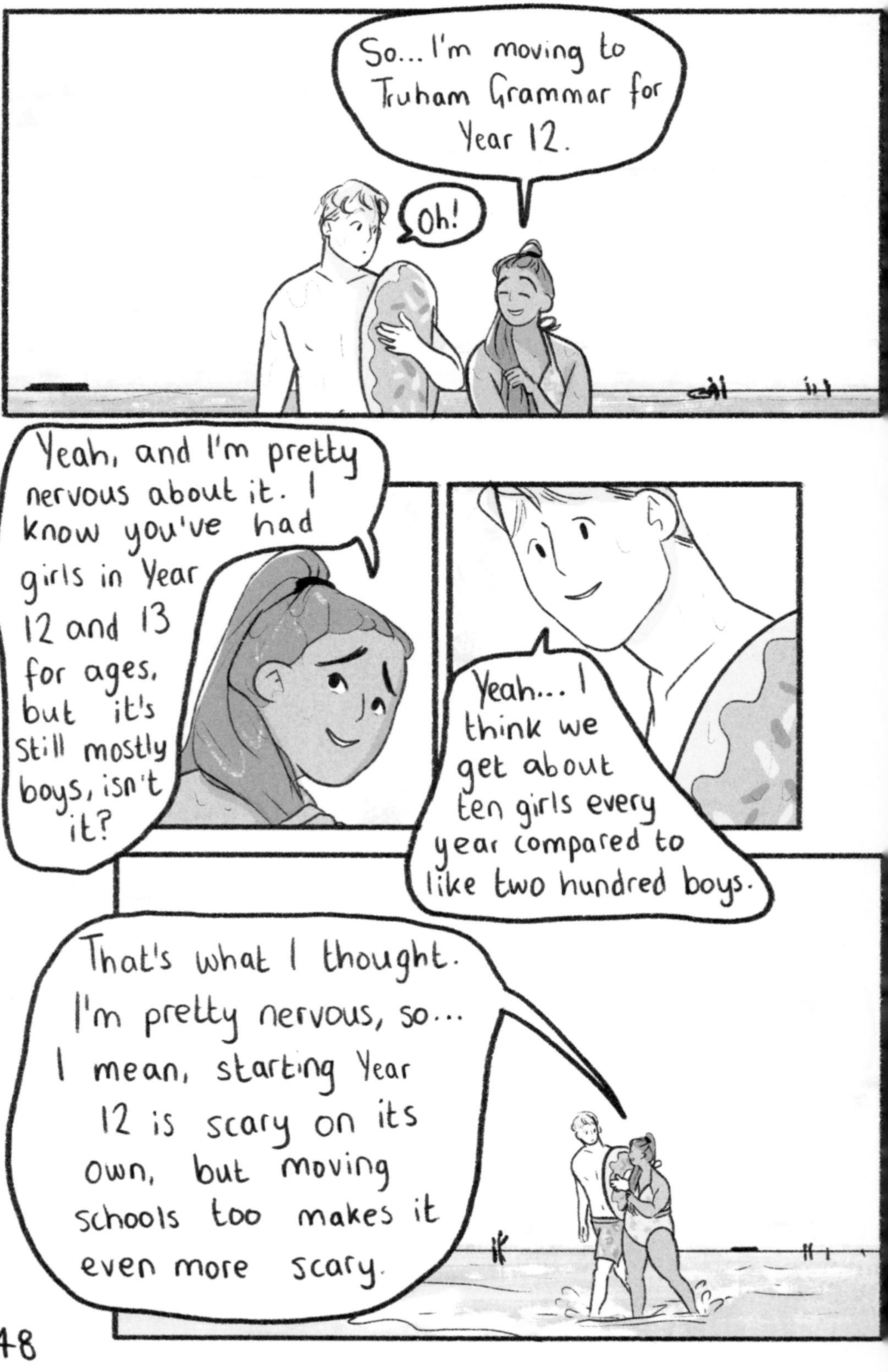
So... I'm moving to Truham Grammar for Year 12.
Oh!
Yeah, and I'm pretty nervous about it. I know you've had girls in Year 12 and 13 for ages, but it's still mostly boys, isn't it?
Yeah... I think we get about ten girls every year compared to like two hundred boys.
That's what I thought. I'm pretty nervous, so... I mean, starting Year 12 is scary on its own, but moving schools too makes it even more scary.

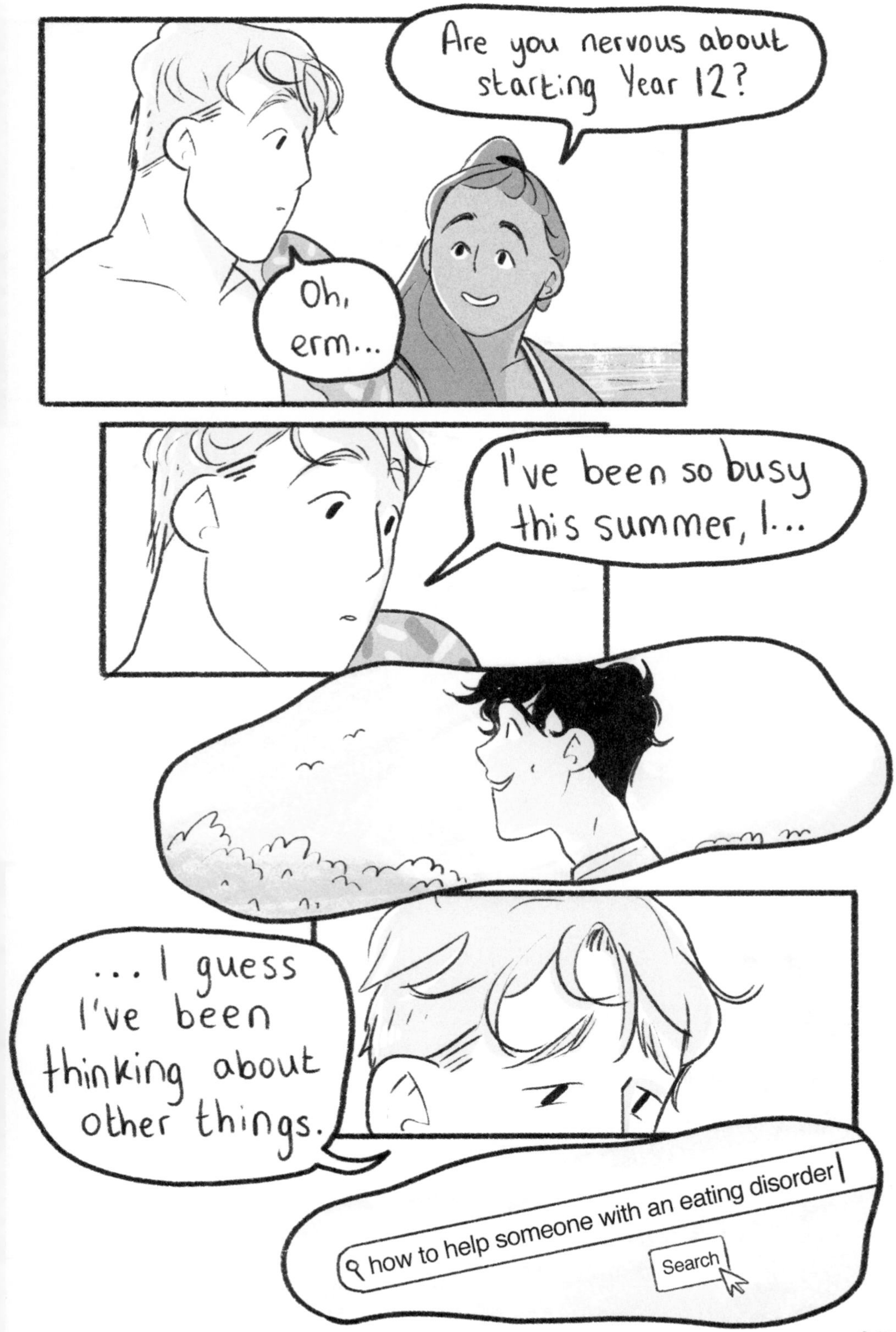

Are you nervous about starting Year 12?
Oh, erm...
I've been so busy this summer, I...
...I guess I've been thinking about other things.
how to help someone with an eating disorder
Search

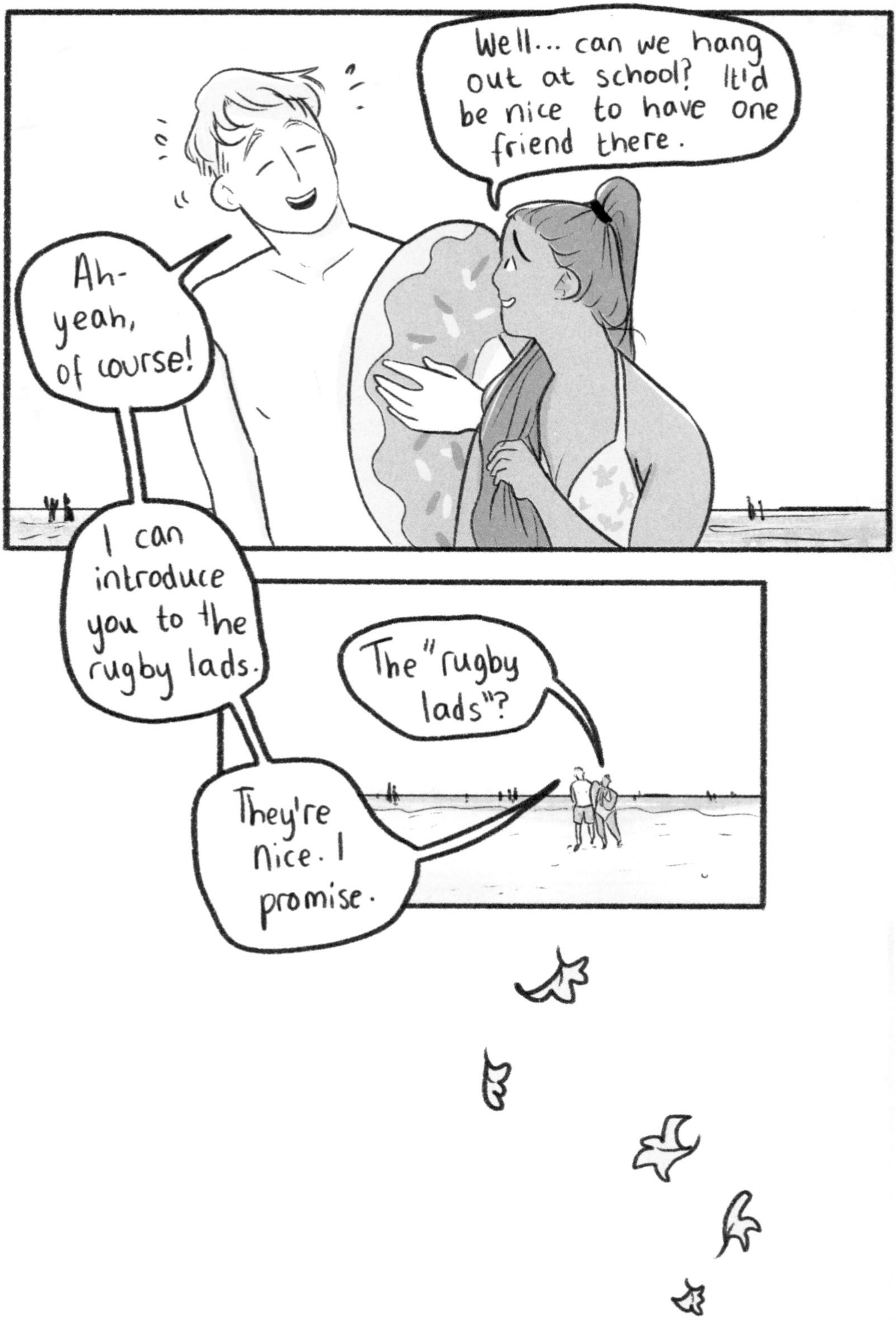
Well... can we hang out at school? It'd be nice to have one friend there.
Ah- yeah, of course!
I can introduce you to the rugby lads.
The "rugby lads"?
They're nice. I promise.

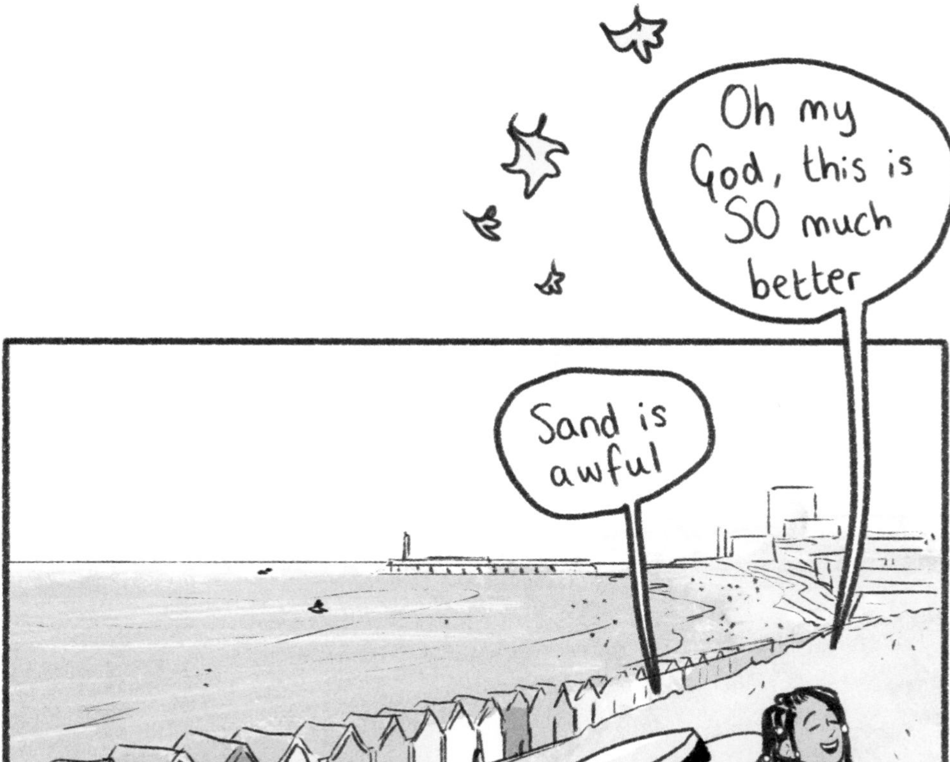
Oh my God, this is SO much better
Sand is awful

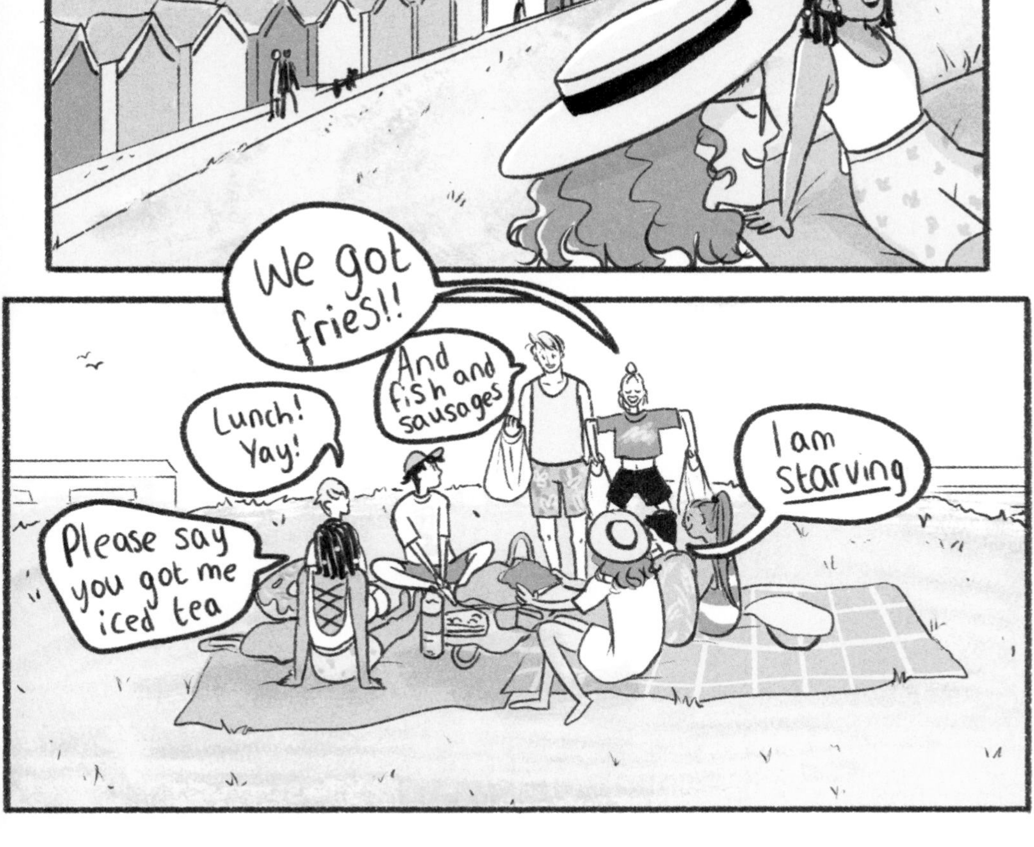
We got fries!!
And fish and sausages
Lunch! Yay!
I am starving
Please say you got me iced tea

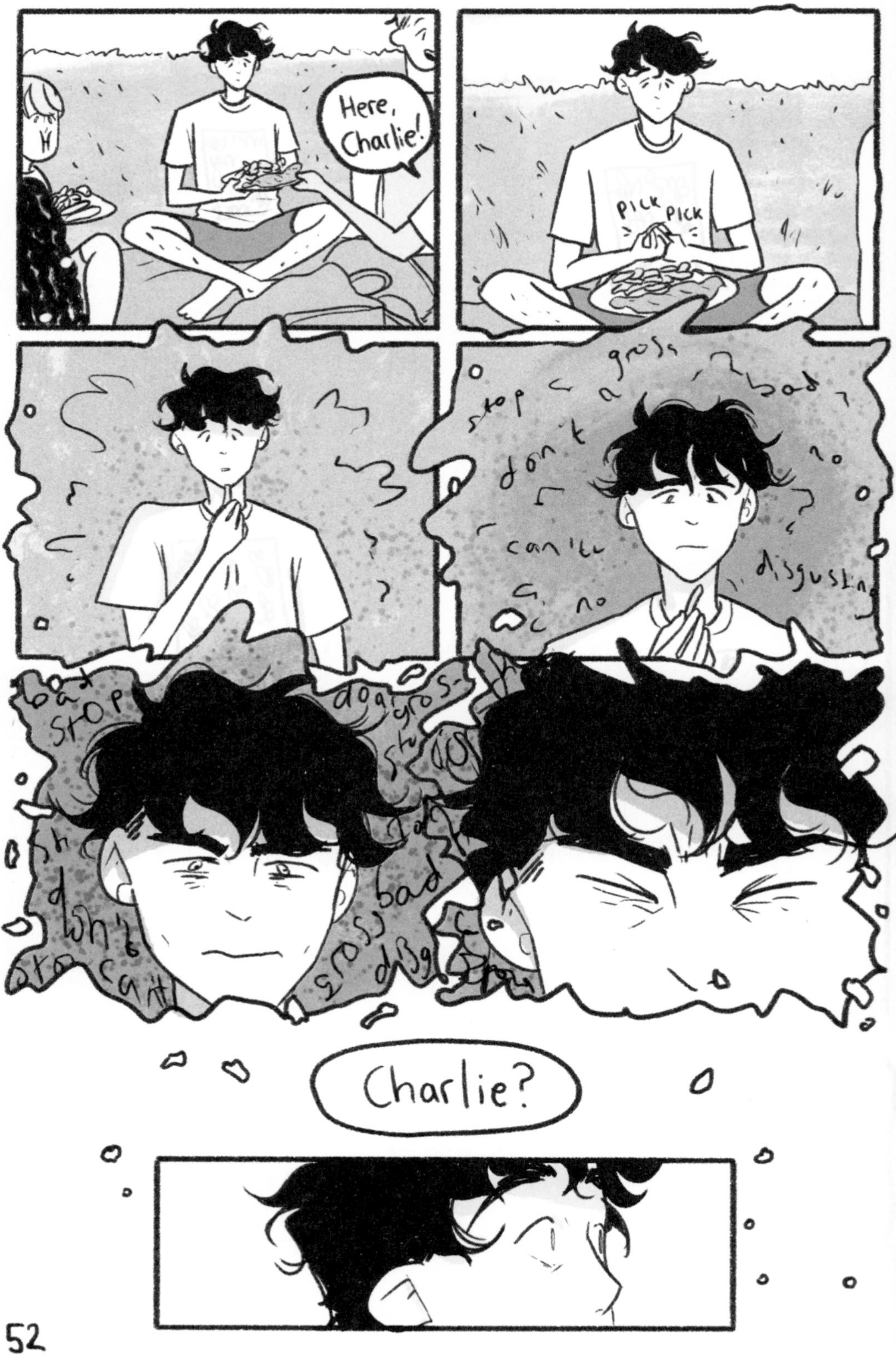
Here, Charlie!
PICK PICK
stop
gross
bad
don't
no
can't
disgusting
Charlie?

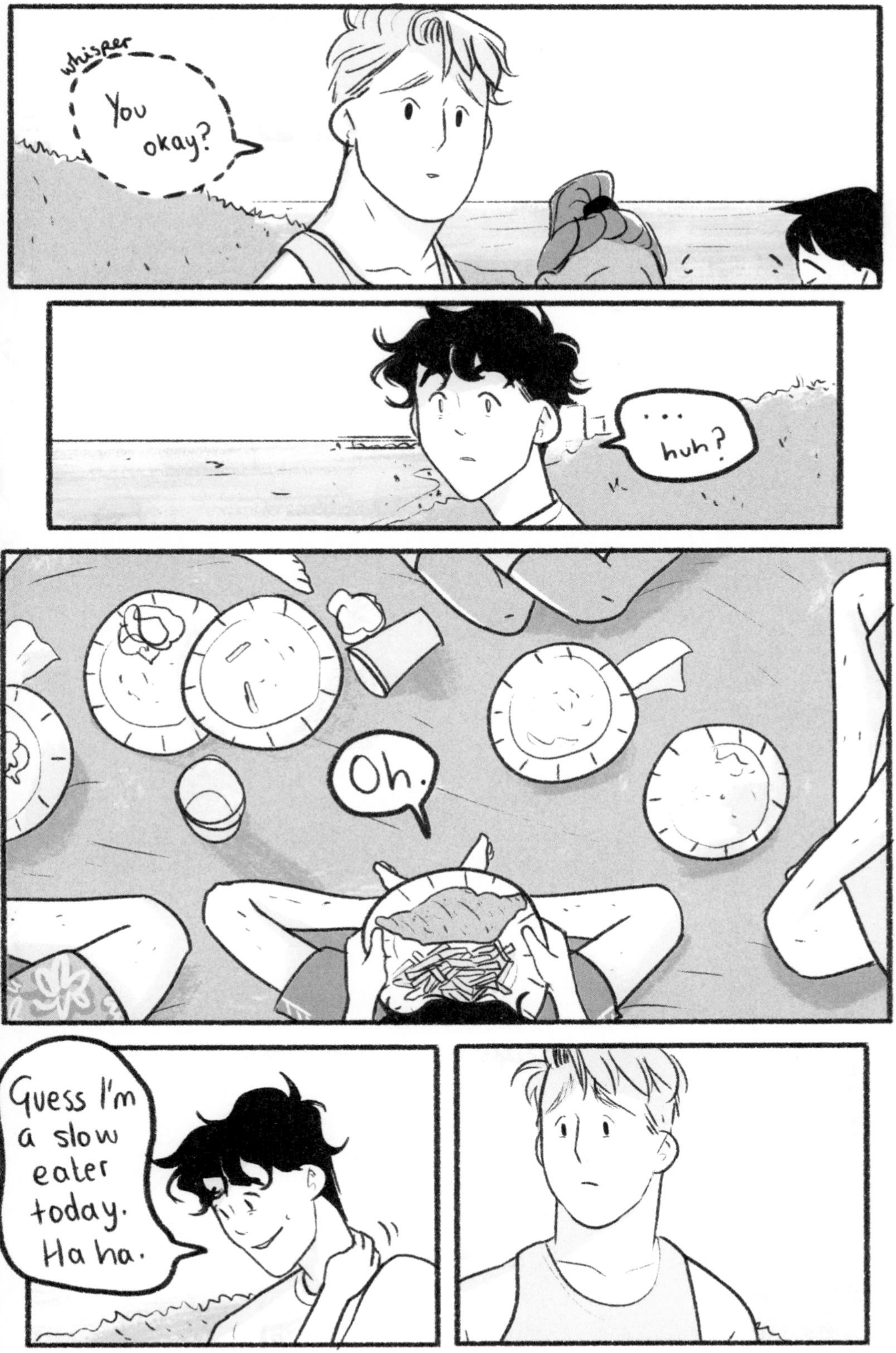
whisper
You okay?
... huh?
Oh.
Guess I'm a slow eater today. Ha ha.

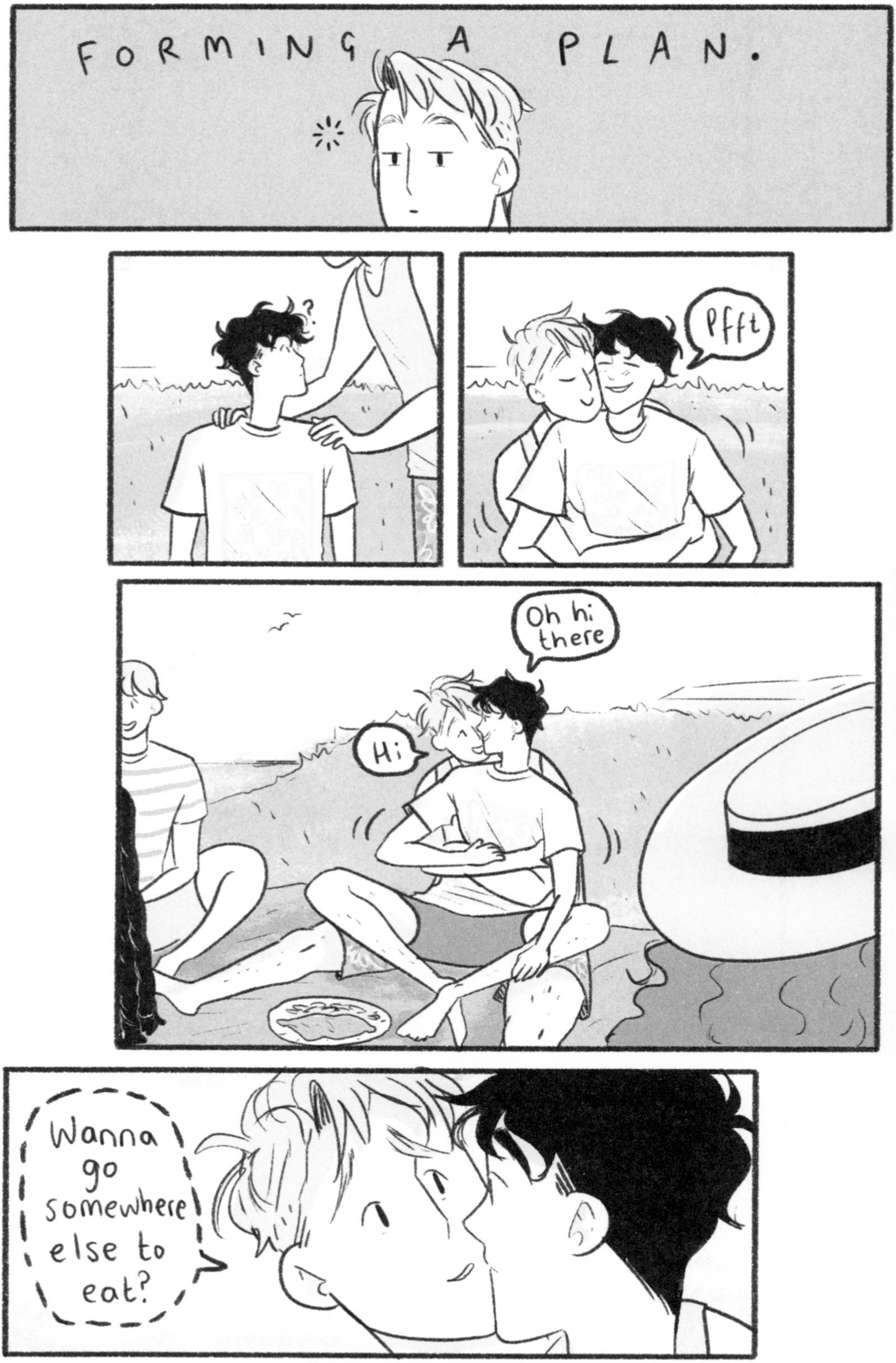
FORMING A PLAN.
Pfft
Oh hi there
Hi
Wanna go somewhere else to eat?

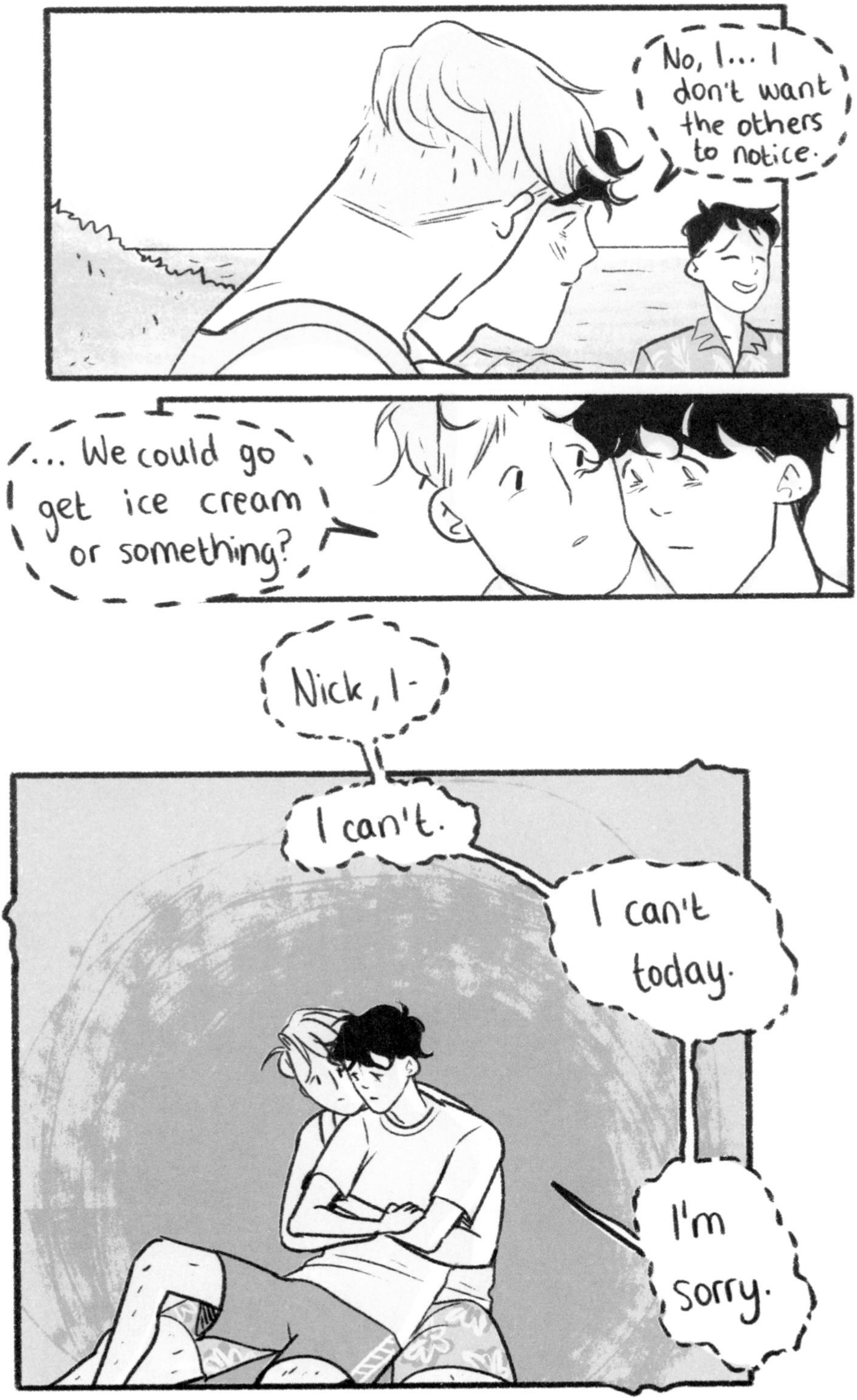
No, I... I don't want the others to notice.
... We could go get ice cream or something?
Nick, I-
I can't.
I can't today.
I'm sorry.

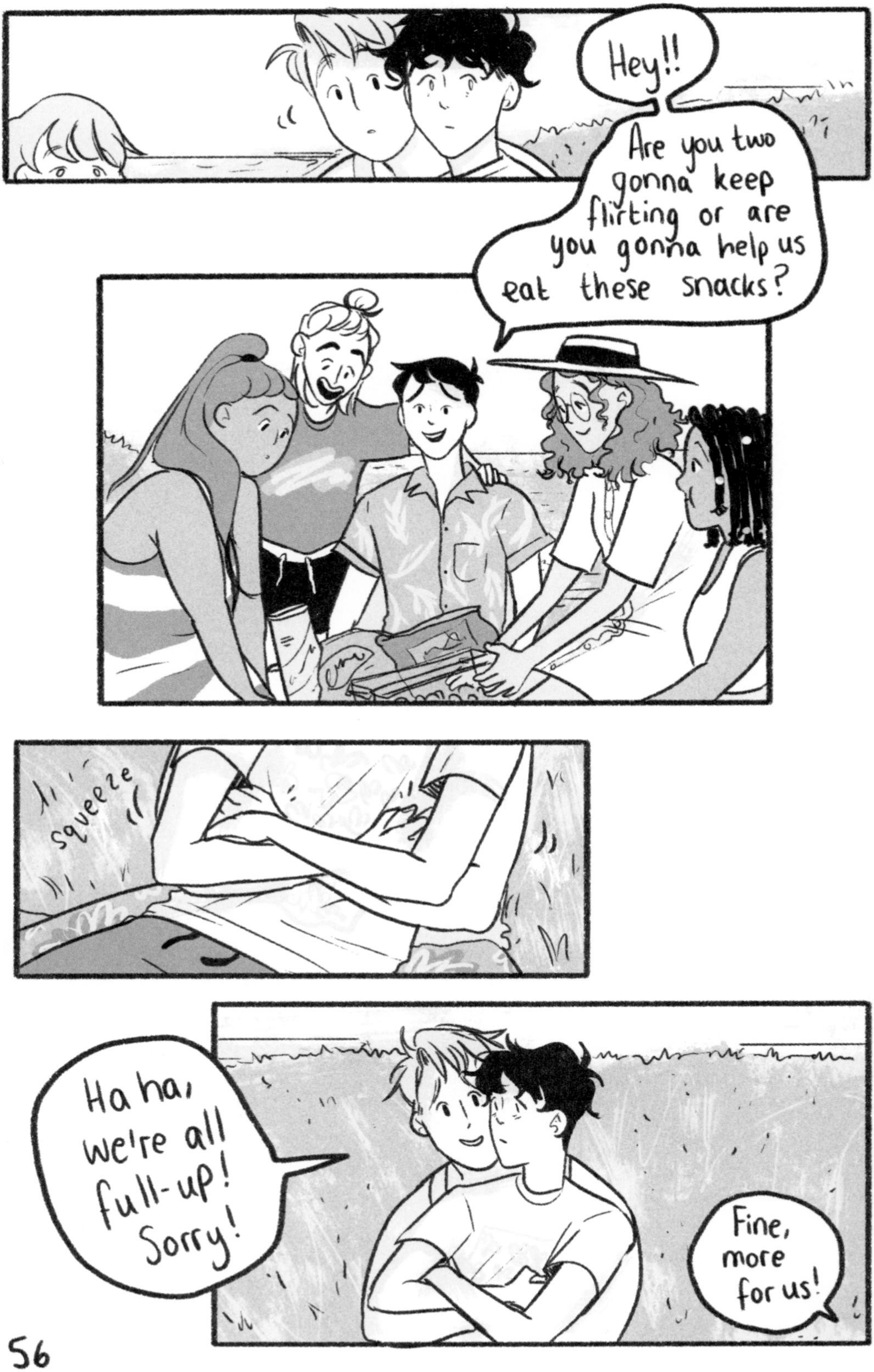
Hey!!
Are you two gonna keep flirting or are you gonna help us eat these snacks?
squeeze
Ha ha, we're all full-up! Sorry!
Fine, more for us!

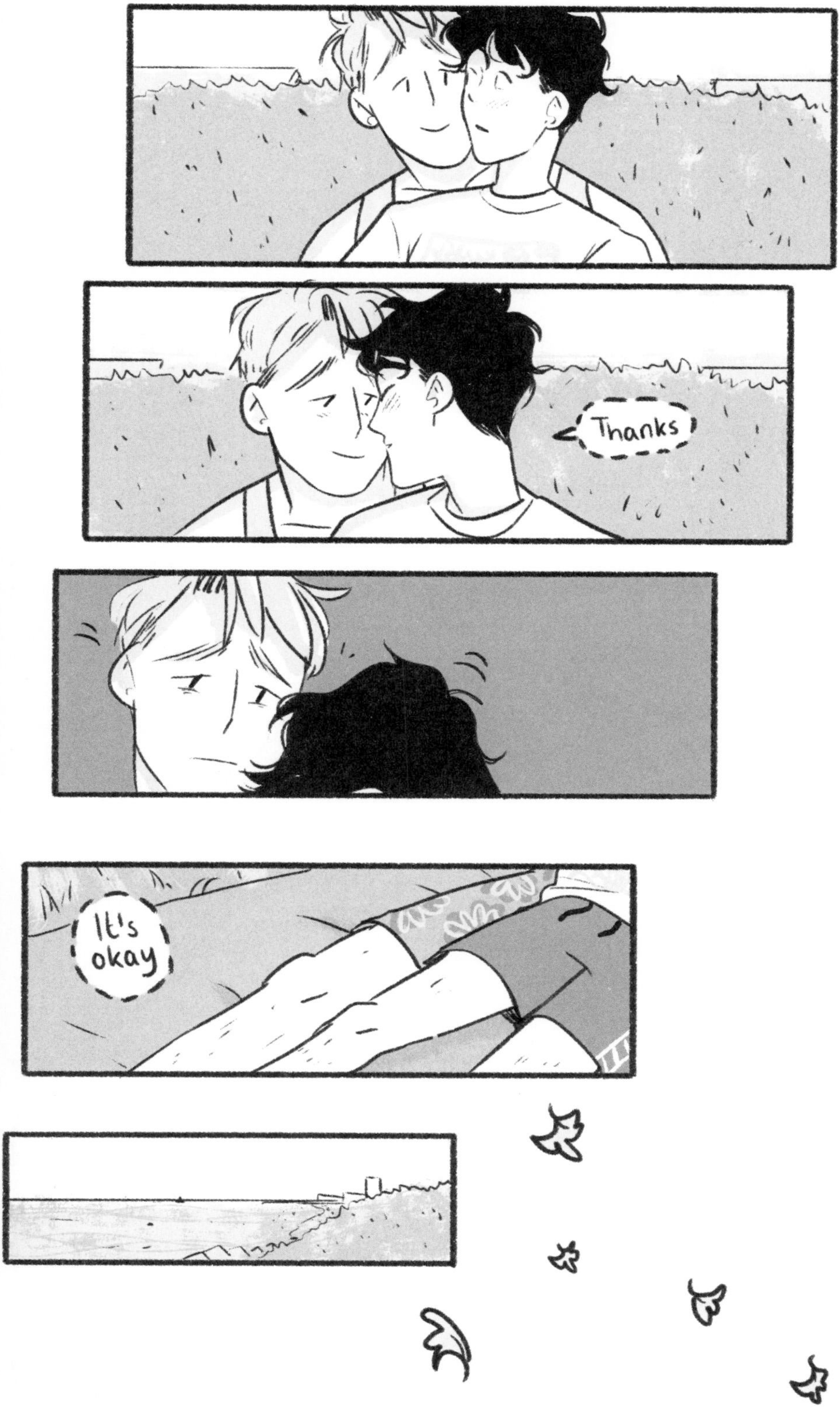
Thanks
It's okay

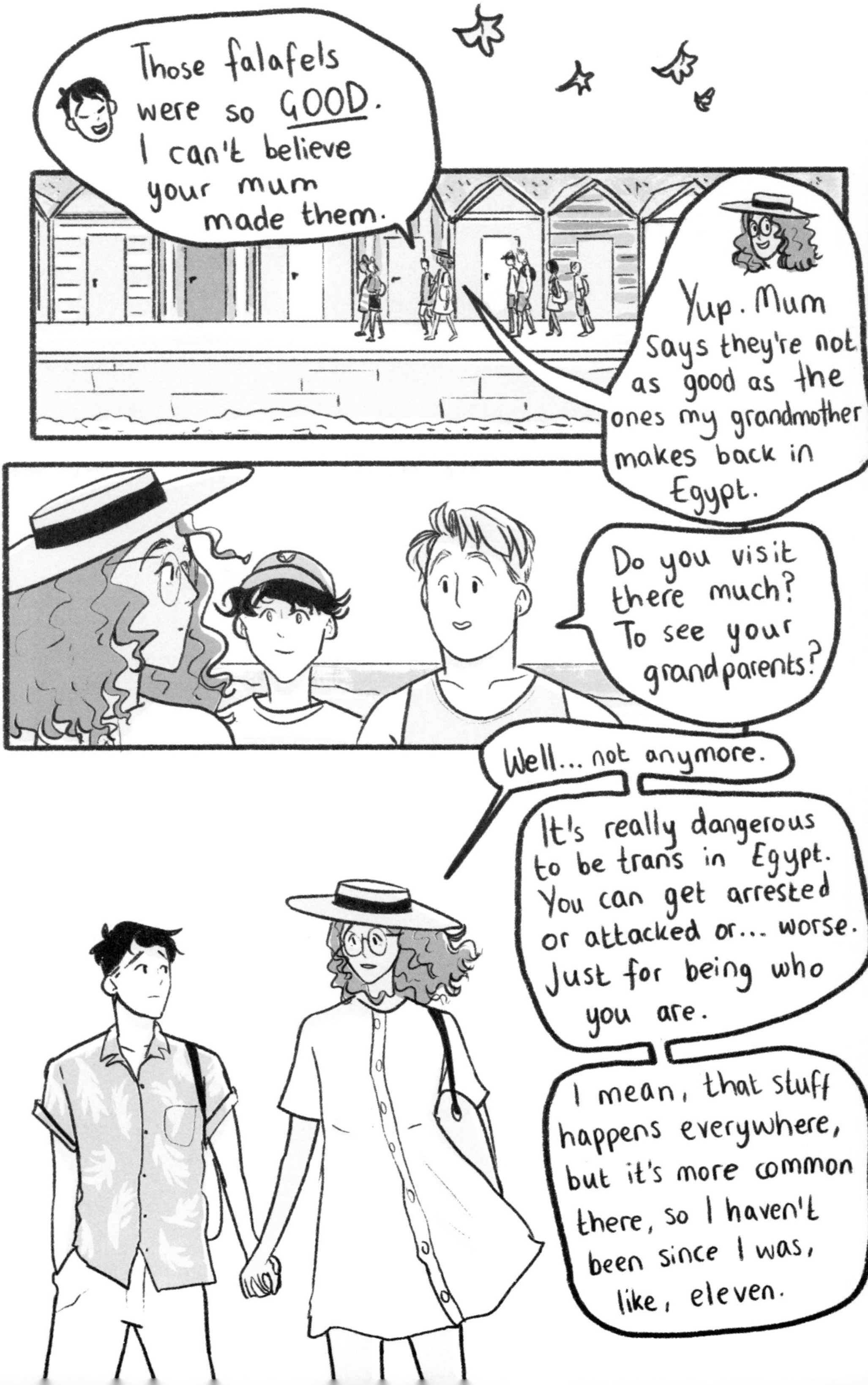
Those falafels were so GOOD. I can't believe your mum made them.
Yup. Mum says they're not as good as the ones my grandmother makes back in Egypt.
Do you visit there much? To see your grandparents?
Well... not anymore.
It's really dangerous to be trans in Egypt. You can get arrested or attacked or... worse. Just for being who you are.
I mean, that stuff happens everywhere, but it's more common there, so I haven't been since I was, like, eleven.

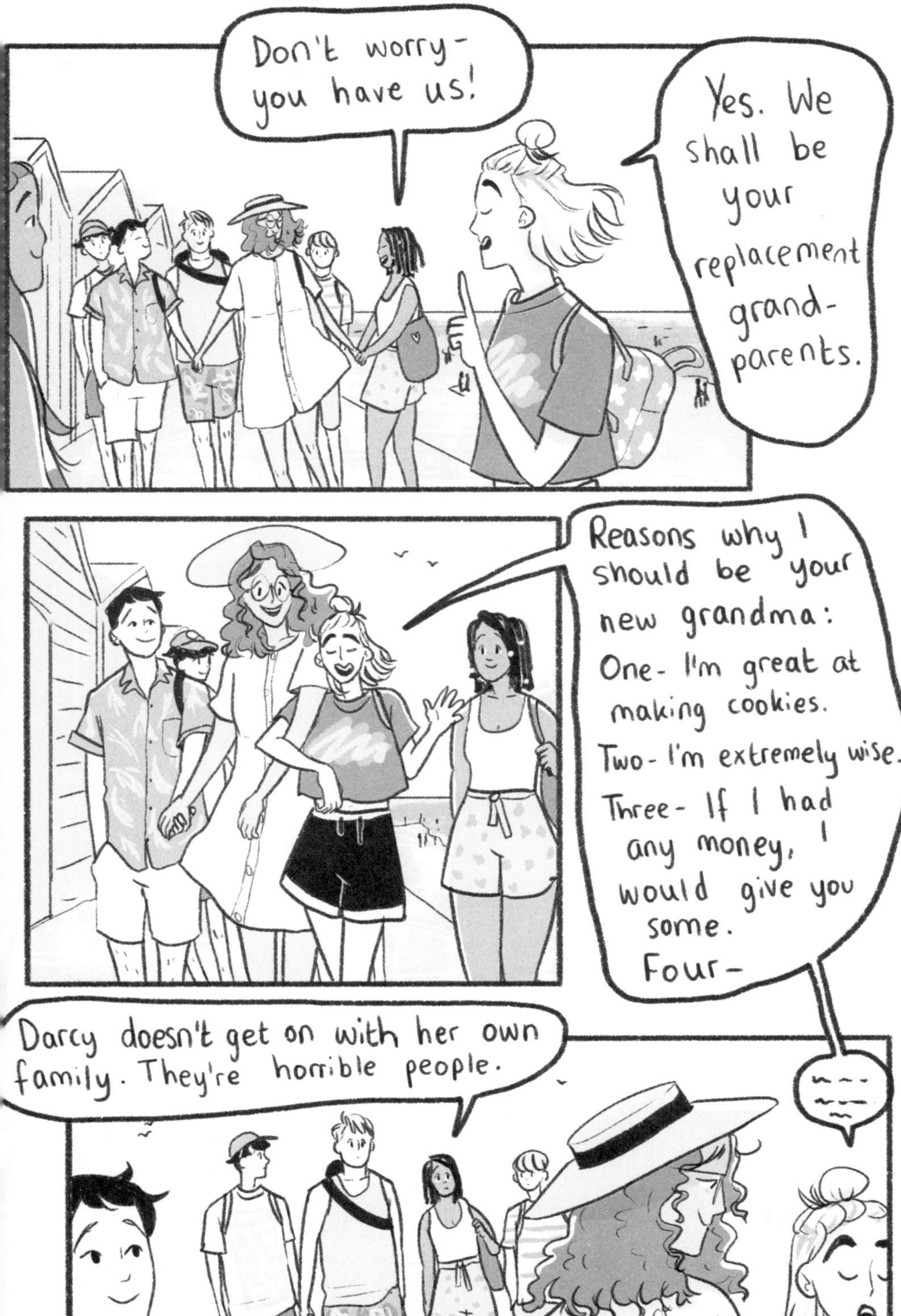
Don't worry- you have us!
Yes. We shall be your replacement grand-parents.
Reasons why I should be your new grandma: One- I'm great at making cookies. Two- I'm extremely wise. Three- If I had any money, I would give you some. Four-
Darcy doesn't get on with her own family. They're horrible people.

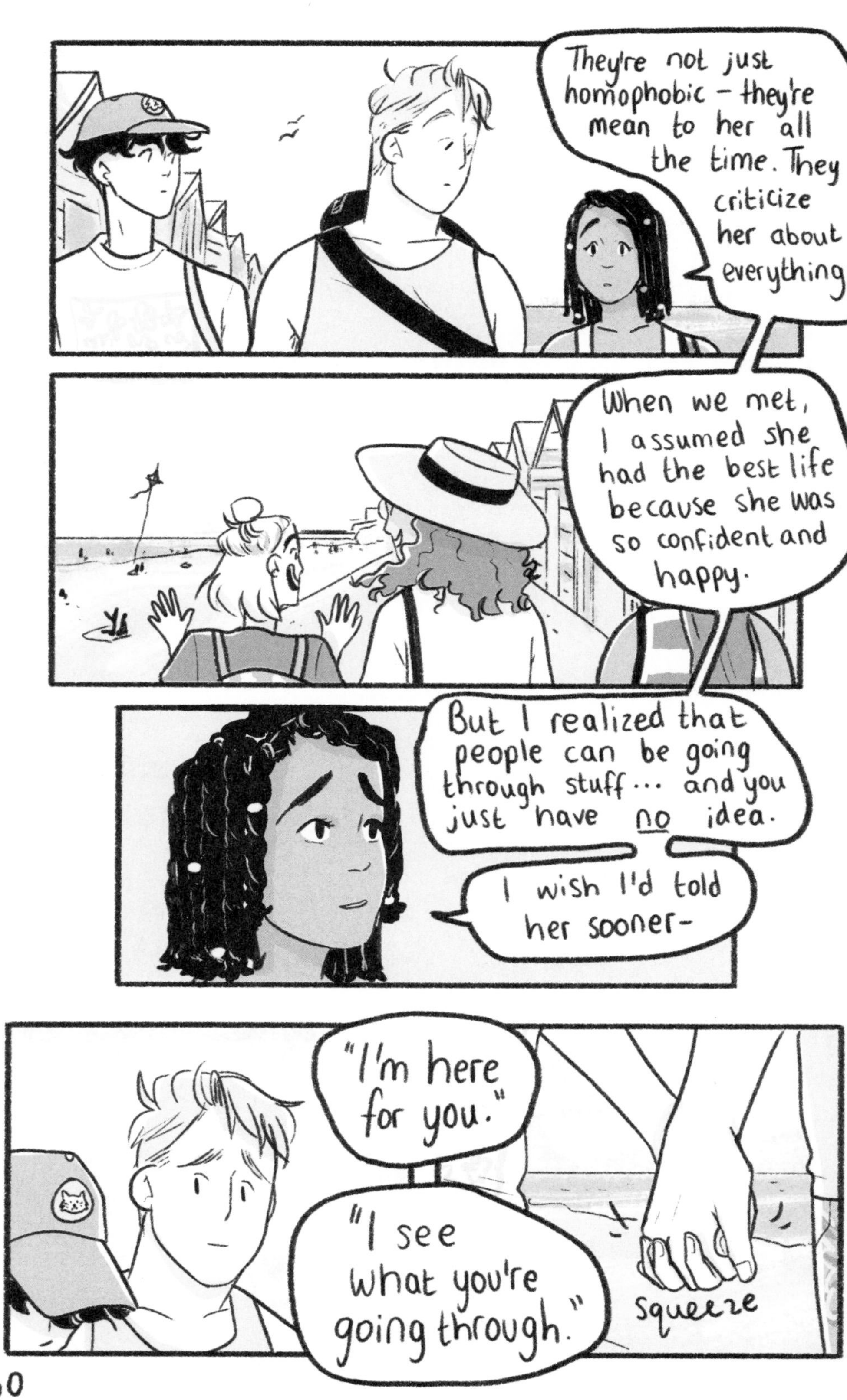
They're not just homophobic – they're mean to her all the time. They criticize her about everything.
When we met, I assumed she had the best life because she was so confident and happy.
But I realized that people can be going through stuff... and you just have no idea.
I wish I'd told her sooner-
"I'm here for you."
"I see what you're going through."
squeeze

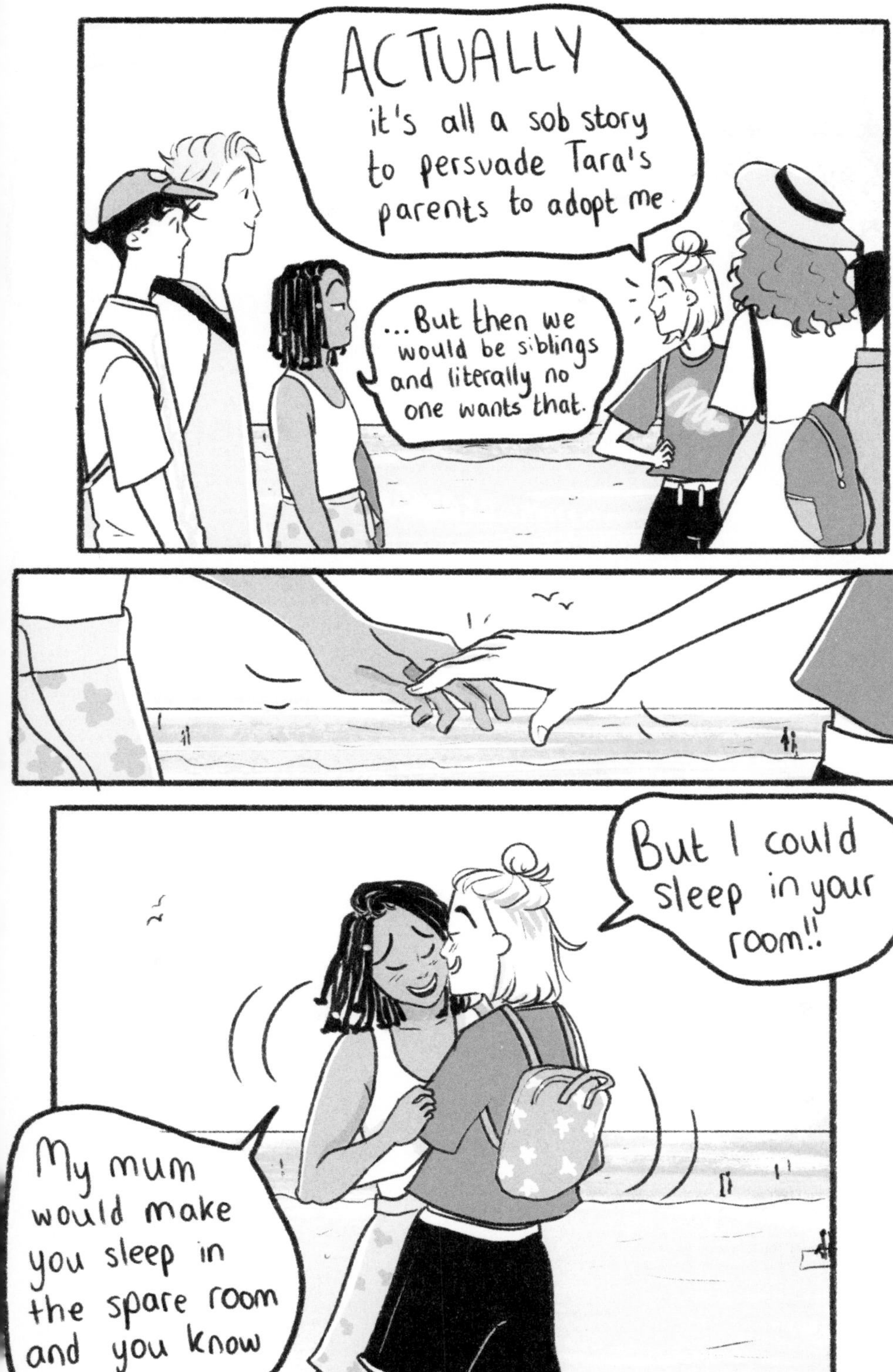
ACTUALLY it's all a sob story to persuade Tara's parents to adopt me
...But then we would be siblings and literally no one wants that.
But I could sleep in your room!!
My mum would make you sleep in the spare room and you know it.

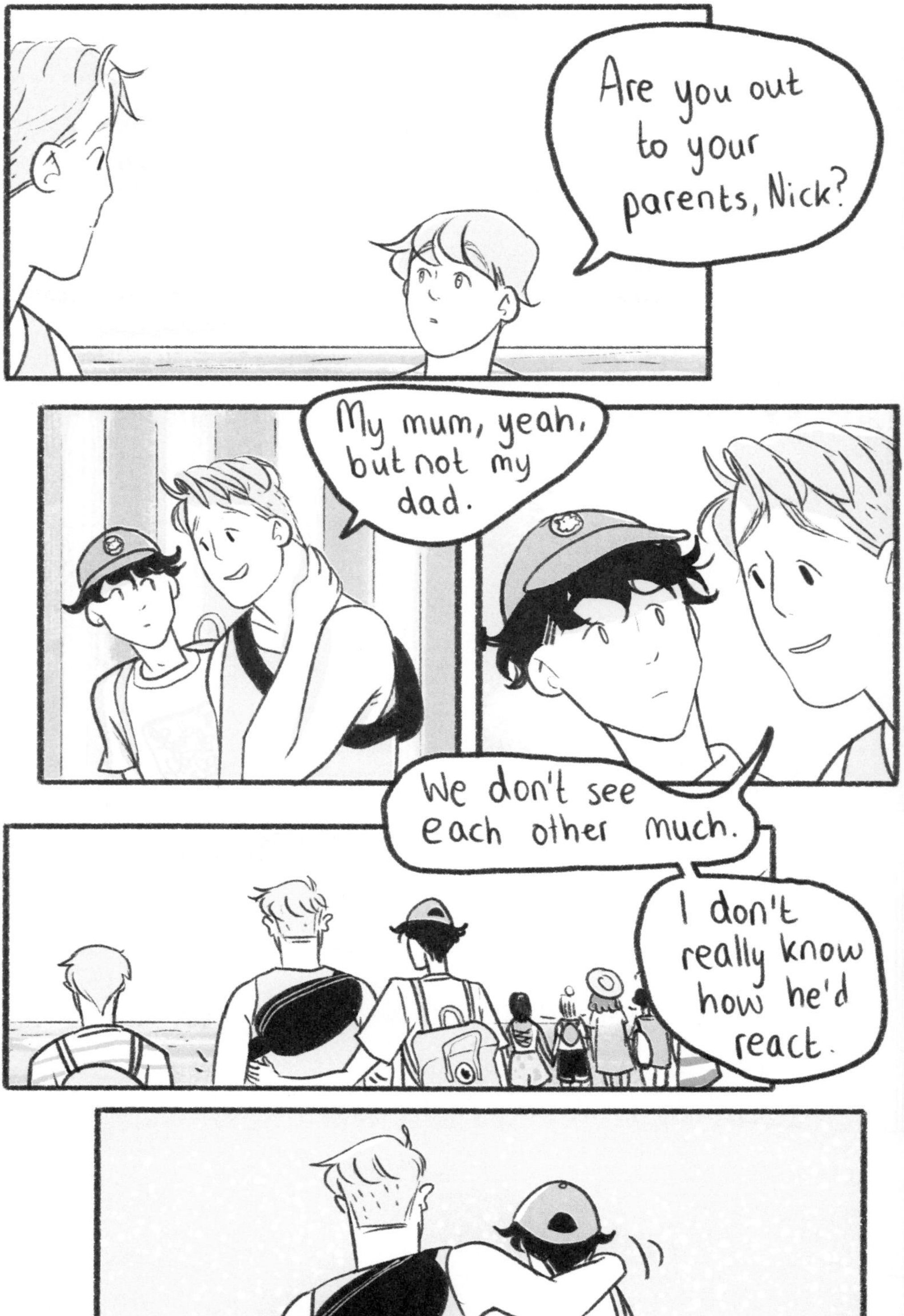
Are you out to your parents, Nick?
My mum, yeah, but not my dad.
We don't see each other much.
I don't really know how he'd react.

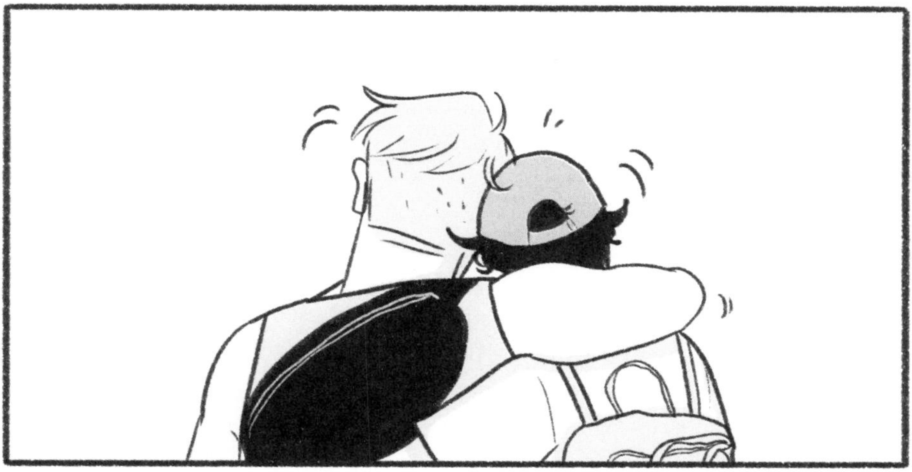

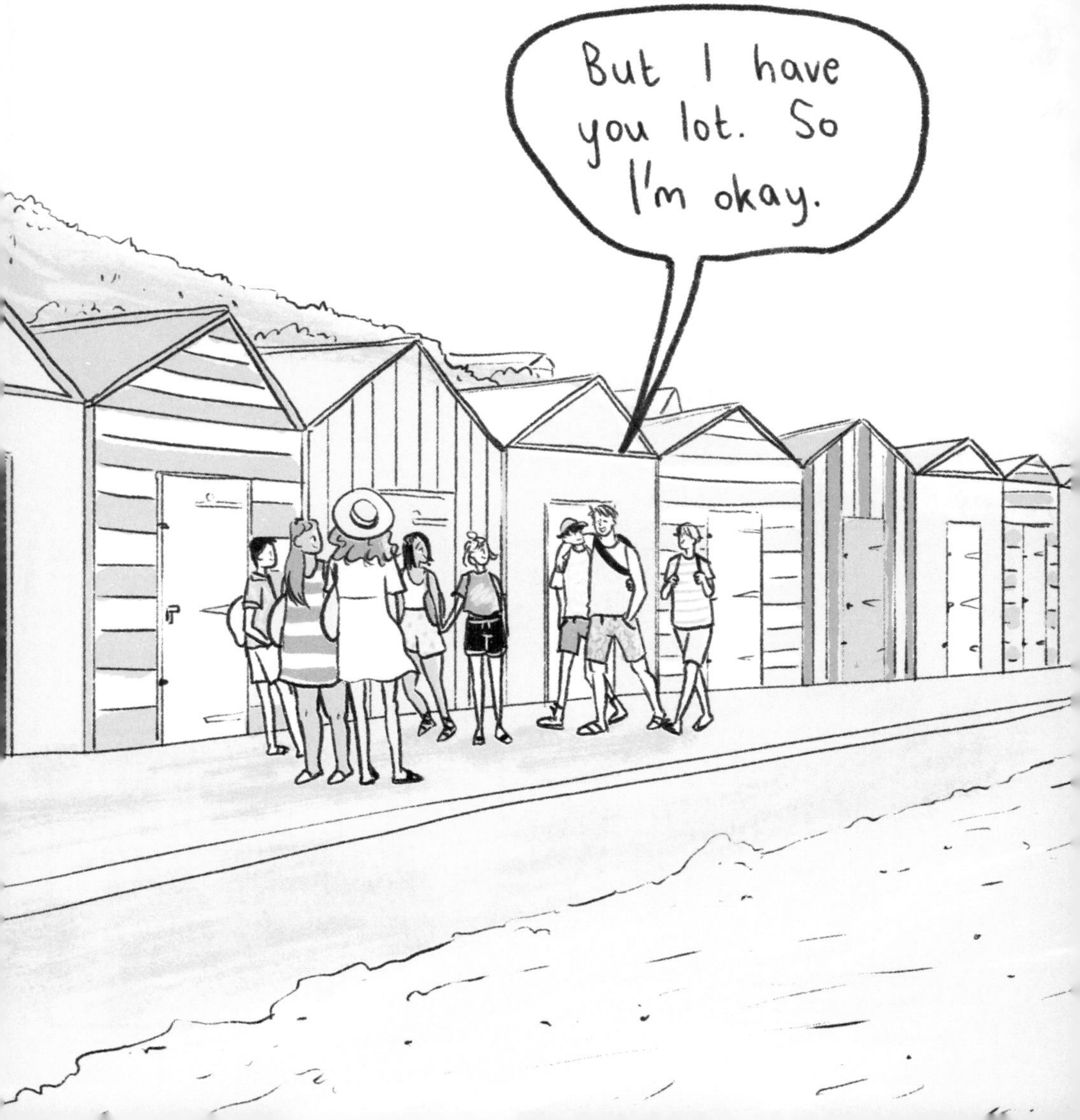
But I have you lot. So I'm okay.

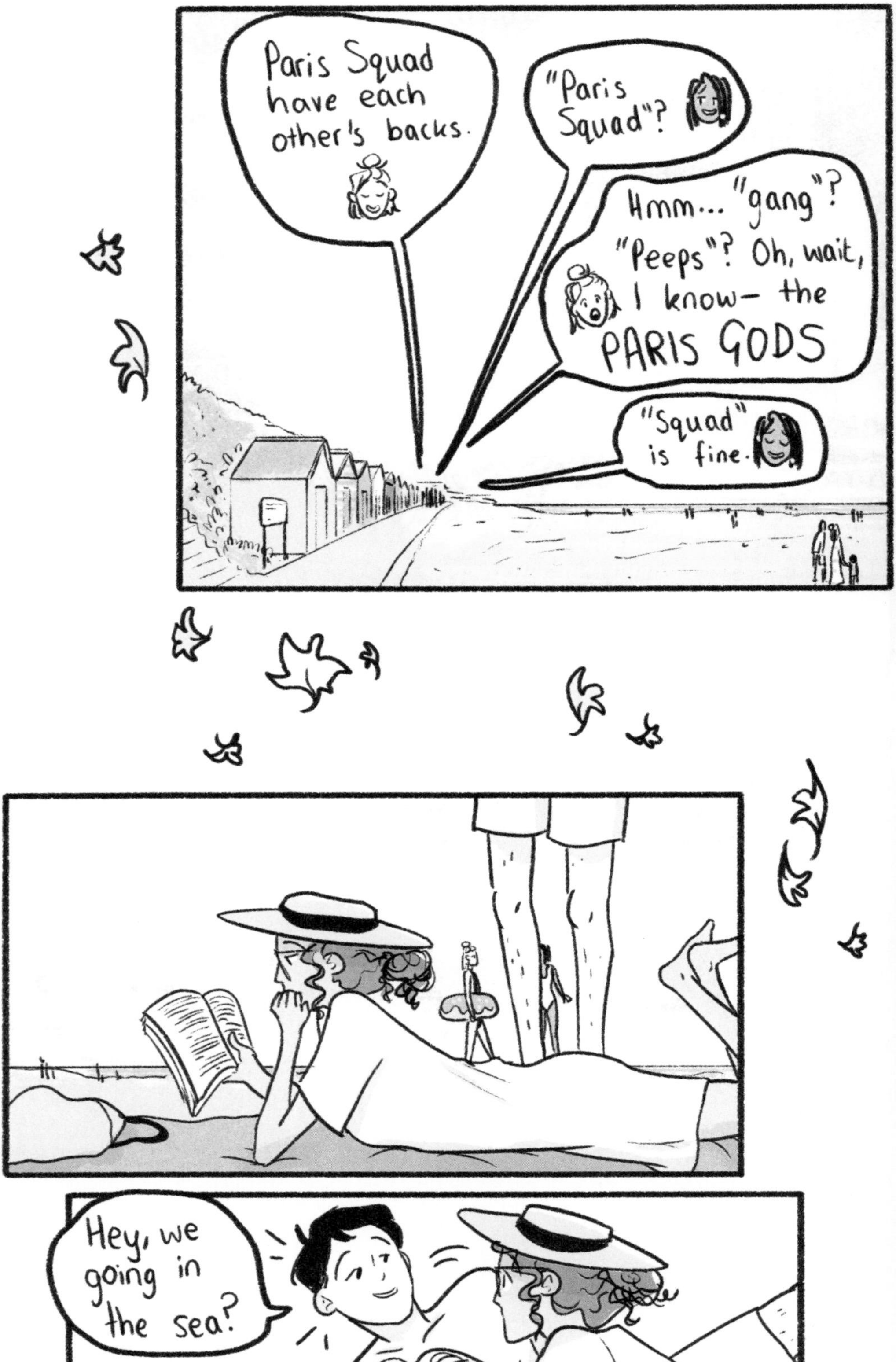
Paris Squad have each other's backs.
"Paris Squad"?
Hmm... "gang"? "Peeps"? Oh, wait, I know— the PARIS GODS
"Squad" is fine.
Hey, we going in the sea?

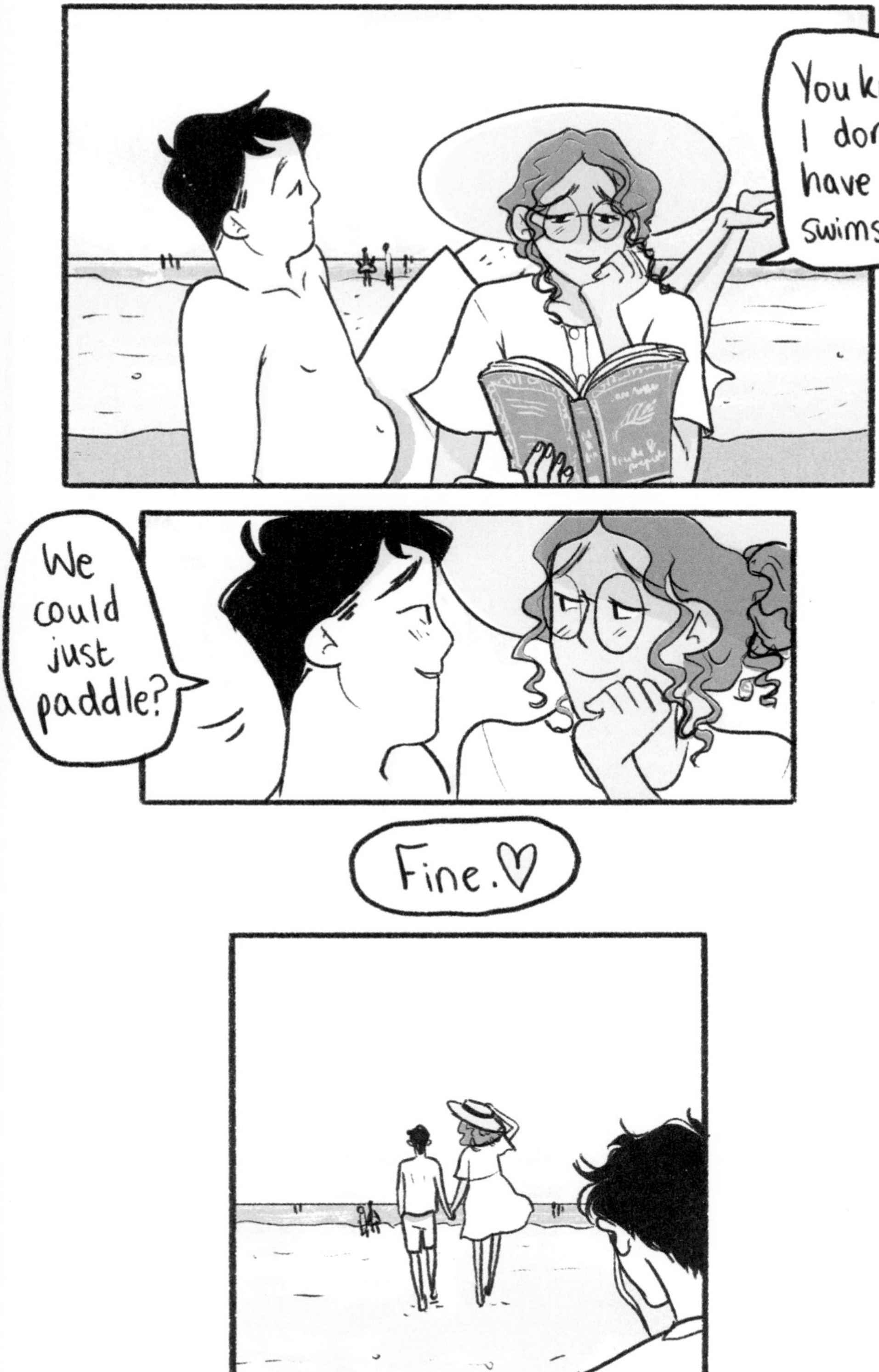
You know I don't have a swimsuit.
We could just paddle?
Fine. ♡

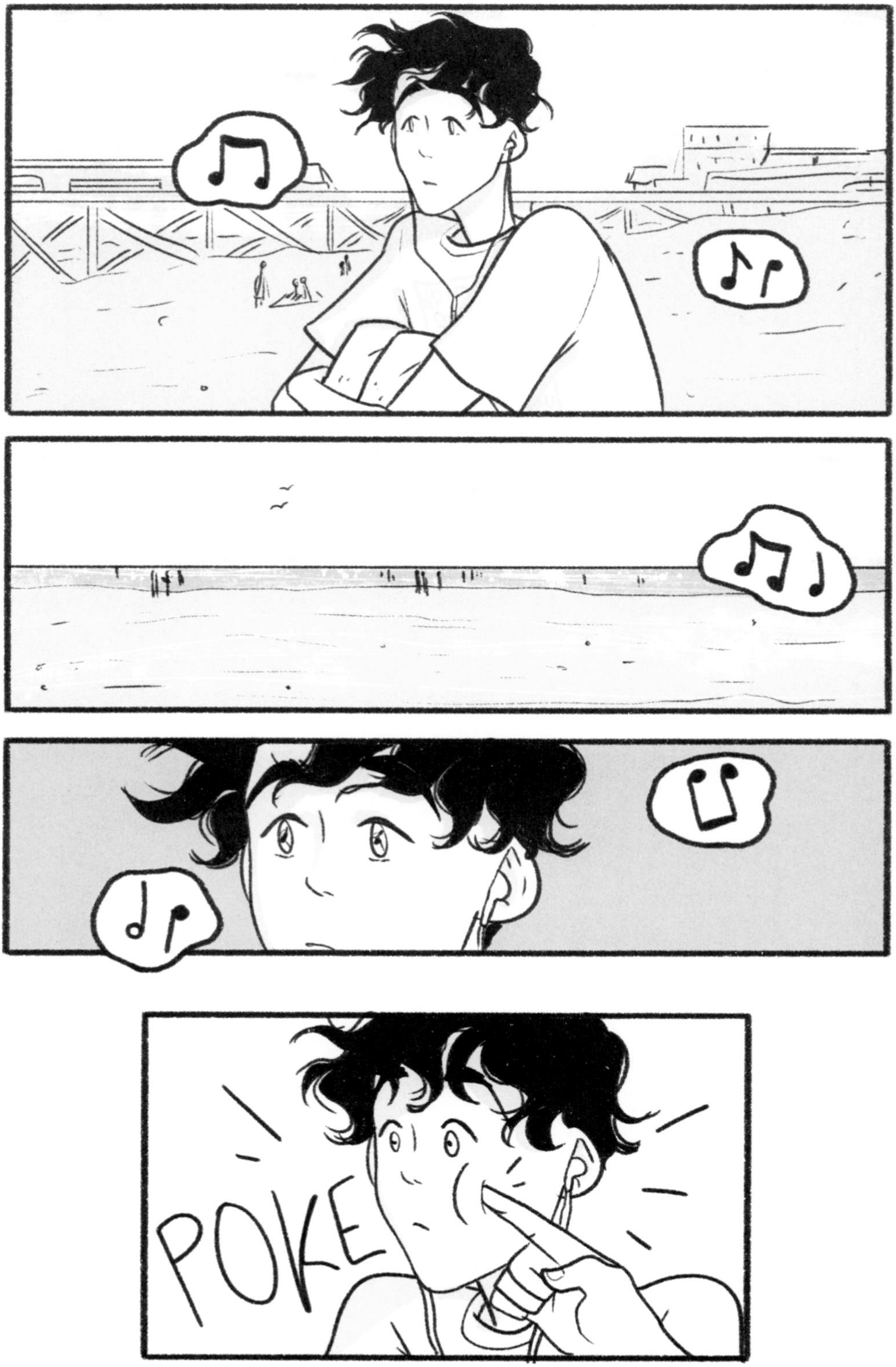
POKE

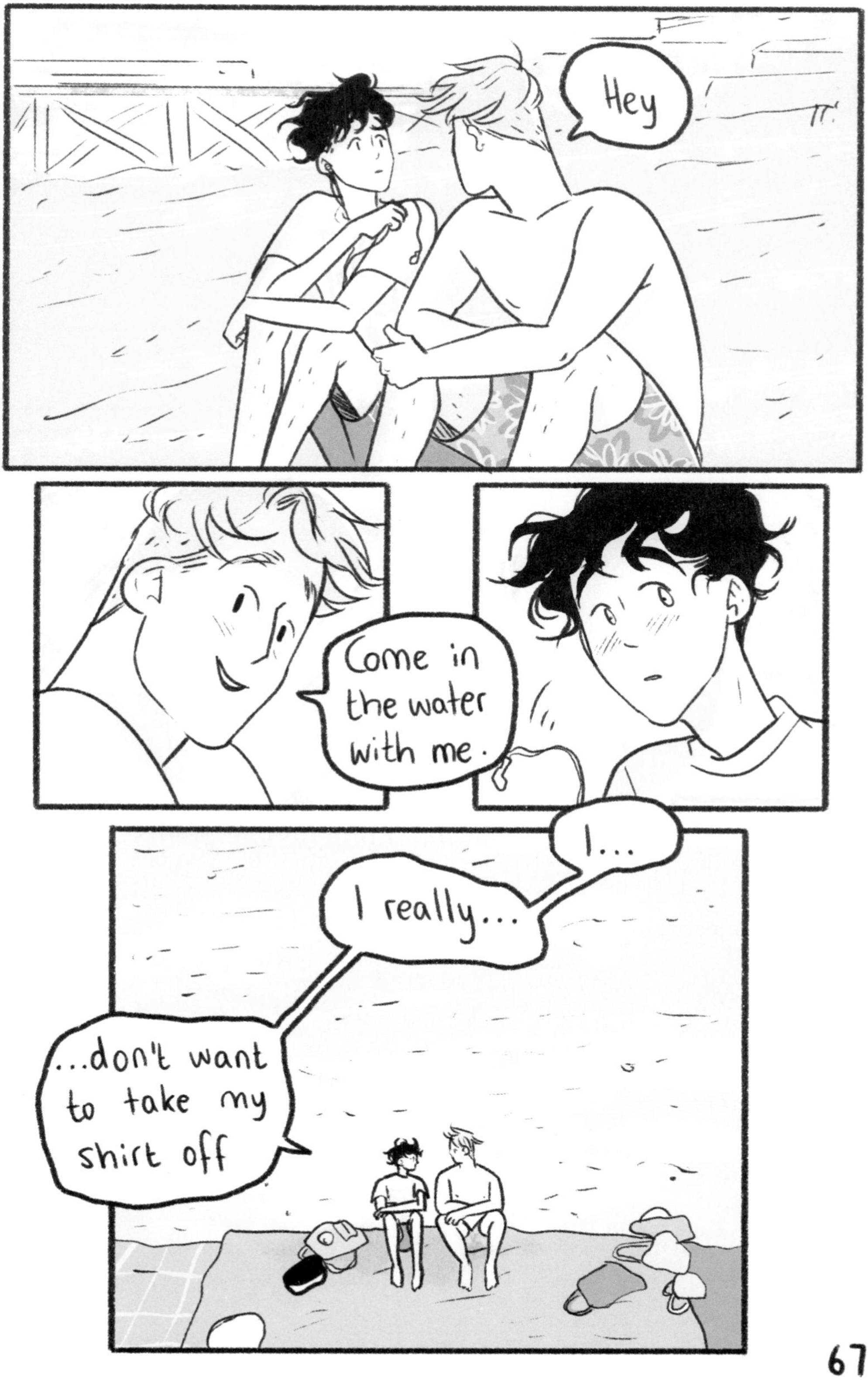
Hey
Come in the water with me.
I...
I really...
...don't want to take my shirt off

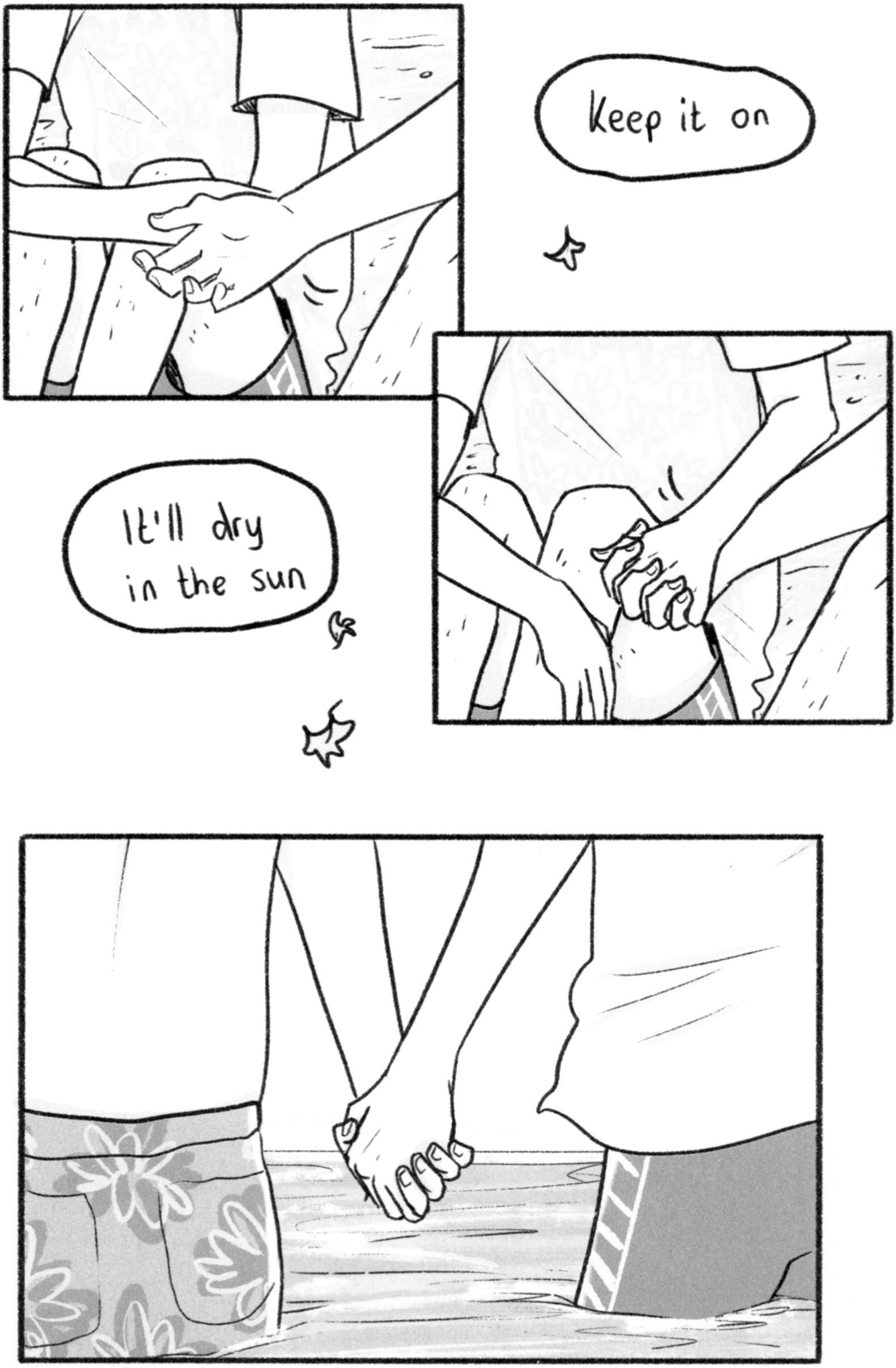
Keep it on
It'll dry in the sun

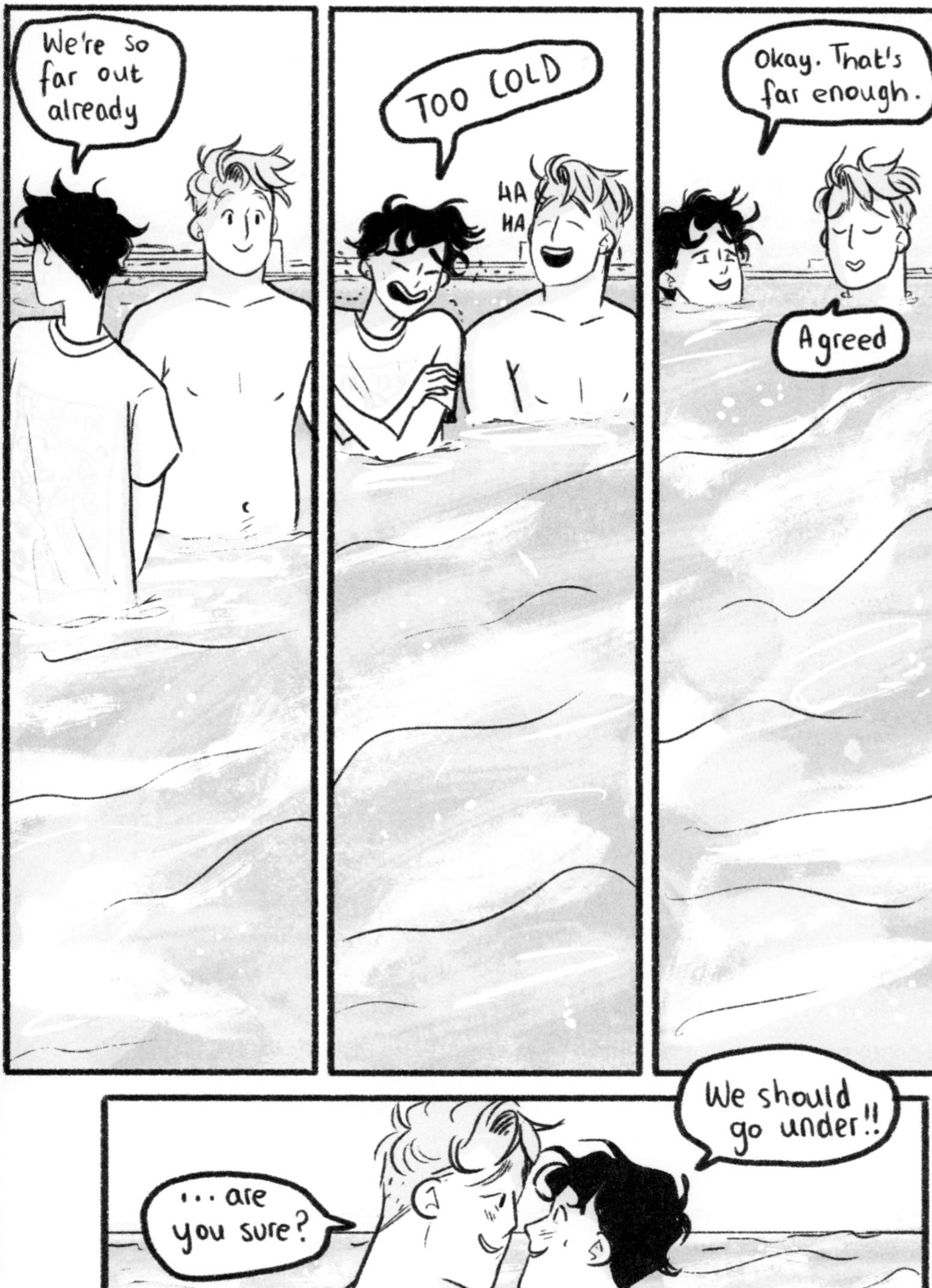
We're so far out already
TOO COLD
HA HA
Okay. That's far enough.
Agreed
We should go under!!
... are you sure?
...no
What if we freeze to death?

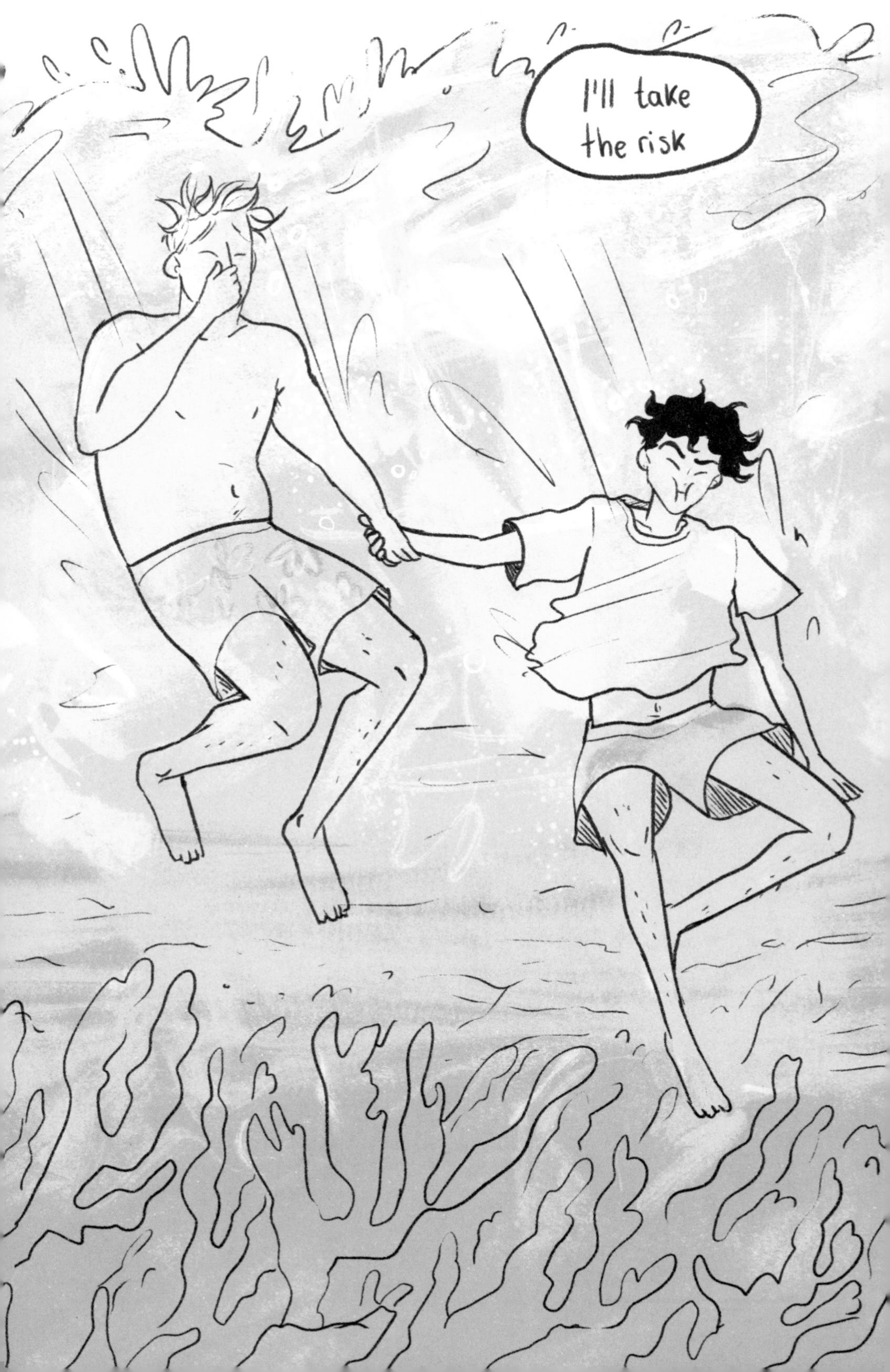
I'll take the risk

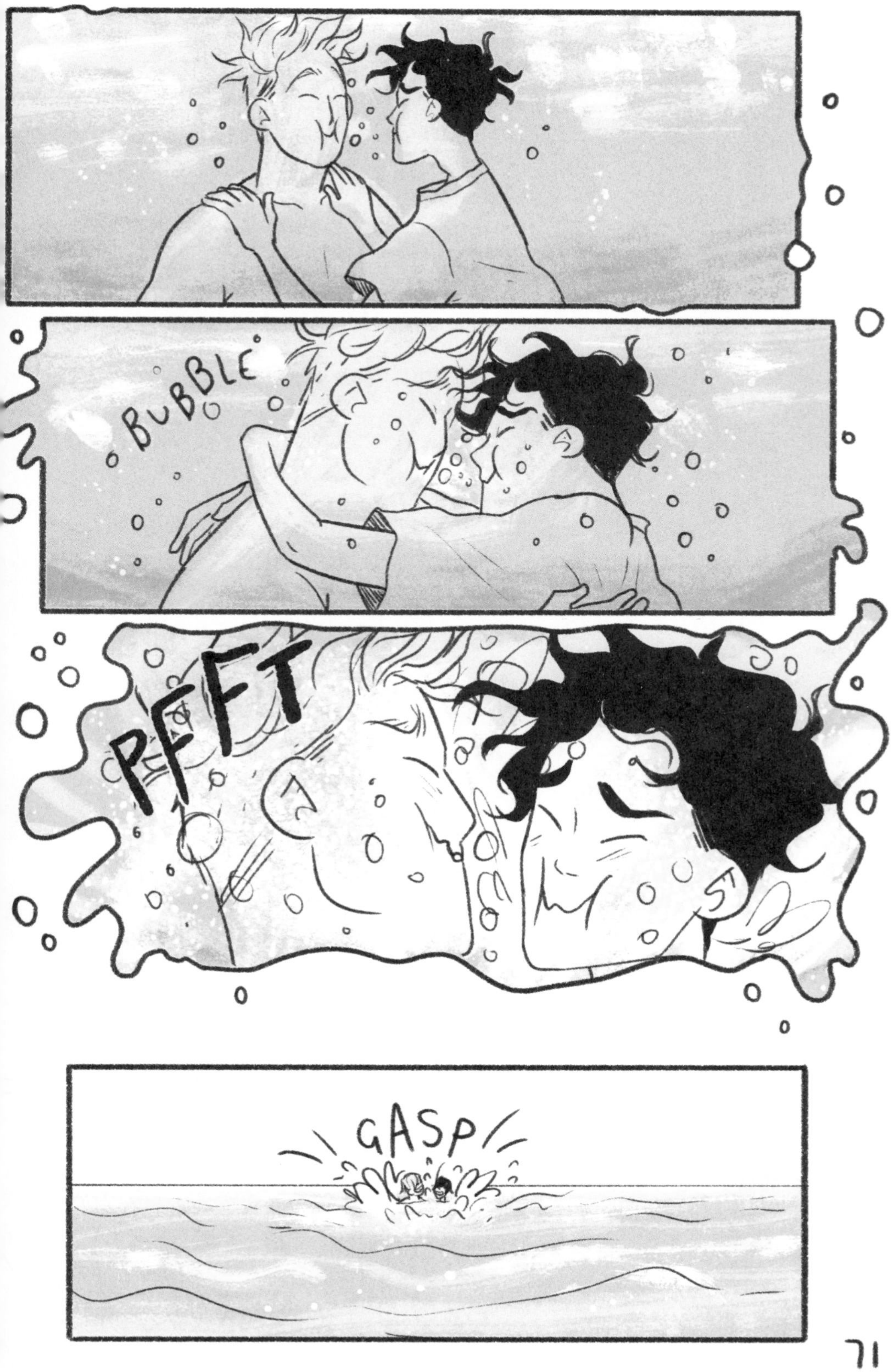
BUBBLE
PFFT
GASP

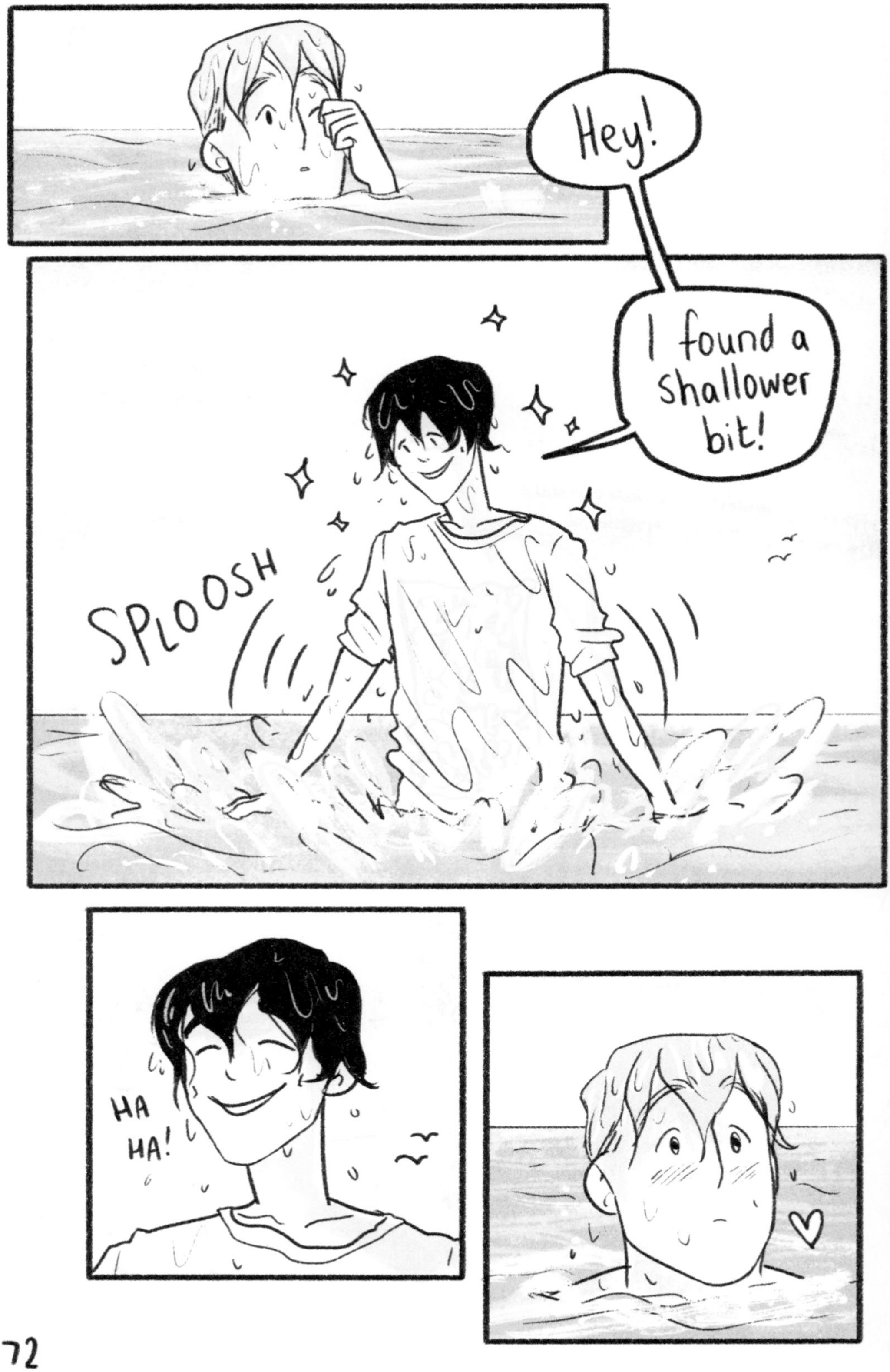
Hey!
I found a shallower bit!
SPLOOSH
HA HA!

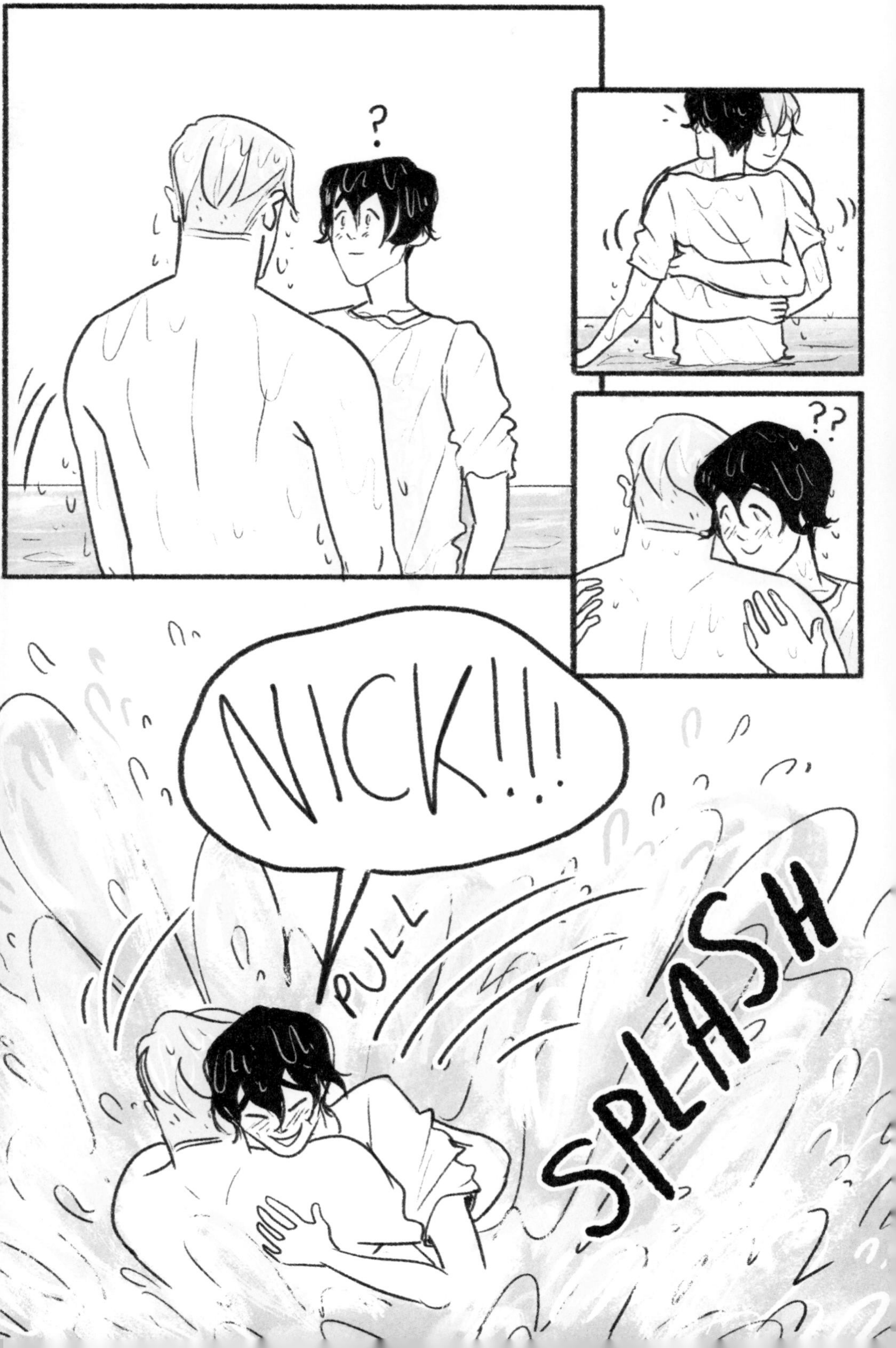
?
??
NICK!!!
PULL
SPLASH

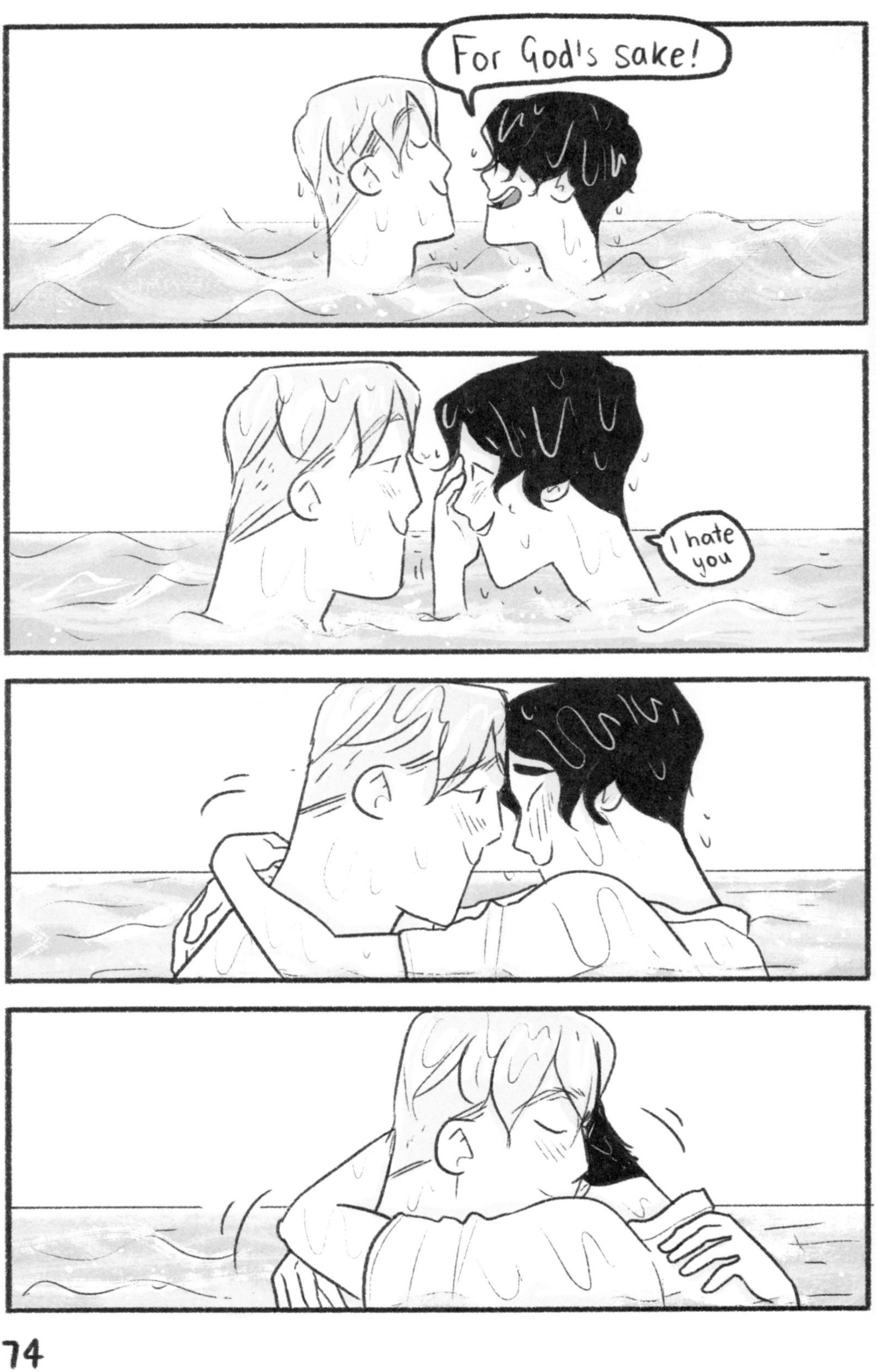
For God's sake!
I hate you

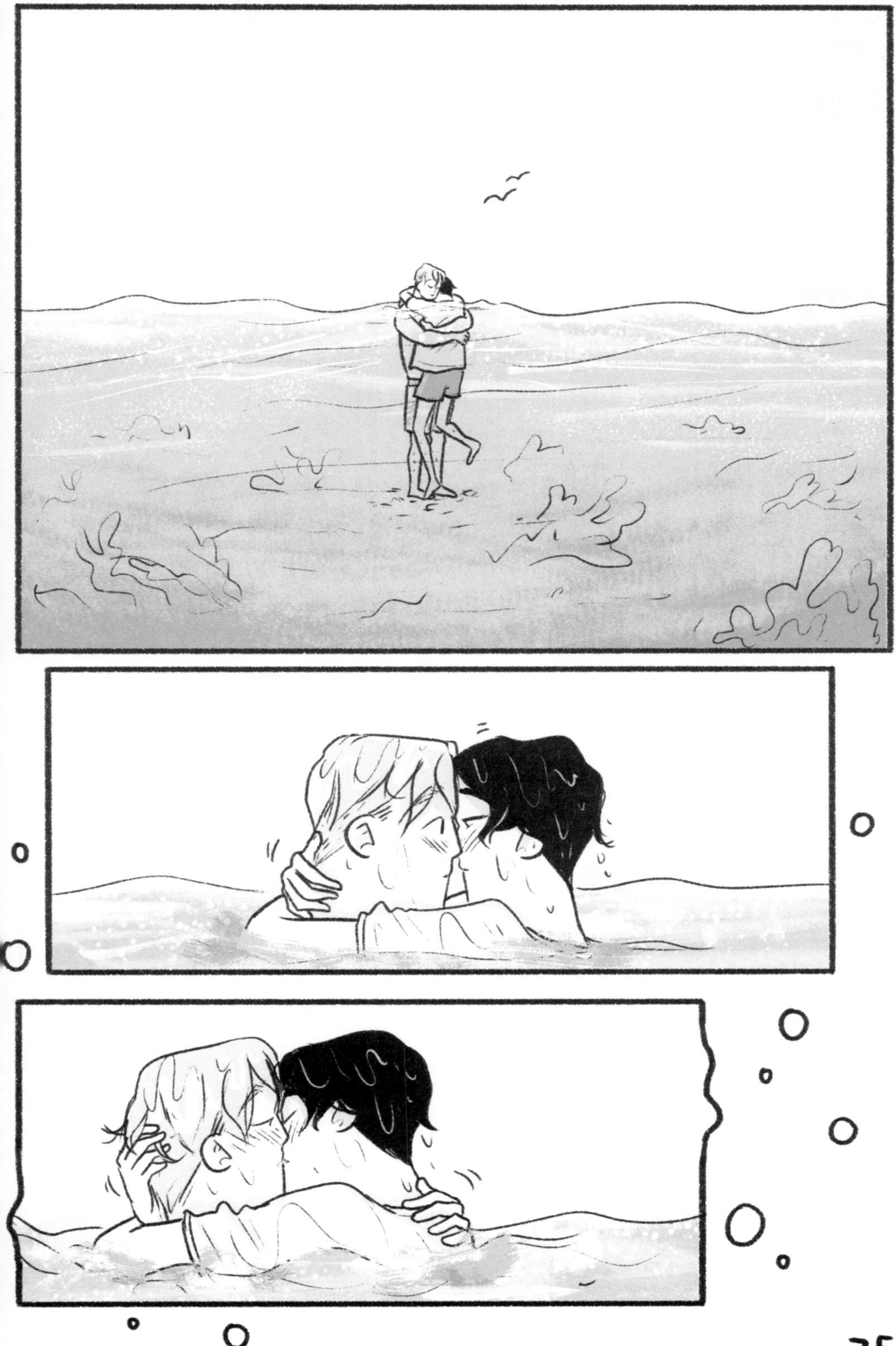

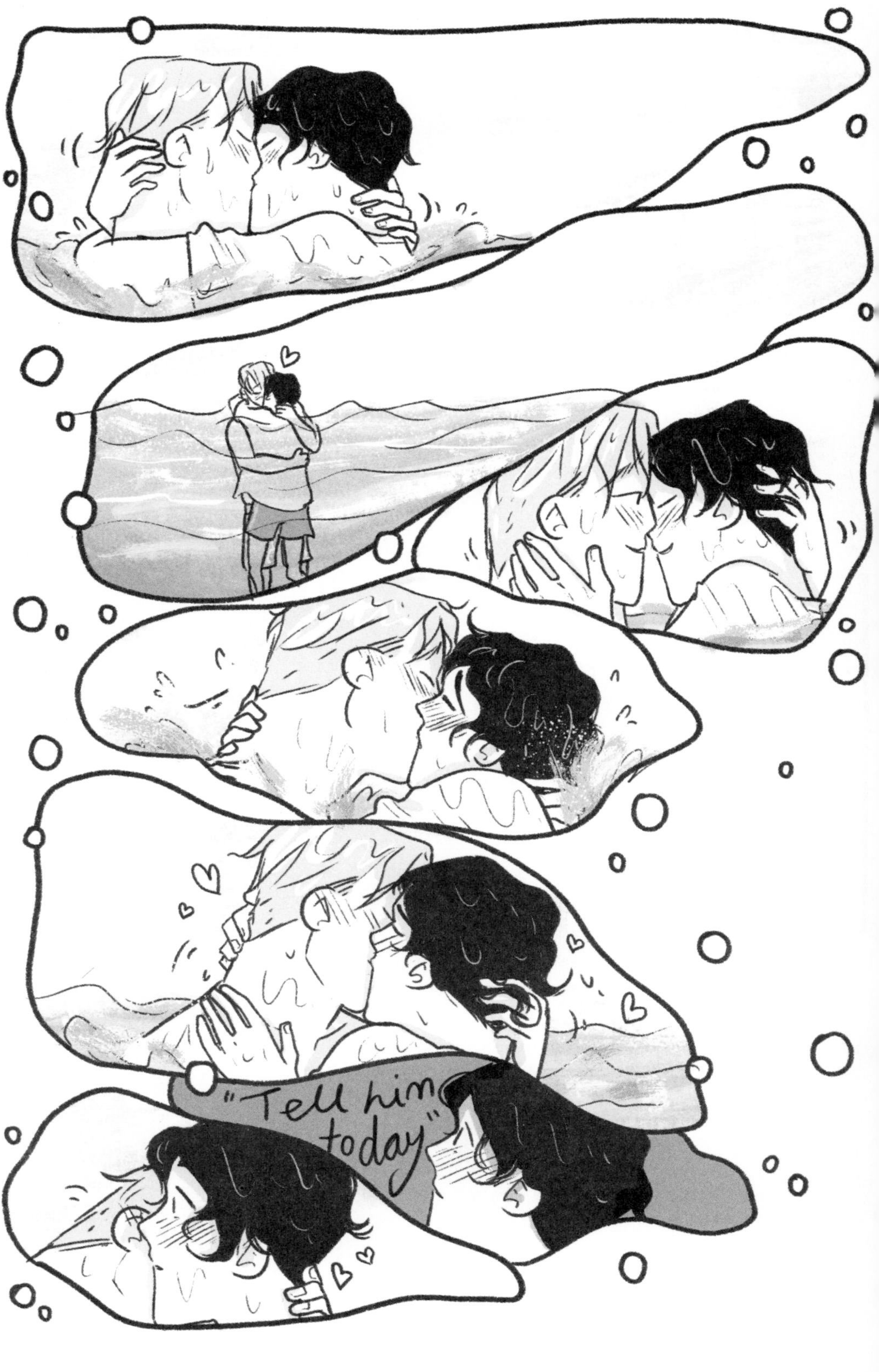
"Tell him today"

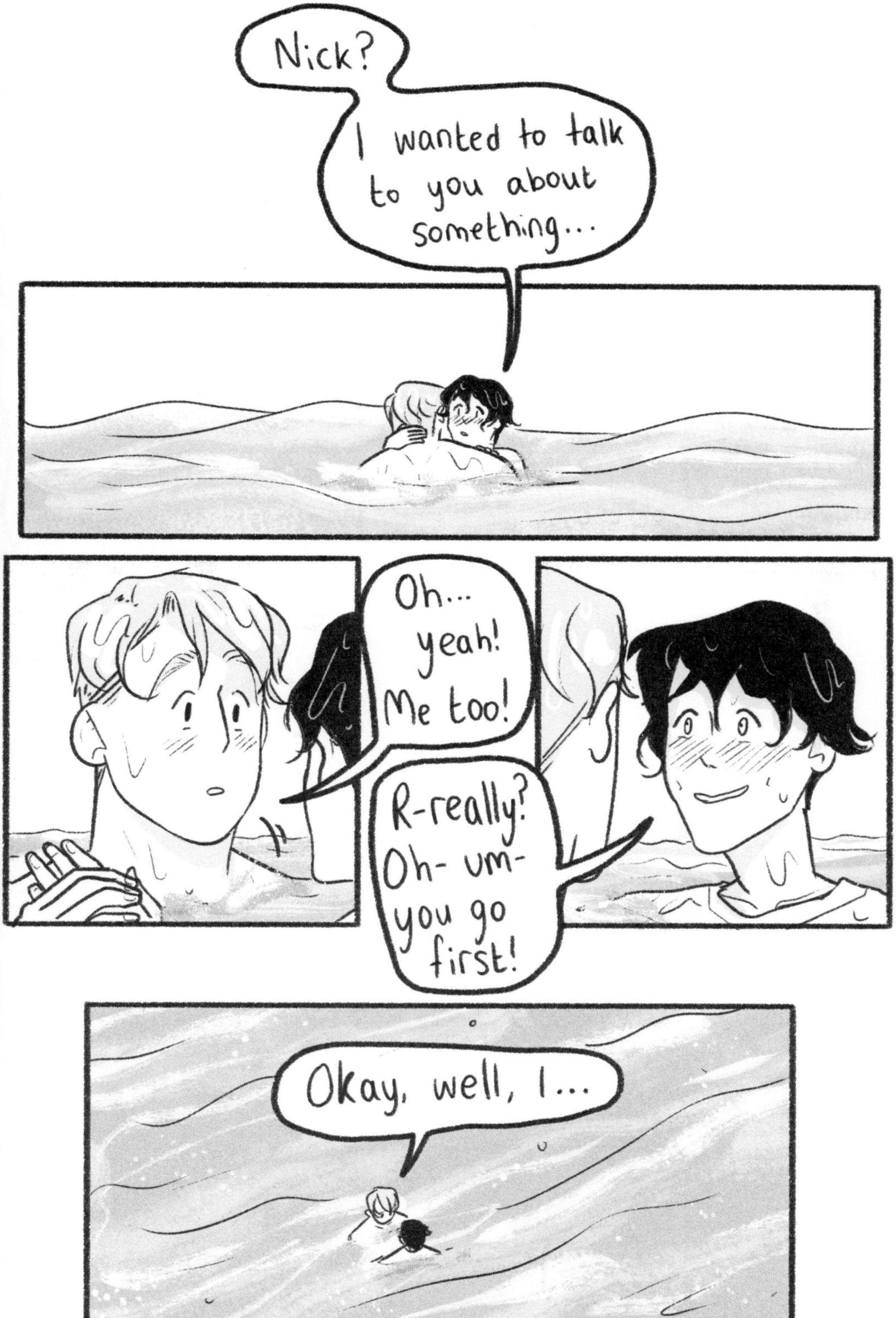
Nick? I wanted to talk to you about something...
Oh... yeah! Me too!
R-really? Oh- um- you go first!
Okay, well, I...

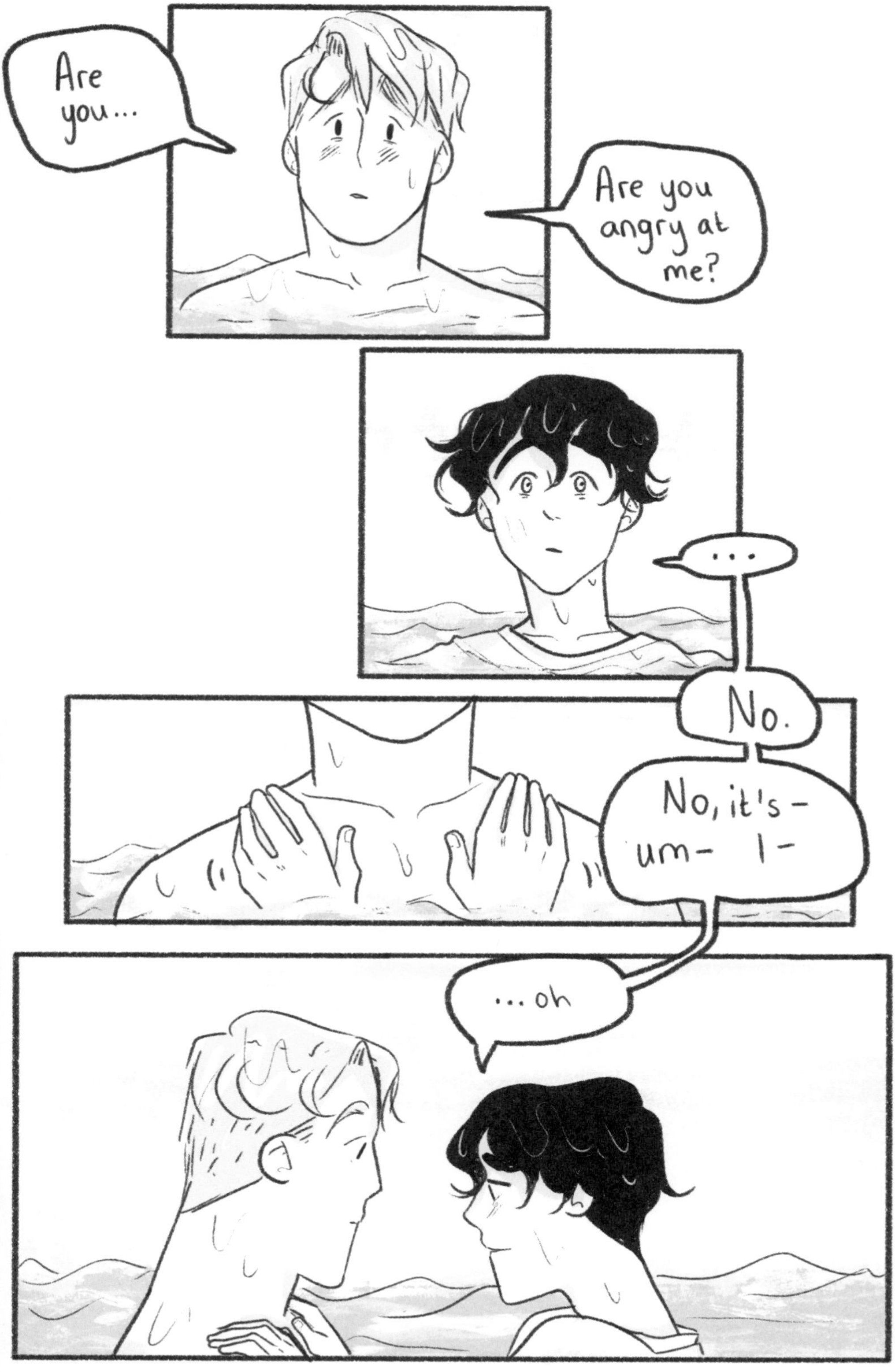
Are you...
Are you angry at me?
...
No.
No, it's - um- I-
...oh

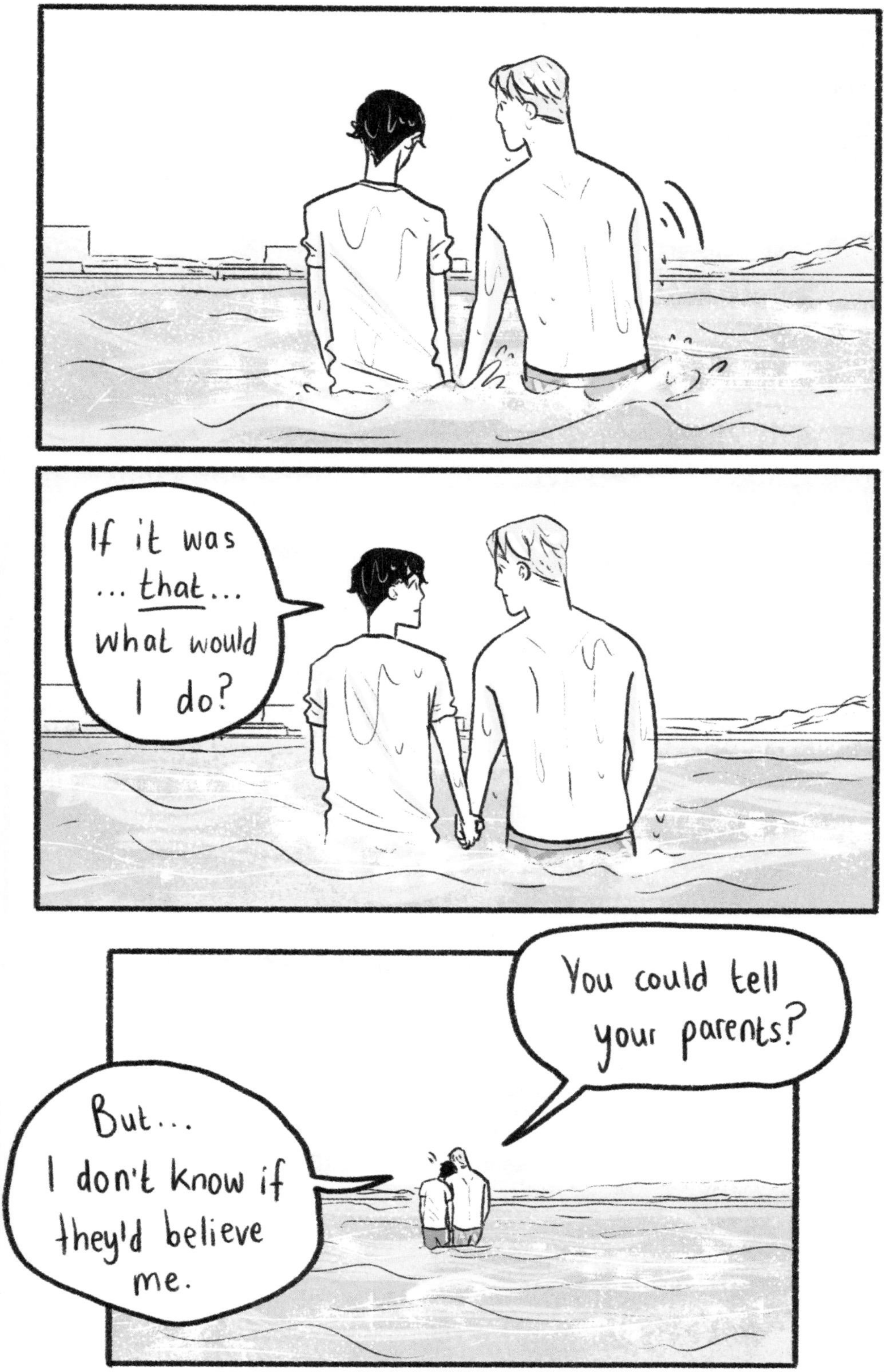
If it was ...that... what would I do?
You could tell your parents?
But... I don't know if they'd believe me.

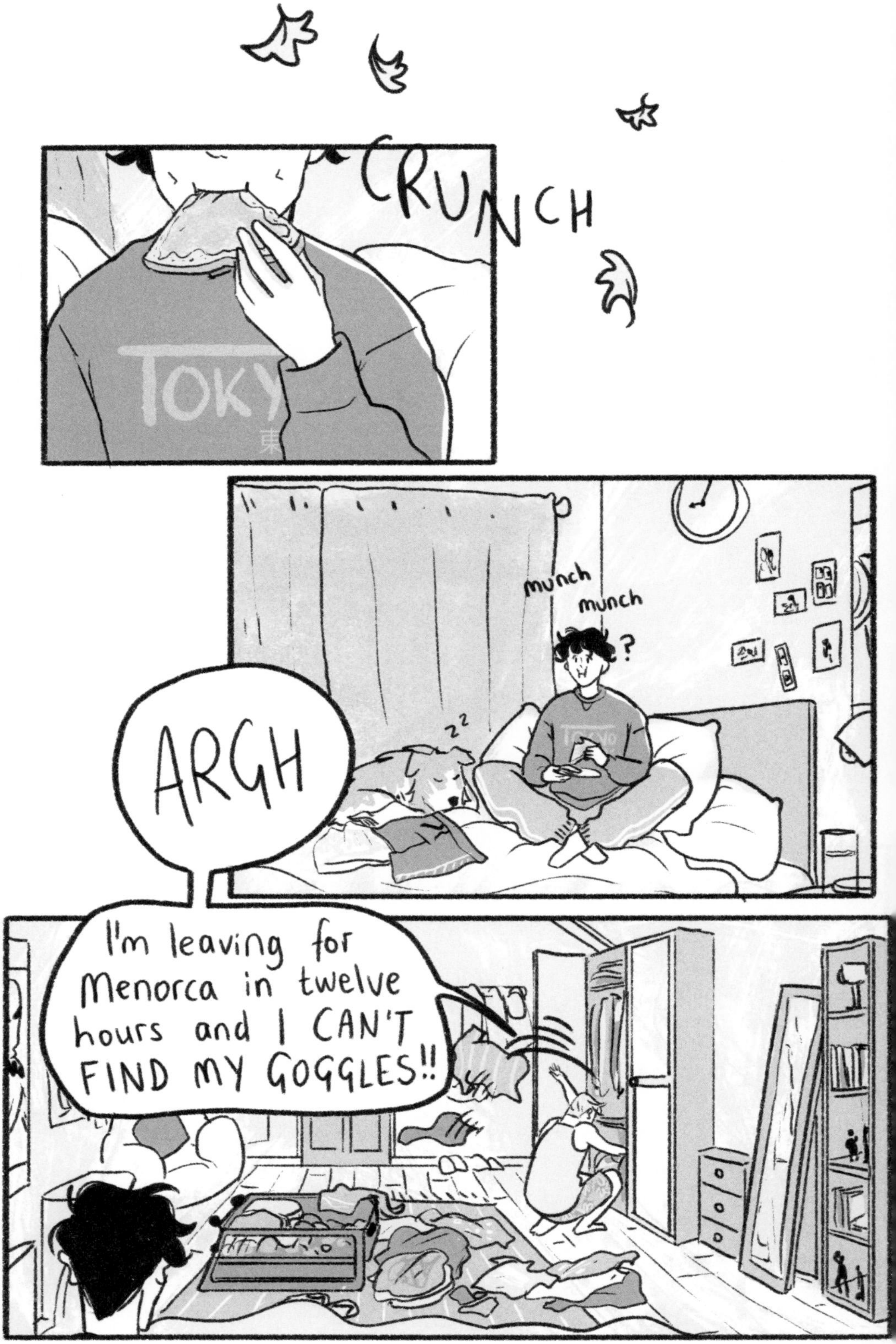
CRUNCH
TOKYO
munch
munch
?
ARGH
I'm leaving for Menorca in twelve hours and I CAN'T FIND MY GOGGLES!!

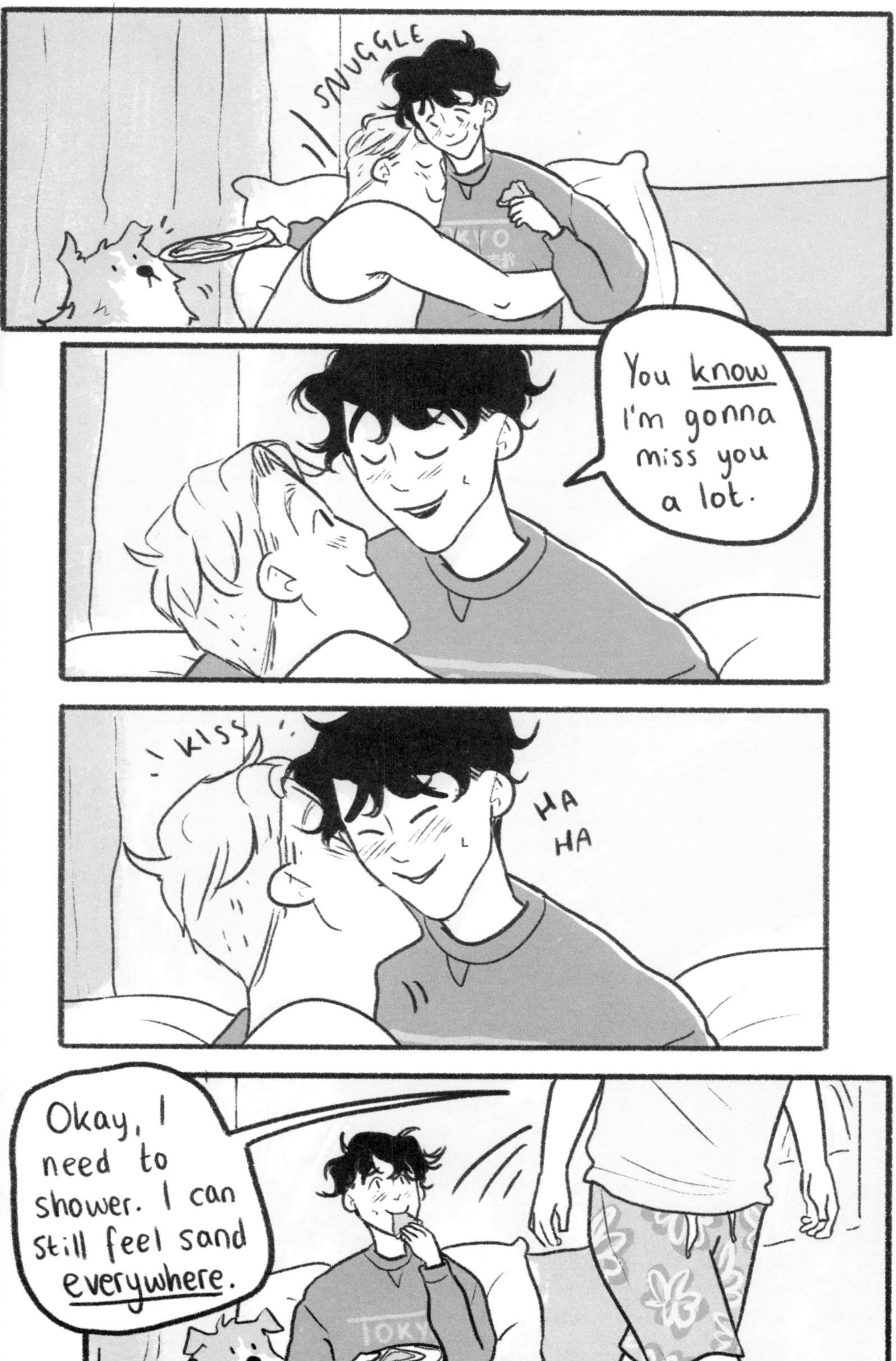
SNUGGLE
You know I'm gonna miss you a lot.
KISS
HA HA
Okay, I need to shower. I can still feel sand everywhere.

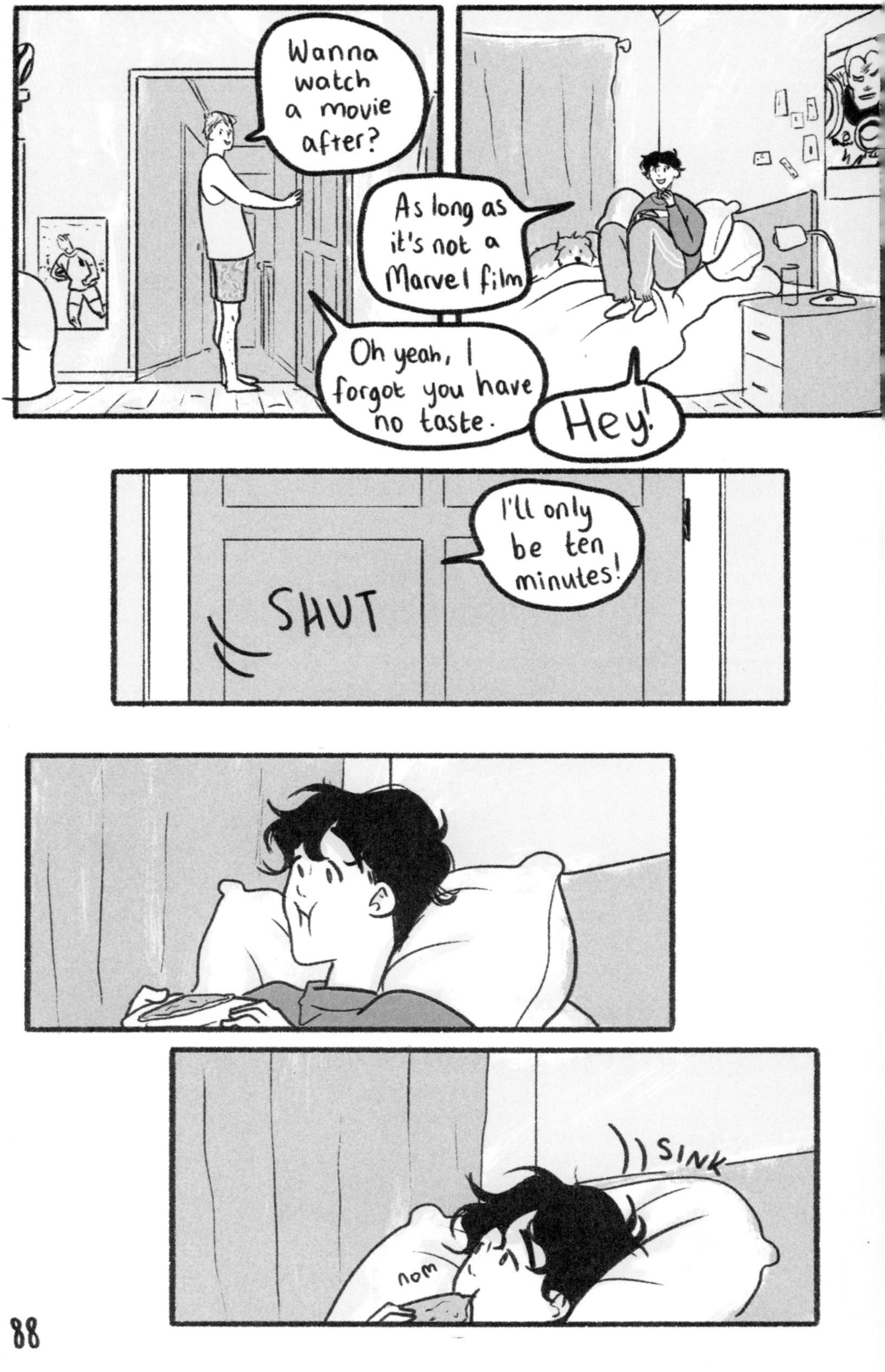
Wanna watch a movie after?
As long as it's not a Marvel film
Oh yeah, I forgot you have no taste.
Hey!
I'll only be ten minutes!
SHUT
SINK
nom

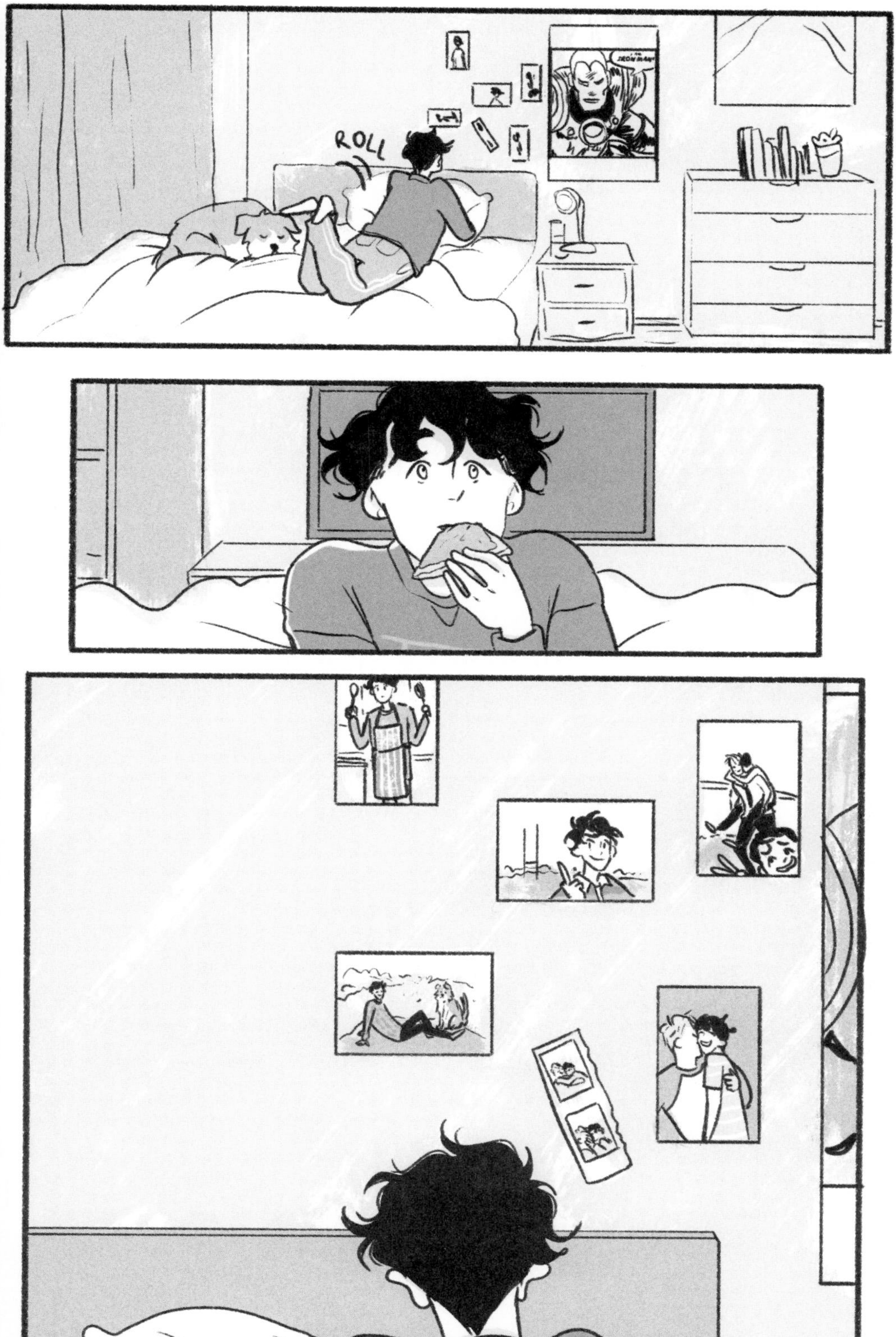
ROLL
IRON MAN!

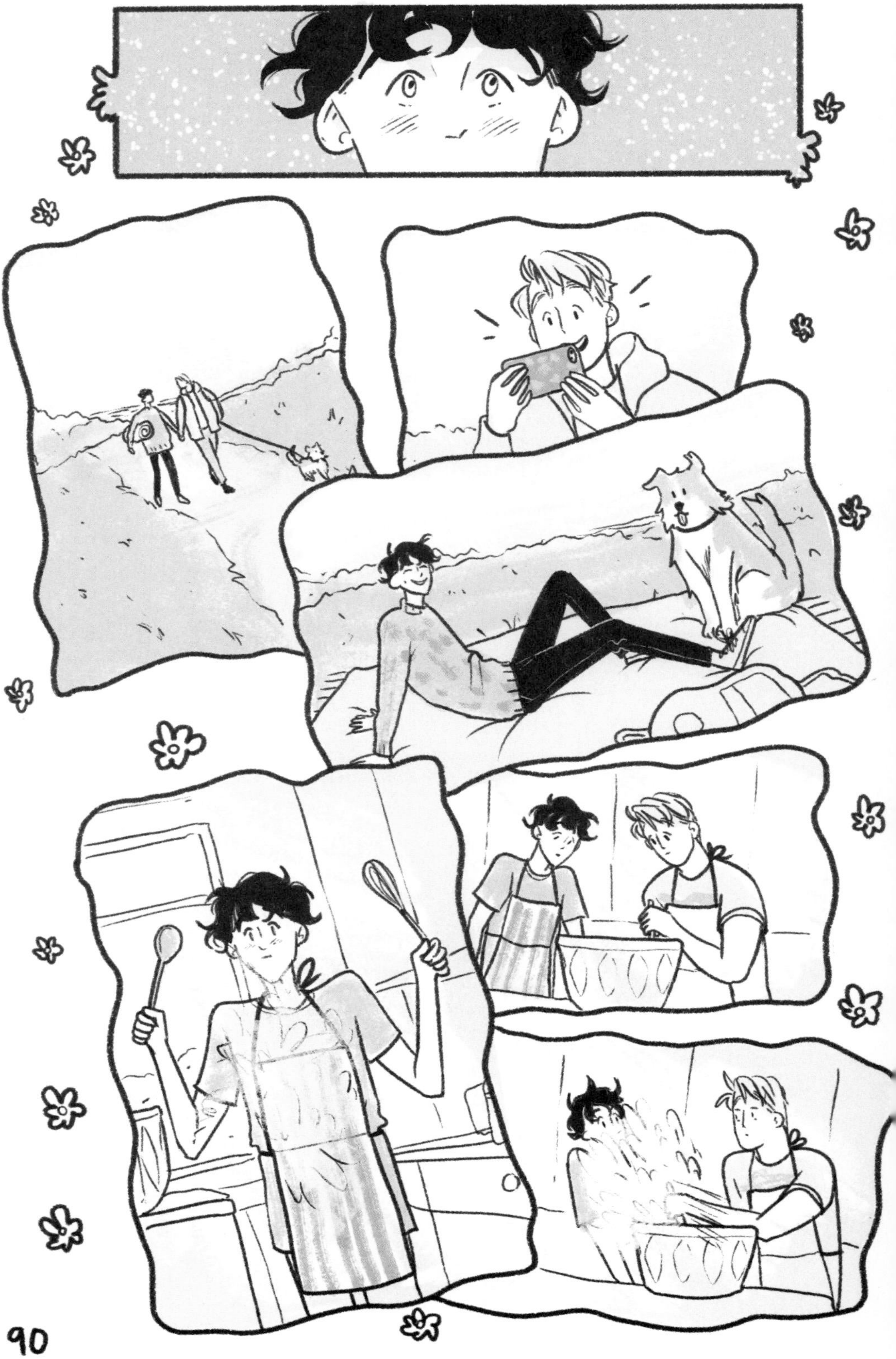

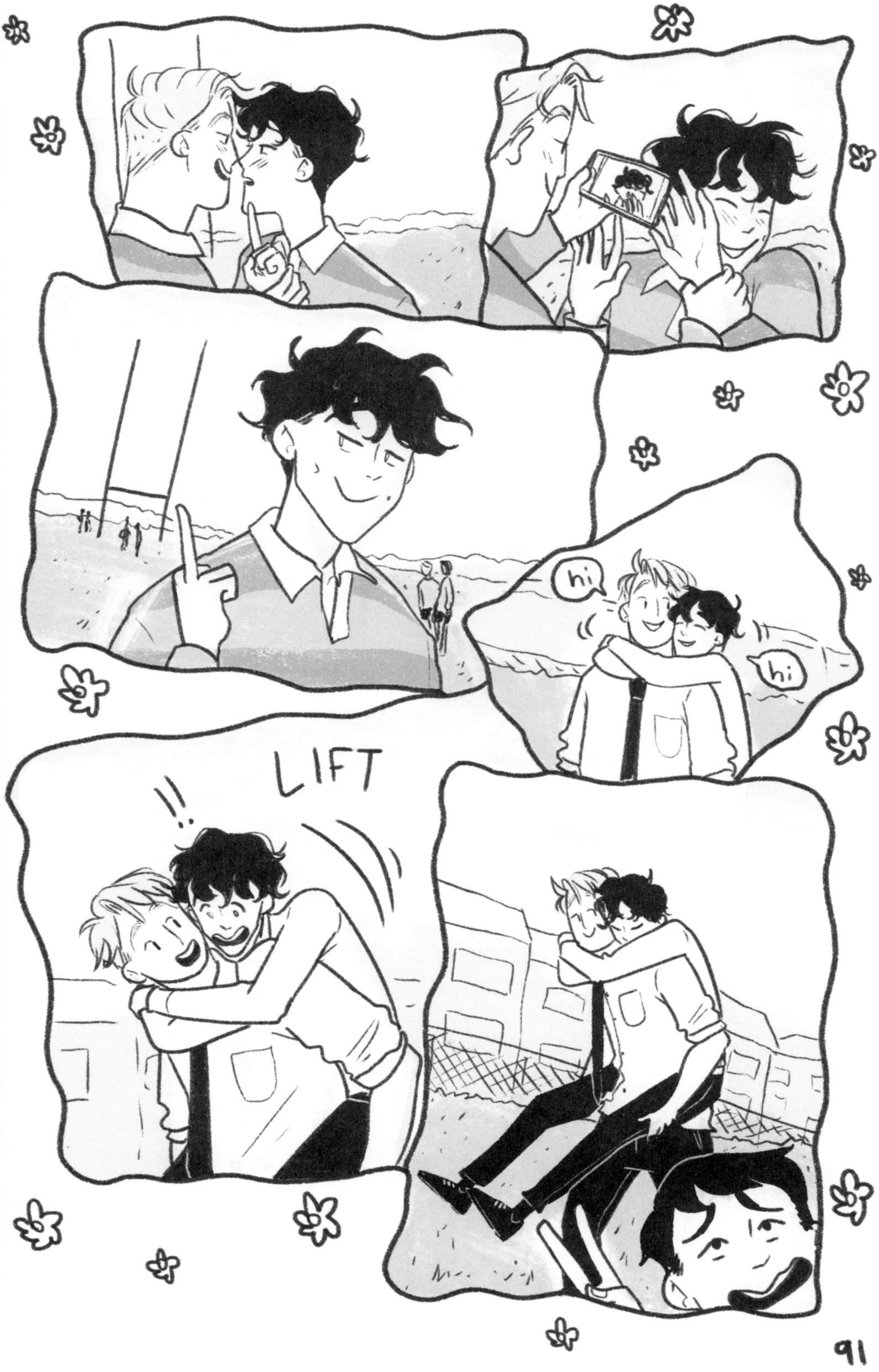
hi
hi
!!
LIFT

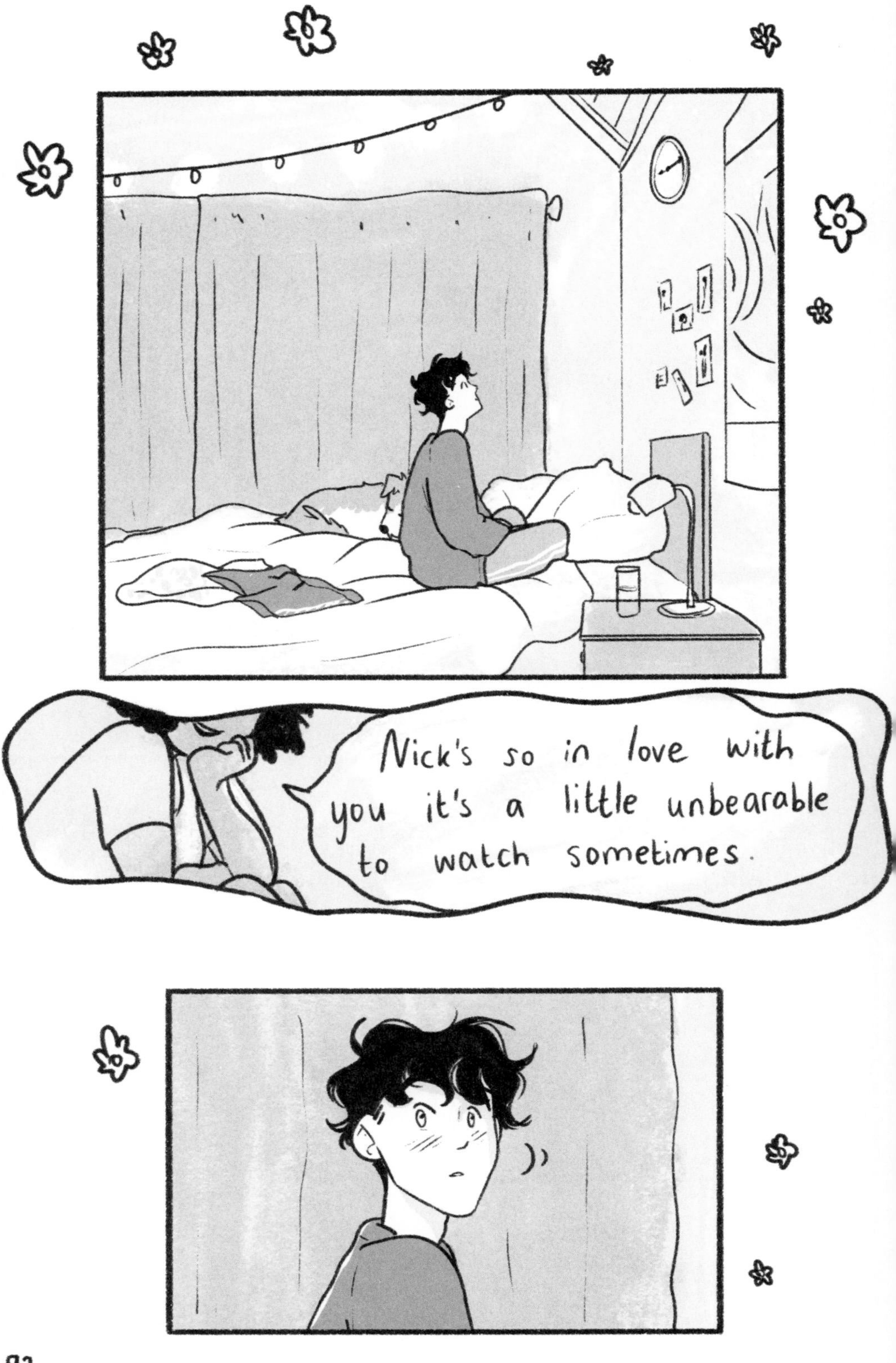

Nick's so in love with you it's a little unbearable to watch sometimes.

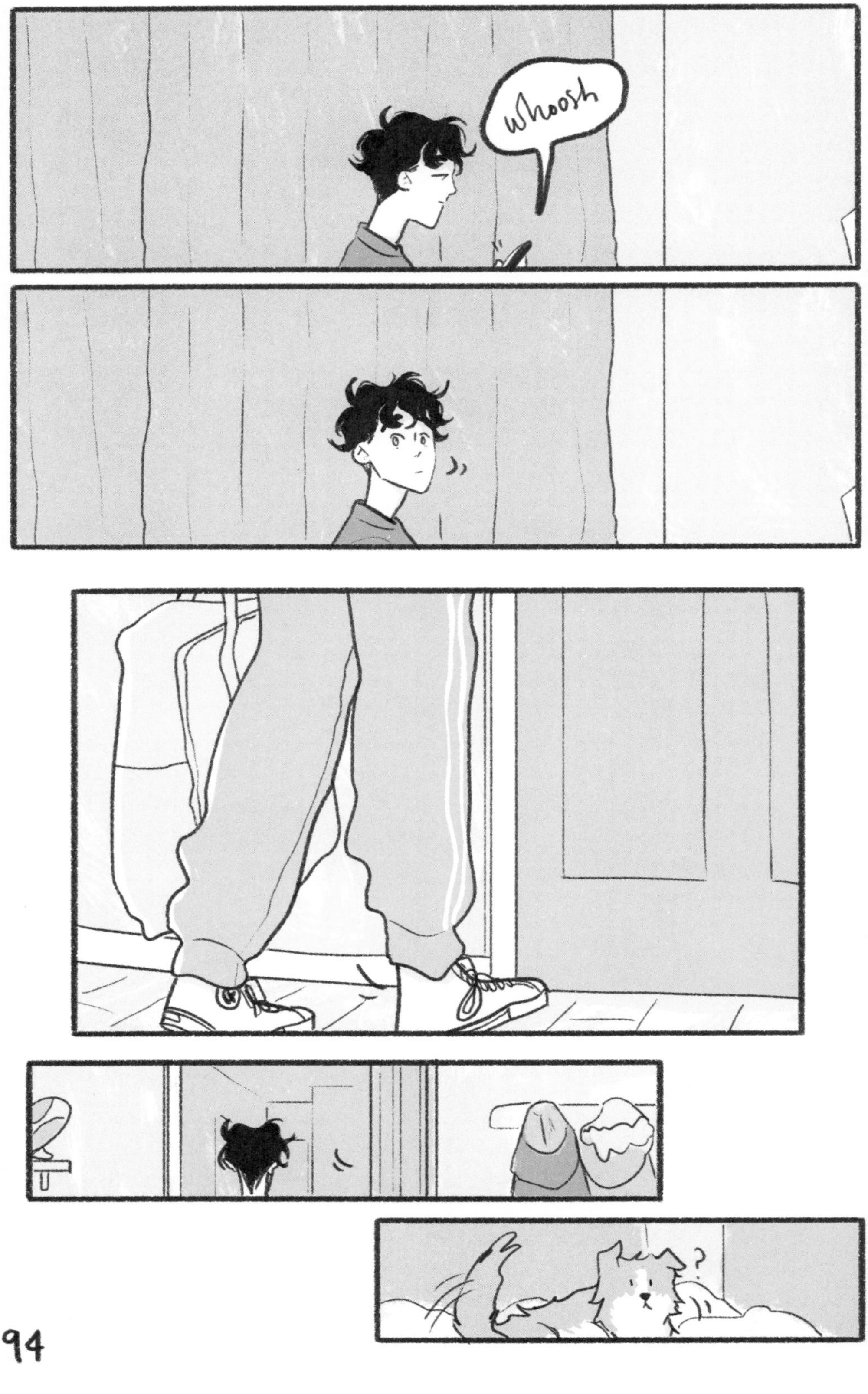
whoosh
?

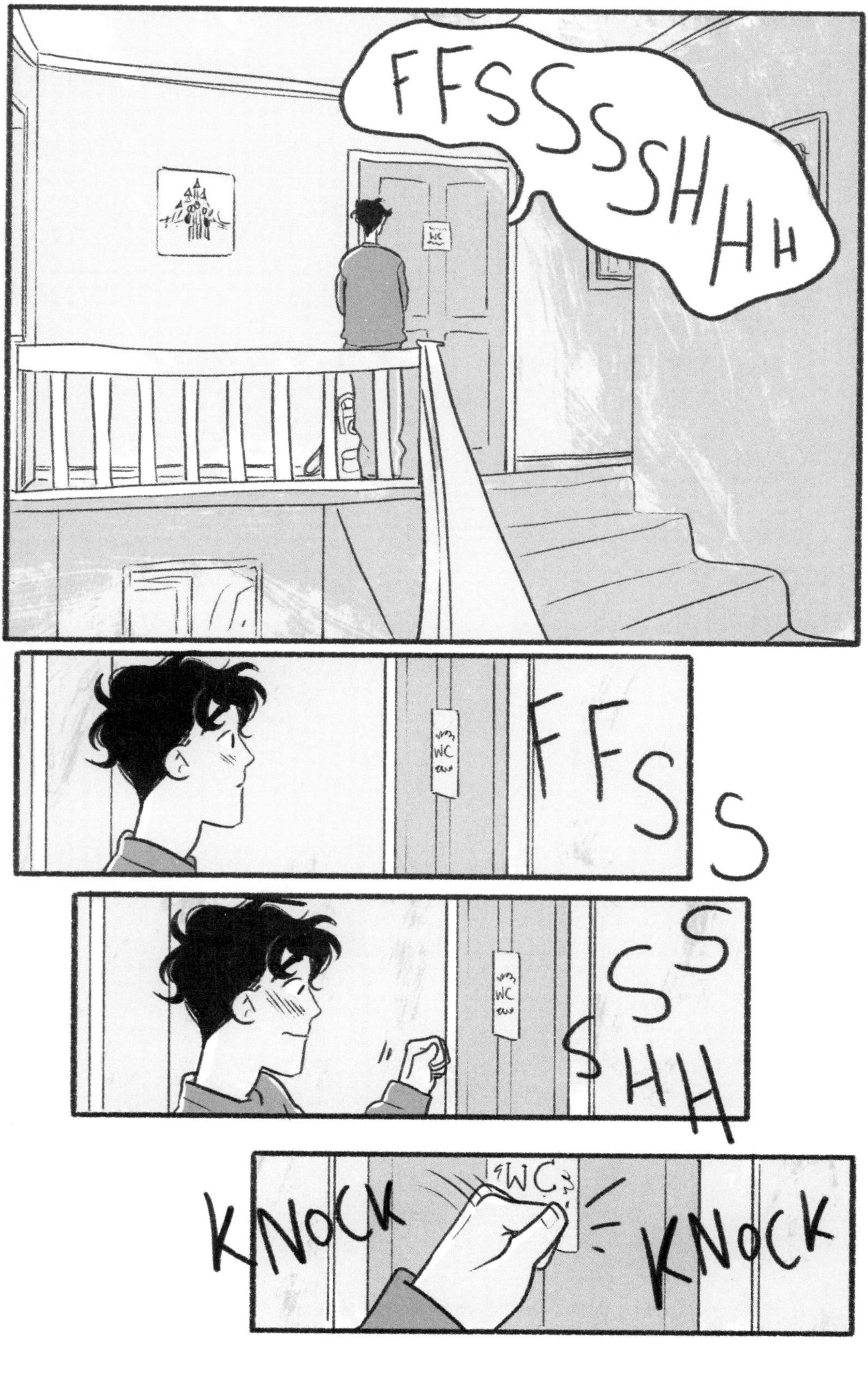
FFSSSSHHH
WC
FFSS
SSSHH
KNOCK KNOCK

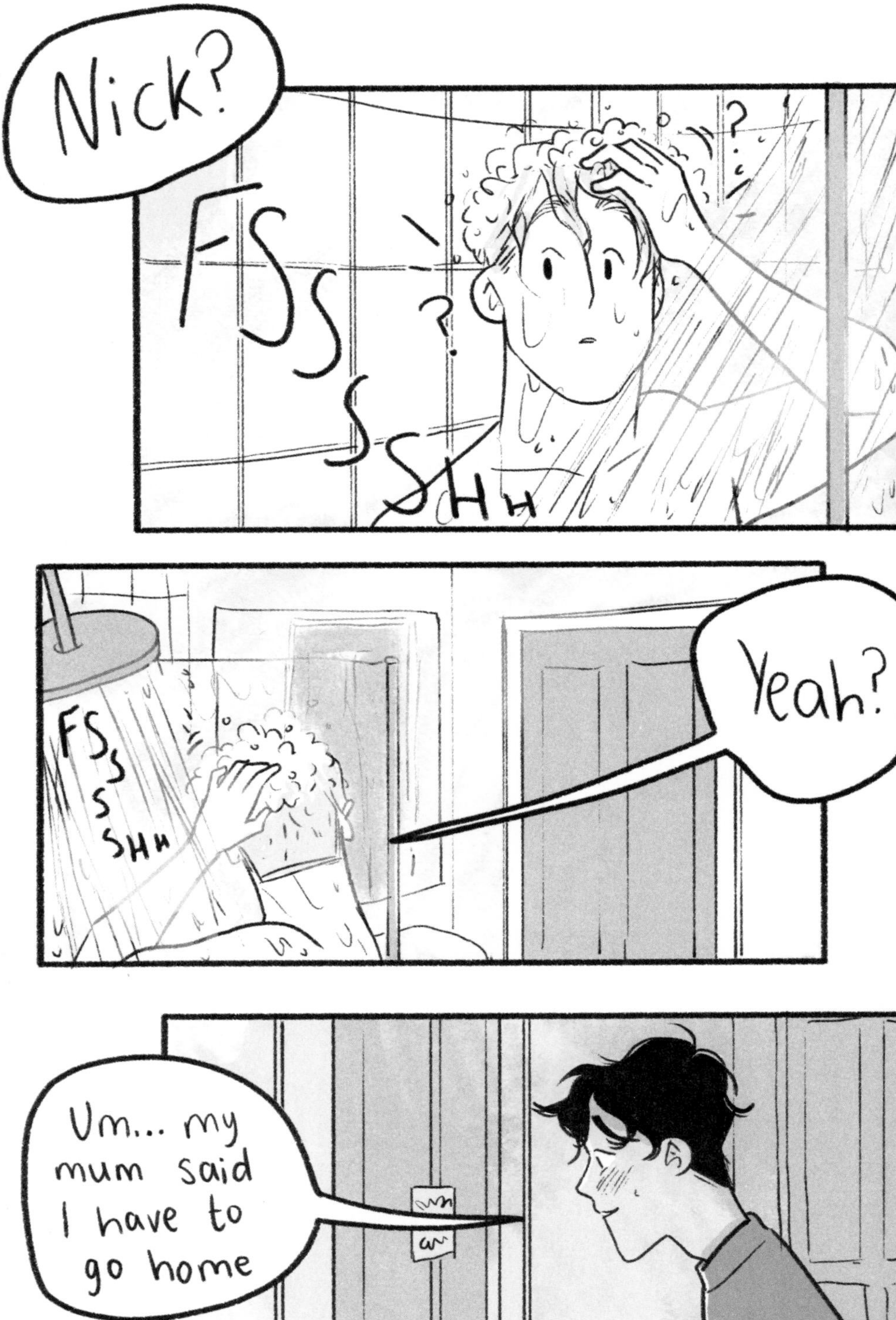
Nick?
FSSSSHH
?
?
FSSSSHH
Yeah?
Um... my mum said I have to go home

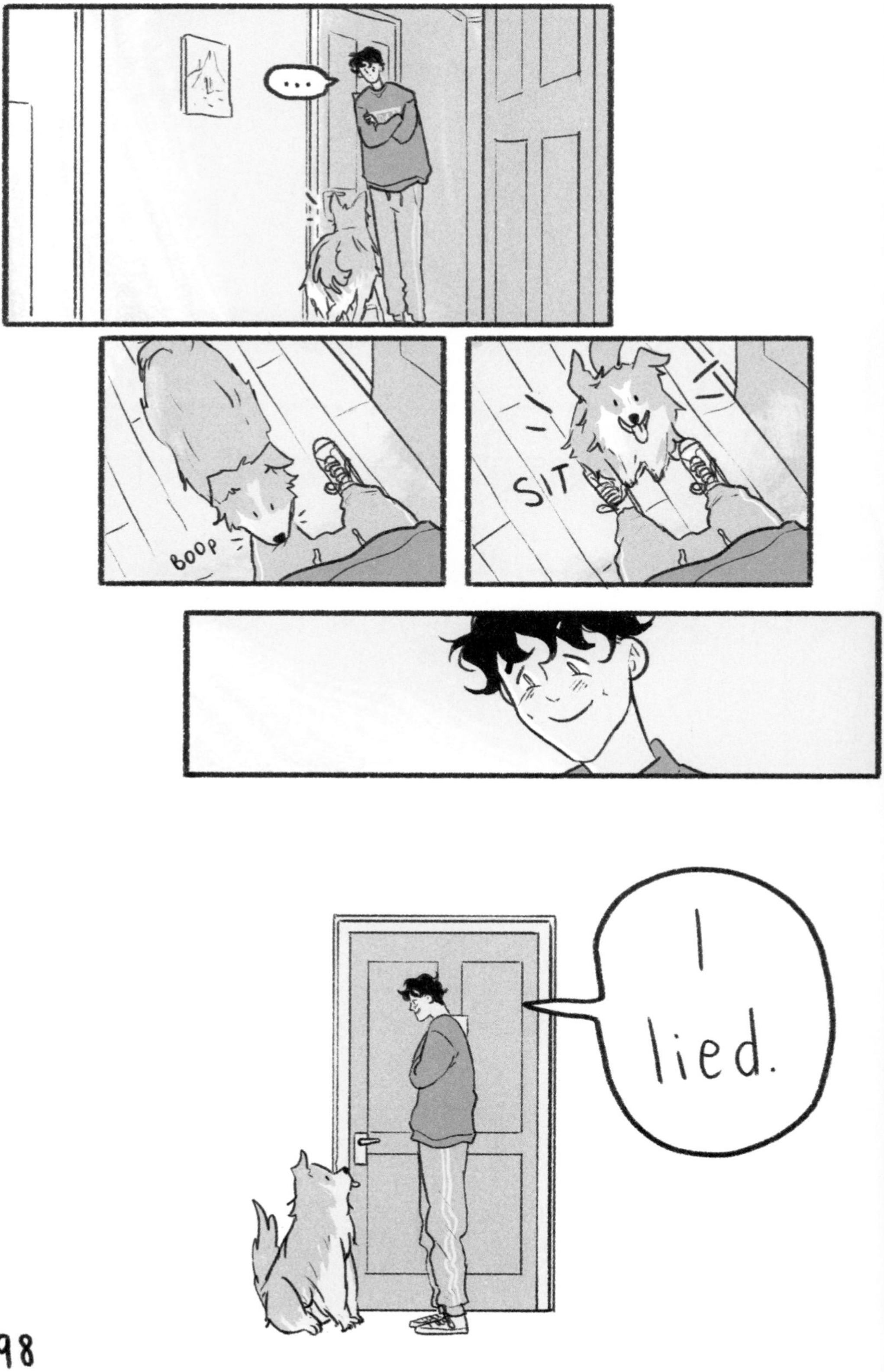
...
BOOP
SIT
I lied.

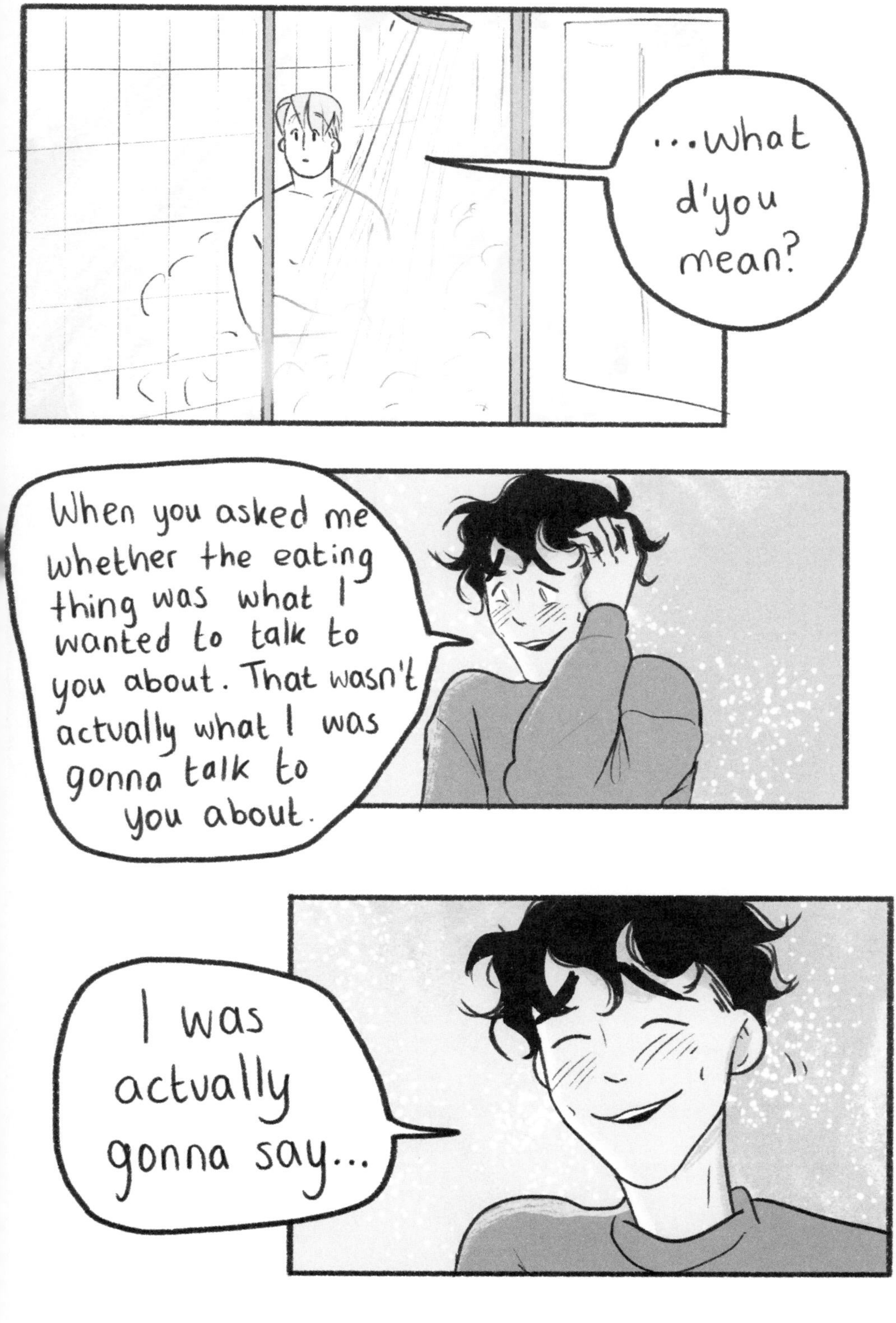
...what d'you mean?
When you asked me whether the eating thing was what I wanted to talk to you about. That wasn't actually what I was gonna talk to you about.
I was actually gonna say...

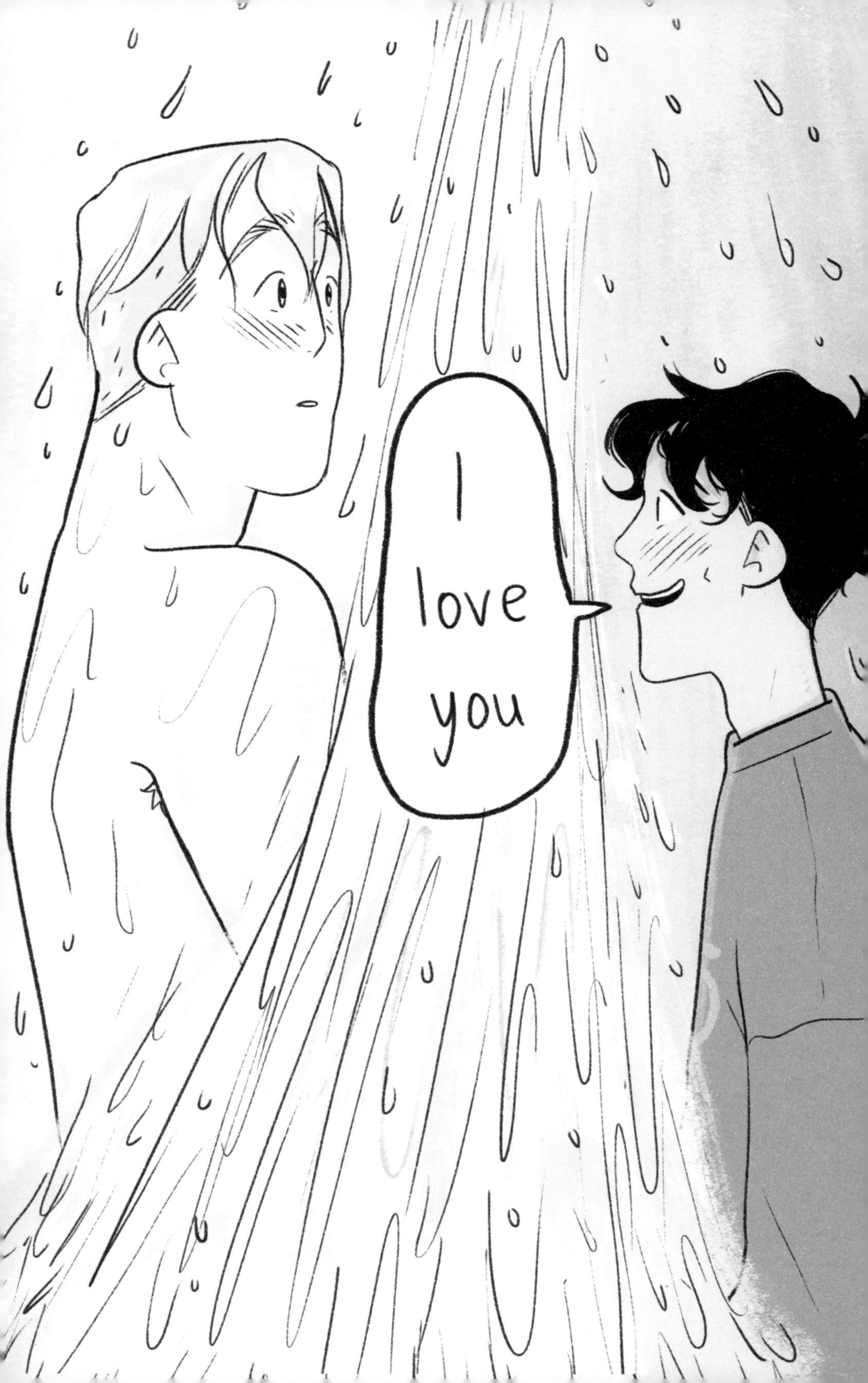
I love you

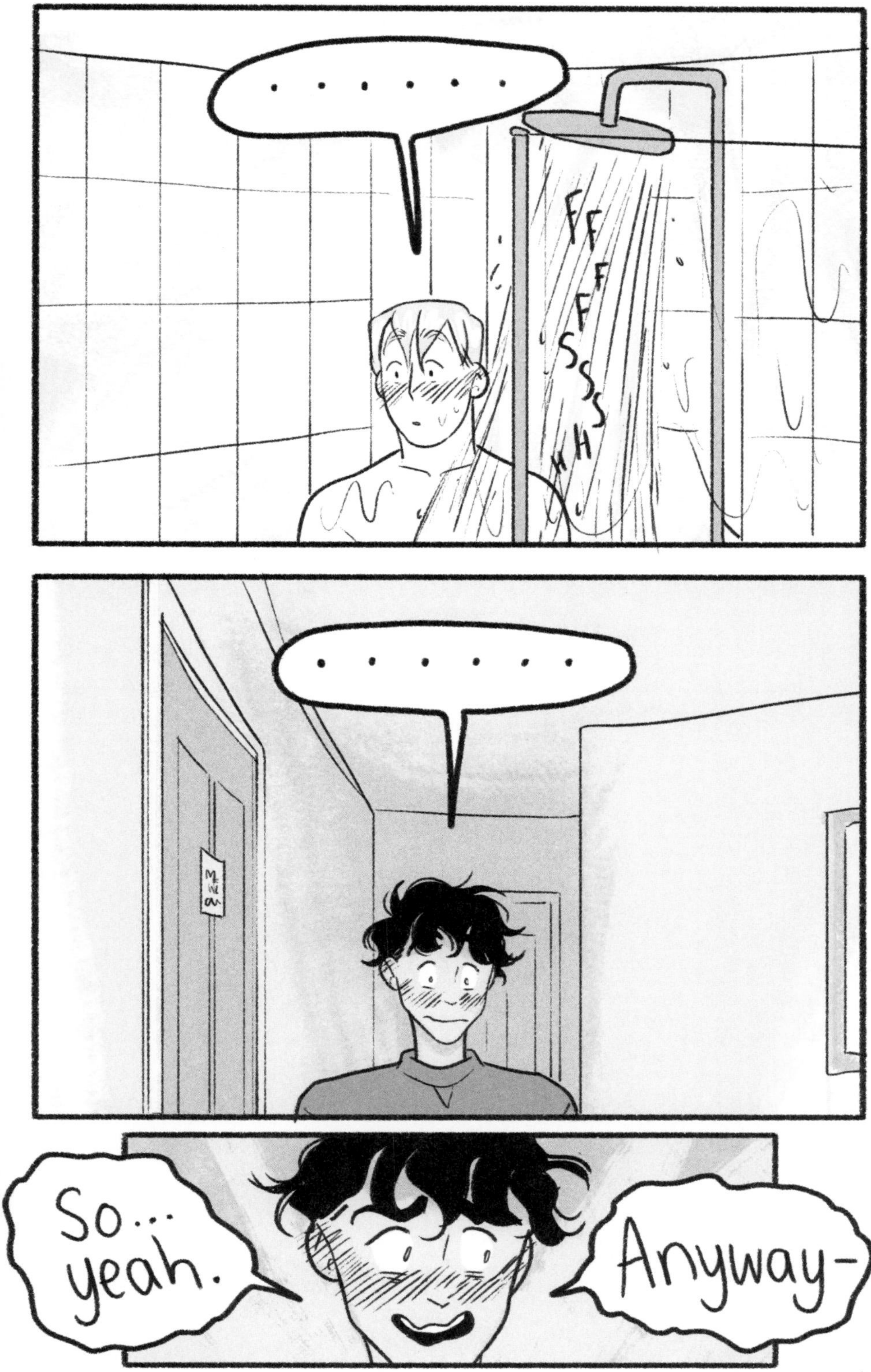
. . . .
FFFFFSSSSHH
. . . .
So... yeah.
Anyway-

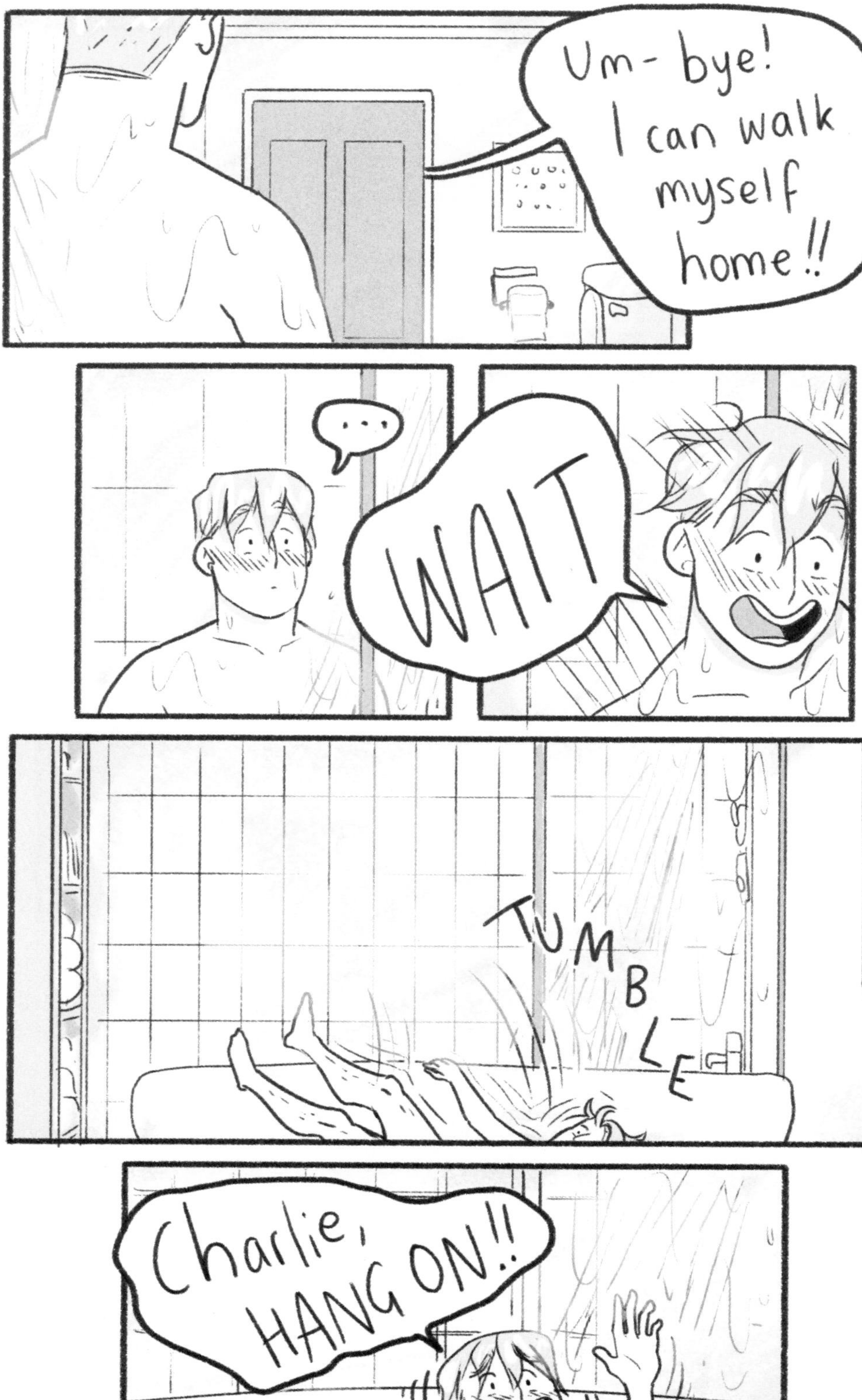
Um-bye! I can walk myself home!!
...
WAIT
TUMBLE
Charlie, HANG ON!!

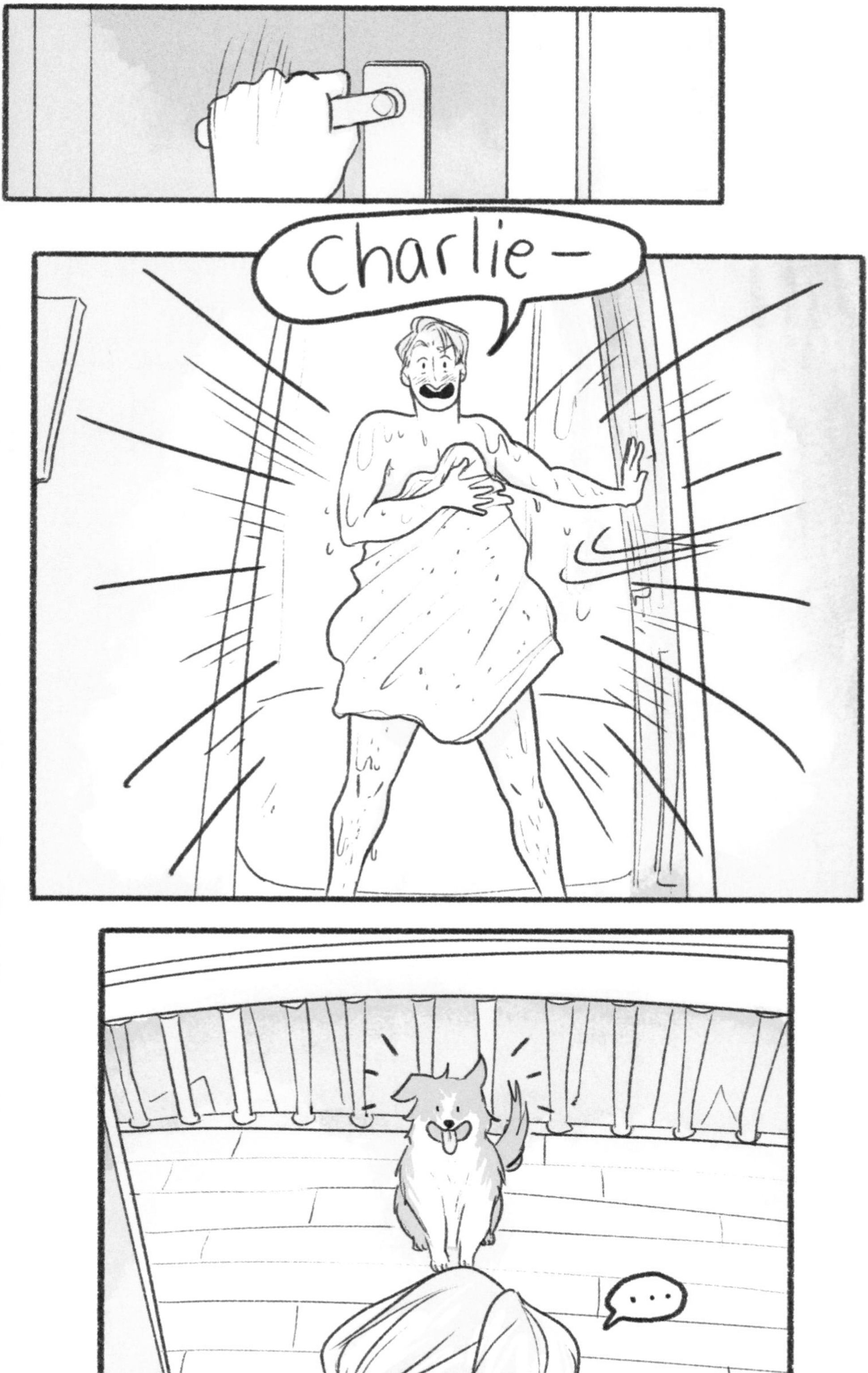
Charlie–
...

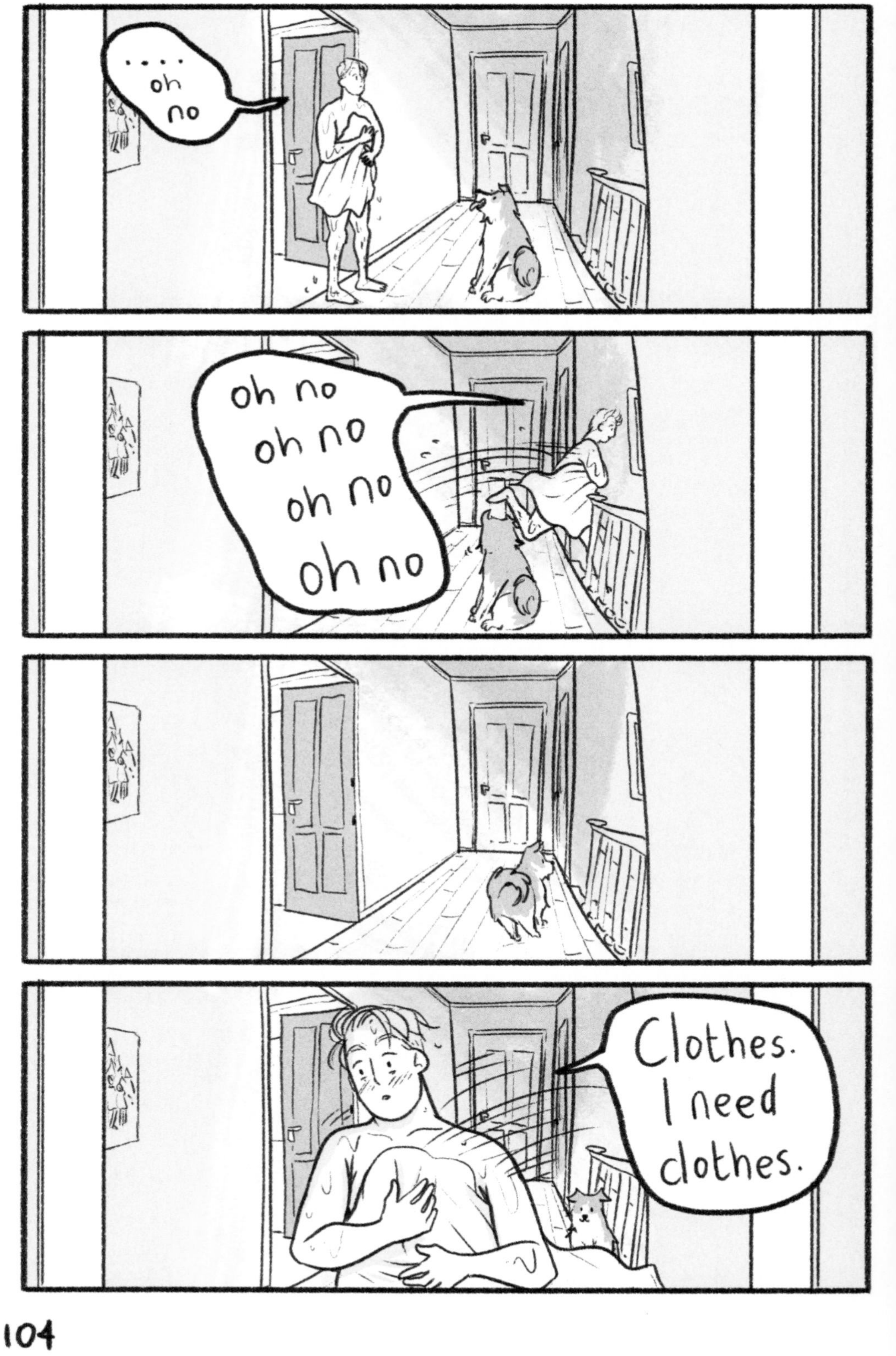
. . . .
oh
no
oh no
oh no
oh no
oh no
Clothes.
I need
clothes.

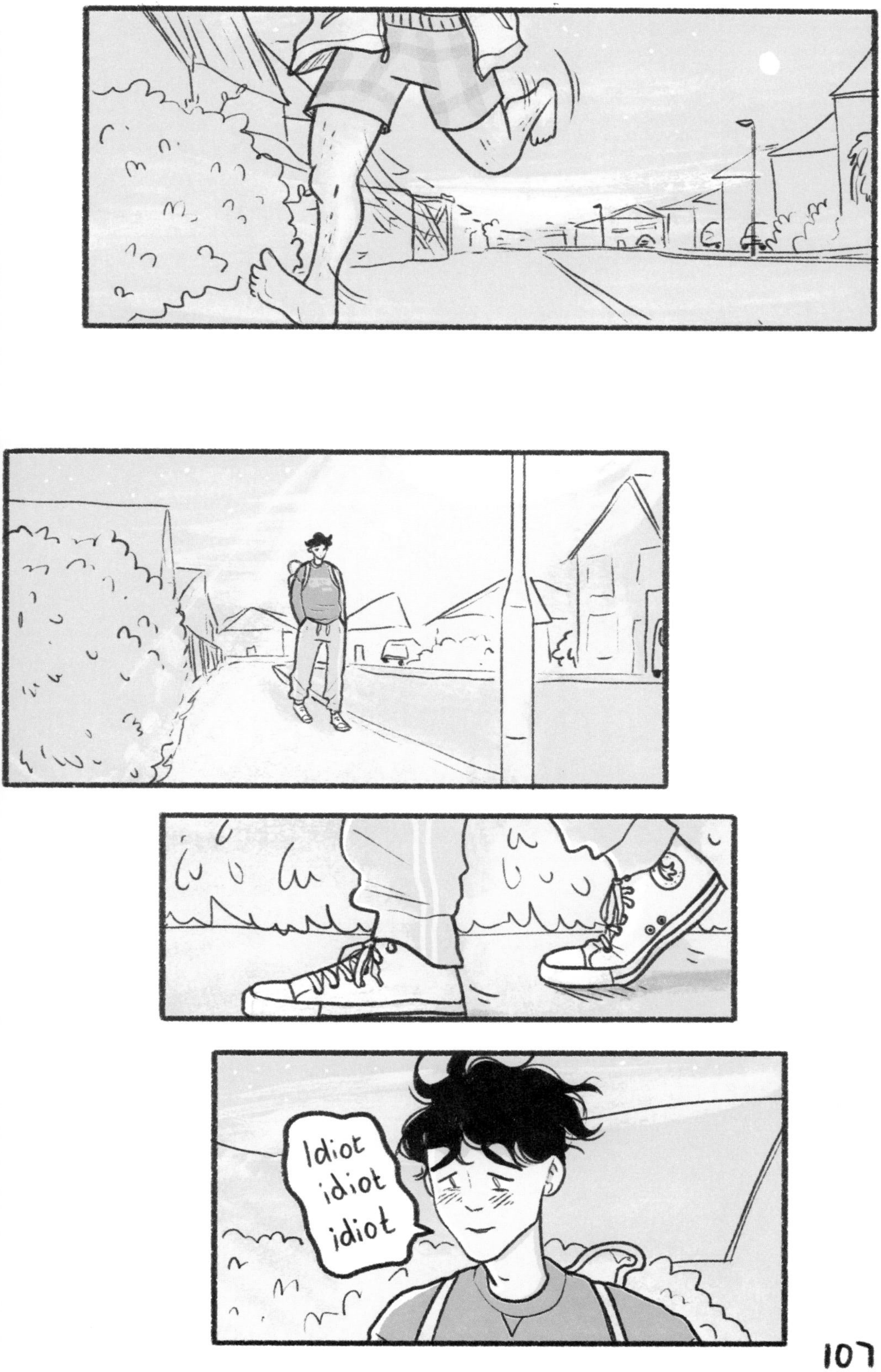
Idiot idiot idiot

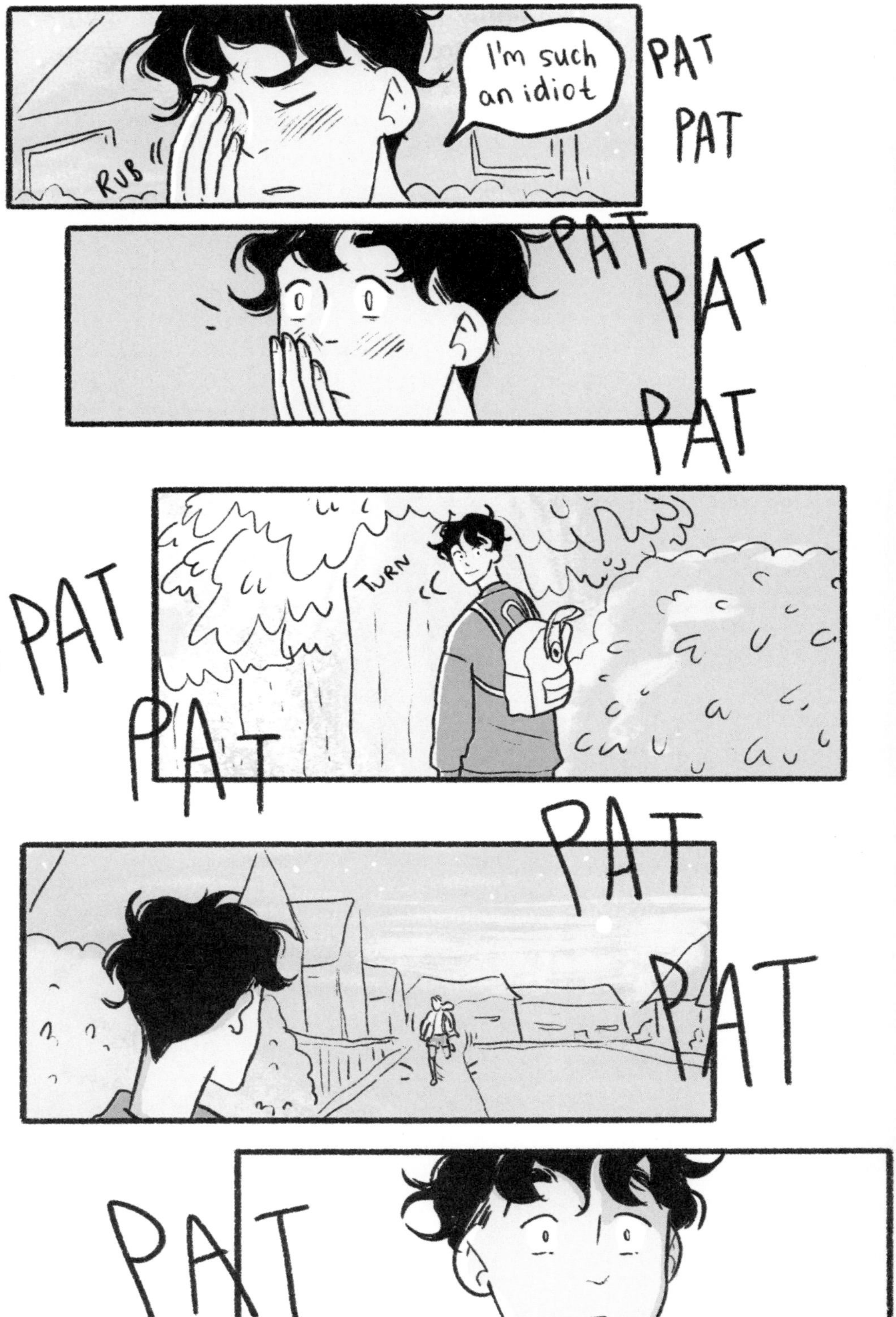
I'm such an idiot
RUB
PAT
PAT
PAT
PAT
PAT
TURN
PAT
PAT
PAT
PAT
PAT

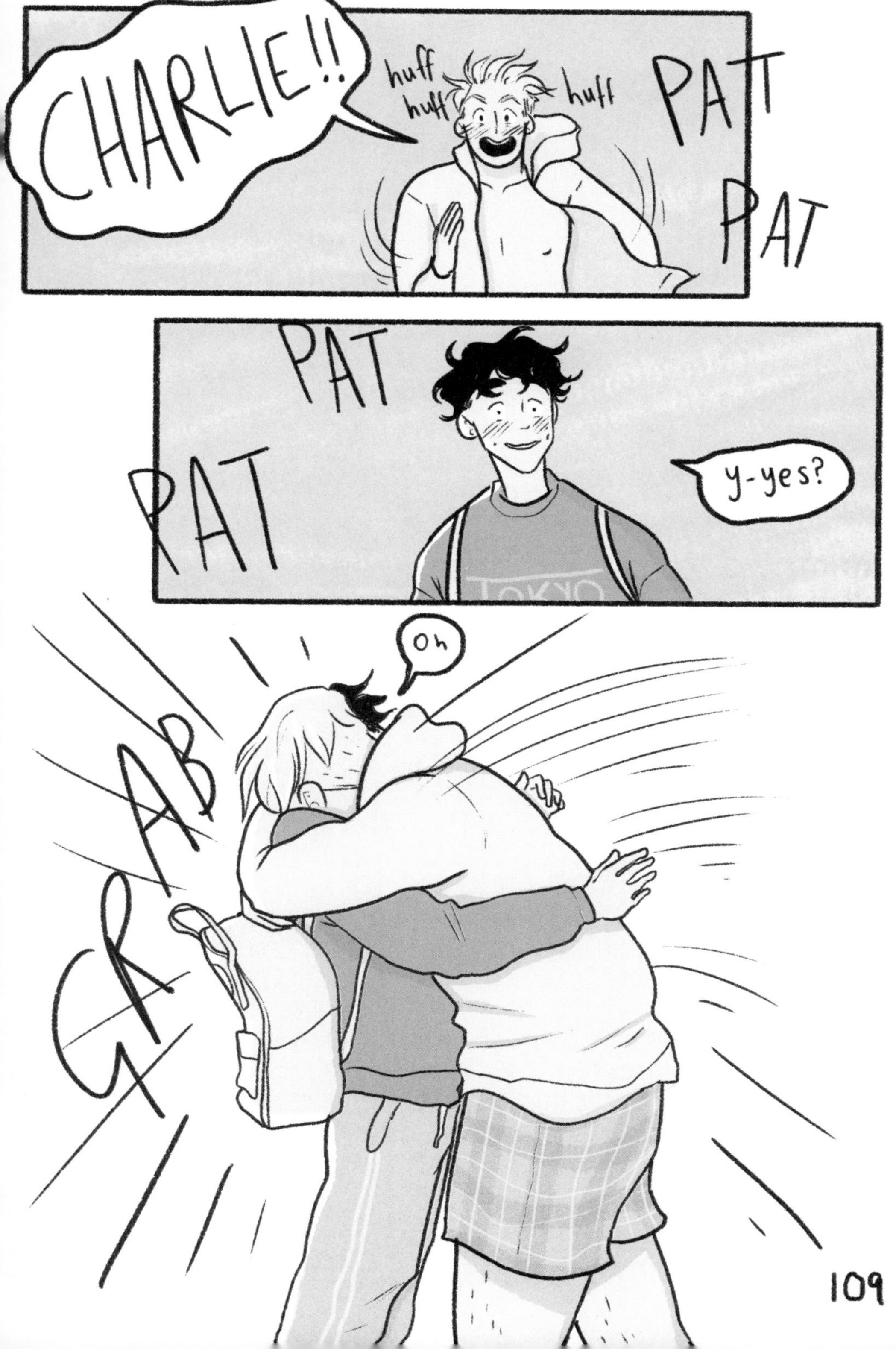
CHARLIE!!
huff huff
huff
PAT
PAT
PAT
PAT
Y-yes?
TOKYO
Oh
GRAB

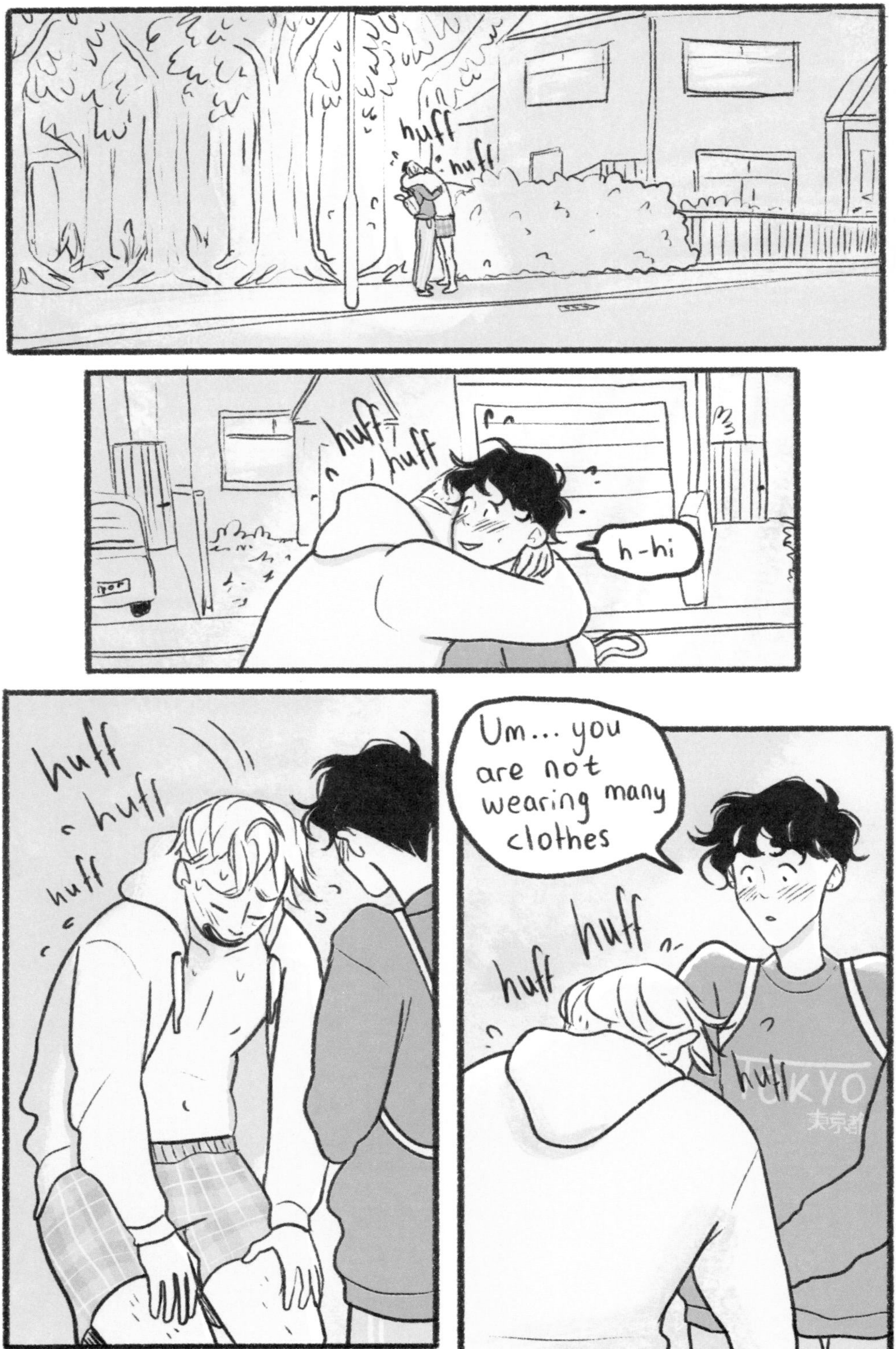
huff
huff
huff
huff
h-hi
huff
huff
huff
Um... you are not wearing many clothes
huff
huff
huff
TOKYO
東京都

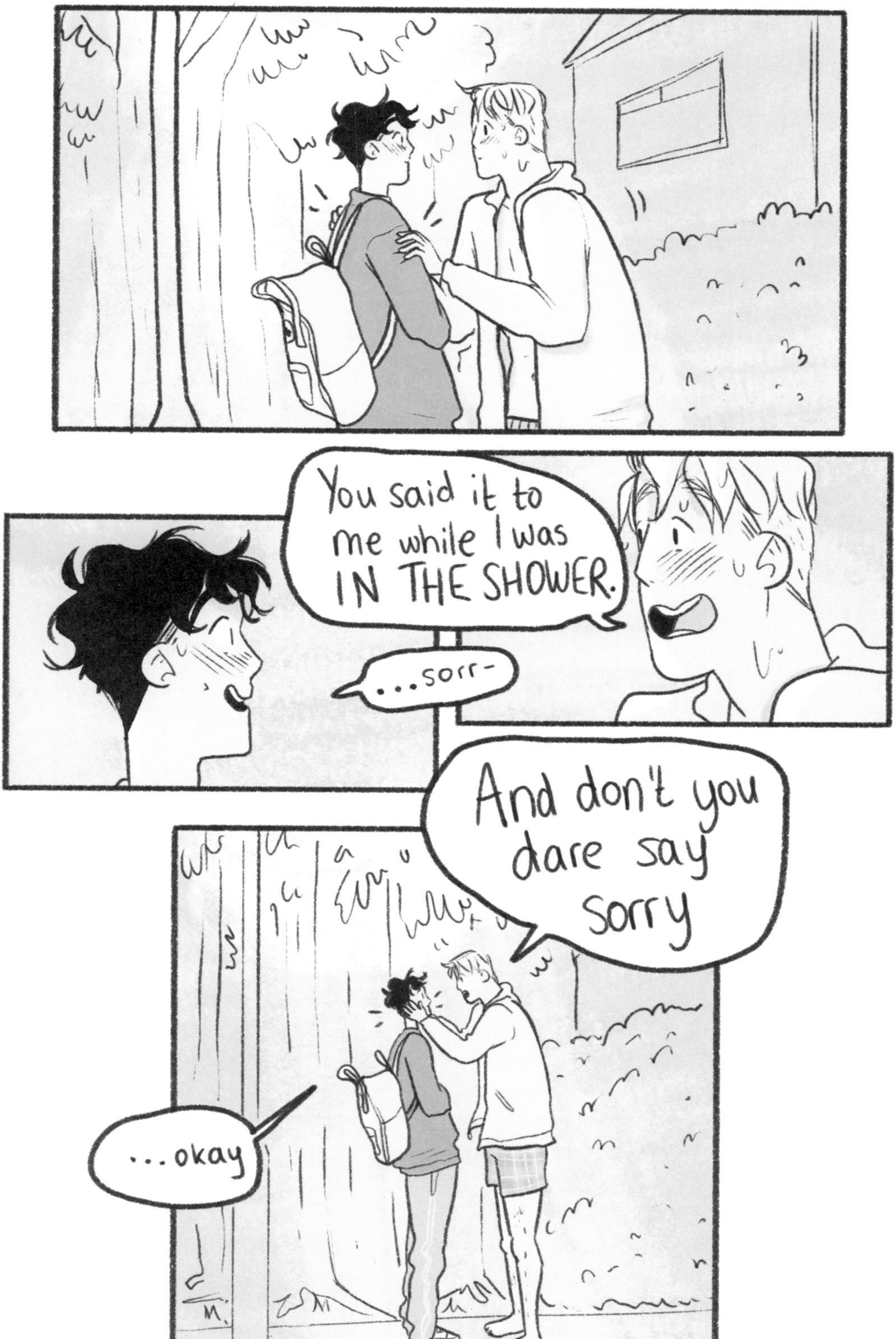
You said it to me while I was IN THE SHOWER.
...sorr-
And don't you dare say sorry
...okay

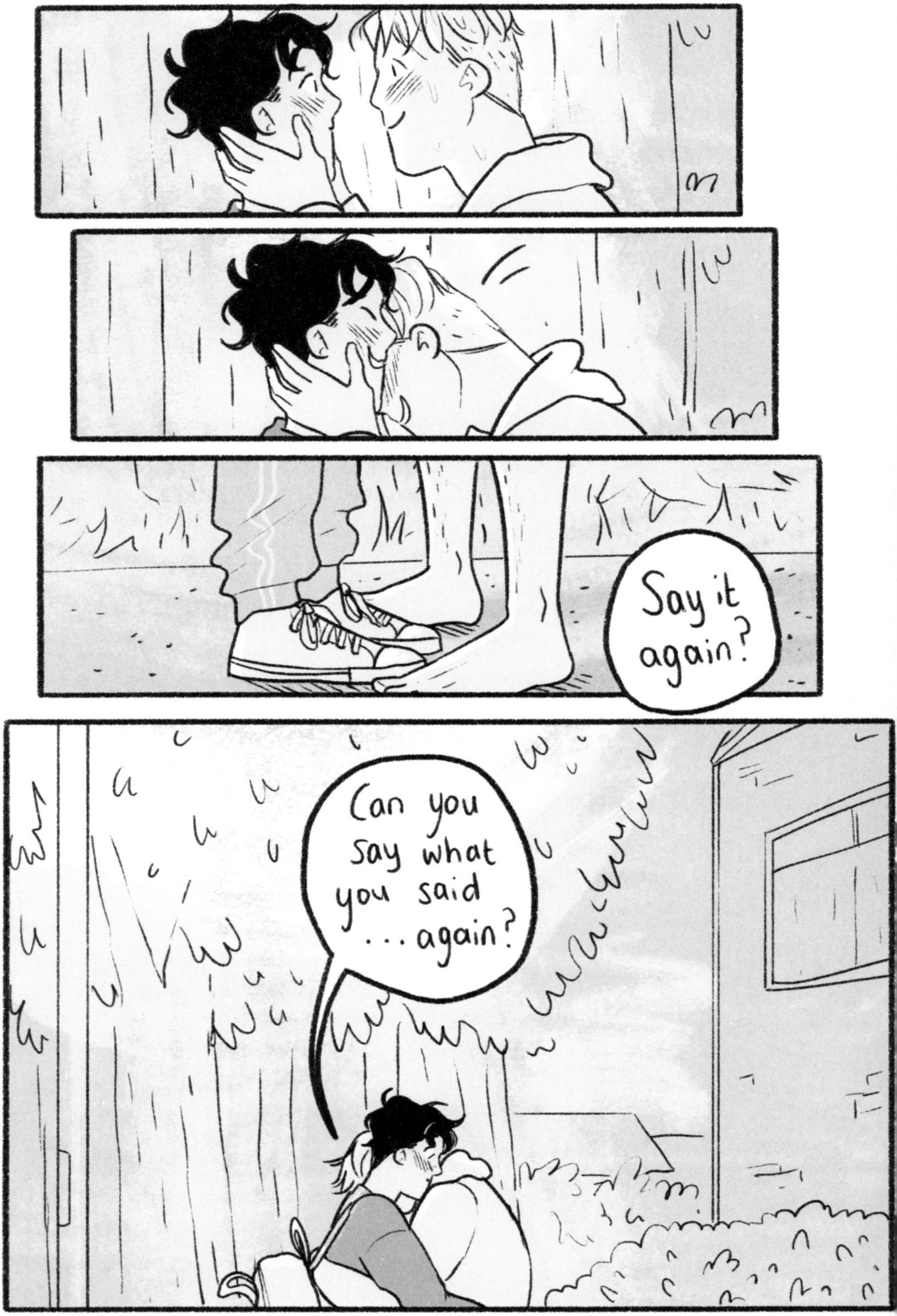
Say it again?
Can you say what you said ...again?

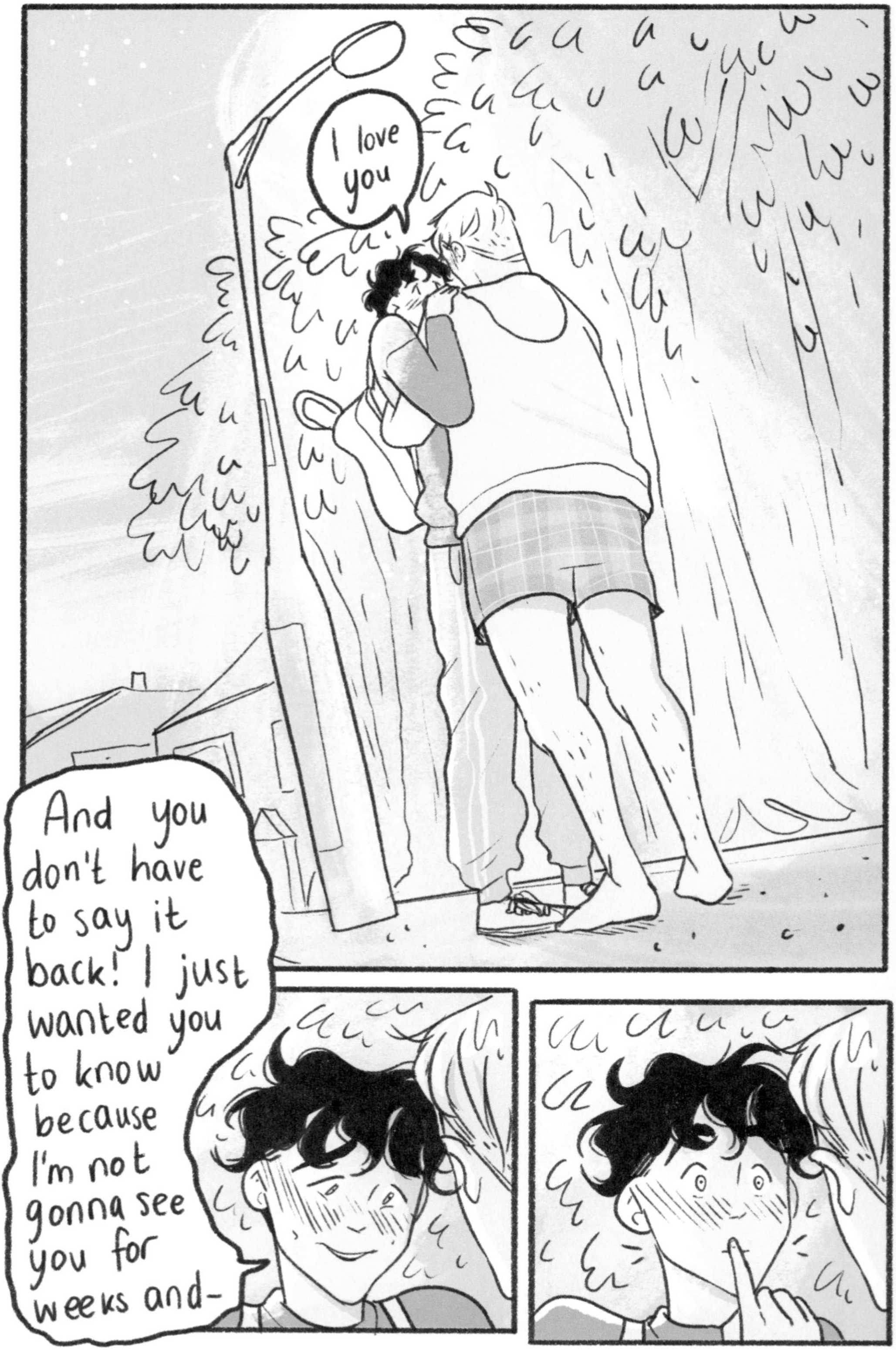
I love you
And you don't have to say it back! I just wanted you to know because I'm not gonna see you for weeks and-

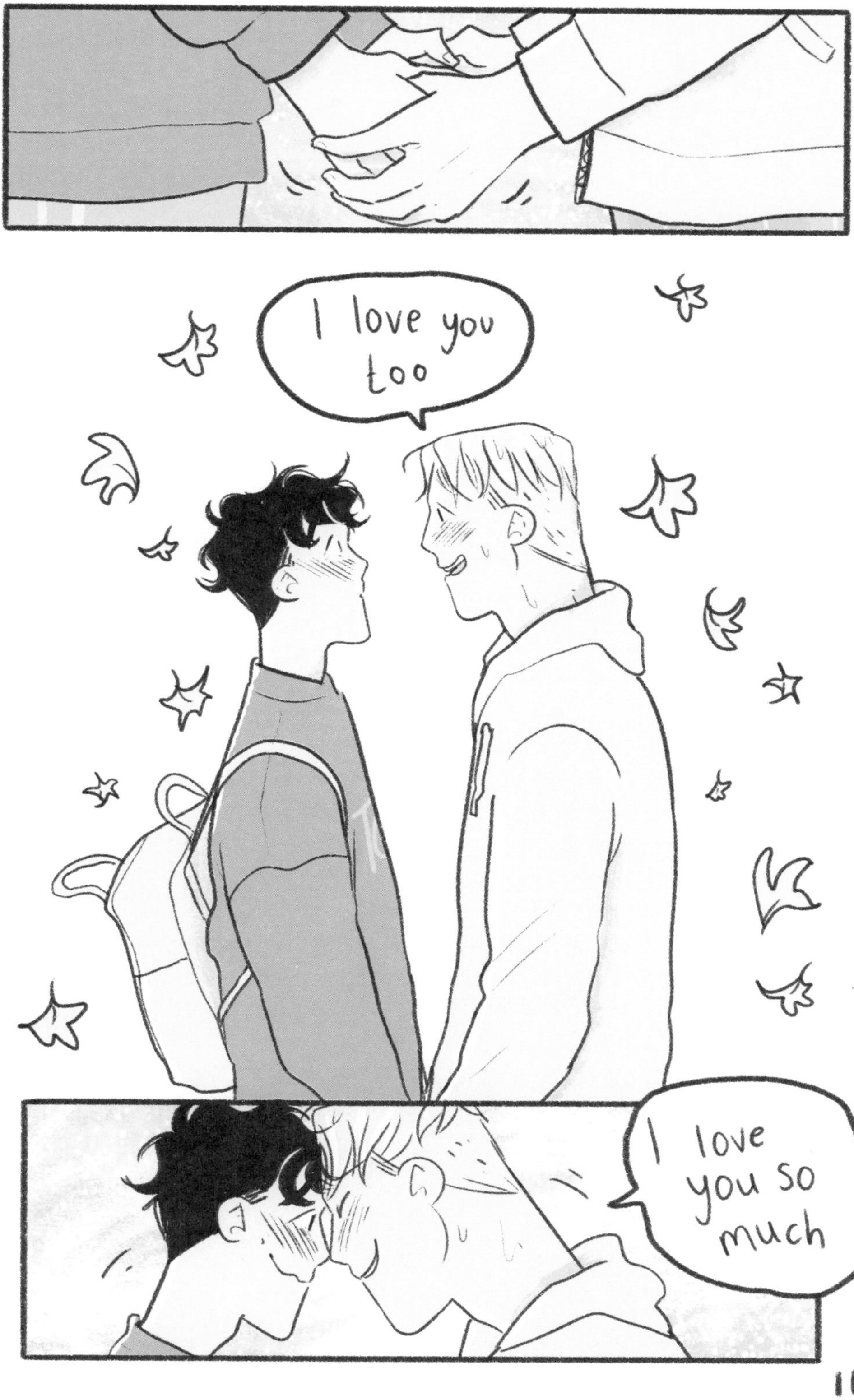
I love you too
I love you so much

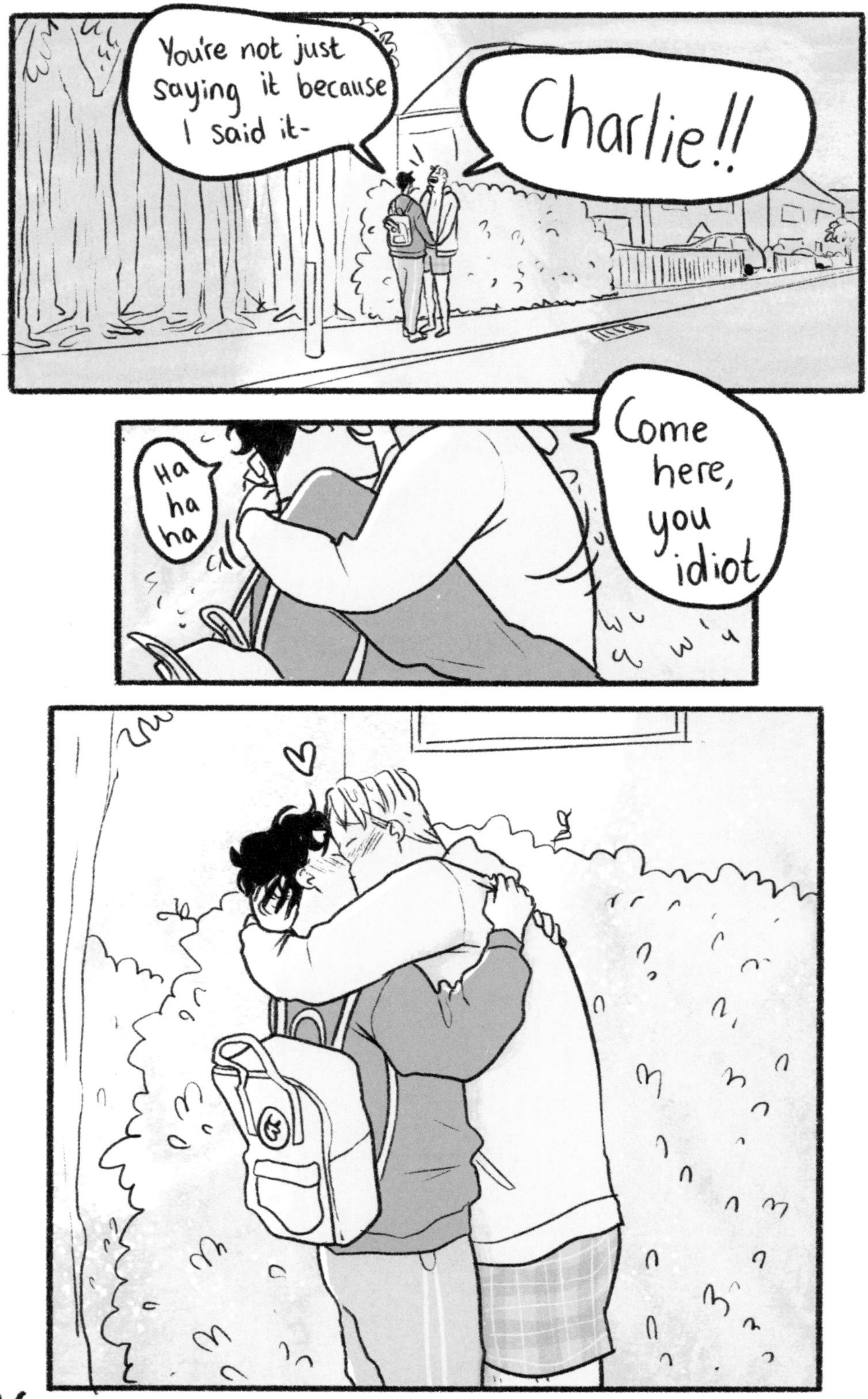
You're not just saying it because I said it-
Charlie!!
Ha ha ha
Come here, you idiot

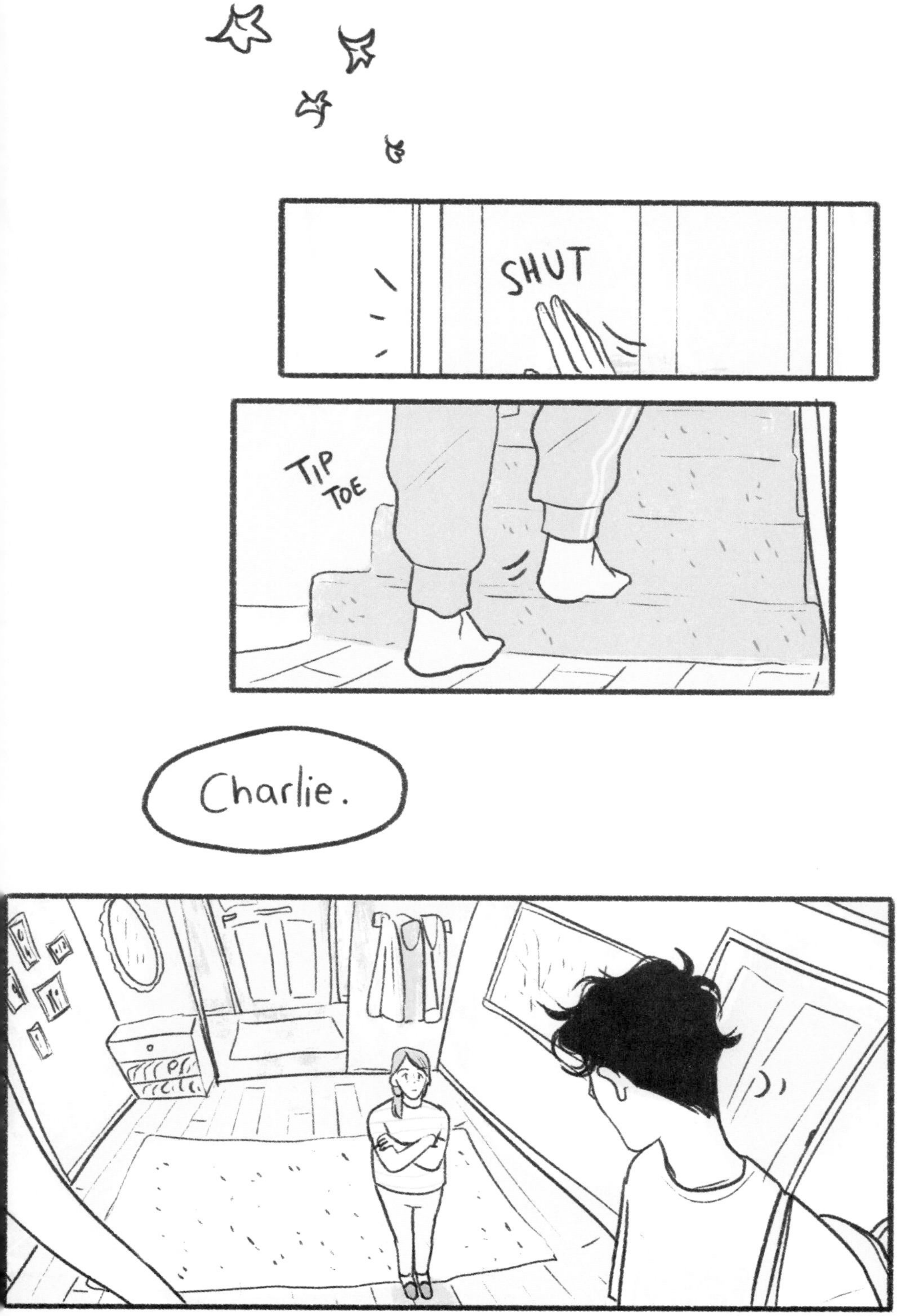
SHUT
TIP TOE
Charlie.

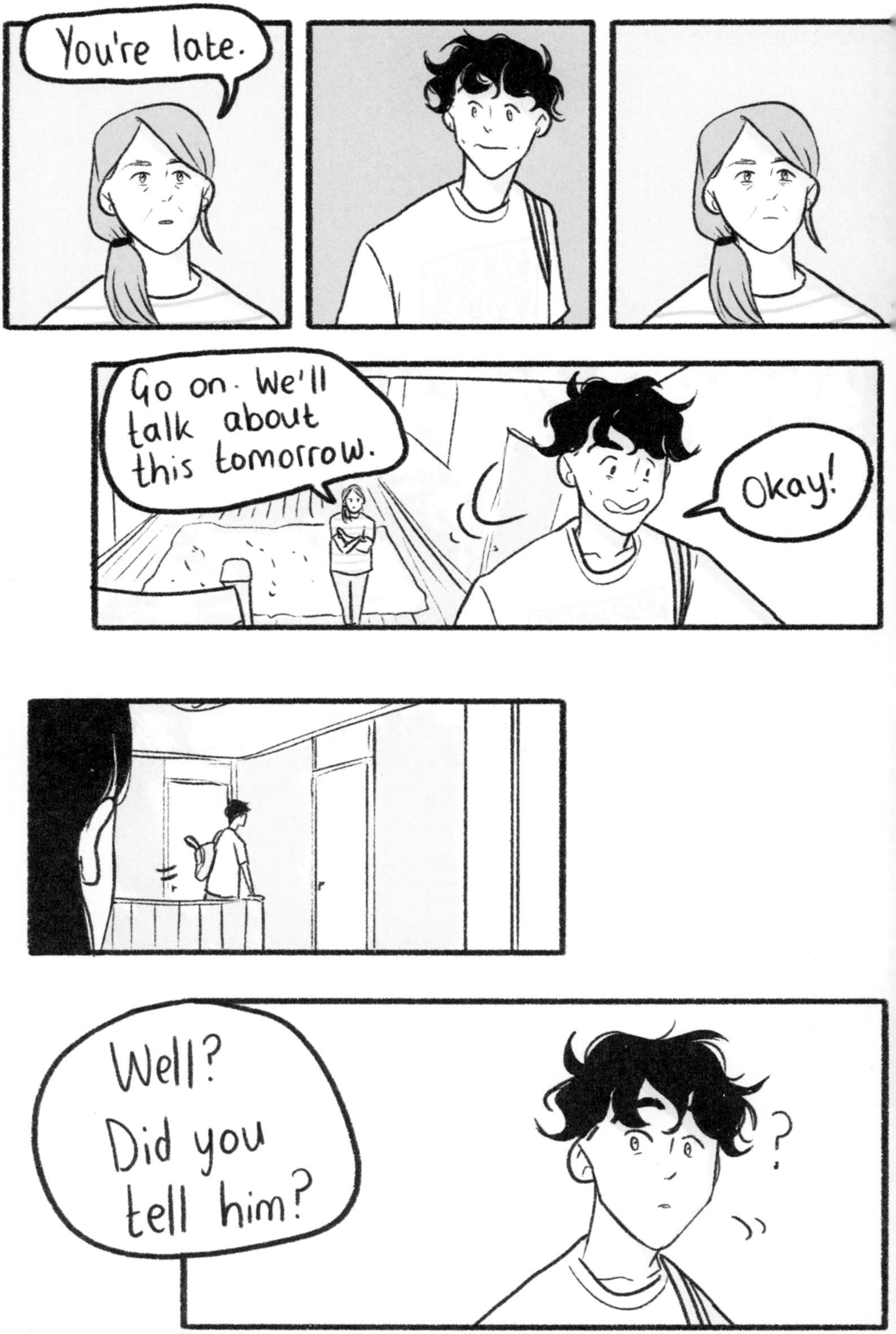
You're late.
Go on. We'll talk about this tomorrow.
Okay!
Well? Did you tell him?

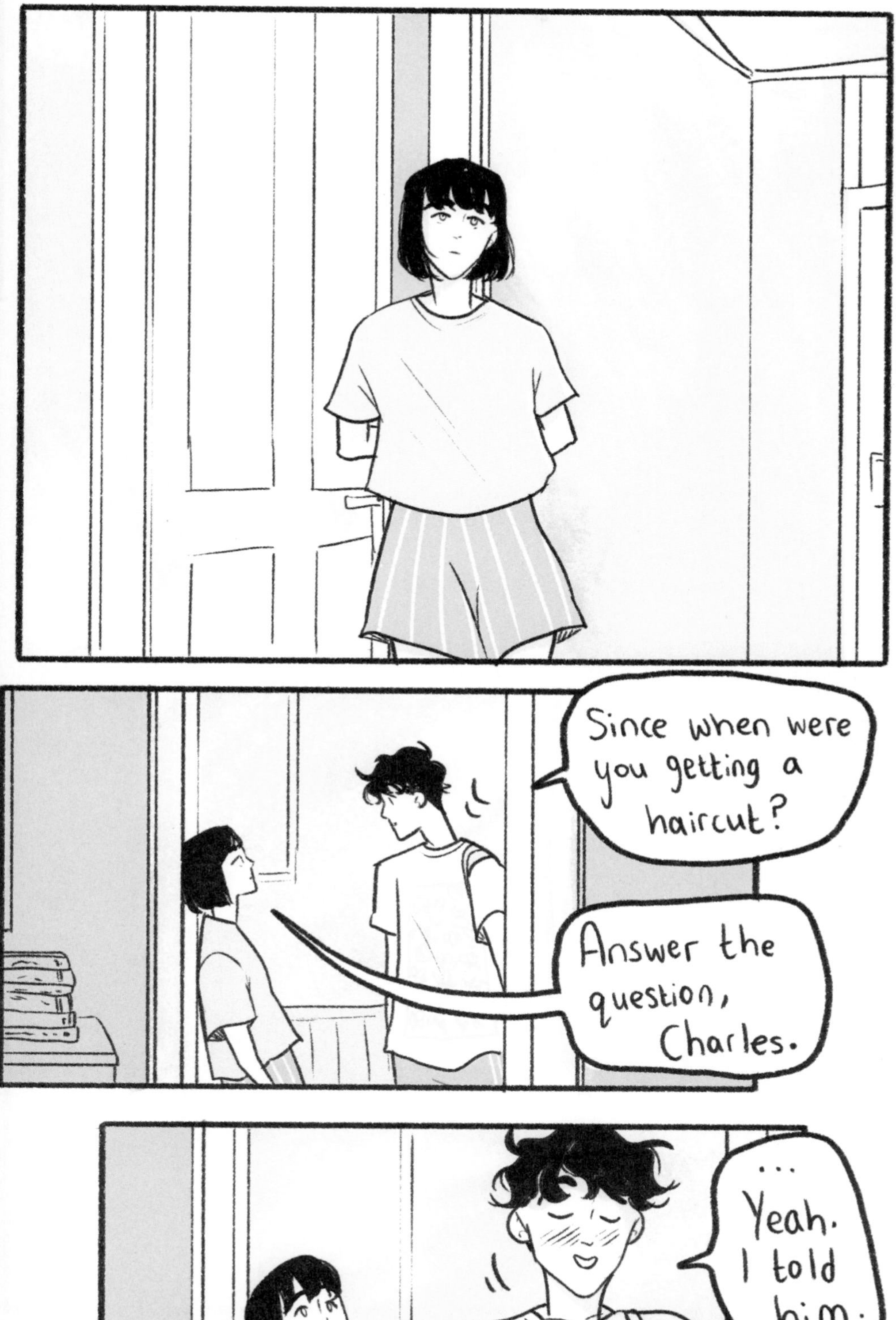
Since when were you getting a haircut?
Answer the question, Charles.
... Yeah. I told him.

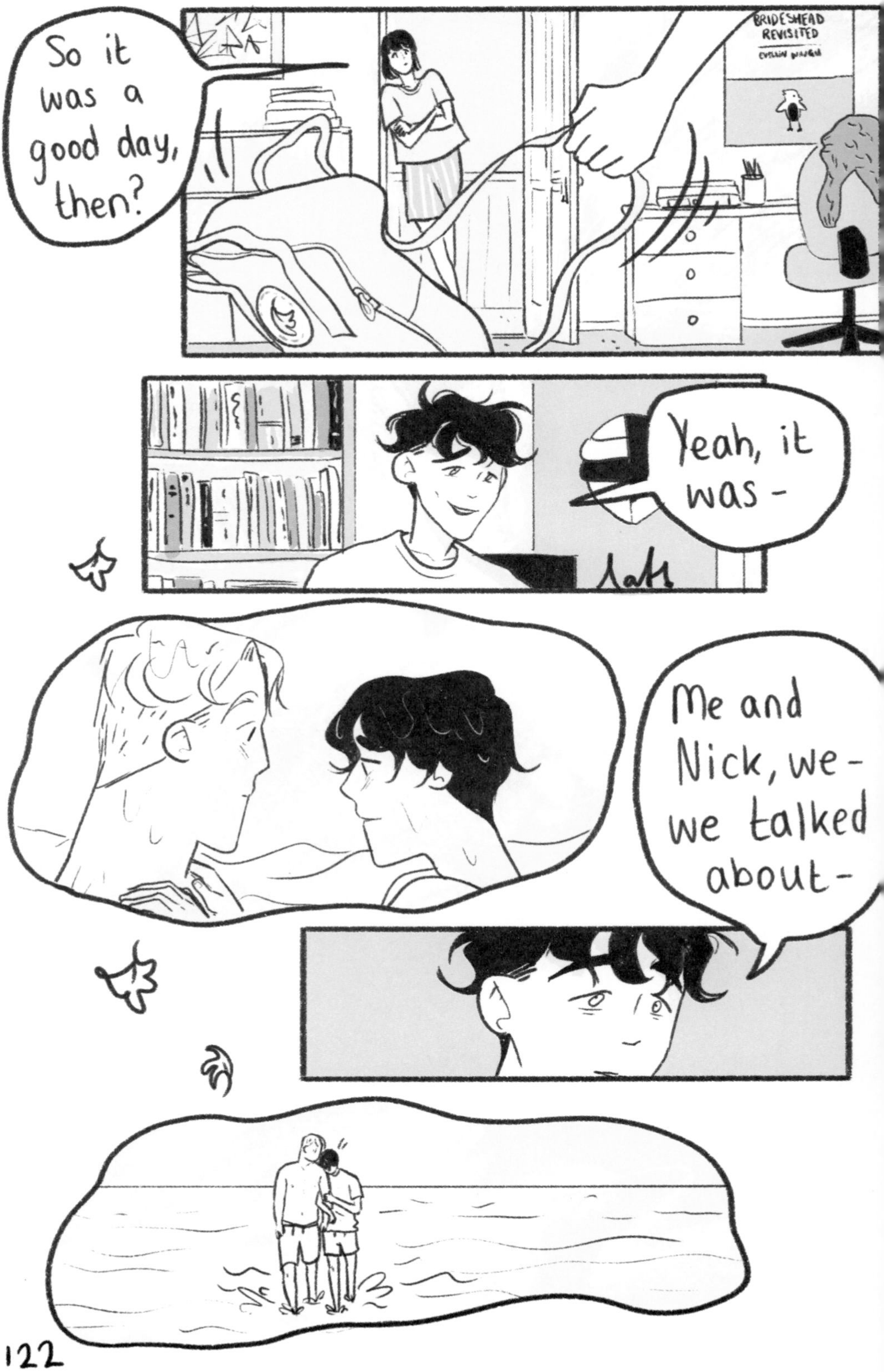
So it was a good day, then?
BRIDESHEAD REVISITED
Yeah, it was -
Me and Nick, we- we talked about-

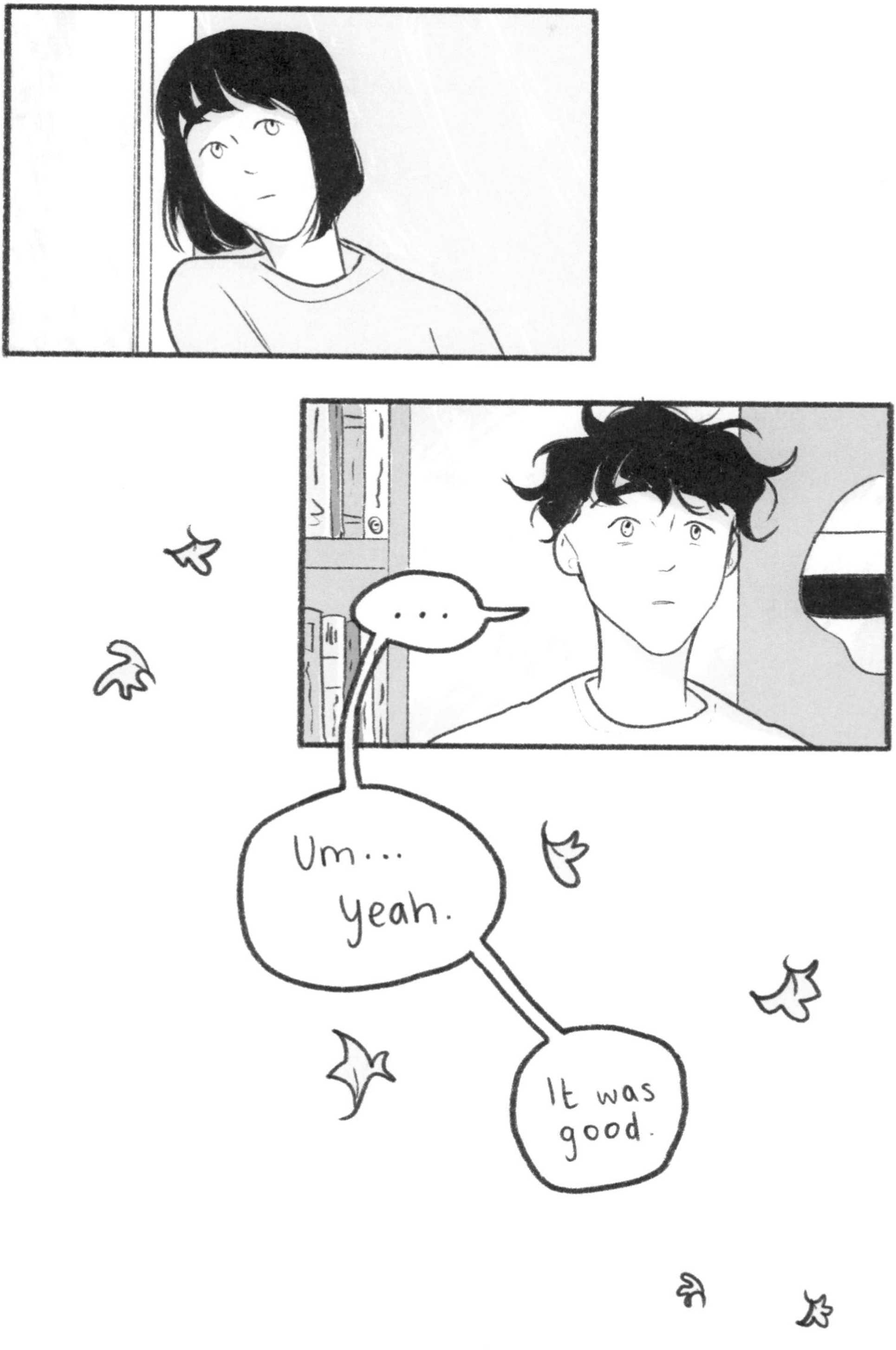
...
Um... yeah.
It was good.

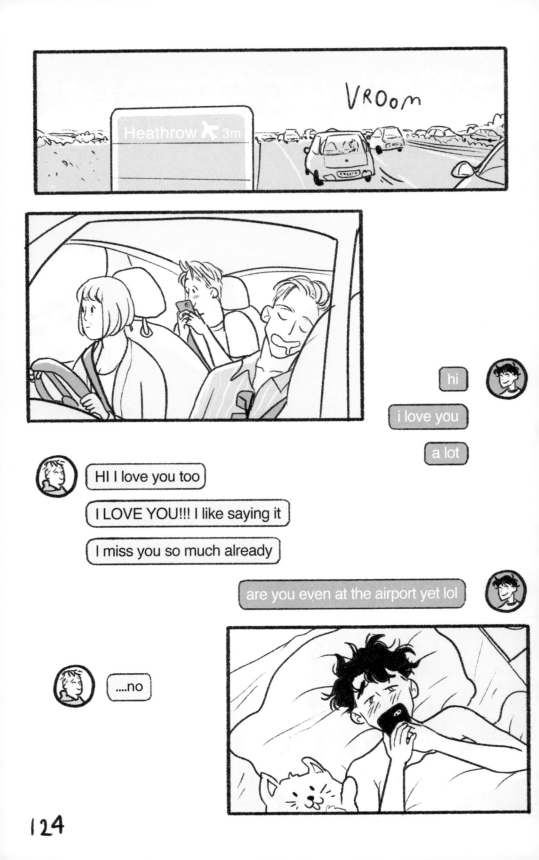

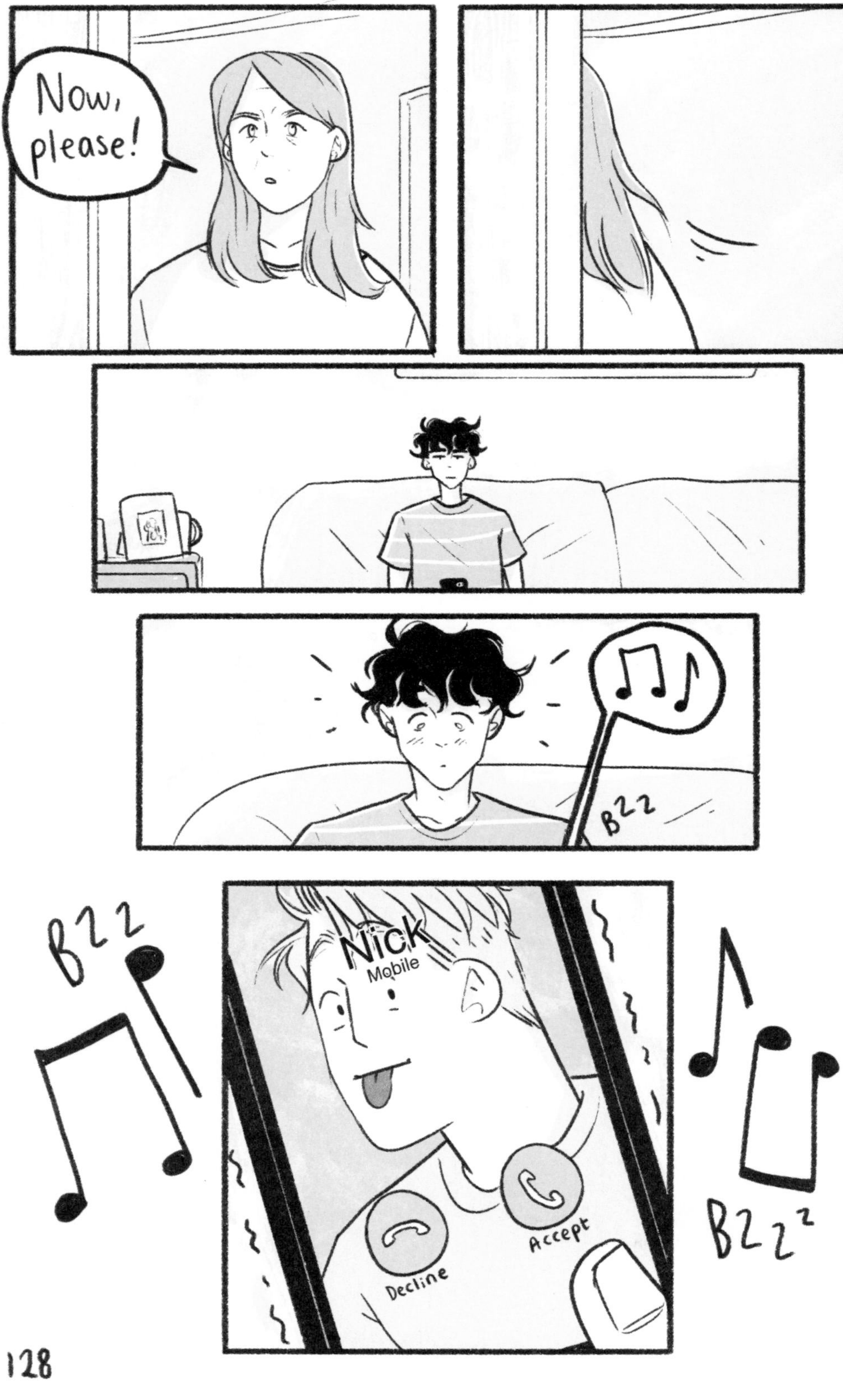
Now, please!
BZZ
BZZ
Nick
Mobile
Decline
Accept
BZZZ

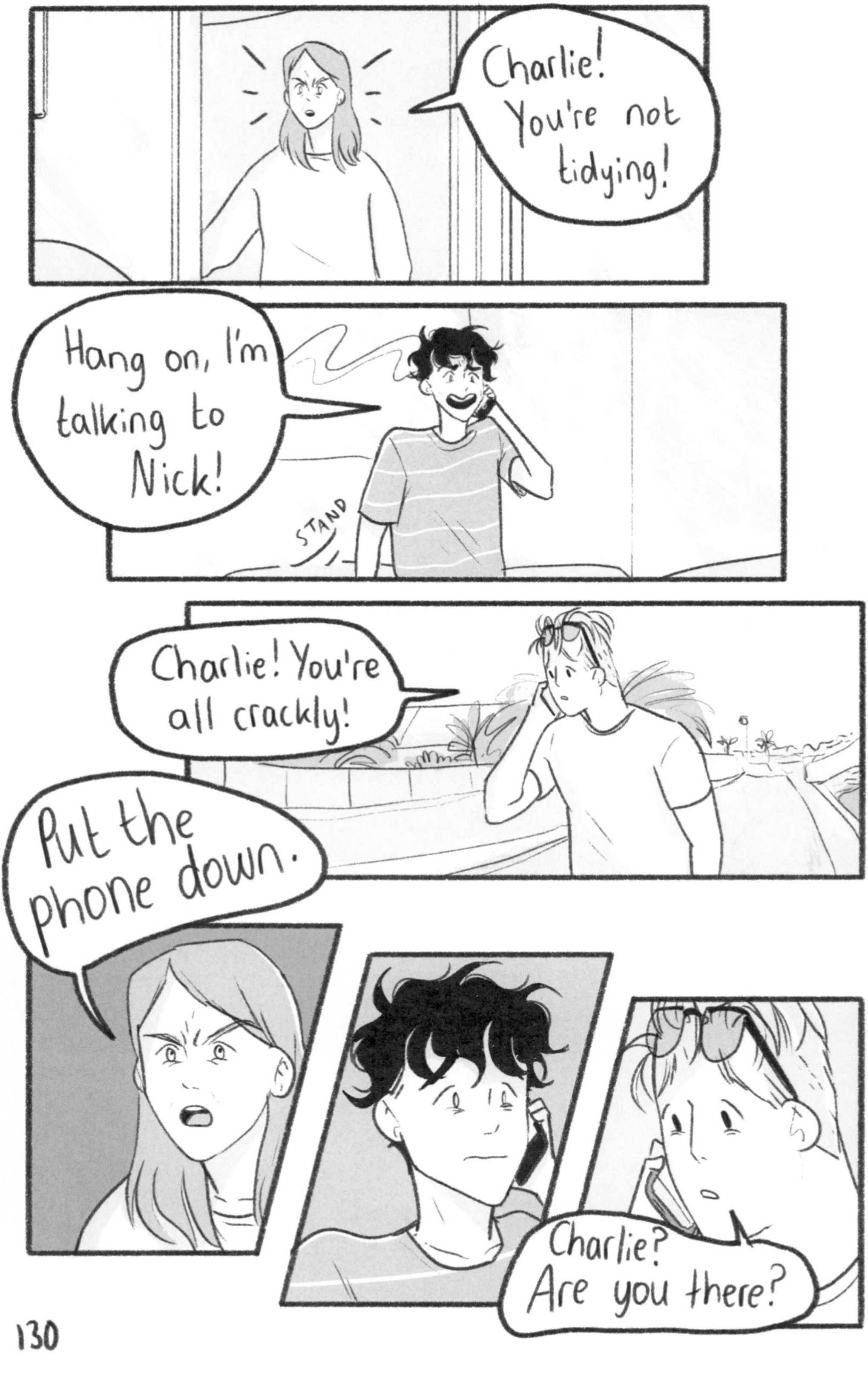
Charlie! You're not tidying!
Hang on, I'm talking to Nick!
STAND
Charlie! You're all crackly!
Put the phone down.
Charlie? Are you there?

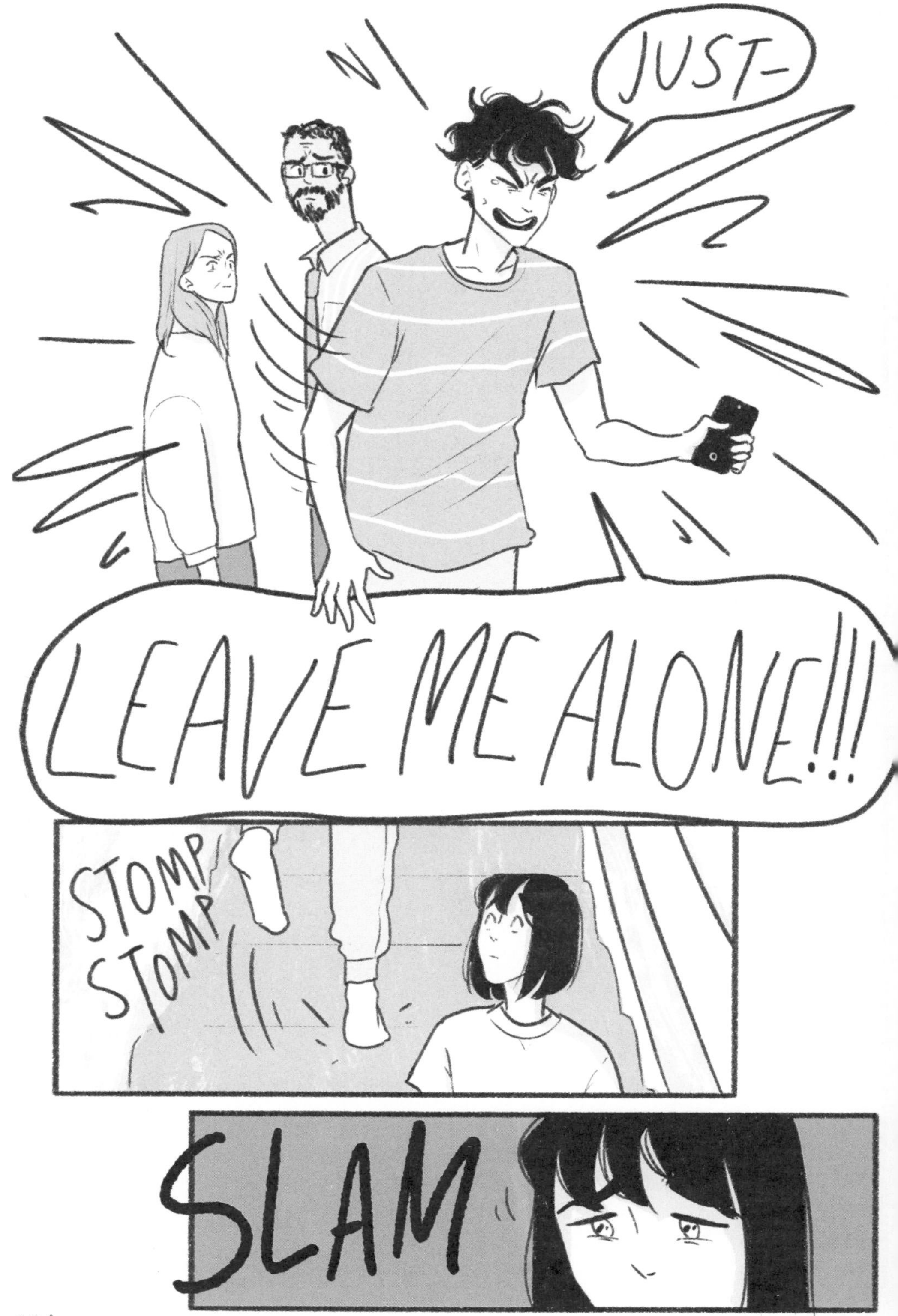
JUST-
LEAVE ME ALONE!!!
STOMP
STOMP
SLAM

Julio, you can't just undermine me like that in front of him.
But you know you were being too harsh.
I just... always say the wrong thing to him.

MUSIC
Ughhhh I think signal is pretty bad everywhere here!!! I hope this message gets through!! I'll try and message you as often as I can! I love you!!!!
it's ok!! i love you too xxxx

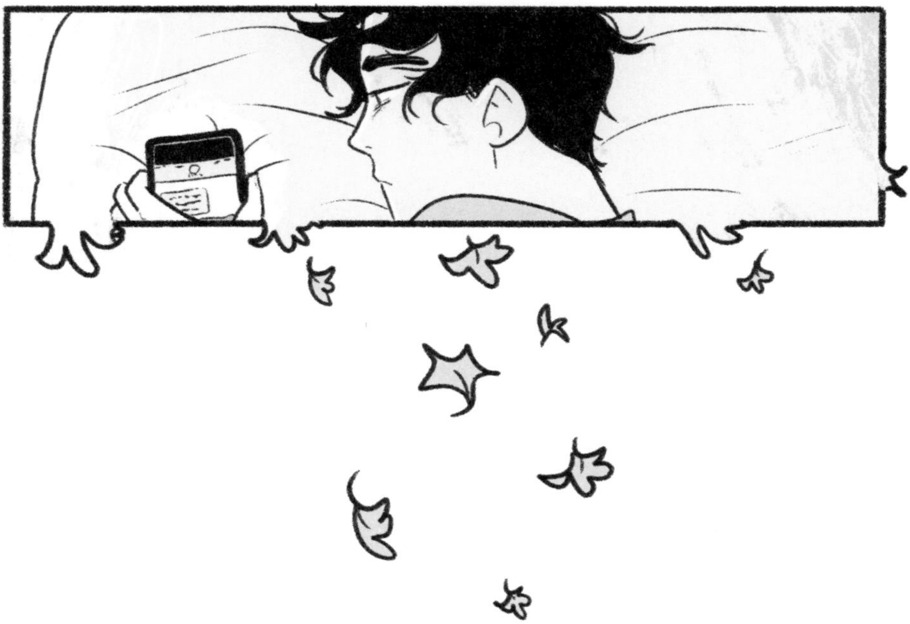

The first week.

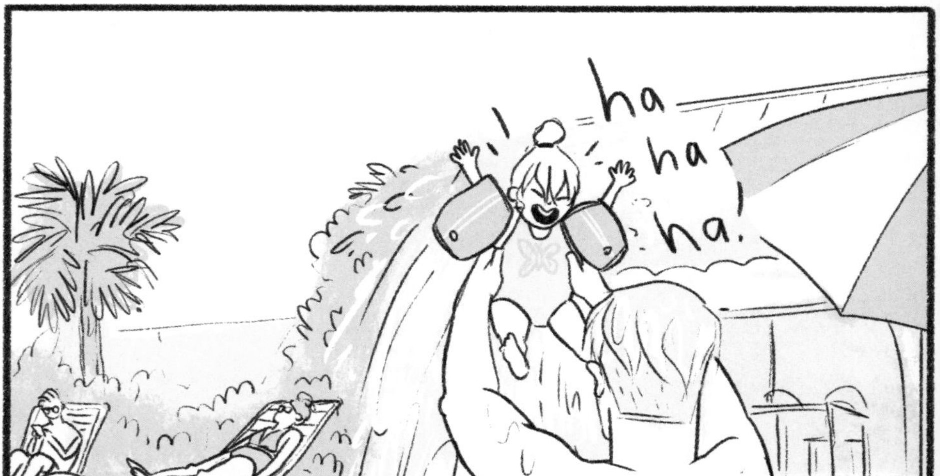
ha
ha
ha!

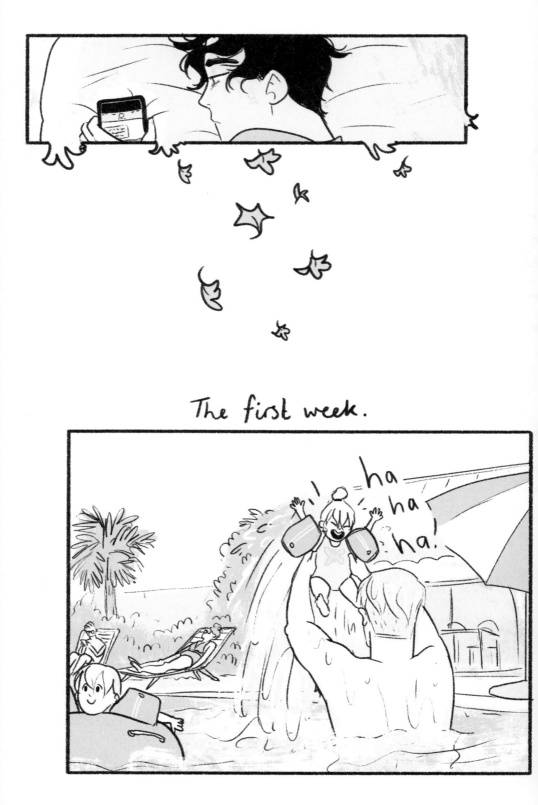

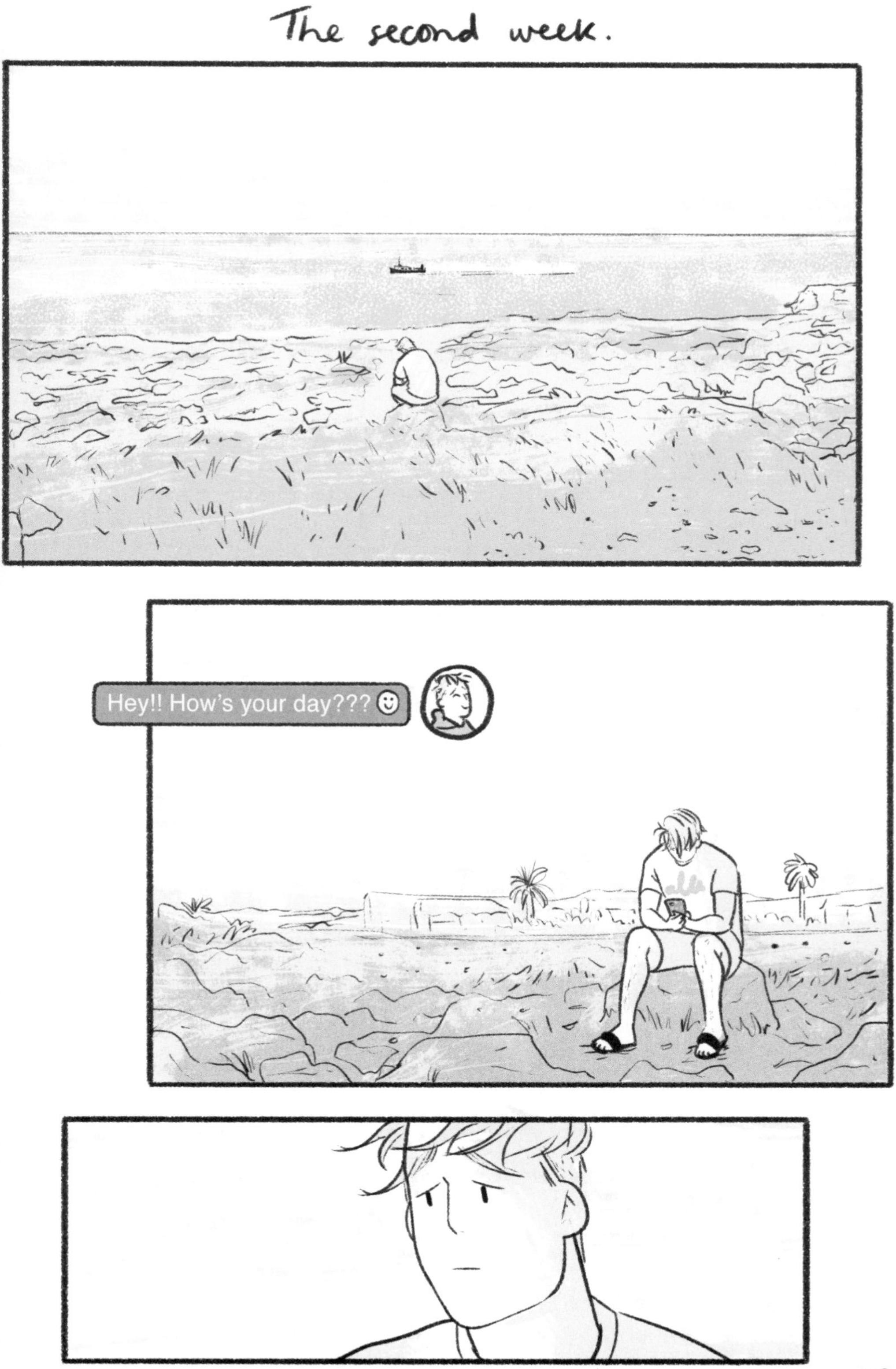
The second week.
Hey!! How's your day??? ☺

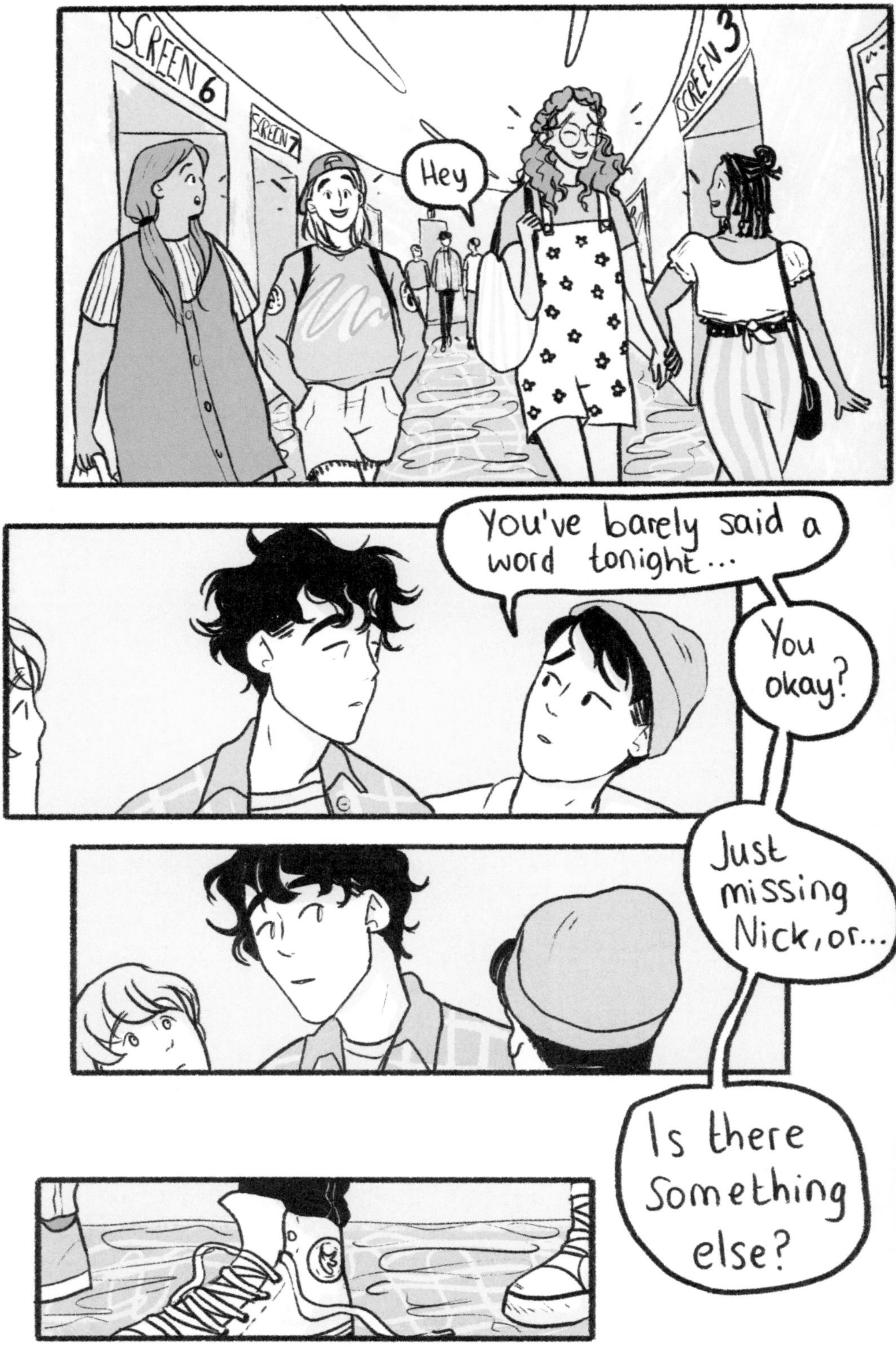
SCREEN 6
SCREEN 7
SCREEN 3
Hey
You've barely said a word tonight...
You okay?
Just missing Nick, or...
Is there something else?

CLATTER
What the f-
David!
What? We're on holiday! Get off your phone!
Just fuck off.
Ooooooh don't throw a tantrum!
You've been on your phone with your little boyfriend nonstop.
Didn't know you gays were so codependent!

143

The third week.

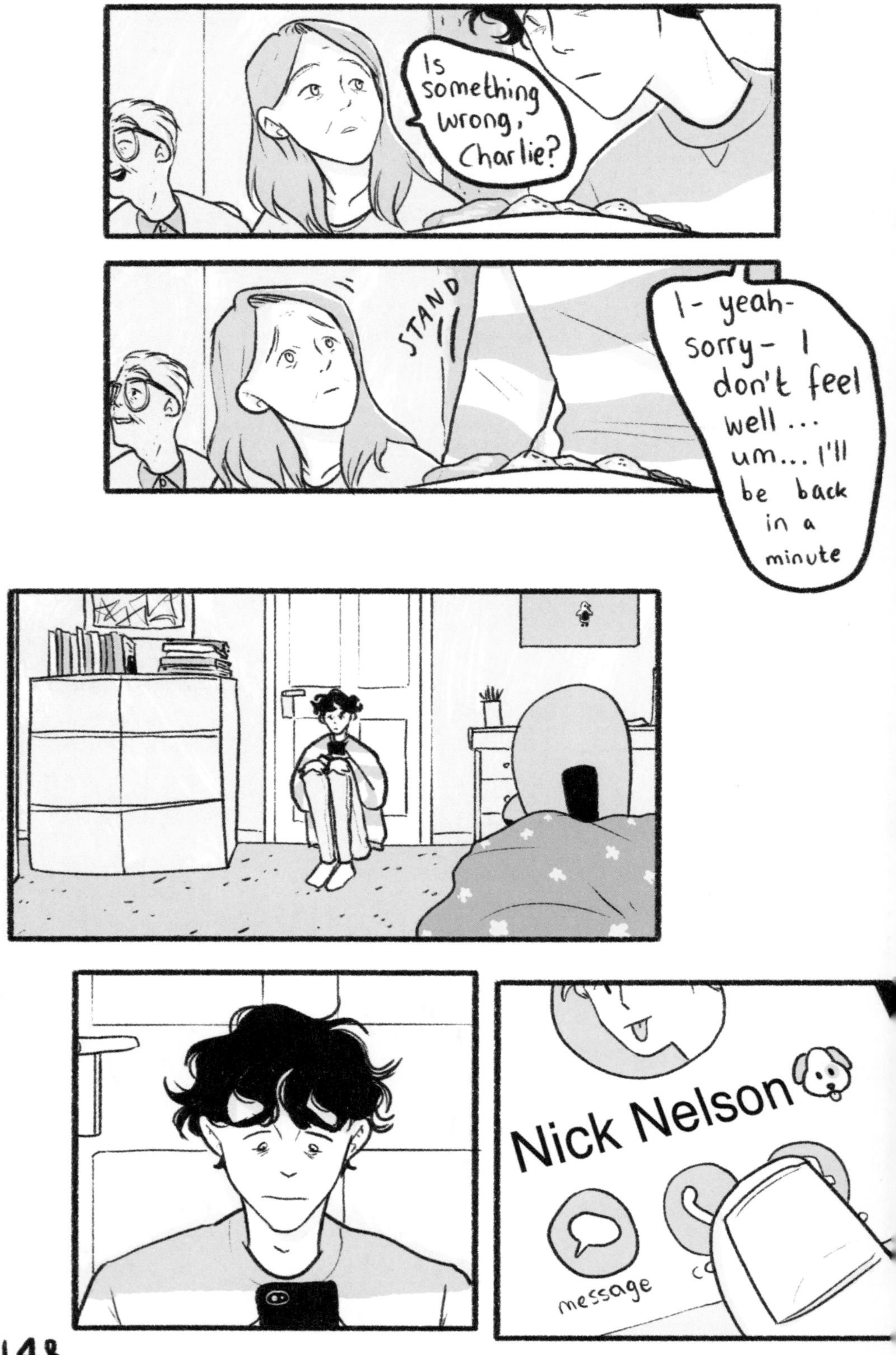
Is something wrong, Charlie?
STAND
I- yeah- sorry- I don't feel well... um... I'll be back in a minute
Nick Nelson
message

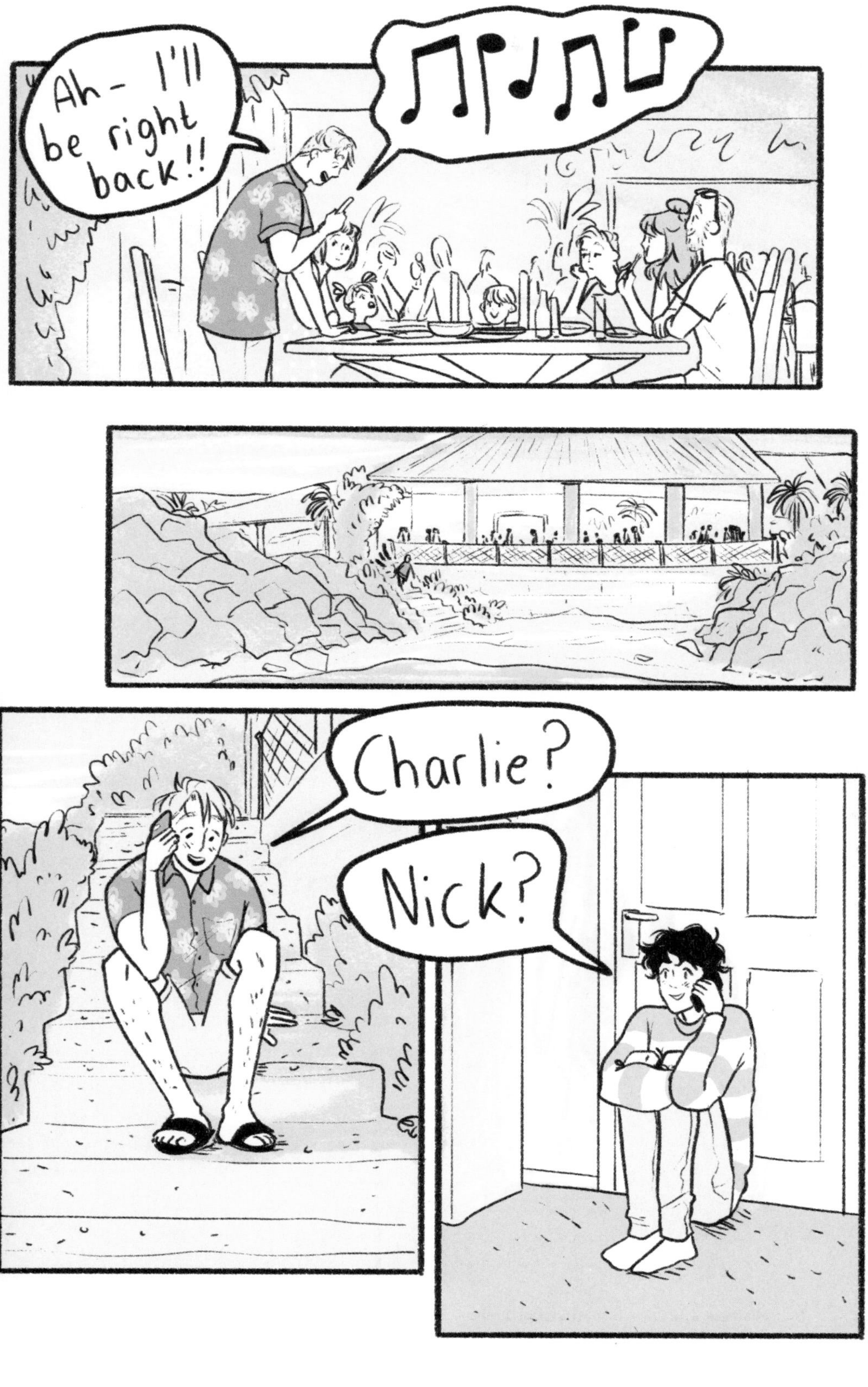
Ah- I'll be right back!!
♫♪♩♫♪
Charlie?
Nick?

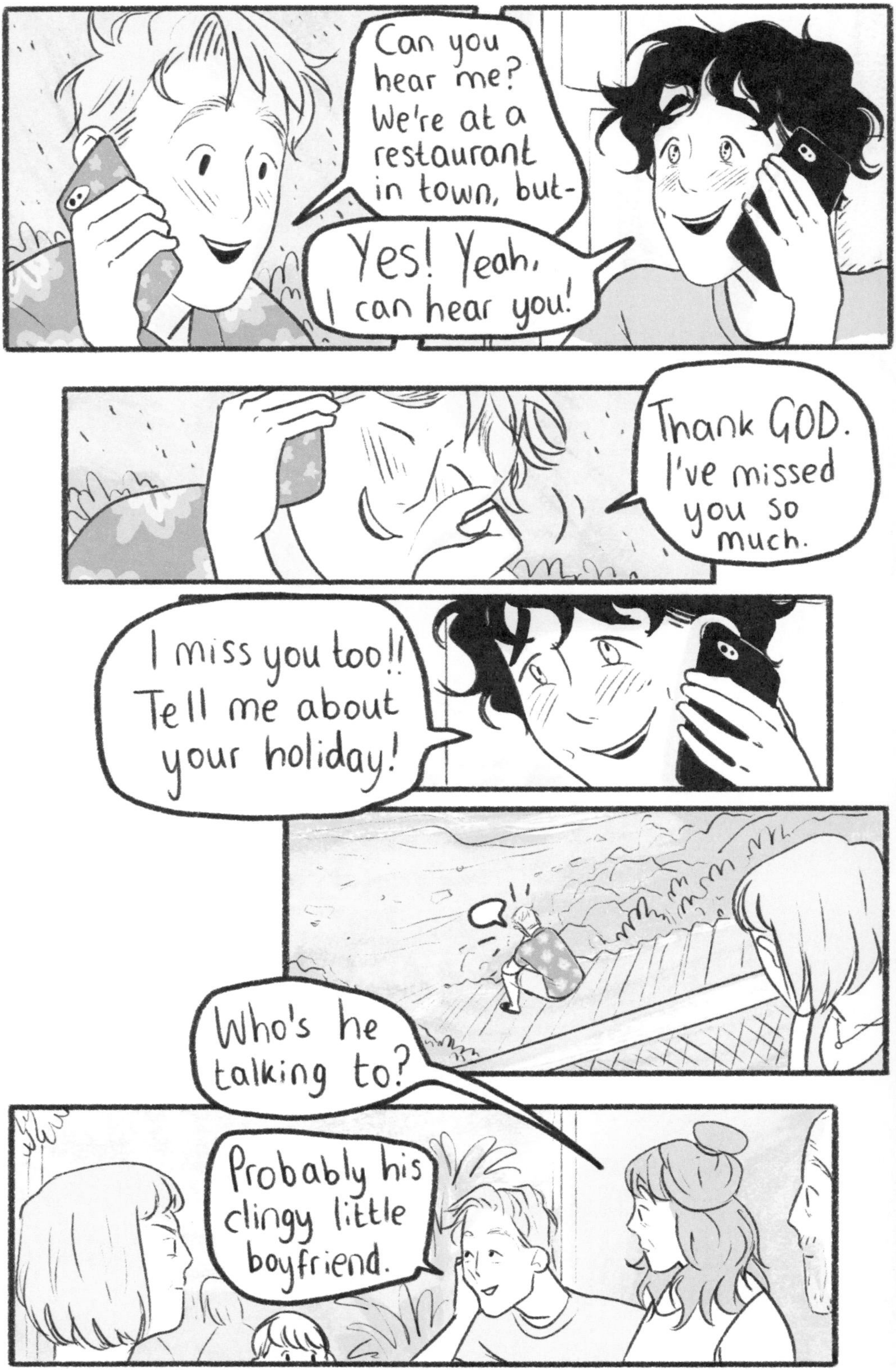
Can you hear me? We're at a restaurant in town, but-
Yes! Yeah, I can hear you!
Thank GOD. I've missed you so much.
I miss you too!! Tell me about your holiday!
Who's he talking to?
Probably his clingy little boyfriend.

151

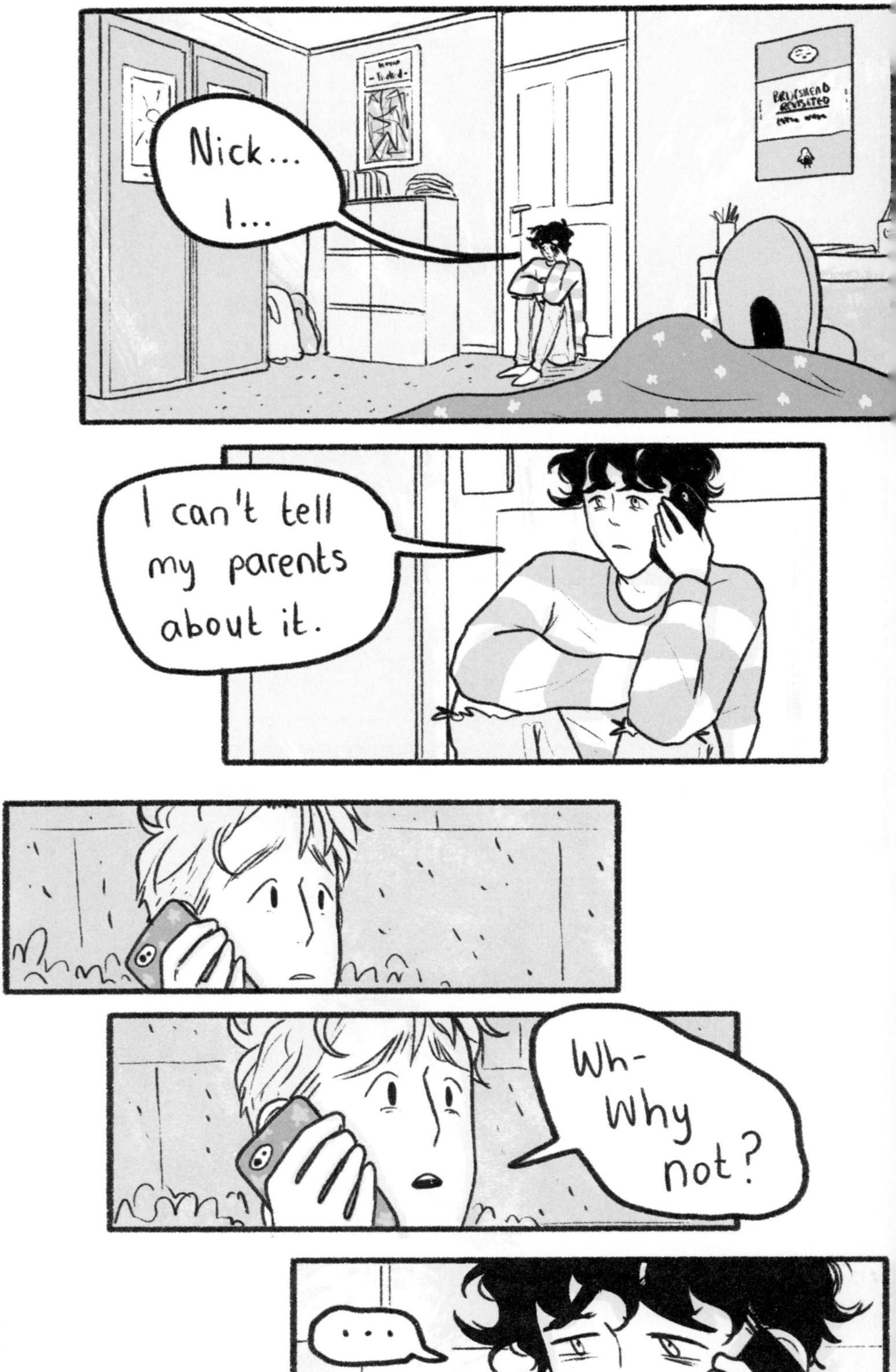
Nick...
I...
I can't tell my parents about it.
Wh- Why not?
...

153

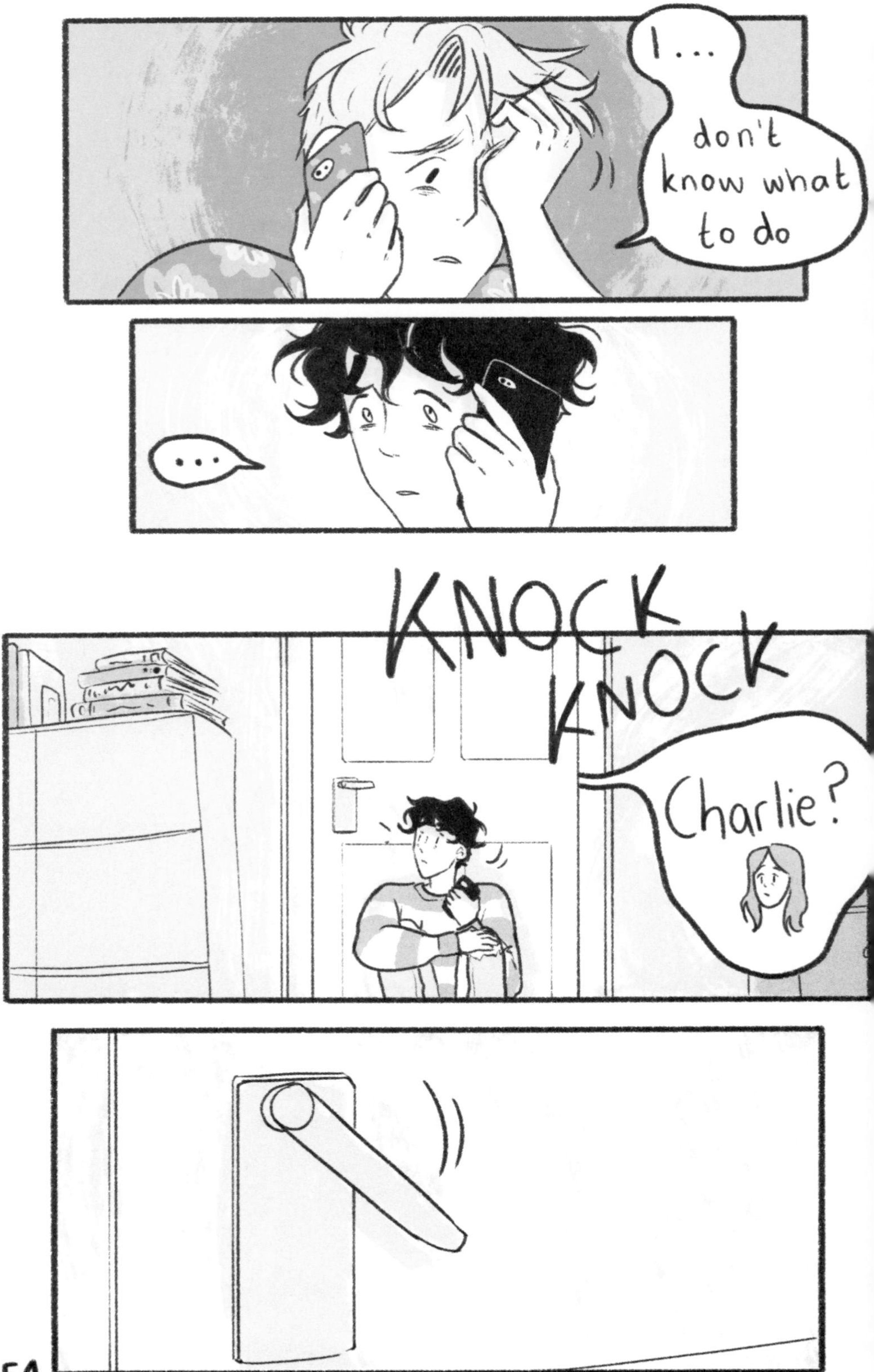
I...
don't know what to do
...
KNOCK KNOCK
Charlie?

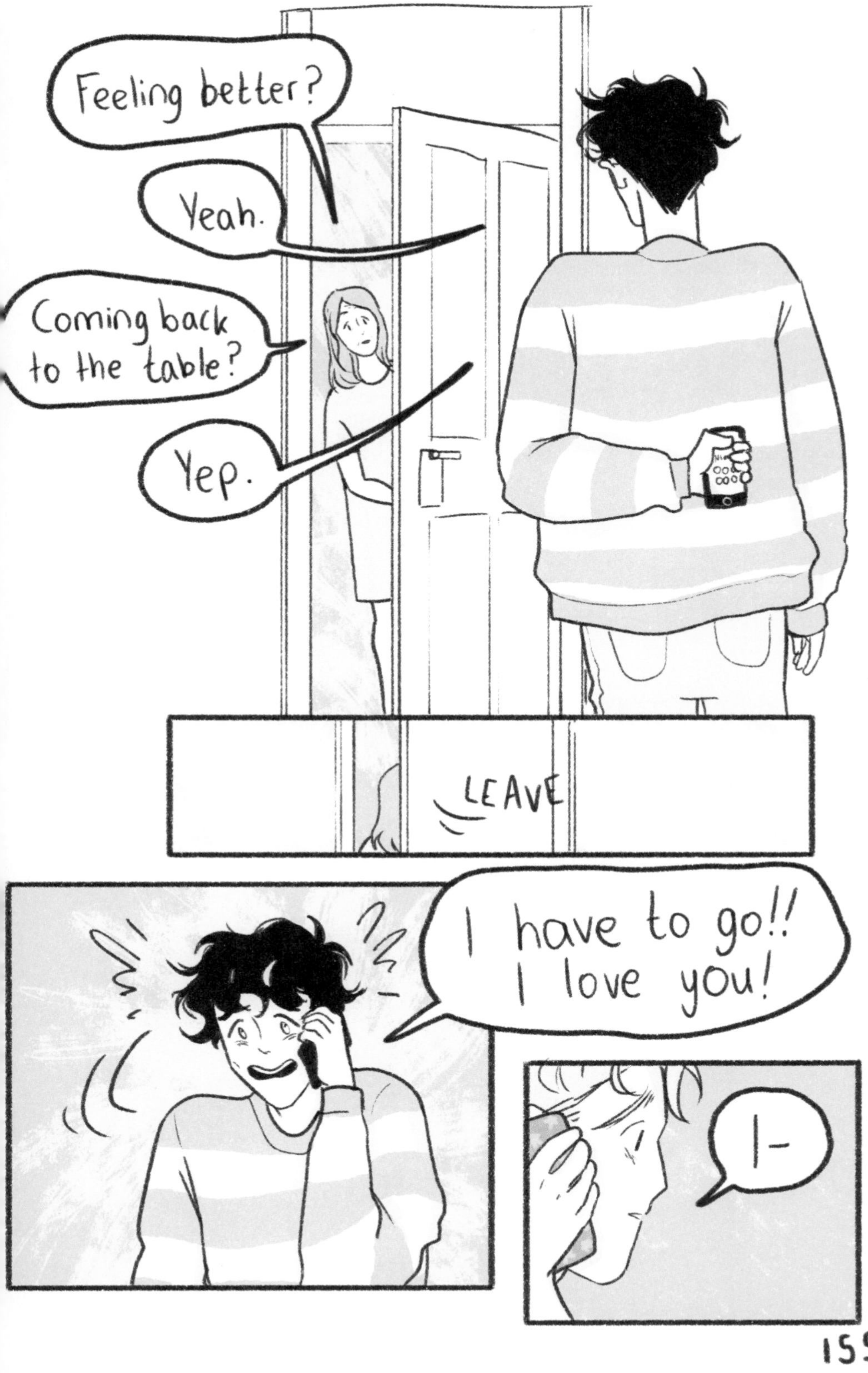
Feeling better?
Yeah.
Coming back to the table?
Yep.
LEAVE
I have to go!! I love you!
I-

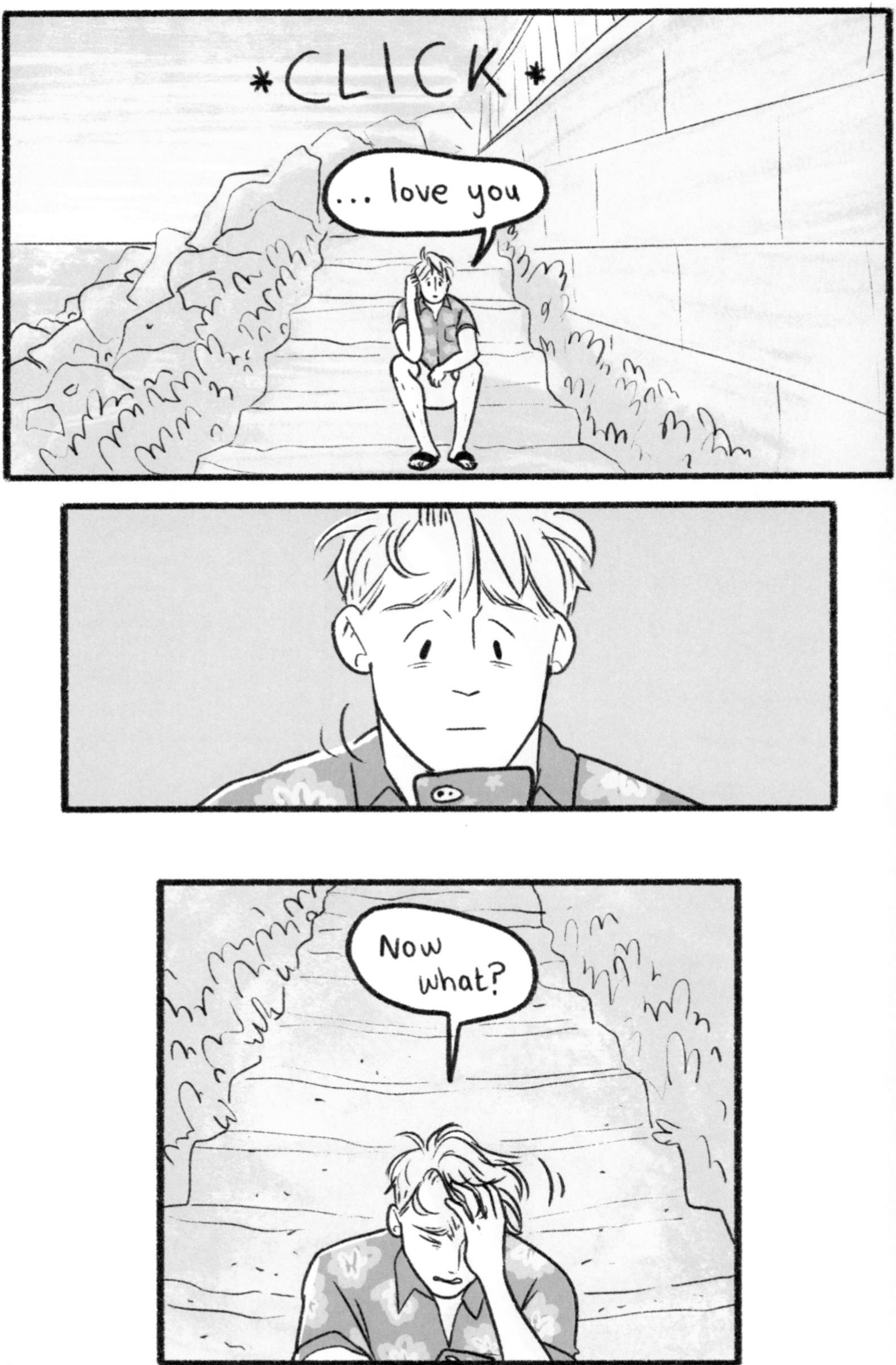
CLICK
... love you
Now what?

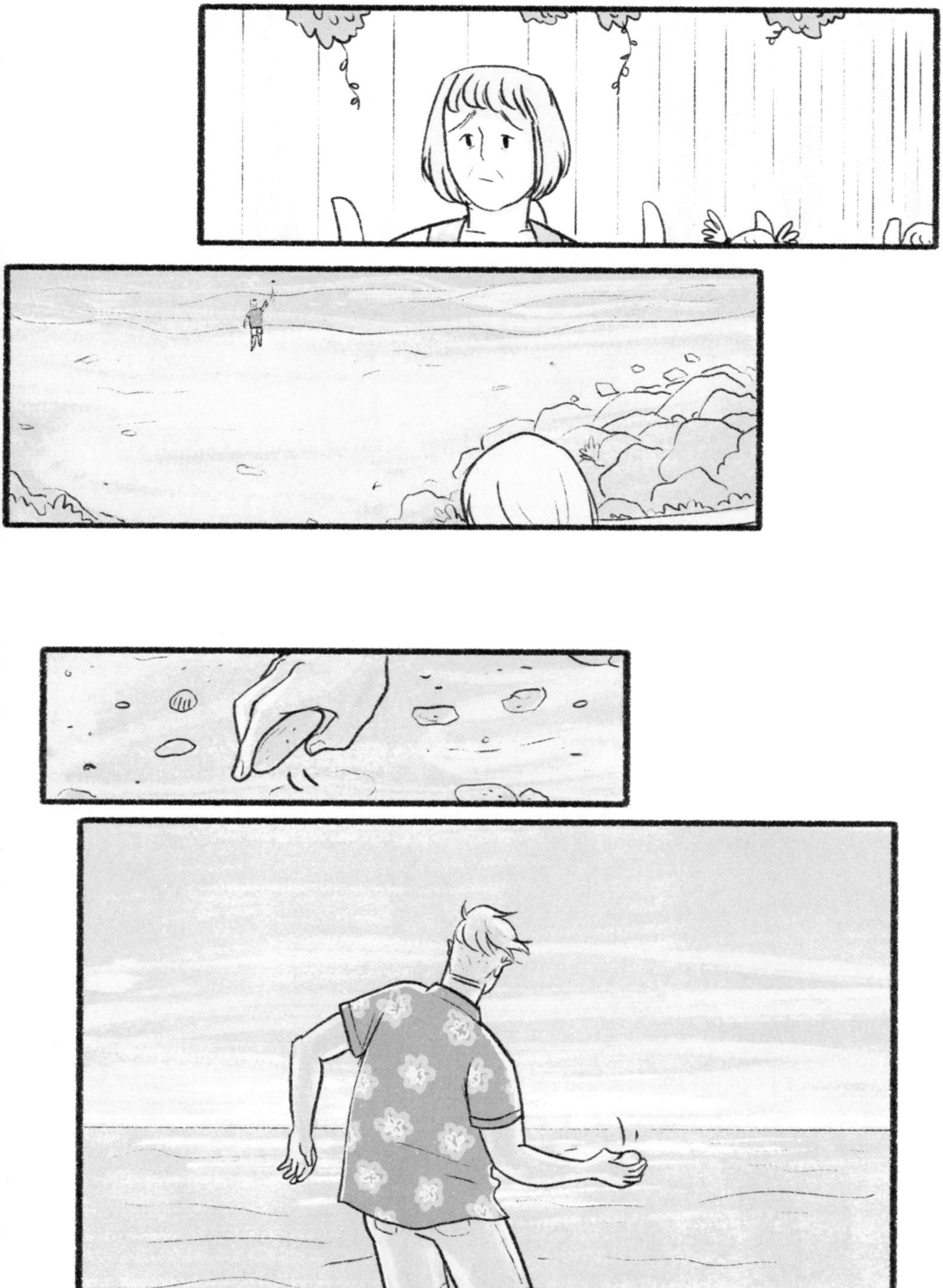

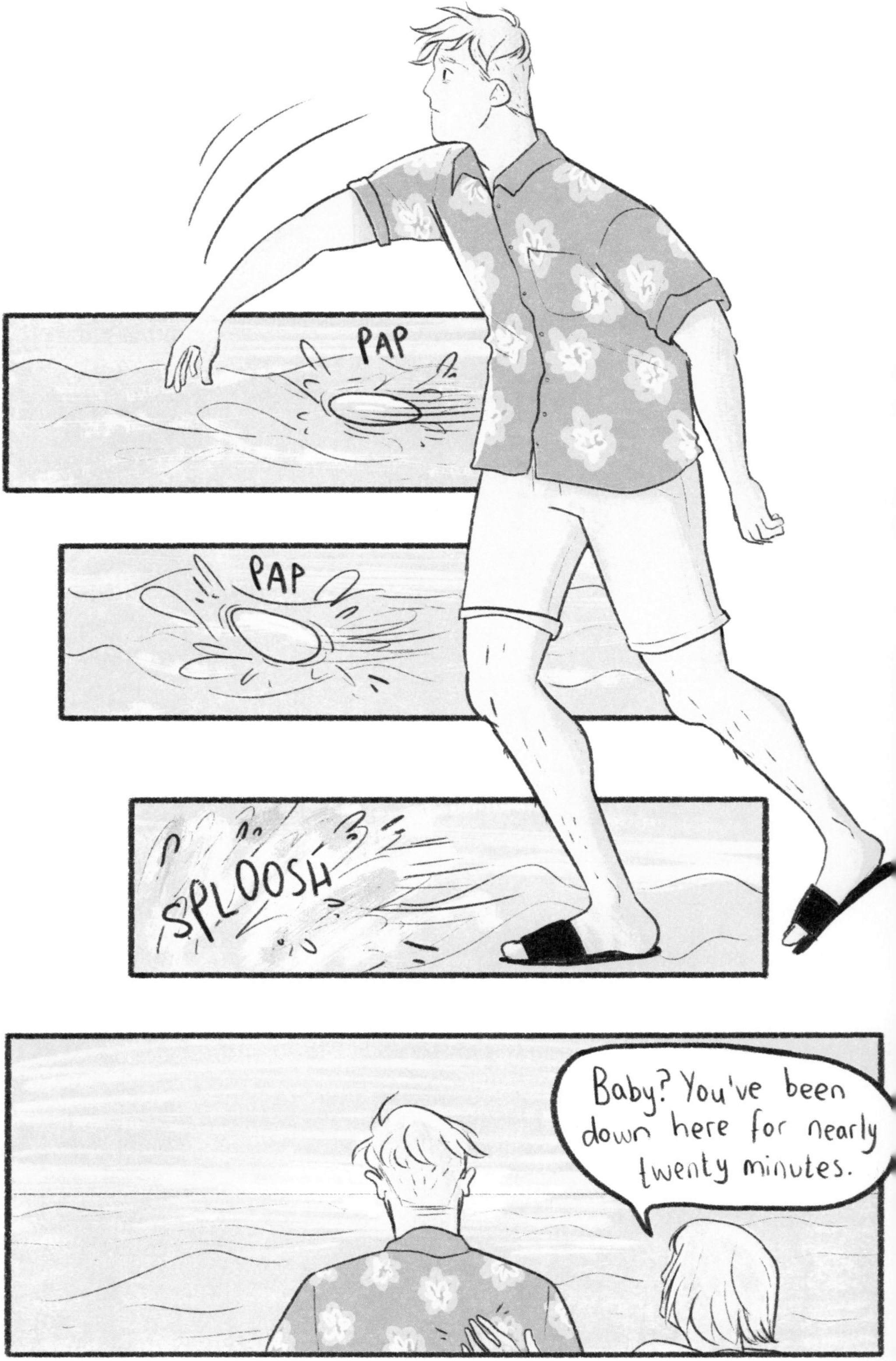
PAP
PAP
SPLOOSH
Baby? You've been down here for nearly twenty minutes.

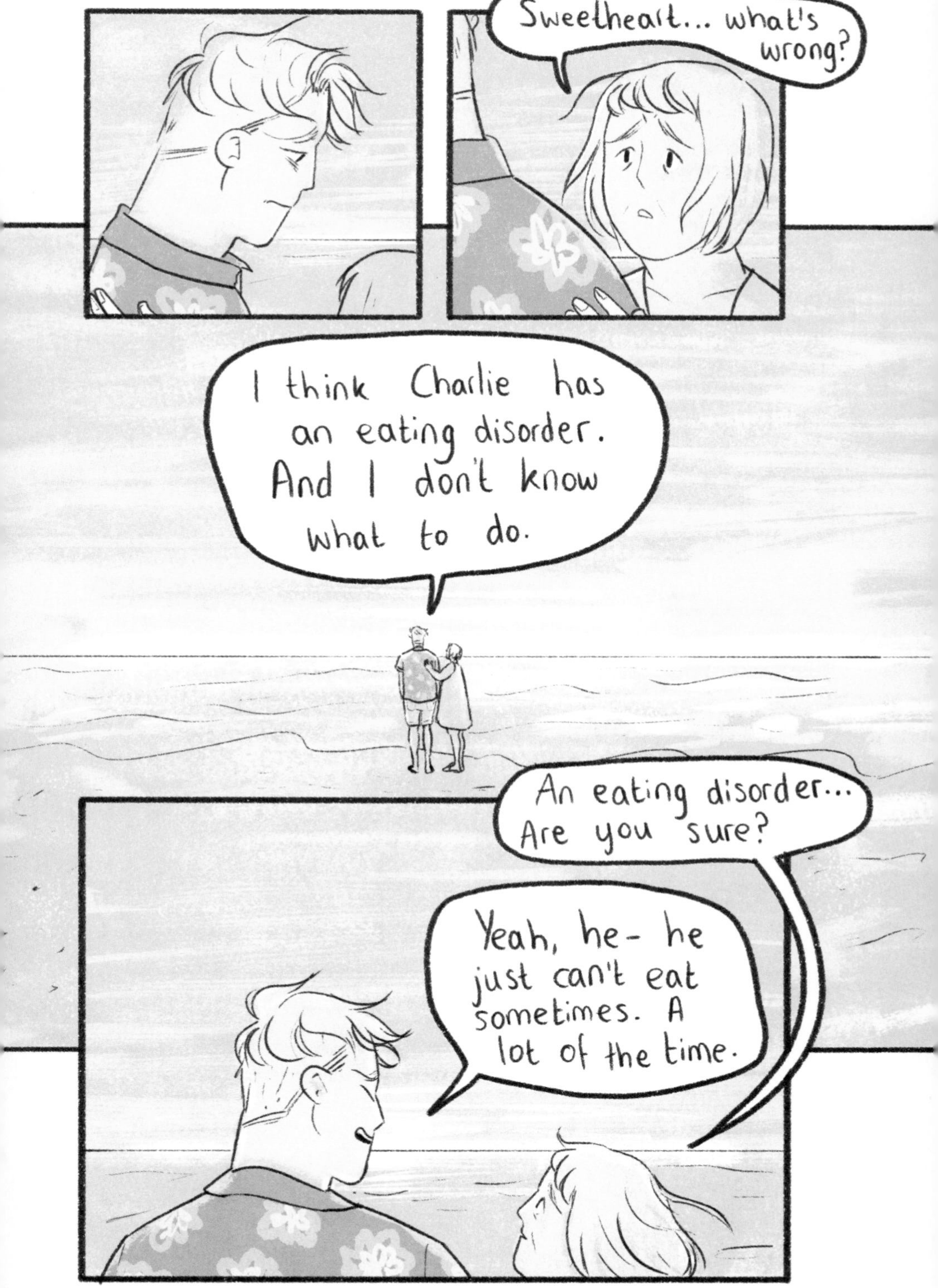
Sweetheart... what's wrong?
I think Charlie has an eating disorder. And I don't know what to do.
An eating disorder... Are you sure?
Yeah, he- he just can't eat sometimes. A lot of the time.

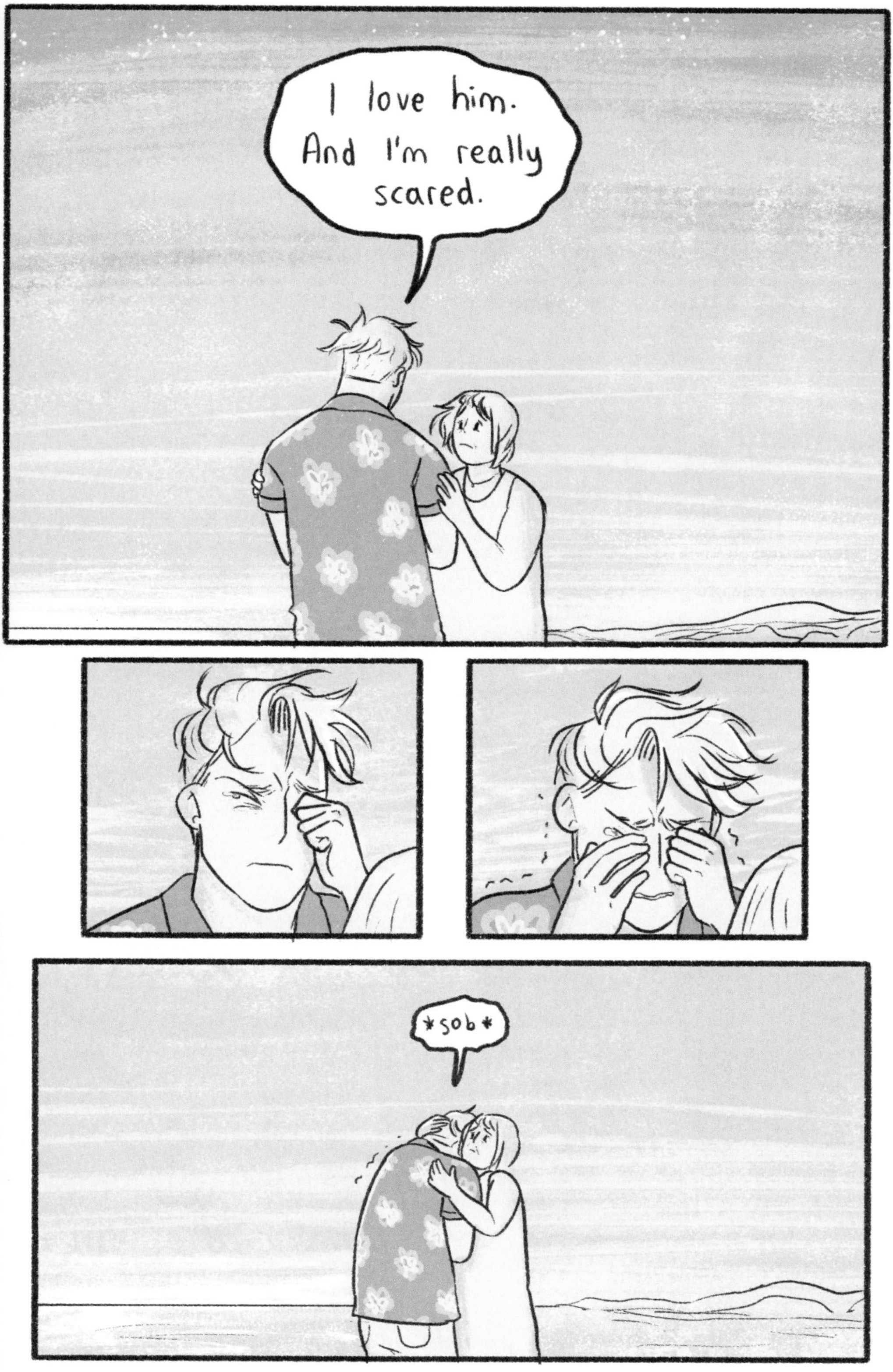
I love him. And I'm really scared.
sob

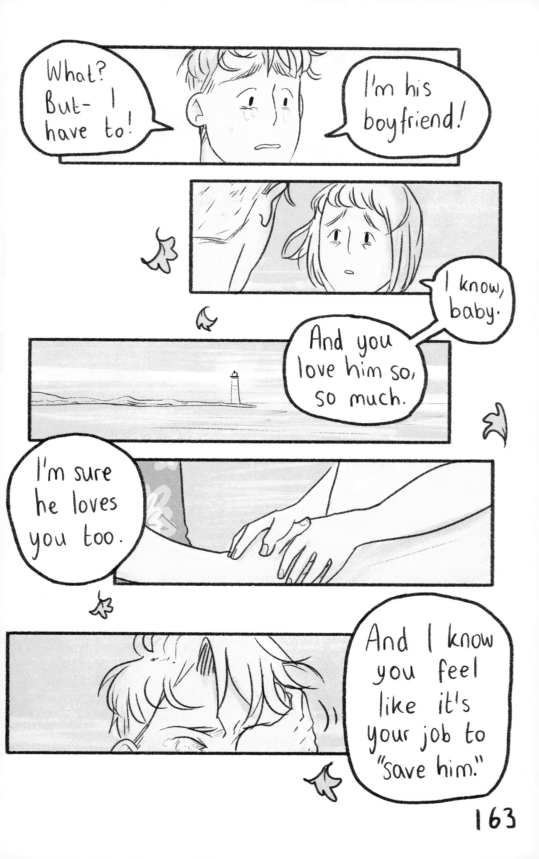

163

He needs help from a doctor or a therapist—

Someone who knows about eating disorders and how to treat them.

How to tell someone you have an eating disorder

It can be scary to talk to anyone about mental health, but sharing your feelings can be the first important step toward recovery. This page will cover:

- Who should I talk to?
- What should I say?
- What do I do if the understa...

Love can't cure a mental illness.

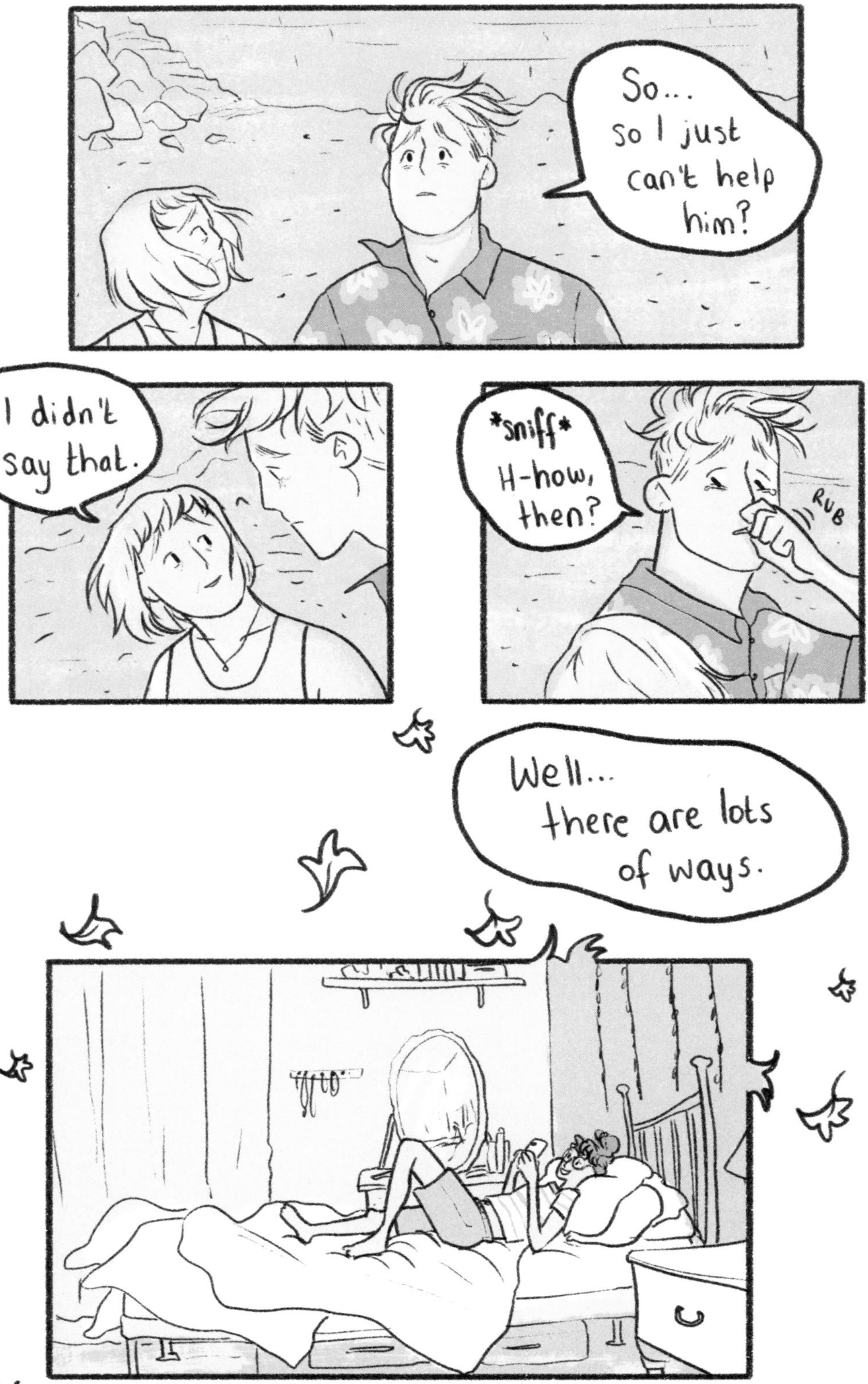
So... so I just can't help him?
I didn't say that.
sniff H-how, then?
RUB
Well... there are lots of ways.

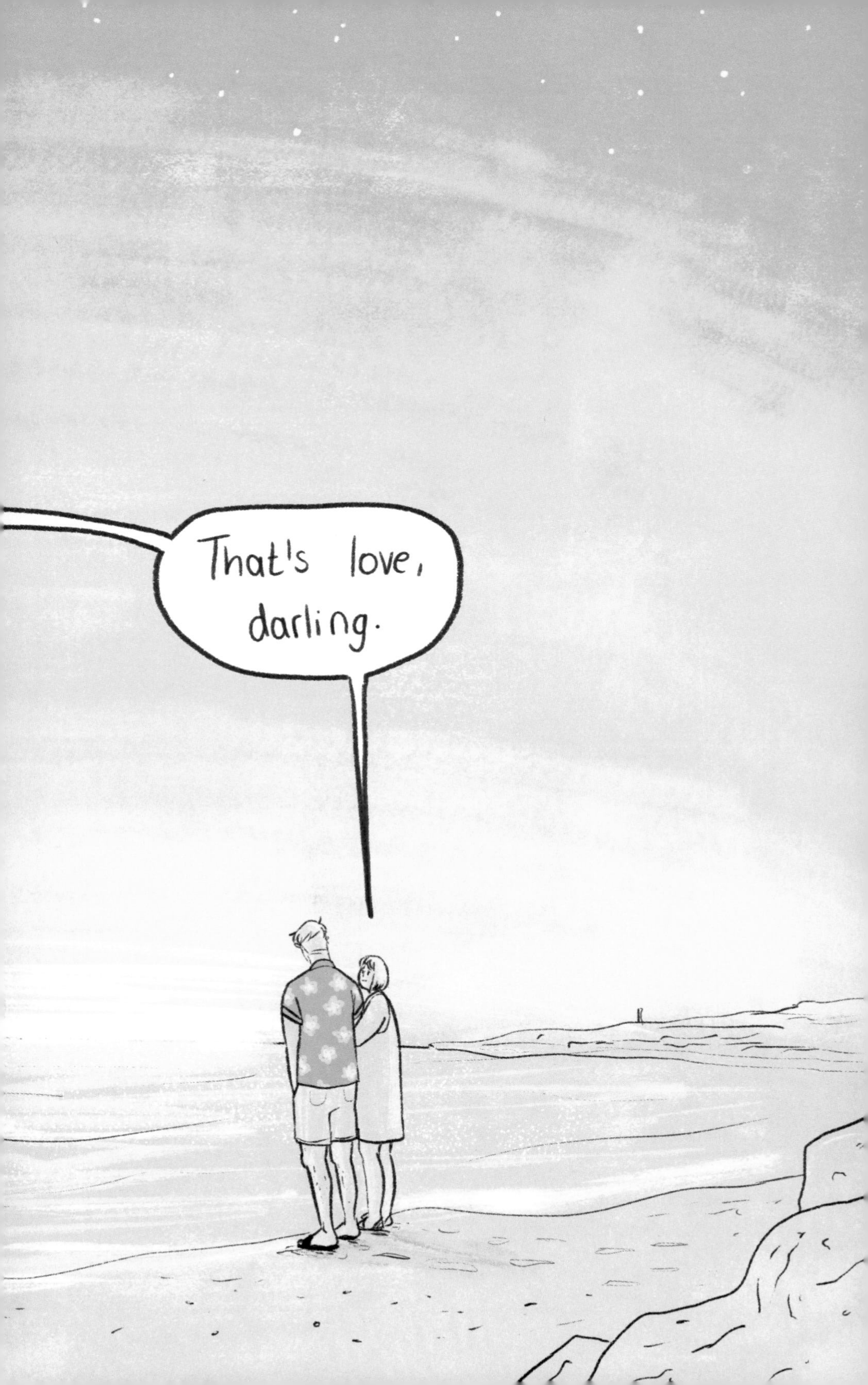
That's love, darling.

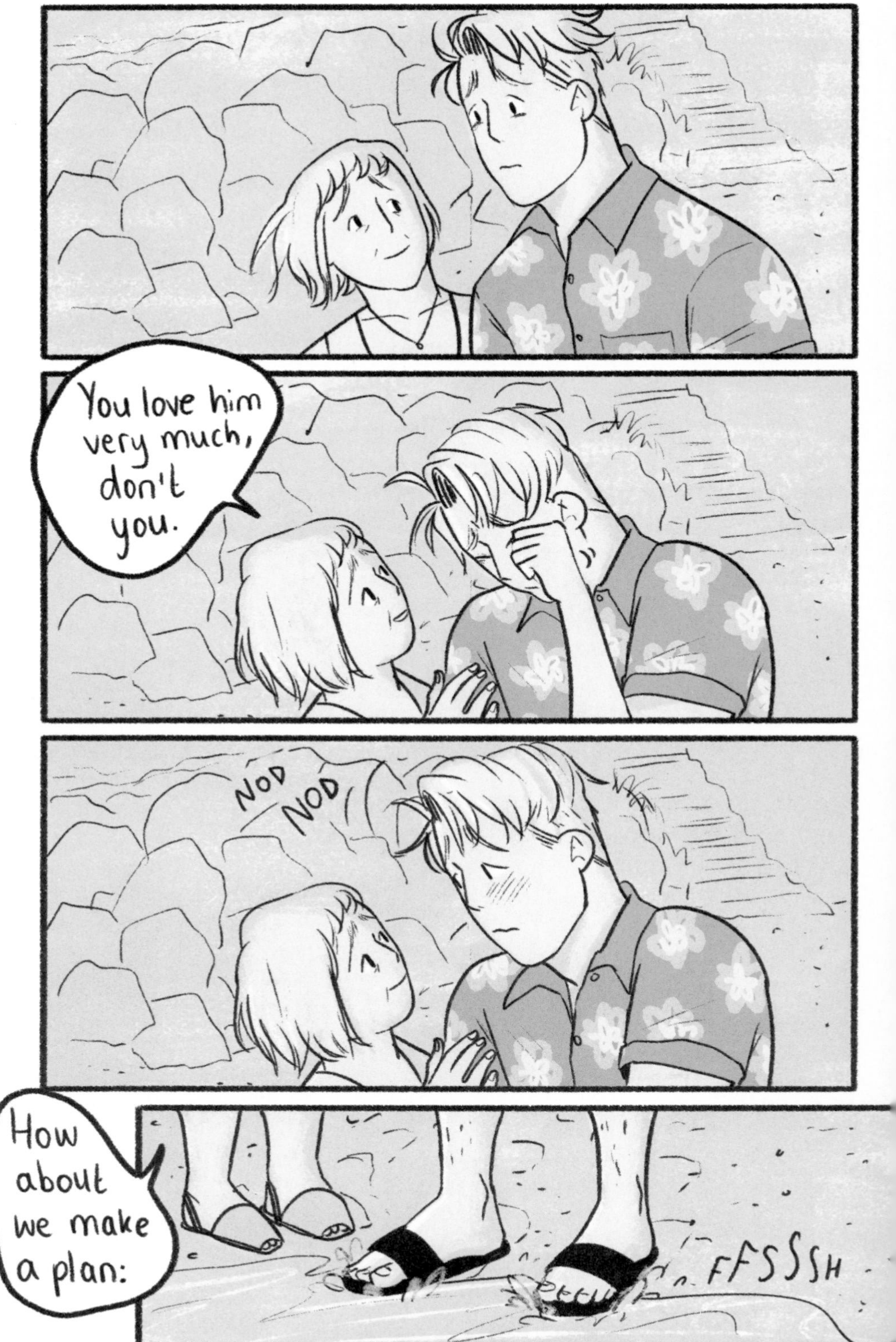
You love him very much, don't you.
NOD NOD
How about we make a plan:
FFSSSH

When we get home, me and you can sit down and do some proper research about how we could help Charlie talk to his parents or to a doctor.
Does that sound okay?
FSSsSsH
Yeah.

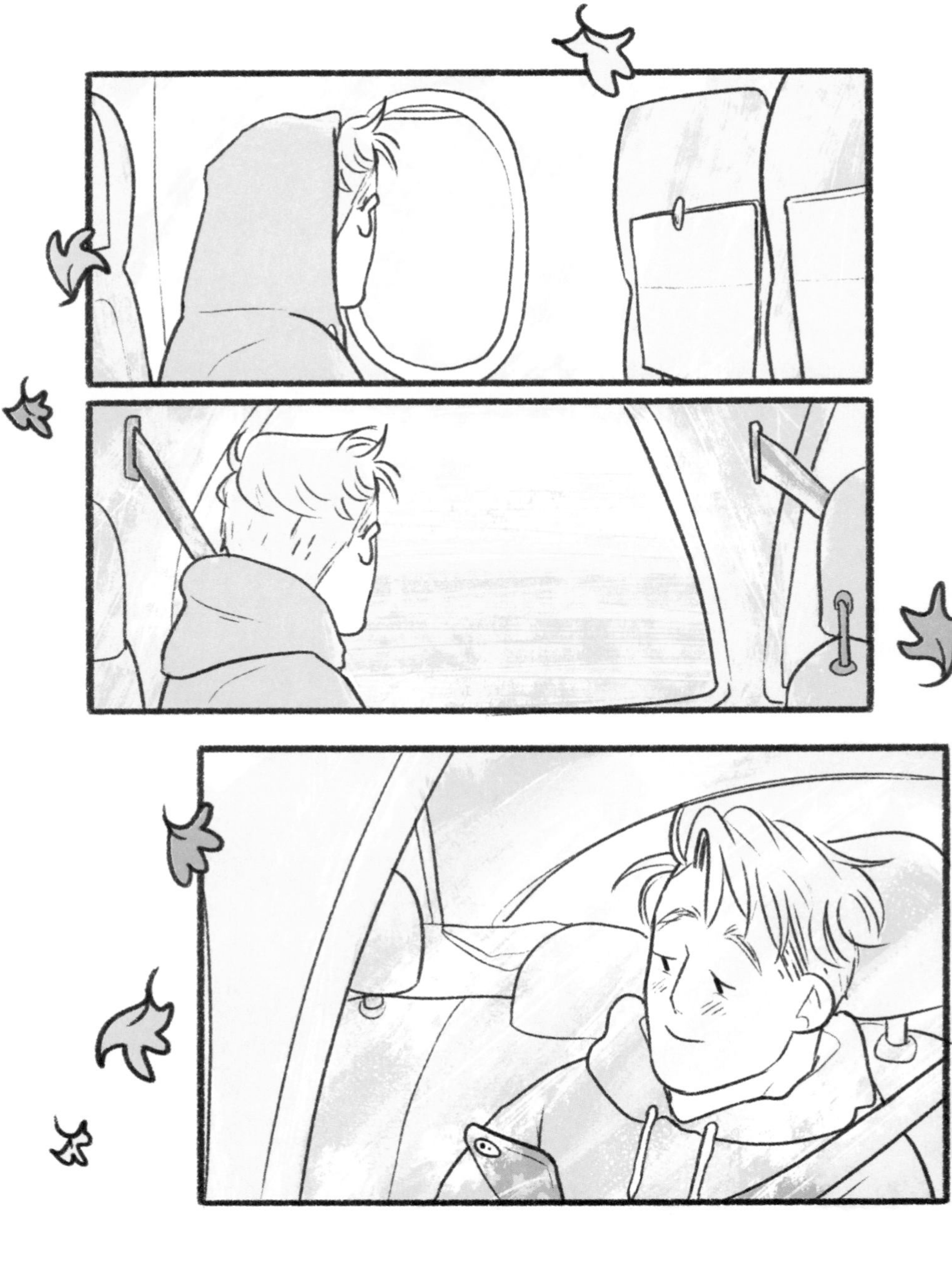

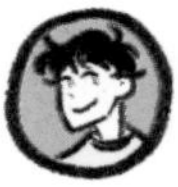

i can't wait to see you at school tomorrow!!!!!!!!

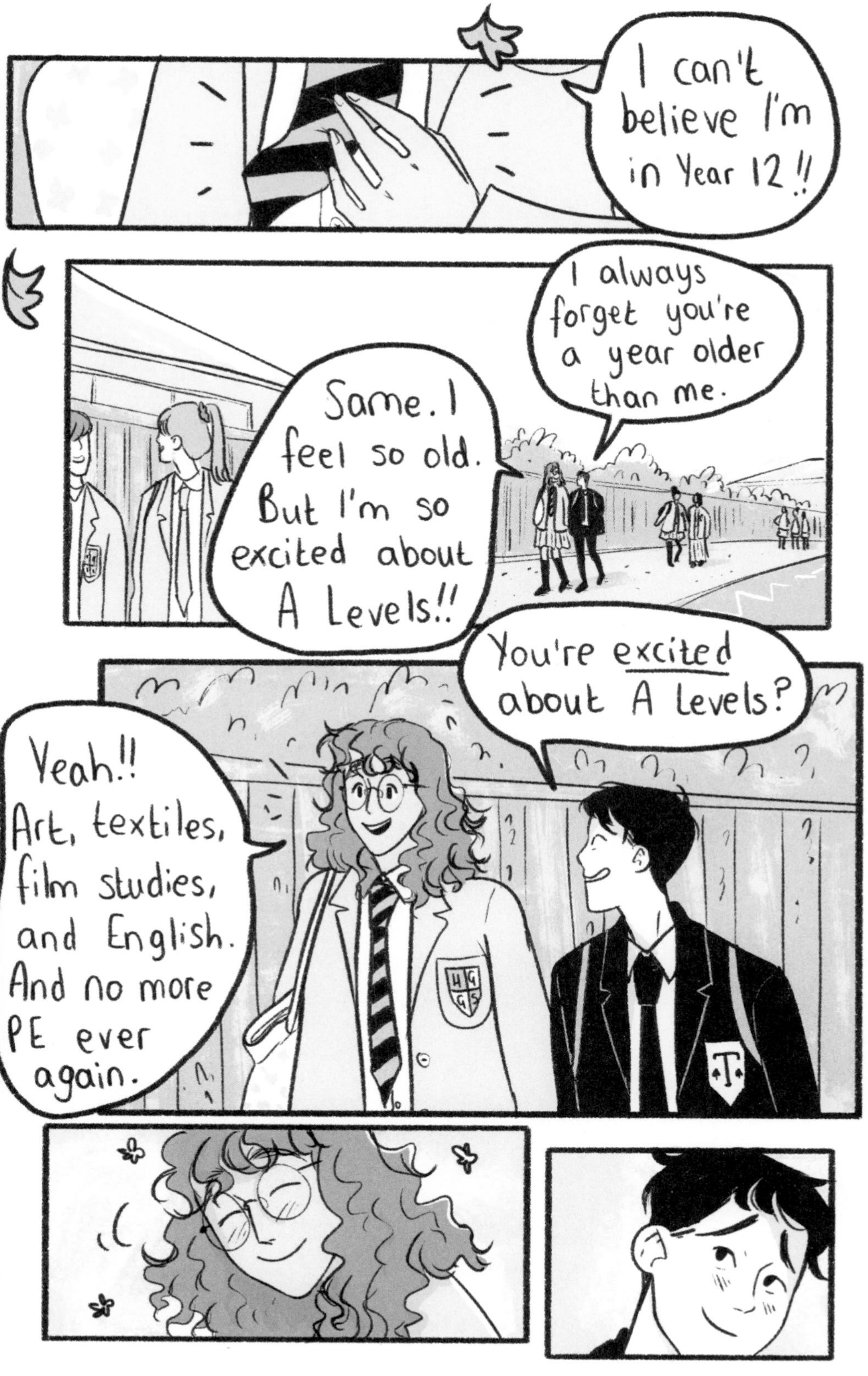
I can't believe I'm in Year 12!!
I always forget you're a year older than me.
Same. I feel so old. But I'm so excited about A Levels!!
You're excited about A Levels?
Yeah!! Art, textiles, film studies, and English. And no more PE ever again.

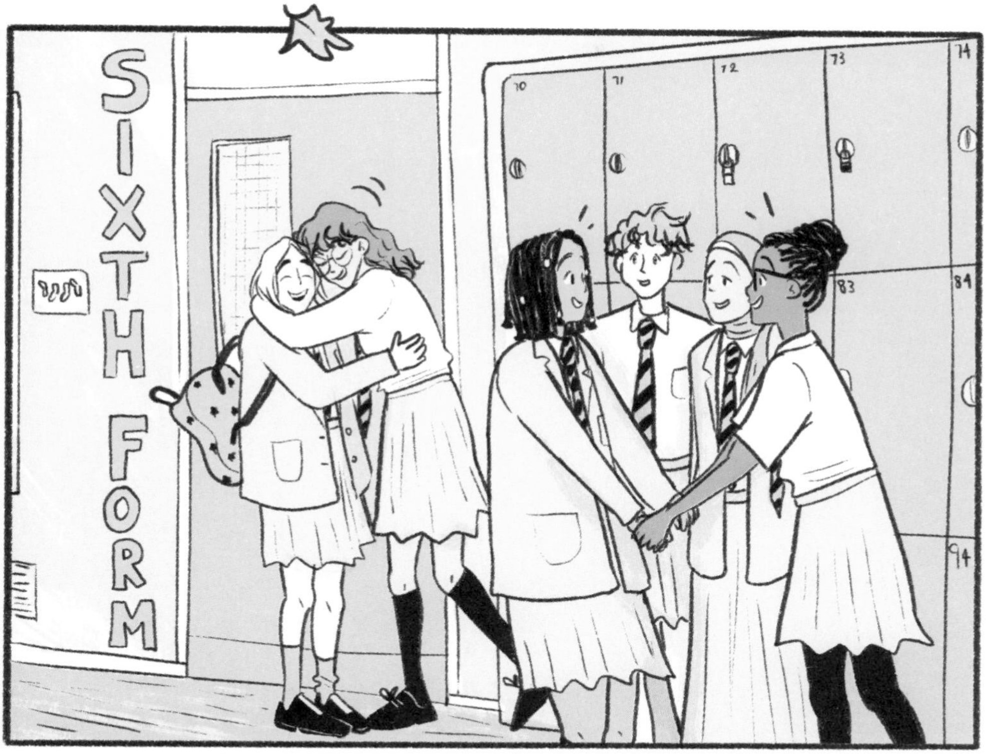
SIXTH FORM
70
71
72
73
74
83
84
94

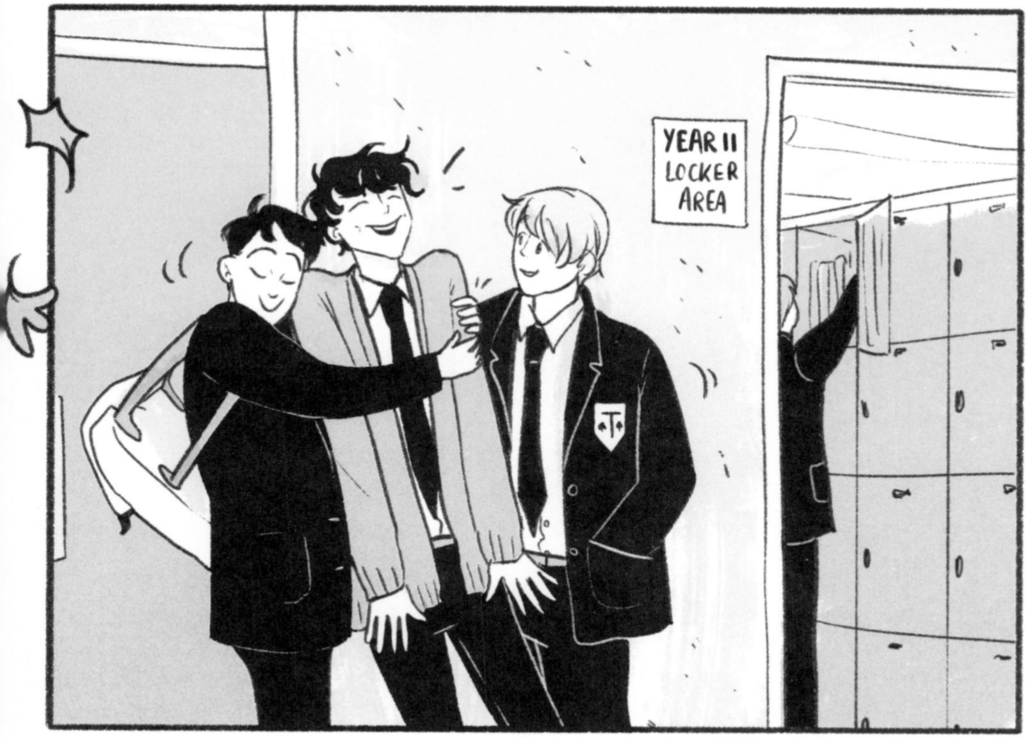
YEAR 11
LOCKER
AREA

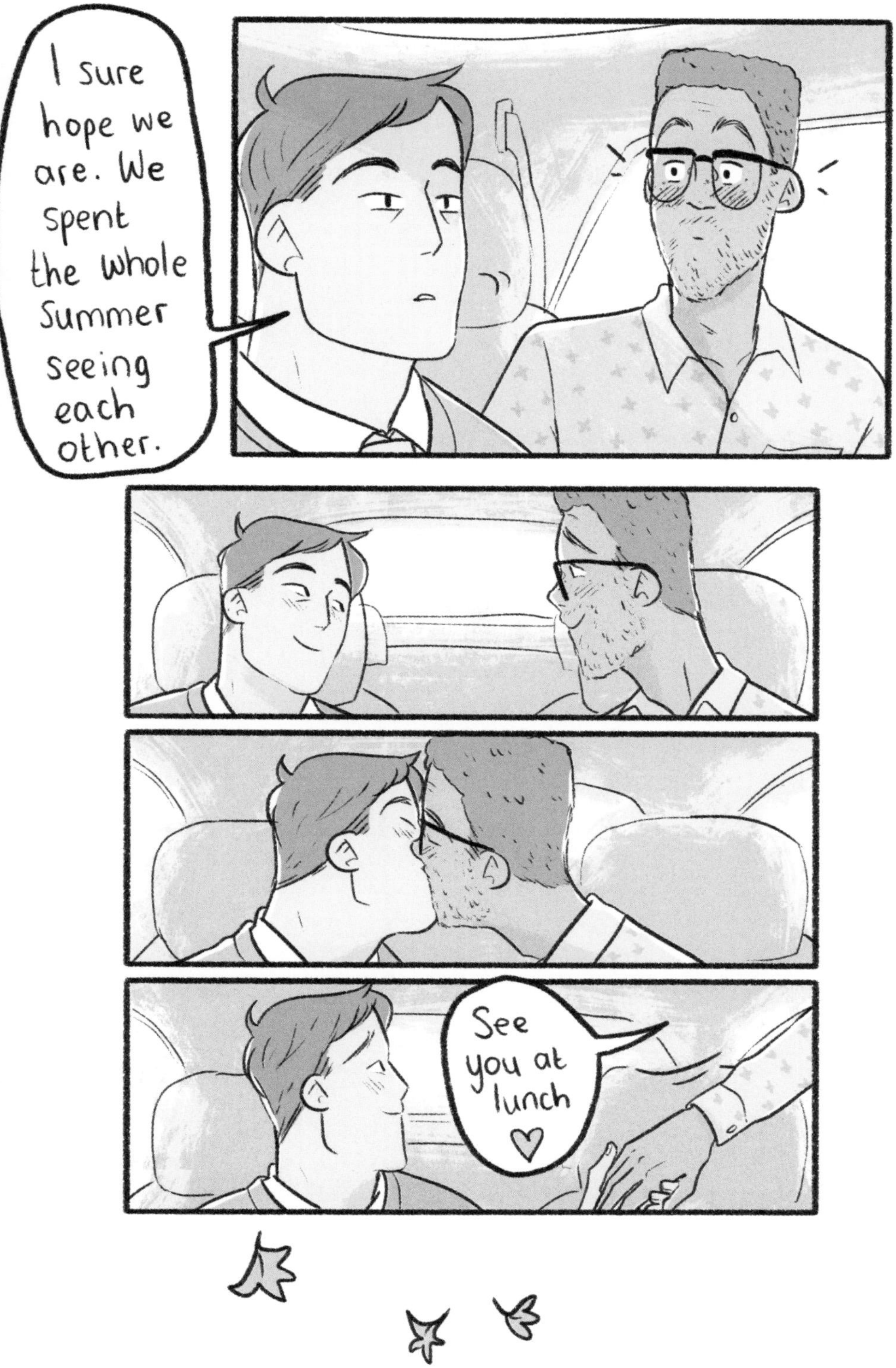
I sure hope we are. We spent the whole Summer seeing each other.
See you at lunch ♡

Name: Nicholas Nelson

Year Group: 12

Form Group: Hamlet 5

A Level Choices:

PSY: PSYCHOLOGY

BIO: BIOLOGY

PE: PHYSICAL EDUCATION

GEO: GEOGRAPHY

PERIOD	MON	TUE	WED	THUR	FRI
1	FREE	PSY	PE	FREE	
2	GEO			BIO	

185

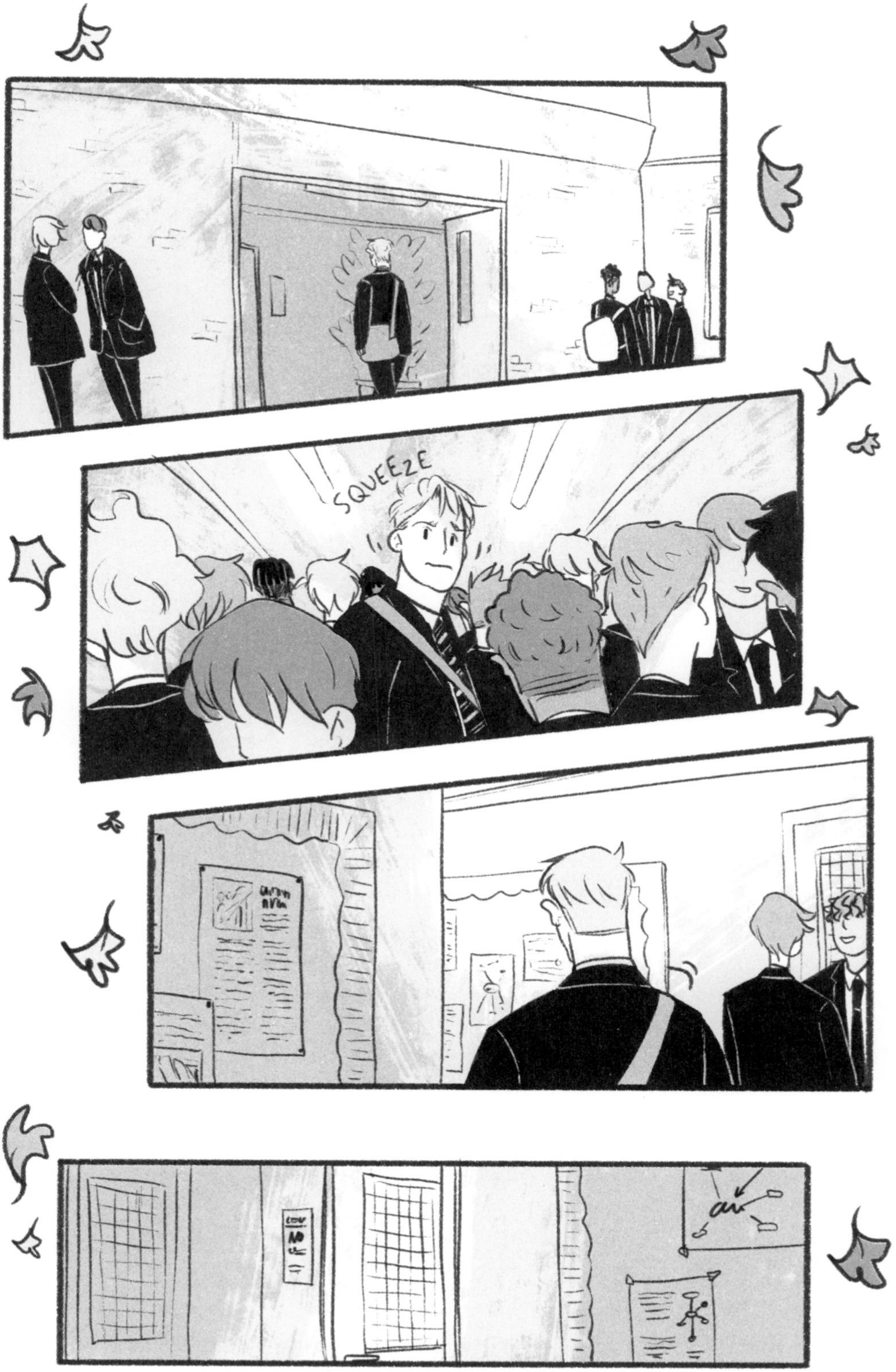
SQUEEZE

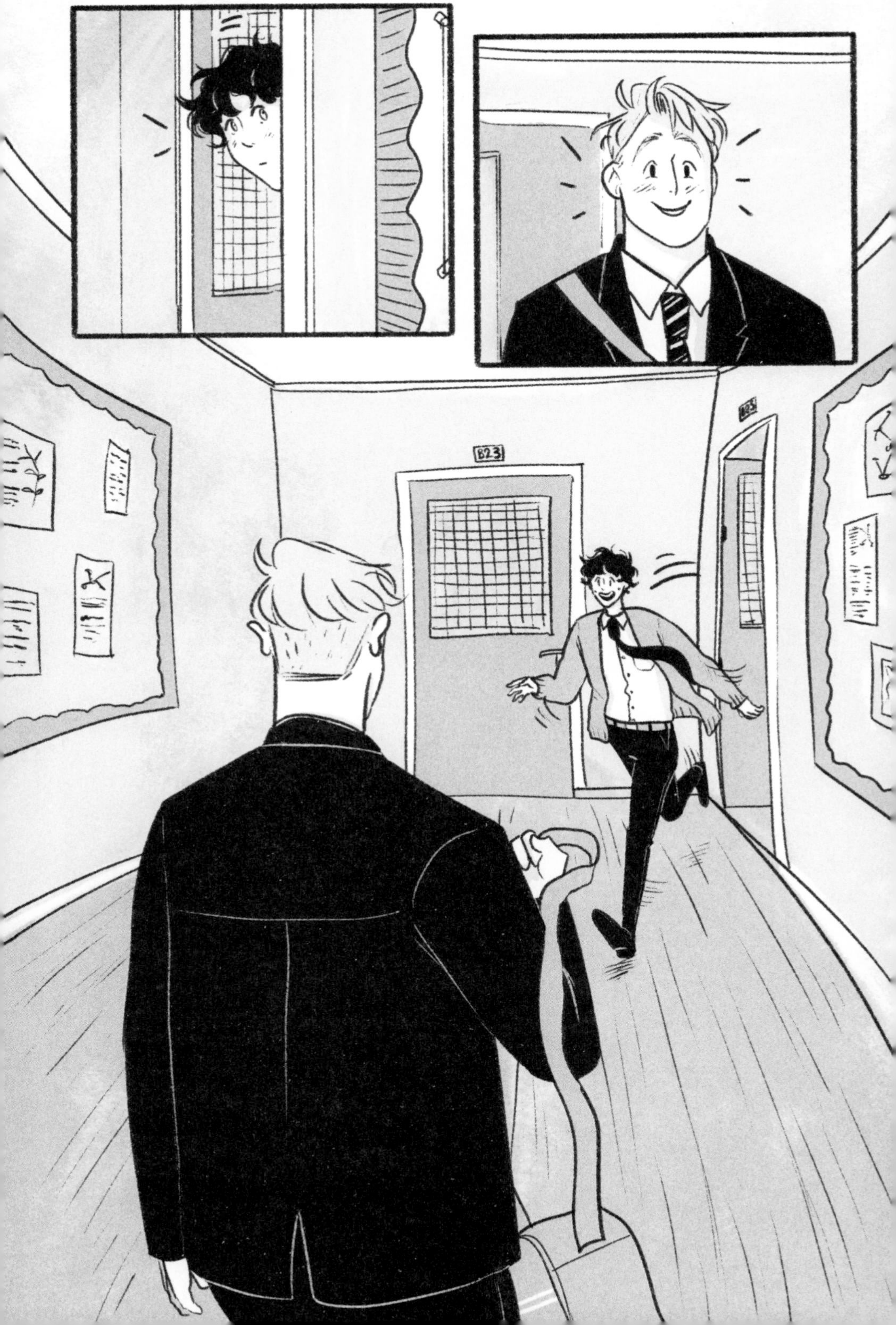
B23

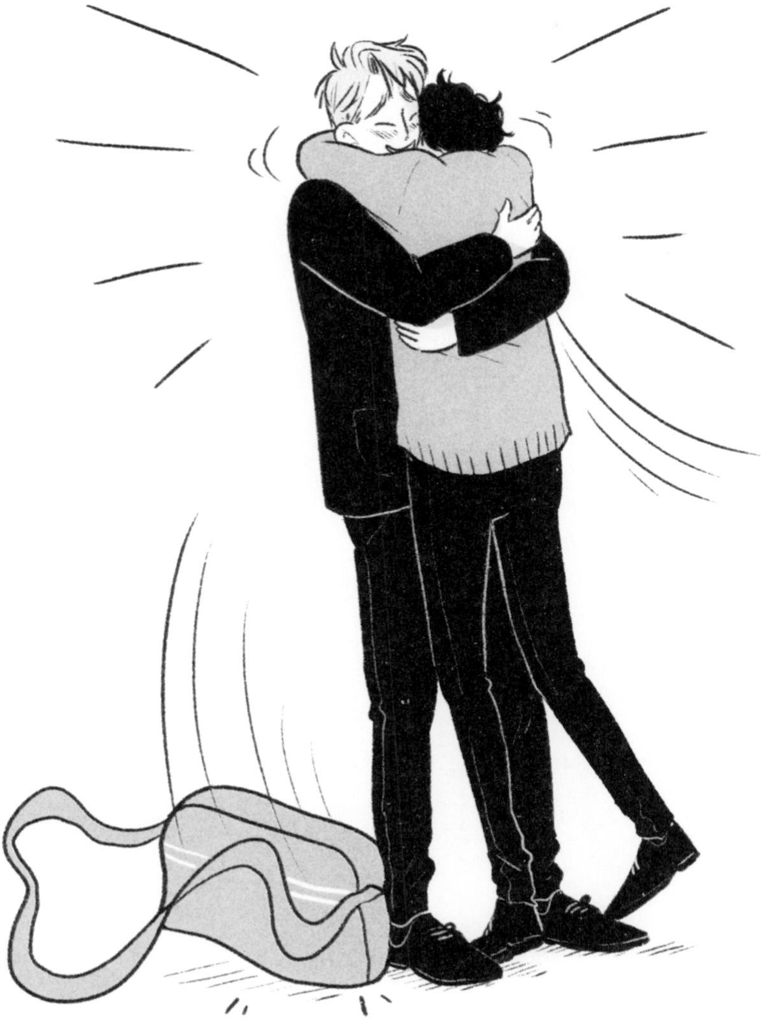

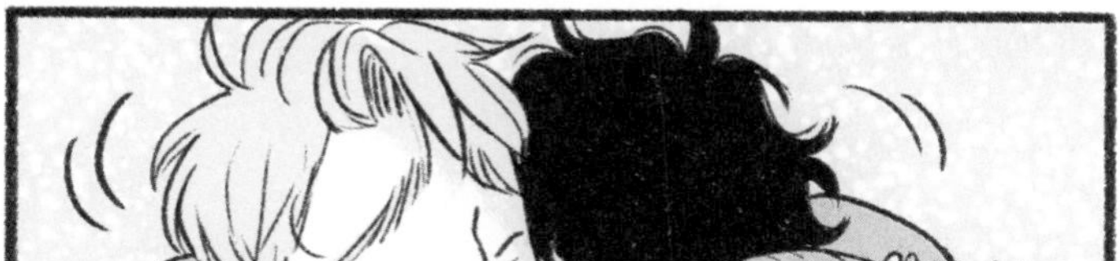

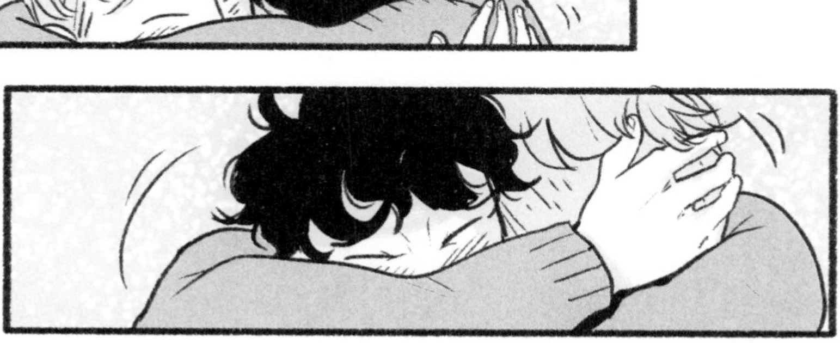

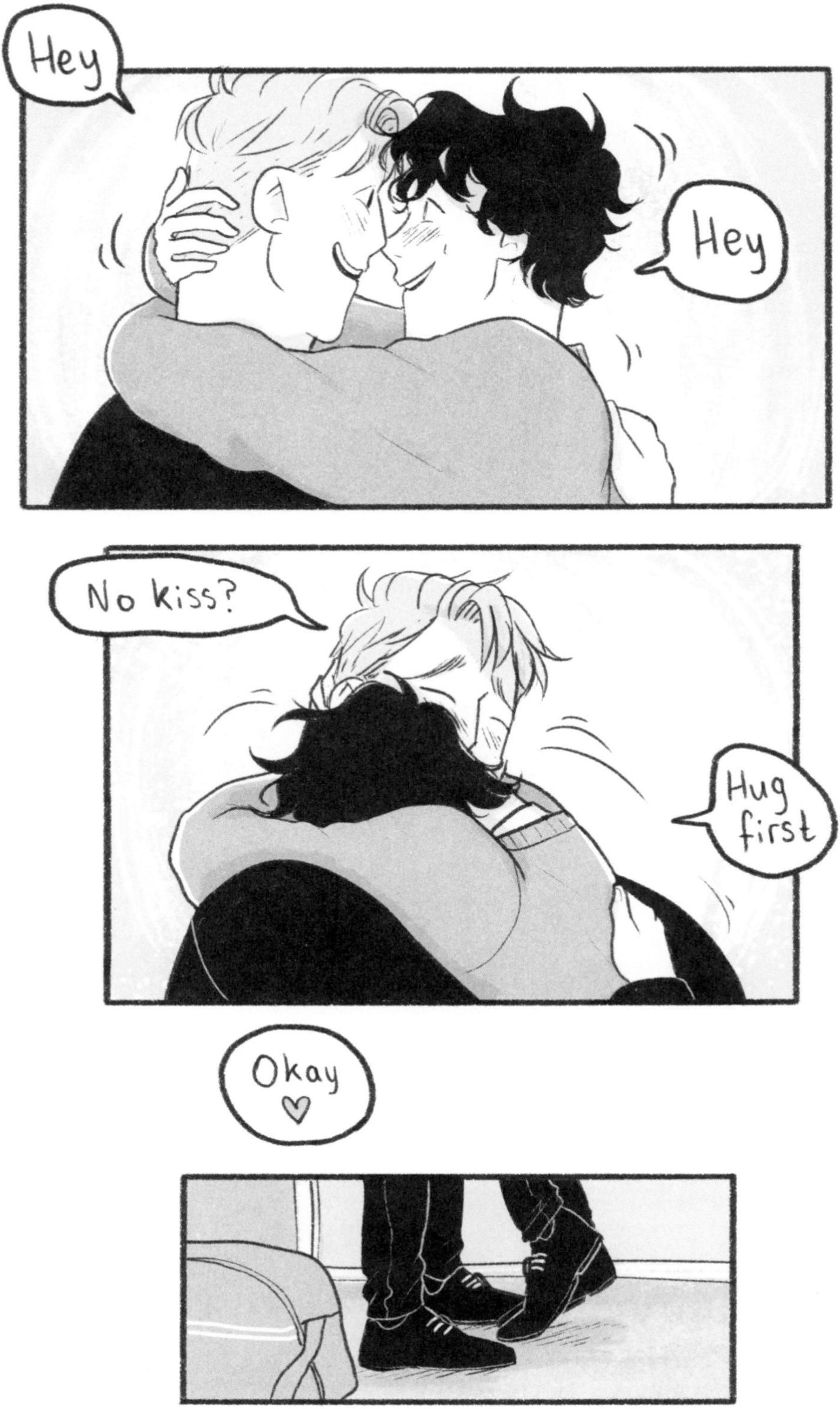
Hey
Hey
No kiss?
Hug first
Okay ♡

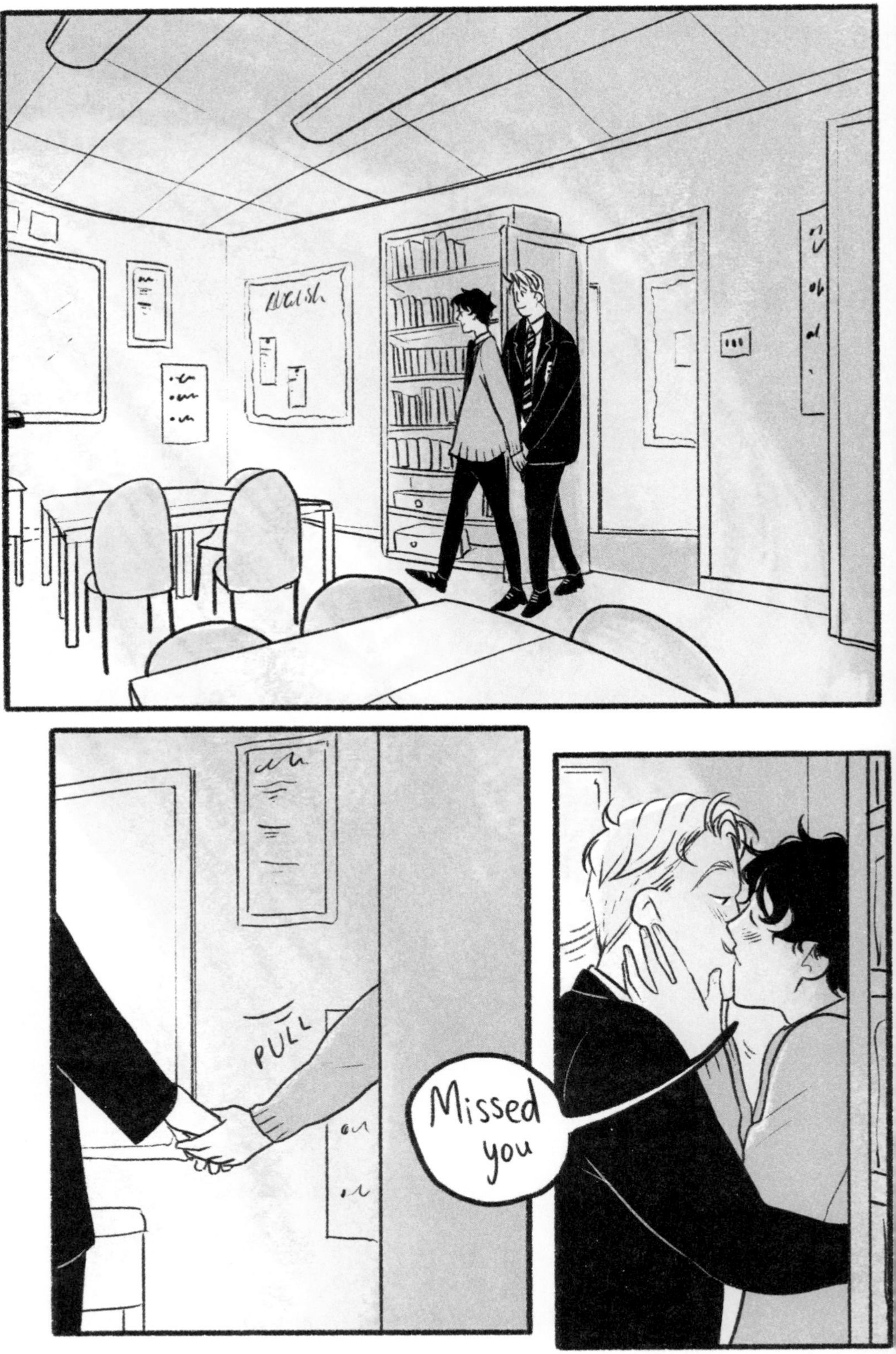
ENGLISH
PULL
Missed you

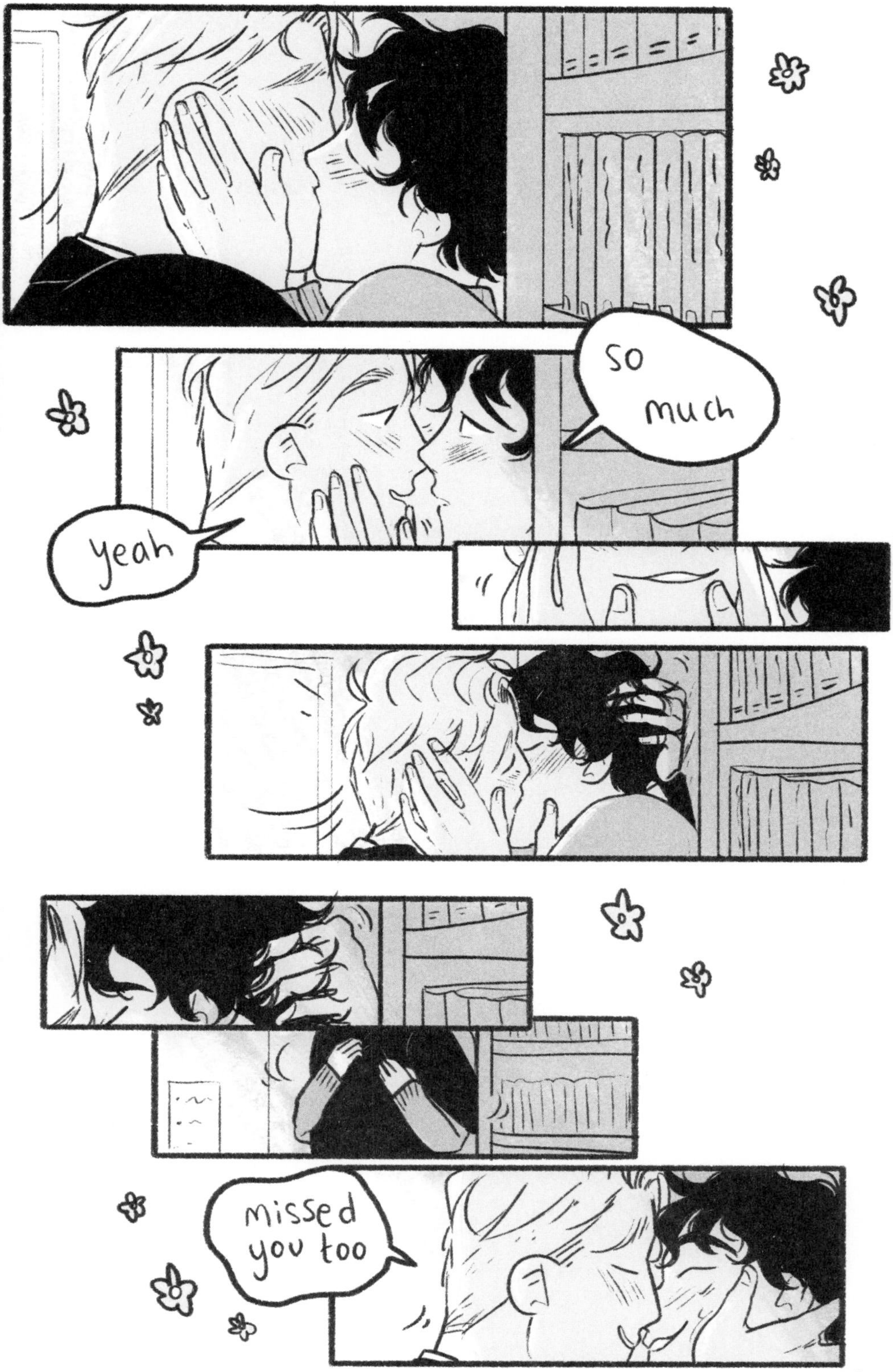
so much
yeah
missed you too

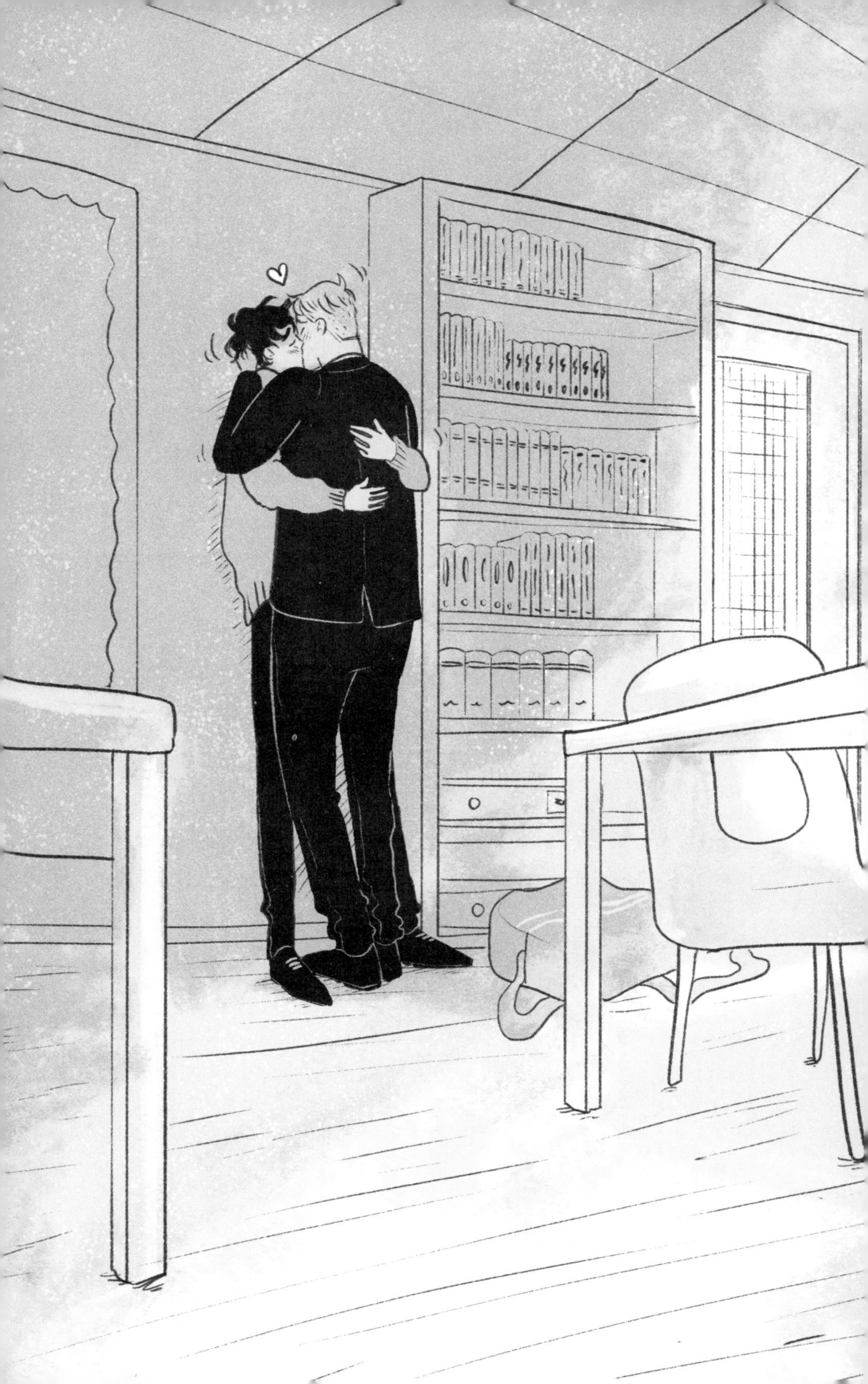

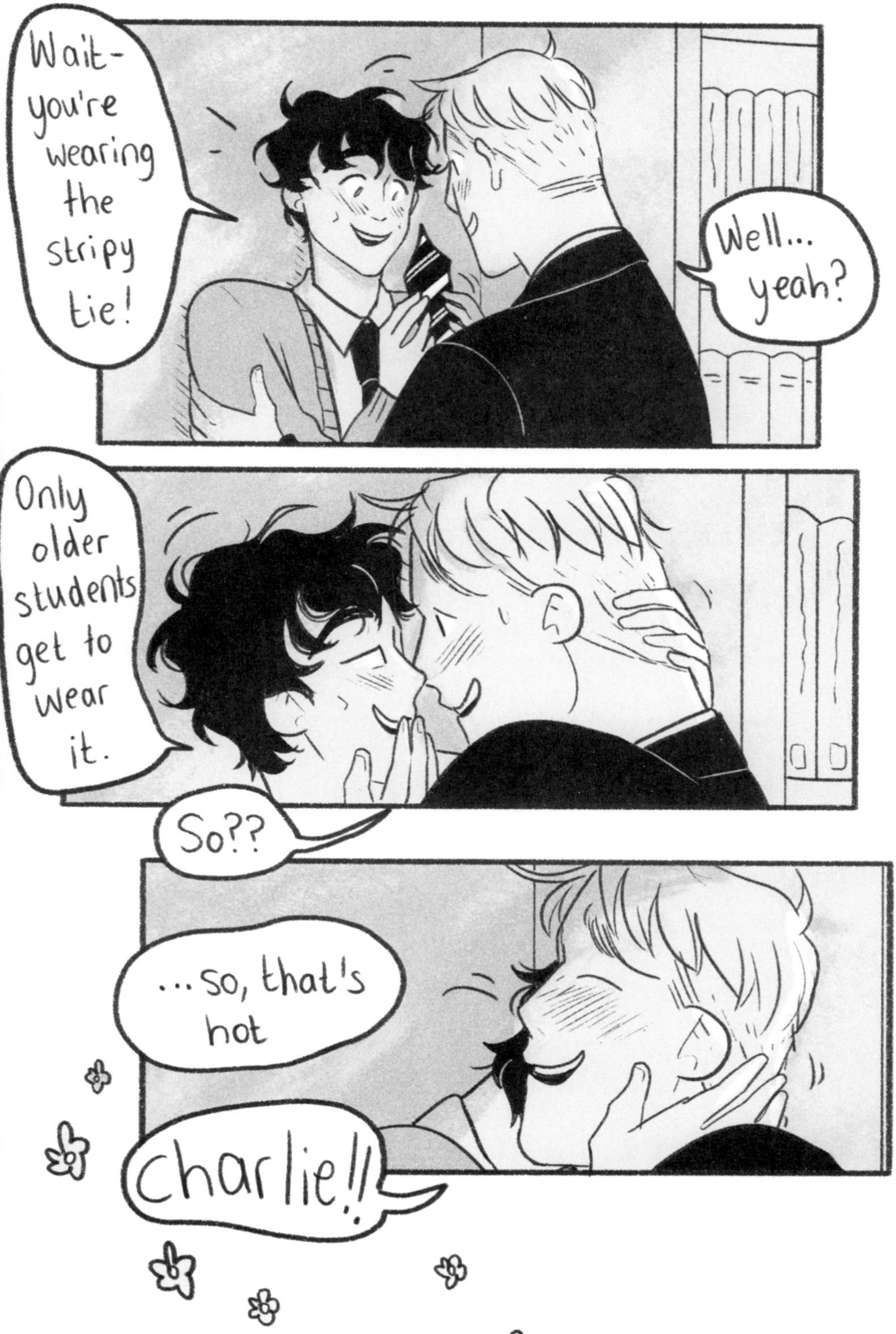
Wait- you're wearing the stripy tie!
Well... yeah?
Only older students get to wear it.
So??
...so, that's hot
Charlie!!

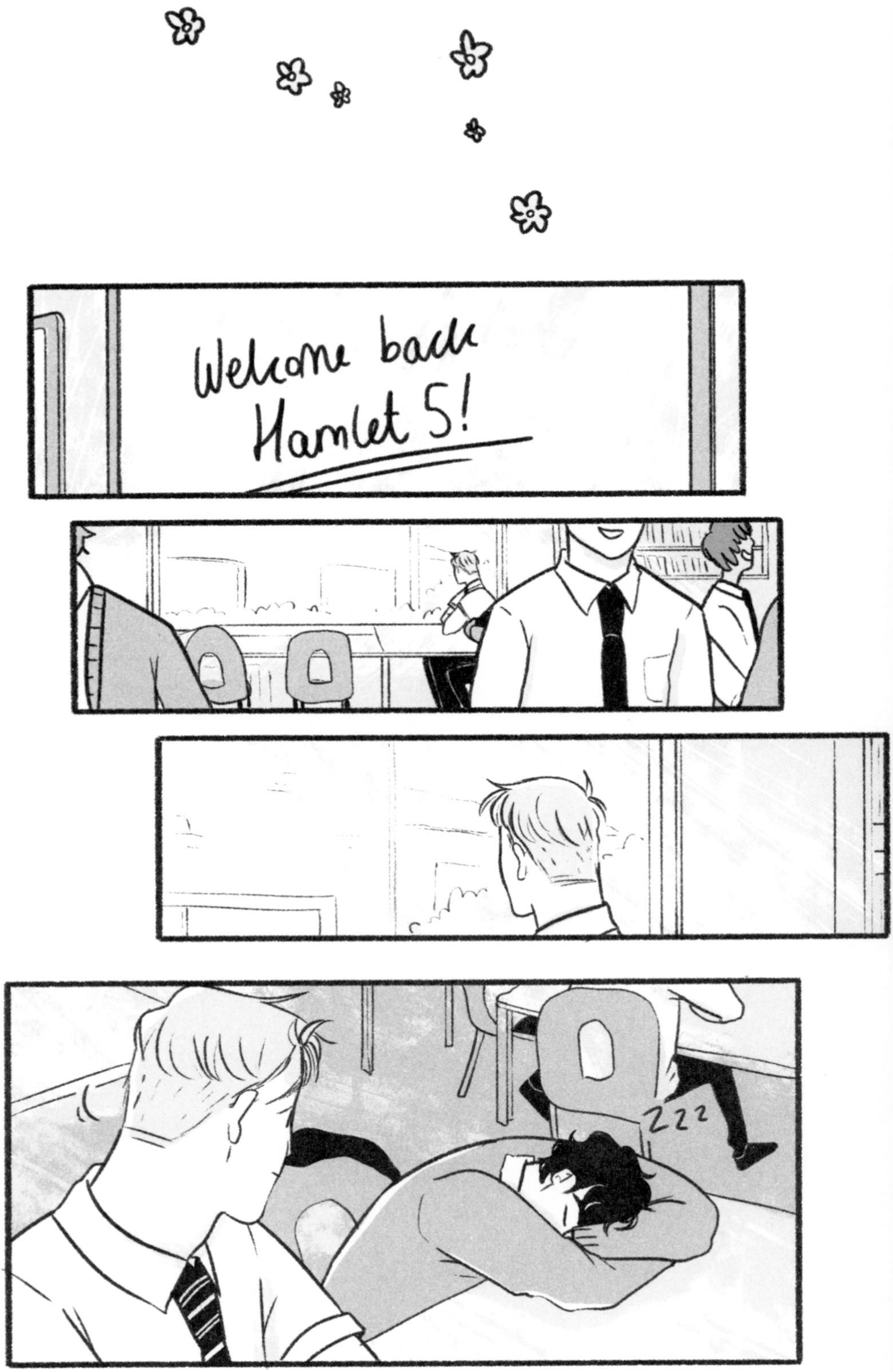
Welcome back Hamlet 5!
Zzz

Saturday

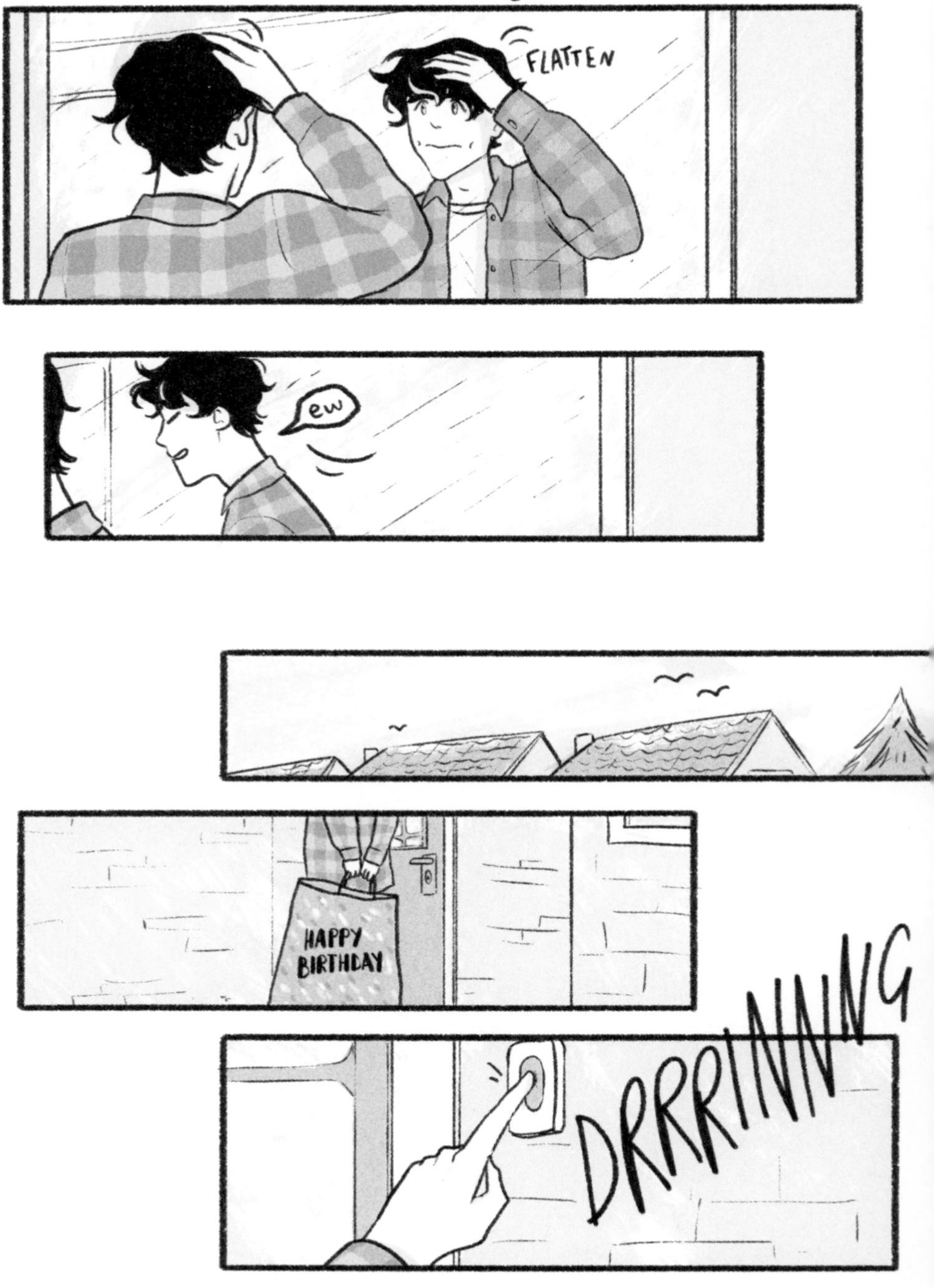
FLATTEN
ew
HAPPY BIRTHDAY
DRRRINNNG

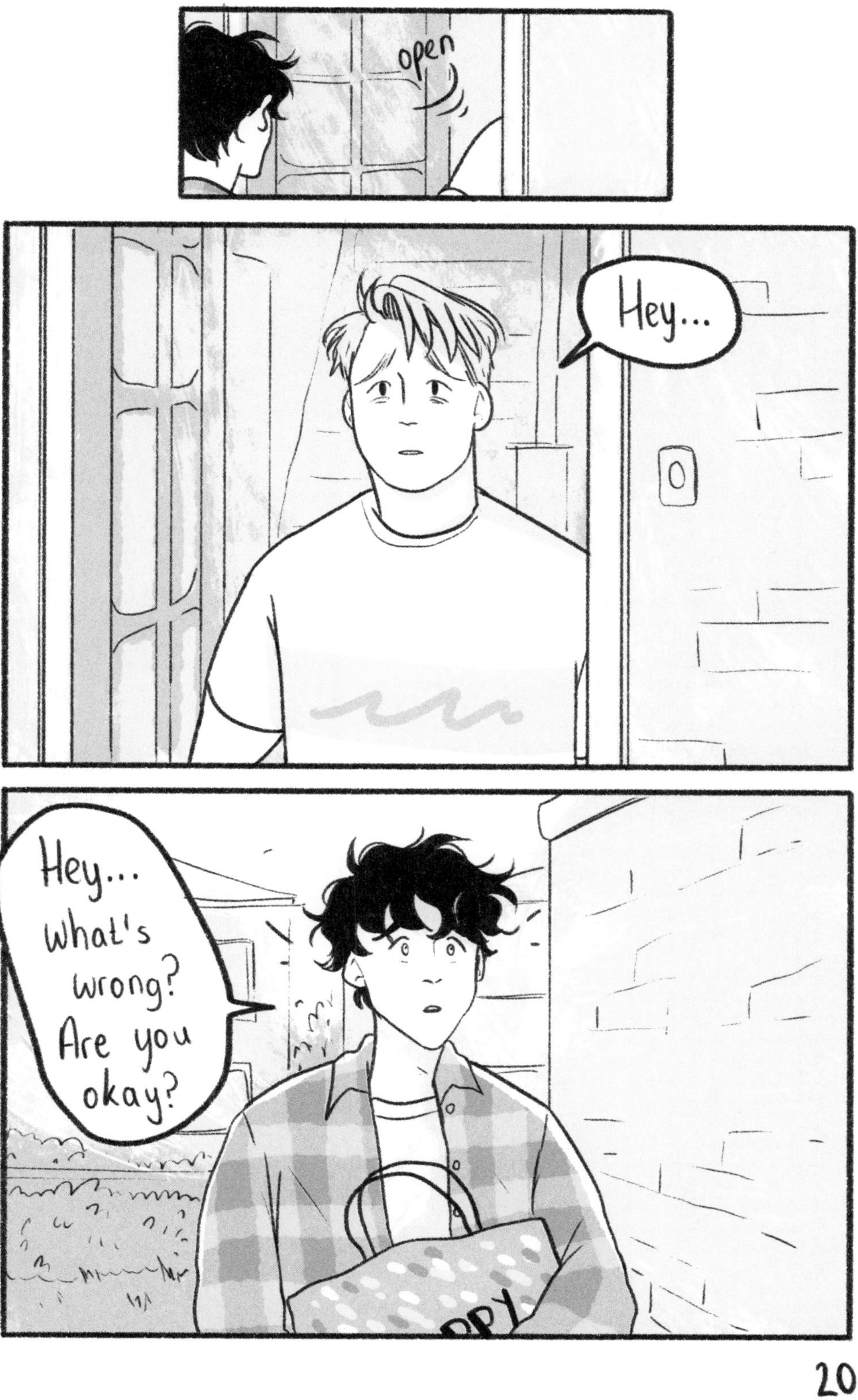
open
Hey...
Hey... what's wrong? Are you okay?

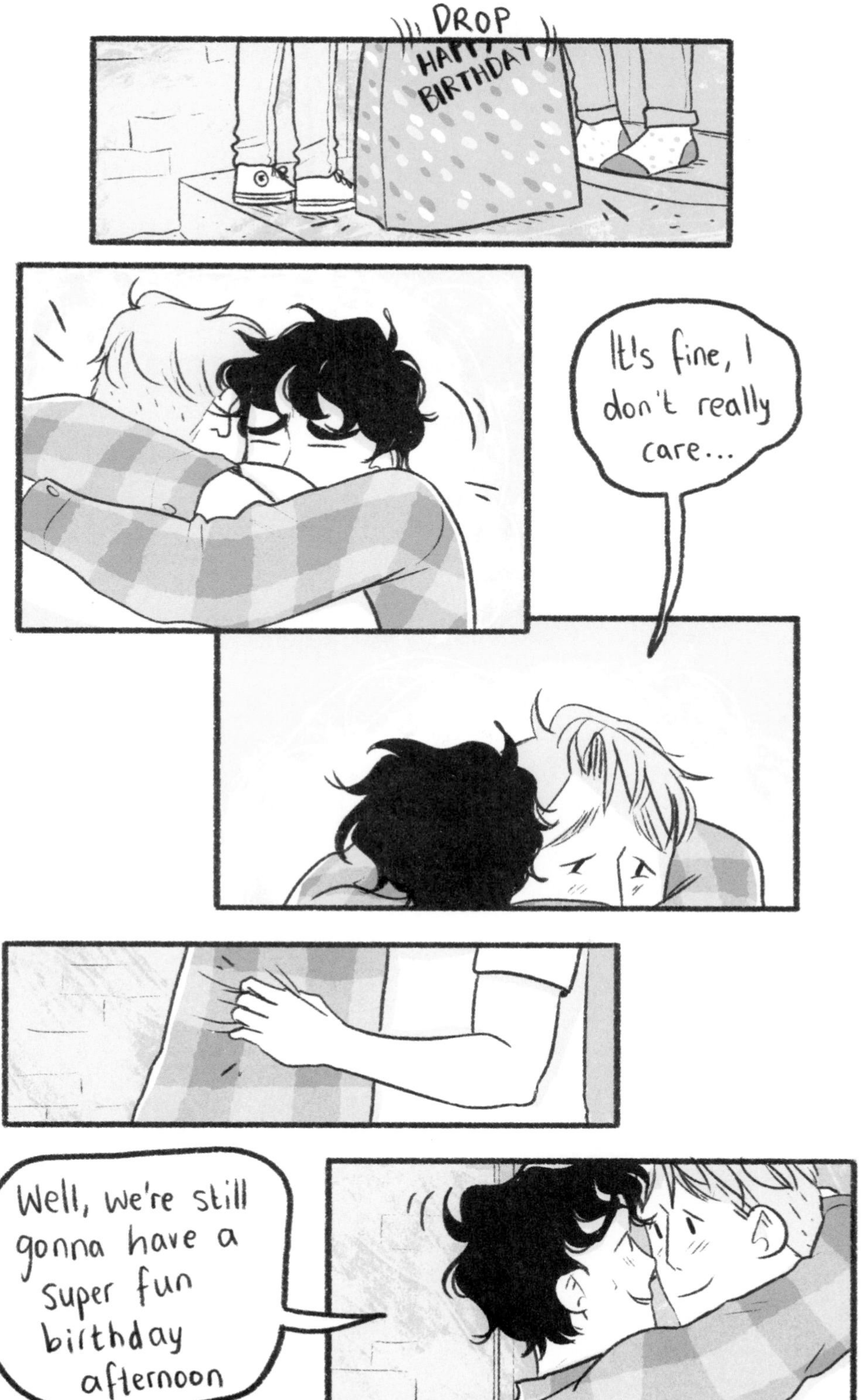
DROP
HAPPY BIRTHDAY
It's fine, I don't really care...
Well, we're still gonna have a super fun birthday afternoon

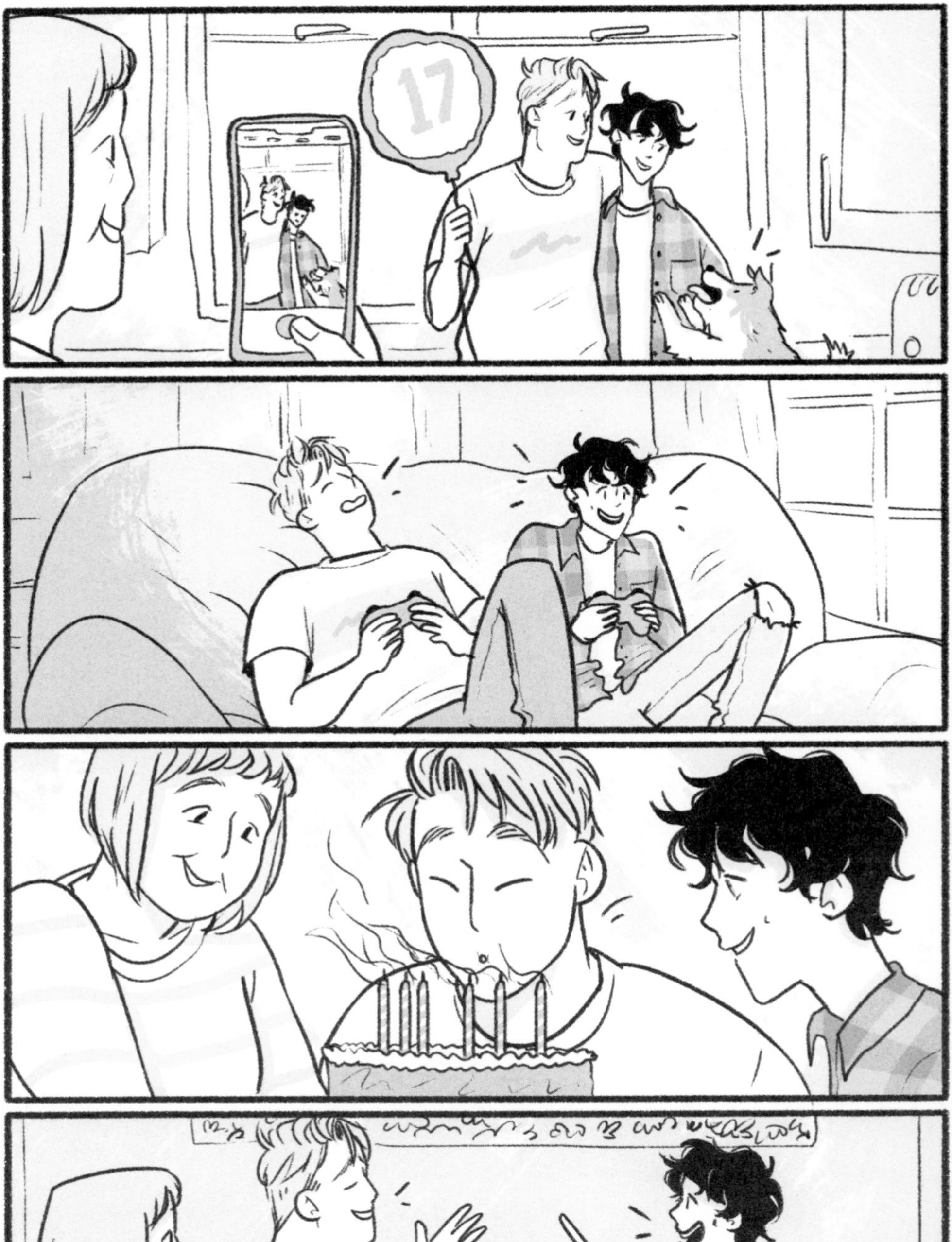
17

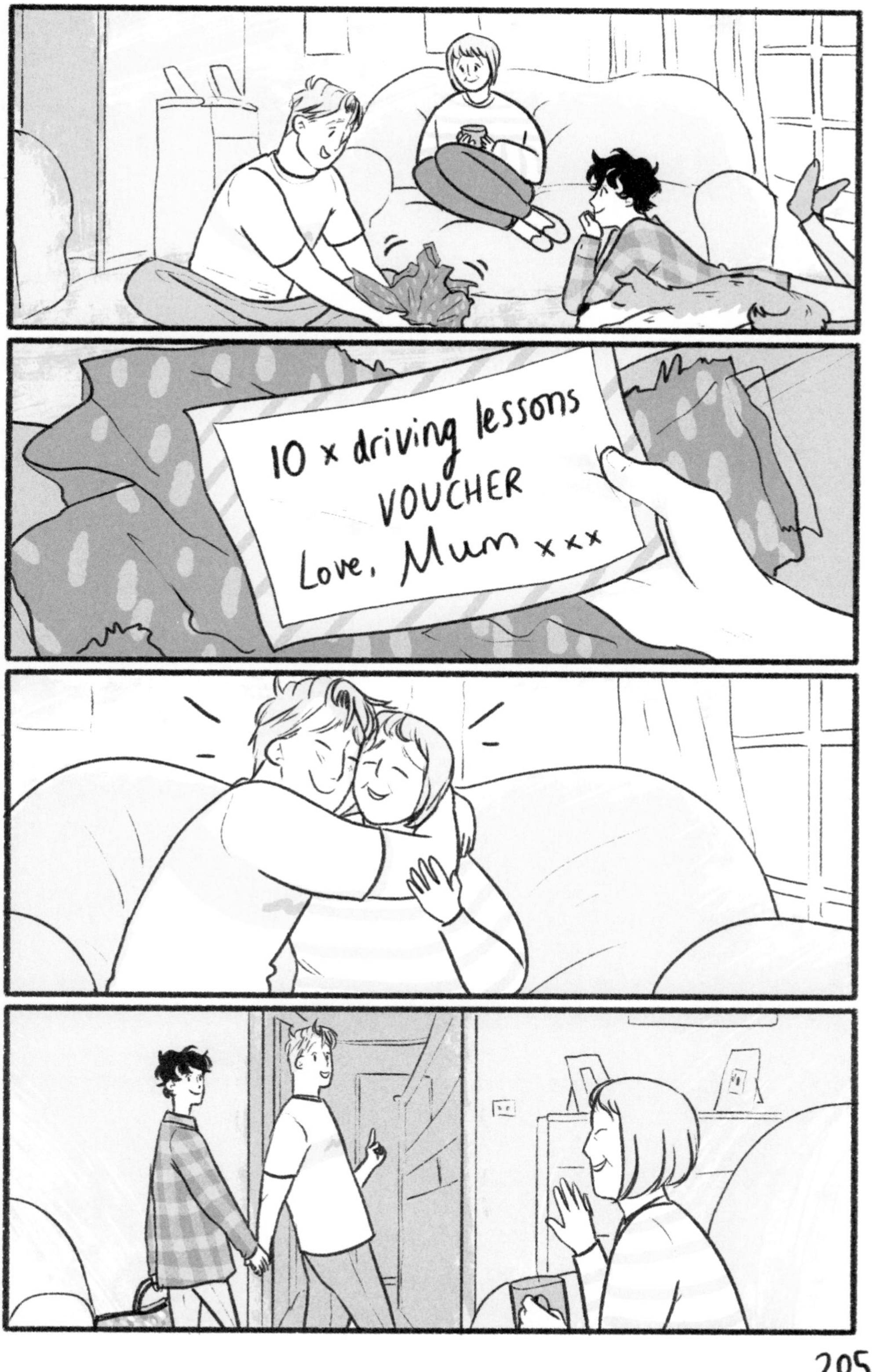
10 x driving lessons
VOUCHER
Love, Mum xxx

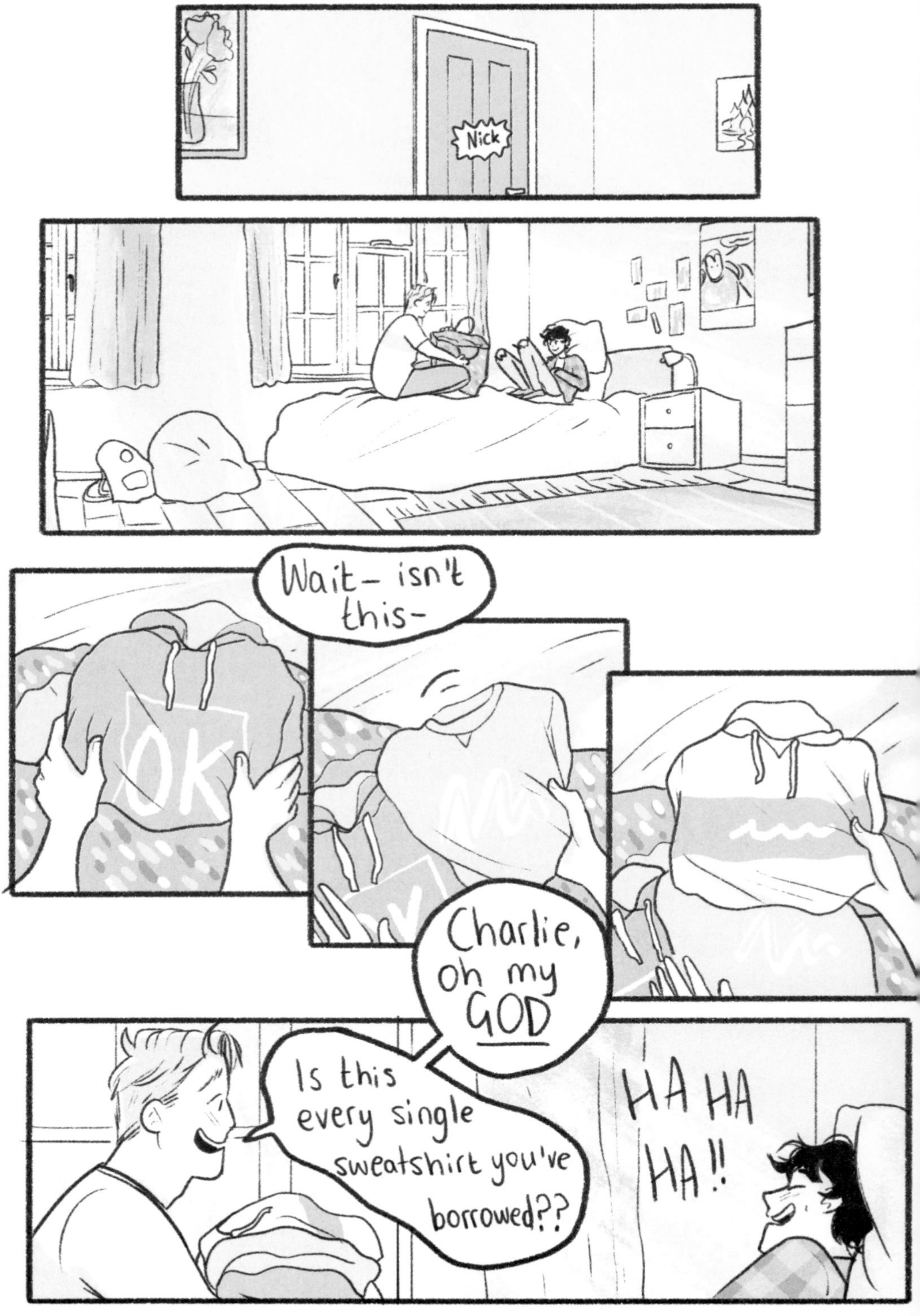
Nick
Wait- isn't this-
Charlie, oh my GOD
Is this every single sweatshirt you've borrowed??
HA HA HA!!

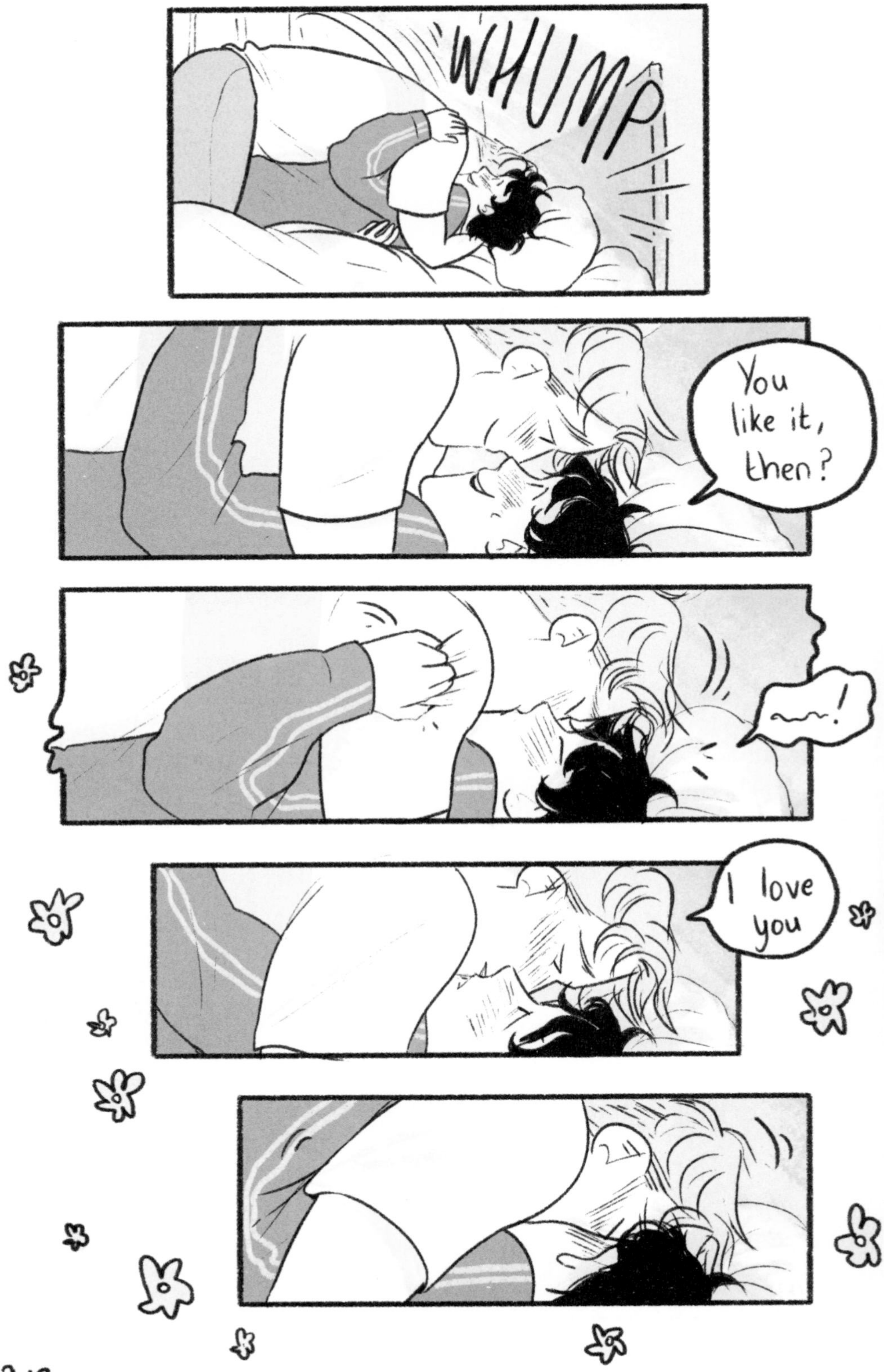
WHUMP
You like it, then?
~~!
I love you

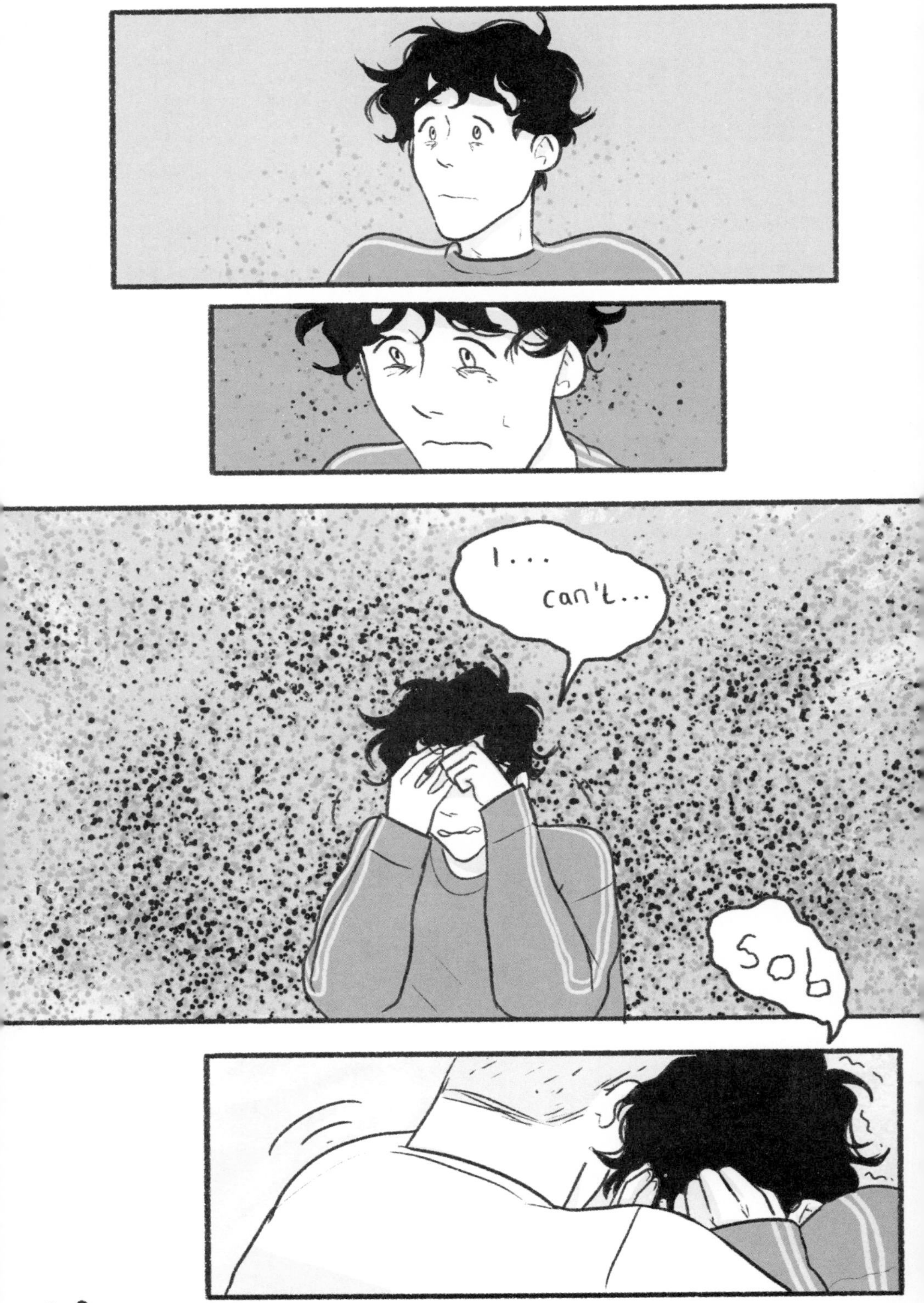
I...
can't...
sob

219

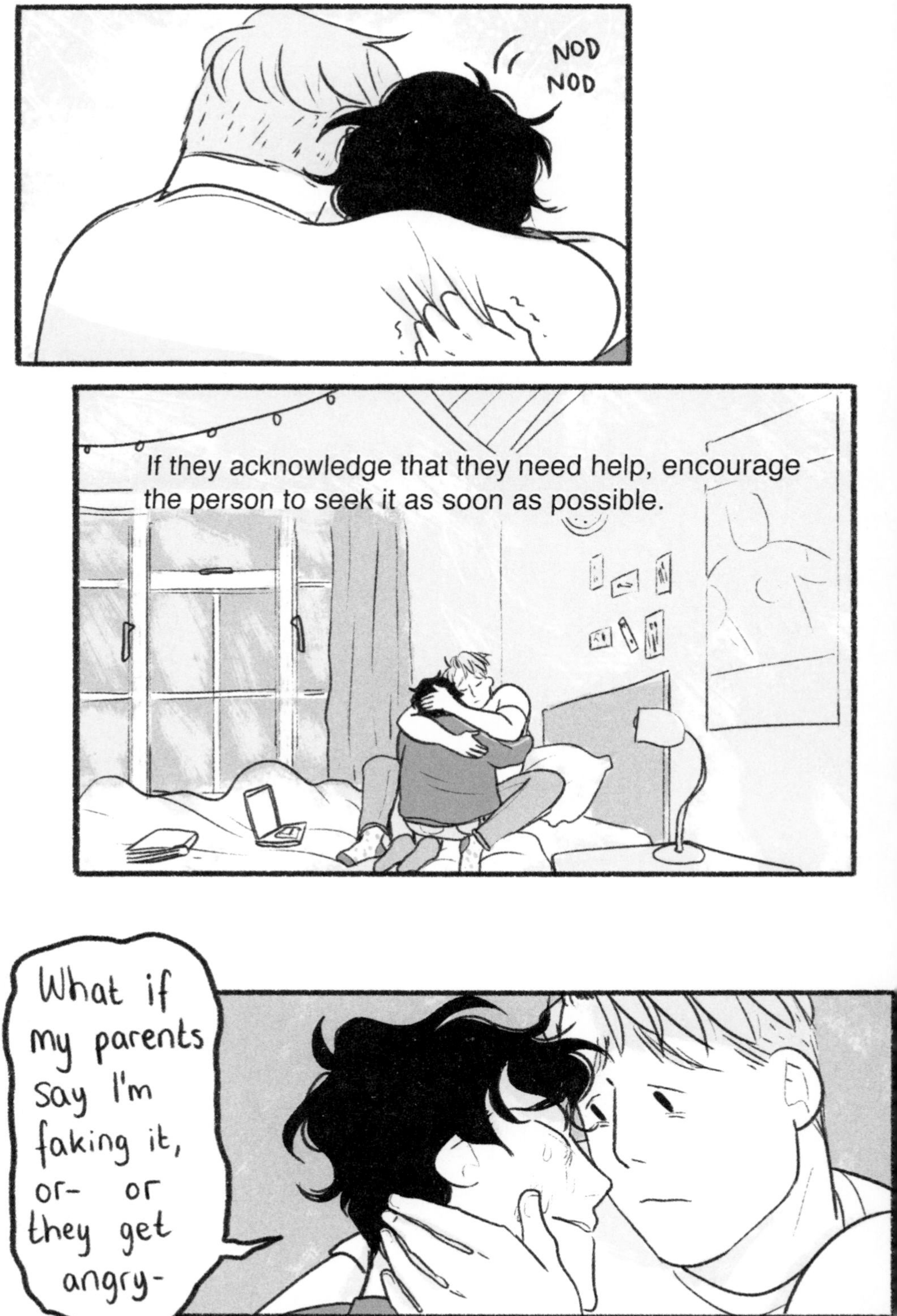
NOD NOD
If they acknowledge that they need help, encourage the person to seek it as soon as possible.
What if my parents say I'm faking it, or- or they get angry-

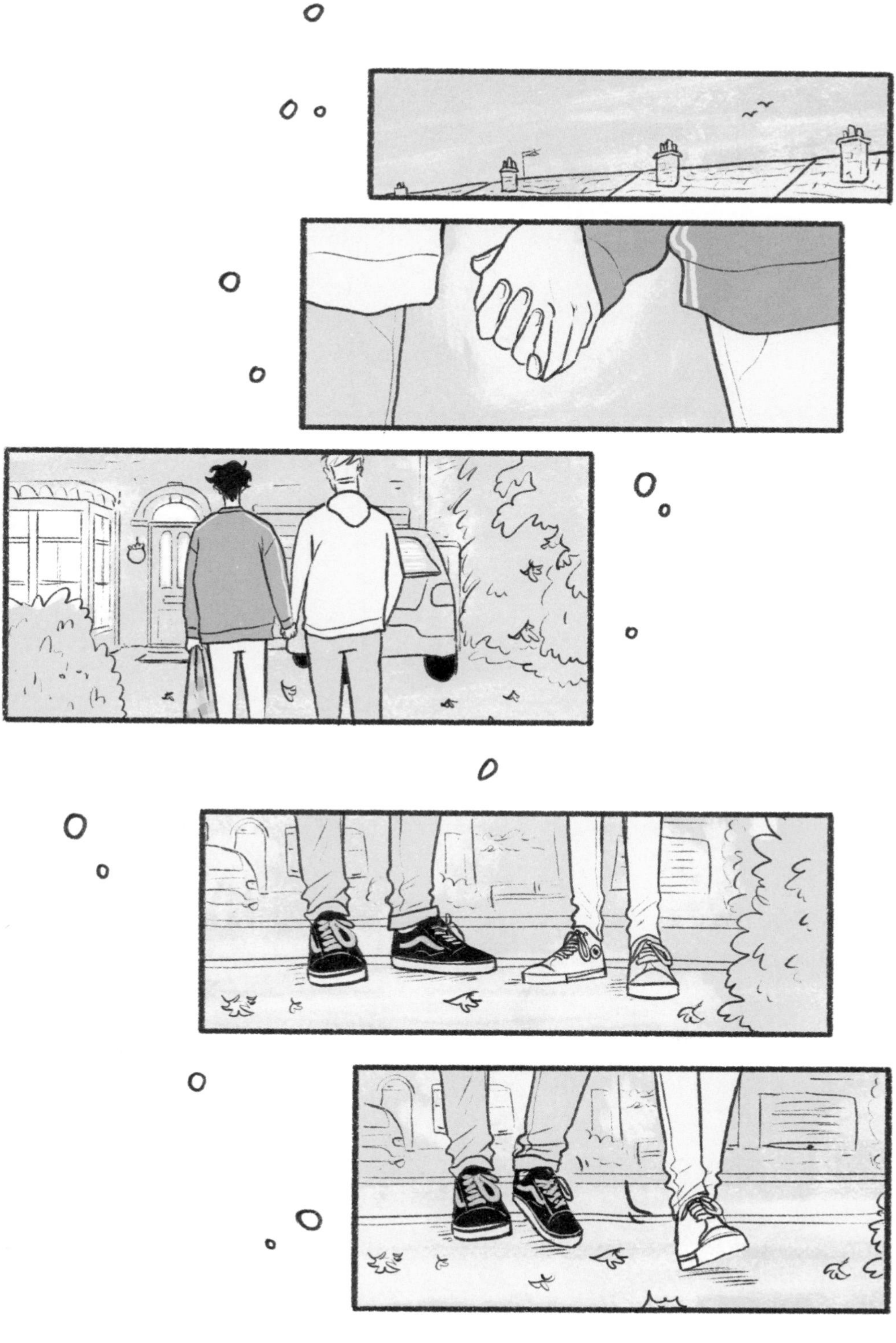

Mum?
Dad?
Charlie?
Oh, Nick... it's a bit late for you to be over, isn't it?
He's not staying long...

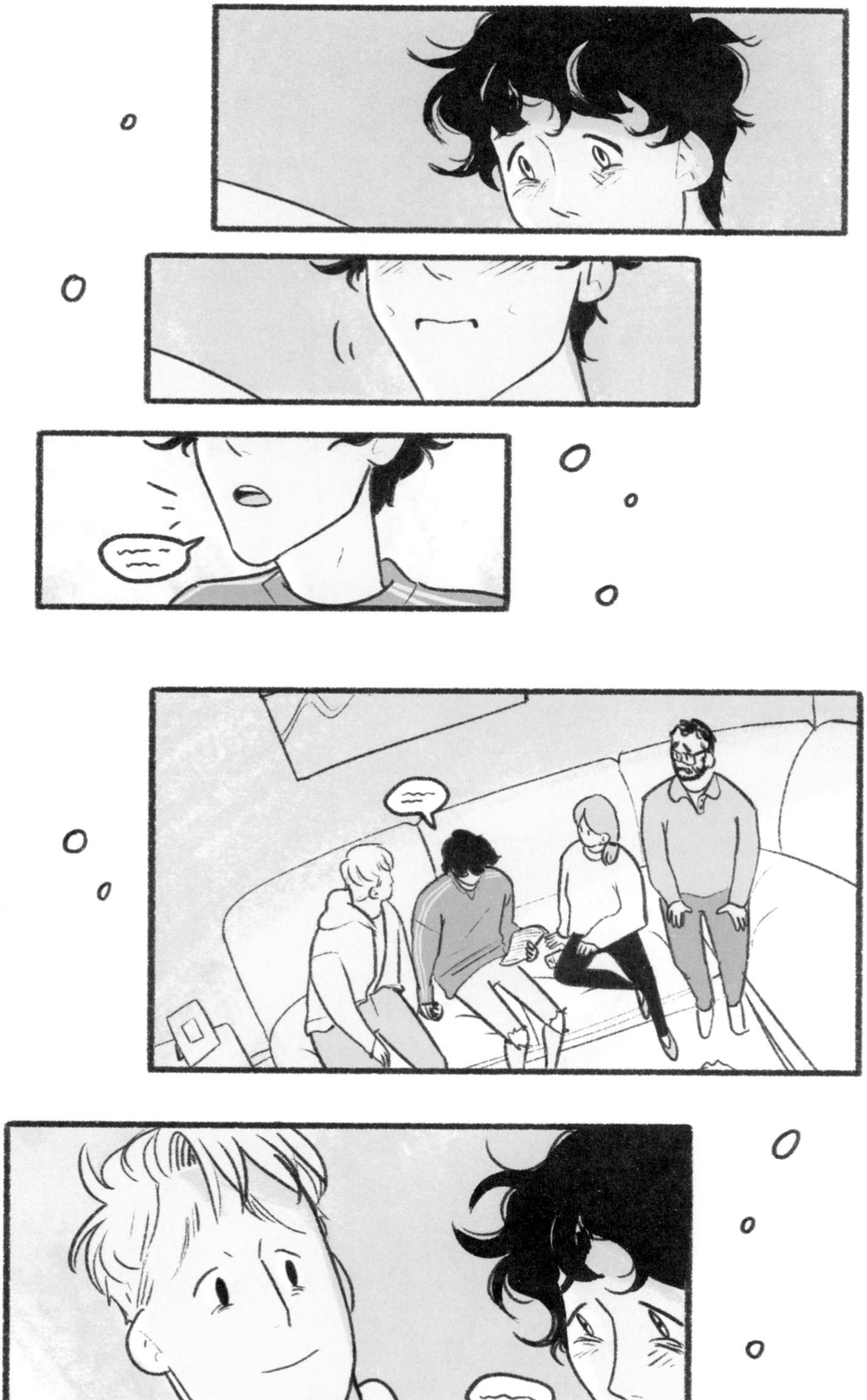

6. JOURNEY

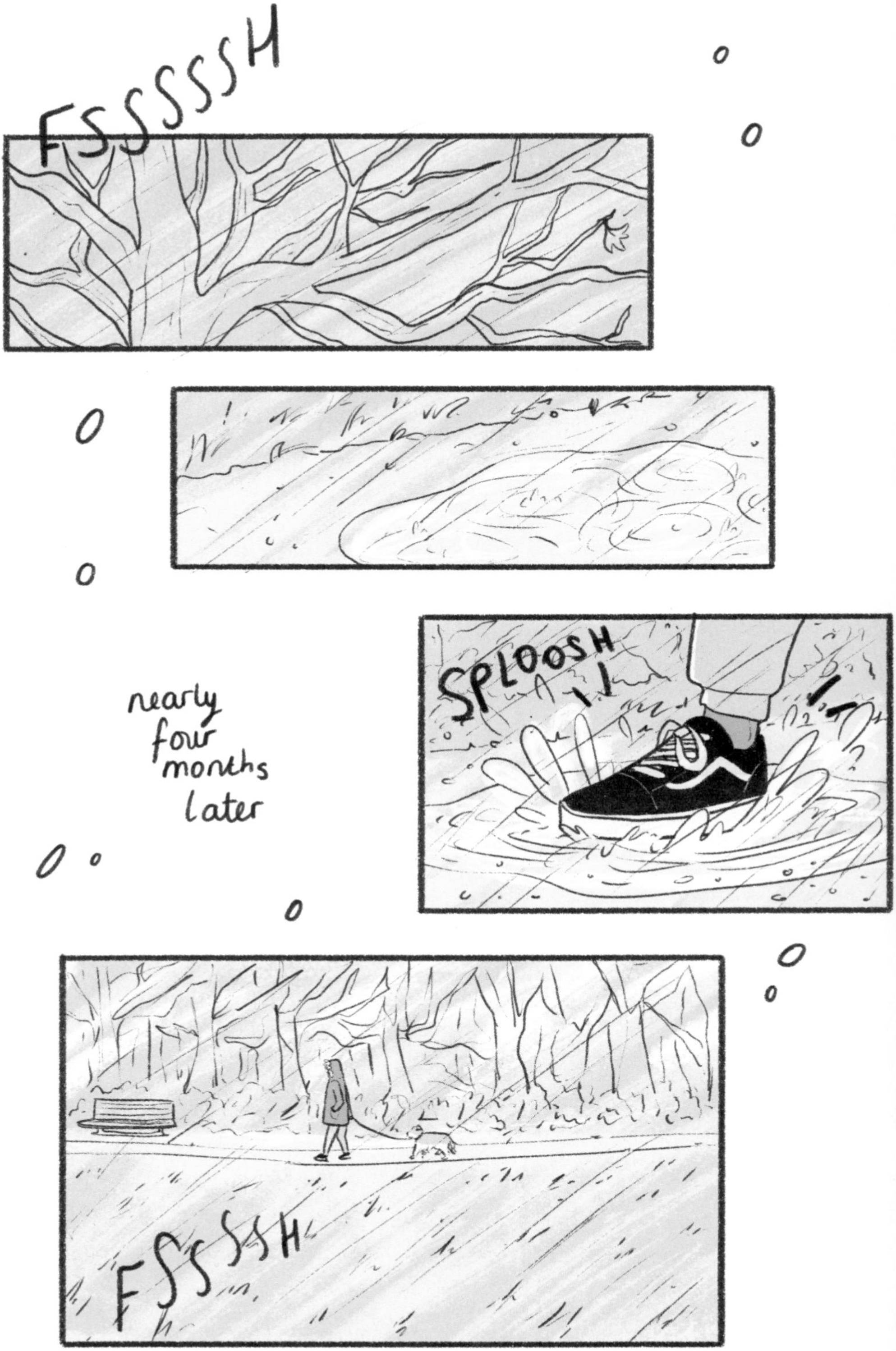

FSSSSSH

SPLOOSH

nearly
four
months
later

FSSSSH

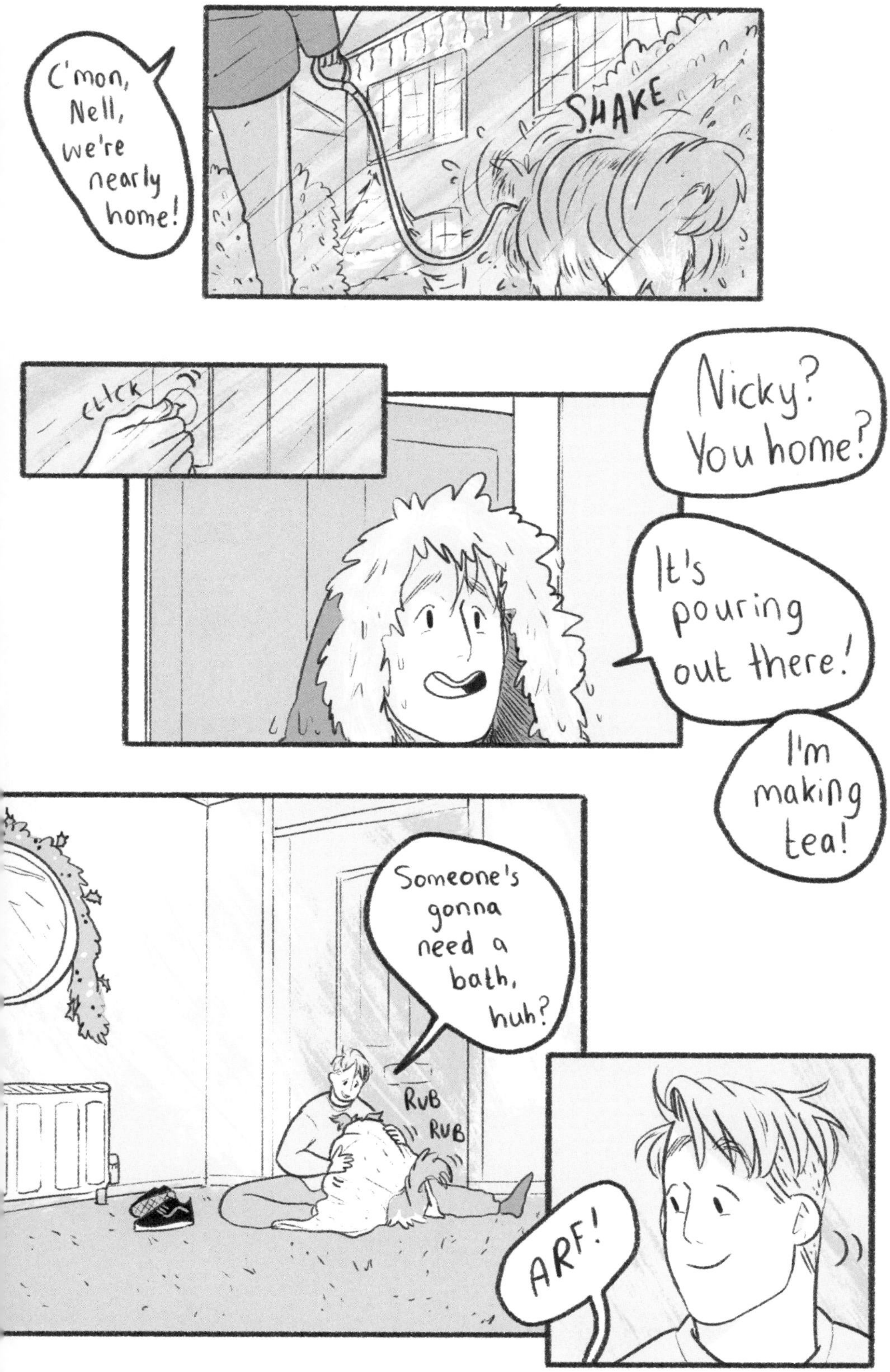
C'mon, Nell, we're nearly home!
SHAKE
CLICK
Nicky? You home?
It's pouring out there!
I'm making tea!
Someone's gonna need a bath, huh?
RUB RUB
ARF!

!
Sorry, Henry, you're still too little for walks!
When's Charlie getting here?
In a couple of hours. We're not leaving for the party till eight.
HAPPY NEW YE
Okay, well, make sure you wait for Gramps and Grandma to get here first, okay? And finish tidying your room!

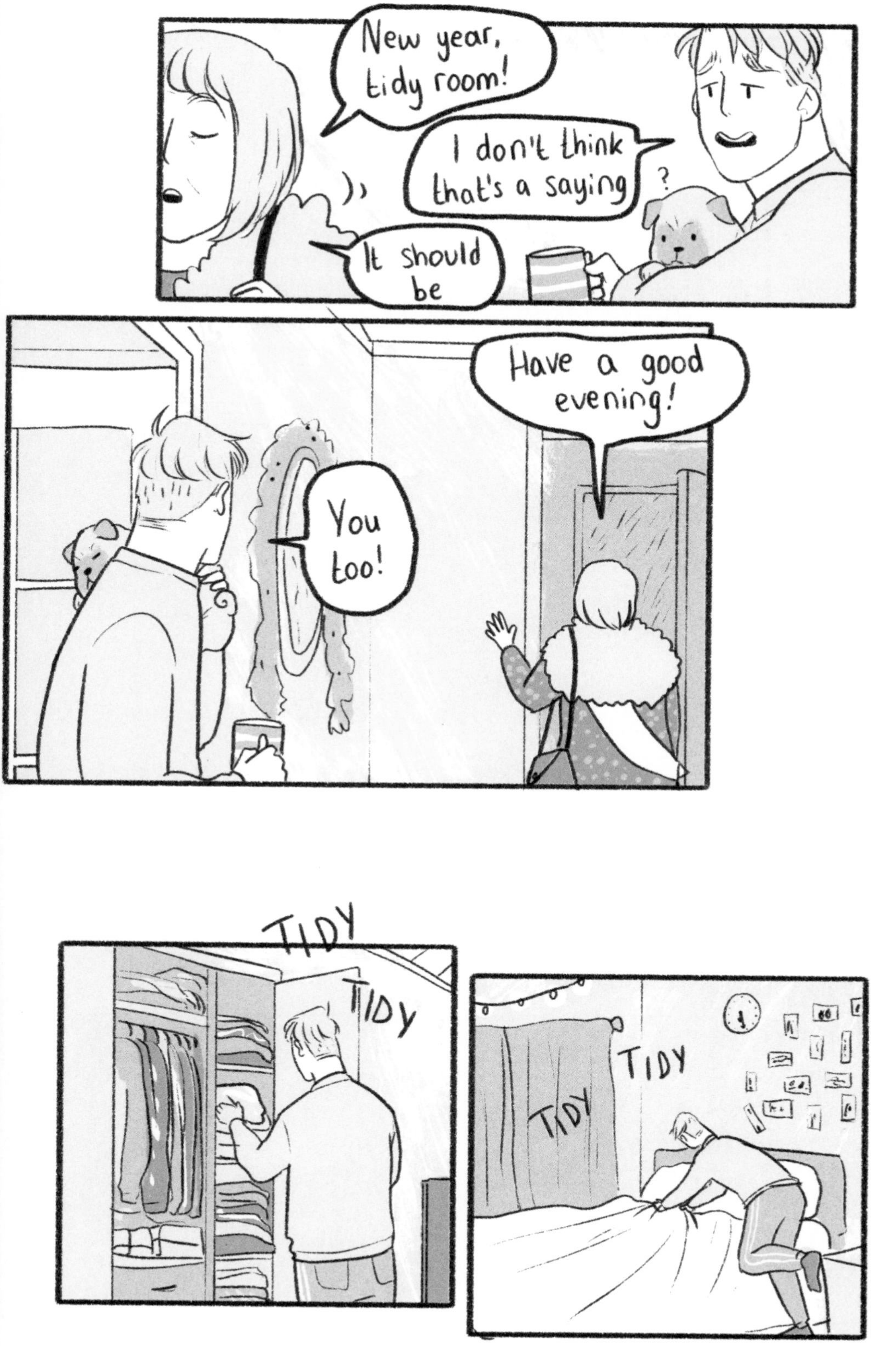
New year, tidy room!
I don't think that's a saying
?
It should be
Have a good evening!
You too!
TIDY
TIDY
TIDY
TIDY

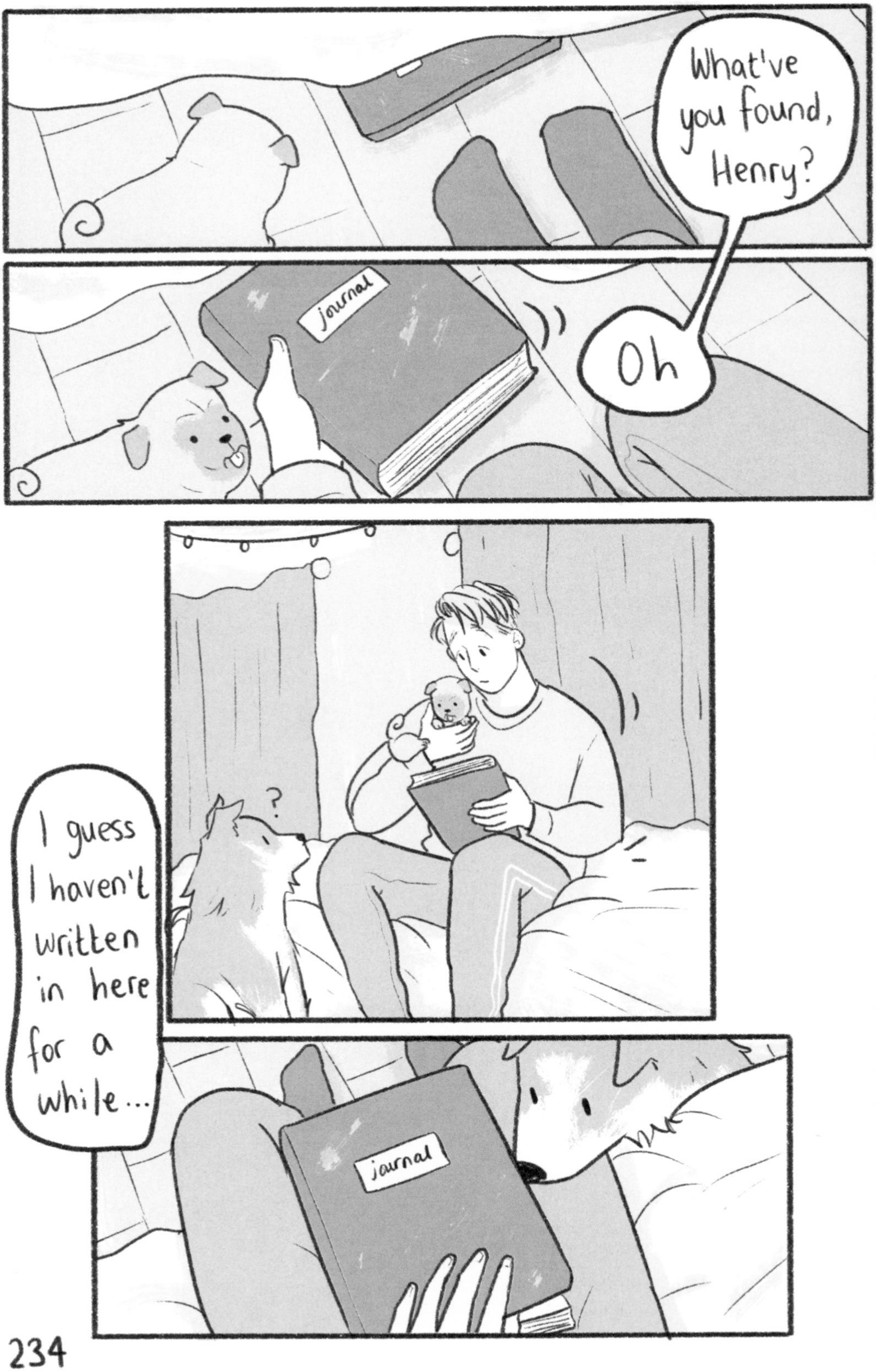
What've you found, Henry?
Oh
journal
?
I guess I haven't written in here for a while...
journal

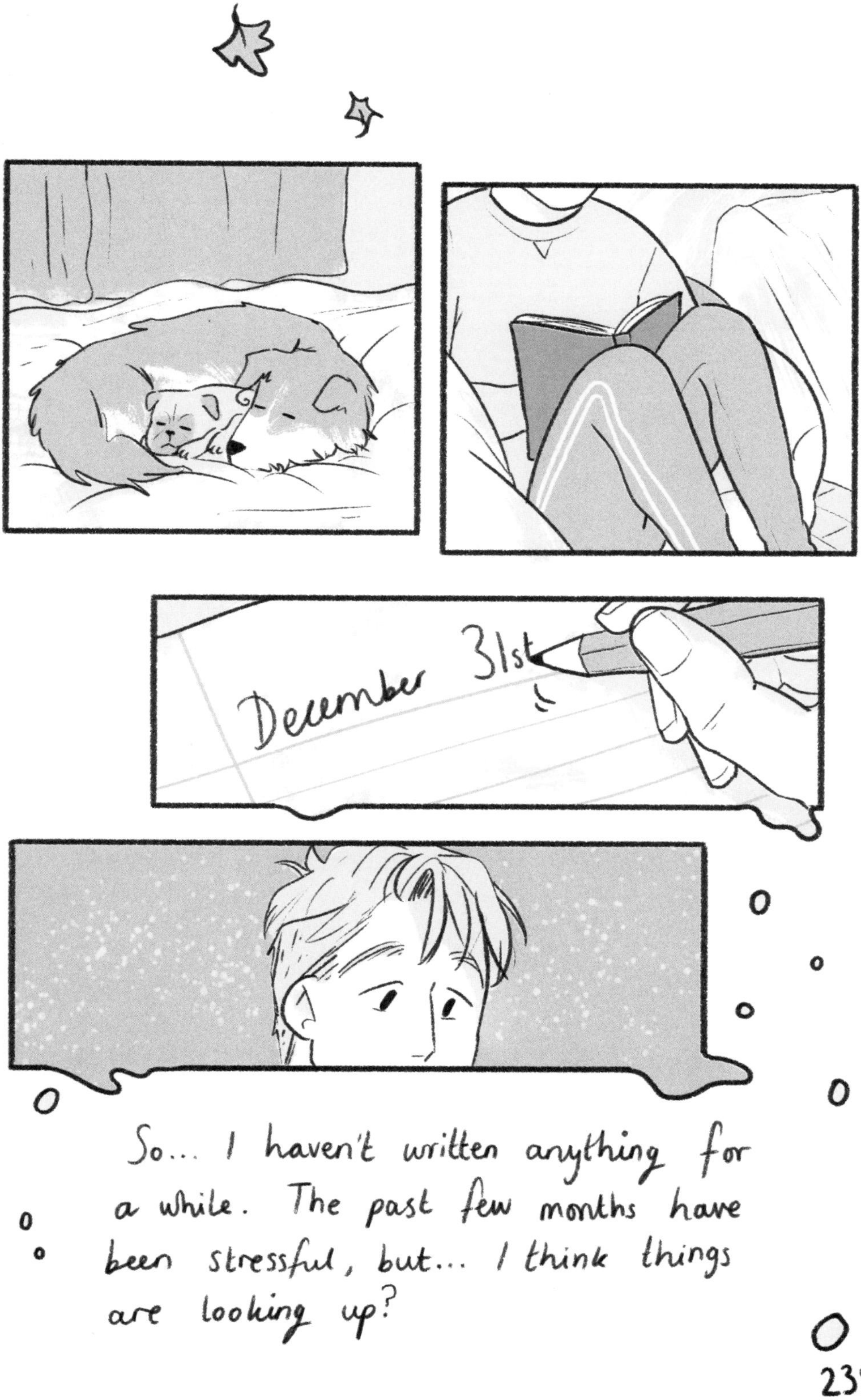
December 31st
So... I haven't written anything for a while. The past few months have been stressful, but... I think things are looking up?

Although- you know that saying that things sometimes get worse before they get better?
Yeah. I think I understand that now.
So back in September, Charlie got an appointment.
SUCCESS!!
9:15a.m.? Great, thank you.
He said he hates going to the doctor for anything. I mean, I can relate.

But this was extra scary.

For obvious reasons.

The doctor was helpful, and referred
Charlie to an eating disorder service, but
the waiting list was <u>so long</u>.

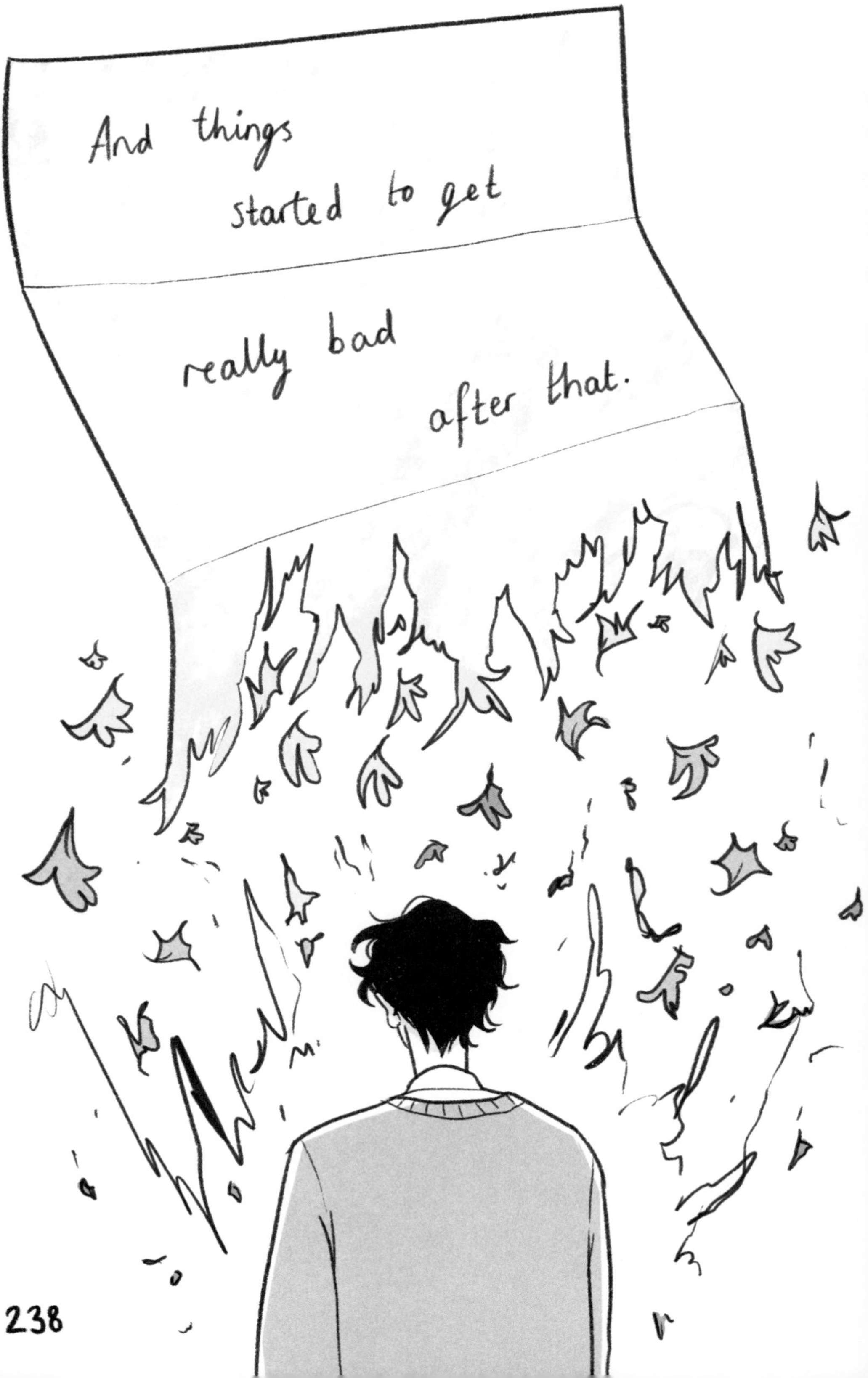
And things started to get really bad after that.

His eating disorder got worse. I could tell, but he wouldn't talk to me about it.

I'm fine

He skipped school a lot, which made his mum mad at him like _all_ the time.

Charlie 🐱

Today

hey, you off school today too?? ♡♡

Read 11:32

His thoughts and behavior about food became... obsessive. It didn't make logical sense anymore. I guess it never did, really. But he'd always lie about it.

I'll just eat at home!

And you know he told me he used to self-harm?
Well, that kind of started again.
Sorry
It's not your fault
I think mostly because of the stress of everything else.
I didn't know what to do except just be there for him.

Charlie's mental health was assessed while he was there, and they told him that it'd be best if he spent some time as an inpatient.

But it was his choice.

Mental Health Treatment In Hospital

Most treatment for mental illnesses is done outside hospital. However, if you are experiencing a mental health crisis, staying in hospital may be the best way to keep you safe and provide you with the treatment you need.

While each hospital is different, this leaflet will give you an overview of what to expect:

- Why might I need to go to hospital?
- How do I access hospital treatment?
- How do I prepare for a hospital stay?
- Can I be forced to go to hospital?
- What happens inside a psychiatric hospital?
- What types of wards are there?
- What happens when I leave?

More information: mind.org.uk

Charlie said yes.

It happened really fast.
I was scared.
He was scared.
Pfft I swear you're getting more emotional than me
Ssh
I mean, I only knew about psychiatric hospitals from movies, and the nearest available space at a ward was a two-hour drive away.

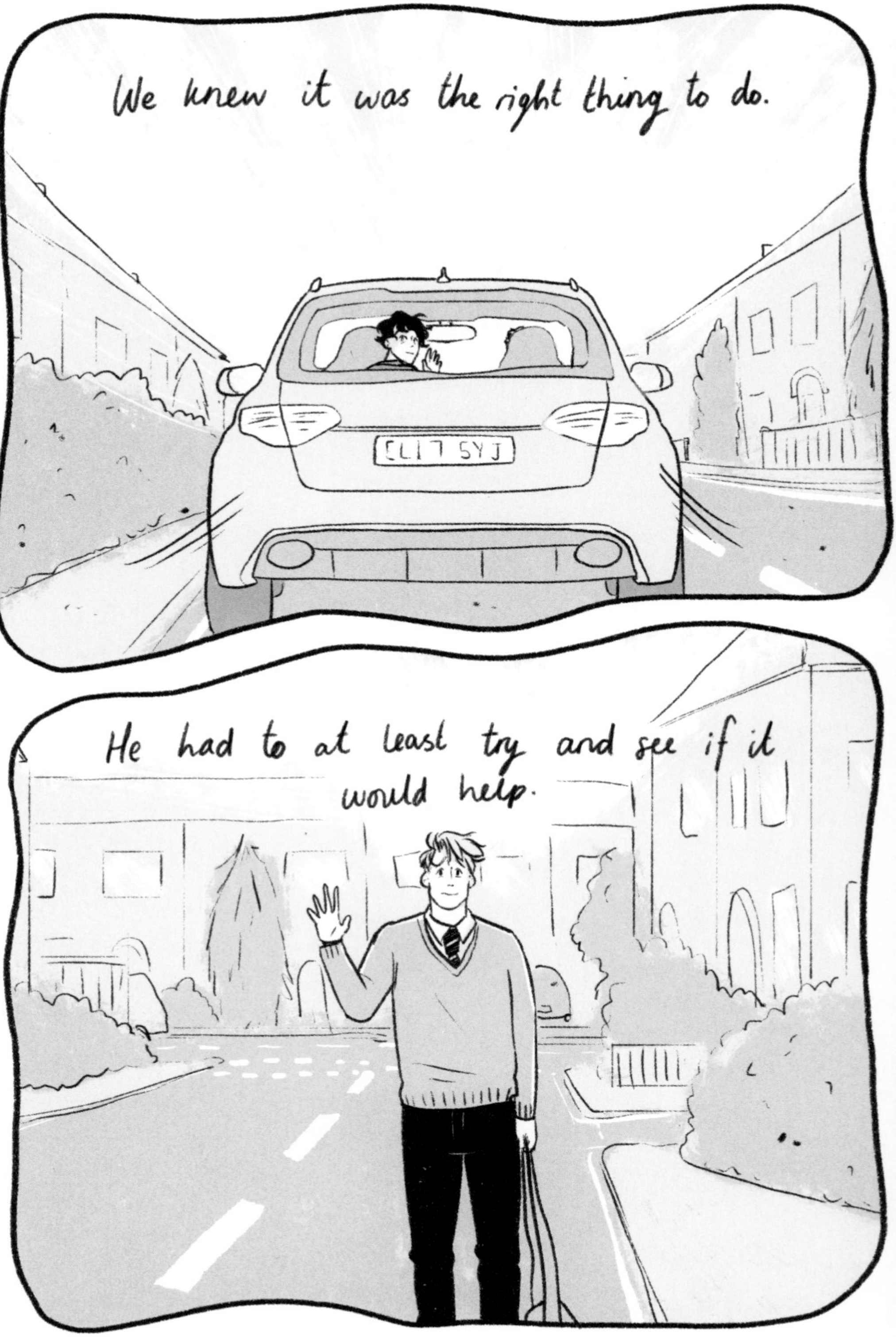
We knew it was the right thing to do.
He had to at least try and see if it would help.

It was weird
being at school without Charlie.
I couldn't stop worrying about him.

We spoke on the phone when we could, and obviously I visited a lot too, but-
I kept wishing I knew how he was feeling all the time.
What is it like in a psychiatric hospital?
Your experience can depend on the hospital you stay at, what kind of treatment you receive, and your feelings about being in hospital.
However, some common aspects of psychiatric hospitals include:
- access to talking therapies and medication
- trained staff on-site to support you
- a daily routine/structure
There are also some potential disadvantages:
- you will be away from family and friends, and visits might only be permitted at set times
- you can't always decide how you spend your time
- staff may need to search you if they
Was he homesick?
Was the treatment helping?
Was it making things worse?
Was he lonely?
Was he bored?
Had he made some friends?

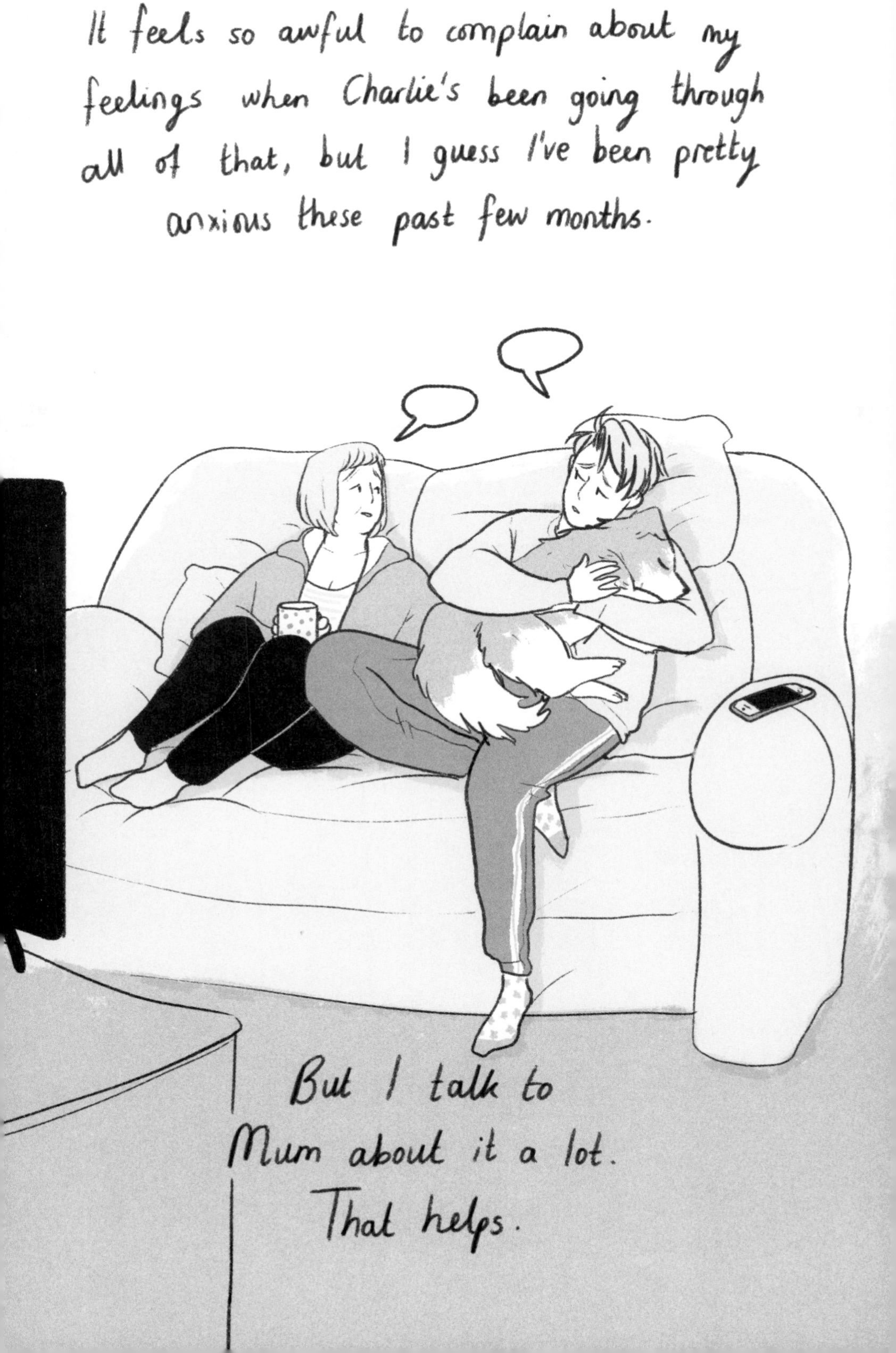
It feels so awful to complain about my feelings when Charlie's been going through all of that, but I guess I've been pretty anxious these past few months.
But I talk to Mum about it a lot. That helps.

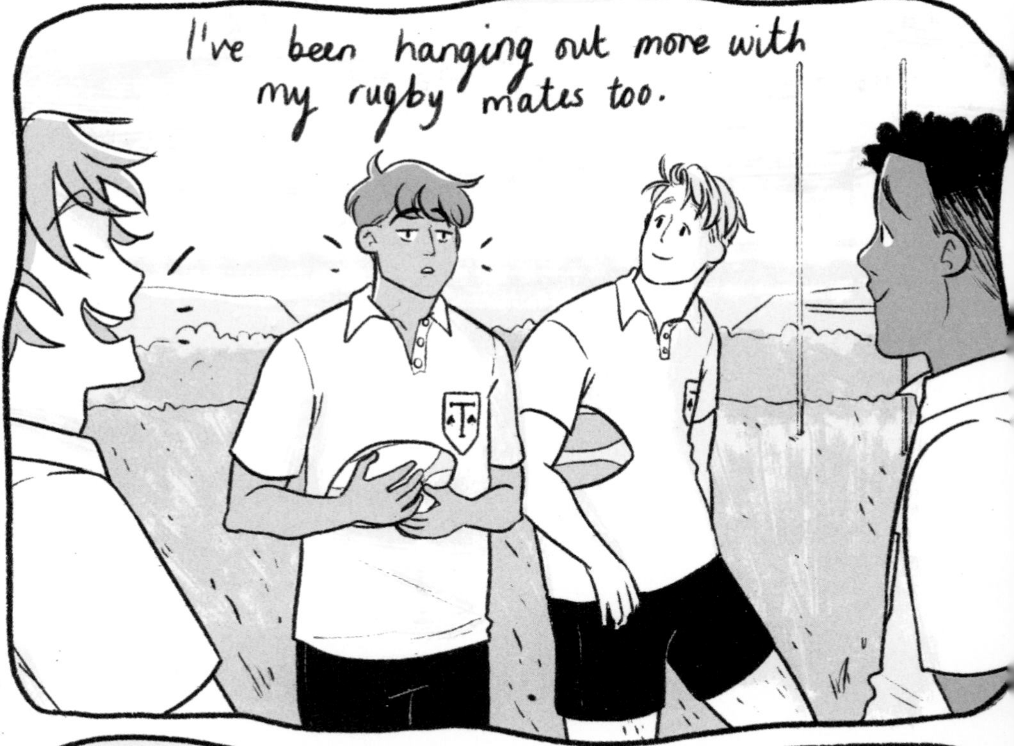
I've been hanging out more with my rugby mates too.

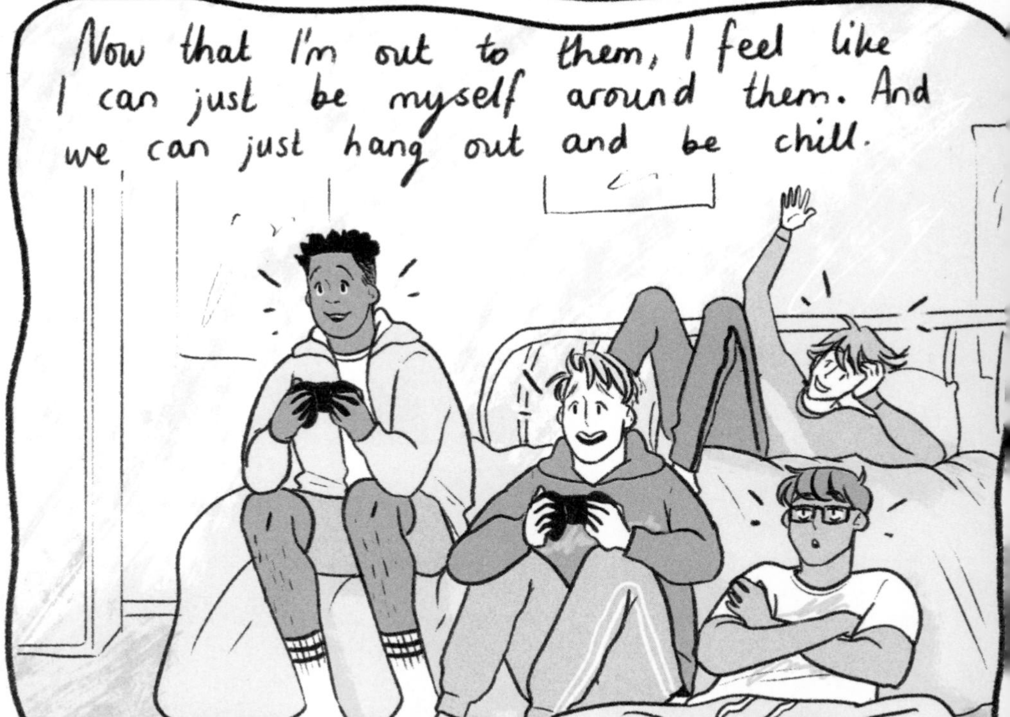
Now that I'm out to them, I feel like I can just be myself around them. And we can just hang out and be chill.

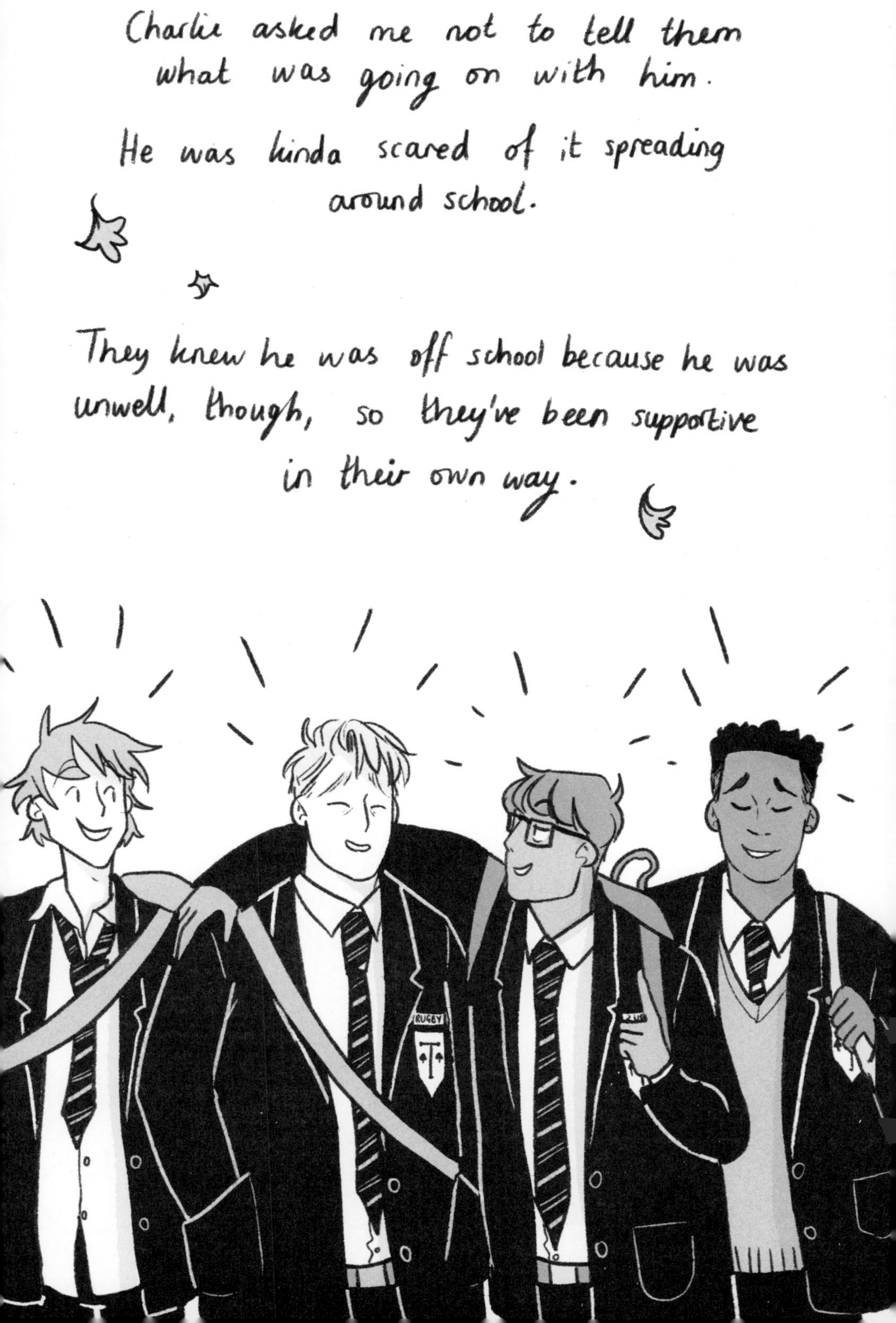
Charlie asked me not to tell them what was going on with him.
He was kinda scared of it spreading around school.
They knew he was off school because he was unwell, though, so they've been supportive in their own way.
RUGBY

Charlie said I could keep the Paris Squad updated.

Elle Argent
darcy did you get the card for charlie?

Darcy Olsson
YEP i got a giant one, it's the length of my arm

Tara Jones
omg

Tao Xu
Nick does Charlie have access to a DVD player???
I was thinking we could send him some fun films to watch

Nick Nelson
yeah he does!!! Good idea, he literally said they don't have Netflix or anything and they've only got movies from like 2005 haha

Tara Jones
I got the gift basket! And some stickers and stuff to make it pretty

Aled Last
i got him some art stuff!

Sahar Zahid
I got him a couple of books!! He said he likes to read so I hope that's okay

Nick Nelson
Do you all wanna come back to mine after school tomorrow?? You can sign the card and we can decorate the gift basket and stuff! also you can come on a walk with Nellie and me if you want!!

Darcy Olsson
I WOULD LIKE TO MEET NELLIE

Elle Argent
i also would like to meet nellie!!!!

Tao Xu
I think we all would like to meet Nellie tbh

He didn't want them all visiting — I think it would have been too overwhelming.
But they still found ways to help.

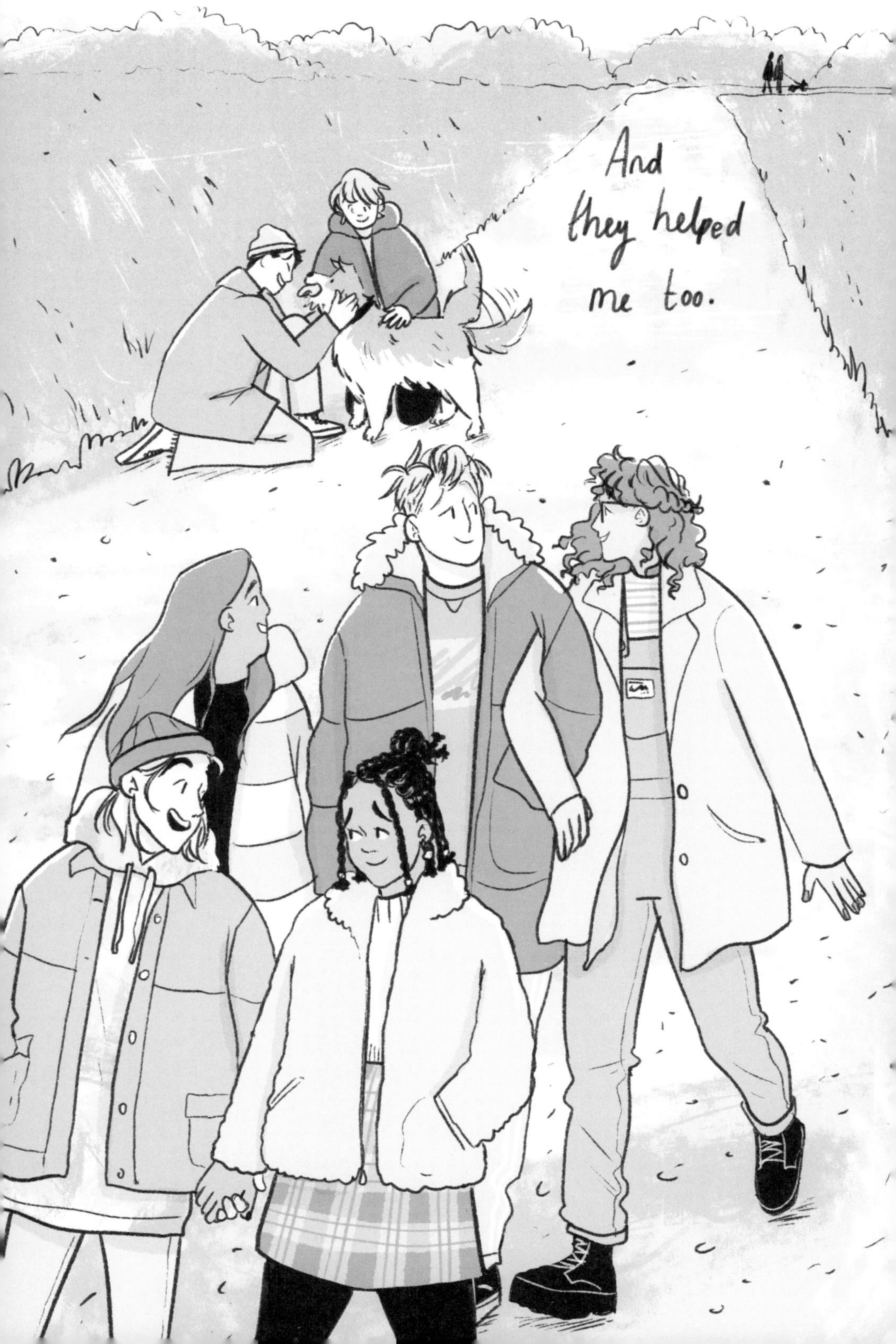
And they helped me too.

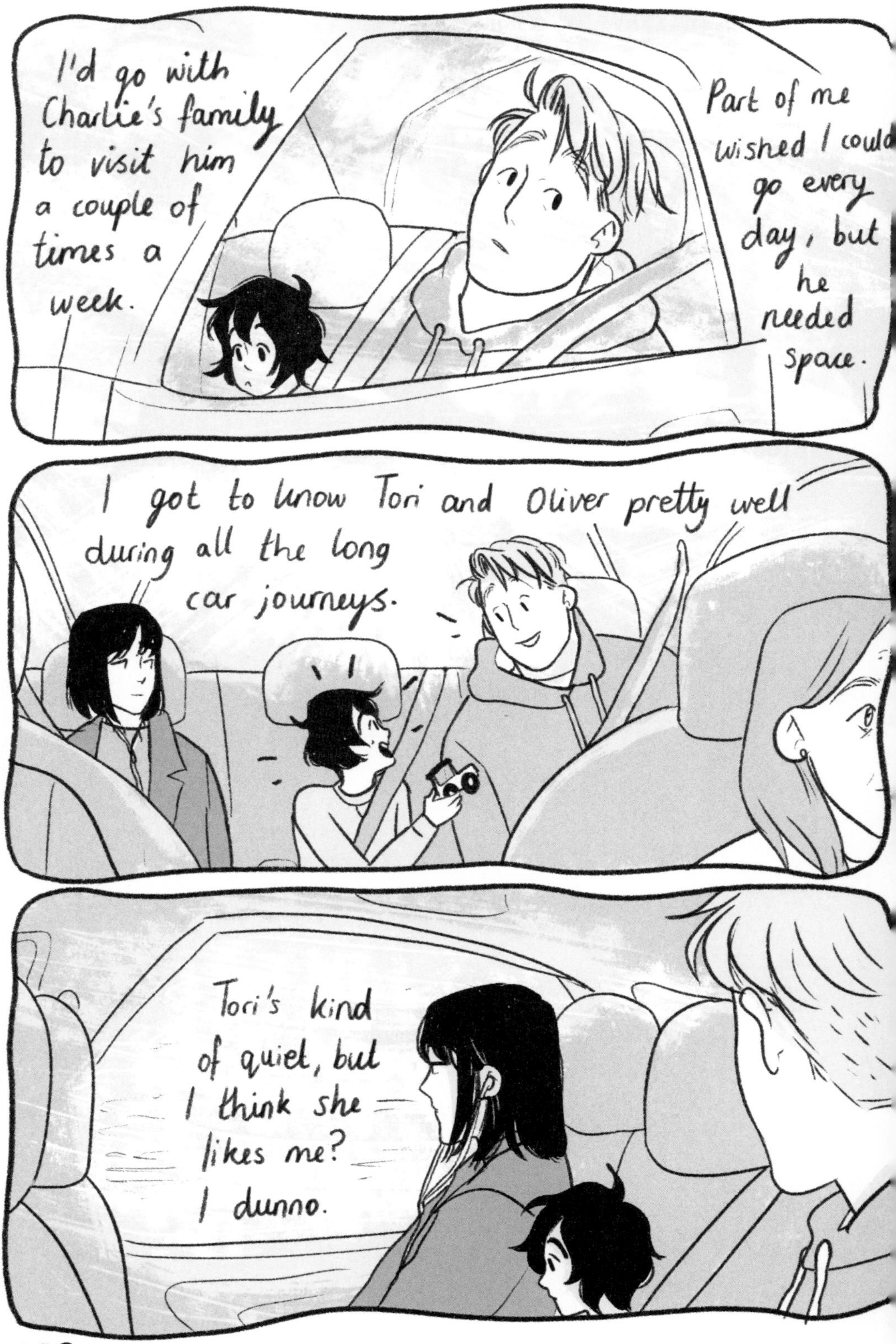
I'd go with Charlie's family to visit him a couple of times a week.
Part of me wished I could go every day, but he needed space.
I got to know Tori and Oliver pretty well during all the long car journeys.
Tori's kind of quiet, but I think she likes me? I dunno.

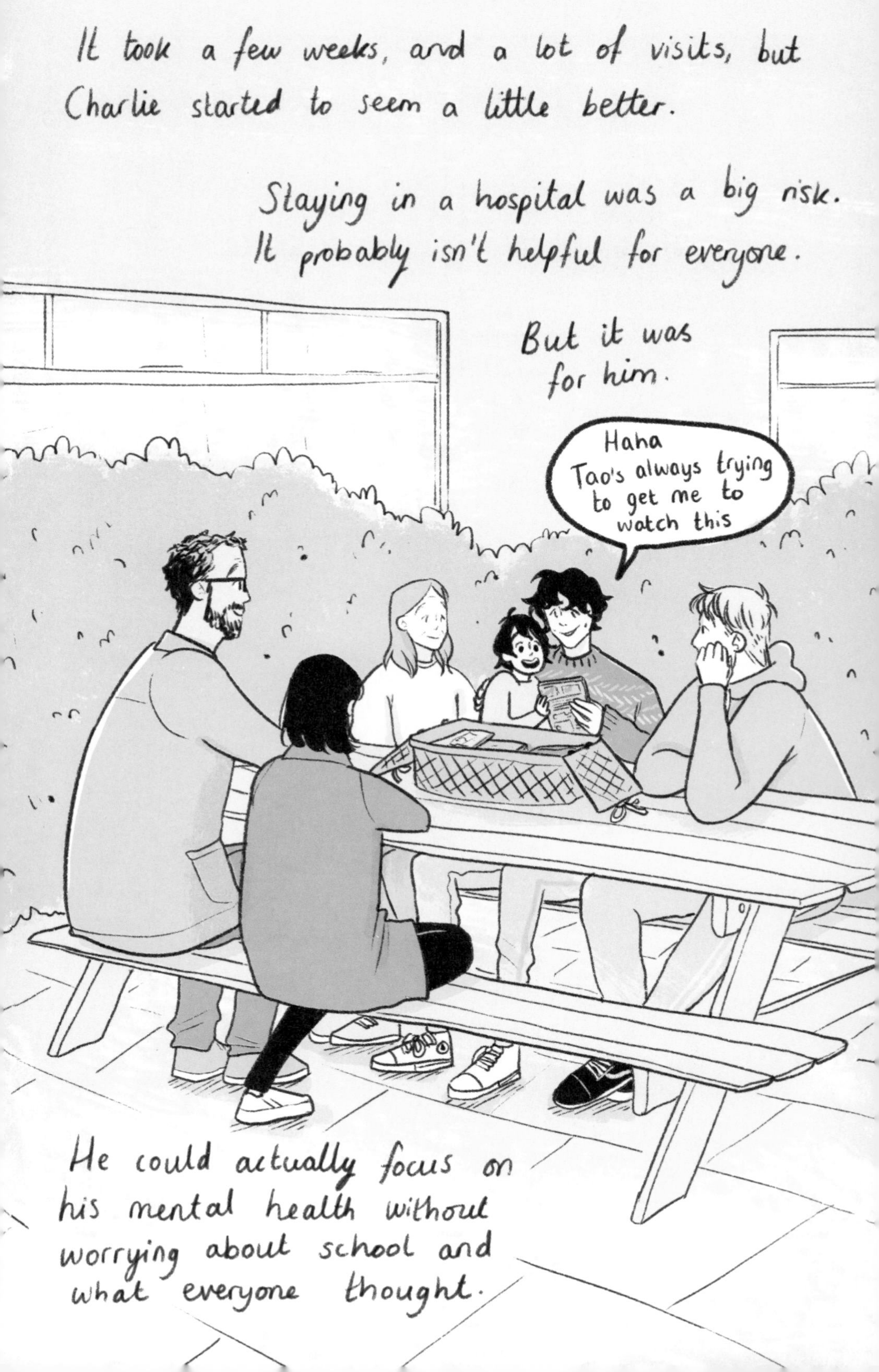
It took a few weeks, and a lot of visits, but Charlie started to seem a little better.
Staying in a hospital was a big risk. It probably isn't helpful for everyone.
But it was for him.
Haha Tao's always trying to get me to watch this
He could actually focus on his mental health without worrying about school and what everyone thought.

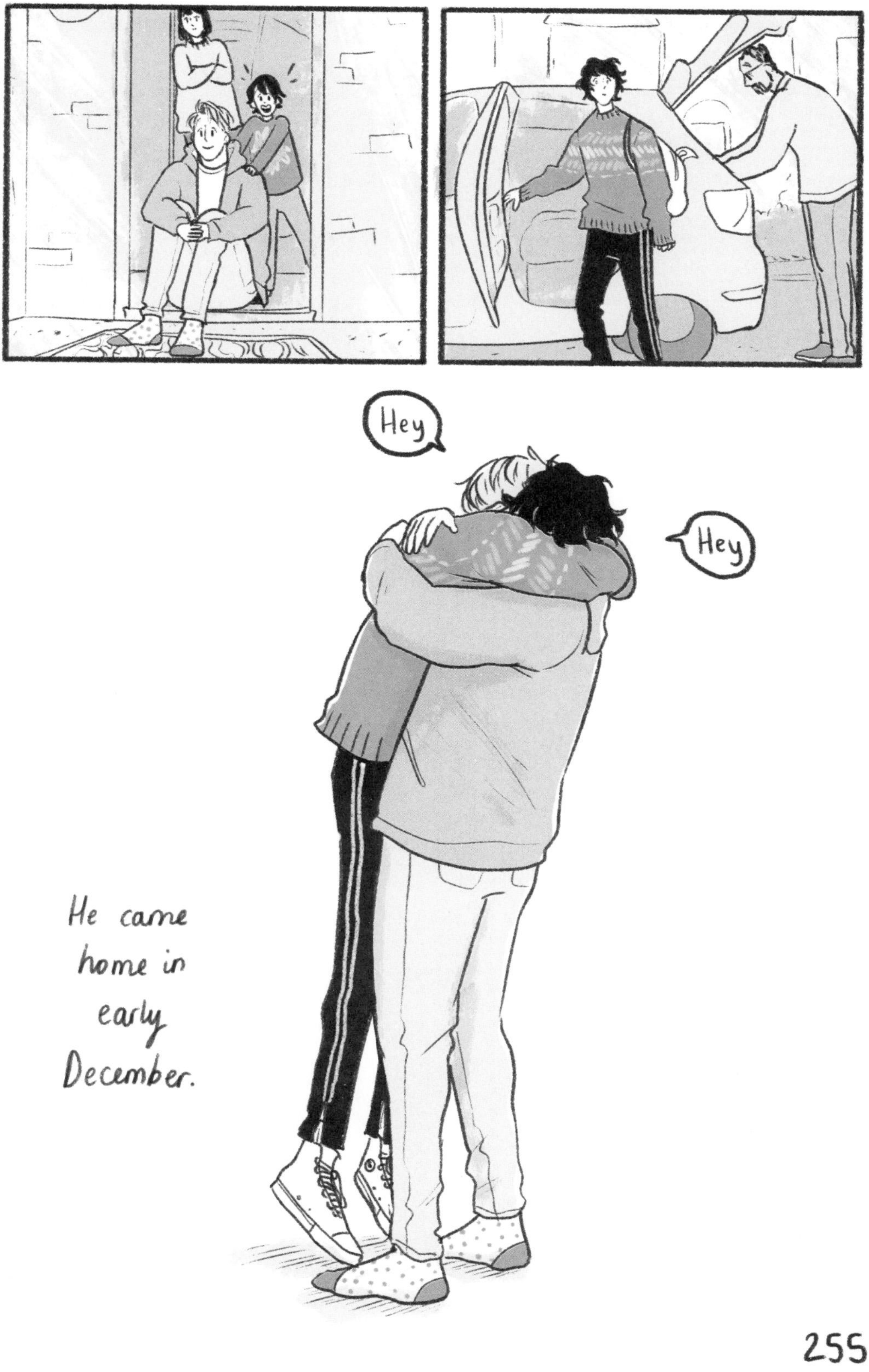
Hey
Hey
He came home in early December.

Just in time for the Christmas season.

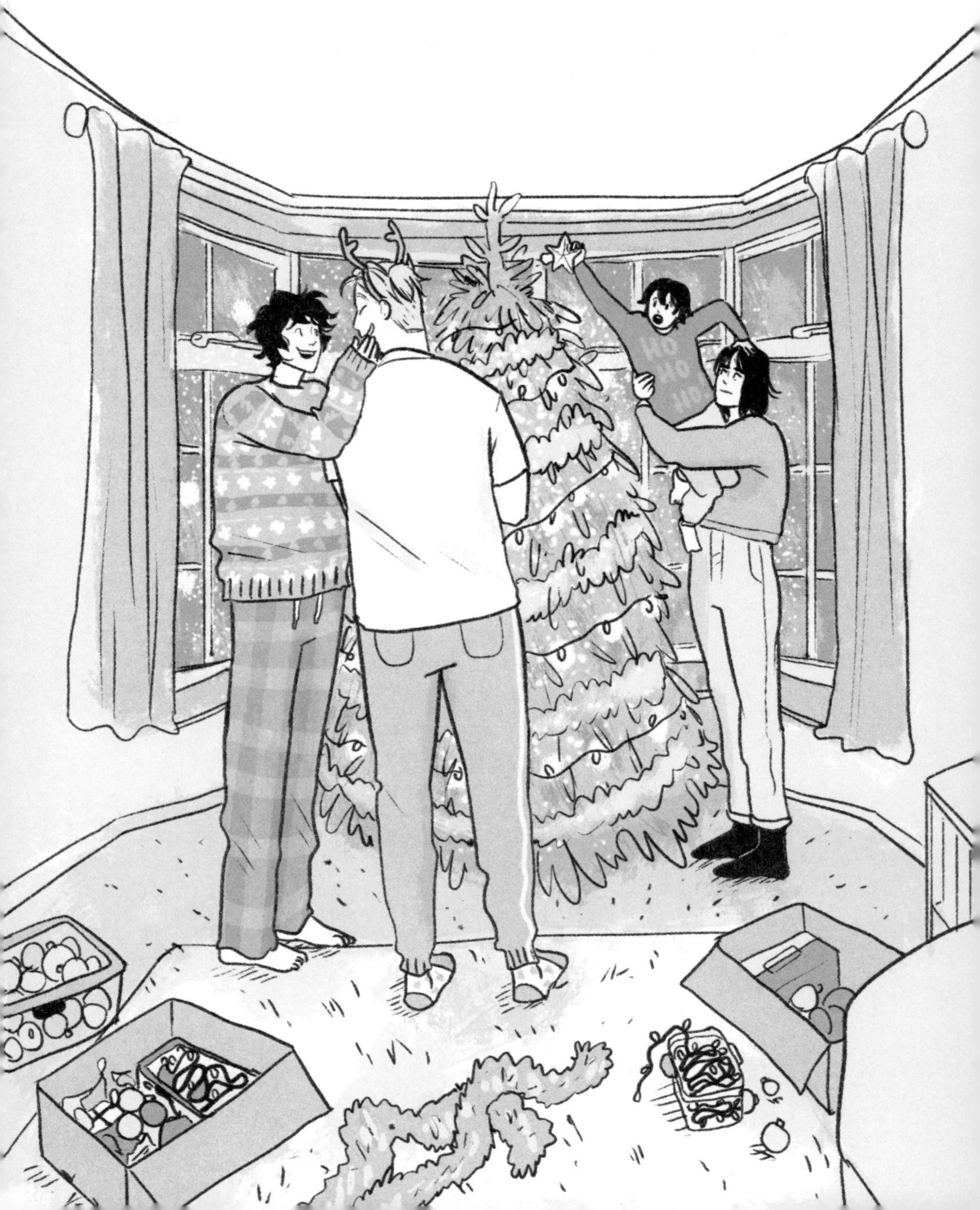
HO HO HO

He's still dealing with a lot, so he stayed off school for the rest of term.

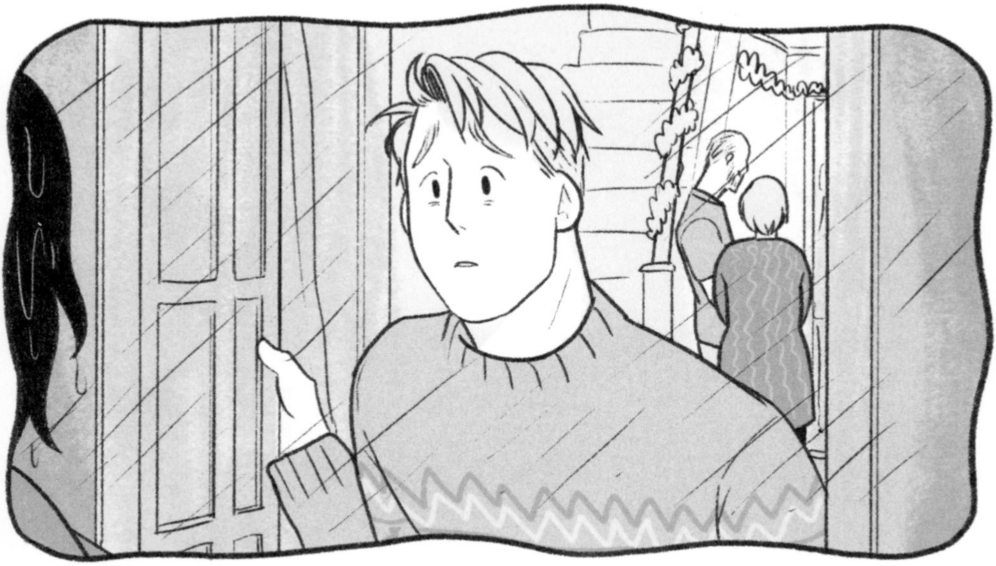

Christmas Day was especially hard. He came over after a big argument with his mum.

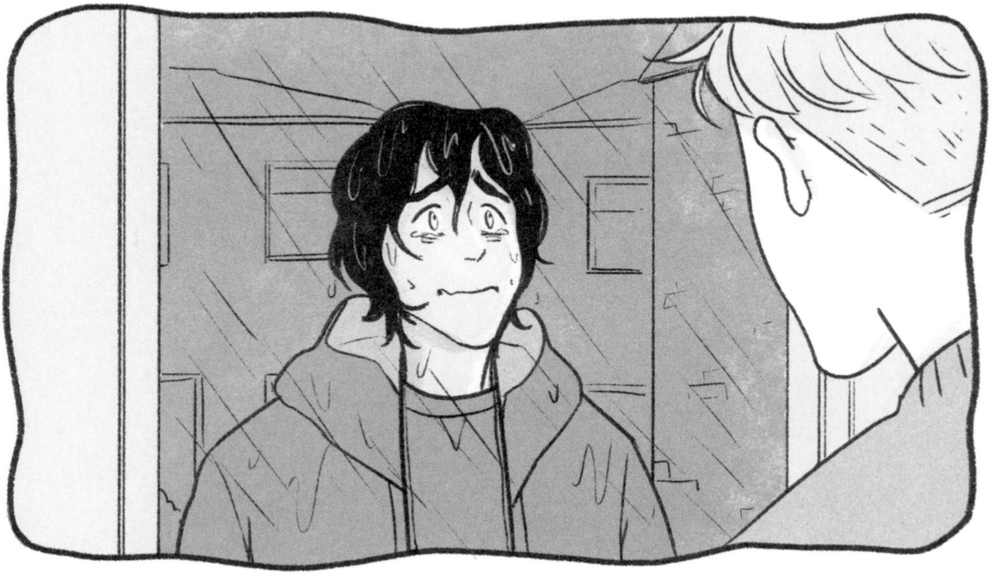

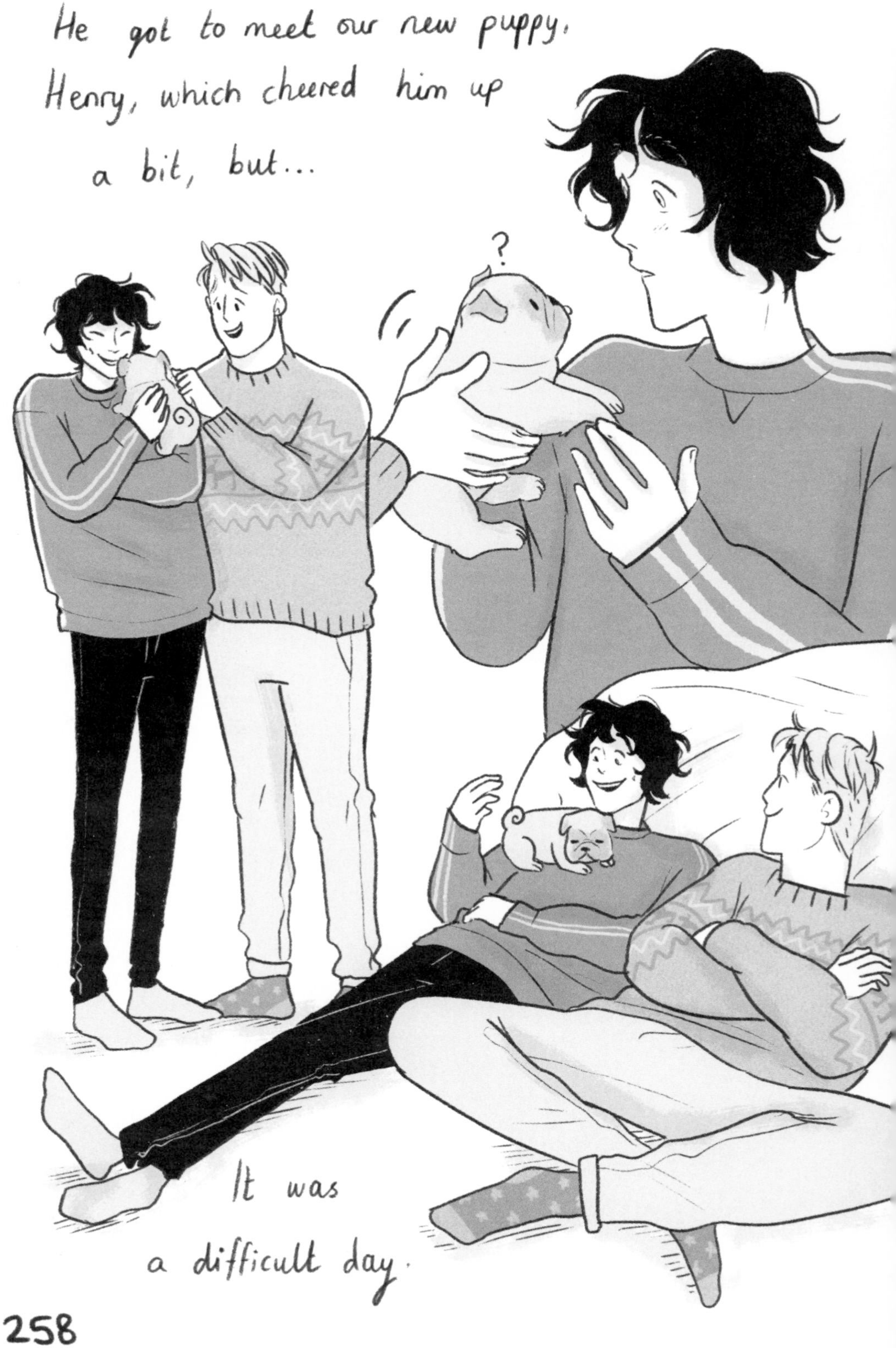
He got to meet our new puppy, Henry, which cheered him up a bit, but...
?
It was a difficult day.

It's not like seven weeks in hospital made him magically okay again.

I know I'm not an expert or anything, but from what I've learned over the past few months, mental illnesses take a long time to go away completely... if they ever do.

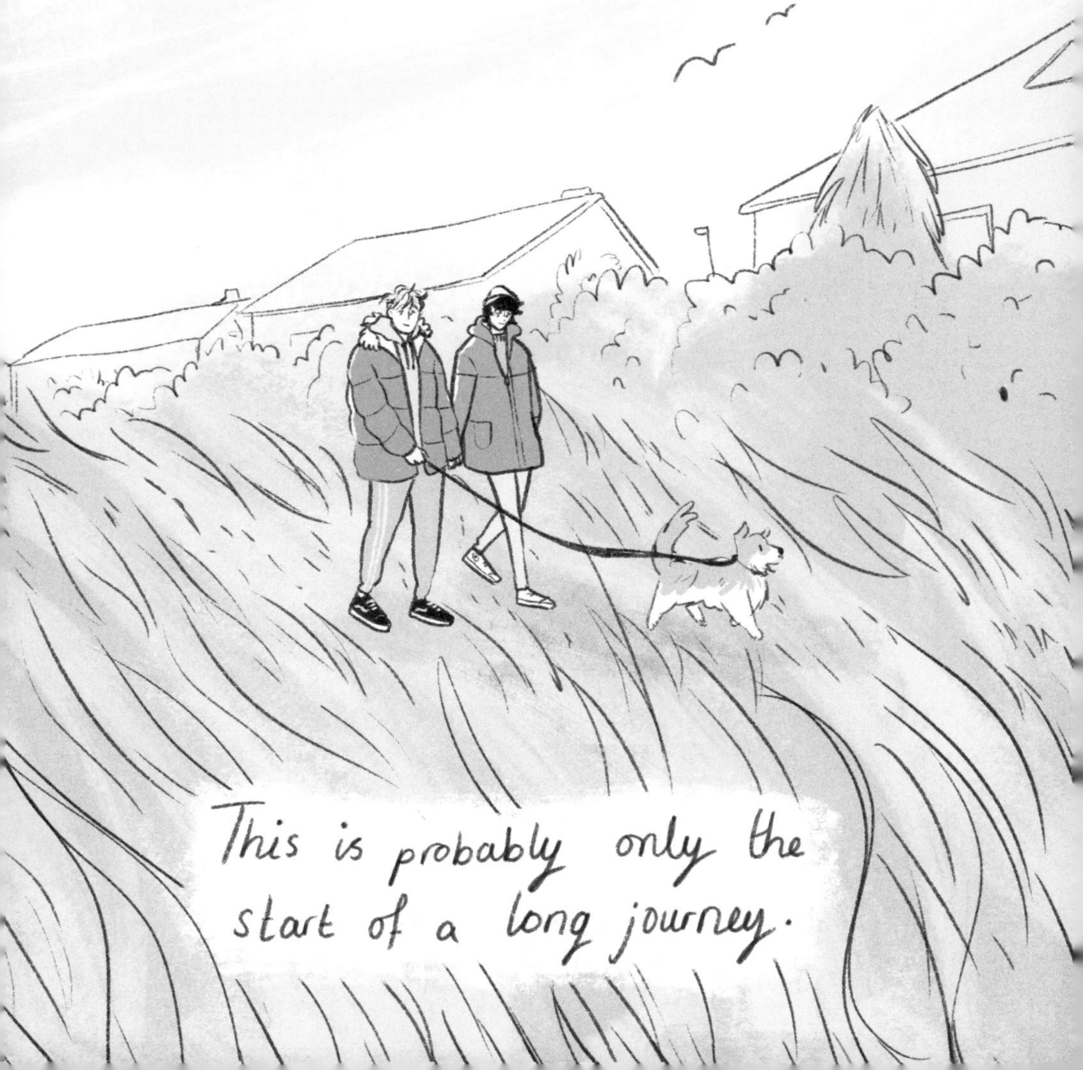
This is probably only the start of a long journey.

But he's definitely doing better.

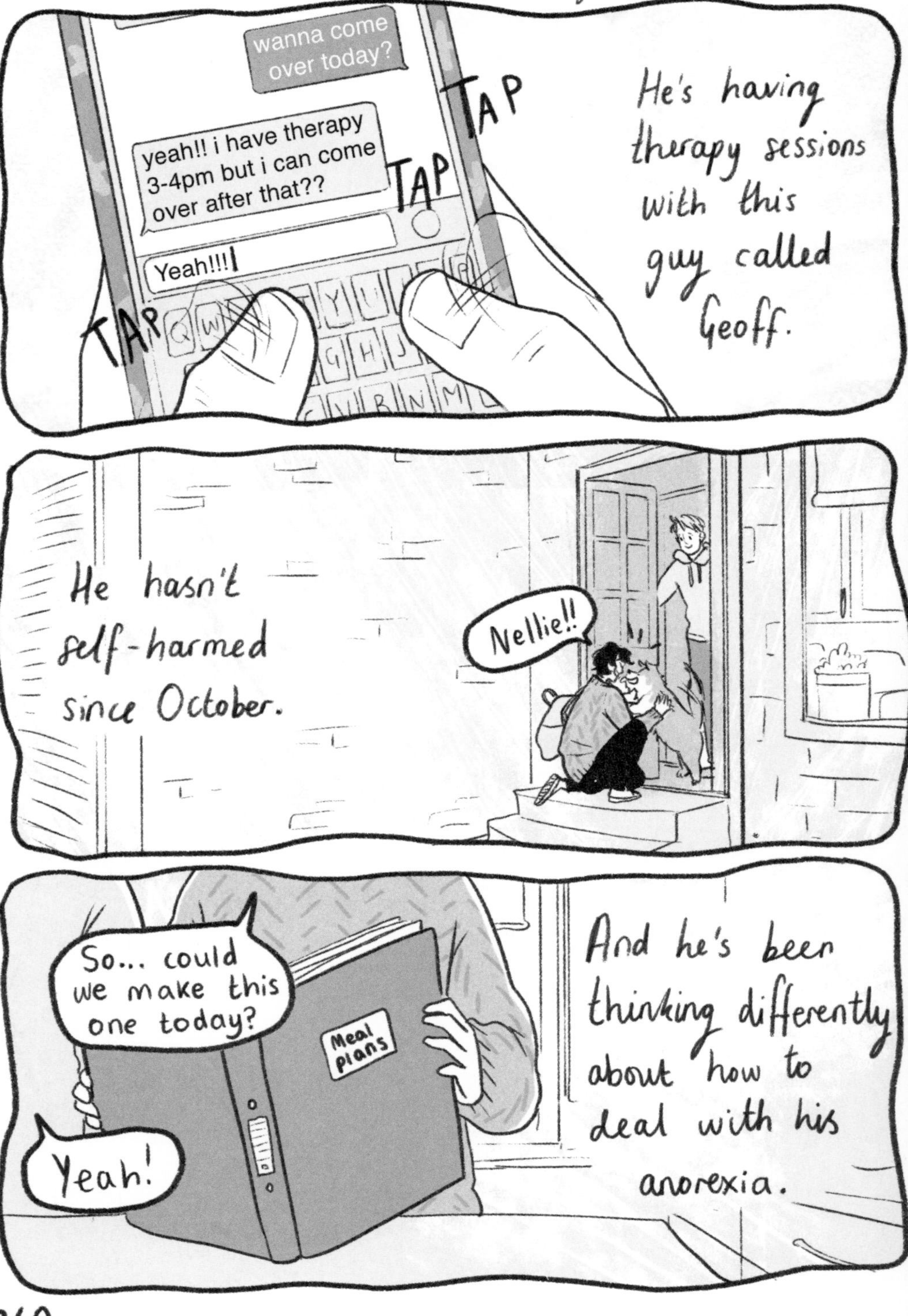
wanna come over today?
yeah!! i have therapy 3-4pm but i can come over after that??
Yeah!!!
TAP
TAP
TAP
He's having therapy sessions with this guy called Geoff.
He hasn't self-harmed since October.
Nellie!!
So... could we make this one today?
Meal plans
Yeah!
And he's been thinking differently about how to deal with his anorexia.

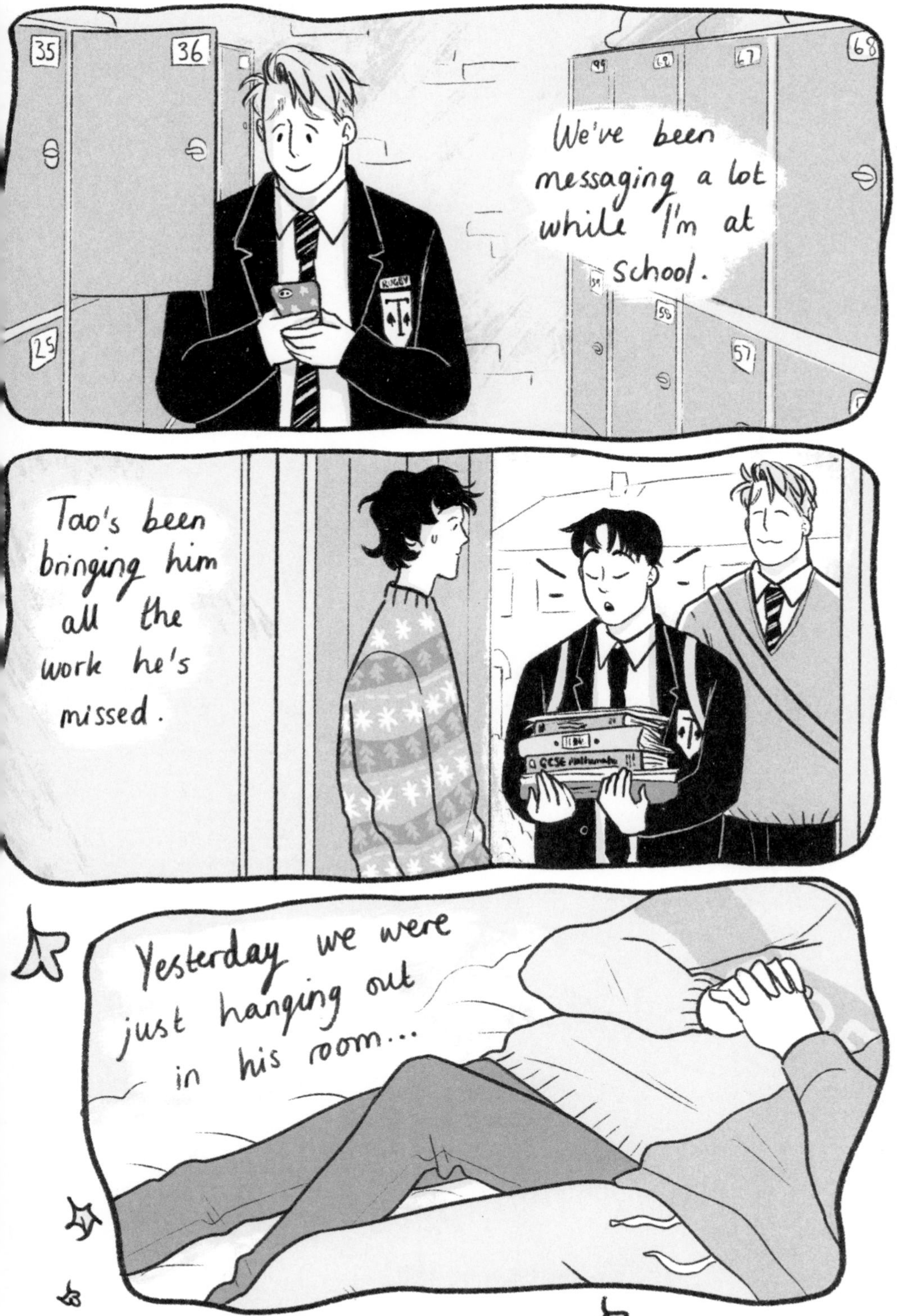
We've been messaging a lot while I'm at school.
Tao's been bringing him all the work he's missed.
Yesterday we were just hanging out in his room...

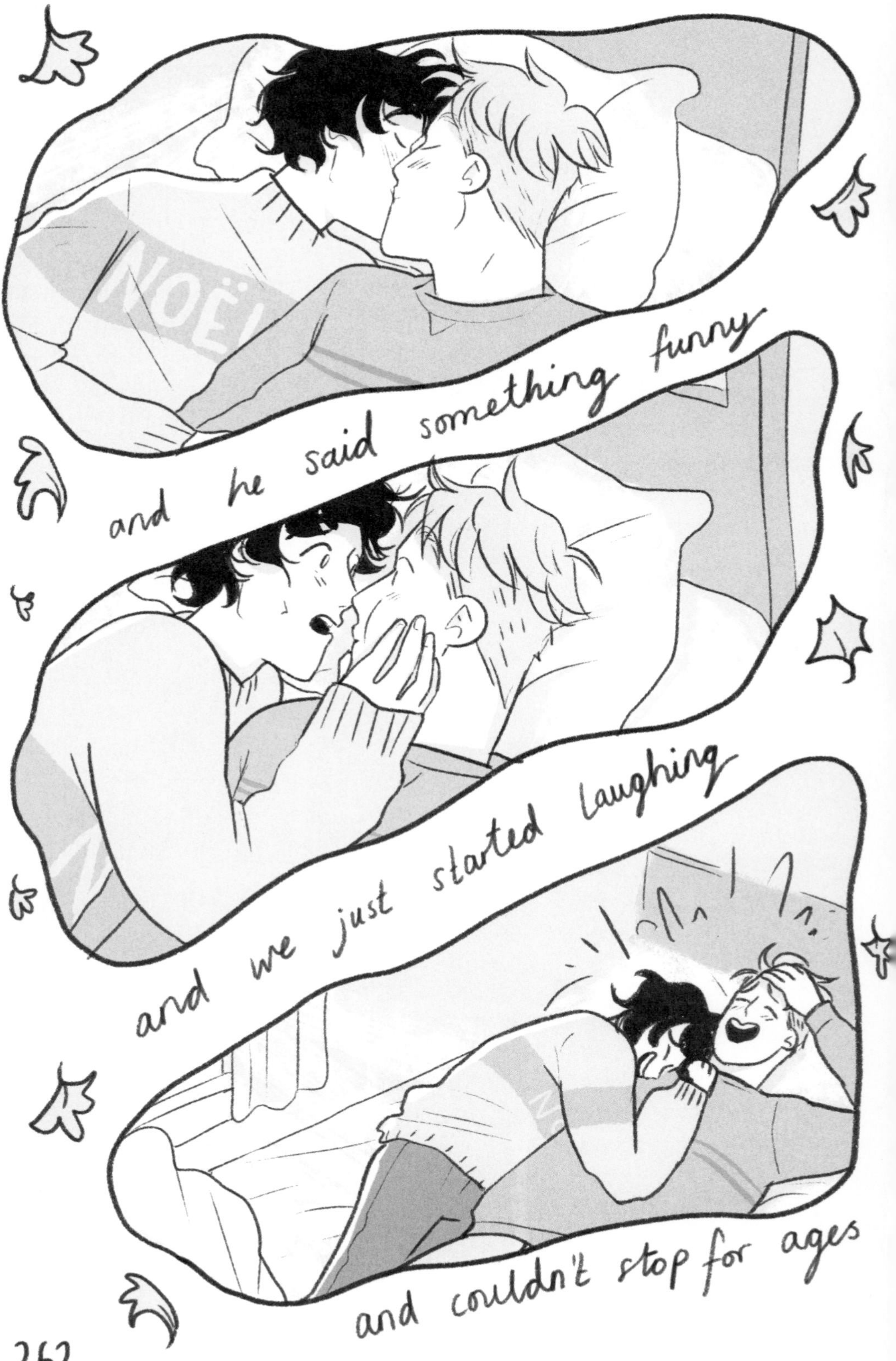
NOËL
and he said something funny
and we just started laughing
and couldn't stop for ages

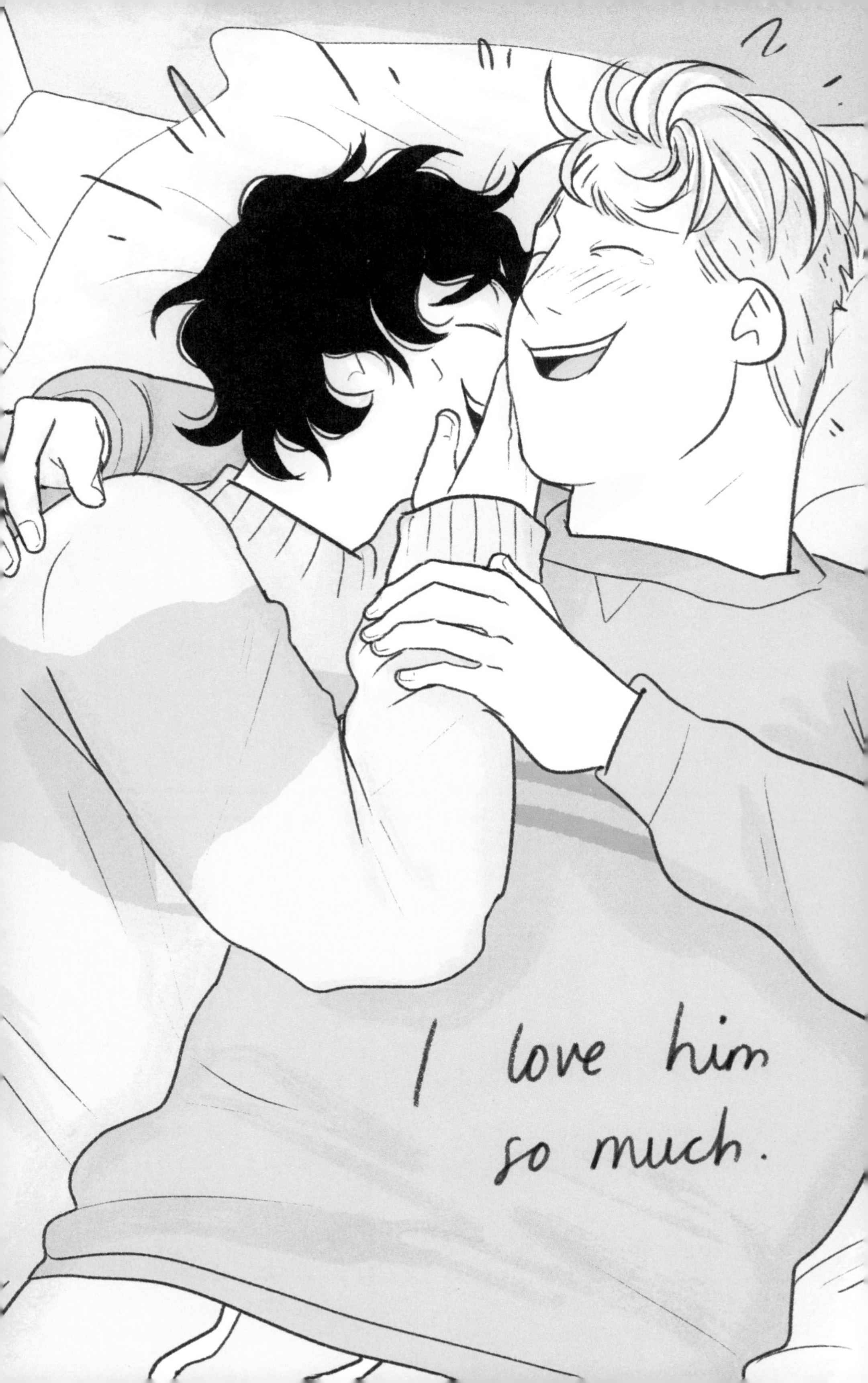
I love him
so much.

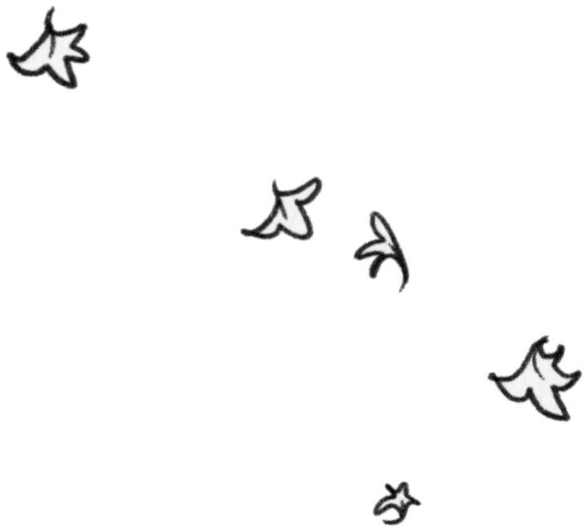

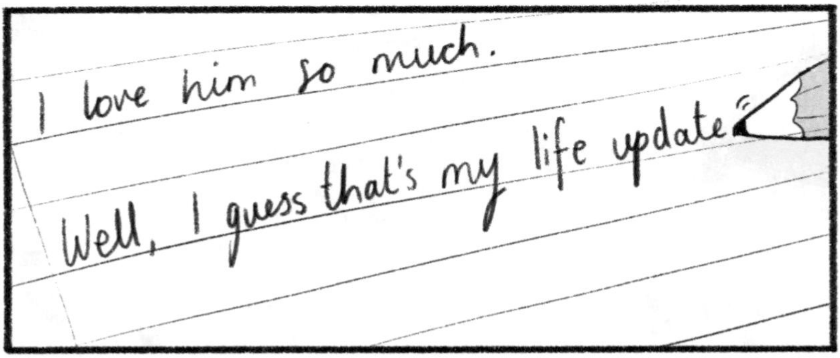
I love him so much.
Well, I guess that's my life update

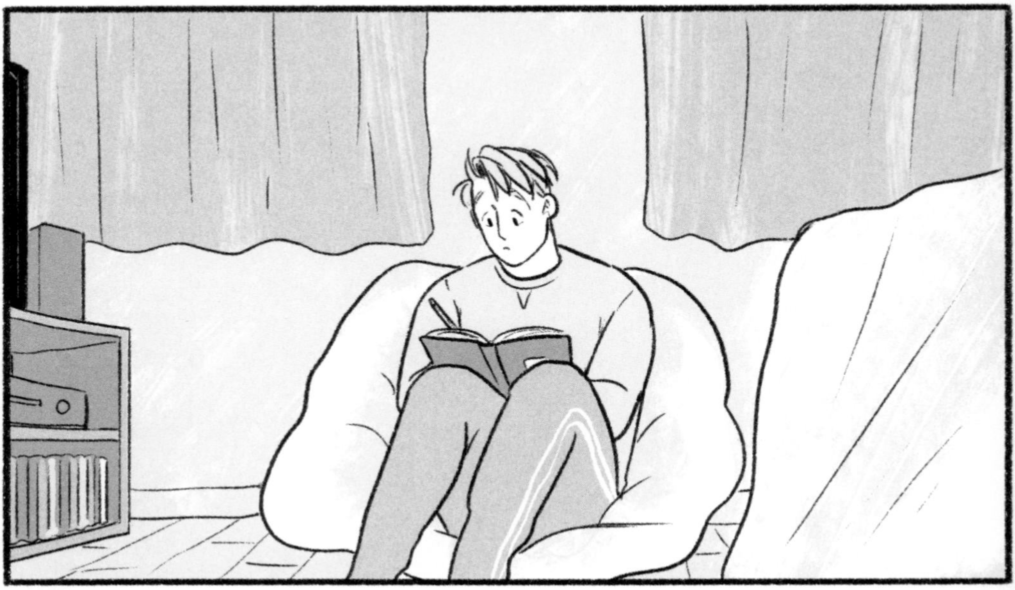

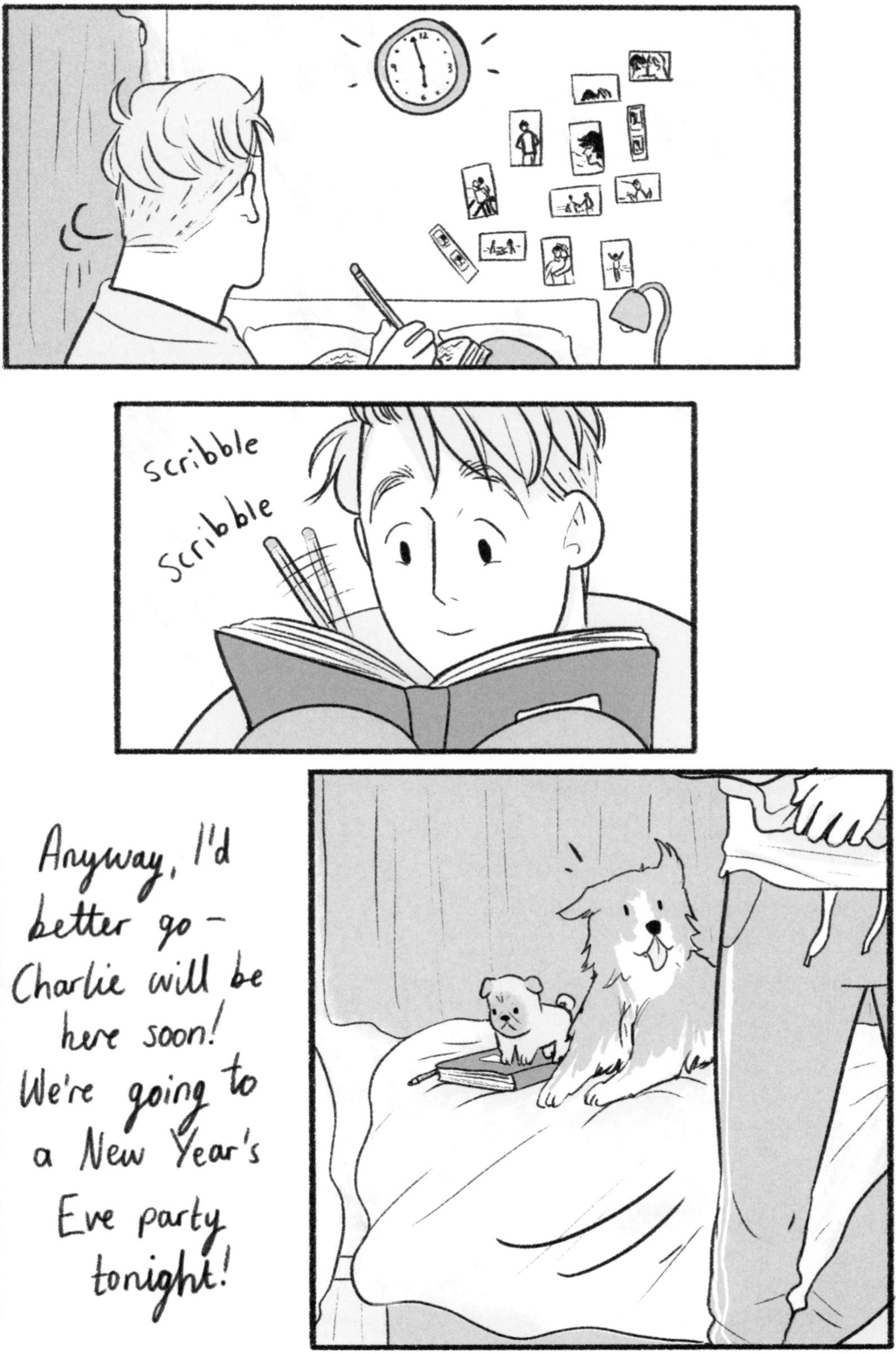
scribble
scribble
Anyway, I'd better go – Charlie will be here soon! We're going to a New Year's Eve party tonight!

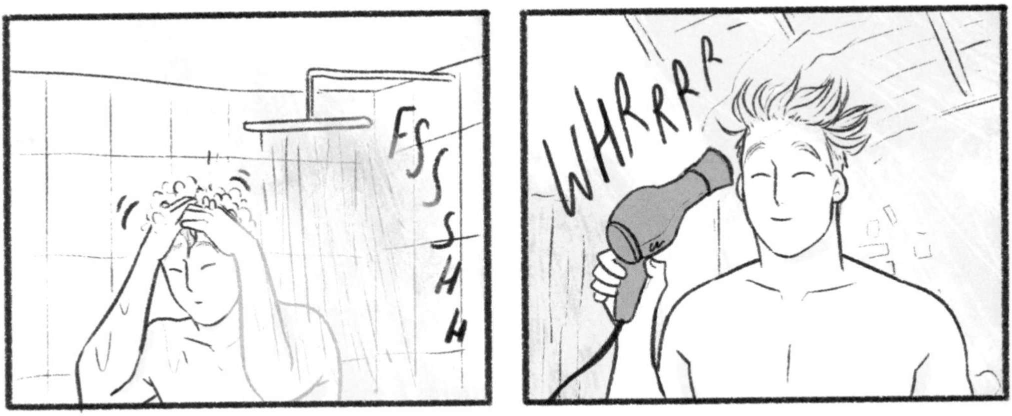
FSSSHH
WHRRRR

A guy in my year is having a big house party with fireworks and stuff.

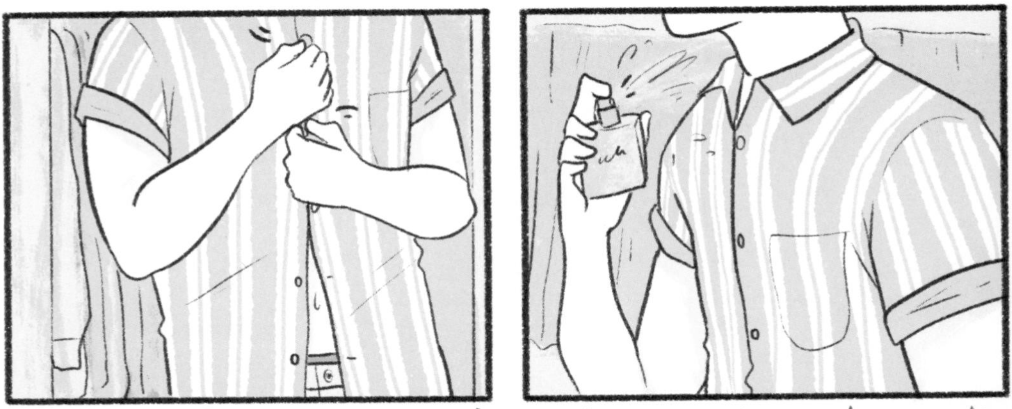

It's the first time Charlie will have been back with a bunch of people from school. We can always leave if it's awful, but I'm excited.

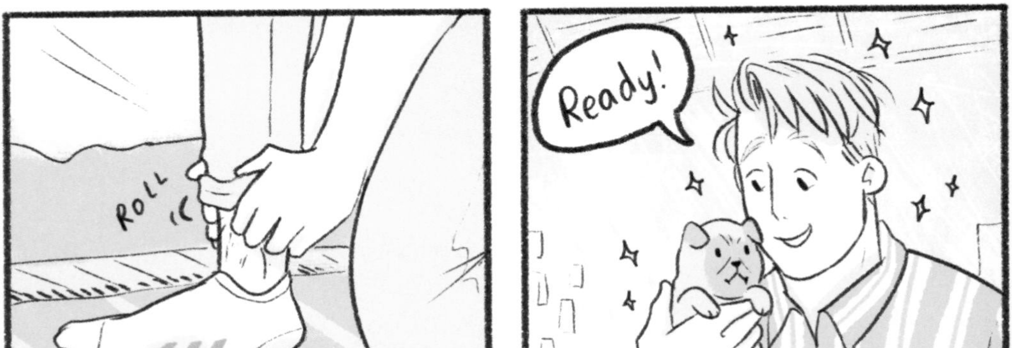
ROLL
Ready!

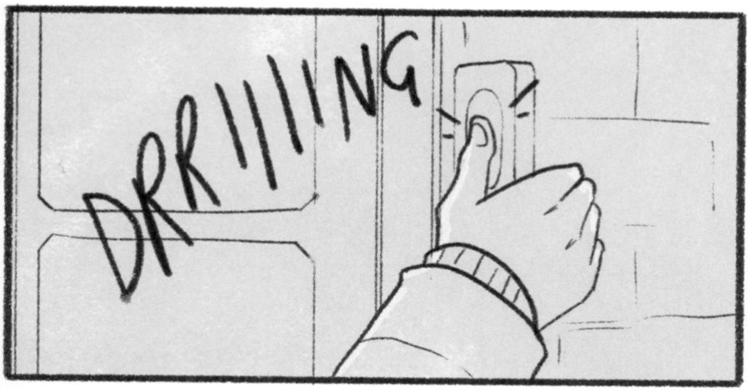
DRRIIIING

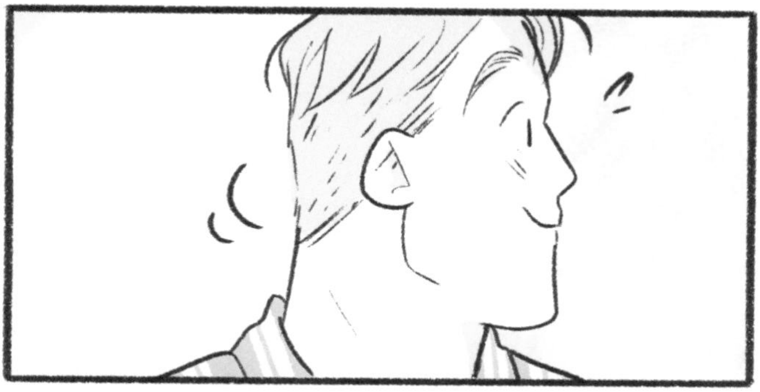

I'm excited to just hang out at a party with my boyfriend.

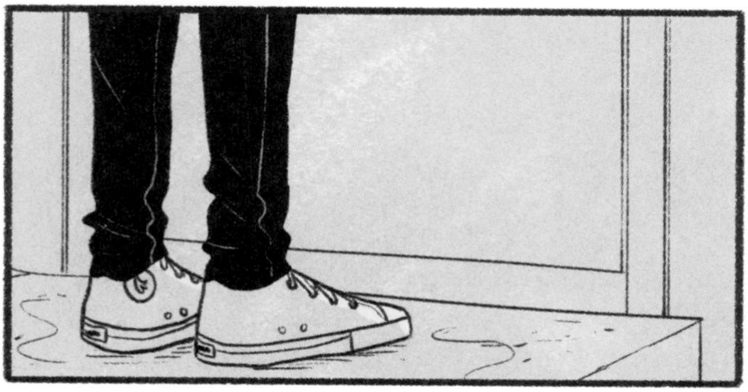

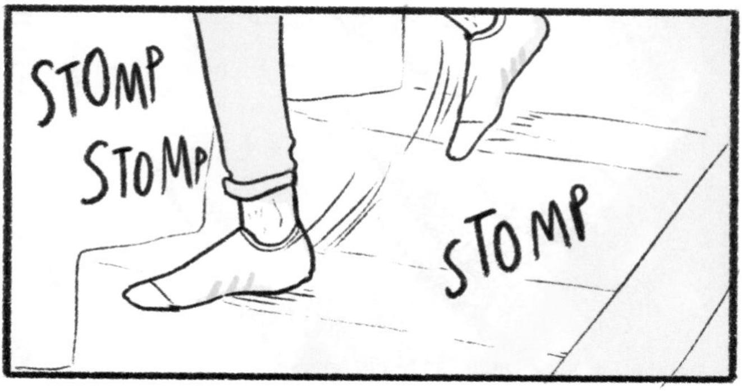
STOMP
STOMP
STOMP

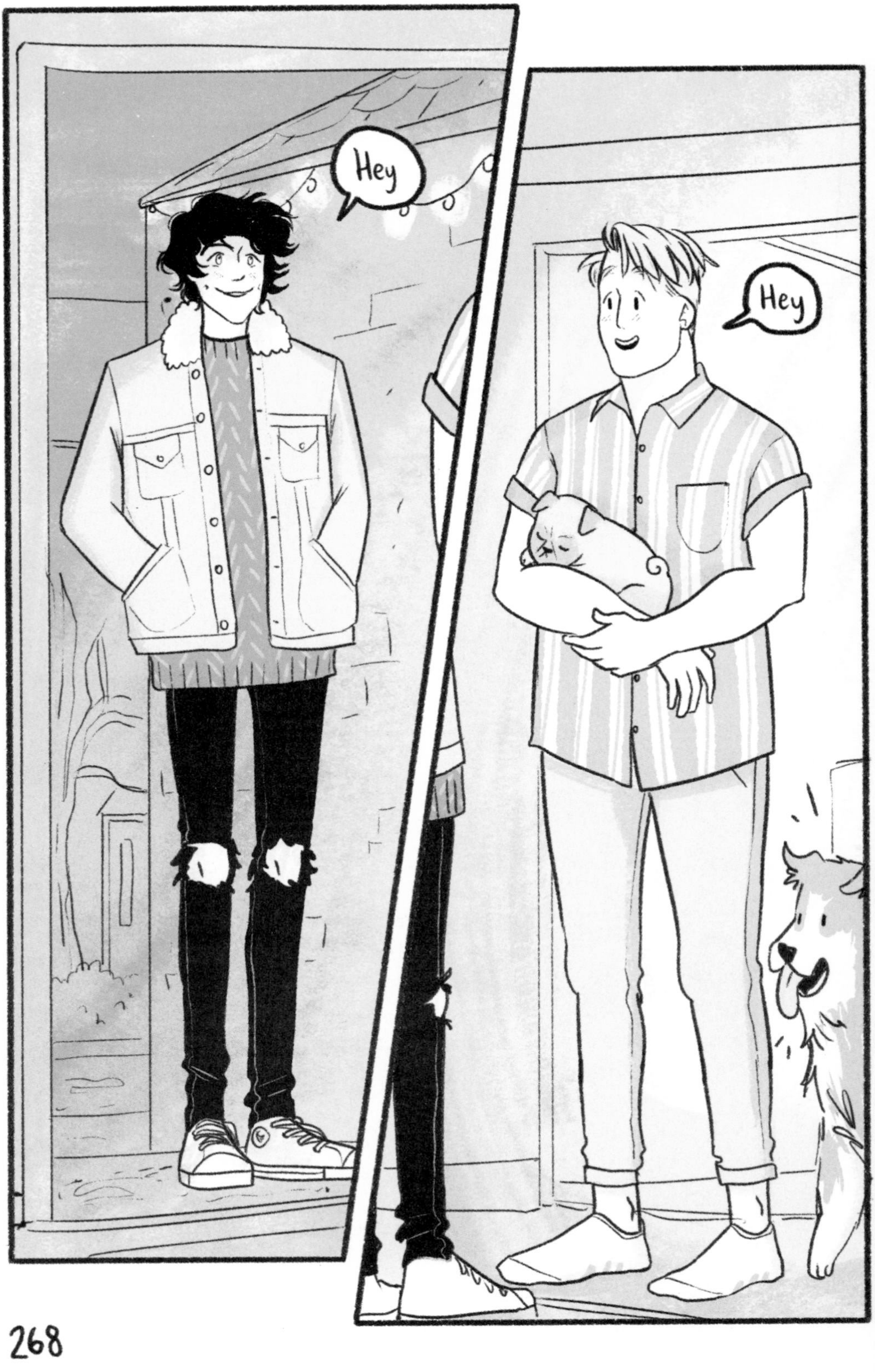
Hey
Hey

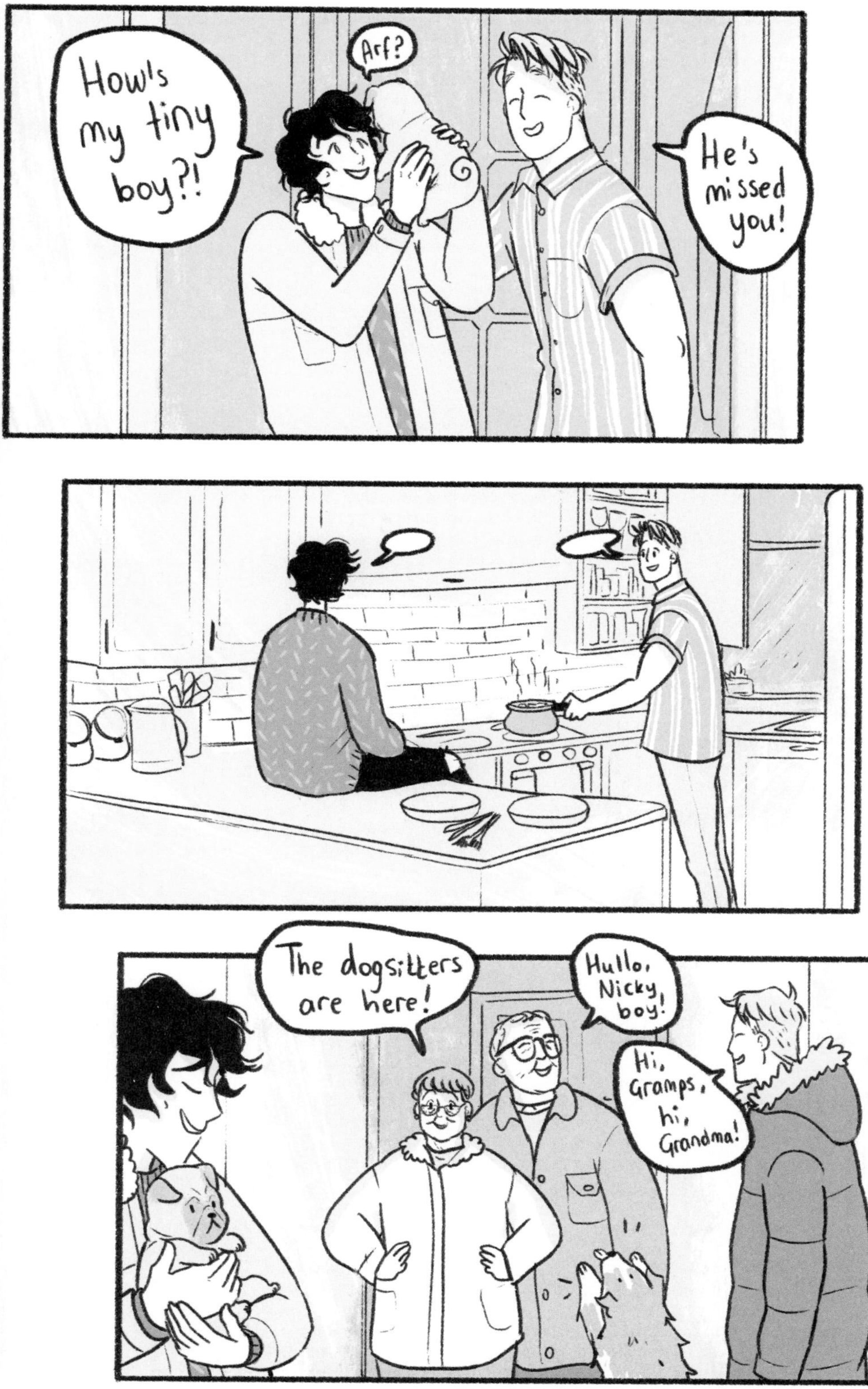
How's my tiny boy?!
Arf?
He's missed you!
The dogsitters are here!
Hullo, Nicky boy!
Hi, Gramps, hi, Grandma!

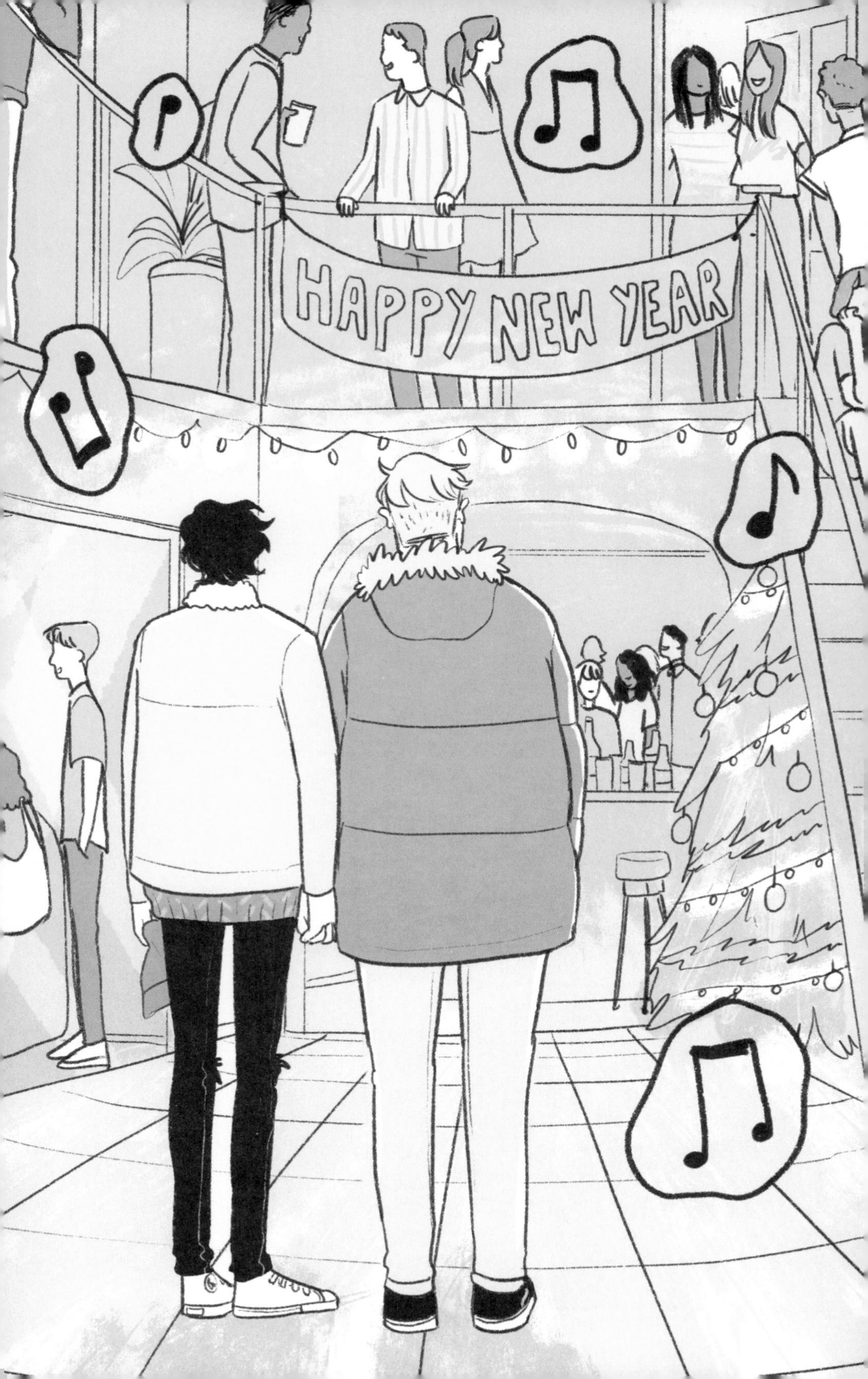
HAPPY NEW YEAR

275

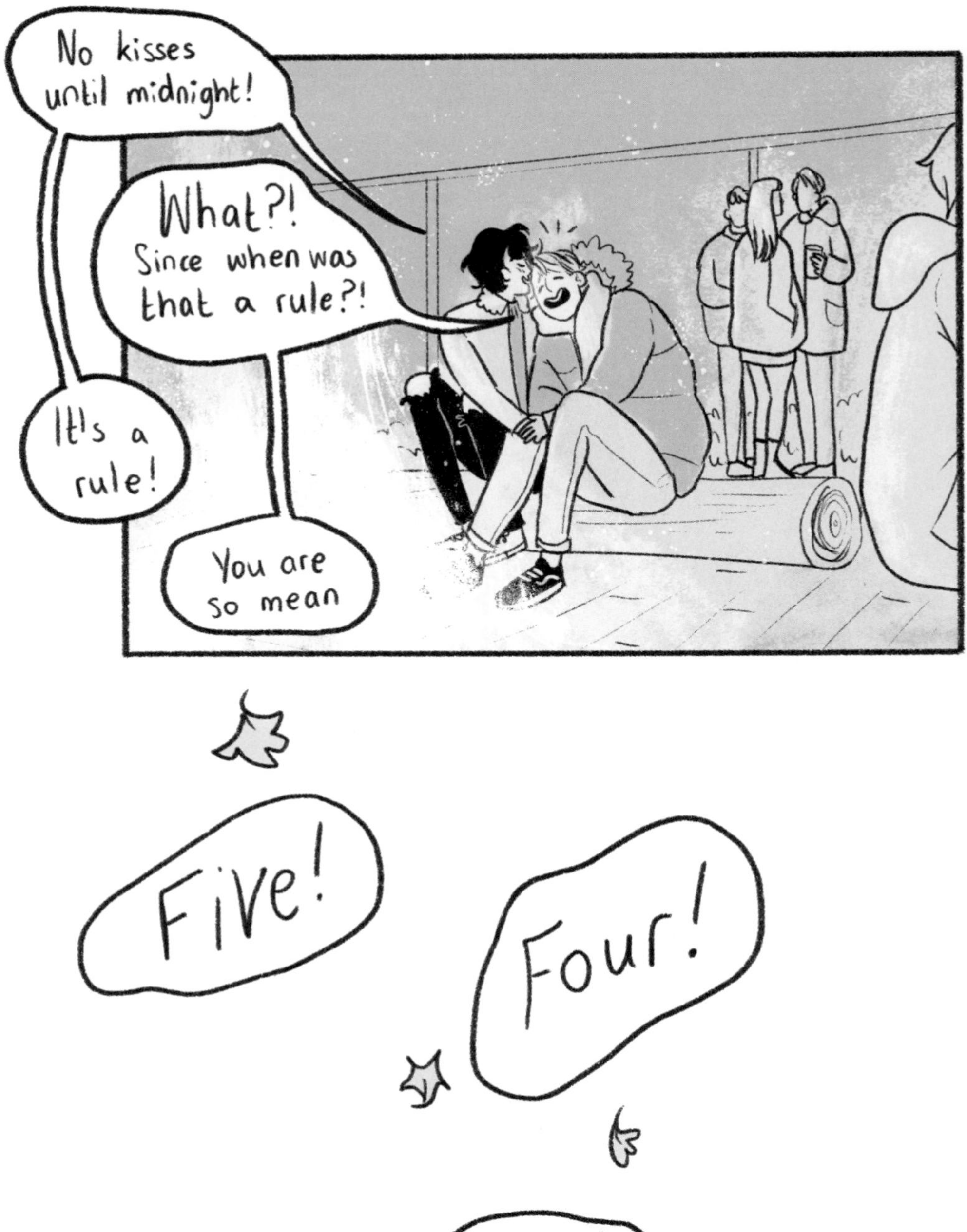
No kisses until midnight!
What?! Since when was that a rule?!
It's a rule!
You are so mean
Five!
Four!
Three!

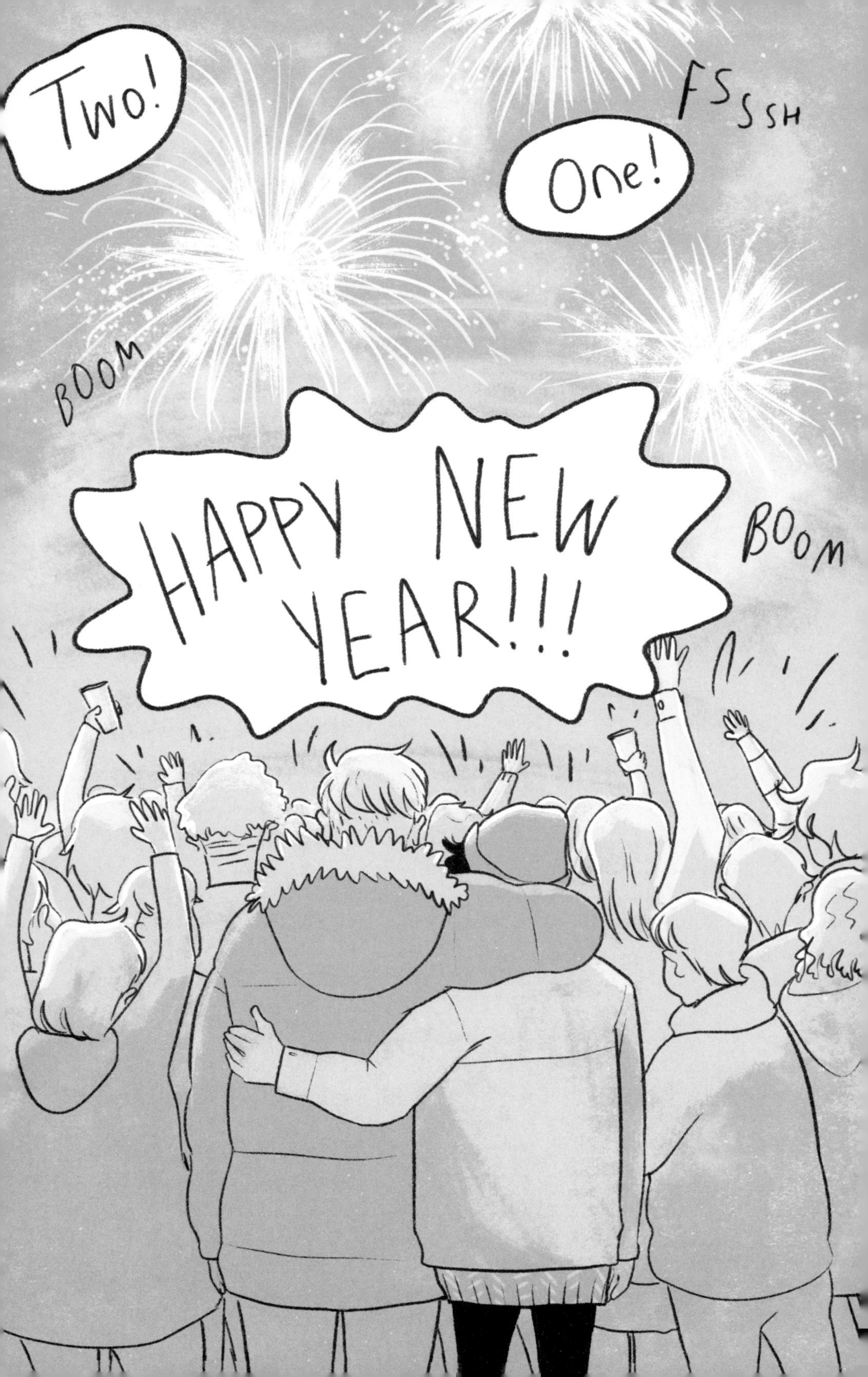
Two!
FSSSH
One!
BOOM
HAPPY NEW YEAR!!!
BOOM

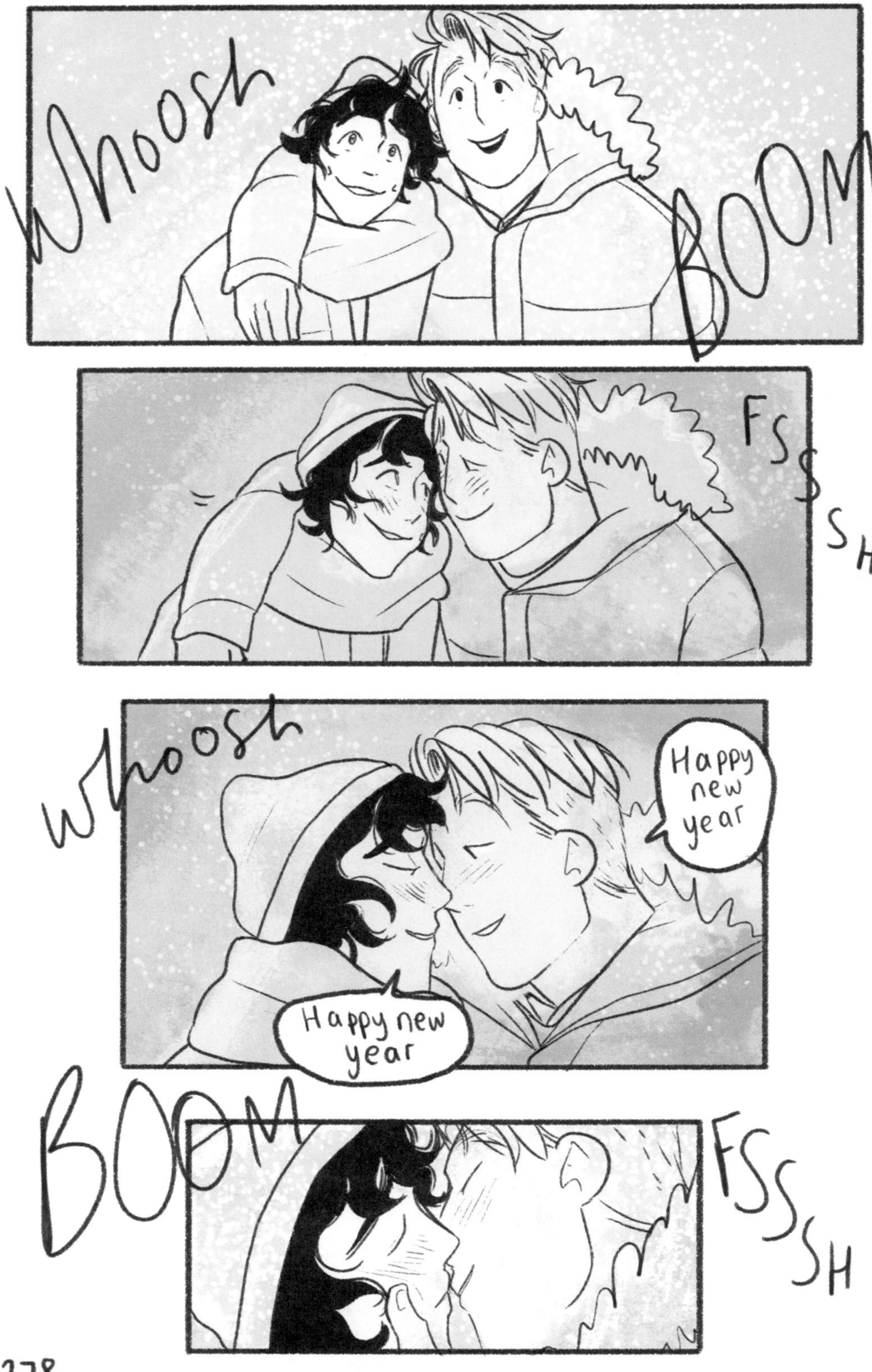
Whoosh
BOOM
FSSSH
Whoosh
Happy new year
Happy new year
BOOM
FSSSH

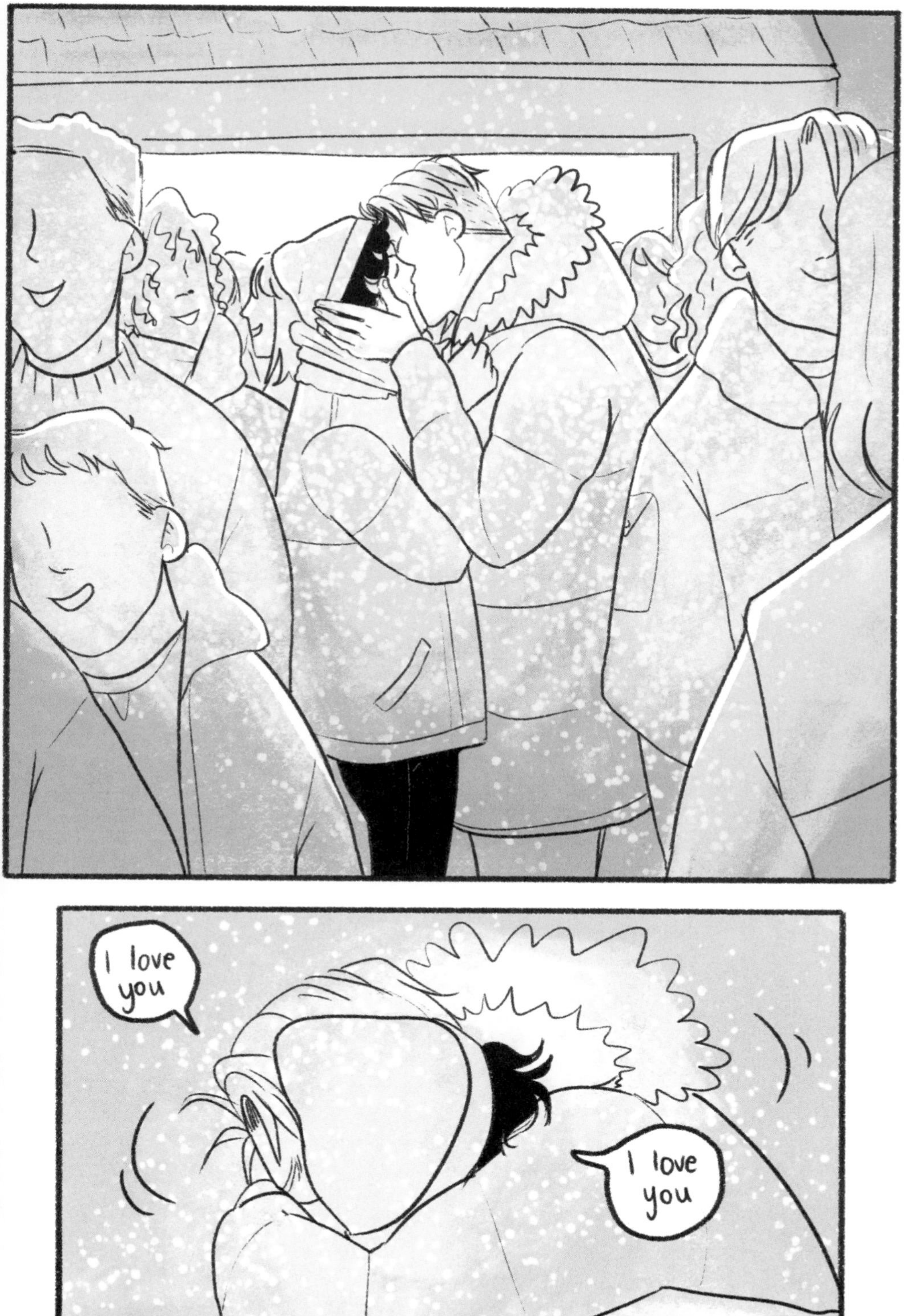
I love you
I love you

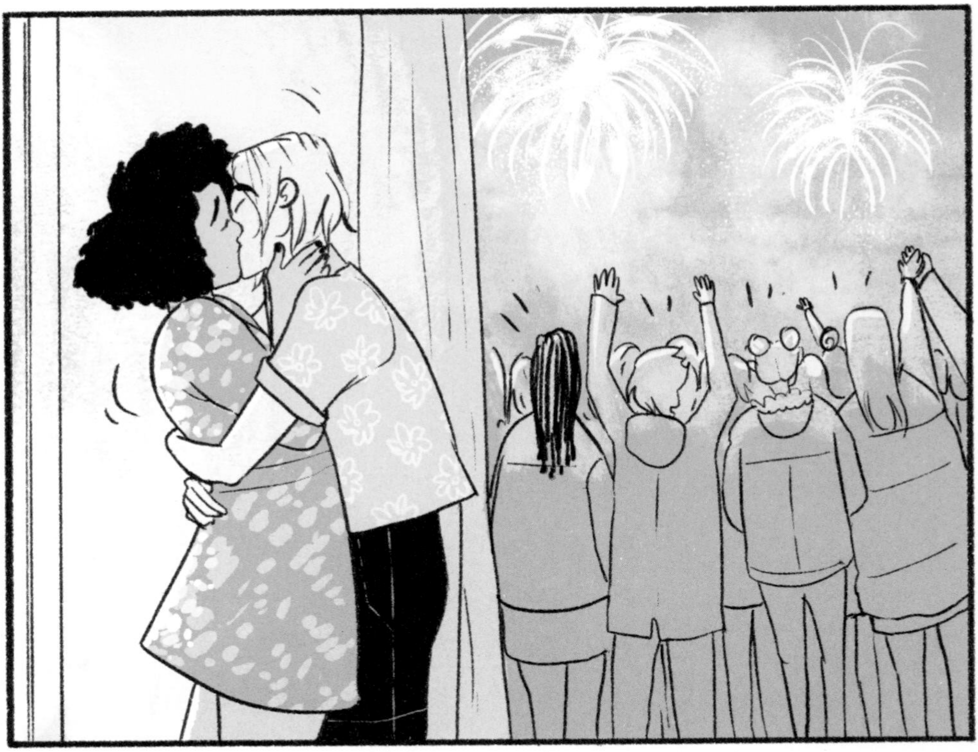

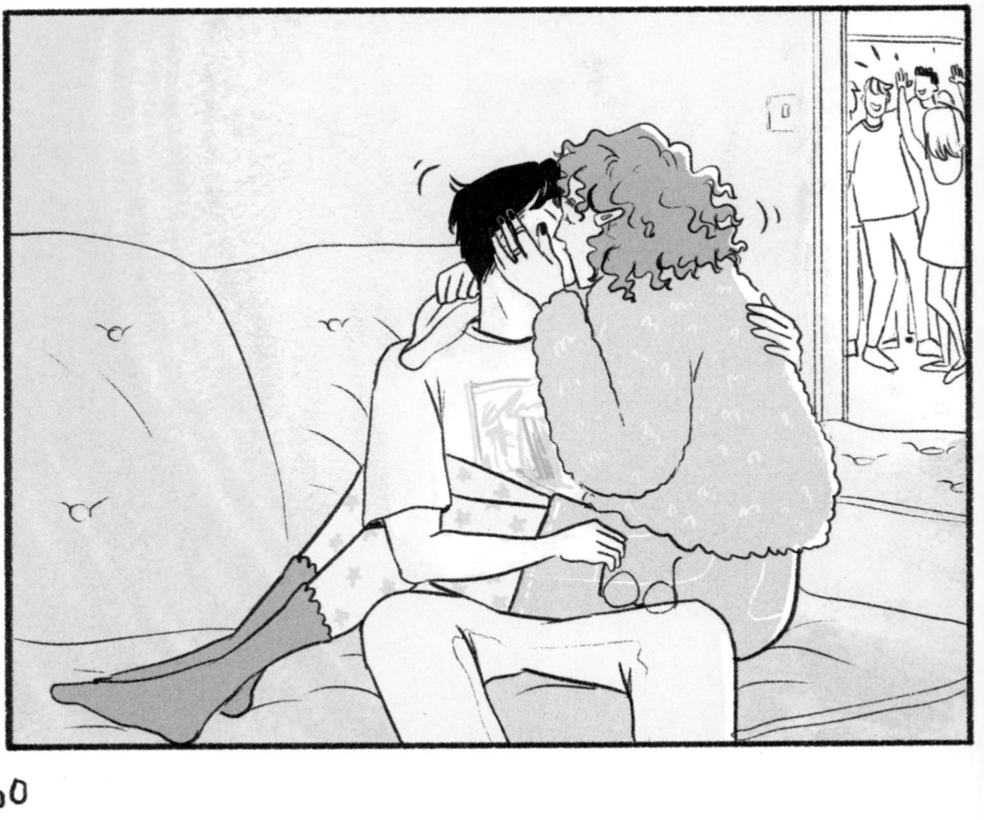

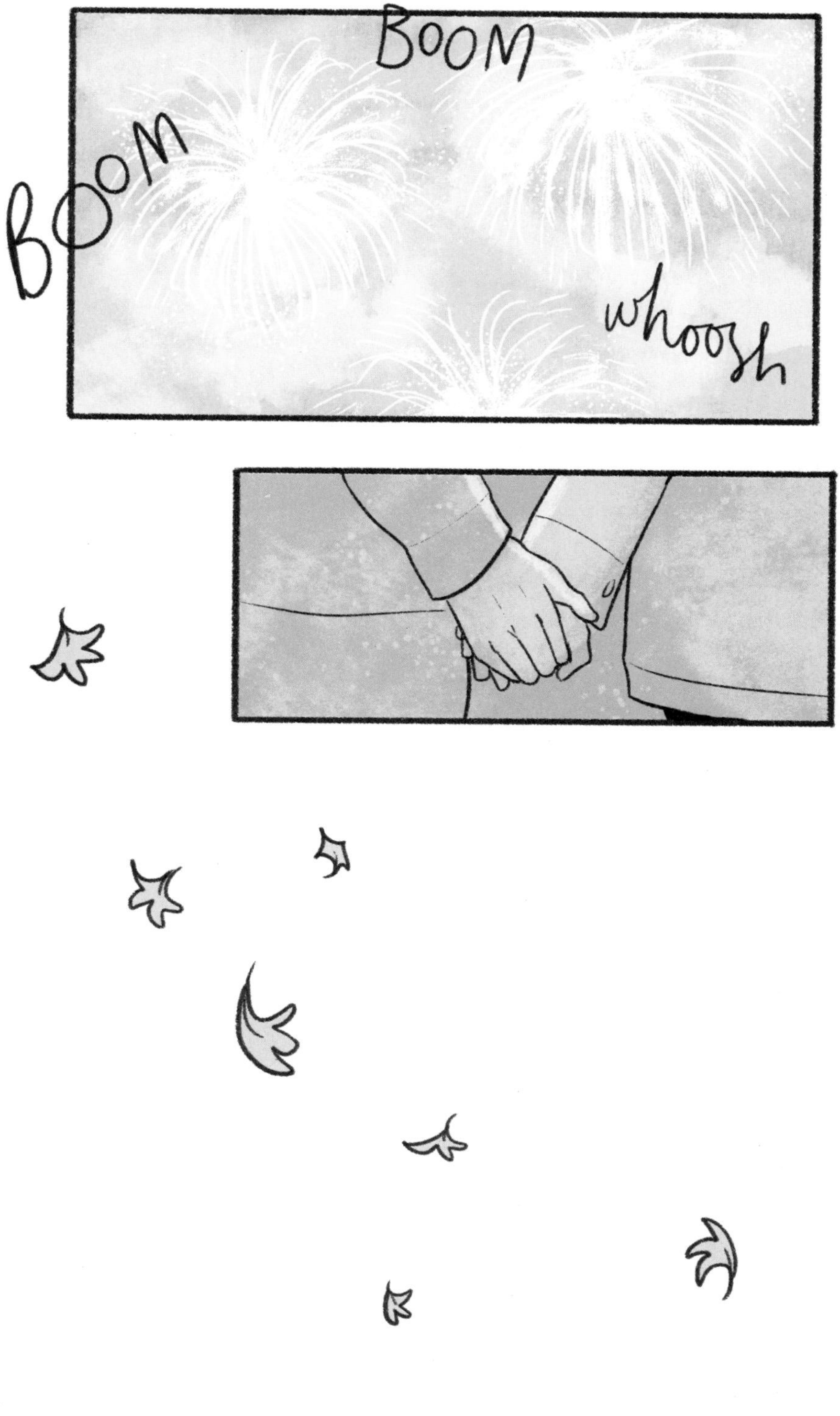
BOOM
BOOM
BOOM
whoosh

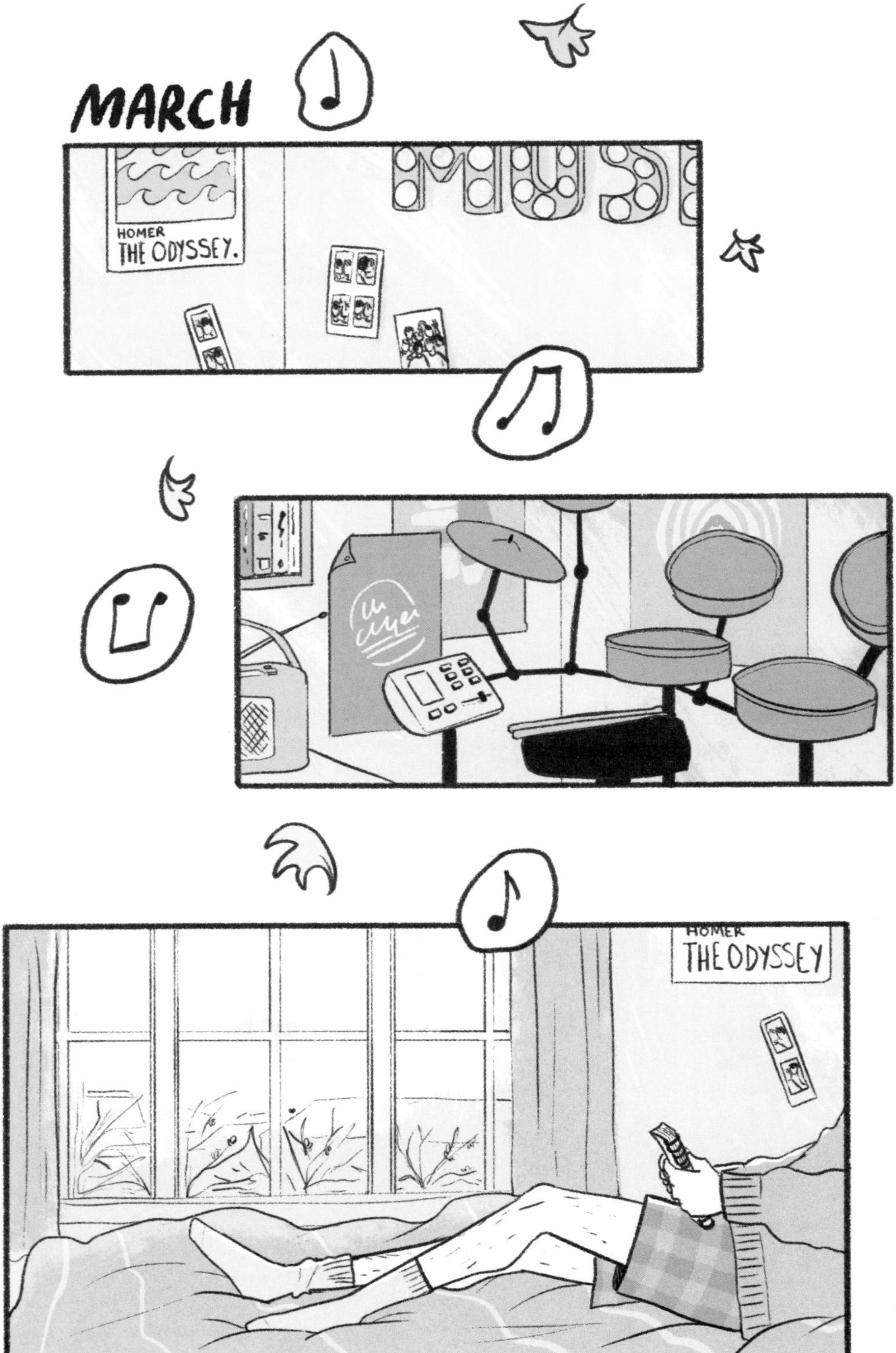
MARCH
HOMER
THE ODYSSEY.
HOMER
THE ODYSSEY

Well, he didn't say I **HAD** to.
He just said it might be helpful.

He's probably
right.

He's usually right,
which is quite annoying, actually.

But I haven't written in here since last
summer, and a lot has happened since then

I can't believe I've been going to therapy for like four months already.

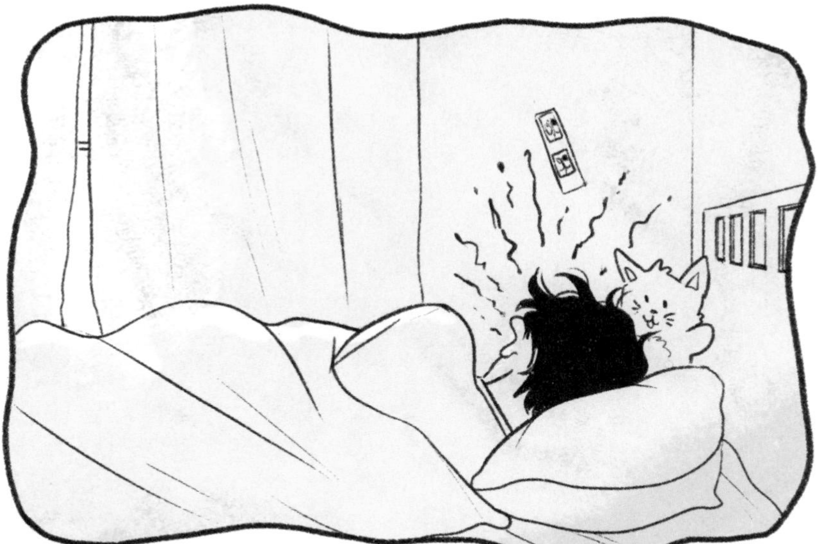

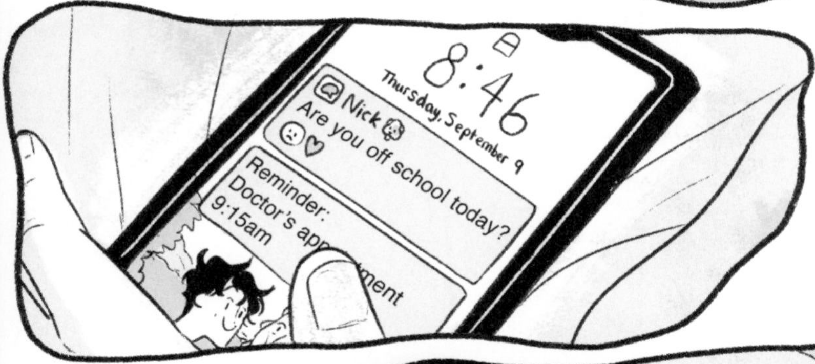
8:46
Thursday, September 9
Nick
Are you off school today?
Reminder:
Doctor's ap
ment
9:15am

I hated the idea at first.

Even though I admitted I needed it.

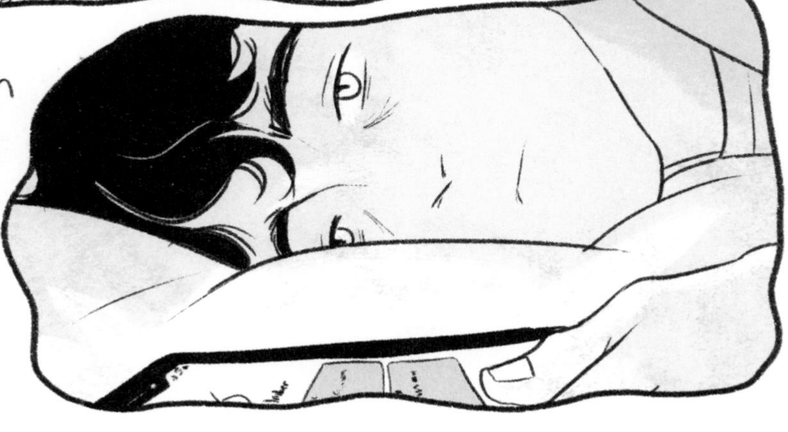

And things didn't exactly get off to a great start, what with the waiting time, and me just spiraling after that.
If you feel you may be su
from mental health problems, seek
rofessional help as soon as possibl
you need to
et out of bed
and sto
eing so lazy
ppointment date: Tuesday, January
e are you off school a
Are you feeling ok? I can
you the math homework
it's due tomorrow and M
ad if you don't
does charlie read the group
chat?? where is he??
disgusting
you keep sk
meals, you
even
harlie please message me
'm so worried about you!!!
don't des
"Mental health waiting ti
children and teens 'danger
nd unhelpful'"
quiry into the latest waitin
need to stay
control or ever
bad an
Things got bad really fast.

Spending a few weeks in a psych ward was obviously not my plan.

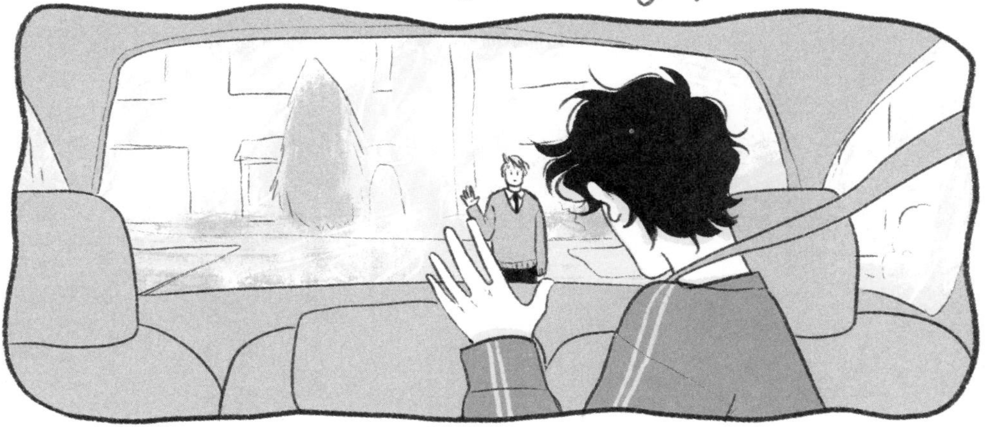

And there were some ups and downs there, sure.

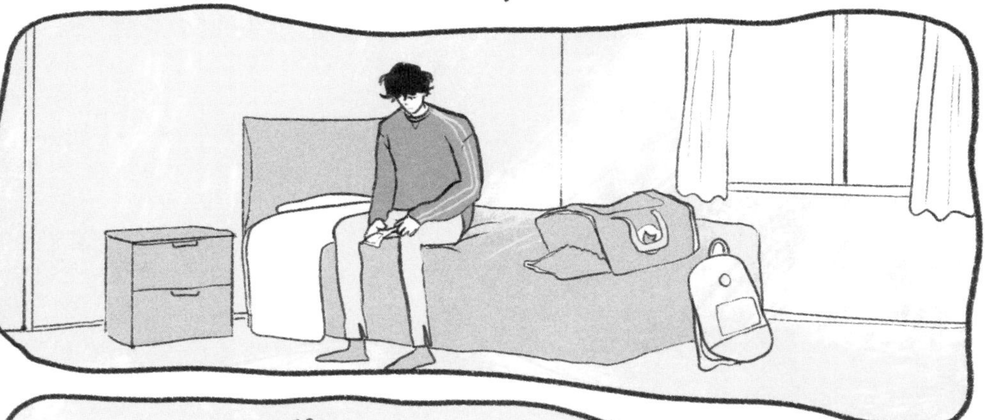

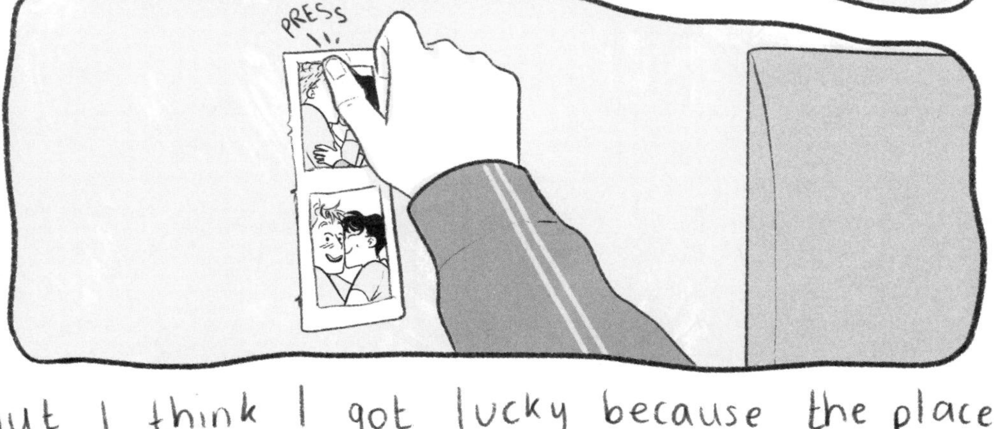
PRESS

But I think I got lucky because the place I went to was actually helpful.

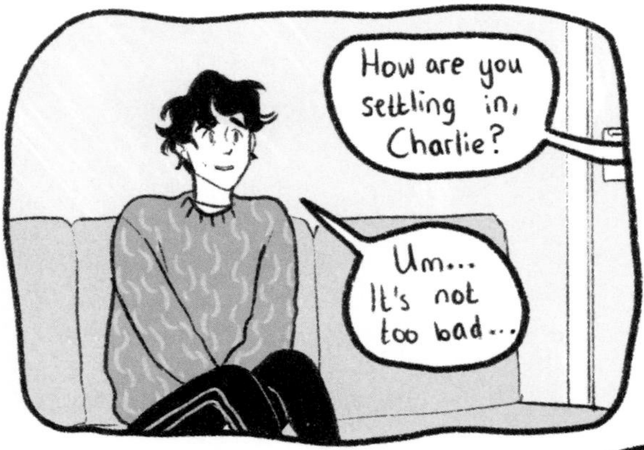
How are you settling in, Charlie?
Um... It's not too bad...

I started therapy there. Not with Geoff, but the therapist was really nice.

I had a nutritionist, too. I know that isn't the case for all psych wards.

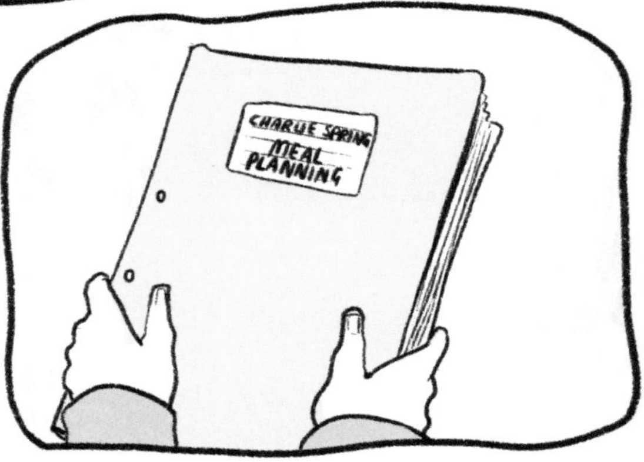
CHARLIE SPRING
MEAL PLANNING

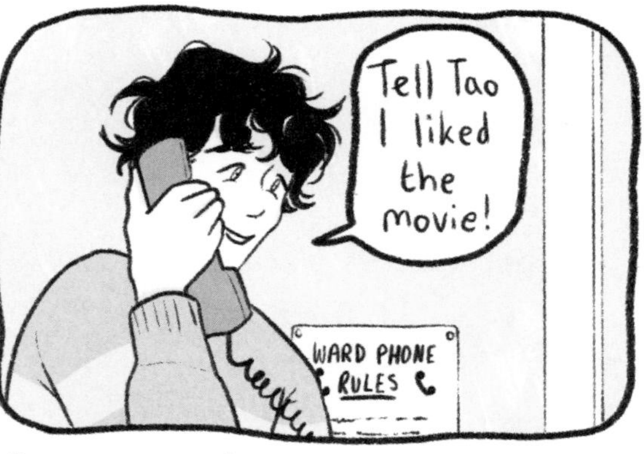
Tell Tao I liked the movie!
WARD PHONE RULES

We weren't allowed cell phones, but I could still call home from the ward phone.

Some of the rules kinda sucked, and some days were awful, but a lot of it was fine. I even made a couple of friends.

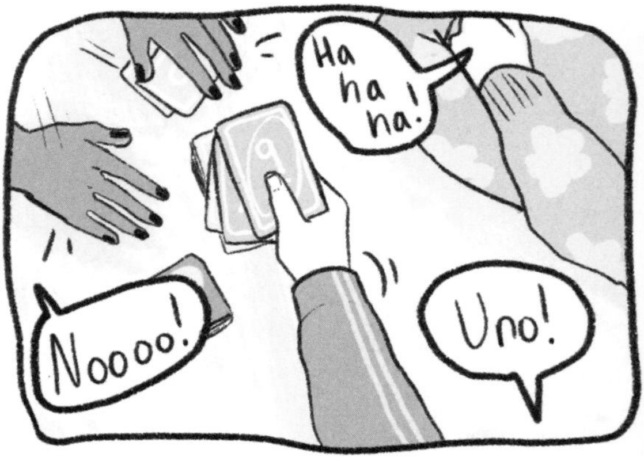
Ha ha ha!
Noooo!
Uno!

At first, I think there was a big part of me
that didn't even want to get better.
That just wanted to keep pretending I
was fine, so I didn't have to put in the
effort to change.

I was so scared of losing control.

Eating was something I could control.

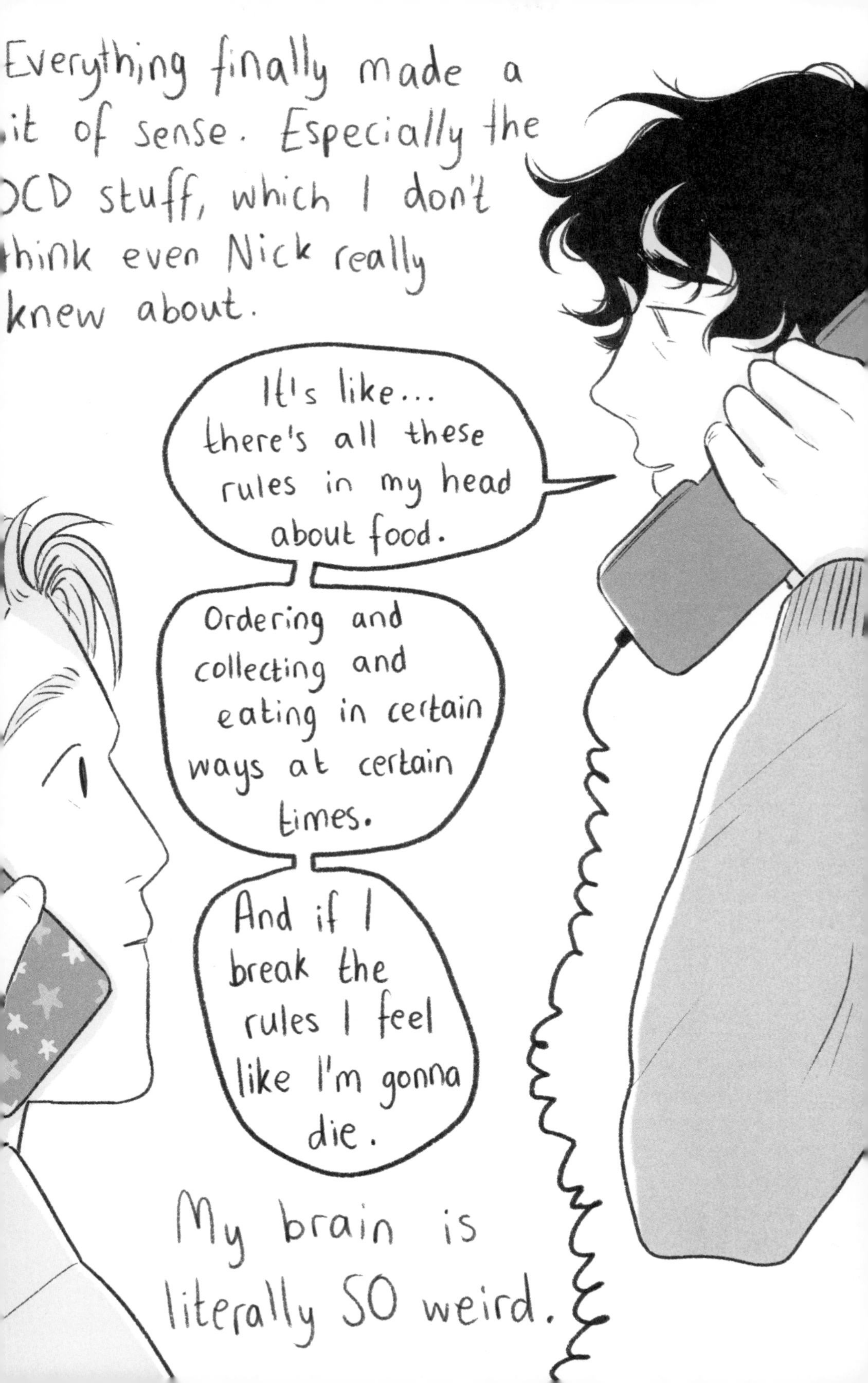
Everything finally made a bit of sense. Especially the OCD stuff, which I don't think even Nick really knew about.
It's like... there's all these rules in my head about food.
Ordering and collecting and eating in certain ways at certain times.
And if I break the rules I feel like I'm gonna die.
My brain is literally SO weird.

Being in hospital didn't make me completely free of mental illness. Not even close.

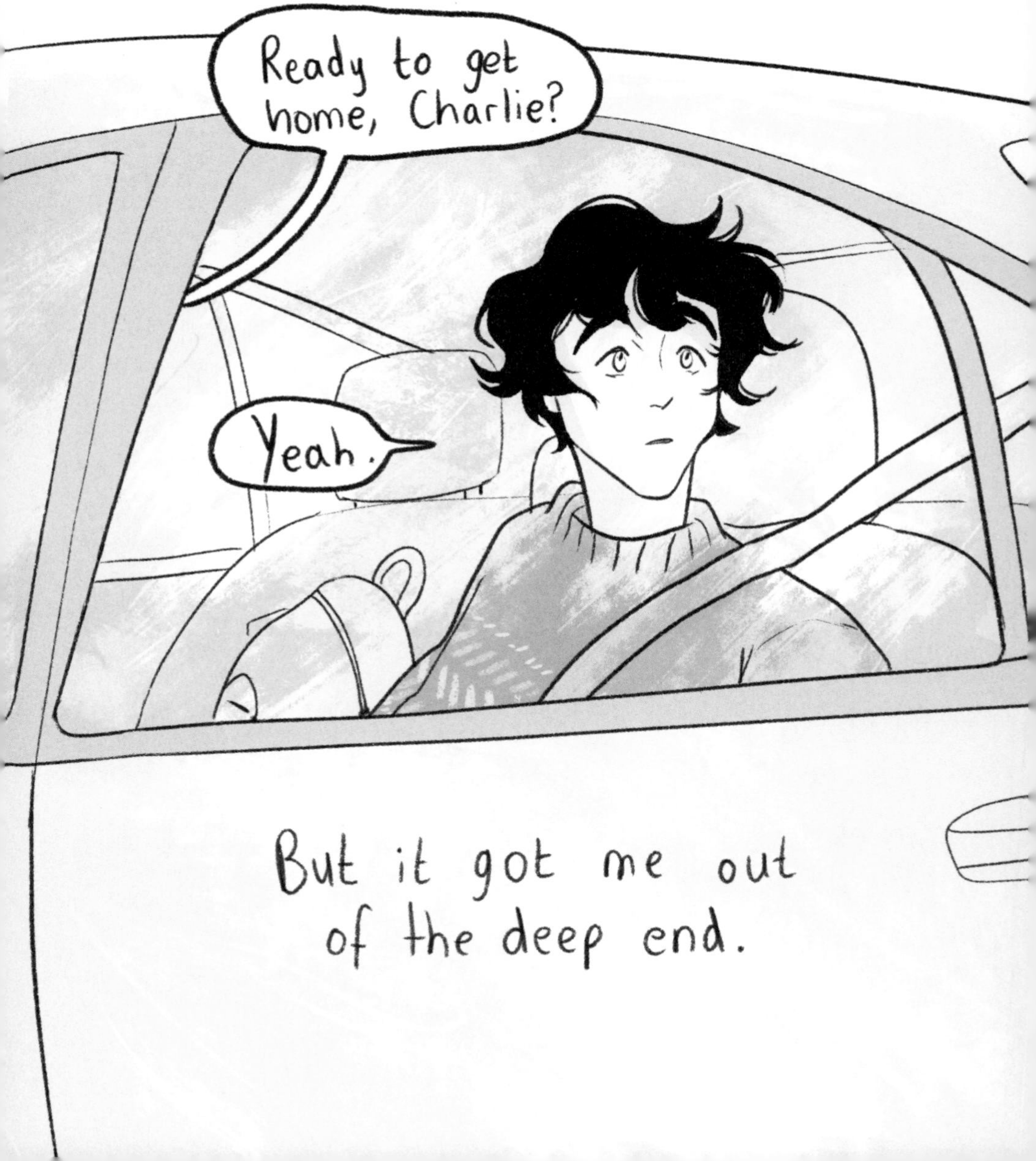
Ready to get home, Charlie?
Yeah.
But it got me out of the deep end.

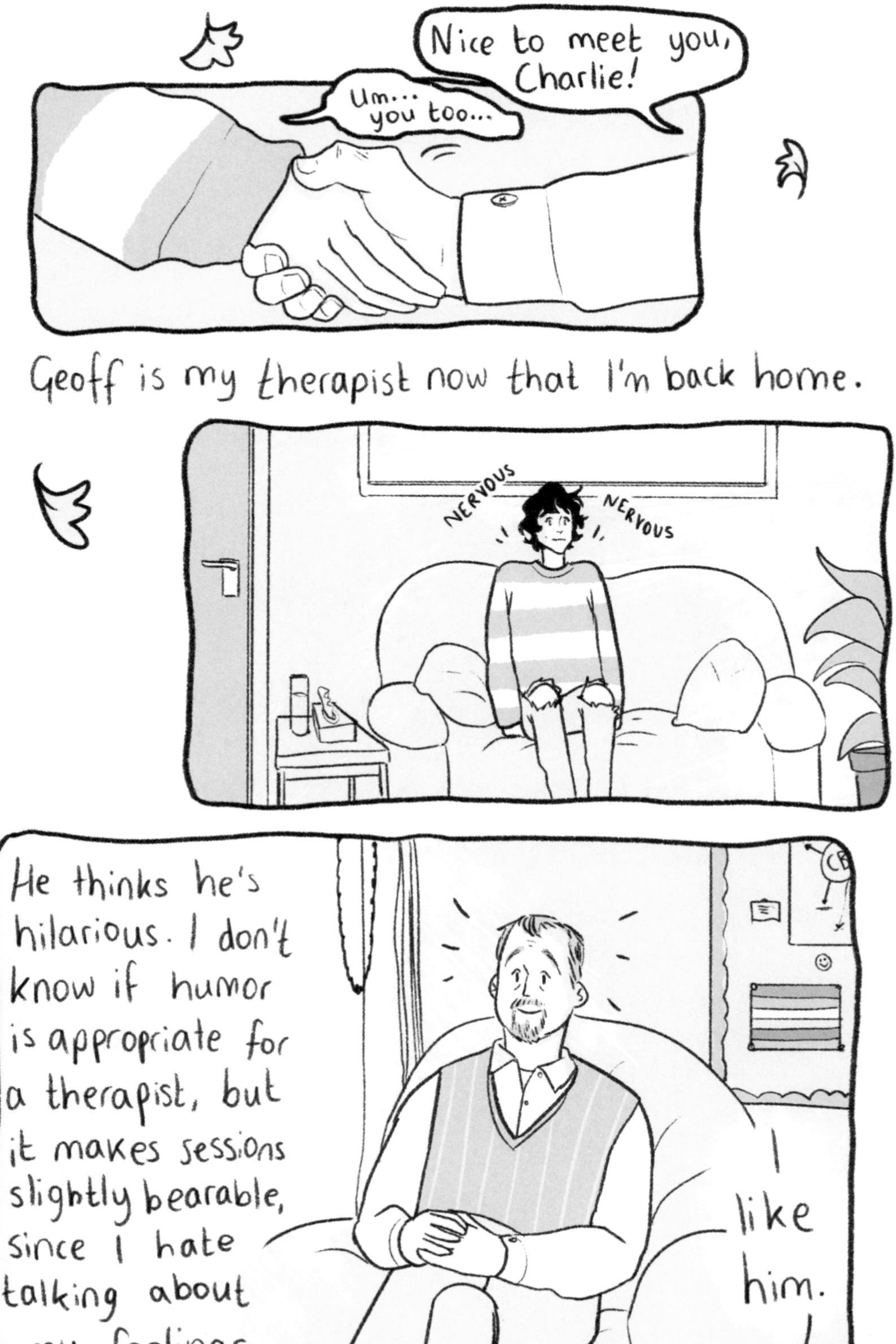
Nice to meet you, Charlie!
Um... you too...
Geoff is my therapist now that I'm back home.
NERVOUS
NERVOUS
He thinks he's hilarious. I don't know if humor is appropriate for a therapist, but it makes sessions slightly bearable, since I hate talking about my feelings.
I like him.

Me and Geoff have talked about what's happened in my life over the past couple of years.

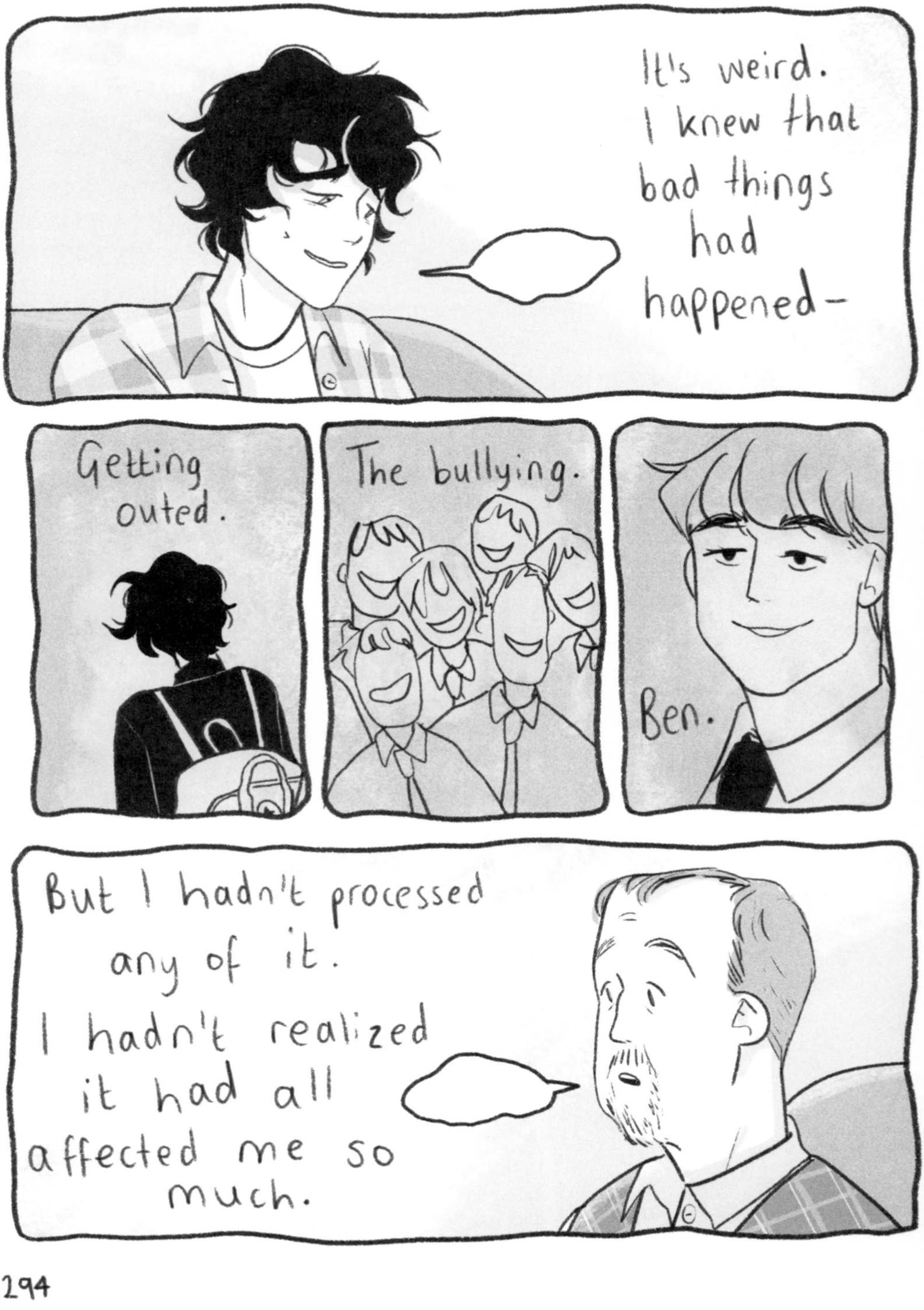
It's weird. I knew that bad things had happened-
Getting outed.
The bullying.
Ben.
But I hadn't processed any of it.
I hadn't realized it had all affected me so much.

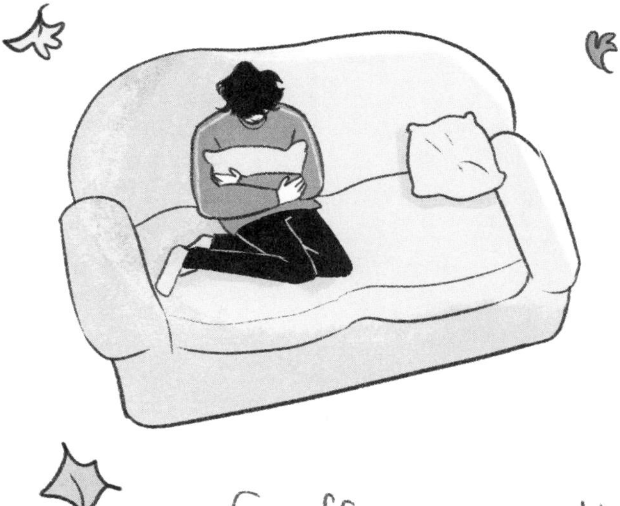

Geoff says it's trauma.

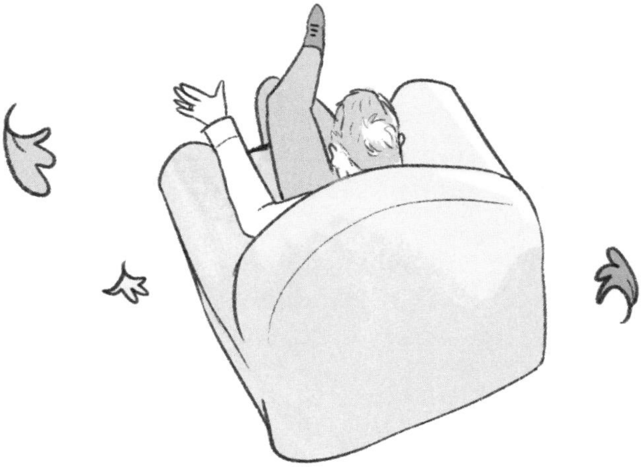

Kind of a dramatic word, I guess, but Geoff says trauma can come from all sorts of things.

Geoff says I'm making progress, but I think I'm realizing now that there might never be an "end".

This could be something that will always be there in the back of my mind, waiting to emerge again and bring all the bad feelings back.

TAP TAP TAP

Some days I'm fine, but others I wake up and I just _know_.

I know that day is gonna be awful.

But Geoff also says the bad days will get less common. And I can just enjoy my life and hardly ever stress out about food.

Some days I think he's full of shit.

But some days I feel hopeful. I guess I'll have to keep trying.

So I went back to school after the Christmas holidays!

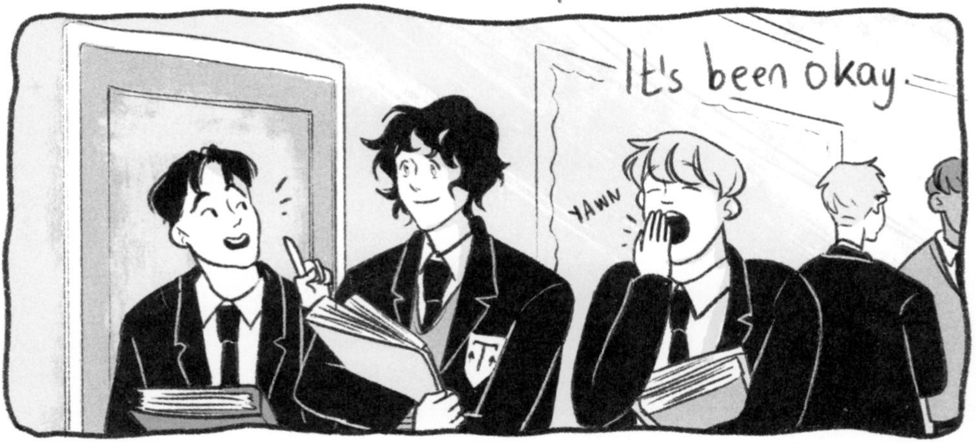
It's been okay.
YAWN

A couple of teachers knew what had happened.

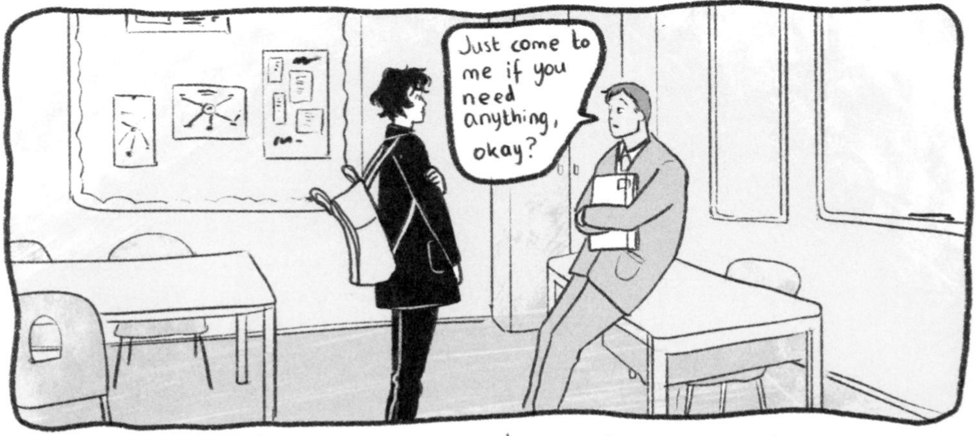
Just come to me if you need anything, okay?

Mr. Farouk and Miss Singh have been really supportive.

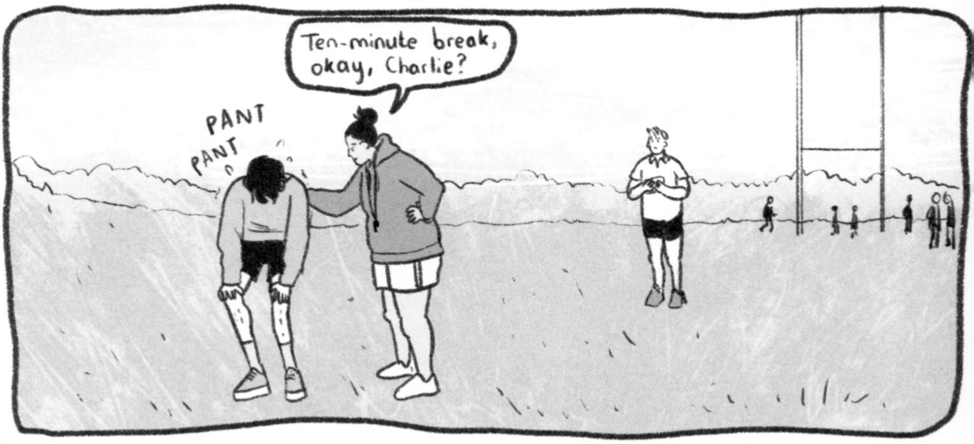
Ten-minute break, okay, Charlie?
PANT
PANT

Especially as rugby has been kinda hard.

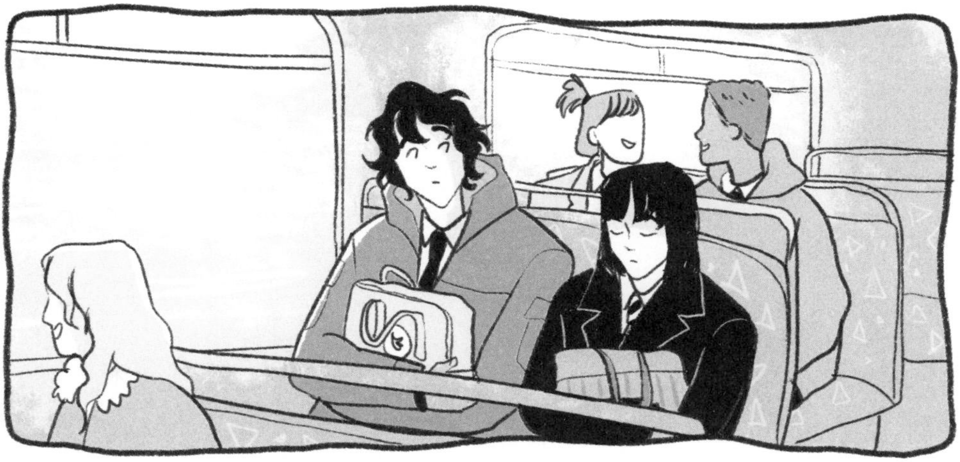

I think Tori feels guilty about everything.

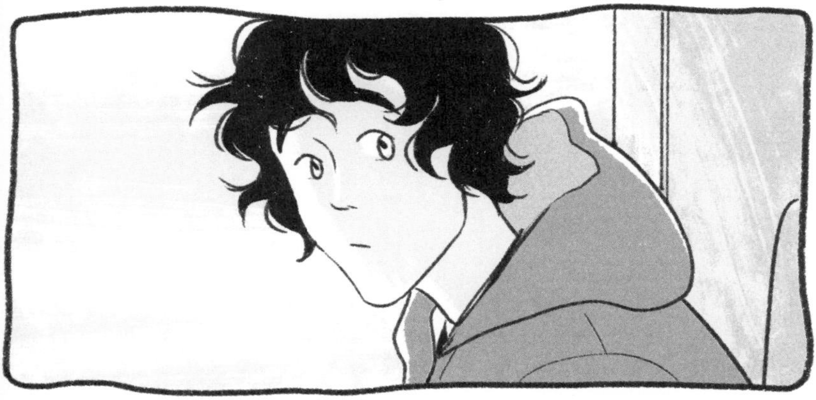

She shouldn't, but...

her mental health hasn't been great either.

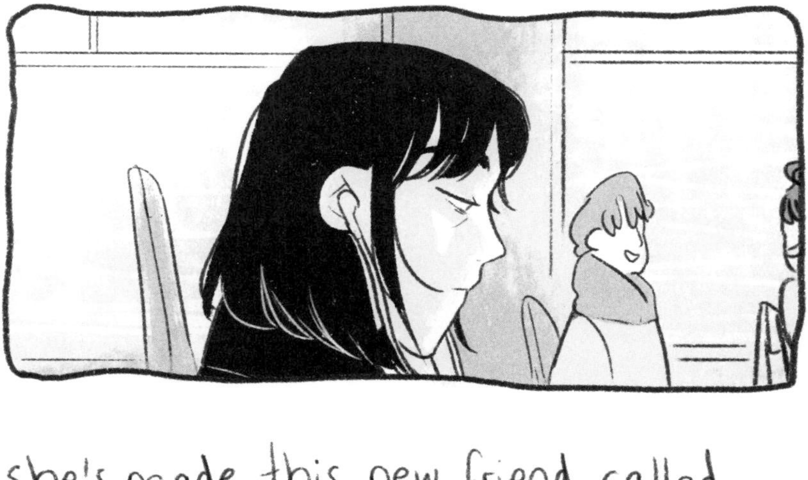

But she's made this new friend called Michael.

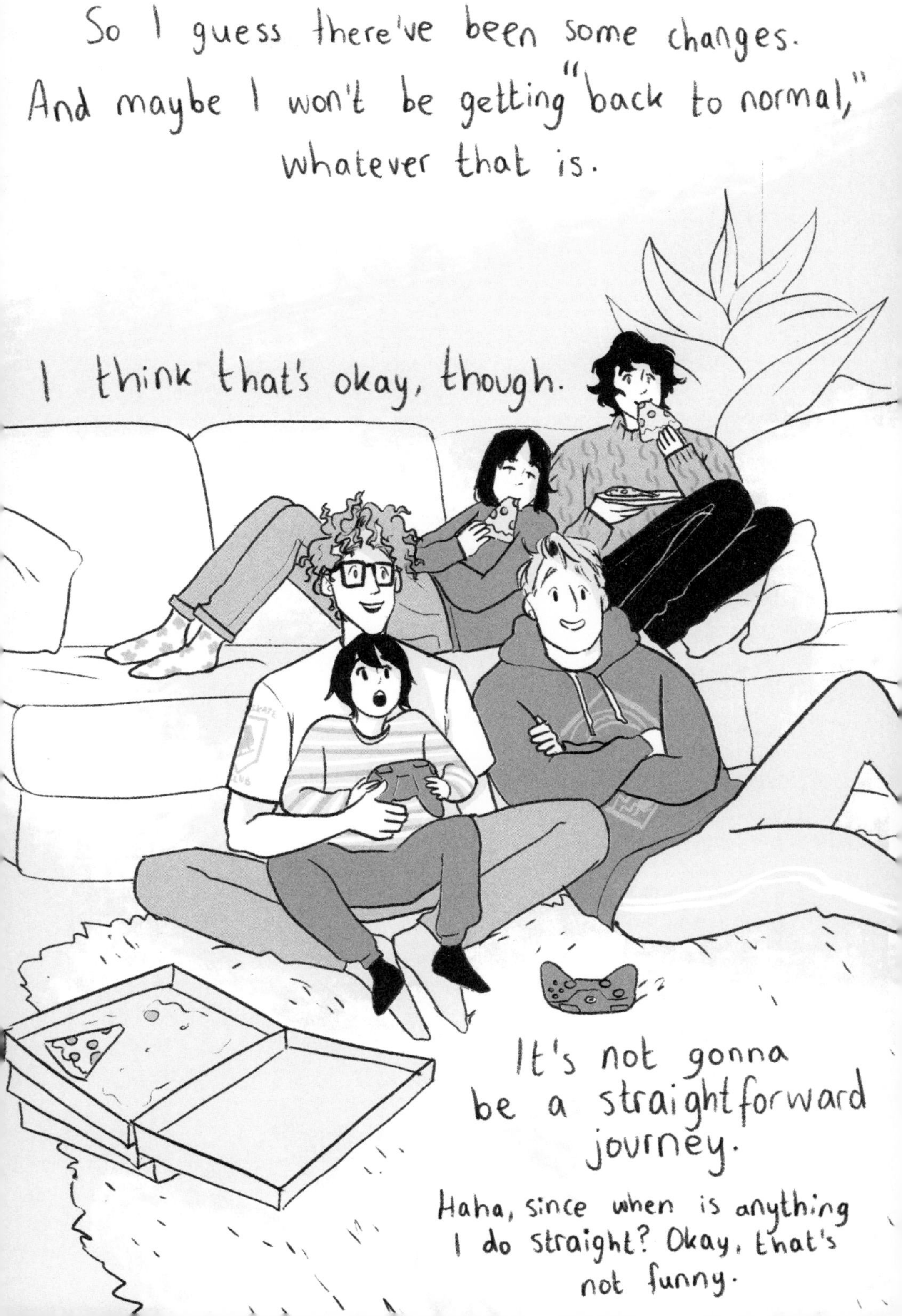
So I guess there've been some changes. And maybe I won't be getting "back to normal," whatever that is.
I think that's okay, though.
It's not gonna be a straightforward journey.
Haha, since when is anything I do straight? Okay, that's not funny.

It wasn't anyone's fault. Relapses happen.
Tori told Nick what had happened, and
he came back later that night.

We
made
up.

Mum and Dad even let him stay over to "keep an eye on me."

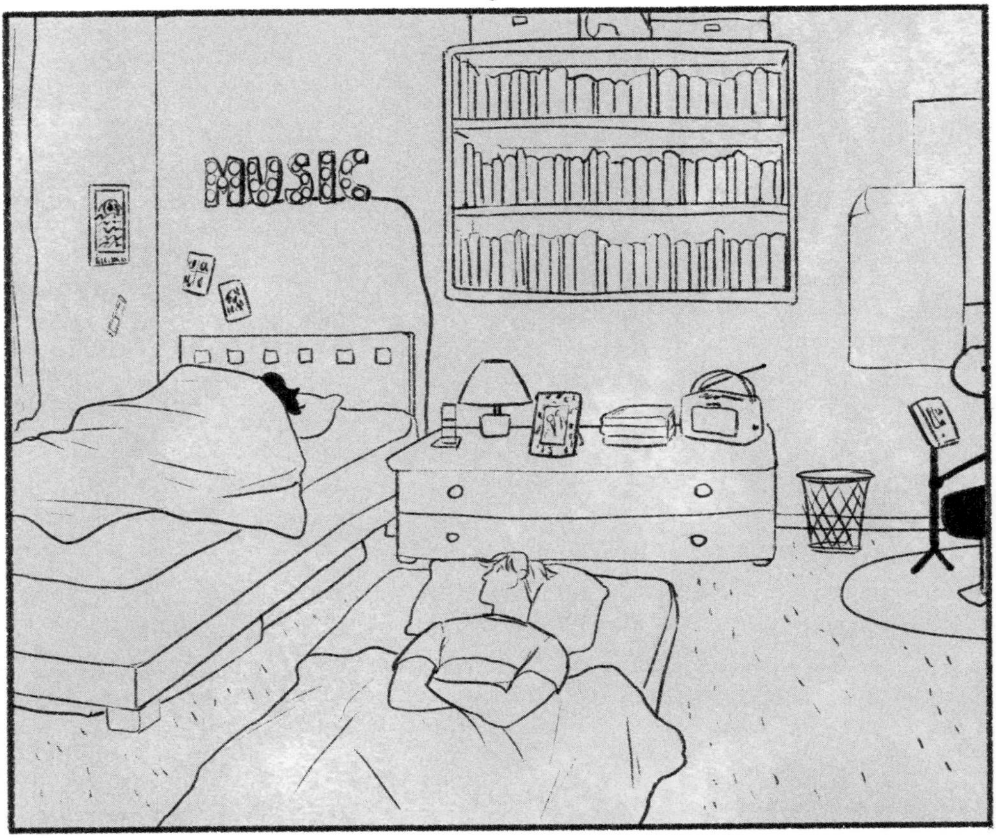
MUSIC

Not really necessary, but I wasn't complaining.

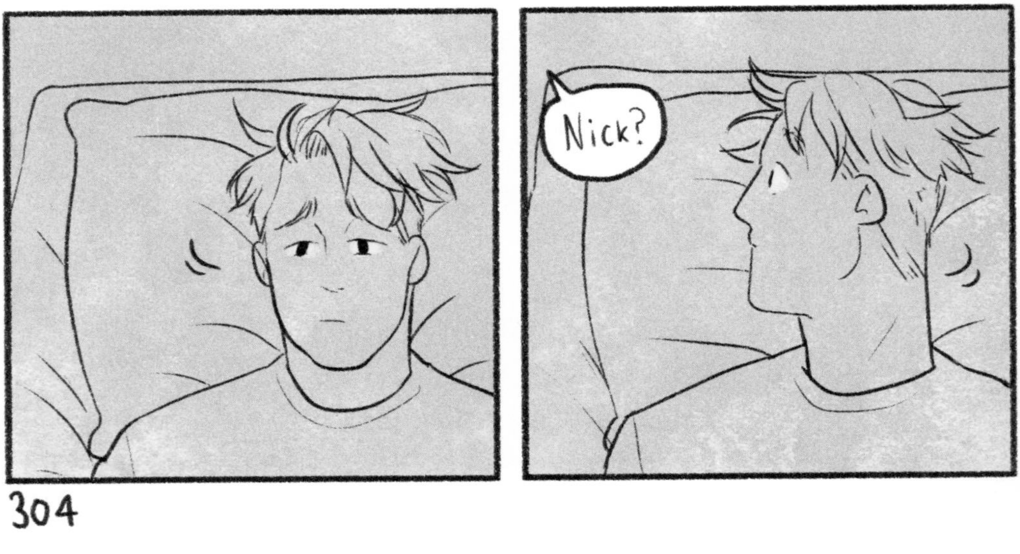
Nick?

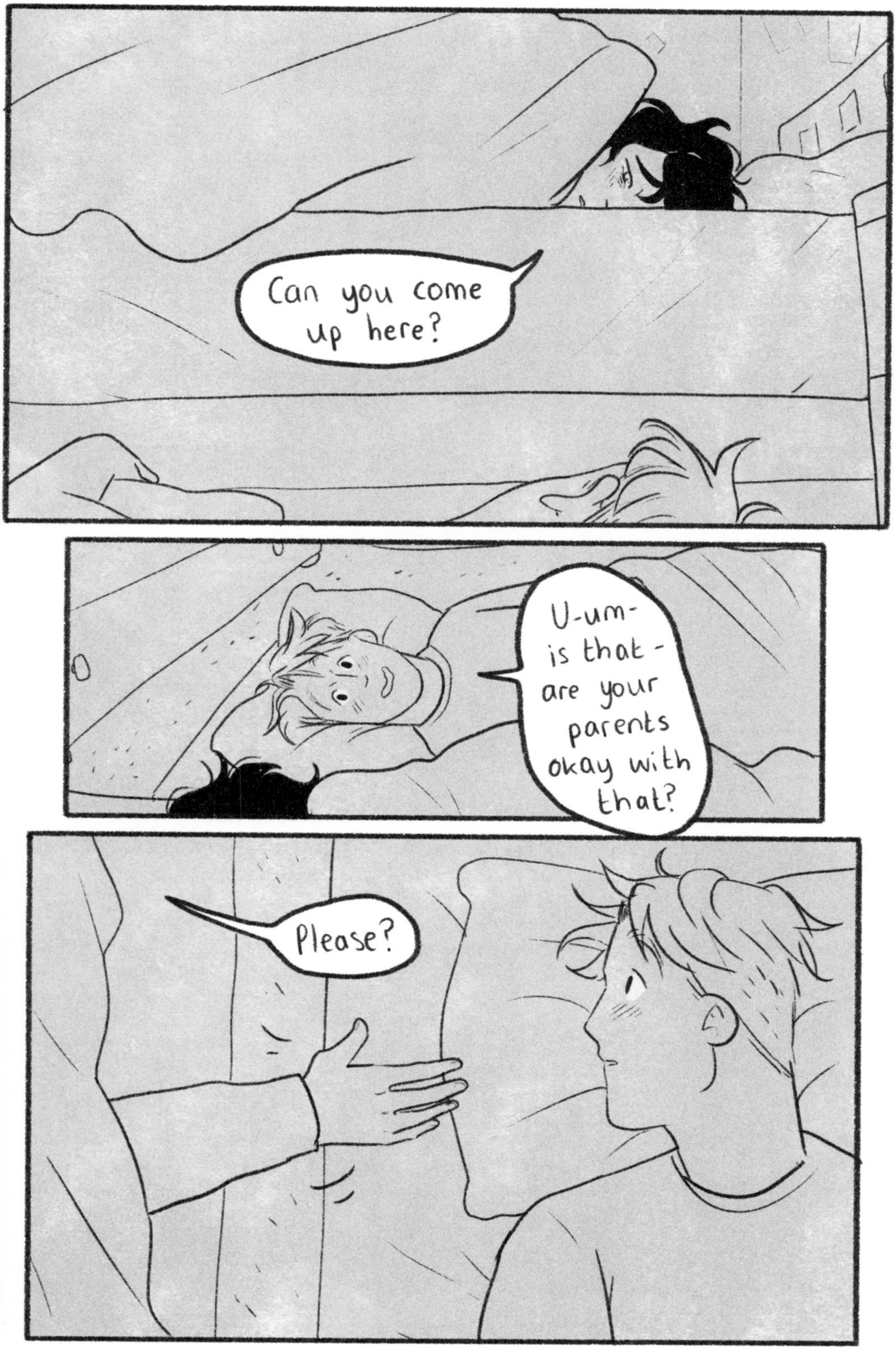
Can you come up here?
U-um- is that - are your parents okay with that?
Please?

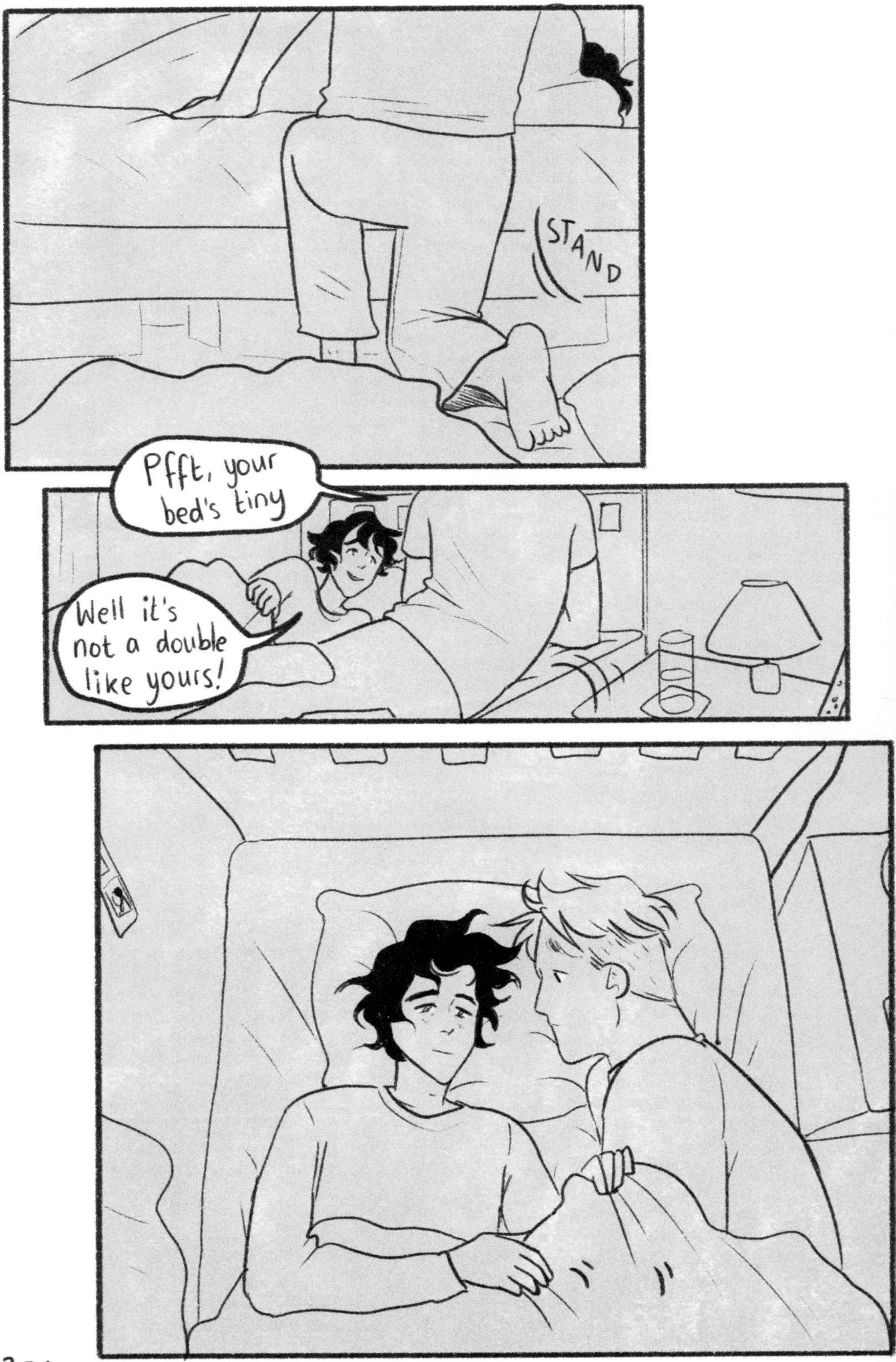
STAND
Pfft, your bed's tiny
Well it's not a double like yours!

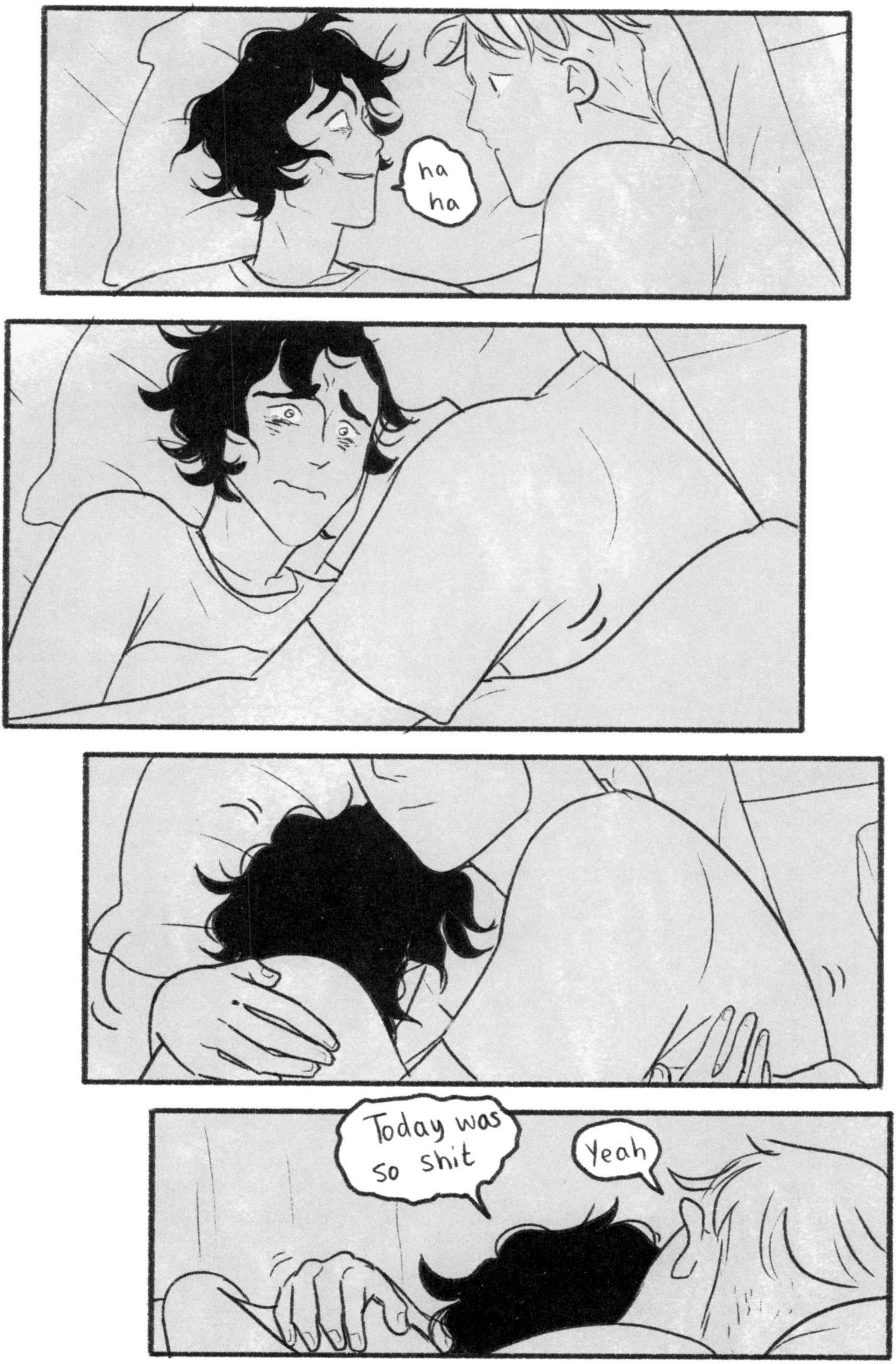
ha ha
Today was so shit
Yeah

I love Nick.

I love Nick so, so much.

But what I've realized through all
of this is that we need
other people too.

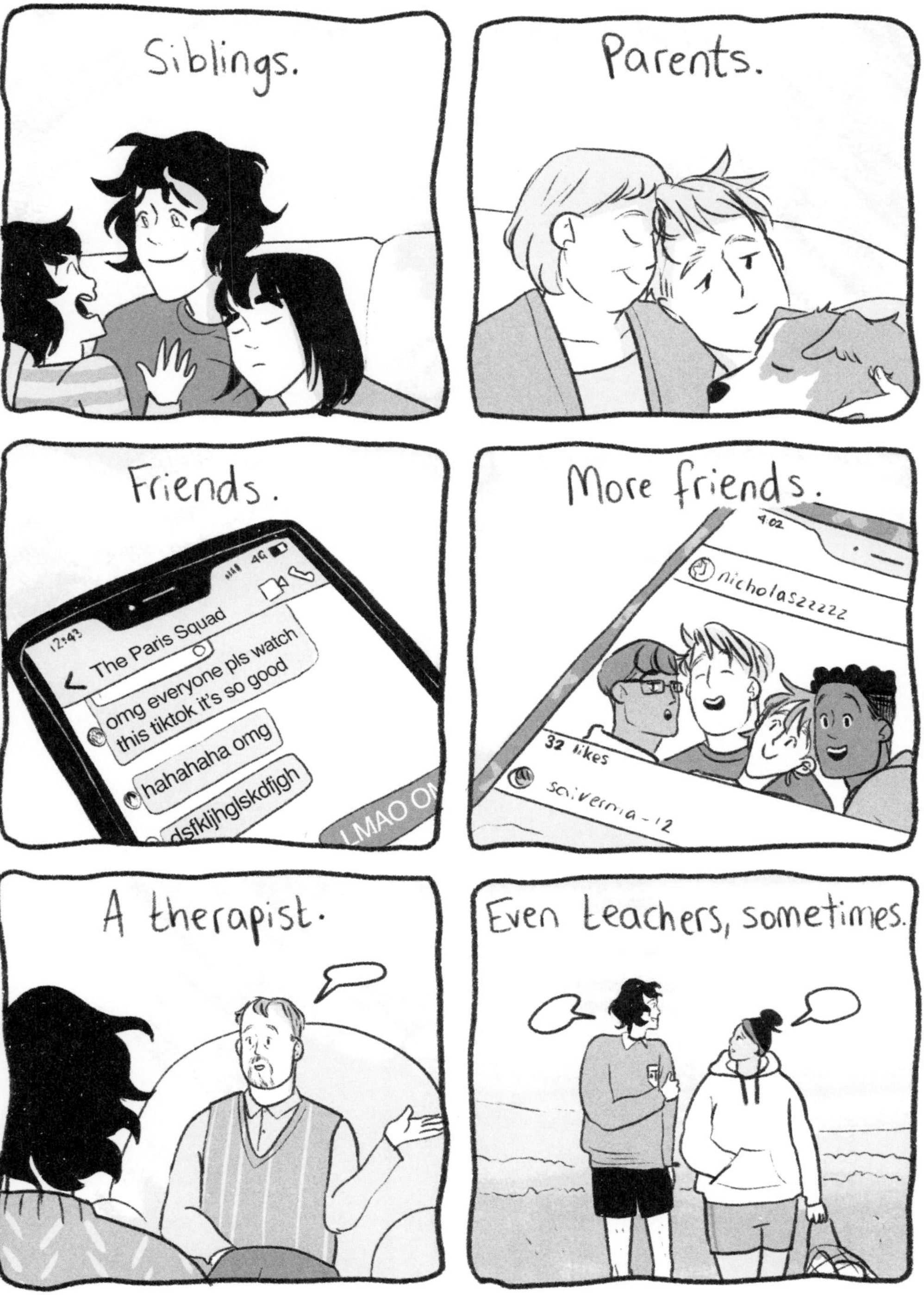
Siblings.
Parents.
Friends.
12:43
The Paris Squad
omg everyone pls watch this tiktok it's so good
hahahaha omg
dsfkljnglskdfjgh
More friends.
4:02
nicholaszzzzz
32 likes
saivernia_12
A therapist.
Even teachers, sometimes.

That doesn't mean our relationship isn't strong.

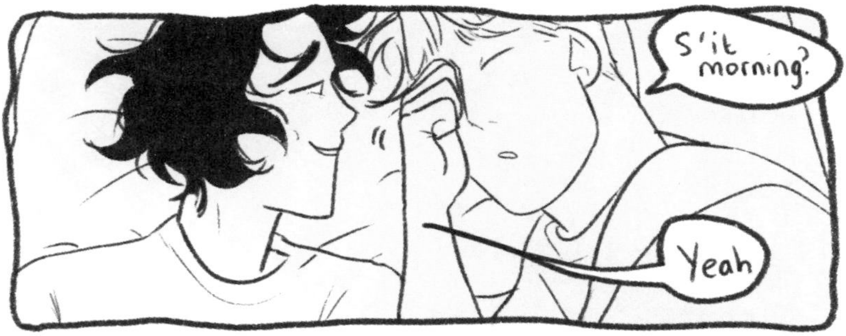
S'it morning?
Yeah

If anything...

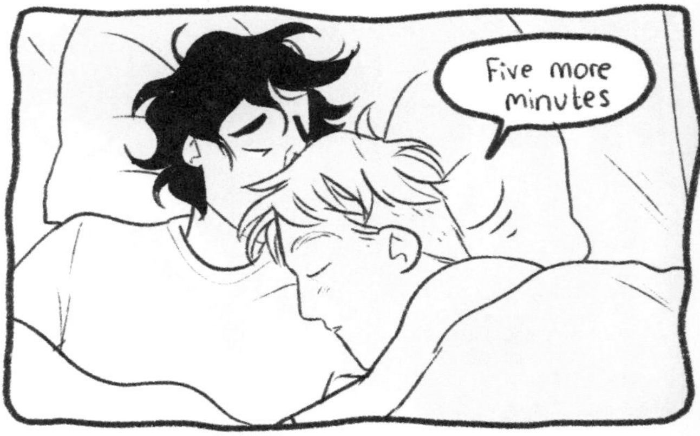
Five more minutes

I think we're stronger now.

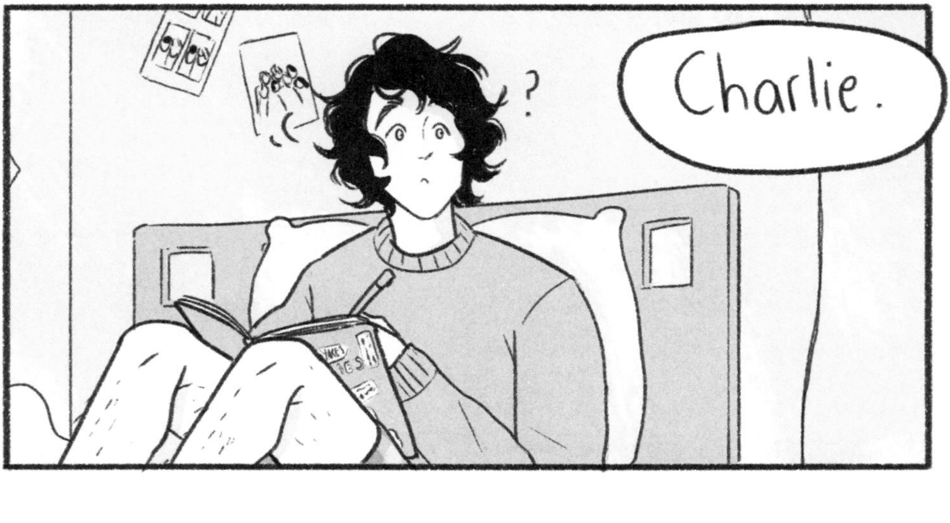
?
Charlie.

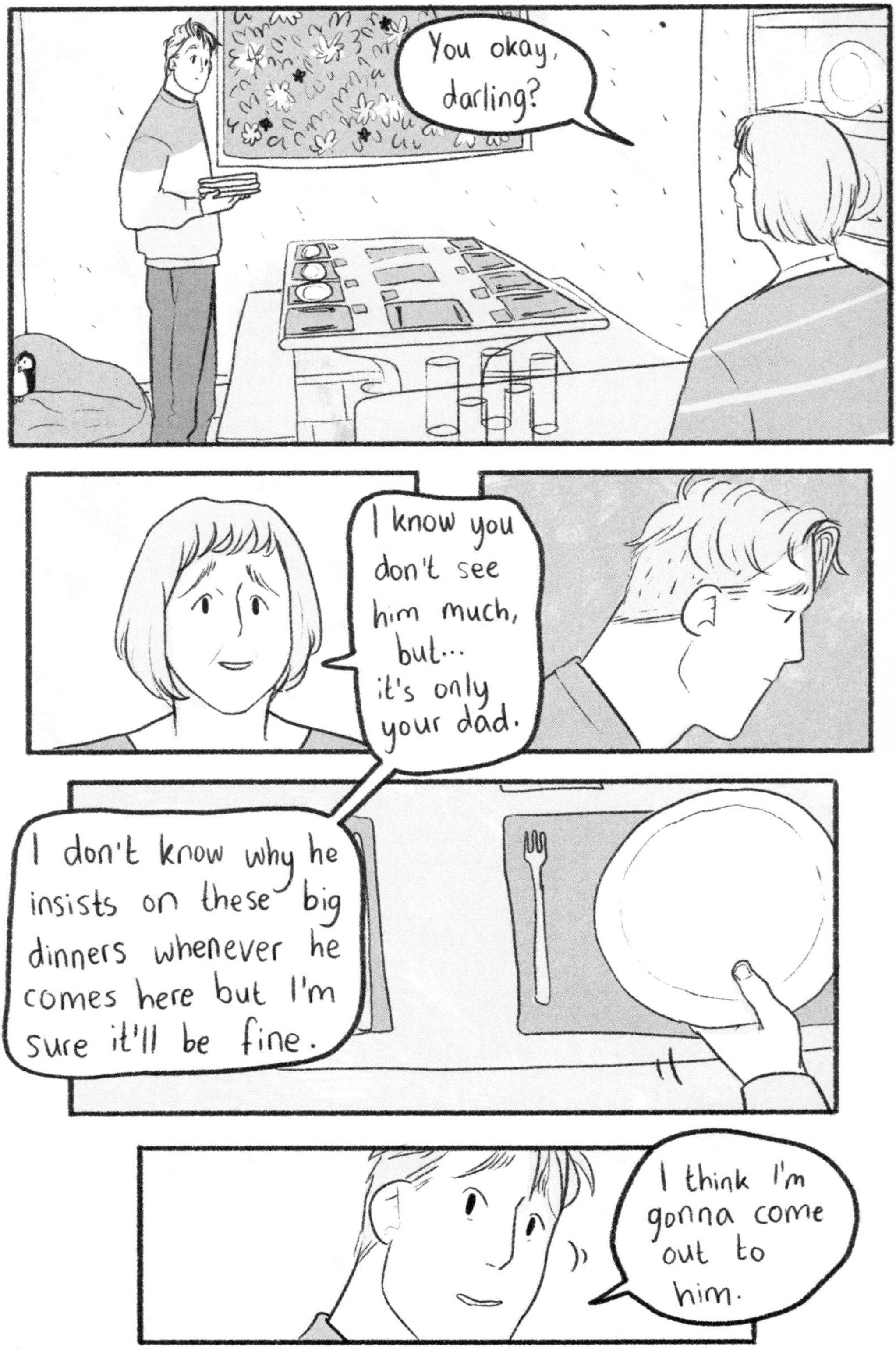

You okay, darling?
I know you don't see him much, but... it's only your dad.
I don't know why he insists on these big dinners whenever he comes here but I'm sure it'll be fine.
I think I'm gonna come out to him.

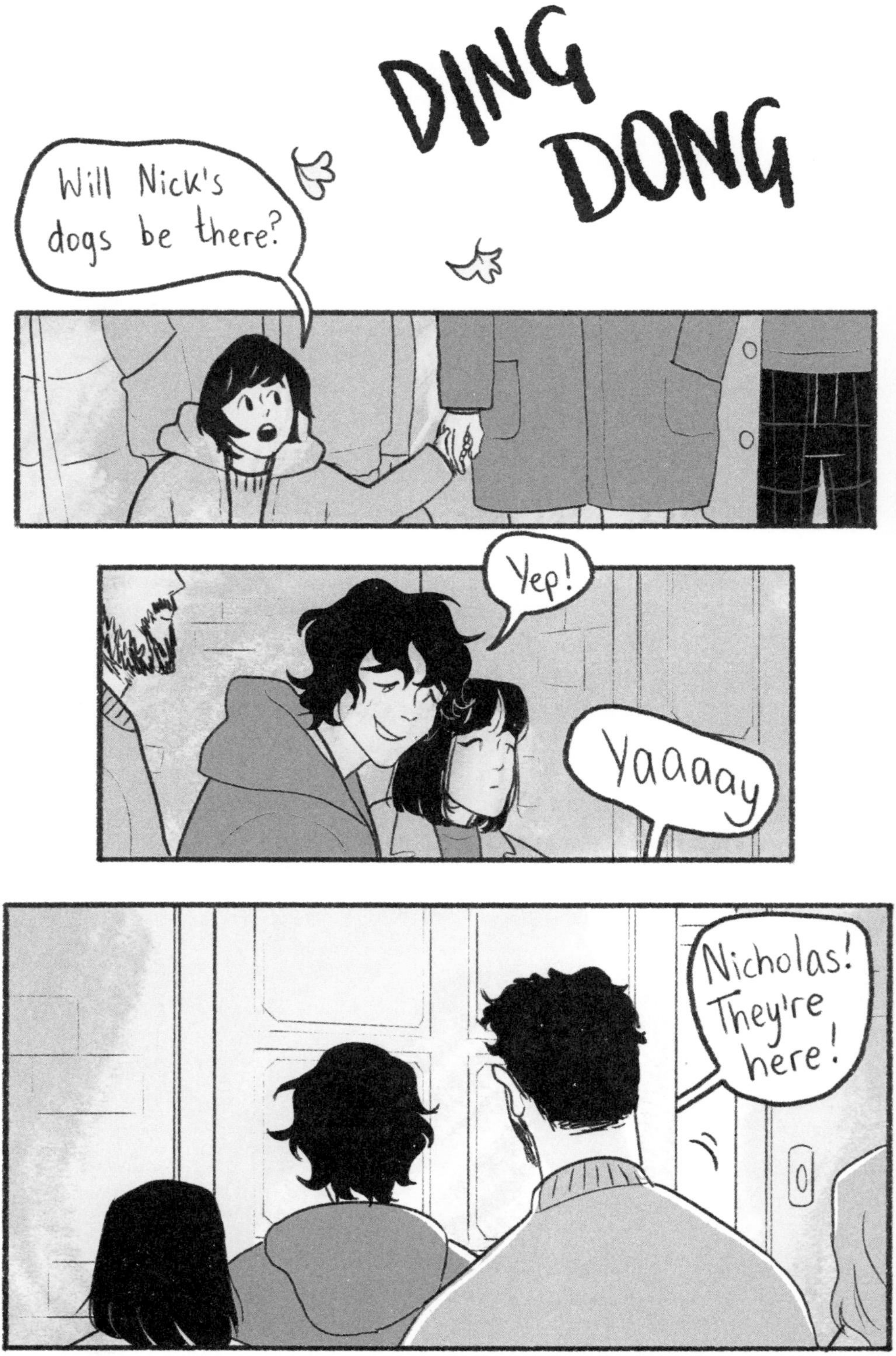
DING DONG
Will Nick's dogs be there?
Yep!
Yaaaay
Nicholas! They're here!

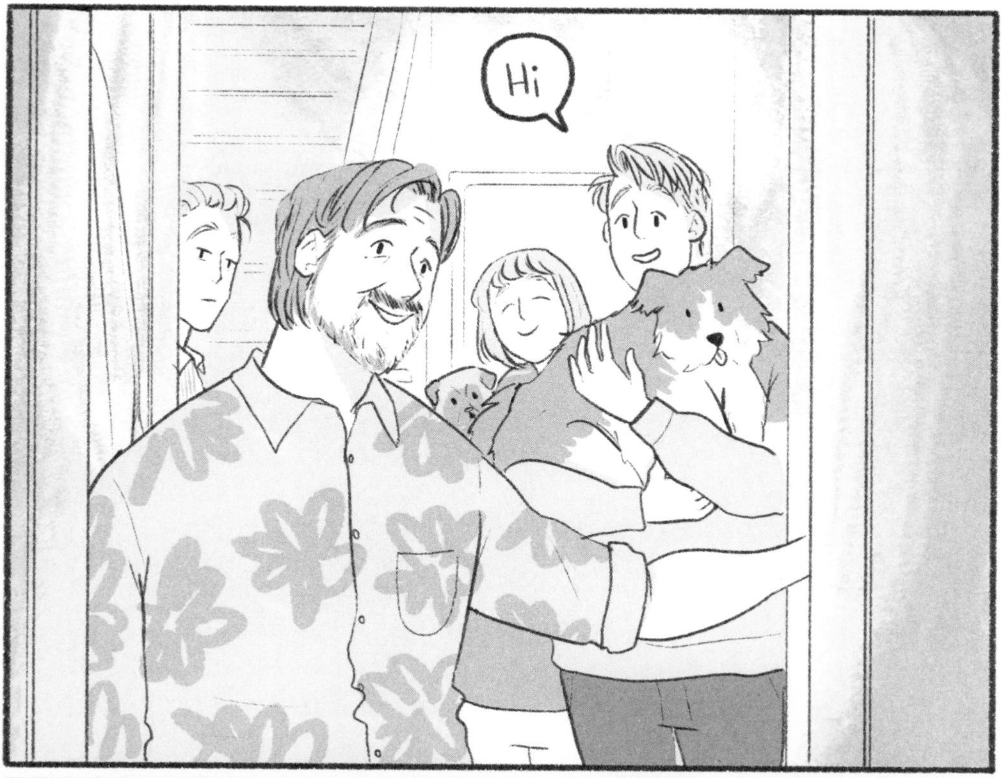
Hi

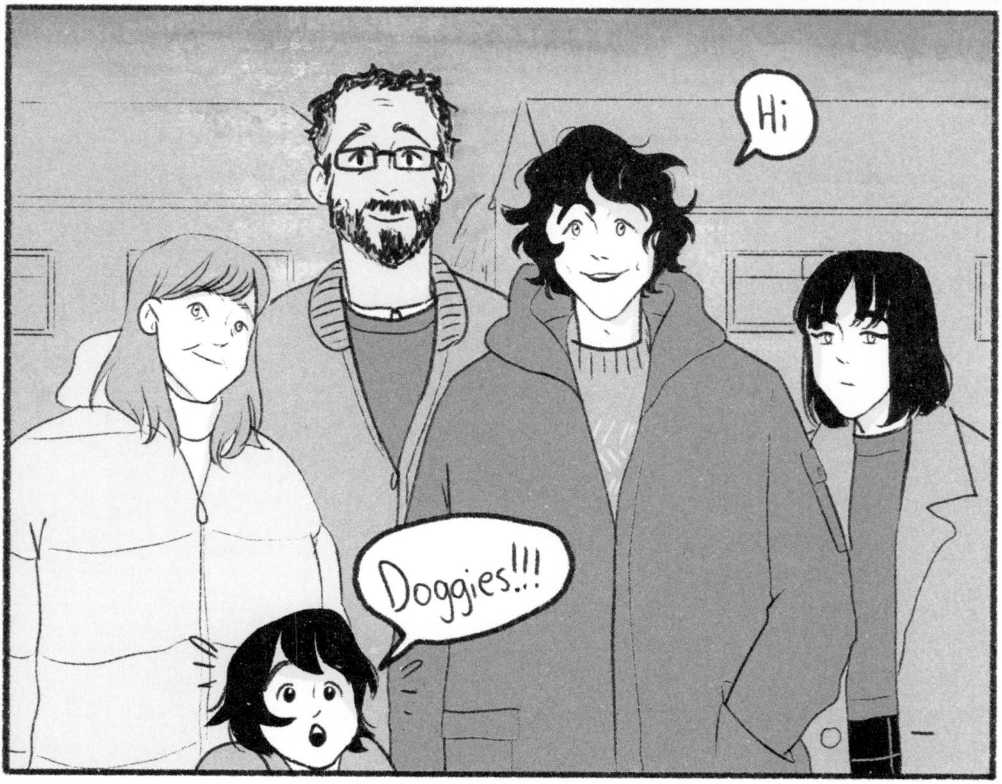
Hi
Doggies!!!

319

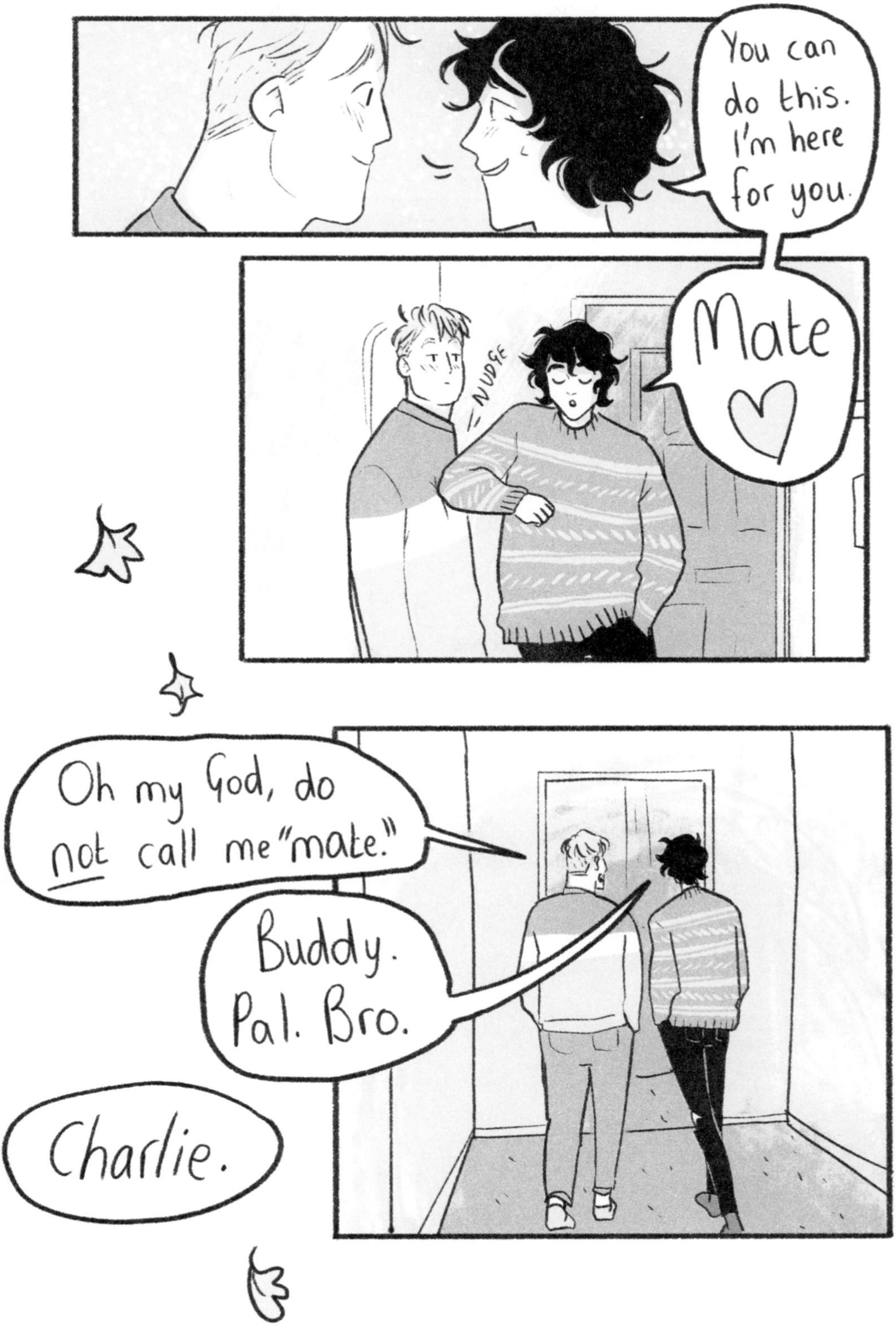

You can do this. I'm here for you.
Mate
NUDGE
Oh my God, do not call me "mate."
Buddy. Pal. Bro.
Charlie.

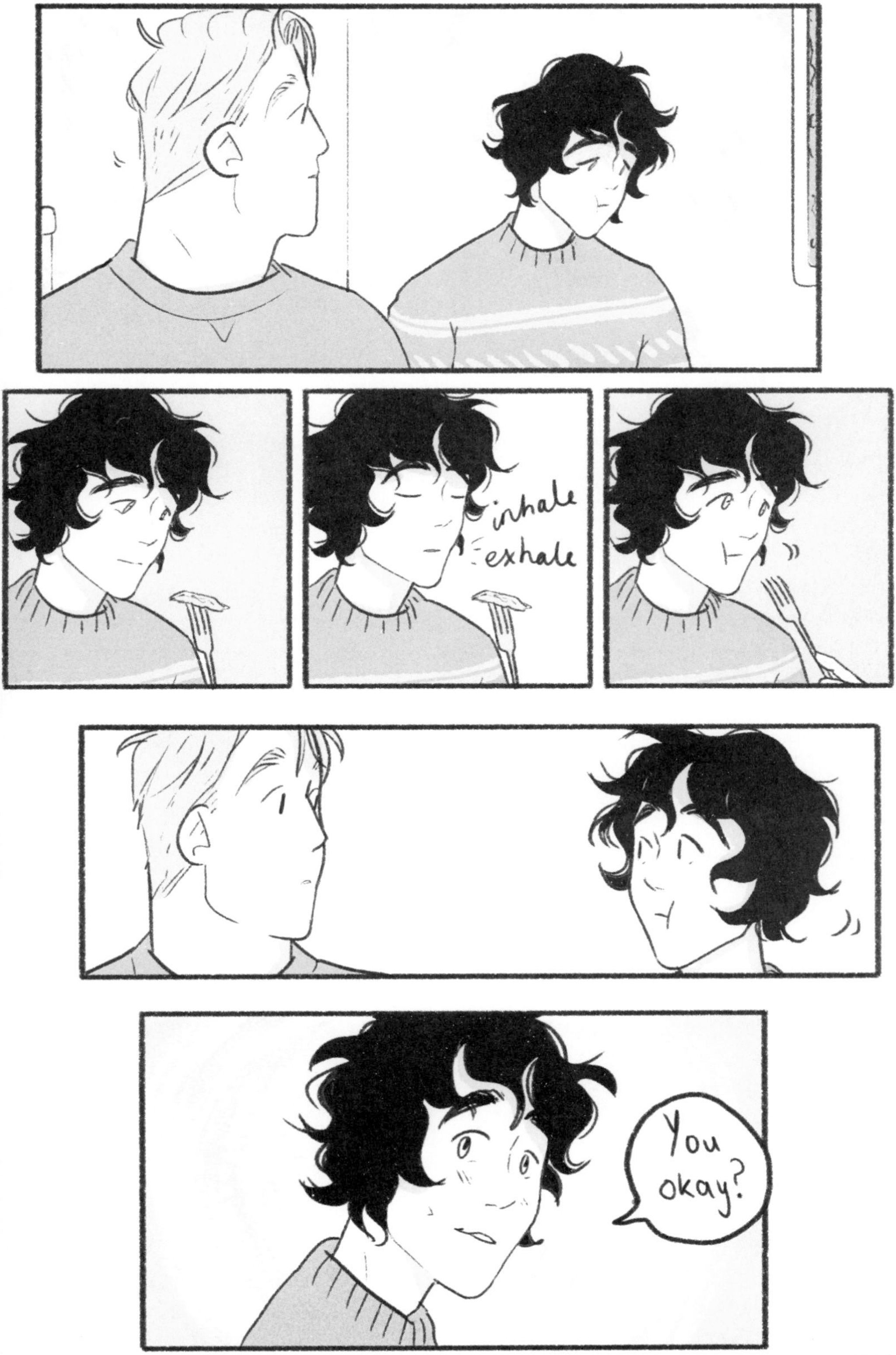
inhale
exhale
You okay?

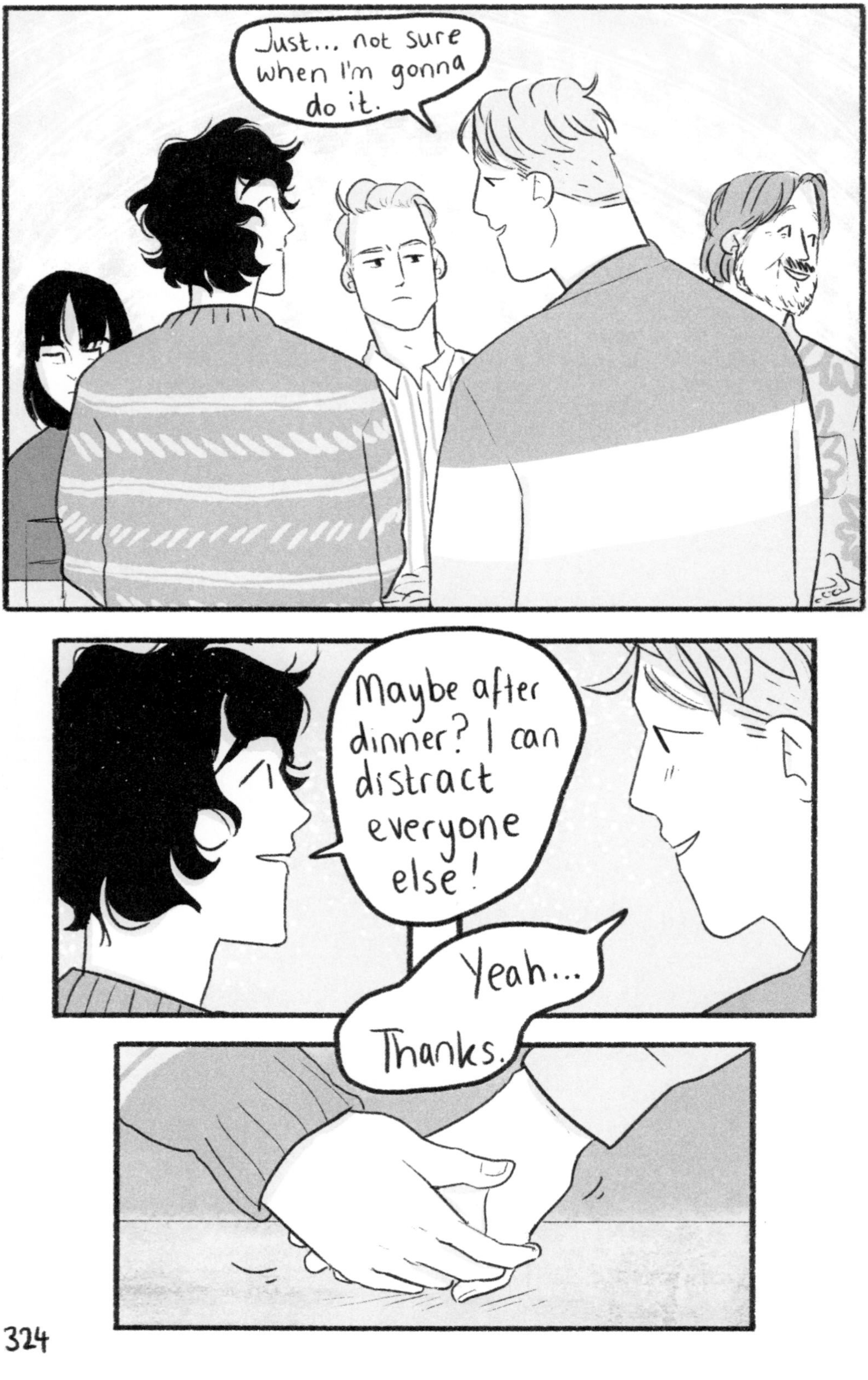
Just... not sure when I'm gonna do it.
Maybe after dinner? I can distract everyone else!
Yeah...
Thanks.

Yeah, Nick was basically obsessed with getting Charlie to join.
Wonder why that was.
You know, the girls love rugby players.
I played a bit of rugby when I was in this country at university. It is a very attractive sport to women!
Have neither of you boys found girlfriends?
...

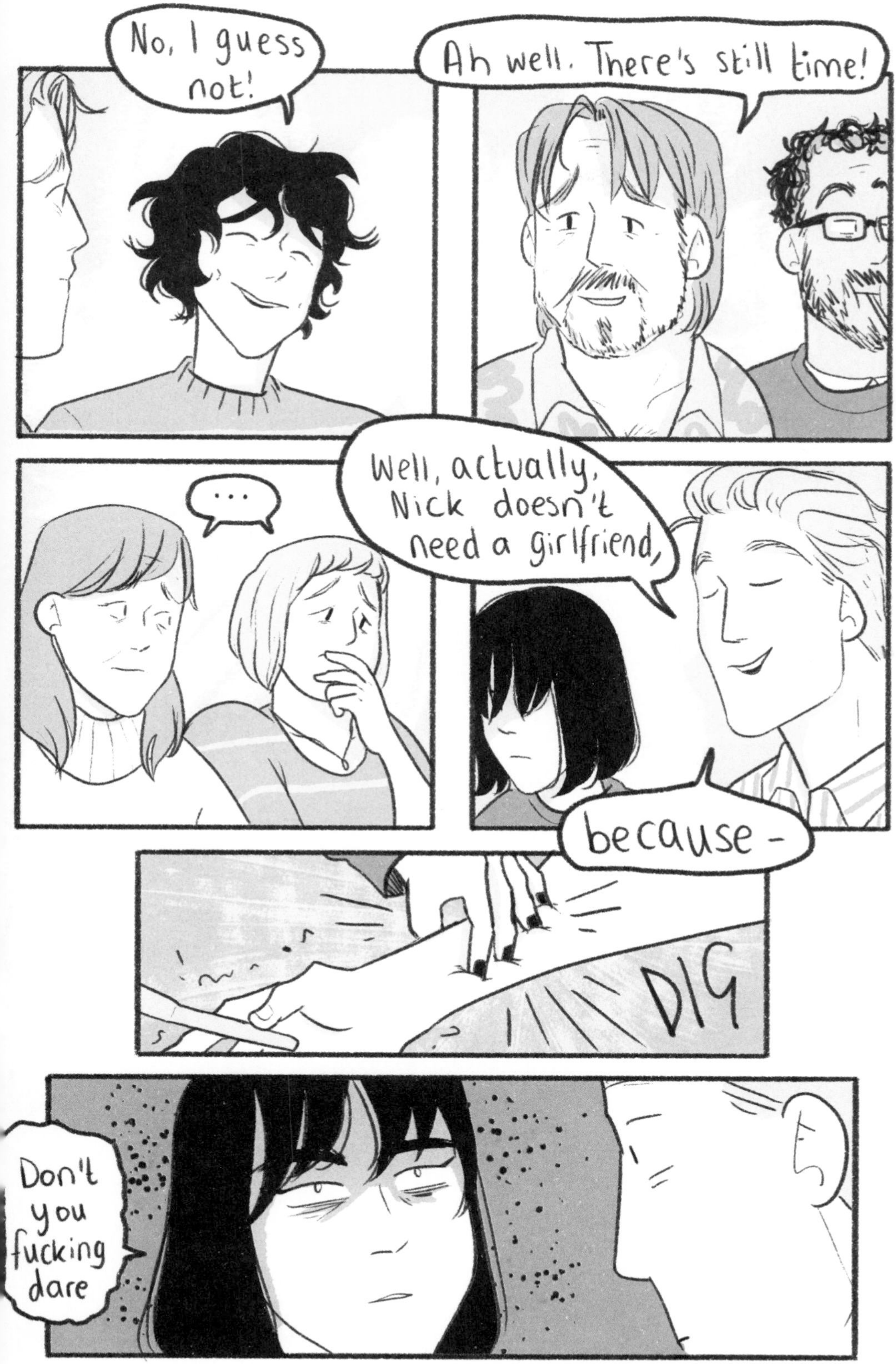
No, I guess not!
Ah well. There's still time!
...
Well, actually, Nick doesn't need a girlfriend,
because -
DIG
Don't you fucking dare

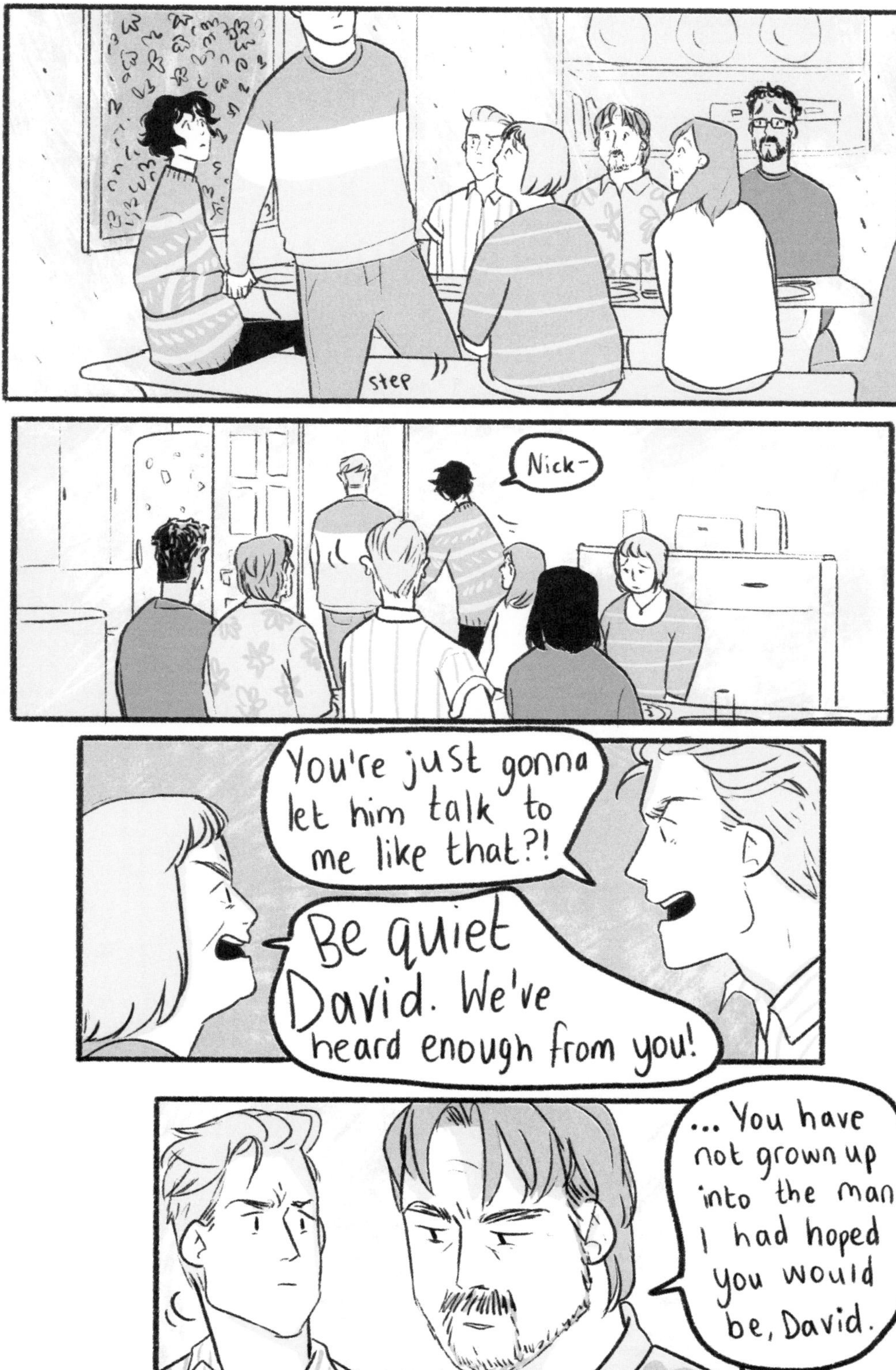

step
Nick-
You're just gonna let him talk to me like that?!
Be quiet David. We've heard enough from you!
...You have not grown up into the man I had hoped you would be, David.

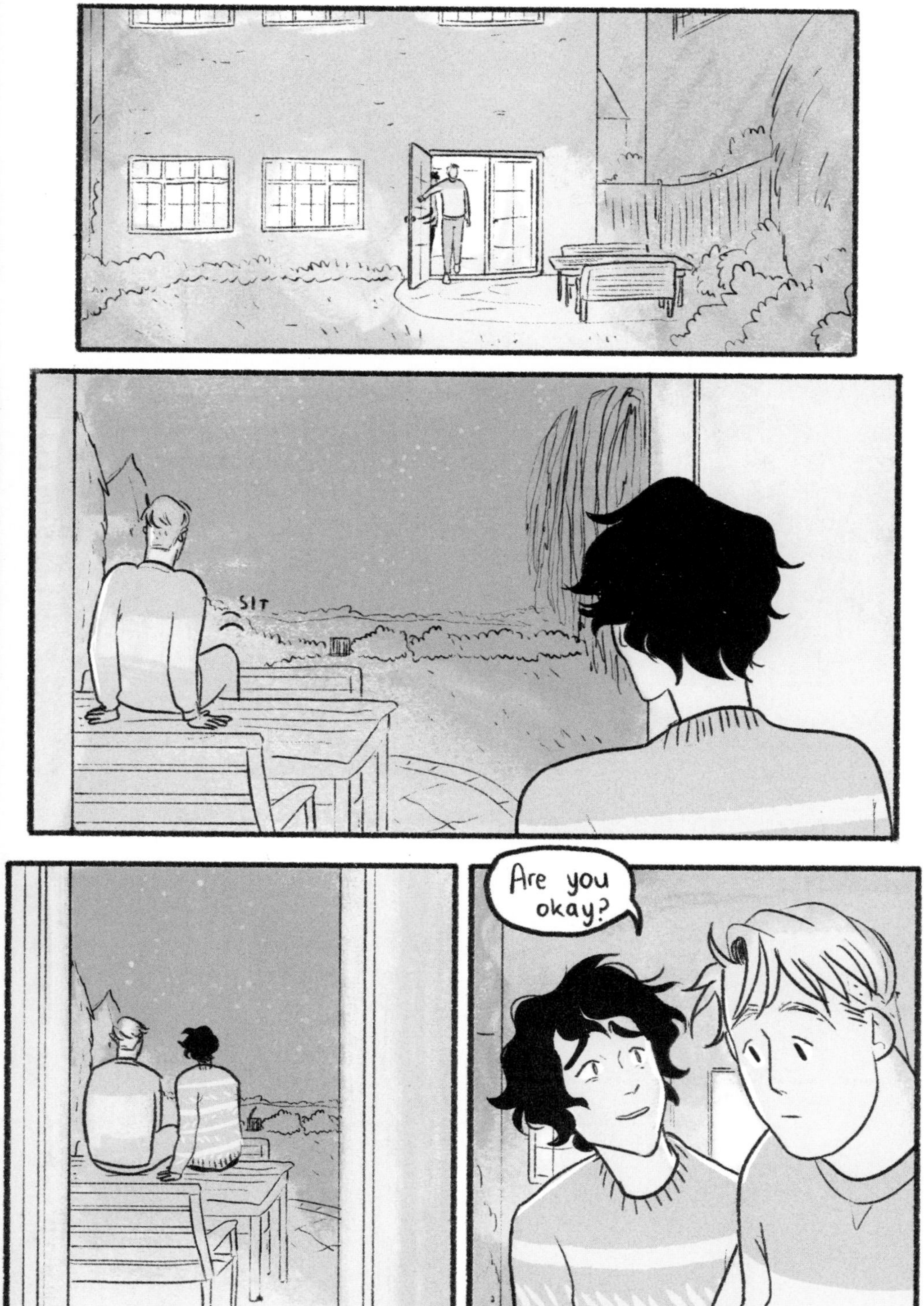
SIT
Are you okay?

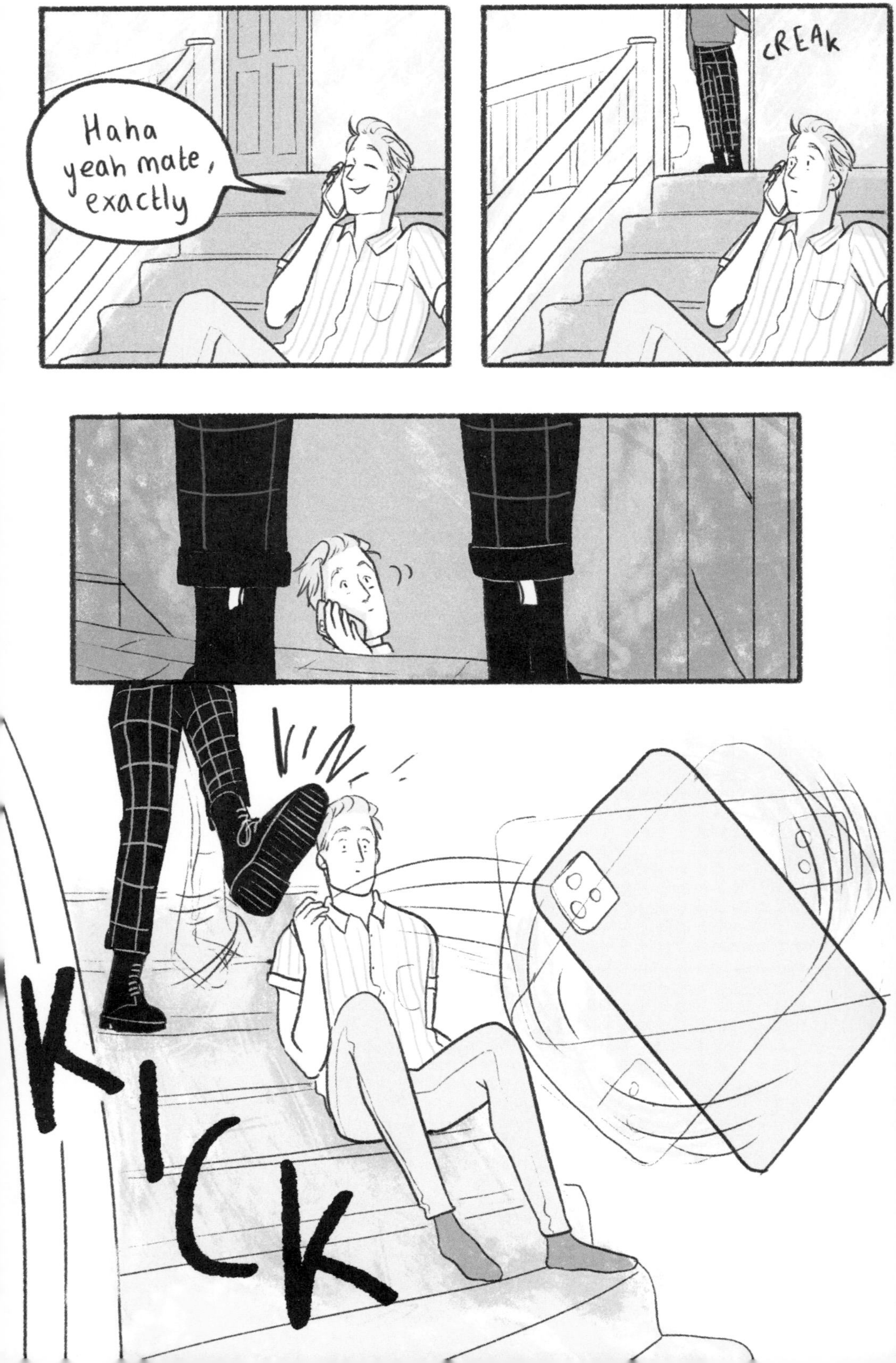
Haha yeah mate, exactly
CREAK
KICK

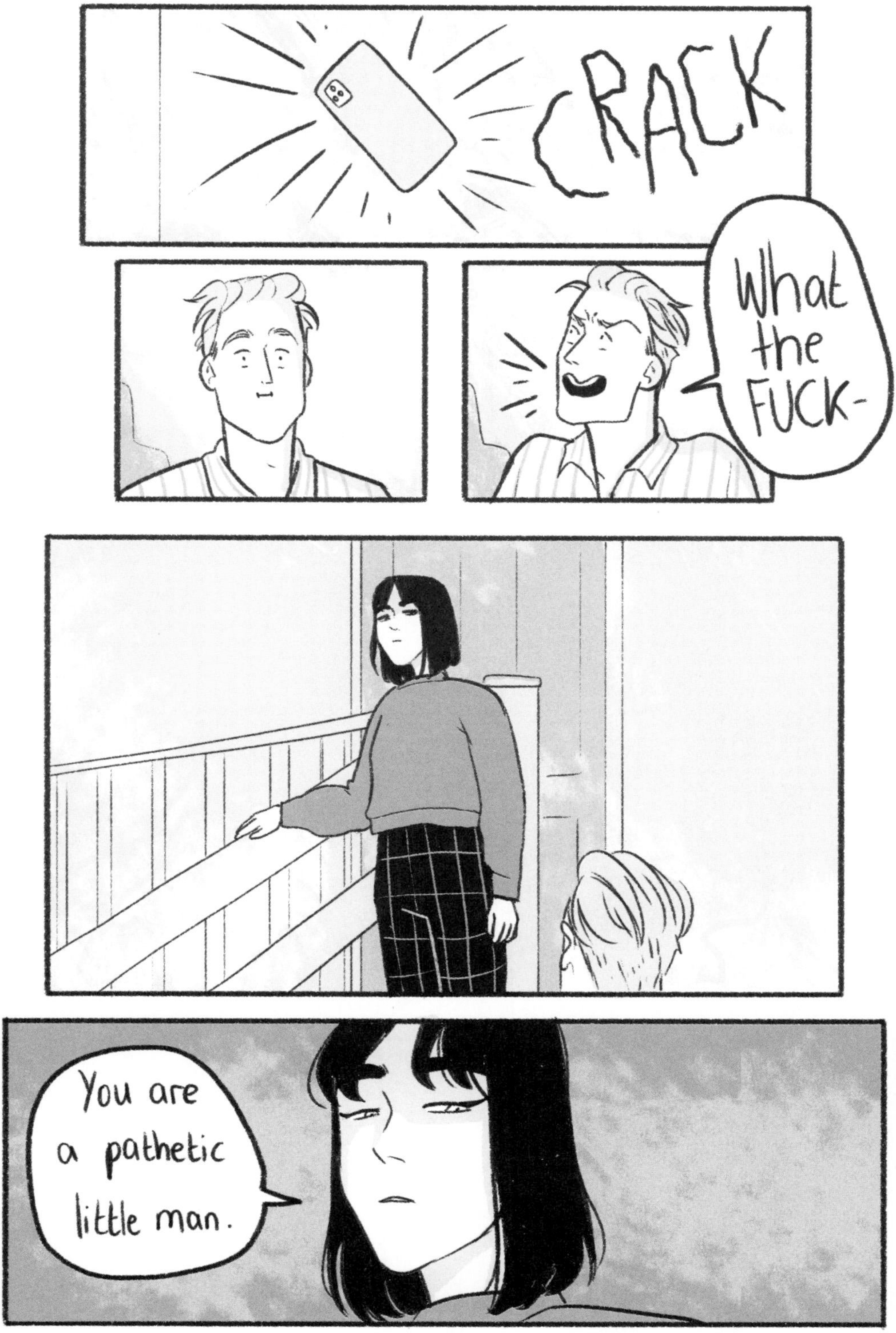
CRACK
What the FUCK-
You are a pathetic little man.

345

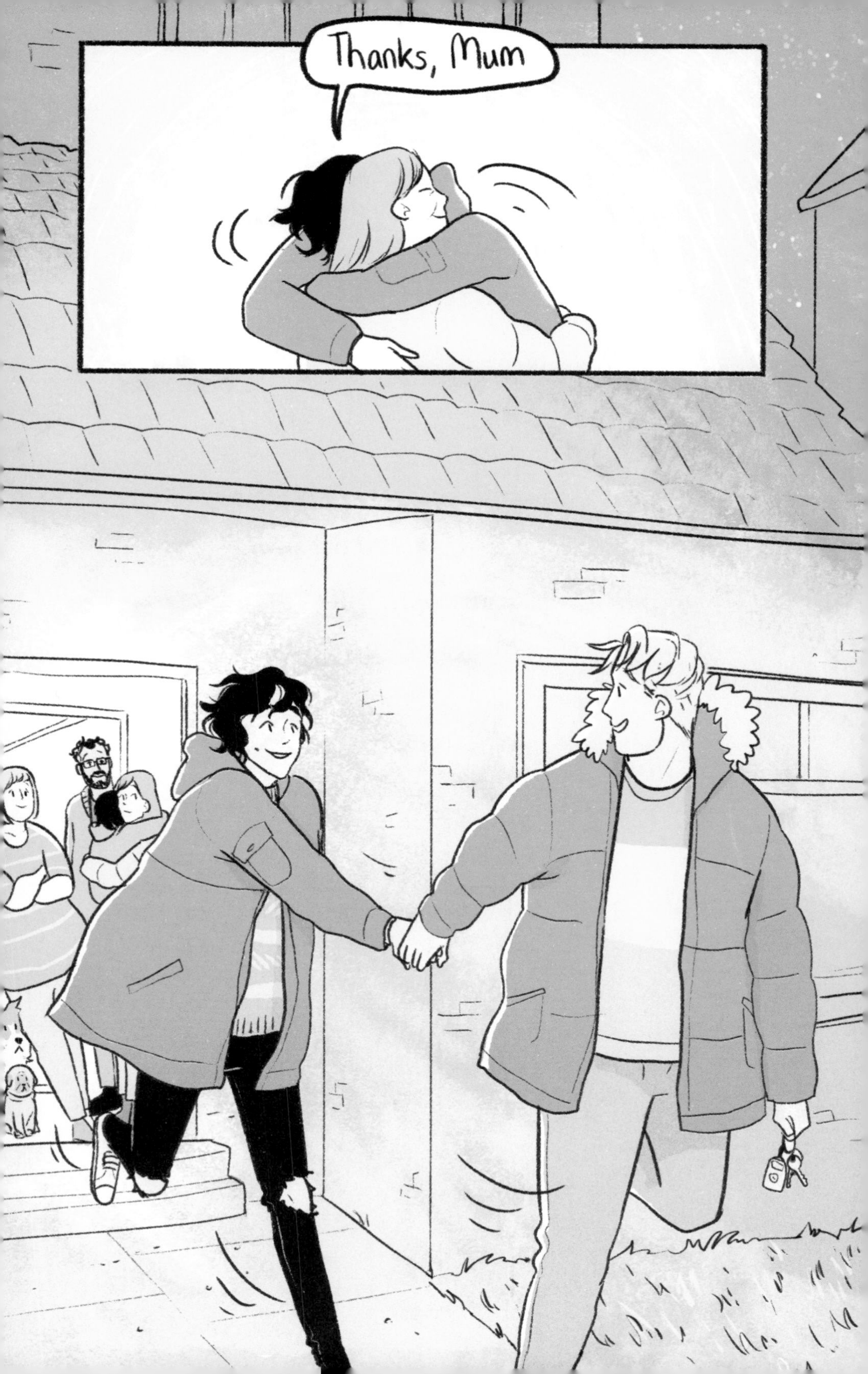
Thanks, Mum

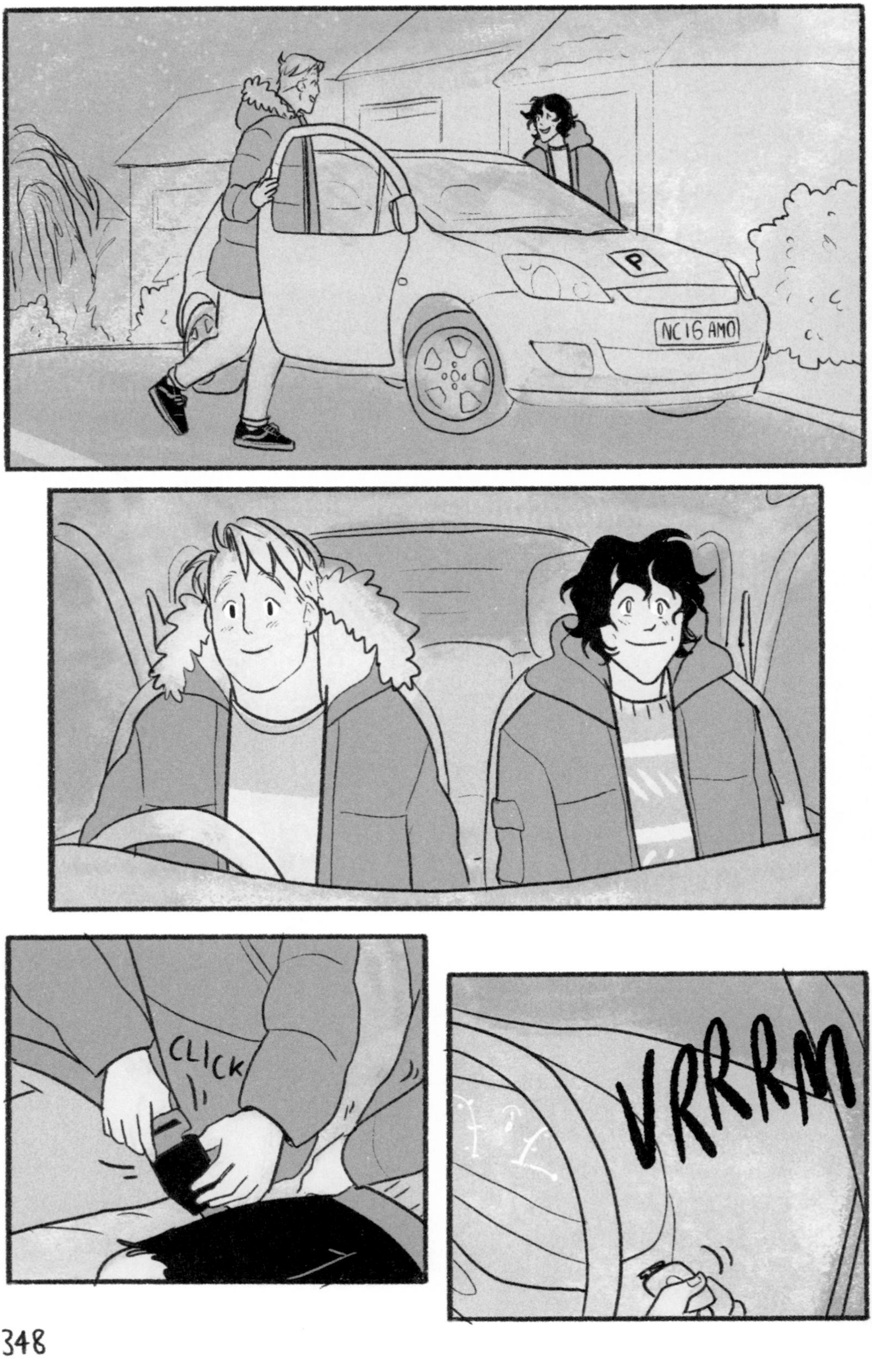
P
NC16 AMO
CLICK
VRRRM

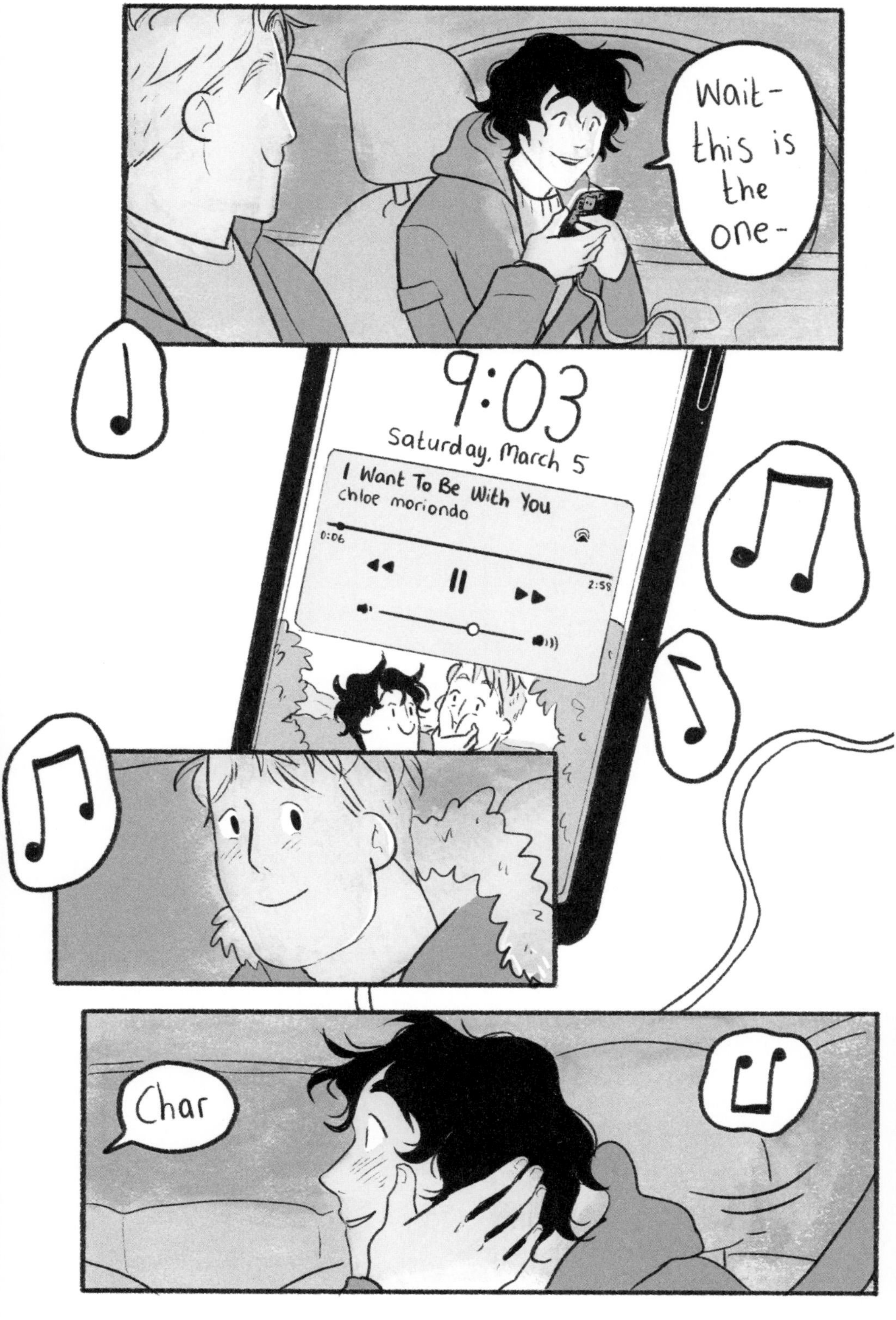
Wait- this is the one-
9:03
Saturday, March 5
I Want To Be With You
chloe moriondo
0:06
2:58
Char

Heartstopper will continue in
Volume 5!

Firsts

A HEARTSTOPPER MINI-COMIC

FIRST KISS

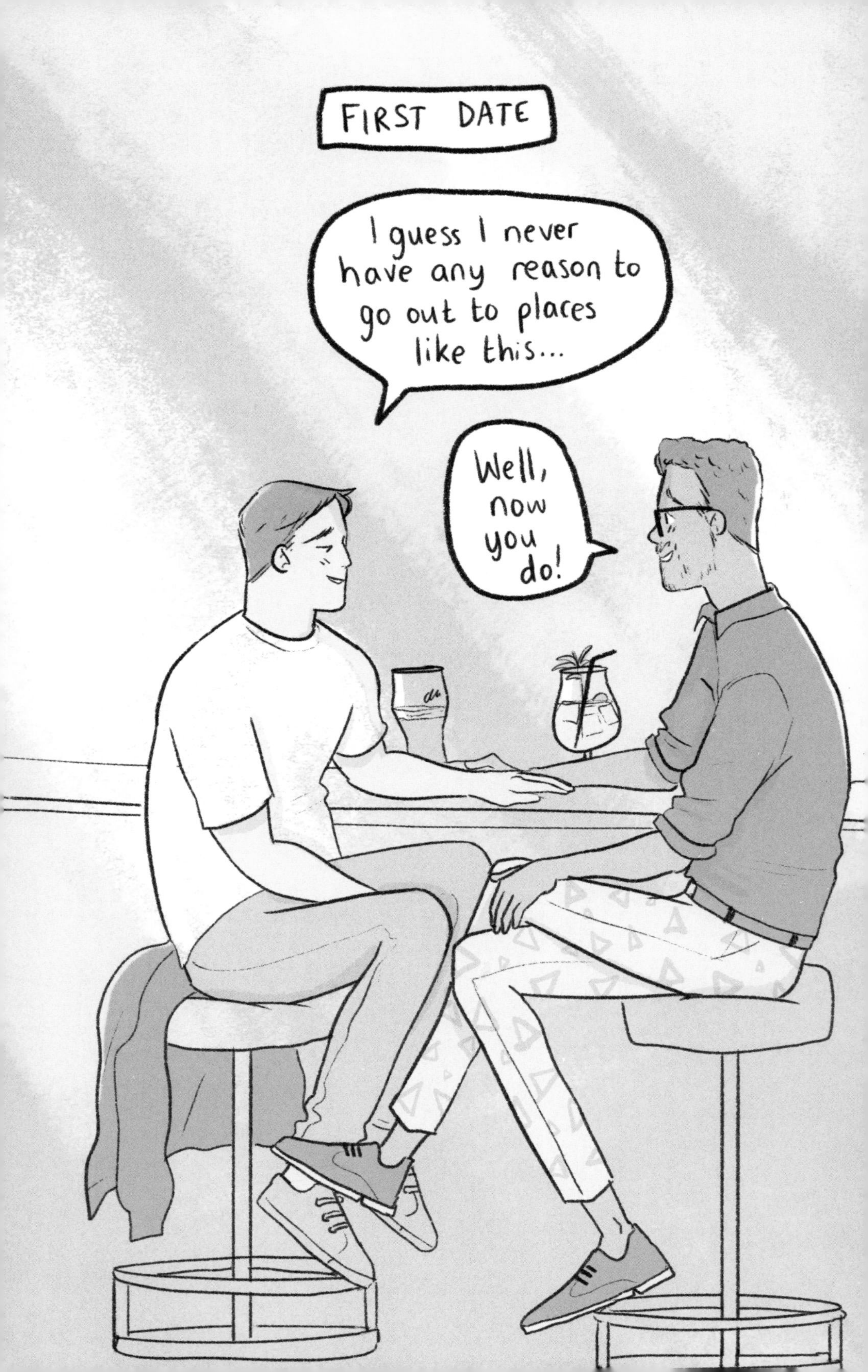
FIRST DATE
I guess I never have any reason to go out to places like this...
Well, now you do!

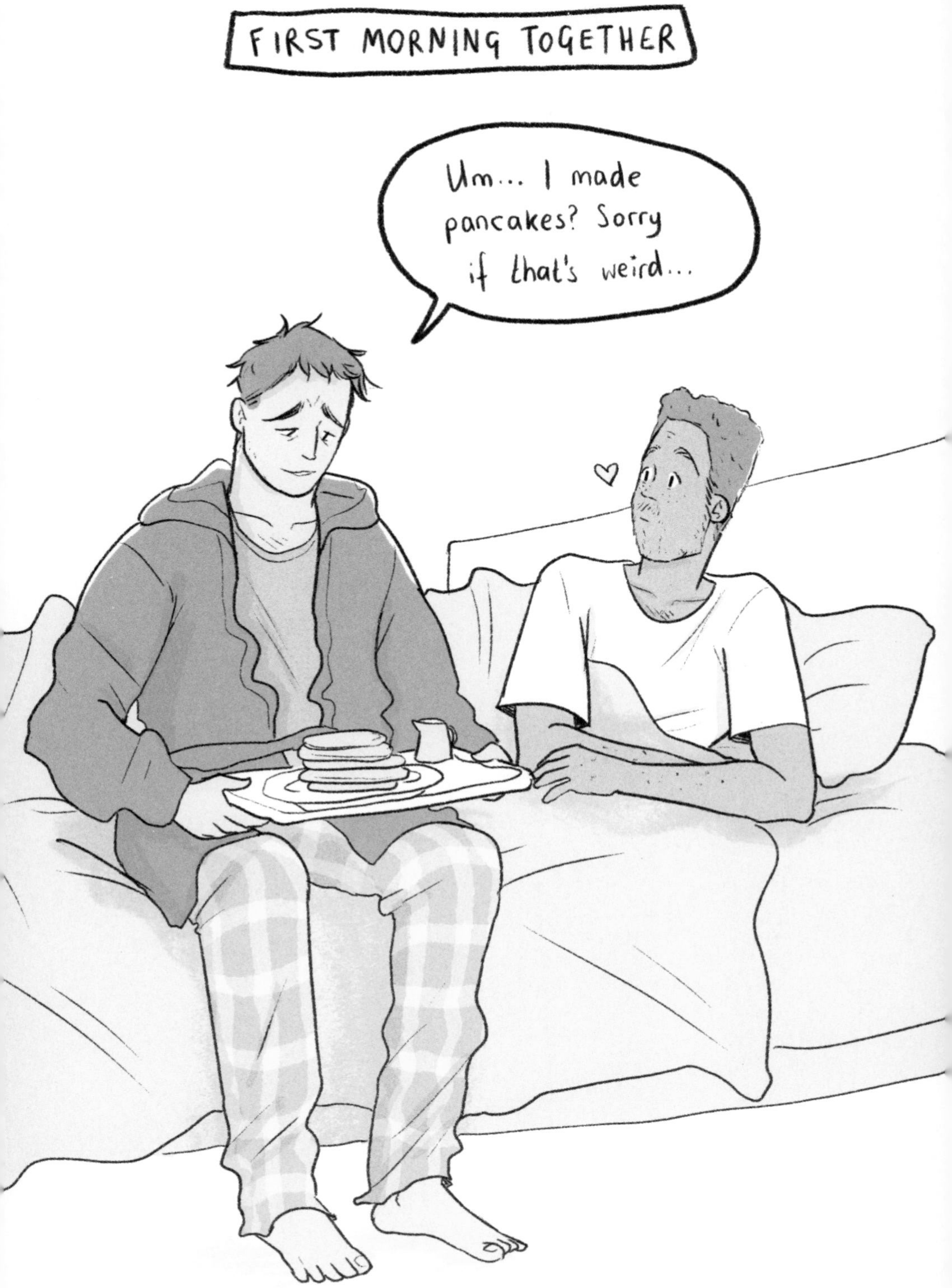
FIRST MORNING TOGETHER
Um... I made pancakes? Sorry if that's weird...

FIRST TIME COOKING TOGETHER

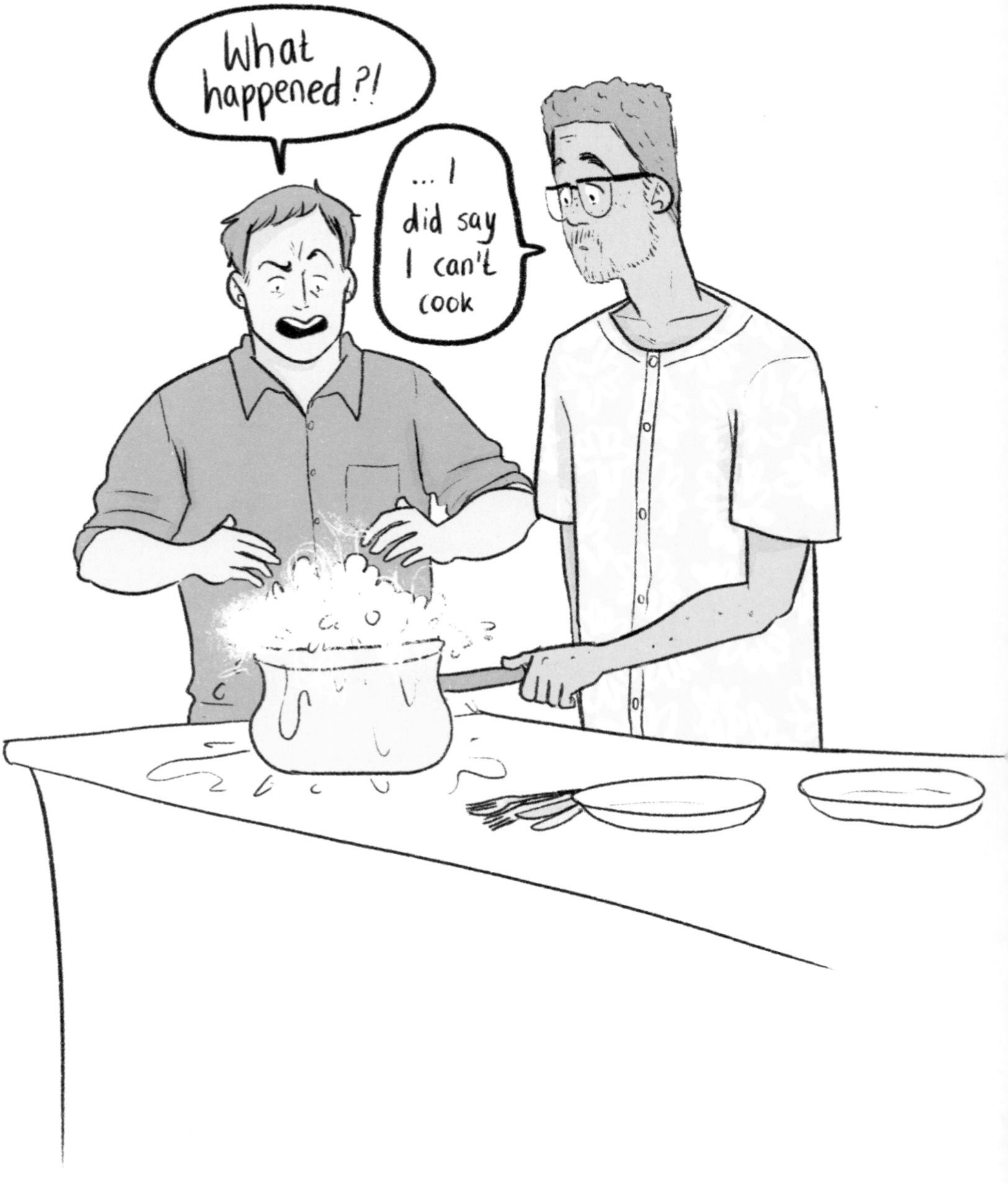
What happened?!
... I did say I can't cook

FIRST SICK DAY

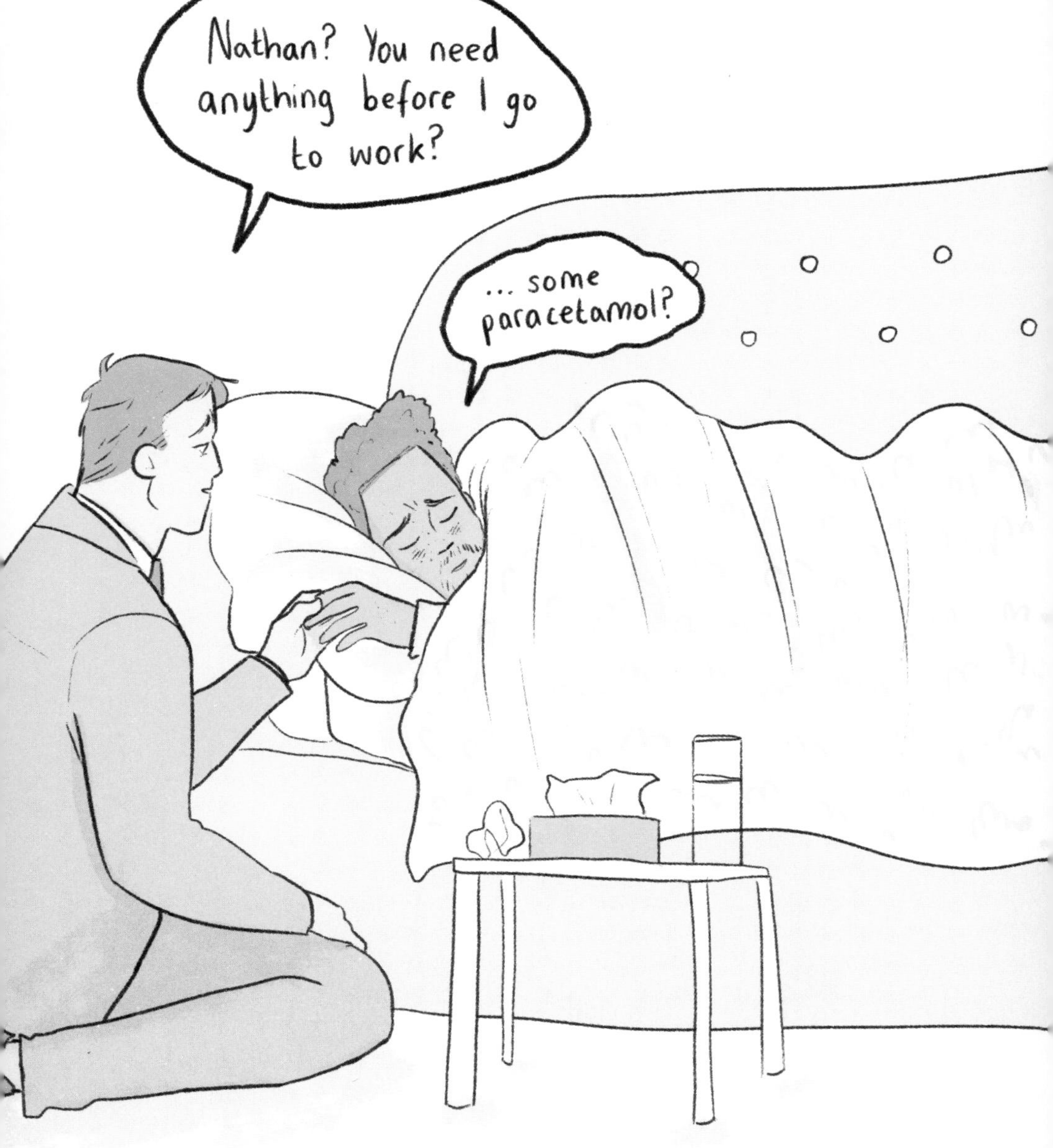
Nathan? You need anything before I go to work?
... some paracetamol?

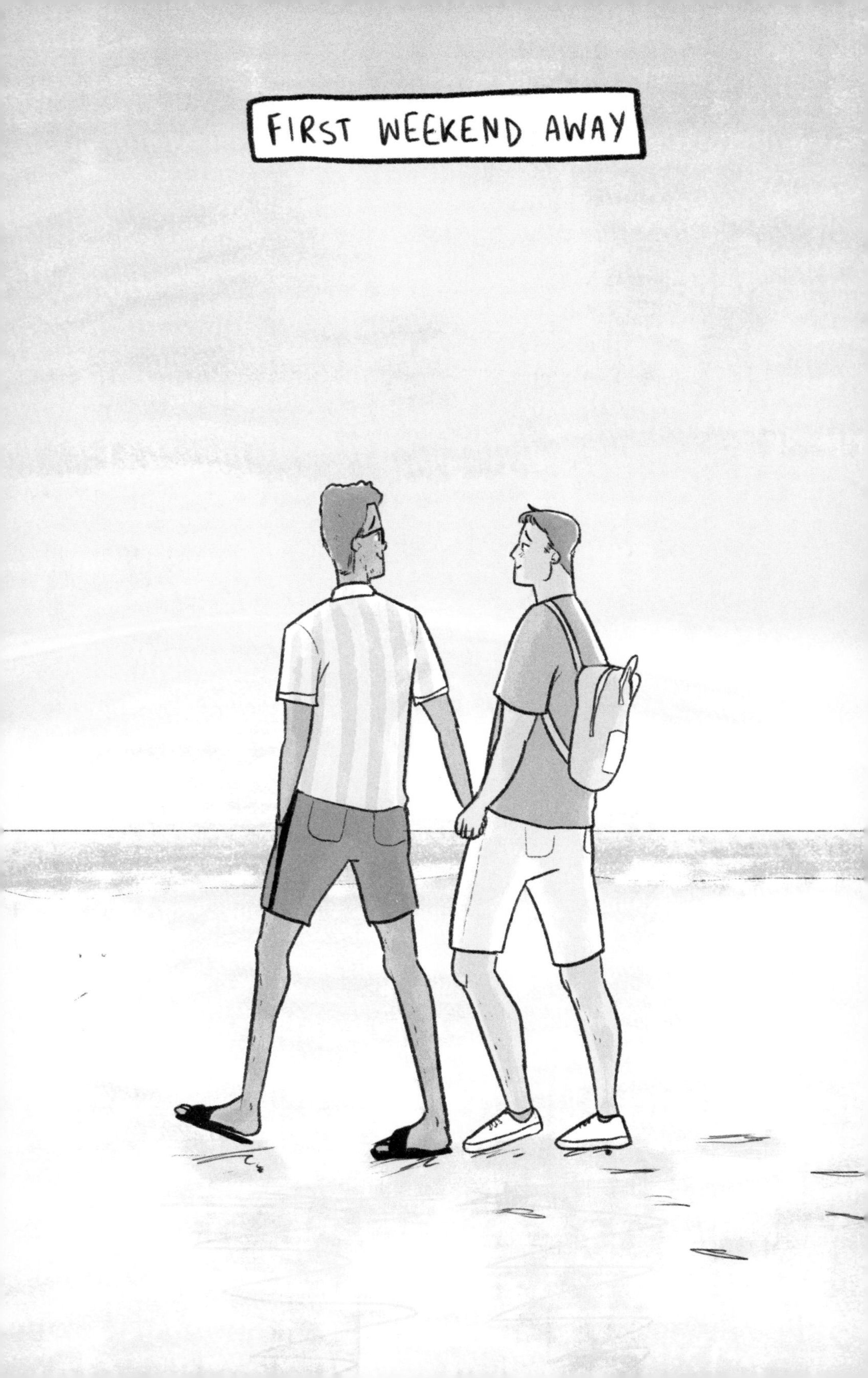
FIRST WEEKEND AWAY

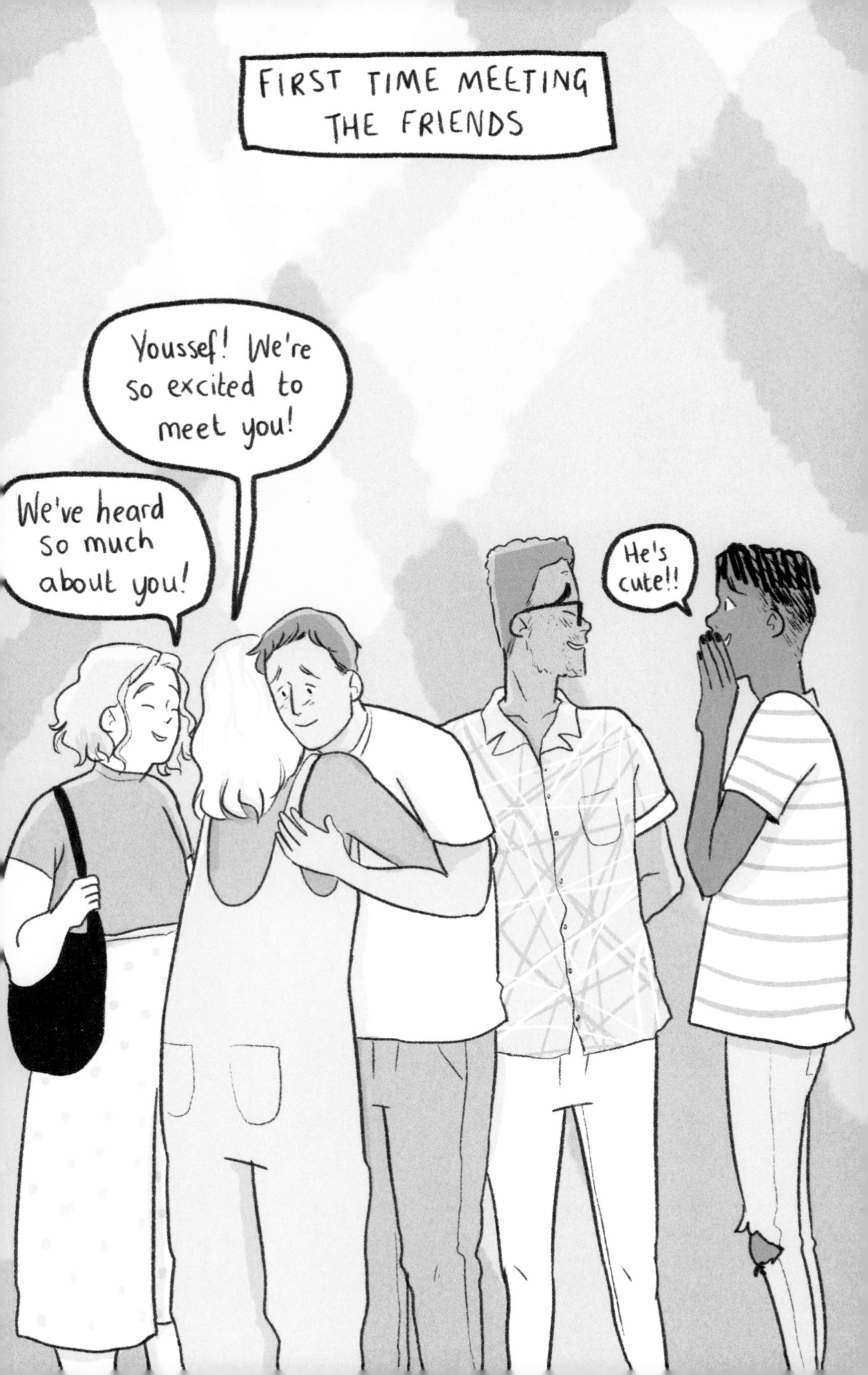
FIRST TIME MEETING THE FRIENDS
Youssef! We're so excited to meet you!
We've heard so much about you!
He's cute!!

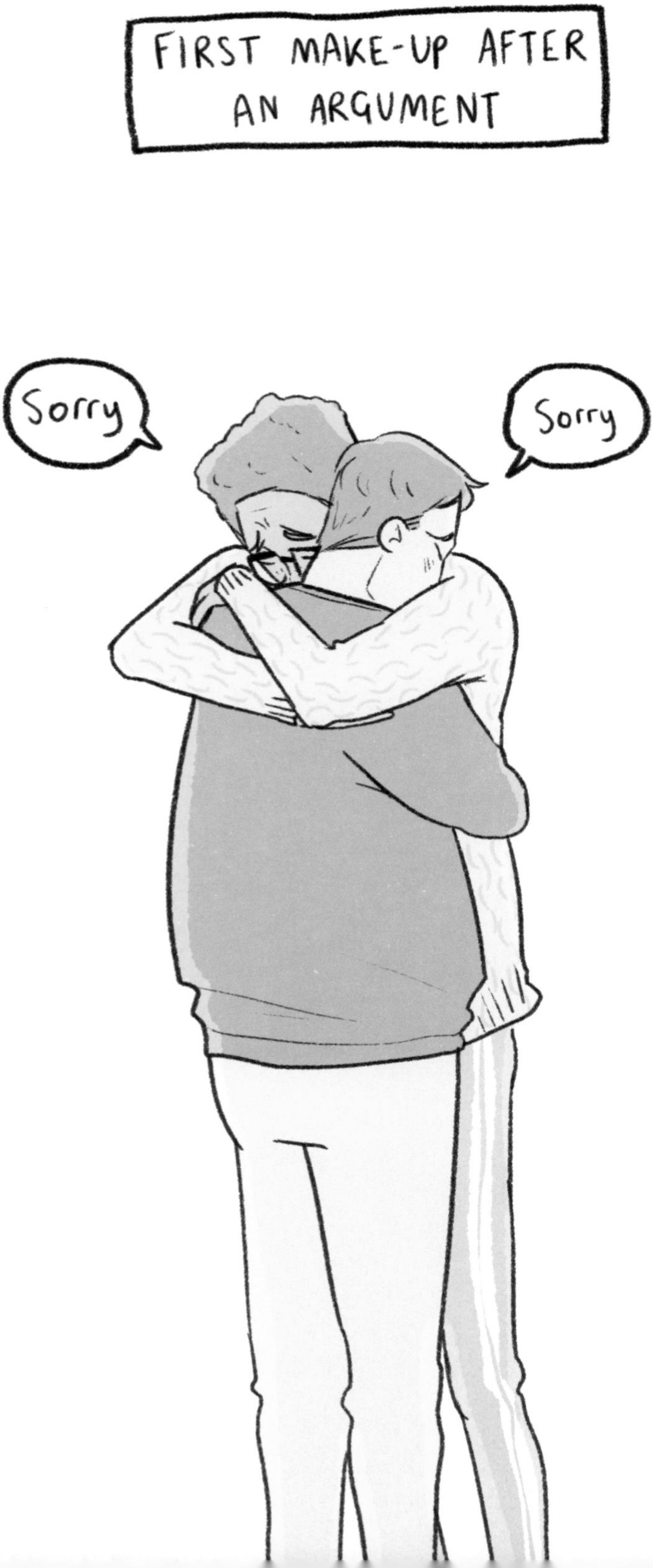
FIRST MAKE-UP AFTER AN ARGUMENT
Sorry
Sorry

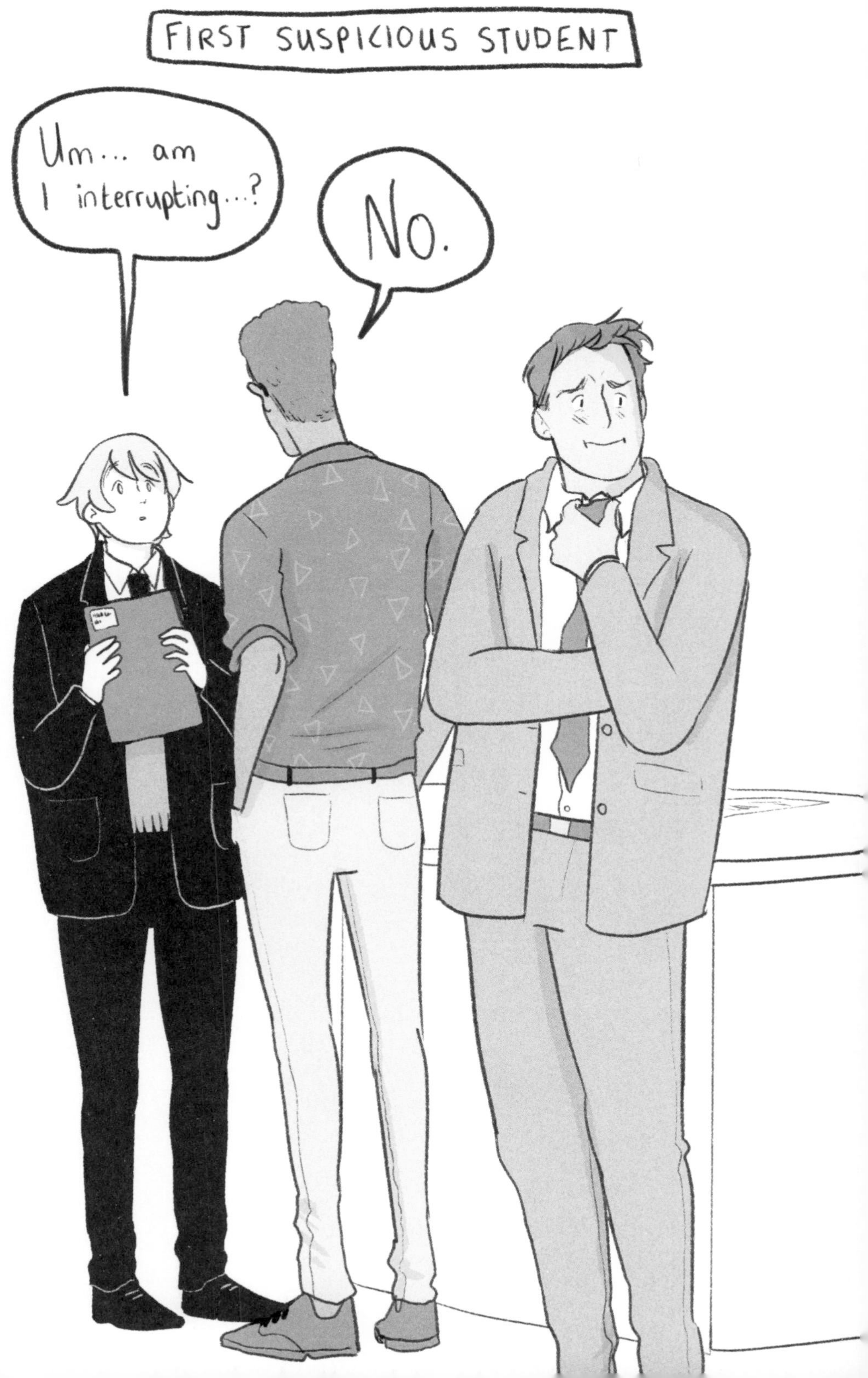
FIRST SUSPICIOUS STUDENT
Um... am I interrupting...?
No.

FIRST "I LOVE YOU"

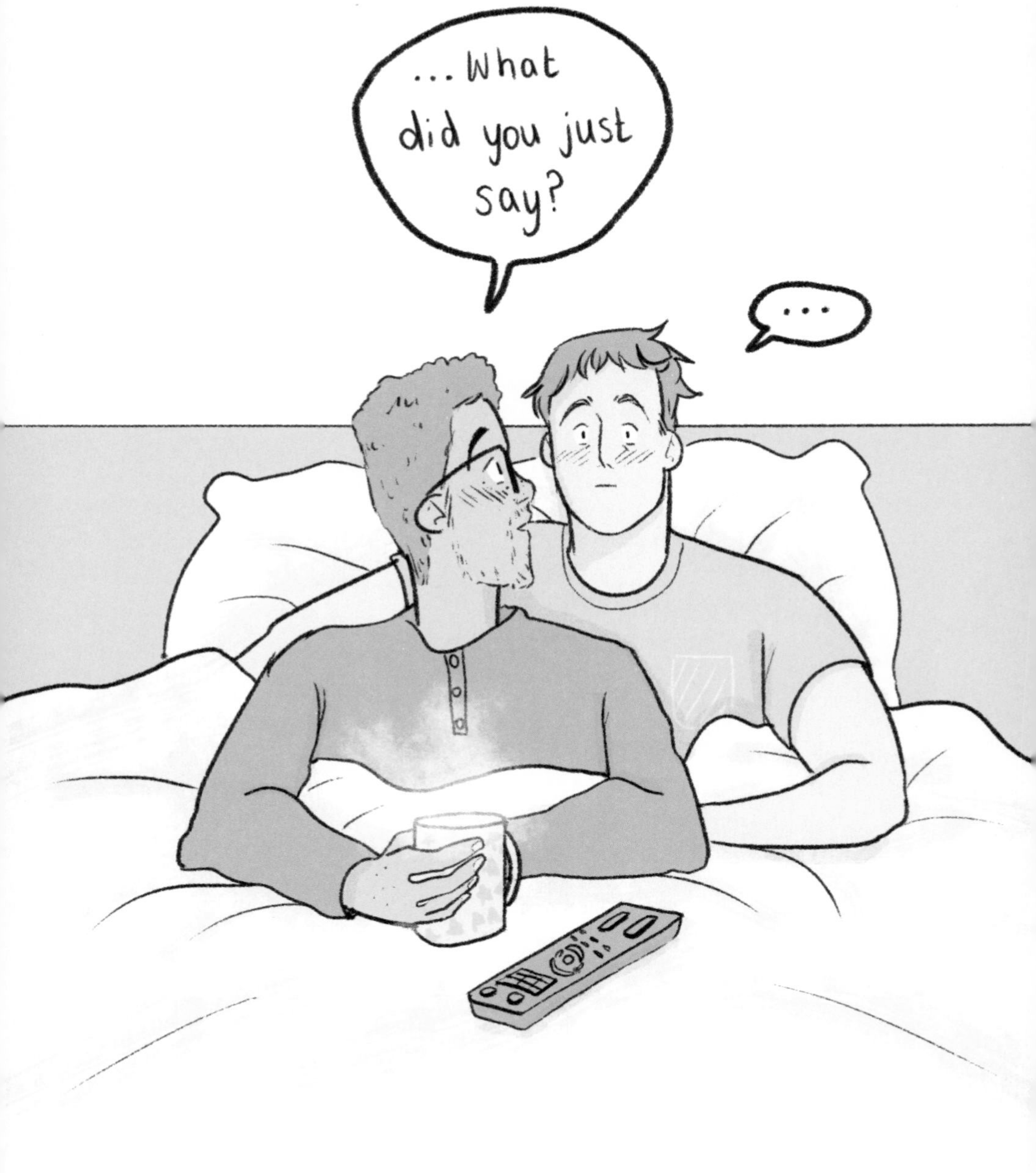
...What did you just say?
...

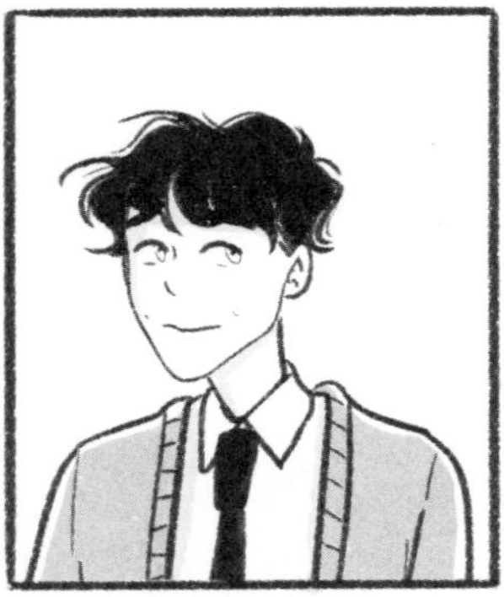

NAME: CHARLES "CHARLIE" SPRING
WHO ARE YOU: NICK'S BOYFRIEND
SCHOOL YEAR: YEAR 11 **AGE:** 15
BIRTHDAY: APRIL 27TH
FUN FACT: I LOVE TO READ!

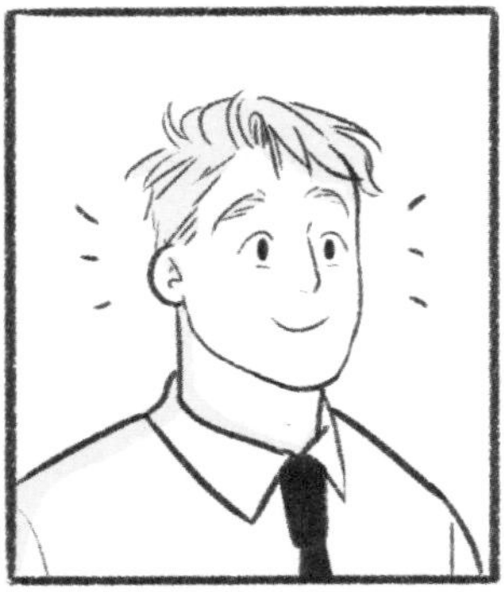

NAME: Nicholas "Nick" Nelson
WHO ARE YOU: Charlie's boyfriend
SCHOOL YEAR: Year 12 **AGE:** 17
BIRTHDAY: September 4th
FUN FACT: I'm great at baking cakes

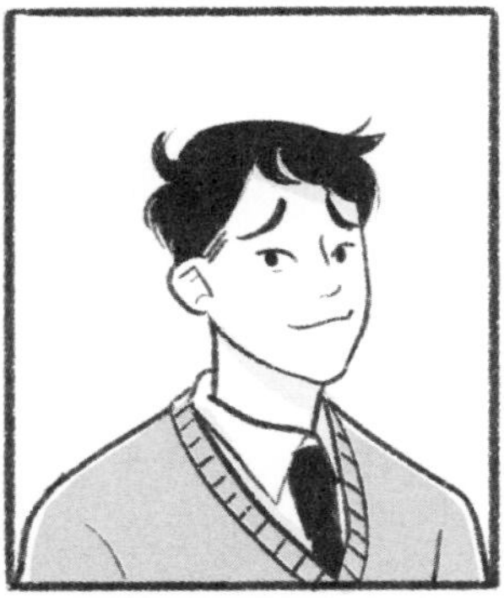

NAME: Tao Xu
WHO ARE YOU: Charlie's friend
SCHOOL YEAR: Year 11 **AGE:** 16
BIRTHDAY: September 23rd
FUN FACT: I have a film review blog

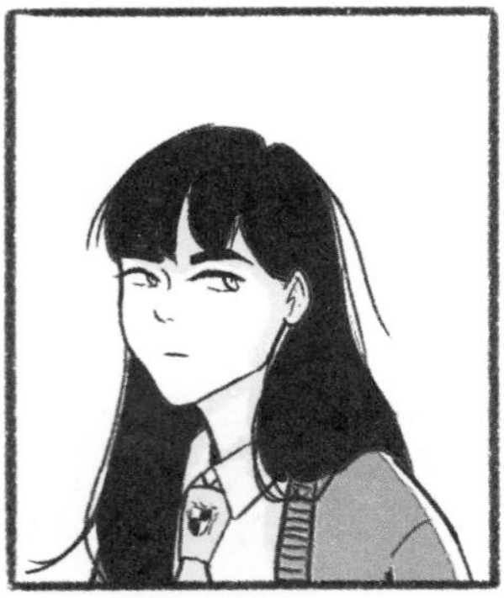

NAME: Victoria "Tori" Spring
WHO ARE YOU: Charlie's sister
SCHOOL YEAR: Year 12 **AGE:** 16
BIRTHDAY: April 5th
FUN FACT: I HATE (ALMOST) EVERYONE

NAME: Elle Argent
WHO ARE YOU: Charlie's friend
SCHOOL YEAR: Year 12   **AGE:** 16
BIRTHDAY: May 4th
FUN FACT: I like making clothes ♡

NAME: Tara Jones
WHO ARE YOU: Darcy's girlfriend
SCHOOL YEAR: Year 12   **AGE:** 16
BIRTHDAY: July 3rd
FUN FACT: I love dance! (especially ballet)

NAME: Darcy Olsson
WHO ARE YOU: Tara's girlfriend
SCHOOL YEAR: Year 12   **AGE:** 17
BIRTHDAY: January 9th
FUN FACT: I once ate a whole jar of mustard for a dare

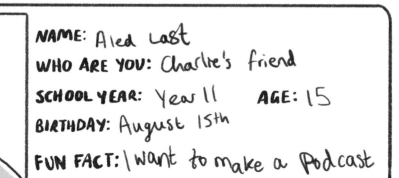

NAME: Aled Last
WHO ARE YOU: Charlie's friend
SCHOOL YEAR: Year 11   **AGE:** 15
BIRTHDAY: August 15th
FUN FACT: I want to make a Podcast

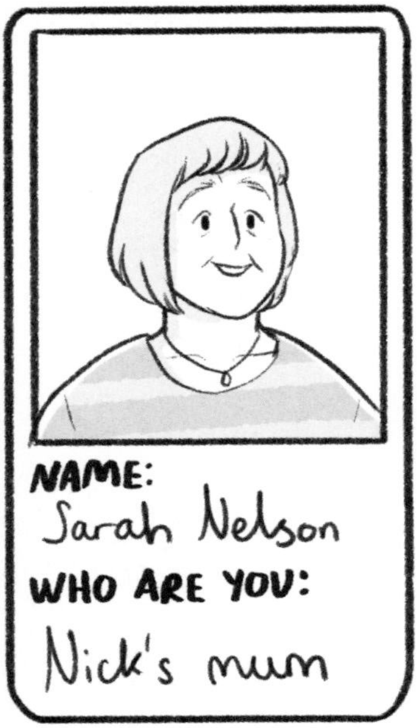
NAME:
Sarah Nelson
WHO ARE YOU:
Nick's mum

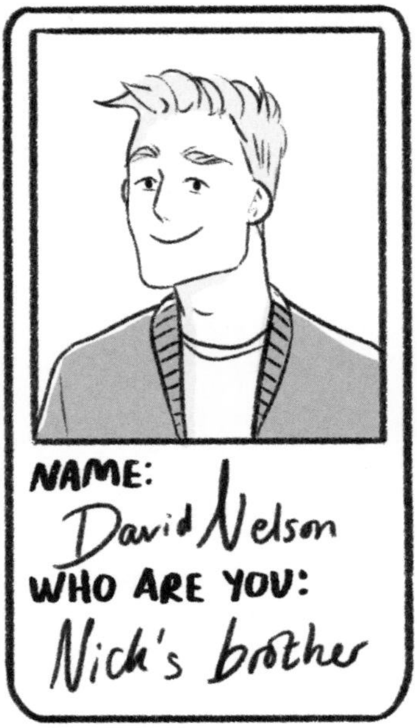
NAME:
David Nelson
WHO ARE YOU:
Nick's brother

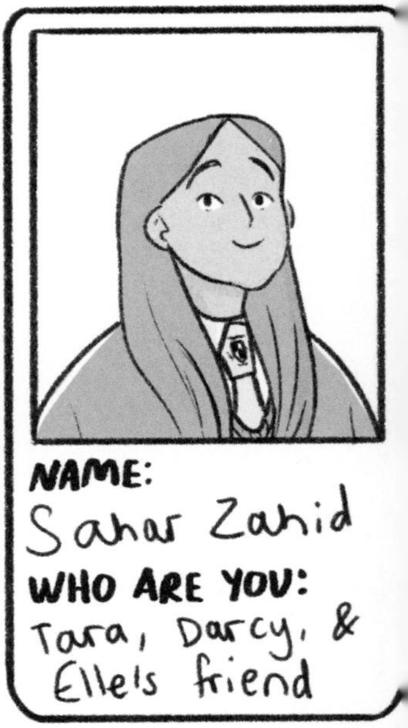
NAME:
Sahar Zahid
WHO ARE YOU:
Tara, Darcy, & Elle's friend

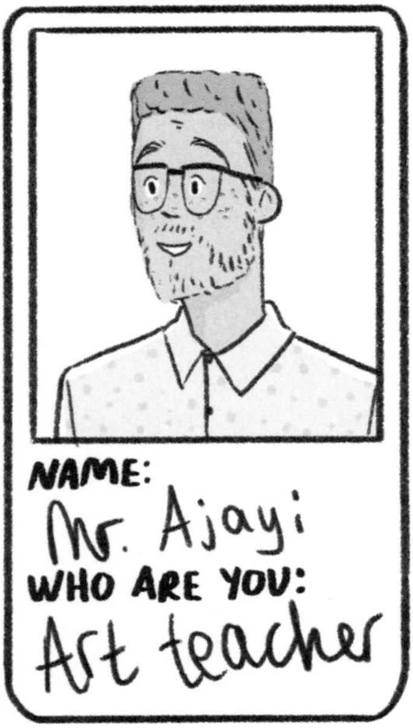
NAME:
Mr. Ajayi
WHO ARE YOU:
Art teacher

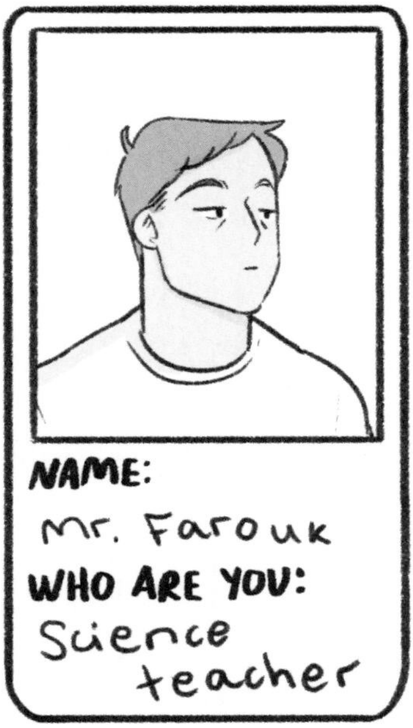
NAME:
Mr. Farouk
WHO ARE YOU:
Science teacher

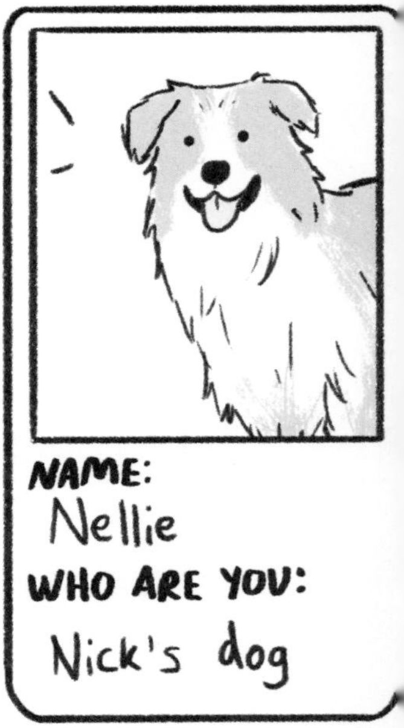
NAME:
Nellie
WHO ARE YOU:
Nick's dog

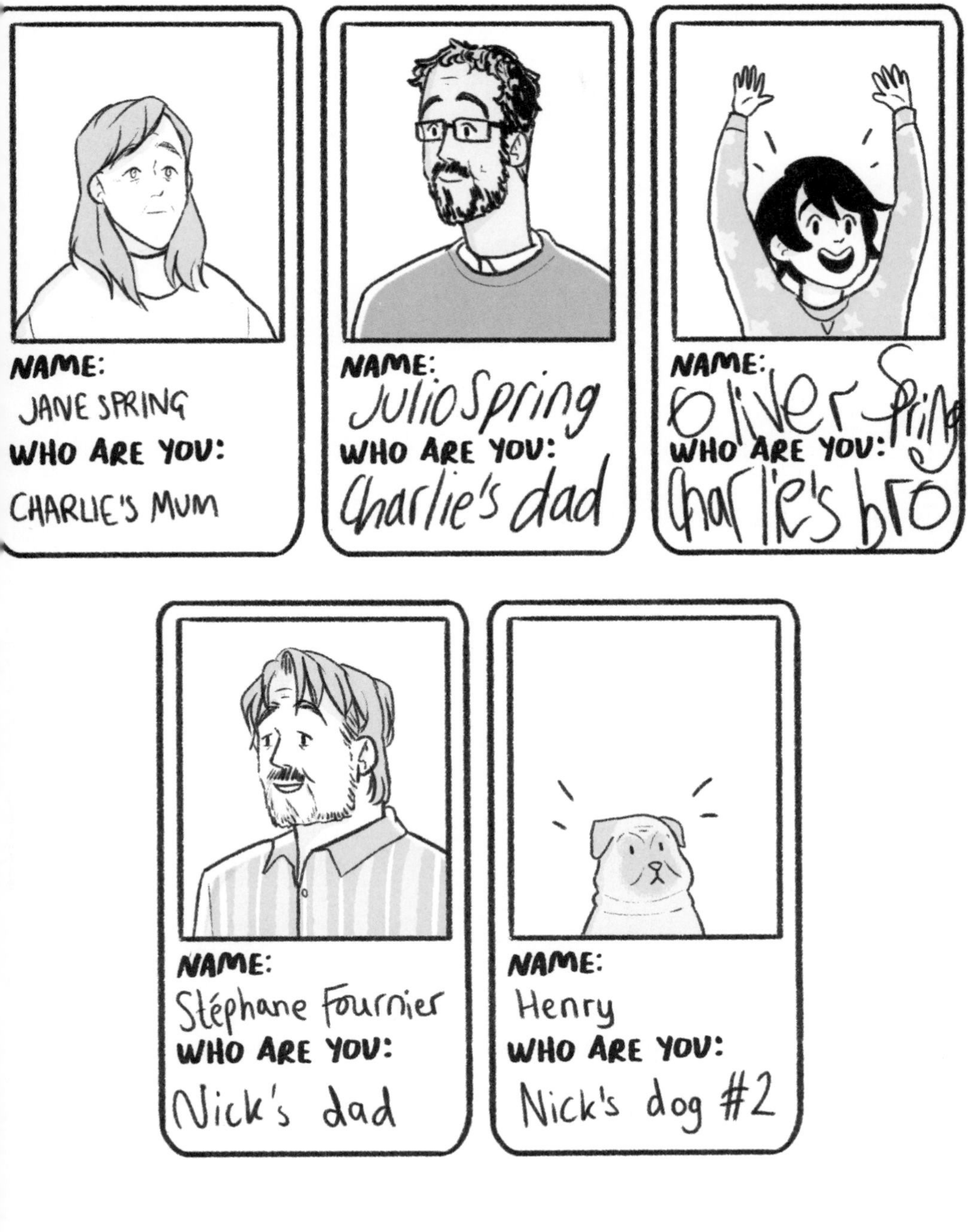
NAME:
JANE SPRING
WHO ARE YOU:
CHARLIE'S MUM
NAME:
Julio Spring
WHO ARE YOU:
Charlie's dad
NAME:
Oliver Spring
WHO ARE YOU:
Charlie's bro
NAME:
Stéphane Fournier
WHO ARE YOU:
Nick's dad
NAME:
Henry
WHO ARE YOU:
Nick's dog #2

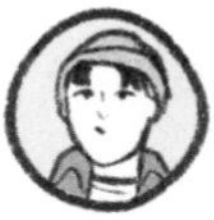

the.xu.tao

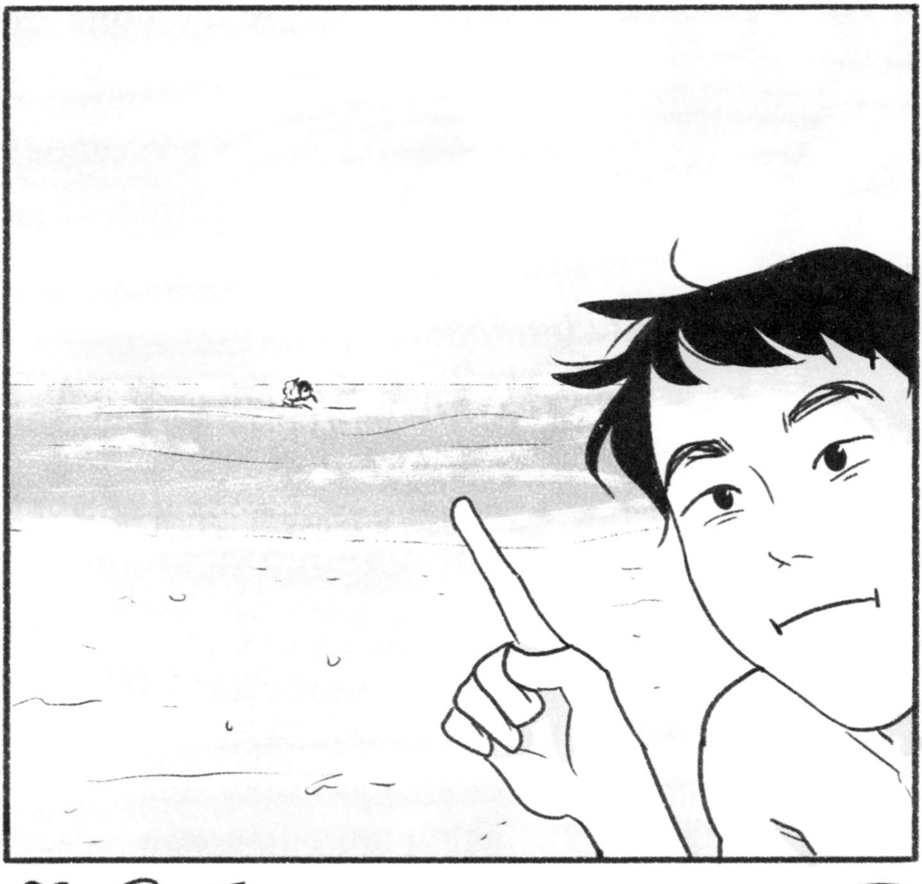

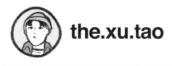

64 likes

the.xu.tao third wheeling

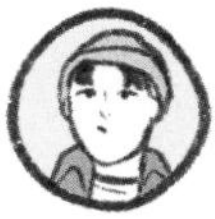

the.xu.tao

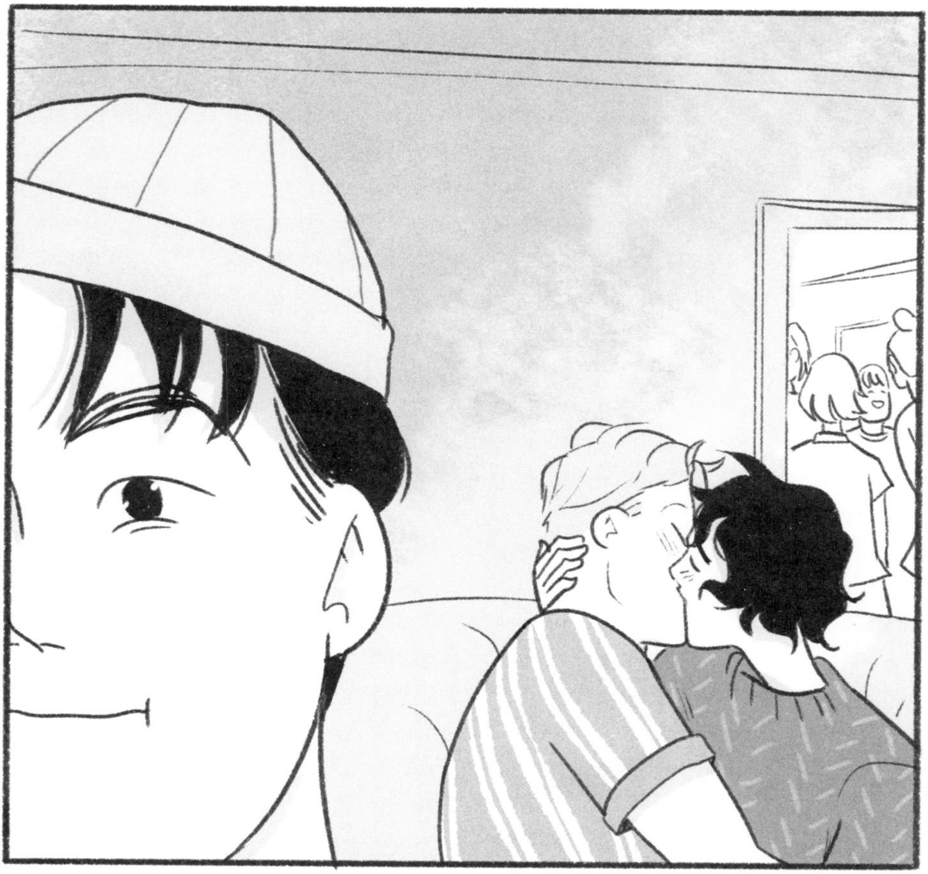

71 likes

the.xu.tao third wheel part 2 (they've been making out for like half an hour)

cfspring why are you so obsessed with me!!!!!
the.xu.tao @cfspring i just ship you two so much
cfspring @the.xu.tao fuck off

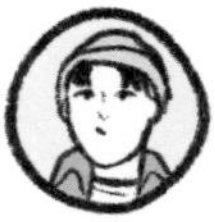

the.xu.tao

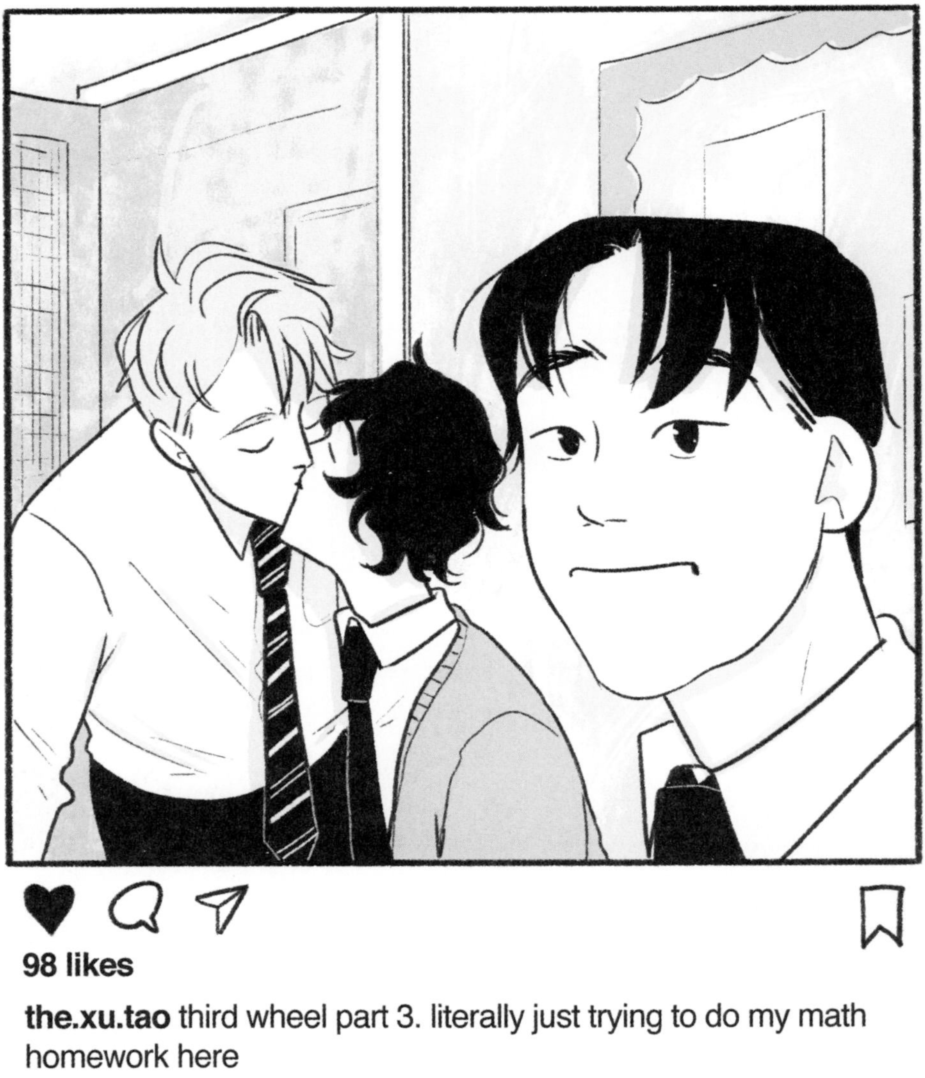

98 likes

the.xu.tao third wheel part 3. literally just trying to do my math homework here

cfspring IT WAS JUST A PECK WE WEREN'T EVEN MAKING OUT

the.xu.tao @cfspring still inappropriate school behavior and i will report you to the authorities

cfspring @the.xu.tao homophobia

cfspring

♥ 💬 ➤   🔖

102 likes

cfspring NOW who's the third wheel huh **@the.xu.tao**

the.xu.tao ...truce?
cfspring **@the.xu.tao** truce

Mental Health Resources

For information, help, support, and guidance
about mental health and mental illness,
please check out the following resources:

National Eating Disorders Association
nationaleatingdisorders.org

Anxiety & Depression Association of America
adaa.org

Heard Alliance
heardalliance.org

The Trevor Project
thetrevorproject.org

Author's Note

Hello, everyone! I really hope you enjoyed the fourth volume of Heartstopper. Can you believe we're already on the fourth volume? I certainly can't!

This volume mostly followed Charlie's mental health journey. I wanted to explore some of his struggles with his eating disorder, but to always show that recovery is possible, and that even though it may not be a straightforward journey, things can get better. But romantic love does not "cure" mental illness, as movies often suggest! This is something Nick learns in this volume. Nick can be there for him, but Charlie has to find his own path to recovery.

So much has happened since the last volume. I got to go on a UK book tour in early 2020, release a Heartstopper coloring book, and was finally able to announce that a TV adaptation is in the works with Netflix and See-Saw Films. None of this would have been possible without all you brilliant, passionate readers. I'm so, so grateful for your support and love for the series.

A huge thanks, as always, to the wonderful team working on Heartstopper: my amazing agent, Claire Wilson, my incredible editor, Rachel Wade, my awesome publicist, Emily Thomas, everyone at Hachette who is a part of the Heartstopper journey, and all the international publishers around the world who are now supporting the series, too.

I know that many of you are sad that the next volume will be the final volume of Nick and Charlie's story. I'm sad, too! But I promise that it shall be magical and heartwarming and full of queer joy.

See you in Volume Five!

Alice x

Collect the Heartstopper series!

"Absolutely delightful. Sweet, romantic, kind. Beautifully paced. I loved this book."
– Rainbow Rowell, author of Carry On
HEARTSTOPPER
VOLUME 1
ALICE OSEMAN

VOLUME
2
HEARTSTOPPER
ALICE OSEMAN

ALICE OSEMAN
VOLUME
3
HEARTSTOPPER

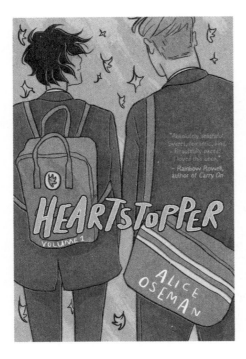

Don't miss this exceptional YA novel about discovering that it's okay not to have romantic feelings for anyone . . . since there are plenty of other ways to find love and connection.

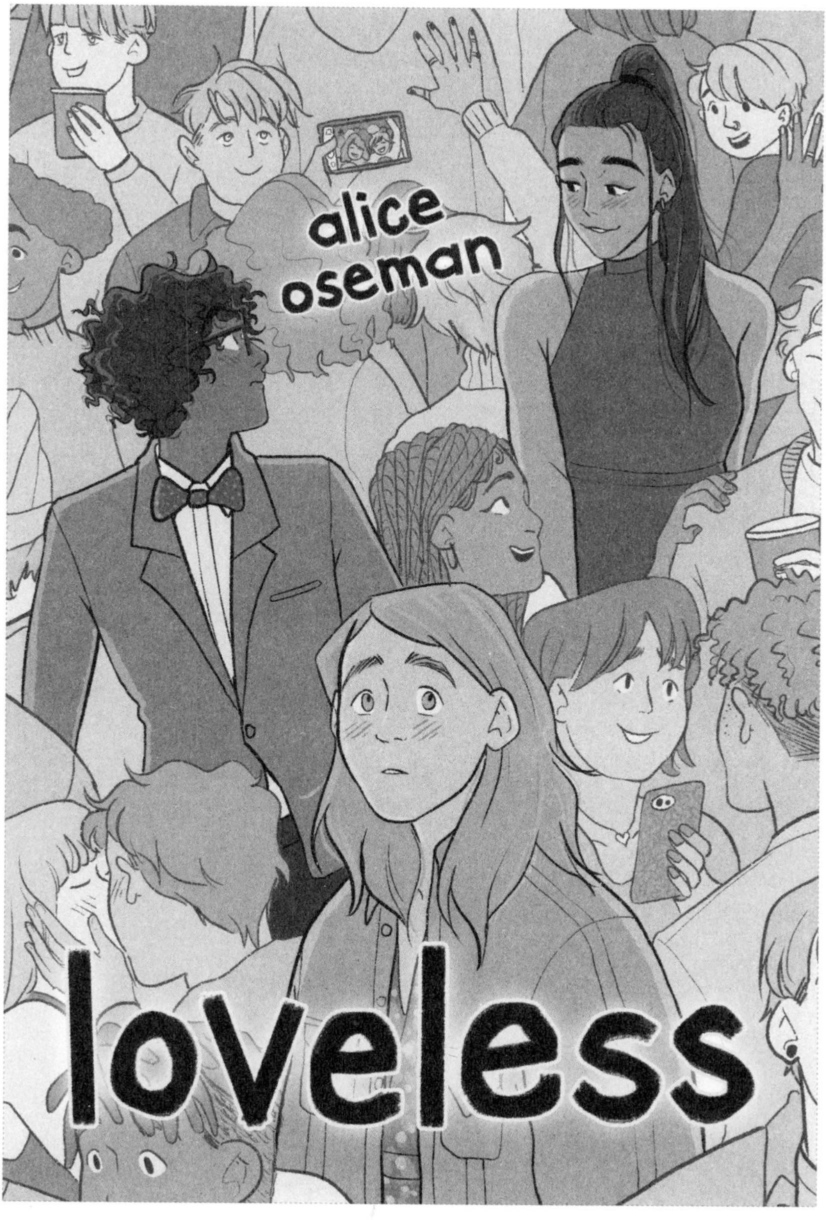
alice oseman
loveless

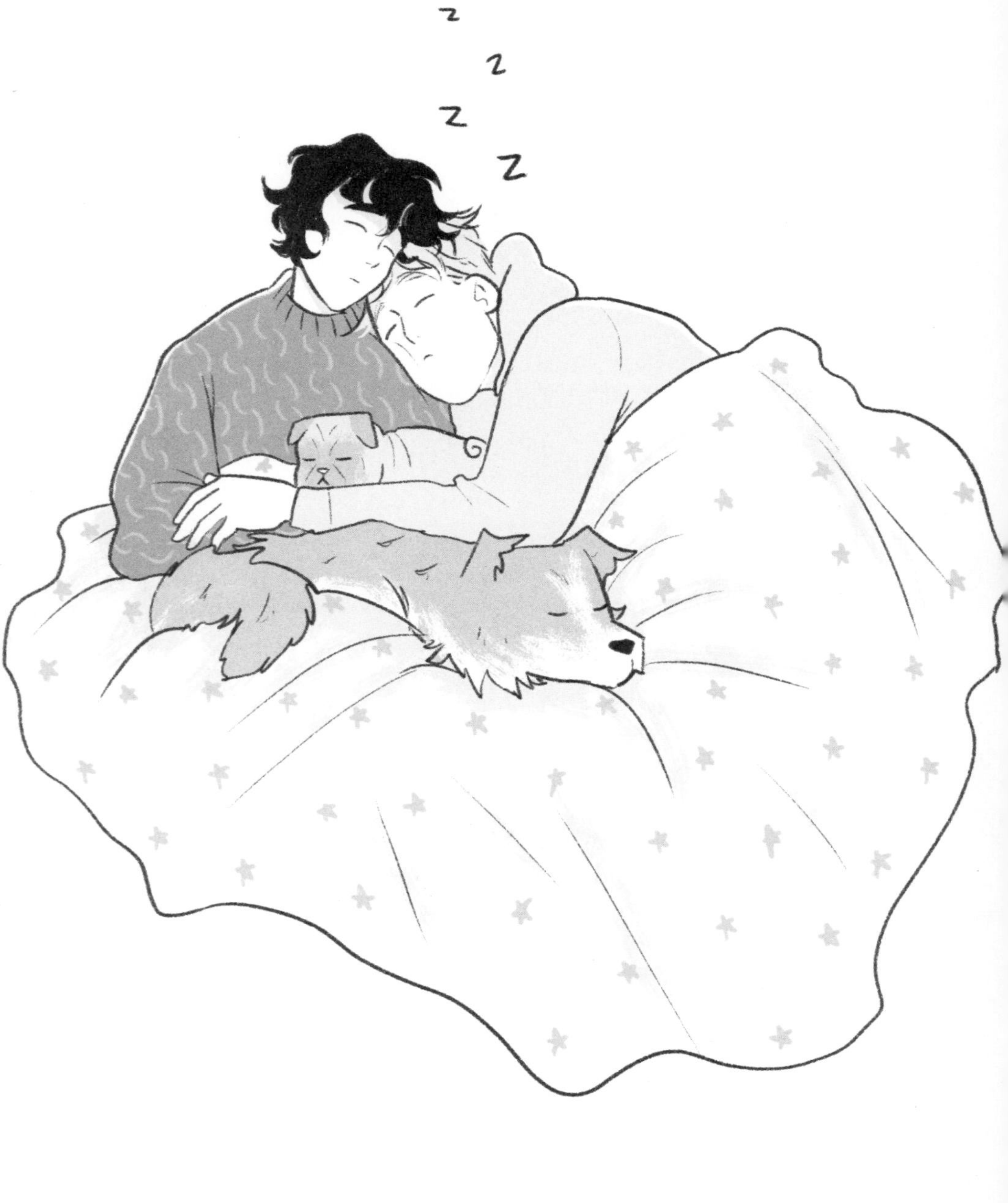
z z Z Z